Masters at Arms

&

Nobody's Angel

(Books 1 and 2 in the Rescue Me Series)

Kallypso Masters

MASTERS AT ARMS & NOBODY'S ANGEL

To discover more about the books in this series, see the *Rescue Me* Series section at the end of this book. For more about Kallypso Masters, please see About the Author.

This is an original publication of Kallypso Masters, LLC
PO Box 206122, Louisville, KY 40250

Copyright 2011, 2012, 2013 Kallypso Masters
Print ISBN: 978-1481222426
First Trade Paperback edition: November 2012
Second Trade Paperback edition: July 2013
Third Trade Paperback edition: November 2013

This book is a work of fiction and any resemblance to persons—living or dead—or places, events, or locales is purely accidental. The characters are reproductions of the author's imagination and used fictitiously. This book contains content that is not suitable for readers 17 and under.

MASTERS AT ARMS:
Edited by Jeri Smith, Booksmith Editing (http://booksmithediting.com/)
Line edited by Carol Ann MacKay, Liz Borino, and Meredith Bowery
Cover design by Linda Lynn
Formatted by BB eBooks (http://bbebooksthailand.com/)
Cover model image licensed through iStockPhotos

NOBODY'S ANGEL:
Edited by Jeri Smith (www.booksmithediting.com) and Meredith Bowery
Line edited by Carol Ann MacKay and Liz Borino
Cover design by Linda Lynn
Formatted by BB eBooks (http://bbebooksthailand.com/)
Cover images licensed through iStockPhotos and RomanceNovelCovers.com, both graphically altered by Linda Lynn

All rights reserved.

Please be aware that this book cannot be reproduced, scanned, or distributed in any printed or electronic form without written permission from the author, Kallypso Masters, at kallypsomasters@gmail.com or at the above address, or within the sharing guidelines at a legitimate library or bookseller. Please do not participate in or encourage piracy of copyrighted materials in violation of the author's rights. Purchase only authorized editions.

WARNING: The unauthorized reproduction, sharing, or distribution of this copyrighted work is illegal. Criminal copyright infringement, including infringement without monetary gain, is investigated by the FBI (http://www.fbi.gov/ipr/) and is punishable by up to five years in federal prison and a fine of $250,000.

Rescue Me Series
Reading Order

Not stand-alone novels
(These love stories can't be contained within one book!)

All four titles are available in e-book and print
(In print and e-book, the first two books are combined into one volume)

Masters at Arms
Nobody's Angel
Nobody's Hero
Nobody's Perfect

Next expected title in series:

Somebody's Angel

Also available in Spanish editions:

Sargentos Marines (*Masters at Arms* in English)
El Ángel de Nadie (*Nobody's Angel* in English)
El Hèroe de Nadie (*Nobody's Hero* in English)

Additional titles will be translated into Spanish as quickly as feasible!

Will these men ever truly become masters of their own fates?

MASTERS AT ARMS
KALLYPSO MASTERS
USA Today BESTSELLING AUTHOR

Praise for *Masters at Arms*

An unconventional but awesome start to a series I look forward to reading. Well done!

~ Eliza Gayle, Author

~ ~ ~

Each of the three heroes is completely individual and has a different grasp of the BDSM lifestyle. Master Sergeant Adam Montague is older, more experienced in life and love; Damián is a gentle soul from an underprivileged home; and Marc is the cocky rich boy who views the female population as a smorgasbord. I found the back-story for each man to be both interesting and well-written enough to make me want to know more.

~ Bobby D. Whitney, Book Wenches

~ ~ ~

Kally takes you on a roller coaster of emotions in *Masters at Arms*. You will laugh, cry and shake your head asking why, all the while leaving you wanting more. And OH you will want MORE!!!

~ Kelly Mueller, Books-n-Kisses

~ ~ ~

Kallypso Masters is a new talent to watch out for and I predict she will quickly become a fan favorite. I am excited to be able to say I'm one of her first fans and hope she remembers me when she makes it big!!!!

~ DiDi Sundance, Guilty Pleasures Book Reviews

~ ~ ~

Setting the reader up for all that is to come, this book took my breath away. I had moments of tears because the story was touching my heart. I had moments where the book was so hot, I wondered if my cheeks were turning red. Finally, I was left absolutely wanting more.

~ Stephanie O., Romancing the Book

~ ~ ~

After I finished this book I literally couldn't wait to go and buy the first book in the series. Reading about how these characters came to be, I got so invested that I now HAVE to know what happens to them! I would recommend this book to anyone who likes men in uniform, BDSM, drama, romance and great characters.

~ Carla Gallway, Book Monster Reviews

Masters at Arms

by
Kallypso Masters

(Book 1 in the Rescue Me Series)

Dedication

This book is dedicated to my pre-publication fans who fell in love with the Masters at Arms—Adam, Marc, and Damián—and followed along on my journey since May 2011. Your encouragement and excitement kept me working to make sure this novel lived up to your expectations. (Of course, the Masters used the flogger and single-tailed whip on occasion, as needed, for motivation, too.)

I also dedicate this book to the men and women in uniform. God bless and thank you for your service. If you are struggling with the aftermath of combat, please find someone to talk with or go to the Wounded Warriors Project, an organization near and dear to my heart. And thank you to your families, whose sacrifices are monumental, as well.

Acknowledgements

There are so many people to thank, and I hope I don't forget any. First of all, my editor, Jeri Smith, of Booksmith Editing. Your keen eye and excellent suggestions have made this book into what it is today, and have led me to improve the story of how these three men formed such a strong band-of-brothers bond. Thanks also for your encouragement. I look forward to working with you on the other books in this series.

To my beta readers and critiquers for the original e-book version, Fiona Campbell Cox, Kristin Harris, Kelly Hensley, Carol Ann MacKay, Kathy McKenzie, Kelly Mueller, Lani Rhea, Kelly Timm, and Kathy Treadway. Thanks also goes to Meredith Bowery who went through the book one more time for me before I put it out in print. And my thanks to Christine Sullivan Mulcair who gave it one more look before going to audiobook format. All of you had insightful suggestions that helped save me embarrassment and made this book and its characters so much stronger.

To Top Griz, a retired Marine Master Sergeant who took me under his wing in spring 2012 and helped me get my Marine Corps references and mindset straight. You made sure Adam didn't say anything but fuck, too, because Marines cuss. They don't say frigging. Just before going to print, Susan Wasek, the wife of a retired Marine Lt. Colonel, gave the book another look and helped me strengthen a couple of parts, for which I'm grateful. Thanks also to Laura Harner, Carol Ann MacKay, and S.A. Moore for their help in getting other general military facts straight. All errors are mine, of course. (Note: Please keep in mind that the military protocols, terminology, and equipment described in this book are from 2002-2005 and may not be the same as those followed or used currently.)

Thanks to my many Facebook friends for encouragement and support. Specifically, my thanks to Elizabeth Leighton, who came up with the title of this book; to Lizzie Walker, who discovered Master Adam's craving for peanut butter; and to Anita Hayes who just knew Master Adam would listen to Aerosmith.

To my wonderful MPs, thank you for lifting me up, making me laugh, giving me delightful inspiration into the lifestyle, and providing me multiple social-networking fixes every day! You're the best! Thanks to Katona Barnes and Lisa Kait, especially for completing the Mistresses Admin 3. We're invincible!

Last, but in no way least, to Cherise Sinclair, who wrote *Club Shadowlands*, the first erotic romance I ever read. Your Doms and subbies are to die for and I hope mine are one-tenth as memorable. Thanks also for your Facebook friendship, mentoring me on various aspects of the lifestyle and writing business, and for your ongoing support and encouragement. Now, please get back to work and finish another story, my dear Alpha Sub. I can't wait for my next visit to Club Shadowlands, Dark Haven, or the Wild Hunt Tavern.

Author's Note

This is an unconventional start to a series, but I wanted to show, rather than tell you about it in snippets later on in the series, the key turning points in the lives of Adam, Marc, and Damián that lead them to be together in Fallujah, Iraq, and to stay together afterward.

While tempted to skip ahead to a favorite hero's book, I caution you to show some discipline for my Masters and read their stories in order, because this is a chronological series and they don't live in a vacuum. They are so interrelated they can't be contained in separate books. For instance, Adam and Karla have major events happen to them in *Nobody's Angel*, even though the main couple in that book is Marc and Angelina. The same is true for Damián and Savannah, who will return in *Nobody's Hero* (Adam and Karla's book), before their romance journey actually continues in *Nobody's Perfect*.

A word of caution about the kink you will read about, too. For those new to the lifestyle, before trying anything in the BDSM realm, please do your homework. You can read books or watch videos about the specific techniques mentioned in this series, but please seek out real-life mentors or experts for the more advanced areas of play. (Go to fetlife.com to find kinksters in your area, but be careful whom you choose to play and interact with.) Be safe, sane, and consensual (or at least be aware of the risks involved) before you meet anyone or try anything.

And if you or a loved one suffers from Post-Traumatic Stress Disorder (PTSD), please reach out to people who have been there and can provide support and advice. For military-related PTSD, contact the Wounded Warrior Project (https://woundedwarriorproject.org/) and other non-government organizations, as well as the Veterans Administration (http://www.ptsd.va.gov/). For non-combat PTSD issues like Savannah's, here are some web sites that can help if you need to talk with someone:

Crisis Services:
http://crisisservices.org/content/index.php/information-resources/

Rape Abuse and Incest National Network:
http://rainn.org/

To Write Love on Her Arms:
http://www.twloha.com/

Now I turn the *Master at Arms* over to your good care. (But, trust me, if you're bad, they can be even more fun.)

Section One: Adam

Prequel to Adam's Story, Nobody's Hero

Night before Thanksgiving 2002, Chicago, Illinois

Joni, you were my anchor. I'm lost without you.

Adam Montague slumped into the seat at the terminal, hoping to catch a couple hours of sleep before his bus left. He looked around Chicago's busy travel hub and saw the autumn decorations scattered every five yards or so. Apparently, going for the homey Thanksgiving look. *Not even close.* Just another shithole bus station, no different from the ones he'd seen a lot of during his early years in the Marines.

Twenty-two years. He'd survived the First Gulf War in 1991 and a deployment to Kosovo in '99. Just when he and Joni started planning for his retirement, some damned assholes attacked the United States, the country he'd sworn to protect and defend. So, he'd put off turning in his retirement papers until he could see how Operation Enduring Freedom went. He'd serve as long as he was useful and needed.

Adam had been deployed to Kandahar twice since 2001. His first tour ended with a medical leave earlier this year after a clusterfuck of bad intelligence led one of his recon units into an ambush with disastrous results. He'd gone in after them and gotten only a few of them out unscathed, but he'd lost two good Marines and managed to get himself injured in the bargain.

So, he'd been home at Camp Pendleton with Joni more than a month last winter as his body had healed. Now he wondered if she'd known about her cancer back then and kept it from him. Would it have made any difference if he'd known? He'd have been sent back to war, and she'd still have had to fight the disease alone. She'd known the deal when she married him. While he was active duty, she'd have to take a back seat to whatever conflict he'd been sent to fight in the world.

His last tour had ended with his hardship leave two months ago when Joni's mother had finally told him Joni's cancer had come back with a vengeance. He hung his aching head and held it in his hands hoping the heels of his hands would quell the throbbing in his temples.

Memories of walking into that bedroom in Minneapolis two months ago flashed through his mind. He squeezed his eyes shut, trying to block it out, but the sight would be imprinted in his mind forever. God, the disease had so ravaged her body by the time he got home, he was afraid to touch her. Then her frail hand had patted the queen-sized mattress and he'd crawled into bed with her and held her in his arms while she sobbed.

Adam raised his head and wiped his hands down his face. Numb. He felt numb, whether from losing Joni or from the two-week bender, he wasn't sure. Probably a bit of both.

He guessed his unit was out of Kandahar by now. Sounded like Iraq would be next on their dance card.

Bring it. I got nothin' left to lose.

Fuck! Stinkin' thinkin' like that would get the Marines under him killed. He wasn't mentally ready to go back, but his orders were to report Monday. He hoped he'd find the intestinal fortitude he'd need by the time he reunited with his unit.

A cornucopia cutout hanging from a fluorescent light fluttered when a blustery wind blew in from the open doors. Joni had always taken so much pride in making their home festive for the holidays. She especially loved Christmas, even though it was just the two of them, well, when he wasn't deployed. She even kept her nativity set and some other favorite decorations displayed all year long for whenever he did make it home. Not that he paid much attention to that. He'd just been happy to see her, hold her, love her, and make up for lost time.

So damned much lost time.

What the hell was he going to do with all that stuff now? He'd call her mother and tell her to do whatever she wanted with it. He had his memories and a few photos—and her wedding ring. Shit, he hoped Joni had gotten rid of their playthings before she'd moved in with her mom. Well, nothing he could do about that now.

Camp Pendleton—or wherever he would be sent—would be his home until he retired from the Corps. He hoped that, by the time he got back in country, whichever Marine Area of Responsibility that would be, he'd have shaken off this black mood that matched the frigid black night outside.

In a way, he couldn't wait to get back. Combat and military life, he understood. What stumped him was cancer. Fucking cancer. Nothing in his tactics or weapons training prepared him to help Joni fight against the insurgent that destroyed her body.

Not that she'd even wanted him to help her fight the disease. By the time she'd let her mom tell him about the recurrence, she was given a month at best. She'd managed to hold out for a couple weeks longer than that estimate.

God, his eyes burned. He rubbed them with a thumb and forefinger, then lowered his hand and clenched his fist. *Damn it, he should have known sooner.*

Joni told him she saw no point in pulling him away from a place where he could make a difference, just to sit by her bed and watch her die. She'd figured he'd have gone stir crazy with the helplessness of not being able to do anything to change the unalterable outcome.

God, he'd kill for another bottle of scotch right now. He looked at the wino passed out on the floor across the room. Adam thought about offering the man a wad of money for whatever he had left in the brown-paper wrapped bottle he clutched to his chest with both arms like a lover.

Adam had held Joni in his arms for the last time, just like that, as she had slipped away from him forever. Before she died, two days short of their twentieth wedding anniversary, she'd assured him she wouldn't have changed a thing in their years together.

Hell, he'd sure have changed a few things.

Togetherness wasn't the best word to describe their marriage. She'd lived with him on base when he wasn't deployed, and they had eight years together after the end of the Gulf War and before he'd been sent to Kosovo. Then came Afghanistan and he hadn't been home much since.

They'd talked about the good times they'd had in the '80s and '90s when he hadn't been deployed to combat zones. Their Dom/sub power exchanges had been total then. But that had been impossible to sustain while deployed.

Fire burned the backs of his eyes. Joni never wanted him to take his focus off the military missions to deal with her "little problems." Like the time she'd totaled the car. She'd taken care of everything herself. He'd been deployed, of course. As always, she'd handled everything perfectly. Except she hadn't told him. Said she was afraid he'd be upset about the car. Hell, he didn't give a shit about the fucking car. He'd just been worried when he heard how close she'd come to being killed.

All of the times she'd needed him—from when she'd held their stillborn son in her arms in 1991 to when she'd fought her last rounds of chemo and radiation this past summer—he'd been fighting battles elsewhere. Long deployments in too many hot spots in the world had come before her more often than he'd wanted. Hell, he'd barely made it home in time to watch her die.

Joni, I'm so fucking lost without you.

He blinked against the burning in his eyes. After her burial, Adam spent two weeks locked in a Minneapolis motel room trying to dig a hole deep enough to bury his sorrows. He'd only wound up in a drunken stupor, not unlike that wino's over in the corner. Joni had told him to lay off the bottle twenty years ago because his excessive drinking scared her. Her father had been an alcoholic. He'd wanted her to be proud of him and had quit for her.

Until now. In the past couple weeks, there'd been a few nights where he'd come out of his stupor clutching a bottle of scotch to his chest.

A lousy substitute for Joni.

But, if he hadn't been due back at Camp Pendleton in five days, he'd be in that hell-hole motel—or buried six feet under beside Joni. He remembered how close he'd come one night, staring down the barrel of his sidearm.

He shuddered and looked around the still-crowded station. He'd been here for several hours waiting for his next connection. With holiday travel in full swing, Adam had known he wouldn't have managed to hop a seat on a flight in time to get to Pendleton by Monday. Maybe if he'd sobered up sooner. No matter. This weekend, the clientele in bus terminals better suited his foul mood. They wouldn't bother him and he fucking sure wouldn't bother them. The last thing he wanted right now was a chatty companion asking if he was headed home to be with family.

He had no family anymore.

Adam leaned forward and held his aching head in his hands. He sure as hell hoped he'd lose the aftereffects of this binge before he got back on base. The colonel would bust his chops if he saw him like this. He had a lot of eager young Marines looking to him to set the example, too.

He just didn't give a shit about anything or anyone right now and didn't know when he would again.

"Can I get you something to eat?"

Adam looked up, flinching at the throbbing in his temples caused by the fluorescent lighting. *Yeah, blame the lights.* He saw a lanky black man in pimped-out orange pants and a robin's egg blue shirt talking to a teenage girl seated across from him. She must have just sat down a few minutes ago, because he'd have noticed her before with her spiked neon pink hair and the most god-awful amount of makeup around her eyes.

Despite the bravado of her flashy hairstyle and all-black Goth outfit, her wide-eyed gaze darted to the pimp, then away. When he slid into the empty seat next to her, she leaned away from him in small degrees, as if not wanting to offend him by just getting up and moving. When the shithead reached out to touch her hair, she squeezed her blue eyes shut and shrank into the chair.

Little girl lost.

Don't let him scare you.

Adam's attention shifted to the shithead. No, Shithead—with a capital S.

"No, thanks. I already ate," she answered in a high-pitched squeak.

Don't be polite. Tell him to go fuck himself, hon.

"How about a drink? There's a liquor store around the corner." He took her elbow, and she shook him off.

"No!"

Better.

"Thanks, anyway, but I'm waiting for my bus to New York."

Aw, honey, don't go and tell him your plans.

"That where you live?"

"No. I, um, have a job waiting." She looked away.

Shit. A runaway. The girl barely looked fifteen under all that makeup. Adam sat up straighter, ignoring the pounding in his head. If that sorry bastard touched her again, he'd rip off his head and shit down his neck.

Don't forget, you have your own bus to catch. He didn't need to be playing hero and winding up doing jail time for assaulting the scumbag.

The runaway pulled her backpack closer to her chest and tried to scoot to the other side of her chair, but the armrest prevented her escape. Like a shark, the pimp moved in on her—the most vulnerable prey he could find here on the night before Thanksgiving.

Her hand shaking, she unzipped a pouch in the pack and pulled out a book. The cover showed a vampire whose fangs were about to pierce the neck of some half-dressed busty woman who looked like she was about to come. While the runaway pretended to read, she cast nervous glances at Shithead. He just continued to stare at her, trying to intimidate her. Succeeding, too. When the pimp reached out to stroke her hair again, she pulled away.

"Please, leave me alone."

Aw, fuck, don't let him see you cry. The tears welling in her eyes tore Adam's guts out. He'd never been able to see a woman cry. Girls either, for that matter.

The pimp hooked his hand around her arm just above the elbow and tried to force her to her feet. "Come on, baby. Let's get outta here."

Anger boiled over in Adam, a sensation he'd been trying to medicate against for weeks. Clenching his fists, he took a deep, slow breath. He fought the need to pummel Shithead into the ground. Hell, as hung-over as he was, Adam wondered if he'd even be able to take the prick down.

But he'd love the chance to work off some of his anger. Damned if he'd sit and watch that scumbag harass a little girl—or worse. Adam stood and took a step toward them, towering over the man.

"I think the young lady asked you to f—" remembering the young girl, he reminded himself to watch his language, "—get lost."

The pimp looked him up and down. "Fuck off, soldier boy. Get your own ho."

Adam's hands snaked out to lift the skinny little prick out of the seat like a sack of potato chips. Obviously, Shithead had no such filter on his salty language. He threw him across the room and watched with satisfaction as the perv slid until he landed against the ticket counter, far from the girl. Adam stood with legs apart, braced for Shithead to make a move against him.

Come on, punk. He'd love the chance to pummel the prick within an inch of his sorry-assed life. Adam clenched and unclenched his fists his breathing fast and shallow.

Waiting.

When the pimp stood up, he brushed himself off and slunk toward the exit muttering something about evening the odds. Adam turned to look down at the girl. *Damn.* Her hands were shaking so badly, he thought she'd pull her book apart at the seams.

Scared to death.

* * *

Don't puke, Karla. Just don't puke.

Karla Paxton's stomach got all weird and fluttery. Her hands began to shake. Then the soldier turned around and looked down at her. The shaking grew worse. What was the matter with her?

At first, she'd been afraid they were going to fight it out right in front of her, but the creep just got up off the floor and walked away. Well, she couldn't blame him. The tall soldier had huge muscles—and obviously knew how to use them.

The soldier had sprung at that skaggy jerk like a mountain lion on a mouse. She'd never seen anyone move so fast. *Especially someone his age.* He had gray hairs at his temples, although the rest of his hair was dark brown—clipped very short, but not as short as Ian's was now. His eyes were bloodshot and kinda sad looking. He must not have had much sleep lately.

Her gaze took in his wrinkled khaki shirt. If Ian's uniform had been wrinkled like that, he'd have gotten in trouble. She looked at his ring finger. Married. His wife must not be nearby to take care of him. Of course, her mom would have made Ian—and probably her dad—iron his own shirt.

When he sat down where the jerk had been a few minutes ago, she shook even more, despite the fact he didn't get into her personal space like that skag had done. Then the heat coming from his body made her feel warm and her hands stopped shaking after a little while.

"You okay, hon?"

Oh, my God. Did he just call me hon?

Not trusting her voice and not too sure about how safe *he* was, she just nodded. He reminded her of Dr. McNeil on *Chicago Hope*. She and her Mom had watched the series all the time until the show got canceled. Karla thought Mark Harmon looked hot but didn't tell Mom that. Mom was always pushing her to notice the dweebs in her class, but they were so immature.

"Where you headed?"

He pulled her back from her thoughts. "New York City."

"Family there?"

Karla looked away. *What's with all the questions?* "No. I need to get away from family right now."

"Someone expecting you in New York?"

She closed her eyes and nodded. "Sure." *No.*

"When does your bus leave?"

"Six forty-five."

He looked at his watch. "That's another seven hours." He sighed as if that was a problem. What was it to him? She didn't need a babysitter.

Then she glanced around at the men nearby and asked him, "What time does yours leave?"

"Four-thirty."

Damn. Why did that make her feel scared again? Well, he wasn't going to talk her out of going. She could take care of herself.

Yeah, like you did with that pimp.

Suddenly, Karla wasn't so sure she wanted to talk with the soldier anymore. No one was going to talk her out of making this trip. She'd saved money all year, working at a bakery near her home all last summer and babysitting until she had enough for a bus ticket and almost fifteen hundred dollars to spare. When she got to New York, she'd get a job at one of the clubs. Someday, she was going to be a star, recording her own CDs and everything.

But she wouldn't tell him that. He'd just nod and say something condescending like "that's nice," and not believe she could do it at all. She was tired of dreaming. It was time to make her dreams come true.

Her stomach growled. She pulled the book and backpack closer to try and shield his ears from the embarrassing sound.

"Have you had anything to eat lately?"

"Sure." Her stomach called her a liar even more loudly.

He chuckled and his green eyes lit up for the first time. The corners of his eyes crinkled into tiny lines turning loose those funny butterflies in her stomach again.

She must *really* be hungry.

"How long ago?"

She tilted her chin up. "I had pancakes for breakfast."

"Come on," he said, laughing. "Let me buy you some dinner." He stood next to her, as tall as the Sears Tower, but didn't grab at her like the creepy man had. He just waited, as if she had no choice but to stand because he had ordered her to go with him. Well, no way was she going anywhere with a stranger. He was too big. She wouldn't be able to fight him off.

Even if I did want to.

Whoa! What was the matter with her? He looked as old as her uncle, who was forty-three.

"No, thanks. I'm not hungry." She opened her book again, hoping he'd take the hint and go away.

When he did just that, she didn't understand why her heart squeezed tight. She looked up and watched him leave, rounding the ticket counter and heading for the exit. *Gosh, he didn't even say good-bye.* And where was his coat? Didn't he know it was freezing cold out there?

Looking around, she noticed a lot of scary people watching her—mostly men. She guessed women were too smart to catch a bus in the middle of the night. None of these guys had eyes that crinkled when they laughed. They didn't smile like they cared about her. They just leered, especially when they stared at her boobs, making her skin crawl as if a bunch of ants had taken over.

She looked across at where the soldier had been sitting and saw a large duffel bag that must belong to him. One of the boob-leering men started to reach down slowly as if to hide the fact he was about to take the bag.

"Leave it alone!" Karla wasn't sure where that voice came from, and then she realized it was her own. The man stopped dead. Wow! "He's coming back soon and, if you know what's good for you, you'll leave his things where he left them."

When the man stood up and walked across the terminal, Karla began to shake again. Only this time, there were no butterflies. Just a feeling like when she'd had the flu last year.

Would she have to deal with creeps like these all the way to New York? Had she made the right decision to run away? Her parents didn't understand how urgent it was for her to start her career now, rather than wait a few years. They just thought she was a stupid sixteen-year-old.

Wait until you graduate from high school, then you can study music at Loyola.

They'd been telling her that since school started. Didn't they realize she couldn't wait that long? Now was her chance. Her music teacher said she had a gift. She didn't need more schooling. She just needed to find a job where she could sing for people who could discover her talent and offer her a recording contract. If she didn't go now, she'd never get there. She'd never be anybody in the music business.

Her parents would be surprised but sad when they woke up tomorrow and she wasn't in her bed. Her eyes burned. She loved them a lot and didn't want to make them sad, but…

"Here. Eat this."

Karla looked up to find the soldier had returned, holding a fast-food bag toward her. She grinned as she stashed her book in her backpack and took the sack from him. *He came back to me.*

As soon as she opened the sack, the smell of greasy burgers and fries caused her stomach to rumble even louder than before. She was too hungry to let it faze her, after skipping lunch today so she could run to the bank and clean out her account for the trip.

"Thanks." She smiled up at him.

The soldier sat down beside her again. Her face grew hotter as he watched her. When she glanced his way, he just smiled and watched as she pigged out on the food. Gawd, she hadn't realized how hungry she was! Feeling a little guilty, she held out the box of fries and offered him some.

He chuckled. "No. They're all for you."

After she'd finished the second hamburger, he handed her a soda. She drank half of it before letting go of the straw and taking a deep breath. Her tummy filled up as if it might explode.

"That was so good. Thanks." She smiled at him again. He really was just trying to be nice. Regardless, she needed to be leery of strangers, even nice ones. But she'd also have to learn to trust some strangers, if she was going to make it in New York. He seemed like a safe one.

Maybe because her brother was in the Army. Ian would have helped out a scared girl, too, if someone was bothering her.

"So, where's home?"

"Here," she answered, without thinking. "But I'm going to live in New York."

"Why New York?"

"They have the best Goth clubs and recording companies."

"So you like to sing?"

"Better than anything."

"What do you sing?"

"Tarja's music mostly." She could tell by his blank stare he had no idea who Tarja Tarunun was. Well, her parents had no clue either. "She's the lead singer for Nightwish." Still blank. "A metal band from Finland."

He nodded. "I see."

No, you don't. But he was kinda cute for pretending he did. She started to crumple up the bag, but his hand covered hers to stop her. A weird tingling moved up her arm, almost like being shocked with electricity. Her heart banged loud enough for everyone in the noisy station to hear.

"Look inside. There's more."

She reopened the bag and moved the crumpled wrappers and empty fries box aside. Like opening a Christmas present. She had a momentary pang of regret, realizing she wouldn't be home to open presents this year.

Oh-emm-gee, pie! She looked up at him. "Apple or cherry?"

"Cherry."

"How'd you know? That's my favorite!" She reached in and pulled out the box.

He shrugged and smiled. His eyes lit up again. "Lucky guess."

* * *

Adam watched her devour the pie in just a few bites. He thought teenage boys had voracious appetites. How she stayed so skinny was beyond him. Of course, she hadn't eaten all day. Maybe he should have bought her more to eat.

Man, her parents must be worried sick.

He regretted that he and Joni hadn't been able to have children. She'd have been a terrific mom. Tamping down those thoughts, he looked at the little Goth girl. She wore too much black. At least her pink hair gave her some color.

"Isn't your family going to miss you for Thanksgiving?" *Aw, hell.* He'd gone and asked one of those fucking nosy questions he didn't want people asking him.

Watch your language around the kid.

She pulled her lower lip between her teeth. "They'll understand."

Doubtful.

After she'd finished the pie, she put her garbage into the bag, except for the soda, and started to get up to throw it away. Adam took the sack and wadded it even tighter, then lobbed it into the open can at the end of the row. *Score!* First basket he'd made since he'd played in high school.

He reached out his hand to her, "We haven't been introduced. I'm Master Sergeant Adam Montague, U.S. Marine Corps. But you can call me Adam."

She placed her limp hand inside his and they shook. "Karla Paxton…the next Madonna." She giggled. "My friends call me…um, well, Karla's good."

He smiled. So naïve. Innocent. He wondered what her friends called her, but wouldn't pry. God, the kid wore her heart on her sleeve. She wasn't going to last long in New York. He worried about her going there and wished he could wake her up with a dose of reality. He'd seen his share of hell in this world and didn't want her to have to experience it.

"I'm sure you've already lined up a place to stay in New York. Right?"

She dodged his gaze. "Well, I figured I'd check in at the YMCA or a youth hostel or something until I find an apartment."

"Where do you plan to live after that?"

"Soho." Her eyes lit up.

Shit. A dreamer. She'd probably seen the trendy neighborhood in a movie or music video.

"There are lots of clubs in Soho I could get a job at."

"I see you've done some homework." *Not nearly enough, though.* "So, what's an apartment in Soho going for these days?" He had no clue, but figured most places in Manhattan would be out of range for a teenage runaway.

"Well…" she began, and then looked away, furrowing her brow. "It's pretty expensive from what I saw on the Web. I'll probably have to find a roommate or two and share expenses."

His gut twisted at the vision of her falling into the clutches of another predator at the Port Authority terminal. Yeah, they'd give her a place to stay all right. *Fuck.* She needed to go back home and spend Thanksgiving with a family that loved her. She didn't seem to be running away from something so much as running *to* something. She just didn't have the patience to wait around to do a little more growing up.

Of course, he'd run away at sixteen himself. He'd had to go through a lot of hell and trouble before he'd found first the Marines and then Joni, both of whom had straightened his ass out.

At least Karla still has family to be with for the holidays.

"Do you have any brothers or sisters?"

"Just one brother. Ian. He's in the Army National Guard. That's why…" she looked down at her backpack and played with the zipper latch.

"Why what?"

She shook her head and smiled, her face flushing.

"C'mon. Tell me." He grinned. So fucking hard to believe there was such innocence left in the world. Certainly not in his world. Not anymore.

"Well," she looked him in the eye, her blue eyes sparkling. She smiled. "That's why I sat across from you. Your uniform reminded me of Ian's."

Khaki looked about the same for either branch. Thank God. Adam didn't want to think what might have happened if she'd sat somewhere else in the station tonight or he hadn't become aware of her predicament in his post-hangover haze.

She sighed. "I miss him." Adam watched as a single tear trickled down her cheek, leaving a trail of watery mascara.

"Where is he?" *God, don't let him be another fallen hero.* They'd lost too many troops in this damned war. He tried to remember if she'd said "is" or "was" in the Army.

"He finished boot camp two months ago. He can't tell us where he is yet."

Adam didn't realize he'd been holding his breath until he let it out in a whoosh. "He's well-trained, I'm sure. Don't worry about him. He'll do fine." *Like Adam could be sure of anything these days.* But military families had enough to worry about without knowing what was really going on.

"I hope so. Are you a hero, Adam?" She smiled at him just the way Joni had done when she sat at his booth in that restaurant in St. Paul. Her short black waitress skirt had shown off the sexiest legs he'd ever seen. She'd confessed later that his uniform had attracted her, as well. She'd called him her very own hero warrior.

Damn it. I don't need hero-worship responsibility right now.

"I'm nobody's hero, hon." Not even Joni's. He hadn't been able to fight the only battle she'd needed him to win for her. *Aw, hell, don't go there again.*

"Aren't your parents going to be upset when they find out you're gone, too?" He hadn't meant to be so blunt and could kick himself when the light went out of her eyes, but at least he'd wiped the hero worship from her gaze.

"They don't understand."

"I'll bet they understand more than you know."

"No, they…"

She gasped as she looked beyond his shoulder. He looked in the direction of her distressed gaze and saw the pimp had returned with a couple of his thugs.

Adam smiled. *Bring it, boys. I've got nothing left to lose.*

Then he remembered Karla and couldn't let them anywhere near her tonight. He turned back toward her.

"Karla, look at me. Now." When she finally dragged her gaze away from the pimp and his scumbag buddies, Adam said, "Go to the ladies room and stay there until you hear me give you the all-clear. If there's a lock on the outside door, use it. If not, lock yourself in one of the stalls." Her blue eyes opened wider. She swallowed hard but sat frozen. Using his master sergeant's voice, he growled. "Now!" She jumped. Her blank stare focused on his face a second before her hands clutched her backpack, and she ran toward the head.

"Good girl," he said, though she didn't hear him.

With Karla out of harm's way, he could devote his full attention on the rat bastards slowly approaching him. He stood and set his legs, preparing for battle. The one on the far left held a switchblade. The one on the right wore brass knuckles. The pimp just wore a cocky smirk.

You may think you have the upper hand, punk, but I'm going to show you different.

"What's the matter, soldier boy? Haven't been able to get into her pants yet? Mebbe I need to show you some moves."

Okay, perv. Now I'm pissed. And not just because you called me soldier.

"Yeah, I'd like to see that."

His CO would be pissed, too, if one of his master sergeants was tossed in jail, so he waited for one of the punks to make the first move. The few people waiting for buses scattered to the other end of the terminal, out of danger. Except for the passed-out wino, but he wasn't in the way.

Adam didn't have long to wait. The man carrying the knife lunged with his body, his weapon pointed toward Adam's gut. Adam answered with a spinning hook kick to the side of the man's head. The knife flew from his hand as he fell to a heap on the floor.

That should even the odds a little bit.

Movement. Out of his peripheral vision, Adam saw the scumbag with the brass knuckles move, expanding the area Adam needed to defend. The first punch headed straight for Adam's kidney. He swung away to evade contact. His two-week bender must have slowed down his reaction time. But at least the impact of the blow landed on Adam's shoulder blade and not his kidney. The scumbag followed with a bare-knuckled blow to his mouth. Adam groaned at the impact.

Focus, man.

Adam stepped back. He needed room. *Swing. Now!* His roundhouse kick landed squarely against Brass Knuckle's ear. The man reeled sideways until he hit the bank of chairs. He sat down abruptly, the expression on his face one of stunned disbelief. Dazed. The man's eyes glazed over as he curled onto his side.

Breathing hard, Adam turned toward the pimp. *Now, prick, it's just you and me.*

Once again, Adam waited for the man to make the first move. Without his bodyguards, he appeared to have lost his bravado when it would have become a fair fight. The pimp backed away from Adam, toward the ticket counter. Adam stalked him like a puma.

With his peripheral vision, Adam watched two of Chicago's finest enter the building with weapons drawn.

"Hands in the air!"

Adam complied, but apparently they knew their usual suspect and one of the officers had the pimp face down on the floor, hands cuffed behind his back, within fifteen seconds. Adam spoke with the second officer briefly to let him know what had happened. He was grateful they only asked for his name and cell phone number. They could follow up with him later if they needed more information.

But Adam needed to make sure Karla was all right.

* * *

Karla huddled in the bathroom stall. She'd locked the stall door in hopes of protecting herself if those guys had come after her. *Yeah, some protection.* The so-called lock barely kept the door closed for privacy, much less safety.

She couldn't stop shaking. Her stomach clenched and heaved. At least there was a toilet nearby if she got sick. But it was awfully dirty in here.

The sounds of the fight outside brought tears to her eyes. Adam had only wanted to protect her and now he could be killed. All because she was stupid and selfish.

I just wanna go home. Please, God, protect him and help me get back home.

"Hands in the air!" Then silence. No more grunts, crashes, or groans. Her heart pounded. She closed her eyes. The rush of blood pounding in her ears blocked out any other sound. Tears streamed down her face.

Please let him be all right. Oh, God, let Adam be all right.

The sound of the bathroom door creaking open caused her to back up against the tile wall. She held her breath, hoping they would think she'd left. *Stupid. They know you're in here, Kitty. They can see your feet.*

"Karla? Hon, you okay?"

The wind gushed out of her lungs. She'd held her breath so long, she gasped for air several times. *Oh my God. Adam!*

"It's over. You can come out now."

She dropped the backpack, fiddled with the wobbly latch, and opened the stall door. "You're alive!"

"You know, I think I am." He sounded surprised.

Relief was short-lived. *Oh, no!* His beautiful face! "You're bleeding!" Blood trickled from his lip down to his chin.

"I'm fine. How are you doing?"

Me? How can he think about me at a time like this?

Maybe he was out of his mind from where they'd hit him in the head. Remembering freshman health class and all the times she'd watched Mom patch up Ian, Karla rushed to the sink and pulled out a wad of paper towels, wetting them with cold water. She blinked away the tears. She'd caused him this pain. If she hadn't run away...

When she turned, she realized she'd never be able to reach his face.

"Kneel down. I need to clean you up."

He waved her hand away, dismissing her. "I said, I'm fine." His tone hurt her feelings. She was only trying to help. After all, his injuries were all her fault.

She remembered the tone of voice her Mom used to get Ian to obey her when he'd been stubborn, even when he had grown much taller than Mom. Karla pulled herself to her full five-foot-six-inch height and straightened her shoulders. "I. Said. Kneel. Down."

That got his attention. He grinned at her in a funny way. Then he knelt.

Oh. My. God. It worked! He obeyed her!

* * *

Adam's mind flashed back to the one and only time Joni thought she'd play the dominant with him. She was so damned cute in her over-the-knee stiletto boots, wielding a riding crop and wearing a black bustier that pushed her beautiful breasts up to the point of nearly spilling out. Well, he'd let her wear the bustier and boots for a while, but wound up using the crop on *her*.

Ah, Joni. I miss you, my precious subbie. How can I go on—?

"What happened to those guys?"

Adam blinked and saw the pink-haired runaway glancing toward the door with worry, as she pressed the cold paper towels against his lip. He drew a deep breath, beginning to feel the pain radiating through his shoulder. "The police have them all in custody. They won't be bothering anyone for a while."

"Where else did they hurt you?"

"One landed a lucky punch to my shoulder." The paper she pulled away from his lip was now stained with his blood. He could have let those thugs put an end to his misery tonight. Instead, he'd learned he hadn't lost the will to fight for what was right. Karla had needed him. He'd answered the call.

She threw the bloody paper in the trash.

"I'm fine." Rising to his feet, he ached in places he didn't know he had. *Definitely getting too old for this shit.* He wet a towel and handed it to her. "You might want to wipe the mascara off your cheeks. I don't want your parents thinking the worst about what adventures you've had tonight."

"How did you know I wanted to go home?"

Good girl.

"Lucky guess."

Apparently, she'd had enough of the exciting runaway life. If she hadn't come to her senses, though, he'd already planned to take her home anyway, kicking and screaming if he had to.

After she'd cleaned her face, he picked up her backpack and slung it over his shoulder with a grunt. *Shit. Was there any place on his body that didn't hurt?* He'd have a bruise on his shoulder blade tomorrow, too. Even his legs and foot ached from his impact punches.

Bring it. He focused on this new pain. Funny, but the physical pain helped the emotional pain to recede a bit, even if it was only a temporary reprieve.

Adam walked up to the ticket counter and waited as Karla got a refund for the ticket she wouldn't be needing—not for a few years at least. The dispatcher announced his bus departure in five minutes. Oh, well. He'd just have to catch the next one tomorrow. He asked when that would be.

"Nine-fifteen."

"Good. Just a few hours behind schedule."

"No, sir. P.M."

Fuck. He hoped he could make it back to Pendleton on time.

But no fucking way was he letting Karla wander the streets alone tonight to get back home. With that wild pink hair, she was nothing but a trouble magnet.

* * *

Karla didn't know what to say to him, so they rode in silence most of the cab ride home. He had to spend another day in the bus station waiting for his bus, all because of her. Was he mad at her? He just stared out the window, looking at the lights of downtown as the cab made its way to her Lincoln Park neighborhood.

Jeez, she'd sure messed things up tonight. Who was stupid enough to run away the night before Thanksgiving? *Only you, Kitty.* She could hear her friends now when she told them about her night.

But Adam had gotten hurt and now she had to face her parents. They weren't going to be very happy with her.

"Why the long face?" He must have gotten tired of watching the scenery pass by.

"I screwed up big time." She couldn't look at him and remind him of how she'd messed up his plans.

"They might be mad at first, but they'll be glad to have you home safe."

Karla chewed her lip as he scrutinized her. Finally she gained the courage to look over at him. Over and up. *Jeez, he was tall, even sitting down.* The street lights illuminated his face—off, then on, then off again. She noticed the cut on his lip was still bleeding, but just a trickle. She wished she'd brought more paper towels.

Adam had fought to protect her tonight. He could have been killed. There were three of them and they'd had weapons! Instead, he'd saved her from whatever that guy had wanted to do with her. Probably rape her, or make her a hooker, or even sell her to a sex-slave operation. She knew about these things. She watched enough TV.

What she didn't know was how she could ever get Adam to forgive her. Well, she'd be home in a few minutes and probably would never see him again. She needed his forgiveness.

"Adam…I'm sorry I got you mixed up in this. And I'm really sorry you got hurt on account of me."

He was quiet for a little while, his eyes kinda sad again. She hated that she had made him sad this time. Then one side of his mouth tilted up in half a smile. The side that wasn't cut. Her stomach clenched every time she looked at his wound.

"I'd do it all over again to keep you safe. Just promise me you won't run away again. Next time, you might not be so lucky."

The cab stopped. She looked out the window and saw they were in front of her house. The porch light was on and Mom's goofy wreath with all the harvest vegetables on it was displayed on the door. A pumpkin sat on the post at the top of the stairs. The big brick house and hokey decorations never looked so good to her before.

Tears spilled down her cheeks. She probably looked like a raccoon again, but she didn't care. On impulse, she turned around and wrapped her arms around Adam, well as much of him as she could reach around. He had the hardest, widest shoulders she'd ever felt.

After a moment, he returned the gesture. Having his arms around her made her feel safe. She wondered what it would be like if he kissed her.

What the hell, Kitty?

He squeezed her really tight, making it hard to breathe. Or was the lack of air the result of her heart beating so fast? She decided to just let him hug her as tightly as he wanted. Ian had hugged her that way, too, before he'd left home the last time. Adam might not get to hug a girl again for a long, long time. Why, she was being patriotic to let him hug her. Although she had to admit selfishly that she liked being held in his arms and wished they could stay like this forever.

He whispered, "Thank you," and she smiled through her tears. His whiskers scratched, tickling her ear.

"Happy Thanksgiving, Adam."

He pulled away. She wished they could have kept hugging. "Same to you, Karla."

He was kinda cute when he smiled that way, without the sad eyes. "Oh, no! Where will you eat turkey today?"

"No problem. I usually have ham on Thanksgiving anyway…" Then his smile disappeared. *Double damn.* She'd made him think sad thoughts again.

"It's probably best if I stay inside the taxi, in case your parents are watching. You have enough problems without having to explain what you're doing hanging out with an old Marine." He smiled. "But I'll wait here until you get inside." Then he grew serious again. "Just promise me you won't run away again."

She nodded. "I promise."

Karla looked down at her backpack. Her throat hurt too much to speak, but, as she opened the door, she turned back and cleared it enough to whisper, "Promise me you'll come home safe."

"I'll do my best, honey." He looked away and repeated in a whisper, "I'll do my best."

Suddenly, Adam's door whipped open and two hands reached inside to grab Adam by the shirt.

"What the hell do you think you're doing with my sixteen-year-old daughter, you pervert!"

Karla leaned over to protect him, but Adam pushed her out of harm's way, as if worried she might be hit by accident.

"Daddy, no! Don't hurt him!"

What was she worried about Adam for? He could have decked Daddy with one hand tied behind his back. Maybe two. But Adam just let himself be pulled from the cab without putting up a fight. Karla scrambled across the seat and exited behind him. Adam stood with his hands at his sides. She moved to wedge herself between him and her dad.

Her Mom came running around the front of the cab and pulled her back. "Karla, get in the house!"

But Karla needed to get to Adam, if he wouldn't defend himself. She'd never seen Daddy so angry.

"Not now, Mom." She brushed her mom's hand aside and went to where Daddy had Adam backed up against the trunk of the cab. Oh, God, he had his fist raised, ready to slam into Adam's already injured face.

"Daddy, don't!" Karla grabbed onto his arm and he stopped to look down at her. "He didn't do anything to me. He rescued me. Twice!"

Daddy breathed really hard. Definitely not in as good a shape as Adam. And yet Adam hadn't even put up his arms in defense. Why not?

Daddy turned to Adam, "Maybe you'd better explain yourself."

Adam opened his mouth, but he'd downplay everything. He was way too modest. "Daddy, he fought off three jerks who wanted to hurt me. He bought me dinner. He's a good man and if you hurt him, I'm going to run away again and I'll never come back!"

Adam looked down at her and she thought she heard him growl. She tried to ignore him, but he wasn't happy with her threat.

"Okay. I'm not going to run away." Both Adam and her father relaxed a little bit. "But on account of me, he missed his bus."

Daddy let go of Adam's now even more wrinkled shirt and stepped back. "You *protected* my Karla?"

"I just did what anyone would do."

"Don't listen to him, Daddy. There were *three* of them! And they had weapons. Adam was unarmed."

Adam glanced away and down at the ground.

"I don't want him to spend Thanksgiving sitting in the bus terminal until tomorrow night. Adam needs a place to stay tonight."

Oh, that got Adam to look at her again! But he didn't look very happy about it.

"Is that true? Do you need a place to stay?"

"No, sir. I'm fine. I've slept in worse places than a bus station."

Karla's mom wrapped her arm around Karla, but her words were directed at Adam. "Nonsense. If our son was in your situation, we'd hope someone would…" Mom's voice always broke when she talked about Ian now. "We'd be honored if you'd come inside."

"He can sleep in Ian's room," Karla offered.

"No, I don't want to impose."

Daddy looked from her to Adam. "If what Karla says is true, it's the least we can do for you for bringing our little girl home." He reached out his hand to Adam. "I'm Carl Paxton. Sorry about roughing you up."

Adam looked down at Daddy's hand for a few seconds.

Go on. Shake it.

When Adam finally reached out, she knew he'd be staying. She let out the breath she'd been holding.

"Adam Montague. Nice to meet you, sir."

"He's a master sergeant, Daddy. In the Marines!"

She wasn't sure what rank that was, but it sure sounded important. When Adam looked at her like he didn't need her help, she just smiled. She didn't have to say goodbye to Adam yet.

* * *

Adam let go of Paxton's hand. The man had a firm grip and an honest face. Karla's parents seemed like good people. What the hell was she thinking, running away from a nice safe home like this? If she were his daughter, he'd tan her hide.

Her dad looked down at Adam's mouth. "You're bleeding."

"It's nothing." Adam licked at his wound. He tasted the iron on his tongue.

"His shoulder's injured, too, Mom."

Karla's mom let her go and came at him like a mother hen. "I'm sorry. Let's get you in out of this cold. Where's your coat?"

Ahem.

Adam turned to see the taxi driver. *Shit.* He'd forgotten about him. He reached for his wallet, but Karla's dad put a hand on his arm. "Go with the girls. I'll take care of this. You've paid enough already." The man pulled several bills from his wallet.

Outmaneuvered and too tired to argue, Adam reached inside the back door of the taxi and pulled out his seabag, just as Karla leaned in the other side to get her things. She looked across the back seat at him and smiled.

Damn. He could see how she wrapped her parents around her little finger. Hell, he had to admit her smile worked on him, as well. He probably wouldn't have been able to tan her hide, either, even when she did deserve it. Her enthusiasm and innocence were sweet. He grinned back at her.

Before he had a moment to think, Karla and her mother flanked him and ushered him up the sidewalk. He looked up the steep stairs to the porch, noticing the pumpkin. Joni would have decorated their porch the same way. *Fuck.* He hadn't thought about his wife much since he'd gotten caught up in Karla's troubles.

God, Joni, I'm so sorry.

Guilt twisted his gut. In an instant, a deluge of two months of painful memories brought his mood back down to where it ought to be. What the fuck was he doing bringing his foul mood into this family's home on Thanksgiving Day? Just what the hell did he have to be thankful for? He turned around to stop the taxi, just as it pulled away from the curb.

What a clusterfuck.

With reluctance, he turned and began climbing the stairs to the porch, feeling each of the dozen steps in his shaky legs.

Paxton caught up with them and opened the door. To his wife, he said, "I'll make some calls to Karla's friends' parents and let them know she's home safe."

Inside, the house was warm. Smelled like cinnamon. Karla's mother led him to the kitchen, where she sat him down on a chair at the table for six. Several pies were lined up on the counter.

"Off with the shirt."

Adam hoped his expression conveyed to her that no fucking way was he removing his shirt. "I'm fine, ma'am."

She just laughed. "Don't go there with me. I'm a nurse. I've seen more naked bodies than you can shake a fist at. Off." Her fingers motioned for him to follow her order. "I am going to take a look at that shoulder, one way or another." When he still refused to move, she added, "Now!" She'd have made a great drill instructor.

Adam looked over at Karla, who seemed to be waiting for a show to begin, her eyes wide open, chin propped on her palm at the island in the middle of the room. No fucking way was he going to let her see his back. He did a half turn in the chair.

Mrs. Paxton seemed to notice his discomfort. "Karla, run up to the bathroom and get me the new first-aid kit. There are some things missing from this one."

He saw the disappointment in the girl's eyes, but she did as she was told. She seemed like a good kid. He unbuttoned his shirt and pulled it off. God, the muscles in both shoulders ached, not just the bruised one. He was getting soft in his old age.

When Karla's mother moved around to check the damage from the back, he cringed when he heard her gasp. "You've seen your share, haven't you?"

"Mostly superficial, ma'am. I survived." Knowing she had a son in harm's way, he didn't add that two of his men hadn't made it out of that ambush alive. She traced a finger over the spot where he had his tattoo, but he let her draw her own conclusions. He wouldn't talk about it.

Adam recalled the ambush outside Kandahar that had taken out half his recon unit earlier this year as they'd tried to establish a foothold in the area. Two men dead, seven injured. Fucked-up mission. His shrapnel scars were reminders of his failure—his inability to bring all his men home. He prayed he'd never have a repeat of that day during his remaining time in the Corps.

Thankfully, she didn't ask. "I appreciate this, ma'am, but it's just a little bruise."

"Please, call me Jenny. And that bruise is going to be more than little. What did you run into?"

"Brass knuckles. Didn't duck fast enough. Getting old."

She scoffed. "From what Karla said, you fought off three guys. I just hope they look a lot worse than you do."

"Yes, ma'am. Two of them do, anyway. The third ran." He needed to assure her that Karla hadn't been harmed or in danger. "I didn't let them near your daughter. She was out of there before any punches flew."

She stepped back to face him. "Adam, we can't thank you enough. When we found Karla's bed empty an hour or so ago—"

Adam heard the catch in her voice and looked up to see tears swimming in her eyes. His gut twisted. He could well imagine her fears.

"We panicked," she finished on a whisper. "The police wouldn't even look for her for twenty-four hours. It's not much, but please know we're forever in your debt."

"Sorry, Mom. It took me a while to—"

Adam looked toward the entrance to the kitchen to find that Karla had come to a dead stop, her jaw hanging open. Her eyes homed in on his naked chest. *Shit, he'd embarrassed her.* He reached for his shirt.

"Come on, girl. Don't just stand there. Get over here." When Karla remained stock-still, Jenny barked, "Now!" Then, to Adam, she stilled his movement to put his shirt back on. "Don't you dare! She's seen her brother's bare chest a million times."

* * *

Yeah, but Ian's chest didn't look anything like Adam's.

Karla crossed the room, holding the kit out to her mom, but not taking her eyes off Adam's muscular pecs and biceps. His skin was evenly tanned, not a single hair anywhere on his chest. She had a whole new appreciation for the anatomy lessons she'd had in health class, because they allowed her a chance to label all of his beautiful parts. Standing so close, the heat radiating from his body became even more noticeable than it had been at the bus station.

Or was it just that her face was overheating?

Her mother worked to open the latch of the new kit while Karla continued her observations. His pectoral muscles bulged, hard-looking nipples protruding from dark brown areolas. Karla just stared at his nips. No, not the scientific term, but that's what her friends called them when they ogled the juvenile boys in their gym class. None of those boys had nips that looked like stone, though. Nothing like Adam's.

She itched to reach out and touch one to see if it was as hard as it looked, but her mother would have made her leave the room if she did that. She wouldn't risk that happening, so she clenched her fists at her sides.

Her gaze went lower. His abdominals were…well… *Oh, my!* So that's why they called them a six-pack. She'd probably be able to bounce a quarter off them if he were lying down. There was this valley between his abs she wanted to lick.

Oh, no, Kitty. Don't think about licking him!

Too late. Her face grew even warmer. What would Adam be like as a lover? Gentle, tender, forceful? Not that she had any experience with lovers or sex. None of the boys her age attracted her; she'd always been more interested in her music career than in dating. But she'd watched lots of love scenes in the movies and on TV. Adam truly had the most beautiful upper body she'd ever seen in her whole life—real or make believe.

"Open this and hand me one of the swabs."

Her mother handed her a cellophane package with two Q-tips inside. With great reluctance, Karla tore her gaze away from Adam's chest, then, realizing how important this was, went to work with a new sense of purpose. If only her hands would quit shaking. She wanted to do this right. What if she didn't and he got an infection and a fever and maybe even died, all because his cut lip wasn't cleaned properly?

Without touching the cotton ends, she handed one swab to her mom and watched her dip it in a bottle of alcohol. Experience had taught her that was going to hurt like a mother.

"This is going to sting," Mom warned.

You'd better believe it. Her mom rubbed the wet cotton over his split lip, holding his chin to keep him steady. Karla wished she could touch him like that. He closed his eyes, but didn't make a sound. Her stomach muscles clenched, as if she were experiencing the pain for him.

"There." Her mom laid the Q-tip on the paper towel she'd placed on the table. "Now let's get some antibiotic ointment on that lip."

Karla saw the tinge of pink on the Q-tip. Adam's blood. Tears sprang to her eyes. He'd been hurt because of her stupidity. She wished there was something more she could do to help him. She certainly couldn't kiss his lip and make it better. Although the thought caused her stomach to flutter again, like it was filled with a flock of butterflies trying to escape. She flushed in embarrassment.

What would her friends think when they heard about her adventures with an older man tonight? And a Marine. *Oh, my!* They would be so jealous, especially when she told them he looked like Mark Harmon. Only Adam acted much more mature and noble than the Dr. McNeil character did.

Her mom brushed her thumb across the red marks on Adam's shoulder. "Not much I can do for the bruising, but I don't think there's a hematoma."

Karla's attention went to the long, thin mark where he'd been jabbed by something with evenly spaced points. Then she remembered that one of the guys he had fought with had been wearing brass knuckles. Her knees buckled at the thought of them tearing into Adam's shoulder.

"Whoa, hon!" Adam reached out and grabbed her elbows to hold her steady. "Not too fond of the sight of blood?"

Her mom scrutinized her, but Karla couldn't take her eyes off Adam. Where he held her arms, a tingle of electricity zinged up to her shoulders and neck, then down to her... *Oh, my!*

"What's the matter with you, Karla?" Mom asked. "You've seen plenty of blood. Ian was always getting patched up."

"I'm okay," she whispered, because of the frog lodged in her throat. He smiled at her and tears slid down her cheeks. He'd taken that hit on his shoulder for her. She ached to press her lips against it, the way her mother had kissed her boo-boos as a kid. Usually, the pain magically went away. She wanted to take Adam's pain away.

He reached up and wiped the tears away from her face with his thumbs. She caught her breath, then totally forgot to breathe for a moment.

"I'm okay, hon. Believe me, this is nothing."

"You should see—"

Adam reached out and placed a hand on Mom's arm. They exchanged a look, as if they shared a secret Karla wasn't in on. Mom nodded. The green-eyed monster of jealousy reared up inside Karla for the first time in her life.

More tears welled in her eyes. Frustration at not being able to touch him, to comfort him, or even to get him to notice her as a woman, gnawed at her. She was just a kid in his eyes. If she touched him the way she wanted, he'd think she was a freak.

But that just made her want to touch him even more.

* * *

Adam tried to stay out of everyone's way on Thanksgiving morning. He'd managed to catch a few hours of dreamless sleep, which was more than he could say for the last few months. Then Karla's relatives had started arriving—grandmother, uncle, aunt, cousins. Adam hadn't been in a huge family gathering for Thanksgiving since he was a kid, and he was feeling a bit claustrophobic.

Her family meant well, but he counted the hours until he could get on that bus tonight and start making his way home to Pendleton. He grabbed his jacket and slipped out the front door, hoping no one would notice. He needed some air. The jacket did little to keep the wind out, but compared with the crowded, overheated house, the fresh air invigorated him. After he'd walked a few blocks, the frigid wind began to seep into his still-aching bones and muscles. He'd known Chicago was windy, but when the gusts were fifty miles an hour and the air temperature barely twenty, it was goddamned frigid.

He didn't know where he was headed until he arrived. Standing on the shore of Lake Michigan, the wind blowing ice crystals from the lake onto his face, Adam braced himself against the gusts. Gray clouds hovered over the surface, much like they did over Lake Superior.

He and Joni hadn't had much money when they'd married and all he could afford for a honeymoon was an off-season cabin rental at a park along Superior. It had been colder than a mother that November, too. Not that they'd wanted to venture out much. They were too busy exploring their newfound mutual interest in sexual bondage and each other's bodies.

Adam got hard picturing Joni tied spread-eagle and blindfolded as he tortured her tits with ice and a feather. She had the cutest damned giggle. He'd tried to use his stern Dom voice, but knowing she couldn't see him, he'd grinned every time she let out her little-girl giggle.

Damned wind made his eyes water. He reached up to wipe the moisture from them, then his mind returned to the cabin. After two days of nothing but sex and sleep—maybe a little food, he couldn't remember—they'd bundled up and ventured out to walk along the icy shore, down to the lighthouse.

Joni was curious about everything and they'd probably spent two hours talking with the lighthouse keeper. Adam accused her later of shirking her wifely duties by delaying their return to the cabin. Her screams of outrage as he reddened her ass during her first erotic spanking had turned them both on so much, they didn't leave the cabin again the rest of the week.

Cold wetness on his cheeks brought him back to the present. He wasn't sure if the dampness was brought on from the wind or his sorrow. He didn't care. No one was around to see him cry. For the first time since learning he was going to lose her, he just let himself feel the gaping hole in his chest where his heart had once been.

Joni had given his heart a safe harbor all these years, but now it was time for him to haul anchor, reset his compass, and shove off into uncharted waters.

"Safe journey, little subbie. We'll meet up again someday."

The wind whipped the words away from him. He hoped they made their way to his dear, sweet Joni, wherever she was. He didn't dwell much on spiritual matters, but believed in his heart he and Joni would reunite one day.

Adam drew a ragged breath and pressed his thumb and forefinger against the bridge of his nose. He was ready to resume his duties at Pendleton or wherever they sent him. While he'd never forget Joni, he'd be able to compartmentalize the memories and pain so they didn't take his focus off the mission at hand. He would never put his unit in jeopardy because he couldn't let go of the past. Until this moment, though, he hadn't been sure he would be able to do that.

A sense of peace came over him. He almost thought Joni's lips had brushed his cheek, the way she did before they curled up with each other and fell asleep. Then he became aware of the icy pellets pounding his face as a lake-effect squall whipped up. He turned around to make his way back to Karla's house.

Standing a few feet away from him, as if on guard duty, shivering inside her coat, stood Karla.

"What the f…heck are you doing out here?"

Her teeth chattered as she tried to answer. He took off his jacket and put it on her to give her another layer of warmth, then wrapped his arm around her, hoping to infuse some heat into her thin body. "Let's get you back home."

"N-n-no, Adam. I have to tell you something."

Adam ignored her and pulled her along toward the house. "We'll talk when we get you out of this squall." She tried to dig in her heels, but he'd have none of it. Damned fool kid needed a caretaker.

He'd been dreading going back into the chaos at her house, but now he just wanted to get her inside as quickly as possible. She'd catch pneumonia out here. They got as far as her front door when Karla wedged her toe against the door and turned to look up at him.

"Wait! Adam, there's something you need to know, and I can't say this inside the house."

Adam tried to block as much of the wind from hitting her shivering frame as he could, but her black-and-pink hair lashed across her face. He reached out and tucked the wild strands behind her left ear because they distracted him from the conversation that seemed so important to her. What in the hell could she possibly have to say that couldn't be said inside?

Karla splayed her gloved hand on his chest, over his wounded heart, and looked up at him with those big sparkling blue eyes surrounded by that god-awful makeup and pink hair. She searched his eyes for a long moment, he didn't know for what.

The scar at the back of his neck set off warning bells—always a sign he wasn't going to want to deal with whatever was incoming. *Fuck.* He hoped she wasn't about to say what he thought she was getting ready to lay on him.

"Adam, I n-n-n-know you have a wife and y-y-y-you think I'm just a kid, but I want to t-t-tell you that...I l-l-love you."

Double fucking damn. He'd need a mine-sweeper to navigate these waters. *Joni, where are you when I need you?* She'd know how to deal with a sixteen-year-old's crush. She'd been surrounded by teenage girls at the Catholic school where she'd taught until last spring. *Help me out here, baby.*

"Hon, I love you, too." *Crap.* That didn't come out sounding right, but surely she'd know what he meant.

When her eyes lit up and she pursed her lips as if expecting him to kiss her, he turned his rudder hard to starboard. She'd definitely taken his words the wrong way.

"Like a *father*, Karla. Hell, I'm old enough to *be* your father."

When tears welled up in her eyes and spilled down her cheeks, his gut turned to mush. He always came undone when a woman cried. But, hell, Karla was just a kid. Why did her tears rip him apart even more? How in the hell had he let this happen?

Now wait a minute there. He'd never given her any indication he wanted to be anything other than a guardian to keep her out of trouble. Fuck, he didn't know anything about teenage girls.

"Look, hon..." *Quit calling her hon, you fucking asshole.* "Look, Karla, I'm an old man. Your life is just starting. I'm sure there are lots of boys who'd—"

"But they're so immature. All they talk about is sports. I don't have anything in common with them."

What the hell did she have in common with an old, worn-out Marine? God, he wished they made tactical maps for situations like these. He was fucking clueless how to fend off this attack.

"Nothing wrong with sports." *Oh, that's profound, jarhead.* Damn. He liked this kid a lot. Didn't want to hurt her for anything. But he wasn't a perv.

Just tell it like it is, man. You've never had any problem doing that before. What's different this time?

She's a kid! And a girl! I don't want to hurt her.

"Look, Karla. I like you a lot, but I don't feel that way about you." When the light left her eyes, he felt like a fucking heel. While the words needed to be said, if it were physically possible, he'd have given himself a good roundhouse kick in the ass for whatever the hell he'd done to make her think he'd welcome this heartfelt declaration. How could he make it not seem like a rejection because there was something wrong with her? She'd make a fine girlfriend and wife for some guy someday. Just not him.

"I still love my wife." *Yeah, that's good. Let Joni pull your prick out of the fire.* He didn't have to tell her his wife was dead. Besides, he did love Joni, in his own way. "You have some growing up to do. I'm sure you'll meet someone one day who can love and respect you the way you should be loved."

Karla tore herself away, opened the door, and ran inside.

He laid his forehead against the cold doorframe. What a fucking mess he'd made of that. Maybe it was a good thing he and Joni hadn't had kids. He'd make a lousy father.

That fucking bus couldn't get here soon enough.

* * *

Karla tried to eat all the food on her plate, but the lump in her throat—and Adam sitting across the table from her—made that impossible.

"Good news, Adam," Daddy said, beaming. "I've managed to get you a ticket on a red-eye flight out tomorrow night. Direct to San Diego. You'll be back on base in hours rather than days."

Karla saw the stricken look on Adam's face. He must be horrified to think of being stuck with her another whole day. Her eyes brimmed with tears and she hung her head down, hoping they'd fall right into her burgundy cloth napkin without leaving an embarrassing trail.

"That's really not necessary, sir. I don't mind—"

"It's done. The least we can do after all you've done for us."

Luckily, Daddy didn't add to her embarrassment by spelling out to everyone at the table why they owed this Marine something. But she and her parents knew. All her fault. A few hours ago, she'd have been thrilled to know Adam would be with her another day. Now she didn't even know what to say or do with him.

Karla had teetered on the verge of crying since Adam had rejected her on the front porch. Of course, she didn't want to break up his happy marriage or anything. But he could have at least given her a little kiss to remember him by. She'd never find anyone like him to love ever again.

Adam continued to avoid looking at her. He didn't eat much either, not even the casserole she'd made for him. Another rejection. More tears.

Grandma began sharing stories about her latest cruise and Karla zoned out until she heard Adam's name.

"Adam, have you ever been to Mexico?" Grandma asked.

"Yes, ma'am. My wife and I went to Cabo San Lucas on a second honeymoon about ten years ago." He cleared his throat. "Beautiful place."

Well, even if he wasn't happily married, he wouldn't wait for you to grow up, Kitty. No, he was so handsome, he could have any woman he wanted. Besides, he didn't even know she existed. Unable to swallow past the lump in her throat, she put her useless fork down. She hoped this nightmare dinner would end soon so she could escape to her room and have a good cry.

Why had she so embarrassed herself on the porch? She needed to make conversation before her Mom hauled her into the kitchen for having such bad manners. Karla looked up at Adam. "I'll bet you miss her a lot."

His eyes got sad again and he looked down at his plate. "More than you'll ever know."

Yeah, he loved her. She was a very lucky lady. As if to keep from having to say more, he took a small bite of her casserole. She smiled.

Mom said, "Karla, your broccoli casserole gets better every year."

Adam looked up at her as he chewed, smiling across the table. "Best I've ever had."

Karla's tummy squeezed tight and she smiled back.

After the dinner plates had been cleared, mom pulled out the Quiddler cards and dictionaries and everyone at the table played. Adam was pretty good at it, but Karla beat him in the last round with the word "domination." That was the best word she'd ever gotten in the stupid game!

The next day went by in a blur, but Karla could never get Adam alone to apologize for her stupid scene. By the time she stood in the airport terminal saying goodbye, tears spilled down her cheeks. Her father already had said goodbye and thanked him, then had to go to his office at the other end of the terminal to check on some emergency.

Saying goodbye wasn't easy. "Adam, please forget what I said on the porch. I was just being a stupid teenager. But I'll never forget you. Thanks for rescuing me."

He shuffled his feet, then seemed to decide something and met her gaze. "Karla, I know you aren't going to understand this, but you're the one who saved *my* life. I'd lost sight of what I needed...what was important to me since...well..."

She thought she saw a glint of tears in his eyes, but none fell. He looked down at the floor again. After a moment, he continued. His voice sounded like he'd swallowed sandpaper. When he looked into her eyes again, those freaky butterflies returned to her stomach.

"If you hadn't shown up in that bus station two nights ago, Karla, I don't know what… I was heading back to combat without the fire in my belly. It's my job to make sure my unit survives its next missions and I…" He rubbed the back of his neck.

She wished she could give him a neck rub to calm him. He seemed so upset. Then his words registered. *Oh, no!* He was going to Afghanistan or Iraq. She was sure of it. That's all she heard in the news now. Ian might be going to one of those places, too. They both might get killed!

Tears spilled down her cheeks again. Good thing she didn't wear mascara. She'd known she was going to cry when she said goodbye, just not how much. Suddenly, it was important that she not lose track of Adam. His wife and family would write to him, but Karla needed to know he was okay, too. He'd become such an important part of her life in the last two days.

"Can I—?" She cleared the frog from her throat. "Can I write to you, Adam?"

His gaze met hers and she thought he was going to say no, then he smiled—another really sad one. She bet he didn't think she'd actually follow through, because she'd acted like such a selfish teenager ever since he'd met her. But she would. Every day.

Well, at least once a week.

"I'd like that."

Before he changed his mind, she reached into her purse and pulled out a treble-clef-shaped writing pad. She wrote his name—well, he had to spell his last name for her—and then his APO address. Ian had an APO, too.

Well, duh, Kitty. All soldiers have those.

She vowed to herself she would also bake goodies to send them both. "Do you like brownies?"

He got that look where he wasn't thinking about her anymore. Then he smiled. "Yeah. With peanut butter."

Karla giggled. She'd never made that kind before, but she'd learn. For her Adam. Maybe she could send him an MP3 recording of her singing. Her music teacher wanted to record demo tapes for her and another student to send to college admissions offices.

"Why don't you write down your address for me, too?" She looked up. He wanted to write to her? "I probably won't get around to writing very often, but I'll write when I can."

Karla scribbled down her address on the next sheet and tore it off to hand to him. She wished Adam would hug her, but he'd been very careful not to get anywhere near her since she'd made a fool of herself on the porch.

But what if she never saw him again?

Karla wouldn't risk never getting to place her arms around him again. She closed the space between them and slipped her arms around his narrow waist. His sides were like steel bands and his heart beat fast against her cheek.

"I'm going to miss you, Adam."

Just when she was about to let go, thinking he wouldn't hug her back, his arms surrounded her and he pulled her into his heated warmth.

Safe. Protected.

Adam. He'd always be her hero.

Section Two: Damián

Prequel to Damián's Story, Nobody's Perfect

September 2003, La Jolla, California

"**H**ey, boy!"

Damián Orlando looked up from bussing one of the isolated booths along the wall of the hotel restaurant to see some rich-looking dude at the booth in the corner waving at him. He did a slow burn at the condescending way the man in the white suit addressed him, but smiled as he'd been trained to do.

In the booth next to the man sat the most gorgeous blonde he'd ever seen. She reminded him of his big sister's Malibu Barbie doll—the one he'd decapitated accidentally while they were playing dragons and princesses as kids.

Her pale skin looked fragile enough to break, like his grandmother's china. She pursed her cherry-red lips. He'd enjoy kissing the lipstick off her full, sexy mouth. The thought of those lips sucking his…

"When you're finished ogling my…date, would you mind asking our server to bring us the top-shelf wine list?"

The Barbie doll looked up at him and he saw the apology in her sad blue eyes. What did she have to apologize for? Her date was the jerk-off.

He looked at the man and clenched his fists. *Fucking jerk-off*. Damián smiled. "Yes…sir."

What was she doing with such an asshole? He shook his head. Understanding crazy rich people wasn't what he got paid for. He turned away from their table, happy to hide his hard-on.

"You didn't have to encourage him, slut." The man's hate-filled whisper carried across the nearly empty room.

"I didn't…"

"Just shut up. If you mess up this deal for us…"

Damián felt himself doing another slow burn. What the hell gave the jerk the right to talk to her that way? And why didn't she tell him to fuck himself up the ass? Hell, Damián had needed no encouragement to stare at her. She was freakin' perfection. But she'd kept her eyes down the entire time he'd ogled her, until right at the end anyway.

Stay out of it, man. You can't get into trouble again.

Damián went out to the patio and found their server schmoozing with some exec from a modeling agency. They'd approached Damián to model for them, too, but he wasn't interested. All of the other restaurant employees were looking for a way out of poverty. He was just happy to have a steady job with predictable hours—and to be out of juvie.

He glanced out at the ocean and breathed in the salty air. The cool evening breeze felt good against his skin. He'd been cooped up in juvie so long, he'd thought his soul had rotted. Now he spent his days cooped up in the restaurant. He was long overdue for a ride up the coast. Laguna Beach always settled him when he got restless.

After getting the server back inside, Damián followed. The dark wood paneling closed in around him again in an instant. While the white tablecloths, fresh flowers, and glowing hurricane lamps on each of the tables and booths helped to lighten the room some, he couldn't figure out why someone would choose to dine inside on such a beautiful Southern California evening. He'd be out on the patio waiting for the sun to set—if he could afford to eat in a place like this.

Damián picked up the dish bin and glanced at the Barbie doll. A tear ran down her jaw as she fiddled with her fork. His gut churned as he turned toward the kitchen. That man had made her cry. His sister, Rosa, had been verbally humiliated that way by her now ex-husband. Then the man had become violent.

Rosa had come close to being put in her grave before Damián forced her to move into his apartment. When Julio had come after her, Damián punched his teeth out—and earned himself two years in juvie for his effort. But he'd do it again. No woman should ever be disrespected like that.

"Keep a low profile and mind your own business, if you know what's good for you." The words of his social worker focused his mind where it belonged. He walked into the kitchen and loaded the dirty dishes into the racks. He sure as hell wasn't going to interfere for a total stranger. Even if her shithead date deserved to be pummeled for his remarks, he knew the man's money would

get Damián's ass locked up so fast, his head would spin. At nineteen, the key would be conveniently thrown down a sewer hole this time.

No way could he afford to get fired, either. He'd yet to make next month's rent money. So, he'd just avoid the jerk-off and his perfect-but-miserable date. He hoped she'd wise up soon and dump him before it was too late. But that wasn't his concern. Just bus the tables.

Rich people sure were fucked up. Damián had grown up in a tiny ranch-style tenant house with too many mouths to feed and too little money. Growing up, he'd thought being rich would solve all their problems. From what he could tell, though, money just brought on a whole new set of them.

He looked at the clock. Three more hours before he got off work. He decided he needed to ride his Harley up the coast. The beach at Laguna called to him. Away from everyone. Just him. The ocean. And his cave.

* * *

Savannah Gentry tried to swallow past the lump closing up her throat. Despite nearly a year of Master's pimping out her body to his high-class business clients and her trying to learn to dissociate from scenes with these men, there were too many to predict their behavior the way she could her Master's.

For the majority of her cognizant life, He had owned and controlled her—mind, body, and spirit. As far as she could recall—and large parts of her life already had been blocked out of her memory—the rape and abuse began soon after her mother left. She was eight. She'd prayed every night for months for Maman to come back and rescue her, but she never heard from her again.

At first, she'd been more angry at her mother than her father. How could she leave her there with such a monster? Although, Savannah didn't remember him being a monster until that night…

She shuddered. Escape had never been an option. Becoming self-sufficient was a pipe dream. Her Master had too much power in Southern California for her to be able to escape Him. And He'd threatened to sell her to a pimp on the streets if she disobeyed. A shiver of fear coursed down her spine. At least with Him she was being tortured by a higher class of clientele, and, when she wasn't being pimped out, she was fed, clothed, even schooled in a fashion.

She watched the busboy clear another table. She felt badly about the way Lyle, her Master's puppet, had treated him. Of course, she had been intensely aware of the busboy's eyes on her. How could she not? He reminded her of the hero in her fantasies, Orlando Bloom. Just yesterday, in her Master's screening room, she'd seen a preview for Orlando's upcoming movie, *Pirates of the Caribbean*. Last night, she'd dreamed he had swung into her bedroom window on a rope tied to who knows what and whisked her away from her private Hell.

Was that why she couldn't take her eyes off the Orlando look-alike across the room? The busboy's shoulder-length hair was pulled into a queue at the nape of his neck. He sported the same goatee and mustache Bloom had had in the movie trailer.

Savannah wondered what his mustache would feel like against her face. Her lips. Her breasts. She was surprised to find she wasn't fantasizing about Orlando now, but the busboy. The way he had clenched and unclenched his fists as Lyle tried to humiliate him, he looked as if he were ready to punch Lyle in his asinine mouth for his ridiculous accusations.

Someone willing to defend her honor. *Well, that would be a first.*

Out of the corner of her eye, Savannah watched as the busboy lifted the heavy bin of dishes. The muscles in his forearms corded and his biceps bulged under his polo shirt. Judging by the front of his pants, they weren't the only things bulging.

And there the fantasy ended. Typical man.

From the first time her father had raped her, sex had equaled pain, control, torture—until she'd turned eighteen and He'd lost interest in raping her. But she hadn't gained her freedom. Instead, He and His junior partner, Lyle, had prostituted her as their pain slut for the past year, using her well-trained masochist's body to solicit new clients for their firm.

For whatever twisted reason, her father had prohibited clients—or even Lyle, for that matter—from penetrating her. They could torture her as much as they pleased. But no intercourse. *Thank God for small favors.*

Why anyone would engage willingly in the sex act was beyond her. She preferred her romantic dream lover, Bloom, over the busboy or any real man. The busboy was like all the rest, ogling her body and becoming aroused without knowing anything about her other than what she looked like. He didn't care if she had a brain in her head. No different from all the men she'd ever known.

All were sadists, getting off on a woman's pain. Ah, speaking of which, into the restaurant just walked her next two clients. Lyle puffed himself up.

"Here they come."

Savannah quaked to her core to think how much Lyle reminded her of her father. She wouldn't be surprised if Lyle was slated to inherit her body after her father died. No, there wouldn't be a "slave clause" in His public will. But she was certain her father would never release His hold over her, even from beyond the grave.

Her lungs clenched, squeezing out the meager amount of air in them. Some days, she actually welcomed death over continuing to exist this way. Ah, the ultimate betrayal of the obedient slave—to execute the body the Master thought He owned. Her only regret would be that she wouldn't have the pleasure of seeing the look on her father's and Lyle's faces as she reclaimed control over her body.

Razor blades? No, too messy. Pills? She'd read that as few as a dozen Tylenol would shut down a person's liver. What would a whole bottle do? Would death be fast? Painless? Well, it couldn't hurt more than what she'd experienced the last eleven years. Yes, when she got home tonight, she would put an end to this miserable existence.

A sense of peace came over her. The time for the ultimate release had come. She smiled, her lips quivering.

"That's good, baby. Smile. You know, I prepared you for these guys a month ago. They're going to love finding your secret. They love shit like that."

When Lyle's words registered, bile rose in her throat. If she'd eaten today, she'd have vomited. Last month, Lyle had restrained her face down on her father's desk in the home that should have been her haven. Her legs had been spread open and secured, while her father's weight held her down so she would remain still enough.

Her stomach clenched into knots as memories of her shrill screams bouncing off the walls in her Master's office resurfaced in her psyche. No one but her Master and Lyle could have heard her. The waves of pain had come so fast, so intensely, she hadn't been able to escape to her safe place. When the pain became too unbearable, she'd fainted. Her Master revived her by pouring ice water on her face. Gasping, she'd returned to consciousness just as the fire began again on the inside of her labia.

Her heart pounded as she remembered returning to her room that night. The raw pain hadn't receded. She'd taken a hand mirror and, lying on her back on the bed, discovered her latest degradation.

Branded with her father's initials.

The branding had healed with much care, but Lyle's sadistic appetites began to frighten her more than her father's. Would she survive having her father's protégé become her Master? Throat suddenly parched, she reached for her water goblet, trying to quell the shaking in her hand.

A heavy weight settled in her stomach as Lyle stood to greet the two Asian men in their matching black-silk suits and starched white shirts—twin-like right down to their black-silk ties. Savannah didn't attempt to stand, because she'd been strategically placed at the enclosed side of the round table. No escape.

The men bowed in sync to Lyle. He ate up their deference to him with a simpering grin. The three exchanged terse introductions. Then, as one, all three turned their attention toward her, the gazes of the clients creeping slowly over what they could see of her body, lingering too long on her breasts. She swallowed down the rising bile and forced a smile to her face.

Lyle motioned for each man to enter the booth from a different side. The short, wiry men slid along the circular leather seat to besiege her, closing in. Smothering. She tried to fill her compressed lungs with slow, deep breaths, but the men reeked of garlic and body odor. She fought the reflex to gag.

As if in synchronized motion again, their hands snaked out to clamp over her knees, then moved upward, under the short skirt of her tight dress. The sadist on her left pinched her inner thigh, forcing a gasp from her.

Savannah needed to prepare herself for whatever these two men had planned for her. Focus. Separate her mind from the scene. Soon she would put this last scene behind her and go home. Then the slave would suffer no more.

She knew the routine. A quick meal, prolonged only if they got off on feeding the slave, then they would take her to the Master's penthouse suite—His because He owned this hotel, just as He owned the slave. Her screams would fall on deaf ears in that isolated wing of the historic hotel. The scene would be videotaped to use as blackmail with the clients later, if necessary.

Just another routine sadomasochism scene for the well-used slave. Lyle, who would wait in the next room, would never come to intervene. The slave would hold off screaming as long as she could, because no amount of screaming would put an end to the slave's suffering. Besides, the slave knew sadists got off on her screams and didn't want to give them the satisfaction of believing they had broken her.

Even after they ejaculated on her, as they always did, the torture would end only when the allotted time had run out. No sense rushing them. Sometimes they became even more sadistic after they'd come. She prayed they'd only paid for an hour, but something told her they'd been able to afford to abuse the slave even longer.

Just be nice to the gentlemen, Savi, and they'll be nice to you. Only the "gentlemen" were never nice to her. Savannah took a deep breath.

The curtain rose on Act Three—the final act.

* * *

Damián stuck his head through the open elevator doors and saw a tray of dirty dishes on the floor outside the penthouse suite. He pushed the cart into the hallway, wheeling it toward the room. He started to bend down to retrieve the tray of dishes when he heard a woman scream in pain from inside the suite.

"Acccchhhhh, God, no!"

Damn. He didn't have a key to the room.

"Lyle! Make them stop!"

Were they screams of passion? Or did she need help? This floor was isolated from the others. He should at least check on her. But he had no way of gaining access to the suite.

"Accccchhhhhh! Rape!"

Mierda. Was this for real or a role-playing thing some *chicas* got into? Sure didn't sound like she was having fun. Damián dropped the dishes into the cart, breaking a wine glass. He pounded on the door.

"Everything all right in there?"

"Fire! Fire! Help me!" The woman sobbed now.

What the hell was going on in there? Damián ran back toward the elevator and pulled the fire extinguisher from the wall, then returned to the door. His heel striking against the handle barely made a dent at opening it. After three more kicks, the door finally crashed against the inner wall.

"Fire! Help!" The screams came from the bedroom. "No more, please!" she begged hysterically.

Damián ran through the fancy suite with its antique furniture and around the wet bar to try the bedroom doorknob. Unlocked. Hoping for the element of surprise, he slowly turned the handle until he felt the tumbler release, then slammed the door open. As it hit the wall and bounced back, he dodged the recoil and rushed into the room.

What the fuck?

The fire extinguisher dropped to the floor. On the bed in front of him, the Barbie doll from the restaurant was trussed up in a grotesque position. The soles of her feet were red. Her naturally blond pussy was splayed open for God and everyone to see. Red, angry welts covered her inner thighs. White nylon ropes suspended her knees in the air, attaching her to the headboard.

Her eyes were closed, but her face was red, with tracks of tears down both cheeks. The sight of her ravaged body tore at his gut.

When he'd first burst in, the two Asians she'd had dinner with had stood naked on either side of her. They'd turned to look at Damián, then dropped some kind of glowing purple globe onto the bed. With frantic hand gestures and short orders to each other in a foreign language, they gathered up the various items on the bed—a quirt, a short bamboo cane, additional rope, that purple globe thing—and stuffed them into their briefcases.

Had they just been into a severe BDSM scene? An ex-girlfriend right out of juvie had been into that shit and had explained to him how it all worked. Damián couldn't get off on hurting a *chica*, so they'd broken up soon after. *Shit, maybe "fire" was the Barbie doll's safeword?* But if she'd said her safeword, why hadn't they stopped?

The men quickly put on their boxers and suit pants, then grabbed their shirts and suit coats and ran out the door. The mud in his brain was clearing and it became obvious to him she wasn't a willing participant. *Fuck.* He ran to the bed, but didn't know what to do first.

She whimpered incoherently, her face turned away from him. Her tits were bound so tightly they had turned bluish-purple. He reached out to untie those ropes first. Tears streamed down her face and she muttered gibberish. Her eyes were closed and her face flushed.

Fuck! Fuck!! Fuck!!! Where'd those guys learn to tie knots?

"Hang on, *querida*. I'll have you out of here in a minute." *I hope. Come on! Untie, God damn it!*

His chest burned as he held his breath, fighting to make headway with the ropes. Finally, they loosened. A few seconds later, she screamed again as blood began circulating to her breasts. Damián wished he could absorb her pain into his own chest, but was afraid to touch her and cause even more pain. He reached for the wrist cuff on her left side and released her.

"Oh, God! Stop!" Her screams left him feeling even more helpless. He'd vowed never to feel that way again once he'd been released from juvie.

"I'm sorry. I know that hurts like hell, *bebé*." He lowered her hand slowly onto the bed and rubbed her shoulder, trying to relieve the stiff and sore muscles. He followed the rope that splayed her thighs open and reached behind the headboard again to find it looped around what felt like an eye hook. He released it, but kept the rope taut until he could grab her battered thigh and gently lay her leg onto the mattress.

Her screams of anguish caused his gut to clench. He was hurting her, but she'd feel better once circulation returned and her muscles relaxed.

He rushed around to the other side of the bed to unfasten those restraints. How long had she been tied up? He'd seen her leave the booth with the three men about an hour ago. Where was the fucking jerk-off in the white suit who'd brought her here in the first place?

Was she some kind of hooker or something? Didn't matter. No one deserved to be tortured like this.

He released the wrist cuff and lowered her arm, then did the same with the ropes holding up her other thigh. Now freed, she cried out and curled her beautiful body into a ball, trying to minimize the pain and comfort herself. He froze, unsure what to do next. Her sobs ripped his fucking heart out.

When she began to shake, his mind engaged again and he retrieved the sheet and blanket that had been tossed on the floor at the foot of the bed. He tucked them around her trembling body, cocooning her in warmth. Even so, she shook from the release of the stress on her body. Endorphins, his ex-girlfriend had explained—like it was a good thing. Maybe it was for his ex, who'd enjoyed that shit. But not for this girl.

"What the hell are you doing in here?"

Damián looked up to see the jerk-off from the restaurant standing in the doorway with his fancy phone in his hand.

"Who let you in here, wetback?"

Wetback? His family probably had been in California longer than this man's.

The man turned to look at the woman. "Savannah, what the hell happened to my clients?"

Savannah. Beautiful, just like her.

"They were hurting her," Damián said. He clenched his fists to keep from bashing in the man's face. The jerk-off knew exactly what had been happening to her.

The man glared at him. "Well, no shit, Sherlock. The bitch gets off on pain—and I get off on making money." So maybe she *was* being paid to do this. The jerk-off looked down at Savannah again. Damián was glad she couldn't see the expression of anger and disgust on his face.

"Looks like neither of us is going to get off today, slut. Get the fuck up!"

When he went to the bed and grabbed Savannah's arm, a gut-wrenching scream poured from her. Damián had had enough. He grabbed the man by the back of his suit coat and pulled him away from her. "Get the fuck out!"

The man stood and addressed him as if he were a bug to squash under his shoe. "Who the hell do you think you're talking to, wetback?"

"Keep a low profile and mind your own business…?"

Fuck that shit. When the man took a swing at his face, Damián blocked it with his left forearm, then rammed his right fist into Jerk-off's soft underbelly. The man doubled over, gasping for air. Damián waited to deliver another blow, but the man reached out for the nightstand and straightened up. He obviously hadn't grown up in Damián's neighborhood. Finished with one blow. Some tough guy.

His voice came out like a wheezing whisper. "You're going to regret this."

But Damián would have had more regrets if he'd let the man hurt her any more.

* * *

Savannah pulled into herself, trying to escape the fiery pain. She could no longer identify one single source of discomfort. Nerve endings over her entire body screamed for relief.

Go to your cave, Savi. I am waiting.

She drifted toward the ceiling, out the window to the balcony, up the coast to the cave where she'd sought refuge so many times before. The waves crashed against the rocks. She walked carefully over the jagged edges, dodging sea urchins. Her flip-flops slipped as she climbed over the sharp rocks.

But this time, he pursued her. Faster. Run faster! He was close. So close. He grabbed her and pulled. *The pain! Oh, God.* She jerked away from him and ran faster. He let go just as she walked under the natural rock arch carved over centuries by water and wind. The sounds of the waves died down. The pain receded.

"Maman!"

Her mother had spread a picnic lunch on a blanket for them to enjoy. When she smiled and held out her hand, Savannah glided forward, her feet just hovering over the sand.

Safe. At last.

Savannah sank to the blanket and took Maman's slender hand. She shivered. The air was cooler than usual inside the cave. Savannah stretched out on the blanket and laid her head in Maman's lap, curling her legs up to her chest. Maman stroked her hair away from her face. She was always brushing her bangs out of her eyes.

A shudder wracked Savannah's body. Maman wrapped her in a warm blanket. Savannah didn't remember seeing the blanket when she'd arrived. She smiled. Maman worked magic. She always knew how to make their time together here perfect.

The waves crashed far in the distance, but they couldn't reach them here. A door slammed.

A door? In her cave?

Savannah's brows furrowed.

"Here, *querida*. Drink this."

She groaned. *No!* How had he found their secret cave? She fought against the man pulling her away from Maman. She sputtered and gasped as water entered her mouth. He captured her flailing hands. Was he trying to drown her? When had the tide come in?

"Shhh. He's gone. Drink the water. It will help. You're safe now."

No, not safe until you're gone. Leave us alone.

She clutched at Maman's dress. "No!" But he pulled her away, dragging her over the sand-encrusted rocks that bit into her skin. Raw. On fire. She fought him, but he continued to tear her from her safe place. From Maman.

Someone screamed in anguish. Then the fiery pain washed over her thighs, pussy, and breasts. She realized it was she who had screamed. A strong, hard body pulled her against him, wrapping a steel-banded arm around her waist and arms, holding her tight.

Claustrophobia. Smothering. She tried to push at him, but his chest was as hard as the rocks on the beach. Only smoother.

"I have you, *querida*. No one's going to hurt you as long as I'm here. Just breathe slowly."

With an effort, she managed to return her breathing to normal, as he'd told her to do. He spoke Spanish. The sadists hadn't. His voice was gentle, oddly soothing to her jagged nerves, despite being a man's.

Her chest hurt so badly, her nipples ready to explode. Ropes, quirt, electricity.

Good God! No, there was no God, good or otherwise. She moaned as images flooded her mind—the purple globe shocking her pussy and breasts. She'd tried so hard not to scream. She hadn't wanted to give the sadists that satisfaction. But the pain. Oh, God, the pain had been the worst ever. She gasped on a sob.

"Shhhh, *bebé*. It's over now."

A strong hand stroked her hair. Comforting, but firm.

Safe.

At last.

Sleep now, Savi.

"Yes, Maman."

* * *

The moment she fell asleep, her body released its tension and she relaxed against Damián. Well, he'd never been mistaken for someone's mother before. He smiled and pulled her closer.

She felt so fragile in his arms, as if he could break her if he touched her the wrong way. Her long, sun-streaked blonde hair was sleek and straight. He wanted to run his hands through it, but didn't want to wake her. Instead, he pressed his face against her hair and inhaled her scent. Flowery. Clean.

An hour passed and she continued to sleep, not moving a muscle. Damián expected the police to arrive at any moment—but no one came. He couldn't move her yet, certainly not on his Harley. Damián eased away from her and went into the sitting room to prop a chair against the suite entrance. He locked the bedroom door. Better than nothing. Might at least keep Jerk-off away from her.

What the hell kind of security did this place have? Hell, he'd busted down her door and no one had come to check. He returned to the bedroom and crawled back into bed beside her. If any of those dickheads came around her again, he wanted to make sure he stood between her and them.

No way would he leave her here alone. He'd take his chances with the authorities, even though he could predict what would happen if they arrested him. Chicanos didn't assault rich white men and get away with it.

He looked down at her again. So defenseless. She needed him. He didn't understand what had drawn him to her, right from the moment he saw her in the restaurant, but he needed to protect her.

She sure as hell didn't make good choices when it came to men. Why would anyone subject herself to this kind of pain and degradation? Was she a call girl? No, he couldn't accept that she was a common *puta*.

"The bitch gets off on pain."

Wrong again. She hadn't enjoyed the pain those men had inflicted on her. So, why had she put herself in such danger? Safe, sane, and consensual. That was his ex-girlfriend's mantra for BDSM scenes, but this one had been none of the above.

Savannah needed someone to look after her.

Well, she isn't going to take a second look at you. Way out of your league, man.

She moaned and turned her face toward him. When she wrapped an arm around his waist, his dick hardened. She licked her full lips and he fought the urge to bend over and kiss her.

Protect her, Damián. No la moleste.

No, she didn't need that from him, too. Just hold her. But if he was going to get rid of his hard-on, he'd better think about something other than the perfect *chica* sleeping in his arms. He steered his mind in a different direction. There was one thing he could kiss goodbye—his job. *Damn.* He didn't want to be homeless again. But, without this job, he wouldn't be able to pay the rent.

Sometimes rescuing women wasn't all it was cracked up to be.

His social worker had suggested he join the Marines. They'd feed, clothe, and house him. Might get his fool head blown off in the bargain. But maybe not. Whatever he was going to do, he needed to come up with a plan and soon.

First, he needed to get this woman home safely. But if home meant taking her back to Jerk-off, then what? He couldn't do that.

Another hour passed. No security. No police. *What the fuck?* Hadn't the man reported him?

The woman slept in his arms as if dead. After she'd turned toward him, she hadn't moved again. If he didn't feel her breath on his chest at the vee in his shirt, he would have tried to awaken her to be sure she was okay.

Damián was content to let her sleep. He'd never again hold something so perfect in his arms. He closed his eyes, giving in to exhaustion. She wasn't going anywhere. Neither was he.

She moaned and his eyelids opened in an instant. What time was it? Still dark outside. He pulled back and looked down at her. She grimaced. Without warning, she began thrashing against him, one fist slamming into his eye socket. Damián didn't try to hold her captive because he didn't need her screaming rape. No way did he have the money or power to fight a charge like that.

"Savannah, open your eyes."

Surprisingly, she did as he ordered, blinking several times as she stared at him. "Orlando?"

How did she know his name? His nametag only gave his first name. When her blue eyes finally focused on him, they opened wider and she scooted away to the opposite side of the bed. Her movements were awkward due to the abuse her body had sustained. She pulled the sheet with her and covered herself.

"Who are you?"

"Damián. Do you remember what happened?"

* * *

The man looked familiar to Savannah, but she couldn't place him. Why had she been sleeping with him? She never slept with clients. But he certainly didn't look like any client she could recall either. And why, if she'd just been asleep, did she want to curl up and escape into sleep once more?

The pain slowly registered. Her body burned from the soles of her feet to her breasts, but she couldn't remember why. Savannah looked around the room. Opulent antique French furniture. Her mother's influence. Tears stung her eyes. The penthouse suite. Familiar. She'd been here many times in the last year.

Then the memory of her last two clients returned.

Ropes. Quirt. Electricity.

Each time she'd managed to separate her mind from the clients' horrific scene, the two sadists had become more relentless in torturing her with whatever device they were using at the time. Sometimes two at once. They seemed determined to keep her mind emotionally invested in the scene, ruthlessly pulling her back into her body to feel each blow, each infliction of pain.

Then one of the men had pulled out his smart phone, spread her private folds, and taken several photos of her shame. They had known she'd been branded. Heat suffused her face. She closed her eyes.

What now? Lyle and her father would be furious. She'd never lost them a client before. Last night, she'd lost two. Her punishment would be severe. She opened her eyes and glanced toward the door. Where had Lyle gone? When would he be back? She supposed her father would send a car for her. They knew they didn't have to worry about her running away. The threat of living a hellish life as a street whore would keep her tethered in her velvet chains.

Savannah began to shake.

"Shhh. It's okay." The man on the bed—Damián—reached out a hand to her, but she pulled her body away. He let his hand come to rest on the mattress between them, as if he were training a dog to get used to him by small degrees. His brown skin contrasted sharply with the white sheets. Exotic. So different from the men who could afford her.

No, he wasn't her client. So who was he? She shivered and returned his gaze, seeing regret, pity. She didn't want or need anyone's pity.

"I don't know you."

"I work here at the hotel."

Oh, Lord! The busboy! She remembered him from the restaurant. How had she come to be in bed with him? Had anything happened? Clearly, she'd zoned out. Had he forced himself on her while her mind was out of her body?

No. The concern in the man's warm-chocolate eyes told her he wasn't a threat. She didn't think so, anyway. His pupils were so large, his eyes almost looked black. Her instincts regarding men were more than a little warped. Something began to melt inside her. The image of him barging into the room last night carrying a...a fire extinguisher? She tried to keep from smiling, but couldn't help herself. So incongruous with the type of rescue she'd needed.

Damián raised an eyebrow, then smiled back. His white teeth against a bronzed face sent a flock of swallows to flight inside her stomach. She giggled.

"What's so funny?"

"You, barging in here last night carrying that ridiculous fire extinguisher."

"*Someone* yelled 'fire.'"

"Well, I read once that no one comes when you yell rape."

His face grew serious. "They didn't—?"

She shook her head. "No. Against the rules." Tears stung the backs of her eyelids. "No one's ever come to my rescue before." She turned away. *Don't let him get inside your head, Savi.* This stranger was even more dangerous than the sadists. He made her feel vulnerable. She needed to keep her wits about her if she was going to keep the walls of her fortress intact.

Until she could get home and put her final plan into motion, she'd do well to remember that men weren't safe or honorable.

But Damián had held her for hours without taking advantage of her. Amazing man.

She looked back at him. "Thank you."

"*De nada.*"

Then she realized what his actions had cost him. "Oh, God. Your job."

A busboy probably needed every paycheck just to survive. She assessed him. He wore a polo uniform shirt—which he filled out better than any polo she'd ever seen—and inexpensive black jeans.

He shrugged, as if it didn't matter. But she doubted he was truly that nonchalant. He'd be fired, if he hadn't been already, all because of her. Unfair. Yet another victim of her father's and Lyle's ruthlessness. His face blurred as tears welled in her eyes. "I'm so sorry to have caused you so much trouble."

He leaned closer. She didn't back away this time, but her heart began beating faster.

"I'd do it again," he whispered. "No regrets, Savannah. No one should hurt you like that."

She closed her eyelids and swallowed. Damián's fingertip brushed away a tear that rolled from the corner of her eye. His hand felt warm against her chilled skin. A jolt of electricity zapped her clit—and not the kind of zap the sadists had delivered either. Her eyes opened wider. No man had ever caused a sexual response in her without first inflicting severe pain or forcing an orgasm.

When he pulled his hand back, she fought the urge to lean toward him. How could she feel so safe with this stranger?

Dangerous. She needed to get away before he got under her skin. Opening herself up to Damián's kindness would just result in even more intense pain when she left him to return to Master. Her life, her body, were not her own.

"I have to get home."

Savannah didn't know what would happen when she got there. Her father would be furious when Lyle told him what she'd done. She looked around the room. Where was the camera? Were they watching her even now? Her skin crawled. Were they waiting for Damián to leave so they could whisk her back to her prison on the hill in Rancho? Her failure would be severely punished.

Again, for a man who espoused no regrets, she did see regret in Damián's eyes. "Why don't you get dressed? I need to go clean out my locker. Can you meet me in the lobby in twenty?"

"Sure." She pushed the sheet aside, but groaned at the pain of moving.

"Are you okay?"

She nodded. "My legs are sore."

"Damn. Let me run downstairs and get the first-aid kit."

"No, really! I'm fine."

"Bullshit. Lock the door behind me and don't open it for anyone but me. I'll be right back."

He didn't wait for her to agree, just left the room. She hobbled over on her sore feet and locked the door behind him, then went to the bathroom to relieve herself. She then washed her thighs with soapy water. At least there weren't any open cuts. Just red welts. She rinsed the washcloth and wiped her legs free of soap, then heard a knock at the door. Her heart thudded until she heard a familiar voice.

"It's Damián!"

She grabbed a towel and went to the door to let him back inside. He administered first aid efficiently, as if he was used to taking care of others.

"Where'd you get your first-aid expertise?"

"I have a niece who's a tomboy. She's always in one scrape or another."

She watched his brown hands against her white thighs as he gently applied antibiotic cream before taping gauze to the insides of her thighs. Then he washed her feet. She hadn't had anyone take care of her needs in such a long time. Not since Maman.

"How does that feel?"

"Better." She smiled. "Thanks, Damián."

"*De nada.* Let me help you get dressed. I'll carry you down the back stairs so we can get out without alerting security."

"You don't have to carry me."

He glanced at her feet, then back at her face. "I'm carrying you."

He retrieved her black dress, bra, and panties from the chair in the corner and helped her dress. She felt like a child and blushed knowing she wasn't. She lifted her arms and he slipped the dress down her torso as she sat on the edge of the bed.

Damián stood back, looking down at her. "Hope you won't mind riding on the back of my Harley."

An image of her legs wrapped around him caused her nipples to harden. His gaze caused them to grow even harder. Her face reddened, then he raised his gaze to her eyes. His grin caused her clit to throb. Oh, Lord. Her breasts had done the talking for her.

"Good, *querida*."

Oh, Savannah, you're so close to ending your suffering.

Don't do anything stupid and screw it up.

* * *

Damián throttled the engine and peeled out of the parking lot. The feeling of control the hog gave him as it responded got the blood rushing through his body in a way nothing else could. Okay, maybe there was something else that could charge his engine. Like the beautiful woman plastered against his back and hips right now. He grinned.

The Harley was the only thing he'd ever been able to call his own. He'd worked for a Harley-Davidson repair shop and saved every penny until he could buy his own used chopper. It had been a total piece of crap when he'd bought it, but he'd restored it himself over the past year and could now interpret every rumble the engine made. He hoped he wouldn't have to sell his baby to make ends meet, not after all the time and money he had put into her.

Savannah's arms held him tight around the waist, her hands pressing into his stomach. He tried not to think about her sexy legs molded against his hips and thighs. His dick hardened. That she'd been game to ride on his bike surprised him. She didn't seem like the type who'd want to get her hair mussed. And she sure as hell wasn't dressed to ride. He'd made her wear his leather jacket, but it barely covered her black cocktail dress.

Savannah sure was full of surprises.

The predawn traffic was light as he rode down Marine Street in La Jolla. Savannah was a natural on the bike, leaning with him as he made turns and lane changes. Now if only he could curb the ache of wanting to bury his dick deep inside her. Between the vibration of the machine and her body pressed against his back, ass, and legs, he felt like he'd explode. *Mierda*. He rolled on the throttle and catapulted them onto the 5. When she grabbed his waist even tighter, he grinned. Damn, she felt good against him.

Palm trees and scrubby evergreens dotted the sides of the road. The Pacific stretched out forever to the west. She'd given him her father's address in Rancho Santa Fe. Not that it was any of his business, but he couldn't help but wonder why someone from a rich neighborhood like Rancho would let men treat her with such disrespect.

He lived in La Colonia where he'd grown up, the Solana Beach neighborhood now known as Eden Gardens. It had sprung up in the shadow of Rancho to house the workers for the wealthy Rancho residents. His Chicano grandparents and father had emigrated from Mexico in the 1930s and worked for Rancho millionaires for decades. His mother, a sixth-generation Californian, had been a housekeeper behind the gates of one of the Rancho mansions. He'd lived in the shadow of the Rancho decadence all his life.

Now he had one of their daughters on the back of his Harley. Wasn't that a pisser? What would her family think when he rolled up at their door to drop her off? He grinned. As much as he couldn't wait to see that, he'd much rather enjoy their brief time together staying in the moment.

She laid her helmeted head against his shoulder and his dick jerked. *Mierda*. Yeah, he definitely needed to stay in this moment. But he couldn't help but wonder what the hell she was doing trusting him, a freakin' stranger, like this. How did she know he wouldn't just take her to some isolated place to rape and kill her? He remembered the torture she'd undergone yesterday. This *chica* had some serious problems with setting boundaries and making healthy choices about men.

Soon he would have her back in her safe little world, thankfully, before they did something she'd regret later. He wouldn't regret anything he did with her, though. No fucking way.

Luckily, her exit was coming up. Soon he'd have her safe at home. He hoped she wouldn't venture out on another escort assignment anytime soon with Jerk-off.

As he came to the end of the ramp, she lifted the visor and shouted in his ear, "Don't take me home yet."

He just about blew a wad in his pants. Whether it was her warm body against him, her sexy voice in his ear, or visions of having her body underneath his, he knew in an instant where he wanted to take her before he let this *mariposa* flit away for good. He'd never taken a *chica* there before…

Don't analyze it. Just point the front tire in the right direction.

He turned left and wove his way through the business and residential districts of Solana Beach, and then became one with the sea air as he accelerated. Riding eighty miles an hour along the Pacific Coast Highway and the 5 always recharged his batteries. He'd begun escaping here as soon as he'd learned to drive. As a sixteen-year-old, he'd made the trip in a beat-up Chevy.

Being locked up in juvie had nearly strangled his soul. When they'd released him, he'd spent about two weeks at Thousand Steps Beach, sleeping on the cliffs at high tide, and exploring the beach and cave at low.

Don't think about that now. You have a beautiful woman plastered against your body, man. Focus.

Damián hoped she didn't mind stairs. He loved how few people frequented this beach—probably because of those daunting stairs. Almost like having his own private beach. He couldn't wait to share the place with Savannah. His heartbeat sped up as they came upon the outskirts of Camp Pendleton.

Wouldn't be long now.

* * *

Savannah's body had never felt so relaxed. She'd have fallen asleep, if not for the fear of falling off his Harley. She grinned. Savannah Gentry riding a Harley hog. *Good Lord.* And in a skintight dress covered in a leather Harley-emblazoned jacket, no less.

She suppressed a giggle. Escape. The feeling was so exhilarating. She never wanted this moment to end. Already, she was in for the punishment session of a lifetime. Might as well do something to earn it.

She raised her head and looked around. The rising sun cast a pinkish tinge over the landscape. The ocean spread out to the horizon on her left. The last time she'd been on the PCH and the 5 just for fun was…don't think about that now. Lifting the helmet's visor again, she took a deep breath of the salty sea air. Alive. She wanted to revel in the feeling of being alive—free—before she returned to her prison.

They were passing through Camp Pendleton because she saw tanks on early-morning maneuvers to the west. How had they gotten this far north in such a short time? They must be flying like the wind. She loved it.

"Where are we headed?" she shouted into his ear, feeling loose strands of his hair whipping against her lips. She felt a zing to her clit. Crazy! She smiled and closed her eyes.

"Laguna Beach. A special place I want to show you."

A niggling memory flashed across her mind. Happy, yet sad. Savannah quashed the memory before it could invade her good mood. *Leave the past in the past.*

She felt like a schoolgirl cutting class, or what she'd imagined that would feel like. Having had private tutors at home, skipping classes was something she had never been able to do. She'd been caned more than once by her tutors for other infractions, though. Some days, she seemed to get in trouble for breathing. More likely, they were just pervs given permission by Master to punish her.

Forget about that for now. Today, you're free, at least for a little while. Lowering the visor, she slid her arms around his waist, her thumbs brushing against his pecs. His muscles were like leather-covered steel. She loved to touch him. The rumble of the Harley motor against her clit stimulated her much better than the butterfly vibrator her father used to force orgasms on her when He wanted to exact that torture on her.

Don't think about Him anymore.

All too soon, Damián pulled into a parking spot across the highway from the beach-access steps. She scooted back on the seat, ignoring the stinging pain in her bandaged thighs. She didn't want to think about that beating anymore. She only wanted to experience this, her last day.

Damián got off the bike first. She expected him to extend a hand to help her off. Instead, he motioned for her to swing her leg over the bike's seat, and then bent down to remove her stilettos.

"We're ditching the heels," he said. He opened the storage case behind the seat, pulled out the beach towel, and stowed her shoes inside the case.

"I don't have any other shoes."

"I'll carry you." He removed her helmet—well, *his* helmet, since he only had the one—and secured it in the compartment with her shoes.

She laughed. "I can walk in my bare feet once we get to the beach."

His hands spanned her waist under the open jacket and he lifted her up as if she weighed nothing. She grabbed onto his shoulders to steady herself, laughing. His muscles corded beneath his black T-shirt.

"I'll carry you again when we get to the rocks, then."

Rocks? She thought they were just going to stroll along the beach. Where did he plan to take her? Curiosity filled her thoughts as she alternated standing on one foot then the other. Seconds after her feet hit the pavement, the cuts she'd endured yesterday on her soles caused her to wince.

Damián handed her the towel and lifted her into his arms. "Oh!" She screamed in surprise and laughed. Holding on to the towel, she wrapped her arms around his neck. Satin on steel. His attention was intent on watching for an opening in traffic for them to cross. She stared at his profile.

His nose had been broken at some point. Had he been an athlete in school or had he been injured fighting? He had a closed-up hole for an ear piercing. No earring. A lock of hair fell over his forehead that she itched to brush back with her fingers. His devilish appearance did strange things to her libido—like ignite it. Strange, indeed.

She was grateful she didn't have to walk after all. It would take a while for her tender soles to heal. He started down the steps and she looked ahead to see where they were going.

A flash of memory caused a momentary bout of vertigo. She held on tighter and looked back up at him, almost expecting to see Maman. No. She was with Damián. She pushed the confusing image back into the recesses of her mind.

The steps went on forever. "My God! Are there really a thousand of them?" She couldn't even see the beach for the overgrown arbor hanging over portions of the stairway. Guilt assailed her for making him carry her. "You can put me down. I can walk."

"I'm carrying you."

His tone didn't invite disagreement, so she held on tight, hoping to ease some of her weight from his arms. Then she worried about putting a strain on his neck. But he didn't even sound out of breath, as though he bench-pressed a woman every day or something.

When he reached the sand and continued to carry her, she nipped lightly at his earlobe and whispered, "Put me down, Damián." His arms tightened around her even more. Lord, she loved the feel of his arms under her thighs and around her back.

Why do I feel at home in the arms of this stranger?

This man who simply made her feel. Period. She'd been numb for so long. How had he gotten past her fortress at all, much less in such a short time? A first for her with any man.

After ten minutes or so, not even winded, he lowered her to the ground, letting her slide down his rock-hard body, allowing her to feel every contour of his chest and thighs. And a very erect penis. Savannah not only felt his erection, but her nipples tightened with the friction of his chest against hers. She'd never been aroused willingly by a man, yet Damián had caused her clit to jolt and her panties to grow wet with little more than a look.

Good Lord, Savannah Gentry was full-blown horny.

Heady with her body's response, she pulled his head toward hers and nibbled at his lips, then sucked on his full lower lip. He groaned and grabbed the back of her head as he deepened the kiss. His tongue dove inside her, claiming her mouth as his. Rather than be repulsed, Savannah's pelvis tilted toward him automatically. He lowered one of his hands to the small of her back and ground her even tighter against his erection.

When she thought her lungs would explode, she broke off the kiss, gasping for air, and laid her forehead in the crook of his neck. His pulse pounded as hard as hers.

"Madre de Dios." He sounded as if he'd run a 25-yard dash.

Now he was winded. She smiled. What carrying her all that way hadn't managed, a kiss had.

Damián reached out to brush a strand of hair behind her ear. "Nice diversion, but we aren't there yet."

Well, she was closer to *there* than she'd ever been before. Then she understood his meaning and looked around. Huge moss-covered rocks dotted the beach leading to an opening in the cliff. A small tidal pool sat at the entrance, surrounded by jagged rocks pounded relentlessly by the foamy waves. To her left were high cliffs with expensive homes barely clinging to their ledges. She was amazed the people living in the homes hadn't claimed this beautiful spot as their own private sanctuary, rather than having it become a public-access beach. In Rancho, the residents would have put up a gate to keep out the riffraff.

A flock of gulls dove at them, begging for handouts. She wished she had something to feed them. When their insistent squawking didn't yield the desired result, they flew down the nearly deserted beach hoping to find an easier mark.

Her feet were soothed by the cold, wet sand. She could probably walk once they got to the soft sand on the other side of the tidal pool. *How do you know there is soft sand on the other side?*

She squeaked when Damián bent down, pressed his shoulder against her stomach, then hoisted her over his massive shoulder like a sack of potatoes. "Hey, put me down!"

"I need to watch my footing or we're both going to be sprawled on those rocks."

The view of his tight ass being brushed by her loose hair sent her stomach into a tailspin. She giggled. She held onto the towel, but didn't know what to hold onto to steady herself. His ass seemed as good a place as any. She slid her free hand into the back pocket of his jeans.

"You'd better move your hands higher or I'm going to drop you here on the beach and have my way with you."

She moved her hands against his lower back instead, holding on to the waistband of his jeans. His hand molded against her butt, holding her steady. Another zing let her know her body was very much aware of his.

She held on for dear life as he began walking. He navigated the rocks peppering the beach below with a sureness of foot, as though he'd been here many times. She looked down at the tidal pool and saw sea urchins clinging to the rocks.

Savannah's heart skittered, then slammed against her chest like a jackhammer. So familiar. She'd come here many times, as well.

In her mind.

"You okay?" he asked, as he stopped.

Her hands gripped his jeans harder than before. She managed to squeak out a "yes," over the steady pounding of her heart. She didn't need to see where they were headed. The jagged archway was the entrance to her cave. Her safe place beckoned them inside. A brisk, cool breeze whipped her hair against her face. She hadn't imagined the wind before when she'd escaped here. Or the strong arms holding her against a hard body.

When he reached the center of the cave, he lowered her to her feet. He looked down at her expectantly, as if proud to show off his special place. Tears spilled from her eyes. Her private cave. She'd never shared it with anyone, except Maman.

Until now.

She almost felt that if she turned around, Maman would be waiting for her, a picnic lunch spread on a blanket. Savannah couldn't bring herself to look.

Maman had left her. She didn't even say goodbye. Savannah still loved her. She just wished Maman had taken her with her, rather than leaving her behind.

Damián's gentle, but firm hand cupped her chin and pulled her gaze upward as he tilted her head back. His brow furrowed and he cocked his head. Concern clouded his eyes. The only man who'd ever cared about her, taken care of her, now wanted to show her *his* special place.

She wanted nothing more than to please him in return, even if there never could be a relationship between them. Tears spilled down her face, bitten by the cool breeze. They could only have this day. This moment in time.

Because someone else owned her body.

Until tonight, when, at last, the slave screwed the Master.

* * *

Damián brushed the wetness away from her cheeks. Tears? Why? "What's the matter, *querida?*"

She shook her head and more tears spilled from the outer corners of her eyes. "Just kiss me," she whispered.

He had no idea what had happened to the mood from when she'd been giggling on the beach, but the hard-on he'd been fighting since last night demanded he worry about all that stuff later. Right now, he held the most perfect woman in the world in his arms. She wanted to be kissed. By him. Before she vanished into thin air, he would give the lady what she wanted.

His head lowered to hers, capturing her lips. So sweet—better than honey on sopapillas. He drew her lower lip between his teeth and into his mouth, sucking gently. When she moaned and pressed her pelvis against his, he decided he wouldn't be able to slow this down. He needed to be inside her. Now.

Mierda. How would he ever last long enough to make it good for her?

His tongue entered her softness, then he sucked her sweet tongue into his mouth. He pressed his hand into her lower back holding her body against his hard-on. With his other hand, he brushed his fingers down her arm, then reached between their bodies to cup her tit. So full. Firm. Her nipple was rock hard even before he squeezed it. Her hips jolted toward his.

Damn. He needed to feel her naked skin against his. To see her beautiful body in this setting, erasing the image of the grotesque position he'd found her in yesterday. He wanted to see her hot and writhing beneath him, waiting for him to please her.

Stepping back, he took the towel from her and spread it open on the wet sand to protect as much of her skin as he could. Then he unzipped his leather jacket with shaking hands and slid it down her arms. Rolling it into a pillow for her head, he placed it near one end of the towel.

He reached down with both arms and pulled the hem of her dress up. She lifted her arms to aid him in removing it. His dick pressed painfully against his zipper. Precum wet his jeans.

Jesús. *Please let me last long enough to make it good for her.*

He reached between her breasts to unhook her black lace bra. Her breasts spilled out and he cupped them. She had bruises from the ropes last night. He hoped he wasn't hurting her. His brown skin against her pale breasts caused his dick to strain even more. Then she skimmed her panties down her legs, careful not to pull at the bandages on her thighs. He throbbed when he saw her natural golden triangle of soft curls.

Mierda. The only thought remaining was how much he needed to bury himself inside her. But he froze, unable to keep from staring at her body. Despite the reminders of last night's torture, she was perfection. Her nipples became swollen, begging for attention. He bent down to draw one hard peak inside his mouth, flicking his tongue against it, causing her nipple to swell even more. She hissed air between her teeth, grabbing him by the sides of his head, causing his dick to throb even harder. His hand cupped the neglected other peak and he rolled it between his fingers. Hard. She gasped, tilting her golden triangle against his zippered fly. His dick pulsated even more.

Madre de Dios, he couldn't wait much longer. Maybe if he kept his jeans on, he'd be able to stretch this moment out. Pressing her down onto the towel and his jacket, he kissed her lips again, his hand skimming lightly along her abdomen as he sought the downy curls between her thighs. His finger stroked between her outer lips and she opened her legs for him. Wet. Her pussy was so fucking wet.

Pulling away, he looked down at her.

"I'm sorry. I can't wait. I need to be inside you."

She smiled and nodded, reaching down to grab his dick through the denim.

He pulled away. "If you touch me like that, I'm not going to last until I get inside you." He quirked the corner of his mouth and shrugged. She released him.

"Open for me, *querida*."

When she spread her wings wide for him, like the beautiful *mariposa* she was, he felt pride surge in his chest. She wanted him as much as he wanted her. How had something so delicate, so perfect, flitted into his life?

Knowing this moment would be fleeting, in more ways than one, he decided to create enough memories to last a lifetime. He changed his next course of action.

* * *

Savannah's clit throbbed. *Please, touch me again.* She'd never asked a man for what she wanted and couldn't start now. She should have helped him take off his jeans, but had been so lost in the sensations of his hands and mouth on her body that all functional thoughts had fled her mind.

Expecting him to take them off himself now, she was taken aback when his head bent toward her pussy. She tried to close her legs, then gasped at the friction of the bandages against her raw skin.

He leaned back and looked up at her. "Did I hurt you?"

She shook her head. It wasn't his fault. Even so, he mustn't look at her there. She felt heat rise in her face. Shame. But he continued to hold her legs open wide. Waiting.

"Please, let me taste you."

Savannah's face grew hotter. He was begging? How could she deny him? No one had ever asked before. It was dark in here. He wouldn't be able to see. She nodded her head and watched as he smiled before lowering himself to her again. When his tongue flitted against her swollen clit, all thought receded. Her pelvis surged toward his mouth.

"Ohh!"

Empowered, he took his finger and wet it against the opening of her vagina, then plunged inside her in one strong stroke. "Yes, Damián! Oh, Lord, yes!" The combination of his tongue and finger was delicious. When another finger joined the first, he moved them in a "come here" motion, which was her undoing. An odd pressure built inside her making her feel she could fly. She bucked against his hand and mouth, simulating intercourse. No, more like lovemaking. There was a difference, she was discovering.

She couldn't hold back. When would he enter her? Then his lips were gone and she felt his eyes on her as his fingers began to plunge in and out of her. "Explode for me, *bebé*. Don't hold anything back."

His tongue returned to draw gentle circles against her clit and she came undone. Her screams of ecstasy crashed against the walls of the cave as wave after wave of pleasure rolled over her. She yanked his head to her, pulling fists full of his hair free of his queue, not wanting the moment to end for anything. But it did. Tears spilled from her eyes. The intense beauty of the orgasm left her feeling fragile. Wanting more.

Feeling lost.

Then Damián stood and removed his jeans. She watched his penis spring loose, large and erect. Oh, Lord. He'd never fit inside her.

Propping himself on his elbows, he pressed his body down against her chest. Smothered. She couldn't breathe. "No!" She pushed him off her chest, gasping to fill her lungs.

Breathe, Savi. He doesn't want to hurt you.

She opened her eyes. Damián looked down at her and brushed her hair away from her face. "What's wrong, *querida*?"

Oh, God. She didn't want him to stop. And she didn't want to explain why she couldn't have him on top of her. "I need to see your face when you make love with me."

He smiled and propped himself up on his hands. Lord, he was so beautiful. He pressed his erection against her sensitive clit. She pulled his face toward hers and met him halfway, kissing his full, wet mouth. Unlike their kiss on the beach, this time she tasted herself on his lips. How strange. He plunged his tongue into her mouth and she felt his penis throbbing against her clit, which responded in kind. Her nipples tightened and budded.

He pulled back, propping himself on one hand. The veins in his arms bulged as he took his penis and rubbed it up and down against her wet pussy lips. Each time he touched her clit, she surged upward.

"Oh, *bebé*. You're so fucking sexy."

The sweet sentimental endearment, coupled with such a crude word, sent her libido into overdrive. She reached down and guided him to the opening of her vagina. "Please. Don't make me wait any longer."

"Oh, shit." He started to pull back. "I don't have protection."

Savannah smiled that he would be concerned, but there wouldn't be time for a baby to grow inside her. The thought of continuing life as she'd known it when Damián took her home tonight was even more unfathomable than yesterday when she'd made her decision to end her life. She only had today and she wanted to experience being made love to more than any other dying wish.

So, she lied to him. "I'm on the pill."

His eyes grew smoky as he balanced himself on both hands and rammed his penis inside her to the hilt. She grunted, feeling as if she'd been split apart.

"I'm sorry. You're so fucking tight." He lay still, waiting for her to adjust to his size. His breathing was shallow and rapid, as was hers. He throbbed inside her, and she tilted her pelvis, taking him deeper. "That's right, *bebé*. Fuck me."

She wrapped her legs around his back, letting her feet rest against his buttocks as she brought him deeper inside. He pulled almost completely out of her, then she drove him home again. Tilting her pelvis, she matched him stroke for stroke. She'd never felt so full, as if the tip of his rod touched her cervix. She reached up and placed her hands on his upper arms, feeling the strength and sinew in his muscles as his strokes grew faster. Harder. Each upward thrust of his penis jolted against her clit. Even though the friction wasn't enough for her to come, she didn't care.

Savannah just wanted to feel Damián possessing her, to feel him claiming her body. Willingly giving her body Damián, she felt empowered for the first time in her life. She'd chosen to be with him.

Then he reached his hand between their bodies, his finger and thumb stroking her wetness. When he placed his thumb on the hood of her clit and used his thumb and finger to massage her, she screamed. "Ohhhh, God!" She closed her eyes. His thumb grazed her clit as he pounded into her vagina. An explosion built inside her unlike anything she'd experienced before, bigger even than the one moments ago. She dug her fingernails into his muscles, panting, unable to catch a deep breath. Dizzy with the sensations roiling through her body, she groaned. So close. She'd never felt such euphoria.

"Come for me again, *bebé*."

At his command, her world flew apart. She screamed as he covered her mouth with his own, capturing her cries of ecstasy and taking them into his body. Her hips bucked against his of their own volition.

"I can't hold back any longer, *bebé*."

"Please don't! Come inside me!"

With a groan, he lowered himself to his forearms and pumped harder. The pressure on her chest caused a moment of panic. Sweat broke out on her forehead. *Breathe, Savi. Just breathe.* Rather than closing his eyes, he stared intently at her. She couldn't look away from his gaze, either. The panic eased a bit. Not completely gone, but manageable. She'd never connected on such a personal level with another human being.

He groaned and the crest of another orgasm rose inside her. Good Lord! Again? So soon? The muscles of her vagina pulsated around him, milking him dry. She closed her eyes and threw her head back in abandon. Her screams of release coincided with his earthy curse as he exploded inside her.

Her body convulsed around him as the aftershocks wracked her body. As she floated back to earth, his forehead pressed to her breast as he, too, gasped for air. She needed to get him off her chest. Smothering.

She threaded her fingers through his hair and grasped the sides of his head to pull him away until their gazes met. He looked disconnected. Lost. *Oh, no!* Hadn't it been good for him? She'd become so used to just letting men do as they pleased with her body—an object, nothing but a receptacle—that she didn't have the first clue how to give back. She'd never been emotionally engaged in the sex act before.

Tears burned against the backs of her eyes. Why couldn't she quit crying? She hadn't given in to tears for such a long time. Now she was crying all the time.

She looked at Damián as he gasped for air. He'd done all the work. Was there something she was supposed to do now? Had she failed him?

"Fucking unbelievable." He smiled.

Oh, Lord. He liked it! A laugh of relief bubbled up inside her. His earthy language turned her on. He could talk dirty to her all day long.

"You can say that again."

"I'd rather do it again."

He remained hard inside her. Worried again, she asked, "Didn't you come?"

"Oh, yeah, *bebé*. But let's do it again before my dick gets the message."

Good Lord! Her prior experience had been with her father, who took hours to be ready to go at it again. Thank God. But she'd never had sex with anyone close to her own age before.

Most days, she felt more like ninety herself. Yet, she'd had three orgasms in a matter of a few minutes. With a stranger, no less! And why didn't she care? Today, she just wanted to feel young, carefree—and alive.

Damián had given her the most beautiful experience of her life. But he only made her want more. She didn't want this day to ever end. She pulled his mouth toward her and just before they made contact, she whispered, "Fuck me."

* * *

An hour later, Damián collapsed onto his back on the wet sand. *Mierda*, he couldn't get enough of this woman. Her screams reverberated around the walls of his mind from her last orgasm. How many was that for her now? Six? Seven? *Madre de Dios*.

When he thought he could string two coherent words together again, he raised himself onto his side and propped his head into his cupped hand. He just stared down at her, his hand playing with the strands of her hair curled around one of her tits.

She smiled up at him, but he saw sadness in her expression. Regrets already?

"What are you thinking, *querida*?"

"I wish we could stay here forever."

Ah, now that kind of regret he could live with. He bent down and kissed her, gently this time. So sweet. Pure torture. He wasn't sure he'd be able to make love again and didn't care. He just wanted to feel her lips, her body, against his. As if ruled by a mind of its own, his hand reached out to cup her firm breast. He couldn't keep his hands or lips off her.

But they couldn't stay here forever. He wondered what she was going to do now. He hoped she wouldn't return to being a paid escort. She deserved a better life than that.

Raising his head again to look at her, he asked, "If you could have any job you wanted, what would it be?"

He watched her teeth trap the corner of her bottom lip between them and she puckered her brow as she thought about the question. Then she smiled and shrugged, as if it were a pipe dream. "A social worker. I'd like to work with abused kids."

Wow. What would someone like her know about abused kids? Well, she certainly was an abused adult. Something like that would require a lot of education. Not that she couldn't afford it.

"So, what's keeping you from pursuing your dream?"

She looked away. "It's too late."

How could it be too late? She wasn't any older than he was. She had to have the time. Look what she was doing now. And money? Hell, she lived in Rancho, after all. If she was so wealthy, though, why was she selling her body? Maybe she was one of the hired help, rather than an owner. Did she have a sugar daddy keeping her? Was it Jerk-off from the hotel? But, if that were the case, then why didn't she have money?

She puzzled him.

If money was the issue, he wished he could help her pay for college. But he could barely support himself. And now that he'd been fired…

"Can't your family help?"

"No." She turned toward him and brushed a lock of hair off his forehead. "Don't ask. It's complicated."

But why wouldn't her family help her make a better life? Damián had come from a supportive, loving family. They didn't have two nickels to rub together, but Mamá had made sure they had food in their bellies, even if they had to eat tamales twice a day. Mamá and Papá had both worked themselves into early graves, making money for the rich bastards in Rancho.

He decided to let it go.

Damián wondered if he'd ever see her again. Doubtful. They were worlds apart. But their bodies sure spoke the same language. Was there any chance they could date?

Yeah, right.

But at this moment, he had her with him. Pulling Savannah into the curve of his body, he molded her against him. Soon, he felt her breathing slow and become more steady. She'd been through a lot in the last twenty-four hours. Her body needed sleep. He hadn't gotten much sleep either, but was too wired to give in.

He'd have to get her back home soon. But what awaited her there? Did she even want to go back? She seemed in no hurry, that's for sure.

Then what? He lifted a lock of hair from her bare shoulder, rubbing its silk between his thumb and forefinger. He'd never dated a blonde before. And he wouldn't be dating this one either. Too different.

Just a few more hours and she'd be out of his life. His head grew heavy and he laid it down on the towel, pressing his forehead against the side of her head. So right. Would he ever hold something so perfect again? He wished…

Fuck! Damián jerked up. He'd fallen asleep. He looked outside the opening of the cave and saw the sun making its descent to the horizon. It would be dark within an hour. He needed to get her home.

Savannah stirred next to him, then looked up with sleep-filled eyes and smiled. His dick hardened. *Damn.* He couldn't get enough of her. She reached up and placed her hand at the back of his head and pulled him toward her.

His lips met hers and tenderness soon turned to flames. She opened to him and he reached for her breast, kneading her soft flesh. What he really wanted was to sink himself inside her again.

Half an hour later, both of them breathing hard and sated, Damián sighed. He stood and reached down to pull her to her feet. She winced again and he remembered how bruised and sore she was after the beating. He hated the thought of anyone hurting her like that again. She reached out and brushed sand off his side.

He turned his finger in a circular motion. "Turn around."

She did so and he brushed the sand off her, as well. Luckily, there wasn't much there. "I think the water might be a little too cold for us to wash more of this off."

"I'm fine."

"The ride back might be a little uncomfortable." He worried about her legs, but the bandages still covered the welts.

"I said I'm fine." Her voice had taken on an edge.

Damián shrugged. Fine then. He picked up her underwear and dress, shook them out, and handed them to her. "Come on. Get dressed. We have to go before the tide comes in."

He couldn't help but notice the disappointment in her eyes. She didn't seem any more anxious to end their time together than he did. No sense prolonging the inevitable, though. They dressed in silence, then he reached for her hand and she tucked it inside his. As he led her toward the entrance, he thought how right her hand felt in his.

Framed by the opening of the cave, the sun touched the top of the ocean on the horizon.

"Wait," she whispered. He looked down at her and saw her skin softened to a pale pink by the glowing sun. Her face was filled with wonder, as if she'd never seen a more beautiful sunset. Well, neither had he, watching its warm rays reflected on her face.

When the orb was but a memory, he turned her toward him. Tears again? Savannah broke his heart. He brushed the tears away with his thumbs, then cupped her face and lowered his mouth to meet hers. Feeling the quiver in her lips sent his dick throbbing again.

He kissed her sweetly, knowing they couldn't stay. The tide would begin to roll in soon. When he pulled away, she smiled up at him. "Thank you for showing me your special place, Damián."

Uncomfortable, he grinned. "I have a new special place now. Wherever you are."

She smiled back, a bittersweet smile. This was goodbye. He lowered his lips to hers, needing one more taste of her before he took her back to her safe gated world.

Then he lifted her and carried her across the rocks to the beach. When he got to the steps, she protested his continuing to carry her, but he'd used these steps as his own personal gym many times. He could have carried her up and down them all day, especially the way he felt after their lovemaking.

Too soon, they were seated on the hog again. His stomach growled. Some date he was! He hadn't thought about food all day. "We should stop and get something to eat."

"I'm fine."

"Well, I'm not." She was way too thin, anyway.

Soon they sat over platters of enchiladas, rice, and beans. Savannah remained silent and barely made a dent in the food. She'd already begun to pull away from him. But he couldn't take her back to a life as an escort, especially when she had so little regard for her own safety.

"You going to be okay at home?"

She looked up from her plate and smiled. The smile didn't reach her eyes. "I'll be fine."

Why did he doubt that?

"That Jerk-off from the hotel doesn't live with you, does he?"

She glanced back down at her plate. "No. He's just a...business partner."

"You need a new partner."

A tear slid down her cheek and onto the table. *Mierda*. He'd made her cry again. He reached out and squeezed the hand holding her fork. "I'm sorry. Just tell me that you're going to be okay when I drop you off."

She nodded, but didn't make eye contact.

"Convince me or I won't take you home."

Her head came up again. A mixture of fear and excitement flickered in her expressive eyes. "I have to go back. But everything's going to be fine. Things have...changed."

Things sure had changed for him, but he didn't understand what she meant. Then she smiled, pulled her hand out of his grasp and ate a forkful of her Spanish rice.

They left the restaurant in Laguna nearly an hour later, when he'd given up on her eating any more. He'd prolonged their time together to its limit. Time to take her home.

Darkness engulfed the 5 as they headed south. He'd put his jacket on her again to keep her from getting cold. When they passed the San Onofre power plant, with its pair of red glowing nipples, he couldn't help but thinking about her breasts pressing against his back, or taking each of her nips in his mouth once more. His still erect dick throbbed.

Not this time, Chico.

Once in Rancho, she gave him directions to her particular gate. Taking the remote from her purse, she opened the wrought-iron entrance to her fortress. As the gates opened slowly, he never felt more out of his element. He half expected St. Peter to be waiting on the other side telling him he needed to park his ass right where it was or, better yet, turn around and head back the other way where he belonged.

She started to take the helmet off. "I can walk from here."

"Like hell you will." He rolled on the throttle and enjoyed the feel of her hands grabbing him around his waist again as he ascended the winding driveway.

He pulled up in front of the mansion, illuminated by a series of spotlights showing off the monstrosity at the top of the hill—although Damián had no idea who could see it with all the trees.

Isolated. She must have incredible views of the ocean on the back side of the house. He wondered why the sunset at Laguna had captured her with such awe when she must see beautiful sunsets every evening.

"Please, Damián! I don't want you to…"

Her hands tightened around his waist as they watched lights turning on from room to room as someone made his or her way to the front door. He had barely cut the motor of the Harley and put the jiffy stand down before she let go and scrambled off the bike. She hurriedly unhooked the helmet and handed it to him.

"Thanks for everything, Damián. This will be the best day of my whole life." She pecked him on the cheek and made a dash for the front door, as if she hoped to get inside before anyone saw him. Did he embarrass her?

Mierda, he wouldn't have guessed that she was like that.

What did she mean by "will be" the best day? She had her whole life ahead of her. How could she know that?

Before she reached the door, it opened inward. Rather than the man from the hotel, a tall, older man stepped onto the fan-shaped flagstone entrance. She lowered her head when he put his hand on her shoulder to halt her. Was this her father?

The placement of the man's hand seemed more familiar than a father would touch his daughter. Her sugar daddy, then? Man, won't he be pissed to learn she'd let someone else dip his wick in her. His crude thought soured his stomach, but if she could just throw away what they'd experienced, then so could he.

"Go in the house, Savannah. Wait in the office."

"Yes, sir."

The man reminded him of the Doms in his ex-girlfriend's porn videos. Was he her Dom? Did she really get off on that pain shit? Then why was he pimping her out to other men? To jerk-off? Those other men?

Her body tensed as she cast a glance at Damián. Tears shone in her eyes. Did he see a bit of fear, as well? His gut clenched. Goddamn it, why did she put up with that crap? Clearly, she'd found sexual satisfaction with him at the beach, and he'd done nothing to hurt her. He wanted to take her in his arms and hold her. Take her away from here. Cherish and protect her.

She turned her body toward Damián, lifting her head just enough to make eye contact and mouthed another *thank you* before veering away to enter the house. Damián watched until he could no longer see her, then turned his attention back to the old man. If the asshole could breathe fire, he'd singe the tires off the Harley. His face was splotchy red, hands clenched at his sides.

"If I ever catch you near Savannah again, Orlando, I'll make you sorry you were ever born."

How'd he know his name?

Well, fuck you, old man. "If she wants to see me, that's her decision."

"Savannah makes no decisions. And I've done some investigating. If you don't want to be charged with assault and battery for that incident at my hotel yesterday, you'll heed my words."

What the fuck? He owned the hotel where Damián had worked? Did Savannah work for him, too? He guessed so. Why? Hell, he didn't understand anything about her. She was the most screwed up *chica* he'd ever met. If she was willing to sell her body so she could live like this, he'd never have anything to offer her.

"Get that contraption off my drive before it leaks any more oil."

His Harley did not leak anything. Pissed, but not wanting to risk an arrest and doing jail time, Damián revved the motor, glanced at the open door Savannah had disappeared through, then peeled away. He turned back to see the black streak of rubber very visible in the overly lit tiled driveway. He gained a sense of satisfaction knowing that, every time her sugar daddy saw that patch of rubber, he'd remember Damián. His spirits lifted a little.

But the haunted look in Savannah's eyes as she mouthed her thanks would be what burned in his memory forever. Had he made the right decision to leave her here? *Mierda*. He should have given her his phone number, in case she needed him. Not that he would have expected her to use it.

Madre de Dios, he hoped she'd take better care of herself.

Damián would just have to hold onto his memories of what had been the most perfect day of his life, with the most perfect woman.

* * *

Savannah sank to the floor, laying her flushed face against the cool tiles. Her stomach continued to threaten to revolt, but she tried to ignore it, knowing there would just be more of the dry heaves she'd experienced for the last fifteen minutes.

What she'd worried about for the past month seemed a certainty now. Two missed periods. Morning sickness.

She was pregnant. Her hand moved lower, from her stomach to the area over her womb. A baby. Tears prickled her eyes, then dripped onto the floor. She had to protect this baby. Who would help her?

Oh, Lord, what was she going to do?

Damián. I need you so much.

She only knew Damián by his first name. She'd tried to get an address or phone number from the hotel's business manager, but the woman wouldn't give out confidential employee information. On former employees, either.

Her Master had beaten her so severely the night Damián had brought her back from their special day at the beach cave over two months ago. If only the torture had ended there. By the time her Master and Lyle had ended the beating, probably because their arms were tired, her Master had had to carry her to her room.

She'd been afraid He was going to rape her again for the first time in a long time. Then He'd told her He wouldn't want to catch a disease from *that spic*. Savannah shuddered. Her Master and Lyle were the only diseases in her life.

Too sore to move for the next couple days, she hadn't carried out her plan to end her life. Then, when she had been able to get out of bed, the possibility of seeing Damián again someday kept her from going through with it.

Not a day went by since Damián had brought her back here that she didn't regret letting him leave without her. But Damián couldn't have known. She hadn't told him what her life here was like. Why hadn't she been brave enough to trust him?

Because of her shame. Thank God he hadn't noticed the brand in the dark cave. She'd never want anyone to see that mark.

But something had changed that day. No, not just something. Everything. She'd begun to live again. To experience life. Damián had roused long-buried feelings inside her. She'd been numb for so long. Opening herself up to the experience of being treated with respect and cherished by a man, if only for a short time, had made her feel worth something more than a body to be used for sex.

As she had guessed, allowing herself to feel had only succeeded in making her punishment even more intense. However, now she had a new safe place to escape to during the beatings. In Damián's arms at the beach cave. The cave wasn't just her imagination now, but a real place, where she heard the waves crashing on the shore, saw the dusky light of sunset, and felt his arms around her.

Magical.

No, safe.

She stroked the skin over her bare abdomen. And now she needed to protect what had resulted from that beautiful day. Sitting up, she pulled herself to her feet by holding on to the rim of the pedestal sink when her weakened legs threatened to give way. In the mirror, she saw that red splotches dotted her cheeks and neck from the strain of the dry heaves. She took a washcloth and wet it with cold water. Holding the cool cloth to her face, she closed her eyes and the image of Damián's face gave her comfort.

She would leave. Today. But where would she go?

Maman. I can't do this alone.

A distant memory flitted across her mind. The Christmas before she'd left, Maman had taken her down to Solana Beach to attend midnight Mass in the Eden Gardens neighborhood. Maman spoke both French and Spanish and loved to hear the Christmas Mass said in one of those languages. Savannah had only been seven then, but remembered it now as if it were yesterday. Maman told her the sermon had been about the Blessed Baby and the importance for members of the community to help young women who were in trouble to find safety and shelter to have their babies. At the time, Savannah hadn't known why having a baby would cause a girl to be in trouble.

And suddenly the answer for herself seemed so clear. She'd go to the Catholic church in Eden Gardens. They would help a young girl they perceived to be "in trouble," even though this baby actually was the impetus Savannah needed to get herself out of trouble. And her Master would never look for her in a neighborhood like that. She'd take on a new name—perhaps the English version of her Maman's maiden name Pannier. Savi Baker. He'd never trace her.

If the people of the Hispanic community were anything like Damián, she'd be okay. Perhaps she could tutor kids or somehow be of help to them while she waited for the baby.

Oh, Damián. I'm so scared. I wish I had your courage and strength.

Section Three: Marc

Prequel to Marc's Story, Nobody's Angel

October 2003, Aspen, Colorado

"Not tonight, damn it." The knock that intruded into his evening was unwelcome. Marc D'Alessio had had an exhausting day trying to juggle what seemed like dozens of crises at the resort and just wanted to be left alone.

He drained his glass of pinot bianco and leaned over to set his wineglass on the oak coffee table. Standing, he walked over to the stereo to turn down Bocelli's *Por Amor*. The lyrics made him uncomfortable tonight for some reason.

The living room of his Aspen apartment was done entirely in earth tones, reminding him of his childhood home in Lombardy. The place usually provided some calm for him after the stresses of trying to run the family business.

So not working tonight.

Another knock. With reluctance, he crossed the living room to open the front door. On the welcome mat knelt a voluptuous Italian woman he recognized immediately, even though her head was bowed.

Ah, shit. Not again.

"I've been very bad, Master Marco."

Melissa raised her head to look at him and smiled. She wore a very low-cut blouse, her breasts spilling from the gaping vee. Two years ago, he'd have dragged her inside, stripped her, and had her ass reddened within ten minutes.

That was before he'd found her in bed with his brother, Gino.

"Look Melissa, I'm tired, I don't appreciate your topping from the bottom. Besides, I thought we were finished playing these games."

She sat back on her heels, straightening her back. A look of sheer desperation crossed her face before she controlled it and reached up to place her hands on the sides of his hips. He didn't help her stand, but perhaps if he had, she wouldn't have been able to rub her breasts across his crotch and chest as she pulled herself to her feet.

Melissa teetered and grabbed his arms for support. Had she been drinking? Not nearly as much as he'd have to drink before wanting to have anything more to do with her.

The woman who had nearly become his fiancée wrapped her arms behind his neck and pulled his face toward hers. "Please, Marco. I need you. No one can satisfy me the way you can."

He doubted she'd waited around celibately over the last eighteen months for him to *satisfy* her again. What the hell did she want? He reached up to separate her interlocked hands and took a step away from her. Big mistake. She stepped into the apartment to follow him.

"Melissa, we're through. We were through six months before what happened after Gino's funeral. That was a big mistake."

Tears filled her brown eyes. She'd always been able to cry at a moment's notice. Her well-manicured hand splayed across his chest. "Marco, we need each other. Gino would have wanted us to be together to comfort each other."

"Somehow I doubt that." Gino didn't share. What was his, was his. And Gino had made it abundantly clear that Melissa was his before he left for Afghanistan. Of course, after their betrayal, Marc had wanted nothing to do with either of them.

She closed her eyes, then gazed up at him again and took a new tack. "Gino never satisfied me the way you could. He didn't understand my need to be controlled."

As if Marc had ever been in control in their relationship. She'd pursued him in college and they'd dated exclusively the year before he graduated. Then he'd brought her home to the resort to meet his family in preparation of popping the question. At least he'd been divested of that notion before it was too late.

Melissa had played Marc for a fool. He'd vowed that no woman would have that kind of control over him ever again.

"Look, I'm going to drive you home. You've obviously been drinking. Someone can bring you back over tomorrow to get your car."

He turned to walk into the kitchen to retrieve his Porsche keys. Melissa pressed her body against his back, pushing him against the dark-gray granite countertop. Her hand snaked out to grab his cock through his pants. She couldn't suppress a moan, apparently disappointed to find she hadn't given him an erection despite her blatant attempts.

"Marco, please. It's always been so good between us." She stroked him, and his long-neglected cock responded.

He spun around and grabbed her shoulders, wanting to push her away. Her pupils dilated. Damn her. If she wanted to be controlled, he could accommodate her.

He wrapped his fingers around her upper arm and guided her back into the living room. She stumbled on the stilettos and he steadied her. Maybe it wasn't that she was drunk, just that she couldn't walk on those damned five-inch heels.

When they reached the tan-colored leather sofa, he turned her around and pushed her hips against the armrest as he eased her torso over until her head was on the seat cushion and her ass high in the air. She turned her head and looked back at him, smiling.

"Hard, Sir. Give it to me hard."

Marc knew he'd hate himself later for letting her top him like this, but right now, he needed to blow off some steam. His life was so damned fucked up. He hated his job, but he couldn't leave it. He owed the family that much. But being cooped up behind a desk all day was killing him. He hadn't been out on the slopes since Gino enlisted.

Managing the resort was killing him by degrees.

He went to the bedroom to grab his toy bag and returned to Melissa, who waited patiently for him to begin. God help him, if she didn't look good to him, draped over the armrest, waiting to be spanked. Well, he definitely wasn't in the mood for an over-the-knee spanking tonight. Too intimate. He reached into the bag and pulled out his riding crop.

When she saw it, her butt cheeks clenched. Her mouth fell open as she sucked air into her lungs.

"What's your safeword, Melissa?"

"Cherry, Master Marco."

"Use it if you need it."

Whack.

Normally, he would have rubbed her ass cheeks before beginning a spanking. He would have planned the scene and gotten his head in the zone, but his thoughts were a jumbled mess tonight. Not that Melissa would notice or care. The flat leather tip came down on her right cheek and she gasped. He watched as the red mark appeared on her olive-colored skin.

Whack.

On the left cheek this time.

He delivered four more whacks in quick succession, alternating cheeks.

"Oh, God, yes!" she moaned.

Damn her for liking it, too. "Quiet!" The next blows fell to her upper thighs. One leg kicked out at him, nearly hitting him in the groin.

"Keep your legs down!"

She put her feet back on the floor. "Sorry, Sir."

The next eight blows reddened her ass nicely. *Dio*, he didn't like taking his pleasure when angry, but his cock throbbed at the sight. He needed to find release. He'd given her plenty of warning, if she wasn't looking for sex tonight, but Melissa had never run cold on him before, and he didn't think she would this time. He reached into the bag and pulled out a condom package. Placing the riding crop on top of his bag, he tore open the foil packet.

"Yes, Master. Give me that big cock."

"I didn't give you permission to speak." He ground the words out between his teeth as he sheathed himself. He most definitely didn't give her permission to speak in porn-flick scripted lines, either. Standing behind her, he reached down to stroke his fingers between her folds. Wet. He spread the moisture to encircle her clit, which protruded from its hood. Her ass bucked and tilted toward him. "Mmm." He rammed two fingers inside her and she moaned, but didn't speak.

Unable to wait any longer, he positioned himself behind her, held her ample hips in place with his hands, and thrust himself inside.

"Oh my God, Master!"

Ignoring her, he battered against her, his balls slapping against her pussy. He nearly pulled out of her, then pushed her legs open wider and slammed into her again.

"Sweet, Jesus! I need to come so badly, Marco!"

"Silence! You do not have permission to come yet." He continued to pound her pussy, then reached down and took her clit between his thumb and forefinger. He squeezed hard. She bucked against him.

"Oh, God! Oh, God! Please, Marco!"

"How do you address me?"

"Master Marco, please. I can't wait any longer!"

"But you will."

"Ohhh! Oh, yes!" As little as she could move with him confining her, she still managed to tilt her hips toward him, allowing him deeper access. "Fuck me, Master! Fuck me harder!"

He thrust until he felt his own explosion nearing. He purposely pictured her in bed with Gino to delay his own orgasm. "Come, now!" As she went over the top, her pussy clenched his cock. He needed to hold out a little longer. He wasn't finished with her yet.

"Oh, God! Ohhh, Marco, yesssss! Don't stop!"

He leaned over her, continuing to stroke her clit even after her spasms had ended. She tried to move her pelvis to evade his fingers on her oversensitive clit.

"Come again."

"No, Marco. I can't."

"Twice you have addressed me as Marco without using my proper title. You owe me two more orgasms." They'd negotiated orgasm torture before, but broke up before they'd tried it. "I. Said. Come. Again." He ground the words out against her ear. With her body restrained under his, he stroked her clit harder, faster. She couldn't escape the pressure he applied. She was trapped.

Just as he was.

Trapped.

"Oh, my God! I'm coming! Oh, shit!" She bucked wildly against him, clenching his cock as another orgasm wracked her body, this one seeming to be more intense than the last. He'd been taught never to promise a sub something and not deliver, but delaying his own orgasm was hell.

He let her breathing slow a bit, then touched her clit again.

"Oh, God, don't! Please, Mar...Master. Enough!"

His fingers stilled. "Do you wish to use your safeword?"

She paused, gasping for breath, then shook her head. He pulled her hair away from her face so he could judge whether she could take another one. He began stroking her clit again. Her cheeks were wet from tears, but her mouth panted as she let the sensations build again. Her mewling sounds told him she wasn't in pain. Not that pain was necessarily a bad thing in Melissa's book of needs.

He stroked her harder. Her screams became incoherent as she bucked against him.

"Open your eyes."

She did as he ordered. He pinched her clit again, then stood up and rammed her with his cock.

"Oh, shit! Oh, Master, please! No more!"

Again and again, he thrust himself inside her, demanding more than he ever had before. He took perverse pleasure in making something so desired feel like a punishment. Not unlike his feeling of being trapped at this resort, staring at the mountains every day and knowing he couldn't walk away from that goddamned desk and enjoy them as he had before Gino had joined the Marines.

He reached down and stroked her clit again as he neared his own climax.

"Oh, ohhh, ohhhhhh, yes! Yes, please! Don't stop!" Her body convulsed beneath him as she experienced her third orgasm in just a few minutes.

Marc found himself breathing hard, as well. He pumped harder, faster. The release as his semen spurted from him caused his legs to go weak. But he continued to pound her pussy until the last spasm of his cock and her vagina ceased. He pulled out immediately and staggered on weakened legs to the bathroom where he disposed of the condom, washed himself off, then got a clean washcloth and wet it with warm water for her.

He looked into the mirror over the vanity. The disgust written on his face brought him to a standstill. Surprisingly, he wasn't disgusted with Melissa, but with himself.

What the fuck was he doing?

He needed to get away—from Melissa, from the resort, from his family.

Far enough away to find himself.

Before this place totally consumed his soul.

* * *

Christmas Day 2003, Aspen, Colorado

"You've what?" Mama turned red. All conversation at the dinner table came to an abrupt halt, quite a feat at a large Italian family gathering. The scrutiny of every set of eyes at the table bore into him, but most especially Mama's. And Melissa's.

"I've joined the Navy." Marc repeated.

"How could you do such a thing?" Mama's voice rose an octave. "Hasn't this family given enough already?"

Marc met his mother's gaze. "Exactly why I need to do this."

In part, at least. If Marc could play some part in the victory over Al Qaeda and the Taliban, Gino would not have died in vain. He'd even passed the test to train as a hospital corpsman. Maybe he could help keep someone else from dying, so he or she could return home to loved ones.

He glanced over at Melissa, whose face was redder than Mama's. If looks could kill, he'd need a corpsman of his own. Why had Mama invited her to the family dinner anyway? She and Gino had barely been engaged a week when he'd enlisted. Talk about a whirlwind romance.

Marc hadn't seen her since that disastrous night at his apartment when he'd totally lost control. He'd talked to the Navy recruiter the next day.

See the world. Whether he was sent to Iraq, Afghanistan, or just another part of the States, it would be far enough away, he supposed.

Seeing Melissa again reminded him of the last face-to-face conversation he'd had with Gino before his brother left home, only to be killed in the mountains of Afghanistan five months later.

Since Gino's death—*Dio*, two months short of two years now—Marc had buried himself in the running of the resort, losing interest in the frivolous pursuits he'd specialized in since high school.

Gino had been the favored son, the one Mama groomed all his life to take over the family business. Always the dutiful one, Gino had gone to Cornell's Johnson School earning an MBA, just as Mama wanted. He'd returned to Aspen and put the degree to use turning the family's ski lodge into a popular world-class, five-star resort offering all of the amenities.

Marc had opted to attend a nearby college and earn a degree in recreation and leisure studies, hoping to come back to the resort to pursue the things he loved, like skiing and camping. He'd lived the life of a carefree playboy—easy job, easy money, easy women. No one expected anything more from him.

Then Marc had invited Melissa to Aspen to meet his family late in the summer following their college graduation. He and Melissa had dated more steadily since his third year of college. Marc's interest in BDSM had been developing for a few years and Melissa had been a willing participant, the first woman his age to have shown any interest in bondage and discipline.

When Marc had caught Gino in bed with Melissa early one September morning two years ago, the brothers had fought, physically as well as verbally. Gino had everything he could possibly want—and yet he found the need to steal Marc's girl away. It wasn't until much later Marc realized Melissa had set Gino up. But Gino hadn't had time to pursue women and fell head over heels for Melissa, proposing to her that day, whether because he loved her or wanted to rub Marc's face in their relationship, Marc wasn't sure.

Neither of them had seen Melissa for who she really was at that point. Gino probably never did. When the Nine-Eleven attacks happened a week later, Gino surprised everyone by enlisting.

Since he'd heard Gino had been killed in action, guilt had plagued Marc over the things he'd said to his big brother that day. Had Gino enlisted for patriotic reasons for their adopted homeland—or because Marc had driven him away with his anger and animosity?

He'd loved his brother, even if they had spent most of their lives embattled in an ugly sibling rivalry. Had Marc driven his brother to his death?

Even though that thought had consumed him every day since February 2002, it still had the power to cause his meal to churn in his gut. He laid his fork down.

Mama's voice brought him back to the present. "You have responsibilities here. Who will operate the lodge?"

Anyone the hell but me.

Lord knew he'd tried. But he and his mother had clashed over every major decision he'd tried to make. Besides, Marc had always been more interested in developing backcountry ski and hiking weekend packages he could lead groups on, not overseeing the day-to-day operations and making sure the payroll and taxes were paid on time.

"I've been showing Alessandro and Carmela how to take over for a couple months now. They're ready for the day-to-day management." His brother and sister took a sudden interest in the lasagna remaining on their plates, afraid of revealing their duplicity in the plan Marc had put into action two months ago when he'd enlisted.

"Unacceptable!" Her Lombardy accent became more pronounced when she perceived a loss of control. She'd grown up in the war-ravaged southern Alps skirting the Po Valley, where Marc and his siblings had been born, as well. The family ran a ski lodge there, but moved to Aspen when Mama had discovered the name of her father, an American Marine in World War II. Marc's grandfather had helped the family get established in this country and all of the D'Alessios were American citizens now.

"Your place is here. You will just un-join." She acted as though her decreeing such would make it so.

"Not an option, Mama. I fly to Chicago tomorrow to begin training at Great Lakes."

Mama's hand gripped her fork and he couldn't help but think she wished it were protruding from his neck at the moment. Her eyes narrowed. "How can you do this to me, Marco?"

The tears welling in her eyes tugged at Marc's heart, but he wouldn't relent. "Mama, I'm not doing anything *to* you. I'm doing this *for* me."

For my country. For Gino.

Papa, Sandro, and Carmela stared at him in disbelief and something akin to awe. He'd never stood up to Mama before. Melissa just looked as if something was slipping away from her grasp.

"Marco," Melissa began, "how can you do this to your Mama?"

Well, that was new. Concern for his mother? *Rich, Melissa. Fucking rich.*

Mama's face became redder with Melissa's encouragement. "This family already made the ultimate sacrifice for America. We need not shed any more precious D'Alessio blood in this war."

But the wrong D'Alessio brother's blood was shed.

If anyone had been expendable in the family, it most certainly would have been Marc. Twenty-six years old and when had he ever done something selfless? Noble? Honorable?

Marc wiped the condensation off his wine glass with his thumb, watching a bead of water trickle down the stem. He'd never admitted to his brother how much he admired him, spending all those years being jealous of Gino's status in the family. He'd never have that chance now.

Marc looked up at her, his gaze locking with Melissa's. She hadn't loved Gino the way he'd deserved. She sure as hell didn't love Marc. Was she just some damned gold digger? He dismissed her, not caring what her motives were.

Then he turned to his mother. "I need to do this, Mama." His voice sounded raspy even to his ears. Marc maintained his gaze with Mama. *You aren't going to win this one, Mama.* When she looked down at her plate. The world shifted on its axis. She'd surrendered.

"Well, at least you haven't joined the Marines," Mama whispered. "I don't think I could bear that."

Gino had served with the Marines. No problem. Marc was tired of trying to compete with his brother. He'd never fill his brother's shoes as a war hero either, unless he got himself killed, which he didn't intend to do. So he'd chosen the Navy instead.

"Just be careful, son," Papa said. "Come home safe."

"I will, Papa." Marc placed his red cloth napkin on the table. "Now, if you will all excuse me, I need to relieve the manager at the front desk for the night shift." Marc had decided he and Sandro would work some of the holiday shifts to give more employees a chance to spend time with their families.

"Sandro, when you're finished eating, you're on duty at the concierge desk tonight."

"I'm finished." His little brother quickly wiped his mouth, probably anxious to escape the tension in the room, as well. "Mama, may I be excused?"

Mama gave him a nod, but her gaze remained fixed on Marc. Without any acknowledgement of Melissa, Marc turned to leave. He felt Mama's and Melissa's gazes boring into his shoulder blades as he exited the dining room.

* * *

Nearly an hour later, Marc placed the phone in the receiver and sighed. He looked across the hotel lobby at the blazing fireplace surrounded by the festive decorations Carmela had orchestrated. Several couples laughed and flirted as they sipped cocktails and beer, gearing up for an evening of sex, no doubt.

Two years ago, he'd partied with the guests after a long day on the slopes giving ski lessons. Marc had never fit into a business-suited world. The guests had treated him like one of their own. He preferred to teach ski lessons during the winter months, lead extreme mountain-hiking excursions the other seasons, and provide his own *specialized services* in his spare time year-round. His gut tightened. He'd given up all three when Gino died.

Right now, though, he had a guest asking for him specifically to handle some emergency in her cabin. Marc picked up the master-key card and put the "Back in a Moment" sign on the reception desk. He told the bartender at the wet bar in the lobby she'd need to cover the desk for a while.

Marc sauntered over to the Concierge desk. "Sandro, come with me. You're going to have to deal with these matters after I leave tomorrow."

At least Sandro showed a knack for the business end of things—and Carmela enjoyed being activities coordinator and working on publicity. They'd do fine. Of course, Mama would continue to pull the strings. She wasn't one to relinquish control.

"You and Carmela have done a great job these past couple months," Marc said as they walked out the service exit. "You're going to do fine."

"Are you sure?"

Marc squeezed his little brother at the nape of his neck. "Hell, yeah, Sandro."

The wind whipped at their faces as they crossed the grounds to one of the more isolated cabins. He wondered what could be wrong. He'd always made sure the resort was maintained to perfection.

Marc knocked and spoke through the door, "Marc D'Alessio!" No answer. He knocked again and heard a woman's voice inviting him to come in. He inserted the key into the lock, turned down the handle, and pushed the door open, motioning for Sandro to precede him.

A couple of steps into the cabin, Sandro came to a dead stop. "Damn!"

Damn was right. Why did he have to have a major freaking problem on his last night? Marc nudged his brother further into the cabin so he could begin to assess the situation.

Oh, shit. On the floor, beside the overstuffed loveseat, knelt a middle-aged woman with brassy red hair and fake boobs, clenching a purple-handled riding crop between her teeth—naked as the day she was born. She also had the nip-tucks to keep everything firmly in place, despite her age.

The woman looked confused as her gaze shifted from Marc to Sandro, then settled on Marc, probably because he was the taller of the two. Her hand reached up to take the crop out of her mouth and asked, "Which one of you is Master Marco?"

Merda. His reputation had preceded him.

Sandro looked at him and grinned. "Is there something you forgot to train me to take over for you, bro?"

Brat.

Marc recalled that week nine years ago when Master Marco had been born. Seventeen, restless, and horny as hell until a sexy, bored cougar he'd given ski lessons to took him under her wing at night for some private lessons of her own design. By the time the week had ended, he'd learned more about bondage and discipline than any underaged kid ought to know. The euphoric feeling of control and power he'd achieved in Dom space had him hooked for life.

In the beginning, the diversion kept him from going stark-raving mad from boredom. Of course, he'd never taken money from the women. They were paying enough to stay at the lodge. He was just…an added amenity.

He'd also drawn the line at having intercourse with them. He had friends with benefits for that, although most of them weren't interested in exploring their kinky sides. Until Melissa. So, Master Marco provided a select few in-the-know resort patrons with whatever level of bondage, discipline, and mild SM kink they chose. He preferred bondage and spanking best, though.

When he met Melissa, he thought he'd found himself the perfect submissive. He'd grown tired of catering to bored, rich older women. Most were anything but submissive. Hell, they'd called all the shots. Having them top him from the bottom was about as sexy as stale wine.

But, shit, he had loved turning their asses crimson red with his firm hand or whatever implement from his growing toy bag they preferred.

But that was then.

Melissa had topped from the bottom, as well. What was he doing to attract such quasi-submissive women? Maybe he needed to take Dom lessons.

He sighed. "I'm sorry, but Master Marco doesn't work here any longer."

Marc politely extricated himself from the indelicate situation and advised Sandro to forget what he'd seen. Master Marco had now officially been eliminated from the amenities offered at the resort.

Someday he'd like to explore the lifestyle with a woman interested in actual submission. As he walked back to the lobby, Marc wondered if he'd ever find such a woman—one he could train himself. One who didn't have a plastic face and a pair of matching silicone boobs.

Focus, man.

First, he had a four-year enlistment in the Navy to fulfill. Maybe in that time he'd become a man he could live with.

* * *

Five months later, May 2004, Camp Pendleton, California

Marc fell back on the rack, too tired to remove his boots. Every muscle in his body ached—some he'd never become acquainted with before. What the hell had he gotten himself into? If he'd known becoming a corpsman might land him in the Marines, he'd never have signed the damned papers. Everyone knew that training with the Marine Corps was more intense than any other regular military branch. He could vouch personally that his Great Lakes boot-camp experience was the bunny slope compared to this.

He heard the rack next to him squeak and looked over to see Orlando. The man had just been through the same maneuvers and exercises and looked ready to go dancing. *Merda*. Marc had no idea how soft he'd gotten at that cushy desk job.

Orlando looked unhappy, as usual. Never saw someone with a more depressing outlook on life. Maybe he could engage the kid in some conversation. At least Marc's jaw muscles were still in working order.

"So, what got you into the Marines?"

Orlando looked around as if perhaps Marc had been talking to someone else, then his gaze zeroed in on him. "Lost my job."

"What did you do?"

"Busboy." He said it as if Marc would look down on him or something. Damn, the kid sure had a boulder of resentment on his shoulder.

"That's hard work."

"It was a living. While I had it, anyway."

Clearly, this conversation was going nowhere fast. "So, where you from?"

"Just down the coast. Eden Gardens at Solana Beach."

Again, he looked as if Marc would make some judgment call. He had no freaking clue what Eden Gardens was like, but it sure sounded nice. When he didn't ask where Marc was from, he just decided to volunteer the info. "I'm from the Lombardy region of Italy, but have lived in Aspen since I was a boy."

"Mmm." Orlando removed his boots and began scrubbing the suede on one of them.

Shit. What the hell could he do to get a response out of the guy? Marc turned onto his side with a groan and propped his head in the palm of his hand. "So, have you ever tied a woman to her bed?"

Orlando's hand came to a stop and he looked up from his boot. Got his attention, at least.

"Once or twice."

Yeah, right. He'd remember if it were once…or twice. But there was a look in his eye that Marc couldn't quite decipher.

"I don't get off on that shit."

"Then you must not be doing it right. Nothing sweeter than the surrender of a submissive woman in restraints."

"Not if she doesn't want to be in them."

"Well, no shit. I'm talking safe, sane, and consensual, good old-fashioned bondage and discipline between consenting adults."

"I had a girlfriend once who was into pain, but I left her. I could never hurt a woman."

"Even if she needed the pain to get off?"

Orlando got a faraway look in his eyes, his hands remaining motionless, holding the boot and brush. "There was this girl last fall who got herself into a really bad BDSM scene. Fucking pissed me off when I found her. She sure as hell wasn't enjoying it." Orlando shook his head. "No thanks."

"Why didn't she use her safeword?"

"I'm not sure she didn't. She was with two guys she barely knew. Not very good at keeping herself safe, I guess." He looked as if he were a million miles away again. Then slowly he began scrubbing the boot.

"Some people don't take enough time to establish trust. Can't have a power exchange if there isn't a firm foundation in trust."

When Orlando silently continued working at the grime on his boot, Marc eased back onto the rack. If he could move, he'd do the same with his boots. Tomorrow morning, he'd have to get up and go through this pain all over again. If he survived reconnaissance training, it would be a miracle.

Gino had gone through Recon Marine training, too. Marc had a new respect for him after a week with this Marine unit. Funny how Marc had tried so hard to avoid going into the Marines—then had wound up in the same damned unit Gino had served in.

Gino hadn't said much about what he was doing. He'd been sent to Kandahar in the early days of Operation Enduring Freedom to help establish the base there. If Marc made it through training, he wanted to talk with Master Sergeant Montague about the firefight that had taken Gino's life. The details they'd been given were pretty sketchy.

But there weren't a lot of opportunities for a corpsman to chat up his master sergeant. Orlando called him Top already, but Marc knew not to ever dare to call his master sergeant "Top" to his face without permission. Funny, but in Marc's past experience with BDSM, Top meant something totally different. But a master sergeant wasn't unlike a Dom, really. Only, in this situation, Marc would have to be the bottom or sub. Not a position he liked to be in.

But he wouldn't be enjoying Dom space again anytime soon. After months of medical training, including A-School, Marc just hoped he'd be able to save the lives of the Marines in this unit when the time came. *Dio*, he didn't want to screw up. They would count on him to be there when they needed him.

Oh, shit. What had ever possessed him to enlist? He'd never carried responsibility like this before in his entire fucking life.

* * *

Two months later, July 2004, Camp Pendleton, California

Iraq. Knowing they'd be shipping out to a Forward Operating Base in Fallujah in a week sure made him want to do a few things before he left. The no-porn, no-sex, no-alcohol rules were going to kill him. He needed to blow off some steam while he could.

Orlando walked into the barracks and dropped Marc's mail on the rack at his feet. Looked like he'd taken the fetish magazine Marc's little brother, Sandro, had subscribed him to out of the wrapper for a peek.

Marc smiled. "Get into a tee and khakis. We're going out."

"Where to?"

"Little place up the coast. You're going to love it."

"I don't think so."

"I do. You need an education."

"More training?"

"Something like that."

Twenty minutes later, they were on the 5 in Marc's vintage cherry-red Porsche 911 Carrera, top down and heading for Los Angeles. He figured that would be far enough off base for them not to run into anyone who would report them up the chain of command. At least they wouldn't find that by-the-book Master Sergeant Montague there. The man had to be about the grimmest, meanest, hard-ass Marc had ever met.

He'd never found an opportunity to ask his master sergeant about Gino. Montague was involved in the firefight that killed his brother, though, and had written a letter to Marc's parents soon after telling them of his regret about Gino's death.

Marc had read the short letter many times after his brother's death, trying to glean some clue as to what had happened, but there weren't many details there. Mostly he'd just shared how honorably Gino had served his unit. Probably just a form letter he sent to all families of the fallen. Maybe someday the two of them would talk about that fatal day in Afghanistan. But not anytime soon.

As the sports car's engine purred, his thumb stroked the underside of the steering wheel. He was going to miss his baby. Sandro had agreed to fly out to San Diego later this week to drive her home—agreed a little too enthusiastically for Marc's taste. He hoped he'd get back from Fallujah before the kid blew the engine.

"Nice ride!" Orlando shouted over the wind blowing around them.

"Thanks. What do you drive?"

"Harley."

Shit! This kid has chick-magnet potential, after all.

"Had to sell it to make rent last year, though."

"Crap. That had to suck."

"Yeah. I'm currently a man without wheels—but I guess it won't matter much after next week."

Marc hoped there would be at least one woman with a military fetish at the club tonight. Even without "Marines" or "Navy" emblazoned on their T-shirts, their high-and-tight haircuts should make it obvious they were military men. Hopefully not too obvious, because they didn't want the MPs to catch them in an off-limits kink club. They'd be so busted.

He also hoped the club provided Dom gear. He'd left his toy bag in Aspen. Wouldn't be surprised if Sandro was trying out his gear, too, the way he'd become so fascinated by the whole Master Marco fiasco. He shook his head.

"So, where are we going again?"

"A little club I heard about."

"What kind of club?"

"Fetish."

"Man, I told you I'm not into inflicting pain on *chicas*."

"No problem. I'll take care of that part. We're tag-teaming. You'll be the master in charge of pleasure. You do know how to please a woman, don't you, Orlando?" Marc grinned over at him.

The kid sat up straighter in the leather seat. "Well, hell, yeah."

Marc's smile widened. Bringing Orlando's machismo into question had riled him up. Being Italian, Marc had been weaned on machismo.

"This place is fairly strict—no penetration except oral, no alcohol other than beer and wine. I know the owner, though. Jerry's a Navy vet who served in Vietnam. He'll make sure we deploy with enough carnal memories to last us for eight months of lonely nights in Iraq. I called and he said he'd find us a fem-sub interested in a threesome." Marc's only hard limit over the phone was that she not be Italian.

"I've never..."

"Hell, Orlando, we're headed into a fucking combat zone. What better time to try a threesome than now?"

Less than two hours later, they were seated in the social area of the club having beers with the petite redhead Jerry had sent over to get acquainted. Bianca seemed to have a thing for Orlando's forearm. She kept tracing her sharp red fingernail along its length, then she'd bat her eyes at Orlando, who for some goddamned reason couldn't quite make eye contact with her.

Come on, kid. She's interested in you, for Christ's sake.

She sighed and looked at Marc. "So, what kind of kink are you boys into?"

Marc brushed a burnished lock of hair back from her forehead to get a better look at her green eyes. "Whatever kind of kink you need, pet."

Her pupils dilated. Marc smiled.

"Well, um, Jerry says I can trust you—or he'll whup your asses." She smiled sweetly to belie the threat. "So, how about leather flogger? St. Andrew's cross? Cunni and fellatio?"

Marc's cock throbbed. She had him at flogger, one of his favorites. Jerry knew and had probably planted the idea. Fucking patriotic of him.

"Mind if I warm up your backside on the loveseat first? The kid here needs to see how erotic spanking is done."

Orlando glared at him, but didn't speak up.

"Sure. Let me go change into something more...appropriate." She smiled and flounced off toward the dressing rooms.

"We'll be waiting!" Marc called after her.

"You don't have to make me sound like a fucking virgin."

Marc turned to smile at Orlando. "Good, then don't act like one. When we restrain her on the cross, I'll let you have first crack at her. Her ass will be pretty sore by then. You can work on her tits and pussy." Marc glanced down to see the bulge in the kid's pants. Yeah, he was coming around.

Fifteen minutes later, as he polished off his beer, Marc looked toward the dressing-room entrance to see Bianca strutting toward them in a short, short plaid skirt and a schoolgirl's white blouse. She held a wooden ruler between her breasts.

Holy shit!

Marc adjusted himself surreptitiously to keep from strangling his cock and stood up.

"You're late, young lady. Mr. Jerry sent you to me for your punishment thirty minutes ago. What do you have to say for yourself?"

Her pupils dilated again as she caught her breath before she cast her eyes down to the floor. "I'm sorry, sir. I was with my friends and just lost track of time."

Marc took the ruler from her and laid it on the table. He had raided Jerry's private toy stash while Bianca was dressing and picked up one of the leopard-print cuffs lying beside the ruler. He handed it to Orlando, then picked up Bianca's hand and extended it to the kid, whose hands shook as he wrapped the cuff around her wrist and tightened it.

"Is that too tight?" Orlando asked.

"No, Sir."

The kid's pants tented at the title. Marc grinned, then he turned her around and pulled her cuffed hand behind her back while he secured the right wrist and clipped the two together. She kept her head bowed, causing his cock to throb even more. He couldn't wait to turn her over his knee. He picked up a borrowed necktie and blindfolded her.

Grabbing the ruler almost as an afterthought, he motioned for Orlando to take one arm and Marc took the other to keep her from running into any obstacles as they led her to a darkened corner. He pointed to the far end and Orlando sat down, then Marc lowered Bianca over the armrest at that end until her head rested in Orlando's lap. He wouldn't be able to smack her as hard with his left hand, but the ruler would sting enough.

Marc lifted her short skirt. *Oh, yeah.* No panties. Her round globes were white and begging for some color. "Tell me why you've been sent to the principal's office, Bianca."

"Because I was talking in class, Sir."

Marc reached out and rubbed her ass cheeks vigorously to get the blood to the surface. Then he indicated for Orlando to do the same. The kid's hand reached behind her to gently stroke her ass. Well, it was a start. At least he was touching her. He motioned Orlando's hand away with the ruler.

Smack!

She gasped in the most sensual way. His cock strained against his khakis. Her left cheek soon displayed the mark of the ruler, holes and all. "Tell me what your mouth should be used for instead."

"Fucking, Sir."

"Good answer." She visibly relaxed.

Smack! The right cheek soon bore a matching welt.

Marc nodded to Orlando indicating her head. The kid moved his hand up past her cuffed hands and traced a path up her arm to her hair.

"Tell me how you want to please us with your mouth, pet."

"By sucking your cocks, Sirs."

Smack!

Smack!

Smack!

"Oh!" The pain and frustration were evident in her scream. The last blow landed across her upper thighs, causing her to squirm. Enough of the damned ruler. He needed to feel his hand against her ass, between her legs.

"Stand!" With his and Orlando's help, she was lifted onto her feet again. The disappointment written on her face told him she thought her discipline had ended.

Not even close, pet.

Marc led her to stand in front of the dividing center cushion, facing her toward the social area where they'd negotiated the scene. He sat down, then reached up and took Bianca by the arm, pulling her off balance.

"Oh!"

"We have you," Marc assured her. Yes, she definitely hadn't expected more. Good. He liked to surprise subbies.

He wrapped his arm around her waist while motioning for Orlando to do the same in front of her thighs. Together they lowered her over both their laps, careful not to overstrain her arms. Bianca was positioned so that her abdomen was over Marc's thighs and her ass lifted in the air, giving Orlando a perfect view. Her calves were across the kid's lap and he reached out to stroke her legs with his right hand.

"How are you doing, pet?"

"Fine, Sir." Her voice had gone up an octave to a high squeak.

"What's your safeword?"

"Red, Sir."

"Use it if you need to." Not knowing how much pain she could take, it never hurt to remind her, before the spanking continued in earnest. Hoping to give Orlando and himself better access to her pussy—he reached down and put pressure against her right knee until she spread her legs for him with some hesitation.

Slap!

He brought his right hand down hard against her pink lower right cheek.
Slap!

Then the left.

Slap! Slap! Slap! Slap!

Continuing to alternate cheeks, he delivered the blows in quick succession until he heard her gasp. "Ow! Oh, please, Sir."

Marc stopped and rubbed the reddened cheeks, watching her flesh jiggle beneath his hand. His cock pressed against her abdomen. "Please what, pet?"

"Please…more, Sir."

"Are you topping me?" He'd had enough of that shit in Aspen.

She stiffened. "No, Sir! I…forgot my place. Please, Sir, do whatever you wish to do to your pet."

"Good girl." He moved her right leg until it slid off their laps and her foot went to the floor, opening her pussy to them nicely. Orlando's hand was making its way closer to the juncture between her thighs. Marc's next blows went directly to that vulnerable area.

Slap!

Slap!

"Oh, God! I mean, thank you, Sir!"

He slid his finger between her folds. Wet. They had agreed that fingers wouldn't break the club's no-penetration limit, so he moved down to slide two fingers inside her. Then he pulled out and his wet fingers pressed against the sides of her clit. She moaned. When he touched the swollen nubbin standing erect from its hood, she bucked against his hand.

"Remain still!"

She groaned and he moved his left hand to her lower back to keep her from moving. Then he delivered his hardest blow yet, against her pussy.

Slap!

"Ow! I…um…thank you, Sir."

Marc decided he shouldn't be having all the fun. He moved his hand away and encouraged "Master Pleasure," sitting like a lump on a log next to him, to take the reins and give Bianca her first orgasm of the evening. The young man surprised him by extricating himself from under her thighs and kneeling on the floor in front of the loveseat. Marc shifted her body to give Orlando better access.

His buddy lowered his face to her pussy and wrapped his arms around her thighs. Marc waited for him to make contact with her sensitive core, and simultaneously pinched her swollen nipple.

"Oh, my fucking God!"

Marc pinched her harder.

"Sir! I mean, oh God, Sirs!! Please don't stop!"

He pinched her again. She was forgetting her place. *Slap!* Her topping annoyed him. "You will ask for permission to come."

"Yes, Sir! I'm sorry, Sir!" Orlando's tongue must be torturing the poor woman. "Oh! Oh! Oh!" Marc grimaced. Her fevered gasps and writhing body sent his cock into conniptions. Shit, he wished he could bury himself to the hilt inside her pussy to get some relief.

"Oh, please, Sir, may I come?"

Marc heard Orlando sucking at her clit, then he pulled away, releasing the swollen nubbin. The kid nodded before taking the tiny erection in his mouth again.

"Yes, you may, pet."

Orlando's head returned to her pussy, shaking back and forth in tiny movements as he tormented her clit.

"Ohhh! Ohhhhhhhh, fuck! Yes! Please…" She moaned, bucking her red ass into the air. Marc's hand landed on her sweet globes. *Slap! Slap!* "Please, yes, there! Oh, God! Oh, God, Yessss! Yessssssss!" Her screams filled the room and Marc had no doubt she'd turned heads throughout the club. *Slap! Slap! Slap!* "Ahhhhhhh! Yessssssssss!"

Her body convulsed on his lap as she went over the top. Orlando's head movements slowed, but he must have continued to lick her clit, because she bucked a few more times against his face, milking every last drop out of her orgasm.

Shit, she would have made an interesting subbie to train. Getting rid of her tendency to top would have been a challenge he'd welcome. But he didn't know when he'd be stateside again. Not fair to make her wait. Someday he'd find the woman who would complete his Dom side.

But, for now, he and Orlando had needs to be taken care of by one smart-mouthed subbie. Orlando leaned back with a pussy-eating grin on his face and a whole lot of her juices glistening against his lips, chin, and nose. Marc nodded and watched Orlando's chest swell.

Well done, man.

Section Four: Bond Forms

The Unbreakable Bond Forms

November 2004, Fallujah, Iraq

Damián hunkered down, awaiting orders. Sergeant Miller signaled for Grant and Wilson to cover the south-facing wall, while he and Sergeant took the east. The insurgent weapons fire seemed to be coming from the east, which made sense based on their recon, but he was beginning to think there was more than one enemy stronghold holding this rooftop in its sights.

Despite being in country four months, this was his first real battle since arriving in Fallujah. Sure, there had been some roadside bombings. Those happened almost every day—and never ceased to scare the shit out of him. Never could predict or prepare for them. But his combat training had really kicked in today. Now, if only they could get out of here with the unit intact.

Damián preferred the earlier days of the battle for this city, when they'd let him use his sniper skills against the insurgents. But the shaky truce limited him to firing only in defensive situations. He knew the insurgents had placed a bounty on Marine snipers. And for good reason.

Their latest intel indicated there was a prime target in a building a thousand yards away and they'd continue to wait until they had a chance at taking their shot. They'd taken turns watching for hours today. Nothing.

Unlike most Marines, Orlando saw the faces of his targets clearly. His high-powered scope homed in on their faces, their eyes, their weapons. And when he hit center mass, even saw the expressions on their faces as they fell dead. One shot, one kill.

But sometimes he replaced their images with those of the Jerk-off who pimped Savannah's body out. Or the two sadists who tortured her. Even her sugar daddy.

Damián sighed.

"He's gone to ground," Sergeant Miller announced after getting the latest radio transmission. He ordered everyone on the rooftop to take advantage of the lull and grab an MRE. It might be a meal ready to eat, but he wasn't sure it was *fit* to eat. At first, he had appreciated being able to eat a hot meal on the run, but if he saw another beef stew MRE as long as he lived, he'd barf. They ate in silence, each of them probably wondering if they'd manage to complete this mission.

Damián's mind wandered back to what had gotten him to this rooftop in Iraq. After being fired from the hotel, he'd tried for weeks to find another job. Nothing. He'd sold his Harley, but not for nearly as much as it was worth. After a few months, when he could no longer make rent, he'd been evicted from his apartment. The only option he could see was to join the Marines.

It hadn't been a bad gig. He liked being a Marine. He'd been afraid it would be like being in juvie hell again—but the discipline and structure here were different. He wasn't just out to survive on his own. He had his buddies to look after, too. He knew they were looking out for him, too. A band of brothers. He glanced over at Lance Corporal Grant, sitting against the other wall. The communications tech temporarily attached to his unit wouldn't take kindly to being called a brother; she was as tough as the rest of them.

He'd met a lot of good friends he expected to keep for life. Sergeant Miller, the blunt African-American from East St. Louis, had fought alongside him on recon and sniper missions since Damián had been in Fallujah.

Grant had become a great friend recently, too. She was easy to talk to. Hard-edged, but honest. He didn't usually have female friends, but she was a Marine first—just one of the guys—and a damned good listener. He'd even told her about Savannah. Damián admired Grant's kick-ass strength. Maybe, being a woman, she had to come across even tougher just to show her worth among the guys.

Grant sure made it clear from the start she wasn't here to be a Marine Mattress—having sex with any and all Marines interested. He liked that about her, not that he hadn't noticed her physical attributes. Blonde, five-nine, muscular build. She just wasn't interested in anything more than friendship with the men in the unit. Said she preferred to top, anyway, and that she couldn't picture any of them tied to her bed. *Hell and hell no!* So, the two of them were just going to remain buddies.

Then there was Doc. Damián smiled. The Navy corpsman he'd roomed with back at Pendleton sure did keep things interesting. At first, the guy had pissed him off royally. Arrogant. Privileged. Driving a freaking Porsche. What the hell was he doing in the military? Certainly not for the stable income, which is what brought Damián to the Marine Corps. But over the months since that night at the sex club, the man—and the Corps—had grown on Damián. His unit couldn't ask for a better corpsman. He'd patched up just about everyone at some point or other. Luckily, only for minor injuries. He hoped that remained true today.

Damián remembered Doc dragging his ass to that fetish club, where he'd learned BDSM wasn't all about violence and inflicting pain. That was just plain wrong. It was about a consensual exchange of power. Having control over another—and yourself. Making sure her needs were met before thinking about your own. He could understand that. Definitely something he might be interested in trying when he got stateside again.

Damián wondered when he'd ever get the chance to be with another woman. He'd sure enjoyed himself with that redhead. He smiled.

"What's so funny?" Sergeant Miller asked.

"Just thinking about what a fucking great life I have in the Corps."

Sergeant grunted. "Yeah, right. I'll bet you were thinking about some sweet pussy waiting for you back in California."

Damián's smile faded.

Ah, Savannah.

He'd replayed the scene at Thousand Steps Beach over and over in his head. He and Savannah had connected so perfectly that day. He'd never been with a woman who turned him on as much or responded to him as well as she had. He thought it had been good for her, too. So, why had she ignored his attempts to contact her? He was in the phone book. She could have called him. She knew his name. He regretted not exchanging phone numbers, but the best he'd been able to do was leave printed messages in the mailbox at her gate. No response.

Well, he'd also staked out the hotel in La Jolla for a few weeks. She hadn't returned, at least not while he'd waited for her there. What had become of her? Had she continued to let men abuse her for money? He gave his head a mental shake. He didn't like to think she'd returned to that life.

No, he preferred to picture her going to college, getting her degree. Maybe she'd go on to become the social worker she'd wanted to be. Help kids who needed her. That's what he hoped…

The grenade came over the wall and rolled to land mere feet from Sergeant Miller's hip. Damián froze. No one fucking moved. He looked over at Sergeant, who just kept eating. He didn't fucking see it. Grant and Wilson kept talking, oblivious, too. After what seemed like an eternity, Damián shoved the Sergeant to move, shouting, "Grenade!" Sergeant bolted up and grabbed Damián's arm, propelling him in front of him. Damián's body moved as if trudging through thick mud. Everything happened in slow motion. He couldn't move fast enough.

Grant and Wilson reacted at last, but too damned slowly. Damián rushed toward them, trying to push them toward the other end of the rooftop. At the last moment, Damián turned to check on Sergeant Miller, who was right behind him. The blast deafened his ears, the percussion of the explosion knocking him backwards, hard against someone. They went sprawling across the roof.

Mother fucking insurgents.

Pressure like a fucking wall had fallen on top of him. His foot was on fire. He opened his eyes and saw Sergeant's head, or what was left of it, lying on his chest. The man's bloody brains showed through the hole in his head. Miller's body lay prone across Damián's chest and abdomen. The pool of blood forming on Damián's chest grew warm. *What the fuck?*

A roaring in his ears merged with high-pitched screams. He realized the screams were his own.

"*Madre de Dios*! No! Sergeant, don't you fucking die!"

He knew Sergeant Miller was gone, but kept yelling at him as if he could bring him back by the sheer volume of his voice. He looked up and watched as Grant and Wilson, on either side of him, lifted the body off him. Damián turned his head away, watching in horrific fascination as Sergeant's blood ran down the rooftop toward Damián's feet, where it mingled with another pool of blood. The one forming around his own mangled foot.

What the fuck happened?

"Corpsman up!" Wilson called.

How could that be his blood? He didn't feel the burning pain in his foot anymore. As he stared, the image blurred. A wave of dizziness caused his stomach to lurch. He was going to lose his MRE. His head slumped back against the warm concrete.

Seriously fucked up shit. Was he going to die here? Dreams of returning home and finding Savannah faded. The sun disappeared into a cloud. Sudden blackness. Damián closed his eyes.

Such a fucking wasted life.

* * *

"Corpsman up!"

Shit. Marc heard the call come from the rooftop of the building across the street. Holed up in the makeshift command headquarters, he grabbed for his pack and a litter.

"We've got your back, Doc," Master Sergeant Montague yelled, then he and several other grunts moved into position near the doorway and windows with their rifles leveled at the buildings where they suspected insurgents remained hidden. Marc ran out of the abandoned house toward the one across the street where the recon team had been staked out for the last couple of hours.

The ratcheting sound of gunfire echoed behind him and from a nearby building as he zigzagged across the street. He dodged the bullets stirring up sand and dust around him. Lucky for him, the stairway to the roof on the outside of the building had a high cement wall he could crouch behind as he made his way upstairs.

When he reached the roof, he stuck his head around the corner to assess the situation. Two Marines down, two upright. Marc stayed low as he crossed the roof and hunkered down beside the one with the worst injuries. A quick check of Sergeant Miller's nonexistent pulse and the damage to his head told him he needed to focus his efforts on the other one.

Two grunts crouched nearby over this one. Orlando. *Fuck, no!* Grant had a white-knuckled grip on the wounded man's hand. His buddy's boot—and foot—had been blown clean off, leaving a bloody stump of bone, tissue, and an exposed artery. Losing blood fast.

Shit. Don't you die on me, Orlando!

"Orlando! It's Doc. You're going to be fine."

The man opened his pain-filled eyes, clenching his teeth to keep from screaming. Sweat broke out on the younger man's forehead. Marc put on his gloves and pulled a tourniquet from the bag. Orlando groaned and tried to raise his head to see the damage.

"Keep his head down!" Marc ordered Wilson and Grant. The last thing he needed was for Orlando to see his foot and sink into shock. He needed to elevate the wound.

Even though Marc was almost seven years older than Orlando, he'd connected with the man during training at Pendleton. Orlando had been so damned serious. Marc had loved finding ways to get him to lighten up. The kid also had a huge chip on his shoulder back then. He'd acted like the whole damned world was against him. It had taken the Corps a while to knock that shit out of him, but you couldn't ask for a better Marine. Marc had been impressed by the strength and courage the man had shown. He was one of the best sharpshooters in the unit, which is probably what landed him on this rooftop in the first place.

Marc applied the tourniquet and bandaged the bloody stump.

"Grenade came over the wall," said Wilson, holding the kid's forehead. "Orlando and Miller saw it first. Orlando shoved Grant and me away. Sergeant Miller took the brunt of the explosion." Wilson looked over at Miller and closed his eyes tightly.

The sergeant was the first fatality the recon unit had suffered. Marc had learned to stay numb most of the time. Since the scene with Gino over Melissa, he'd never been one to show much emotion, so it hadn't been hard to do. He wouldn't even try to process the loss of Miller's life for a while.

Focus on the living.

Marc checked Orlando for other wounds, but didn't find any visible ones, not that this one wasn't serious enough.

"How bad, Doc?" Orlando spoke through gritted teeth, his lips whitened by the effort not to scream. Despite the kid's bravado, he looked scared shitless. The young man was about to get a lesson in maturity no one should have to learn. If it didn't kill him first.

Marc tried to remain calm, even though his heart beat so fast he was sure Orlando heard it. He doubted the surgeons would be able to reattach the foot, but as his corpsman, he'd do his damnedest to keep him alive until they could take over. If Orlando was lucky, the amputation site would be low enough not to cause too many problems later on.

"Your foot's pretty banged up. I'm going to hook you up to an IV and we'll have you medevacked out of here in no time."

"Will I lose it?" he whispered, as if afraid to put the idea out there too loud for the universe to act on.

"The surgeons will do all they can." He needed to get Orlando's focus on something more positive. "You'll probably be going home soon."

Orlando tensed in pain, gripping Grant's hand even tighter, before his body slumped against the rooftop, his head lolling to the side. The kid began to shake. Shock. Marc inserted the IV needle and adjusted the drip then heard the hiss of an incoming RPG round.

Instinctively, he shielded Orlando's chest and head with his own body, spreading his arms out to cover as much of his wounded buddy as he could. The rocket hit the wall beside him, taking out a section of the cement structure. Chunks of cement slammed into his back and side, stinging the skin where he didn't have protection from the SAPI plate.

Fucking sitting ducks.

Marc shouted, "Let's get him off the roof!"

"Sure thing, Doc!"

"Staging area's across the street. I'll send up a 9 Line request." Marc knew it could take up to ten minutes for the medevac chopper to arrive. "Then we'll come back for Miller."

As Marc made the call, he gasped for air. *What the hell?* Two grunts loaded Orlando onto a litter, picked it up, and started for the stairs. Marc rose to his feet to follow, but felt a crushing weight against his side and chest. He tried to catch his breath, but couldn't fill his lungs.

He managed to fight the pain and take a few steps before his vision blurred. The pain in his side was so fucking sharp, it inhibited his ability to breathe. Gasping for air, he watched the rooftop stairway swim before his eyes. He pitched forward into blackness.

* * *

Adam wondered why his last tour had to be so fucked up. If he could get his unit out of Fallujah without major casualties, it would be a miracle. While the Coalition Forces seemed to have the upper hand, there were many more bloody days ahead before they'd be able to claim the Sunni stronghold. He just wanted to finish up this deployment and get everyone home in one piece. He was getting too old for this shit. As soon as he got stateside again, he'd retire.

The hiss of an RPG round brought him back to full alert. The blast looked like it had hit the rooftop where he'd stationed his recon team. *Fuck.* He needed to get up there.

He turned to Captain McGuire, as he put his helmet on and adjusted the strap. "We're going to pop smoke, sir, until we get them down off that roof." The smoke screen would provide much-needed cover. He then cautioned the grunts remaining behind to be careful about firing blindly through the smoke onto anyone in the building's exterior stairway, in case the wind blanketed the area.

When the smoke grenades detonated, Adam thanked God the wind had died down, because the white smoke probably would stay in place long enough to get everyone to safety. He ran across the street and hunkered down in the stairwell and began to climb toward the roof.

Seconds later, Wilson and Grant rushed down the stairs bearing a litter. *Fuck.* Adam stood ready to provide cover fire for them. Who'd gotten hit? The Captain and the remaining Marines inside the staging building also peppered the area with gunfire as Adam followed the grunts with the litter back across the street. Once inside, he looked down at the unconscious Orlando.

"Doc radioed for the 9 Line Medevac, Top," Grant reported. Even though he didn't want any of his Marines to be injured, he thanked God it hadn't been Grant. He wasn't sure he could live with himself as it was for placing her in this much danger.

Now he needed to get Orlando on a chopper out of here. Adam looked through the doorway, expecting to see his corpsman. And where was Miller? No sign of anyone else coming off the rooftop.

"Where's Doc? Miller?" Adam barked.

"I thought Doc was right behind us. Maybe he stayed with Miller, Top," Wilson said as he covered Orlando with another blanket. "Miller didn't make it."

God fucking damn. He'd lost another Marine. "I'm going back over there."

"I'm going up with you, Top," Grant said. Before he could stop her, she grabbed another litter and started across the street.

Adam followed, providing cover. He needed to get to Doc. The corpsman's job was to save lives. He'd be upset about losing Miller, even if he couldn't have prevented it. Although Doc had been trained to use his rifle, the corpsman wouldn't be thinking about protecting himself right now. No Marine left behind.

They headed across the street, insurgent gunfire spraying bullets at them as they ran. At the top of the stairs, they turned the corner and found Doc lying face down. A few feet away lay Miller, his head blown apart.

Fuck. He'd get Miller out of here as soon as he took care of Doc.

Doc's right side was covered in blood that had soaked into his digitals and had begun to pool by his outstretched arm. His medical bag lay beside him. Several pieces of shrapnel had embedded themselves deep in the back of the SAPI plate, but some must have entered the side of his torso where the plate didn't provide protection.

Doc gasped for air.

"Get the scissors out of his bag!" Adam ordered as he surveyed the damage.

God damn it! A chunk of cement and steel protruded from the side of the corpsman's chest, under his arm. While Grant rooted in the bag, Adam reached out and placed his hand on Doc's shoulder. "Hang on, Doc. We'll have you out of here in no time." Adam accepted the scissors from Grant and cut the digitals away, being careful not to jar the projectile.

No telling how much of it was buried in his chest or which organs had been damaged. A number of small pieces of shrapnel were embedded in his skin, as well. Pressing the push-to-talk button on his shoulder mic, Adam shouted, "Wilson! Check the ETA for the 9 Line. Doc's in bad shape." Adam didn't know if Doc had even gotten off the request before he'd collapsed.

He took a bandage from the bag and cut it to the center, then pressed it on the skin against the wound around the metal, sealing the wound as best he could without shifting the metal protruding from his side. He hoped.

The radio squawked. "Three to four mikes," Wilson reported.

"Doc! Stay with me!" He hoped the man had those three or four minutes. Blood trickled from the corpsman's mouth. The steel projectile must have punctured his lungs. Adam was fucking helpless.

To his surprise, Doc gave them a thumbs-up sign. He'd thought the man had been unconscious. Then Adam heard the Blackhawk approaching. *Thank you, Jesus.*

Small-arms fire reached a fever pitch around them. His other units must have located the insurgent holdout. He hoped there were no more casualties. This had been the worst battle his unit had fought this entire deployment.

Another clusterfuck. He'd almost gotten them all home safely this time.

Wilson arrived a few moments later leading the medevac team. Adam backed away from Doc's side as the medical team set their own litter and supplies down, unloading the instruments they'd need to save Doc's life. *Please, God, don't let me lose D'Alessio.*

His mind flashed to Kandahar. Another D'Alessio. Fucking Christ, he needed to check and see if there was a connection. He'd gotten so used to calling this one Doc, he hadn't thought about the two men having the same surname. Maybe his mind hadn't wanted him to process the name and be reminded of one of the two men he'd lost in that ambush.

Shit. Could Doc be related to Gino D'Alessio?

Adam watched helplessly as they listened for lung sounds in Doc's chest. "Pneumothorax, maybe even hemopneumothorax. Let's just load and go!"

As the medevac team prepared Doc for transport, Adam motioned for Wilson and Grant to help him load Miller's body. They carried the litters down the stairs, Doc's going down first. Four other grunts brought Orlando's litter from the staging area. The kid lay unconscious. Thank God for small favors. At least he hoped he was just unconscious.

At the chopper, Adam watched helplessly as two of his men were loaded, to be taken to the Combat Support Hospital. He surrendered Miller's body to them, as well, for transport to the Marine morgue at the same location. Another angel.

God, don't let me lose any more of my Marines.

While You're at it, get the rest of my unit the fuck out of Fallujah in one piece.

* * *

"Orlando?"

Marc's throat was raw. His chest burned as if a fire-breathing dragon had taken up residence there. The nurse looked down at him with a puzzled look on her face.

"What, sweetie?"

"How's Orlando?"

"I don't think we have a patient here by that name, but I'll check when I get back to the desk. Maybe he's already been taken to Landstuhl." She put the blood-pressure cuff around his arm and inflated it. When he opened his mouth to ask another question, she admonished, "Don't talk." After she recorded the information in the chart, she said, "You'll probably be heading to Germany yourself in a few days. We're just waiting for your lung to re-expand fully before we fly you out."

Pneumothorax. That explained why his chest hurt so badly. He didn't remember anything other than trying to stabilize Orlando. The nurse stuck a thermometer under his tongue. Marc closed his eyes. Keeping them open required more energy than he could muster. Why was he so damned tired?

"Your master sergeant came by to visit earlier. I told him you'd probably be up to having visitors tomorrow."

Marc didn't even know where "here" was. Must be the CSH in Fallujah, if Montague was here. His eyelids grew so heavy he didn't try to open them again, even after she pulled the thermometer out of his mouth.

"Temperatures up a little." The nurse patted his forearm. "That's right, sweetie. You just get some sleep and let your body heal. A hemopneumothorax isn't anything to mess with."

Hemo, too? Blood in the lungs. *Merda*.

When he awoke again, the room was dark. Marc wasn't alone, but didn't know who sat in the corner until he heard him speak.

"'Bout time you woke up." Master Sergeant Montague moved his chair closer to Marc's bed.

Marc smiled. "Getting lazy in my old age, Top." His voice sounded raspy and weak.

Montague grunted. "Don't tell me about old." Marc looked at his master sergeant and thought he did look older than the last time he'd seen him. Dark circles under the man's eyes told of sleepless nights. Worry. Or worse.

Miller. Oh, *Dio*, they'd lost Miller. But what about Orlando? The others? Had anyone else died? Is that why the master sergeant had come to visit him personally? Marc couldn't form the words to ask.

"How you feeling?"

Marc shrugged. His chest didn't burn as much as it had earlier.

"You've been out of it a couple days. Quite a fever. They said they'll keep you here until they know there's no more infection."

Marc nodded. Even that small exertion made him tired. He tried to take a deep breath, but couldn't quite fill his lungs. He closed his eyes and took several shallow breaths, fighting the panic over feeling smothered all the time. Why didn't Top tell him about Orlando? Had the kid made it?

Christ, he had to know. "How's Orlando?" he whispered.

Montague ran a hand through his hair. Marc's heart hammered, reigniting the fire. Oh, *Dio*, no! He took several more shallow breaths, trying to regulate his heartbeat and relieve the stress on his heart and lungs. Was he ready to hear the words he'd been dreading since he'd come to?

"I should have said something sooner. I'm sorry. They couldn't reattach the foot."

The breath Marc had held whooshed out, releasing some of the burning from his chest. "He's alive?"

Montague's eyes opened wider in surprise. "Oh, hell, yeah, Doc. Shit. I thought you knew that much."

As best he could, Marc breathed a sigh of relief.

"You did great work. You always do. Grant told me you shielded Orlando and took the brunt of the mortar attack yourself."

Marc looked away. If someone had told him a year ago he'd have been prepared to lay down his life for another, he'd have said they were crazy. But for the first time in his life, with this small band of Marines, he felt a part of something so much bigger than himself. A noble cause. A desire to think of his buddies before himself.

The master sergeant looked away and rubbed the back of his neck. "I don't know why I didn't make the connection sooner. You're Gino D'Alessio's brother."

"Yeah." Marc had been wanting to ask Montague about him since before they deployed, but there never had been an opportunity.

Fire burned the backs of Marc's eyes. He closed the lids before he embarrassed himself. He'd always wanted to know the details about how Gino had died. Now, he needed to know how he'd lived and fought. Had he wanted to serve?

He opened his eyes and stared at Montague a long moment. "Top, was Gino a good Marine?"

Montague looked down at the floor, unable to maintain eye contact. His voice was a harsh whisper. "Damned fine Marine. One of the best men who's ever served under me." He looked up at Marc. The pain in his face took Marc's breath away again. "I'm sorry I got him killed."

Marc didn't understand. It was an ambush. Bad intel. How could that be the master sergeant's fault?

"I trusted the wrong people." His Top looked down at his hands. "We'd worked with these Afghan soldiers for months. They swore we had friendlies in the village. I led my men into a fucking ambush. Called for air support. No gunships available. Called for Hotel Echo…" he said, referring to high-explosive artillery shells. "Nothing. I should have made sure those things were in place before we went in. I shouldn't have trusted anyone."

Would Gino have been alive if there had been backup? Maybe. But the master sergeant wasn't to blame for the lack of it. Marc knew enough about the insanity that takes place in a combat zone to know those things just happened sometimes. You can't predict and plan for everything. You couldn't know who to trust. The enemy and the US-backed foreign military all looked alike. Infiltrators were common.

"I don't blame you, Top."

The master sergeant reached up to rub the back of his neck again. "Your brother was one of my best." He glanced up at Marc. "I'm not just saying that to make you feel better, either. He was my lead scout in the recon unit.

When we drew gunfire, he and another member of the team hunkered down behind some boulders. They returned fire. But we were taking it from all sides. From the village. From the caves in the cliffs above us. Total clusterfuck."

He paused, looking down again, deep in thought. Then he looked back at Marc. "Clearly, you're brothers."

Puzzled, Marc furrowed his brow. "I don't understand, Top."

"When an incoming mortar round dropped on them, your brother shielded his buddy from the blast. Just like you did for Orlando."

Marc could see the scene as if he were there. Tears welled in his eyes and he turned away. Gino, the brother he'd admired growing up, who had done everything right. Gino who loved serving as a Marine. Gino who had even died right, saving someone else. Images of his big brother's body being blown apart by flying rock and debris as he'd tried to protect someone else forced Marc to place his arm over his eyes, hoping to block the image out. No such luck.

Marc regretted that they'd fought over some damned woman the last time they'd been together. He'd never again let a woman come between him and the ones he loved.

Had Gino been with Marc on that rooftop a few days ago, guiding him in how to honor the Reconnaissance Marine's Creed? Regardless, he felt a bond with his brother he'd never imagined he would experience again after Gino had been killed.

Montague reached out to grasp Marc's forearm and squeezed, bringing him back to the present. Marc had to know one more thing. He lowered his arm and looked at his master sergeant. "Did he succeed?"

The older man looked thrown off by his question, then realization dawned and he smiled. "Hell, yeah. Sent his buddy home to his wife and newborn baby. If you'd like to meet them sometime when we get stateside, I'll hook you up."

Marc had to clear his throat to speak. "I'd like that very much, Top." How soon would he be shipped home? Would this injury put an end to his service? "I'm not ready to go home yet, Top. You think they'll let me return to the unit after I recover?"

"Above my pay grade. What'll you do if they send you home?"

Marc knew the chances of remaining on active duty were slim. He thought for a moment about his options. "Guess I'll go back to Colorado. Not sure what I'll do once I get there."

"Why not go to school and train for something in the medical field? You're damned good at it, you know."

"Maybe. I'll think about it."

The worry lines on the man's face relaxed a bit. "I'm retiring after this tour. Maybe I'll just follow you to Colorado. My wife always loved the mountains there. Still thinking that's where I want to go, even without…" His master sergeant looked down and twirled his wedding band. "Thinking I'll move to Denver and start a fetish club."

Marc wasn't sure what the appropriate response would be, so he remained silent. Was the man joking? No, he was dead serious.

"Well, maybe I'll just join your club. I was known as Master Marco back in the day."

Montague laughed. "Thought you might be like-minded. Saw you and Orlando at a fetish club in L.A. just before we deployed."

Oh, shit. They were lucky they weren't busted. Then again, if their master sergeant was there, too…talk about a "Top." Marc grinned.

Montague grew serious again. "My wife Joni and I talked about owning a club. Those years between the Gulf War and Kosovo we had a total power exchange." He remained lost in the memories.

Marc had never found a woman willing to do a long-term power exchange with him. He realized he hadn't even come close with Melissa.

Could he ever open himself up to another woman? Everyone thought the Dom in the relationship had the power, but that was nonsense. The sub held all the power. He'd like to find a woman he could trust completely.

The master sergeant continued, breaking into his thoughts, "We wanted to show others how satisfying a Dom/sub relationship could be for the right couples. Planned to live off my pension and open our house up for weekend classes and play parties."

"I'd like to meet her someday."

Adam looked at him, pain filling his eyes. "I lost her to cancer two years ago."

Shit. "I'm sorry to hear that, Top. I didn't know." Maybe that explained something about why the man had been such a hard ass in those early months after Marc had joined the Marine unit. He sure didn't seem like one once you got talking with him.

Silence fell between them. Uncomfortable, Marc blurted out, "Until I sort out my future plans, I'd be happy to help you get the club started. I'll need a diversion."

"I might just take you up on that." Montague stood. "Now, get better so you can get home and start living again."

Marc hadn't started to live in the first place until he'd joined the Navy and then been assigned to the Marines. If he was discharged, would that end? The thought of what lay ahead scared him. He'd changed since enlisting. He wanted his life to stand for something. He definitely had no plans to work at the family's ski resort. No, he was going to make a difference in some way.

Damned straight.

But doing what?

* * *

Two months later, January 2005, Landstuhl Regional Medical Center, Germany

"Grenade!"

Grenade. Move. Damn it, move! Damián slammed his body against his buddies, trying to push them away before the damned thing went off. The world exploded. Blood. Pain. So damned much pain. Grant and Wilson standing over him. Damián tried to get up. What had fallen on him? Dizzy. Sergeant Miller. Where was he? Damián opened his eyes and saw the man's bloody brains spilled over his chest.

"Madre de Dios! No! No! No!"

Damián jolted awake from a dead sleep, his screams reverberating through his ears. Sweat trickled into his eyes. His heart pounded like a sledgehammer, igniting a responsive throbbing in his right foot. The lingering effects of his nightmare receded by slow degrees, but the pain in his foot persisted. He sat up, shoving the sheet aside, and reached down to massage away the ache.

Thin air. He stared at the bandaged stump above where his foot should be.

Fuck.

He closed his eyes and slumped back against the pillow and sheet, both of them cold and wet from his sweat. How many times would it take before he stopped reaching for something that wasn't there? He'd left the damned thing behind in Fallujah. But the phantom pain taunted him every time he fell asleep.

Damián stared up at the ceiling. What in the hell was he going to do when they sent him home? They'd told him he'd be taking rehab in San Diego for a few months. But what were they rehabilitating him for?

Would he ever be able to ride his Harley again? Hold down a job?

Carry Savannah to their Laguna cave?

Well, he didn't have to worry about that one. He'd had dreams of returning home to her as a man, and then finding Savannah and convincing her she belonged with him. He wanted to take care of her, slay whatever dragons pursued her, and love her the way she should be loved...

But he wouldn't be carrying her anywhere ever again. He wouldn't saddle her with a cripple, even if he could find her. She deserved a whole man—nothing less to match her perfection. He tucked away the memories of their one idyllic day at the beach. Those images would have to last him the rest of his life.

He should have just fallen on the grenade and been done with it. Why hadn't he? A hero would have done that. They'd pinned a goddamned Purple Heart on his chest a few days ago, but he'd stowed it away in his seabag. All he'd done was get wounded—and let a man die. Why did he need a fucking reminder medal for that?

If he'd been a true hero, he'd have saved Sergeant's life. The man had a wife and three kids back home. *Fuck.* Just months from returning home and he'd been killed by a fucking hand grenade. So damned senseless.

Dios, *you took the wrong Marine home.*

Damián heard a squeaking wheel and looked up. "Doc? What are you doing here?" The corpsman wore a hospital robe that barely fit across his shoulders. He wheeled an IV pole that kept veering away from him. Each time, he'd pull it back in line.

Damián had heard what the man had done to save him from further injury. Doc had taken the very shrapnel in his chest that might have finished the job for Damián. Another wasted opportunity. Another man became a casualty because of him.

"Just got here this morning. Took me a little longer to get out of Fallujah than you." Damián watched as Doc's gaze roamed over him, head to foot...and stub. His gaze stopped to linger there a little longer, then returned to Damián's face. "Wanted to see how you were doing."

"Can't complain." *Not out loud, at least.* "How about you?"

"Coming around. Should be headed home in a week or so if the infection doesn't come back." Doc took a series of shallow breaths as if the exertion of walking and talking had taken a toll on him.

"Take a load off, Doc."

"Thanks." He pulled the chair closer to the bed. "How about you? Any news on when you'll head home?"

Home. He had no home to go to anymore. He'd always dreamed about having a home with Savannah. But that dream had faded one November day on a rooftop in Fallujah.

"Nah. They say I'm headed eventually to Balboa Naval Hospital near Miramar for rehab."

The two remained silent for a moment. Doc broke the solitude and asked, "Then what?"

Stunned by the question, Damián just sat there and stared back at him. He really had no fucking clue what he'd do after that. He didn't even see himself finishing rehab. What would be the point? Damián shrugged.

"Don't you have a girl waiting for you?"

Damián looked away. "No. There was one once, but she was out of my league."

"You're a Marine now. You're going to find you're in a league of your own. You'll have women falling at your feet."

Damián met Doc's gaze and said, "Foot, you mean." He pointed at the stub.

"Nobody's perfect. You have a lot more going for you than looks and a body. The right woman will overlook shit like that if she really loves you." Doc ended his speech by sucking several more breaths into his lungs.

Damián wished the man wouldn't get so riled up. No way would he change his mind. First chance he had, he'd put an end to this miserable life. When Doc caught his breath, he asked, "Does she even know what's happened?"

"No. We haven't kept in touch."

"Maybe if she knew..."

"I don't even fucking know where she is!" Damián regretted his tone as soon as the words came out. "Sorry, Doc. I'm sure for her it was nothing more than a day of hot sex with a Latino on the beach. Let's just drop it."

"Orlando, you have more integrity, courage, and honor than anyone she'll ever meet again."

Those words burned in his craw more than any others. "I was just in the wrong place at the wrong time. I didn't do anything courageous. Sergeant Miller is dead. You got wounded trying to save my sorry ass. You guys are the heroes, not me."

Damián's chest hurt now, too. He put his forearm over his eyes to hide the embarrassing tears that sprang from nowhere. "I'd like to get some sleep now." He knew his voice sounded ungrateful, but didn't care.

"I'll see you later."

Madre de Dios. I wish everyone would fucking leave me alone to just rot and die.

Courage? Integrity? Honor? No fucking way. He was nothing but a lousy Chicano scared shitless. What the hell was he going to do now?

* * *

Marc slowly made his way back to his room. Sweat broke out on his forehead and his legs shook at the effort. Just this short excursion left him feeling as weak as a runt-of-the-litter *gattino* refused its mama's tit. When would he experience the simple pleasure of filling his lungs with air again?

His talk with Orlando haunted him. The kid was fucking wrong if he thought women would never want him again. Maybe that one girl had broken up with him, but that was before he'd been serving with a Marine. Women loved Marines. Especially heroes like Orlando.

Right now, Orlando's feelings of hopelessness worried Marc the most. He needed to get through to him before the kid was shipped back to San Diego. Chances of seeing him again after that were slim.

He'd talk with the nurses to be sure they stayed on top of the man's depression. He knew they were monitoring him already. Depression was common for an amputee. But Orlando meant a lot to him. They'd trained together to be recon Marines. They'd even played hard together. He remembered the redhead at the L.A. fetish club. Orlando didn't need a foot to please a woman.

Dio, he didn't want the kid to become another suicide casualty.

Marc entered his room and saw his bed ahead of him, hoping he'd get there before his legs gave out. So fucking weak. So close…

"Marco!"

Mama? Marc turned slowly to find both of his parents standing in the doorway.

Shit.

"Mama? Papa? What are you doing here?" They had a business to run. This was the height of the skiing season. His mother came toward him. *Dio.*

"When we heard you were injured…" Were those tears in her eyes? She reached up and stroked his cheek, and he just marveled at what looked like real tears streaming down Mama's plump face. For him?

"We've been waiting for you here in Germany…" Her voice cracked and she wiped her tears with the back of her hand.

"Waiting for you to get out of the hospital in Iraq," Papa finished.

Marc noticed the dark circles under both their eyes. Their clothes looked as if they'd slept in them. How long had they been waiting here? Why hadn't they booked a hotel room?

"I'm fine. You didn't have to come all this way."

"They said you almost died," Mama said.

Who told her that? He hadn't been that bad off.

"They said you saved a man's life," she said, then smiled, her mouth quivering.

Marc turned away. He sure as hell wasn't a hero. The heroes were people like Miller and Orlando. Like Gino.

"I was just doing my job, Mama."

"Well," said Papa, "we want you to know we're proud of you, son. The whole family is so proud of you."

Marc looked from one to the other. While having them be proud of him wasn't his goal or even anything he cared about, for some strange reason, the words made him feel better. Then Mama wrapped her arms around him. She hadn't done that since he was a little boy. He'd always been in trouble and was more likely than his brothers to be punished. Marc put his arms around her shoulders and hugged her in return.

"I hated that you joined the military, Marco. But that was just because of Gino… I didn't want you to…"

Marc pulled away to look down into her eyes. Tears streamed down her face and she did nothing to wipe them away this time. Papa wrapped an arm around her, too, obviously as stunned by her emotional state as Marc was.

"Mama, you won't believe this, but I'm actually serving with Gino's unit. With his master sergeant even."

"No!"

When Mama looked as though she'd collapse, he and Papa grabbed her by either side and guided her to the only chair in the room. Marc was careful not to dislodge his IV. He hadn't told her before because he didn't want to remind her he'd become a Marine, but needed to tell them what he'd learned.

"Master Sergeant Montague told me about Gino. Mama, Papa, Gino was a real hero, a brave Marine. He saved a man's life."

His mother rocked herself. Seeing her exhibiting such maternal emotions shook Marc to the core. She'd hardly cried when she'd heard about Gino, at least not in front of him. Something inside his chest broke, as loud as if his rib had cracked. He'd never thought of her as being vulnerable. Of course, Gino was special to her. His brother always had been her favorite one. For good reason. He'd never given Mama any trouble.

Easier to love.

Marc hunkered down beside her chair, but his legs began to shake and his lungs grew tighter and tighter. He wanted to comfort his mother, but his head grew light. When he gasped for a breath, Mama looked up, "Marco, you must get into bed!" She motioned for Papa to help her get him to the bed. They guided him there, and Marc collapsed against the pillows as he tried to catch his breath. Damn. He hated feeling so fucking weak and helpless.

"Go get the nurse, Papa," Mama said, lifting his feet into the bed and pulling the sheet up over him.

Between his gasps for air, Marc said: "No nurse, Mama…I'm fine…Just moved too fast…Hard to catch my breath still."

But Papa had already left for the nurse's station. Marc could have pointed out that there was a call button, but instead focused on catching a decent breath.

"Here, take a sip of this." Mama held a straw to his lips and he sucked down the ice-cold water. Even something as simple as that left him shaky.

"What's up, Doc?"

The blonde nurse who had checked him onto the floor bounced in and quickly checked his pulse.

"Just a little dizzy and short of breath. Moved too fast."

"Well, hon, you'd better stay in bed a while and save those moves for later." She wiggled her eyebrows and he smiled. She'd been flirting with him since he'd arrived this morning.

"Yes, ma'am."

"Your parents have been camped out all night waiting for your flight to get in. You got away from them while they were out to get a bite of breakfast."

Marc's chest squeezed tight, but not from the hemopneumothorax. "Yeah, we were just…catching up now."

Her smile faded as she helped him to sit up in the bed and pressed her stethoscope against the middle of his back. "Take as deep a breath as you can for me without hurting yourself."

He did the best he could, although it was anything but deep, then he felt the familiar hitch in his side.

"Good enough for now. I'm going to torture you with the spirometer later, though, so you'd better rest up. Don't want you catching pneumonia on top of that hemopneumo." She helped him lie back down against the pillow. He grunted from the exertion.

"Maybe we should leave and let you get some rest," Papa said.

"I want to stay," Mama said to him, then looked down at Marc. "If you don't mind, Marco. I promise not to upset you again."

"You didn't upset me, Mama. I'm glad you're both here, but I'm afraid I won't be much company. It's all I can do to keep my eyes open."

Mama pressed her warm fingers against his forehead and drew them down over his face to close his eyelids. "Just sleep, my son. We'll be here if you need us."

The next thing Marc remembered was opening his eyes and seeing that Papa had found himself a chair, and he and Mama were huddled together with their sleeping heads leaning on one another, hands clasped together.

Sweet. He couldn't picture himself growing old with a woman. He liked women too much to settle for one. Besides, you had to let your guard down if you were going to let someone that close. He didn't want to be that vulnerable to a woman ever again.

He turned away. For now, he'd like to get stronger so he could see if the blonde nurse was all talk and no action. Somehow, though, he pictured she might be the one into wielding the whip.

Regardless, he held onto the dream of finding that perfect little subbie to work with. Maybe he'd find her at his master sergeant's BDSM club.

* * *

Five months later, June 2005, Balboa Naval Hospital, San Diego, California

Adam rubbed the back of his neck, trying to ease the crick he'd gotten on the flight from Denver, as he walked down the hallway beside Doc. "Any change?"

Doc gave him a sidelong glance and shook his head. "None. He's got no fight left. Won't let anyone visit. Not even his sister. Does the bare minimum with the therapy staff. Won't wear his prosthesis."

They walked slowly down the hallway toward Orlando's room. He didn't want to walk too fast, in case Doc had any lingering effects from his collapsed lung. "Sounds like he needs a swift kick in the ass."

Marc smiled and glanced at him. "That's why I called you, Master Sergeant."

Adam grinned. "It's Adam. I'm retired."

"I've tried to get through to him for the last couple weeks. He's fucking stubborn. But next week, I start classes to train with the search-and-rescue squad. I have to get back to Denver tomorrow."

When they reached the room number they were looking for, Adam stopped and glanced over at him. "Good choice, by the way." Adam was proud of how far the kid had come from the cocky SOB who had joined his recon unit as their corpsman to someone who could lay his life on the line for someone else. "You'll make a fine SAR worker."

The younger man looked down at the floor. For a once-arrogant man, he sure didn't take compliments well. Maybe he wasn't arrogant at all, just hiding some past hurts. "Anyway, I'm glad you called me out here. Hate to see the kid discharged just to go do some damn fool thing because he hasn't gotten his head on straight yet."

"You and me both." Marc reached for the door handle to Orlando's room before pausing. "I'll wait out here. He's sick of seeing me. Good luck."

Adam nodded and entered the room to find the blinds closed and the room in near darkness. No wonder the kid was depressed. He marched to the window and opened the blinds full force.

"What the fuck? I've told you to keep them closed!"

Adam turned and came around the bedside curtain to see Orlando shirtless and stretched out on the narrow mattress, the white sheets bunched around his waist. His dog tags hung against his brown chest, buried in a diamond-shaped tuft of black hair.

"You talking to me, grunt?" Adam tried not to smile as the kid practically came to attention while lying flat on his back. God, he missed having that kind of power over people. Couldn't wait to get his club started. At least, he'd have submissive women responding to him like that again. Even better.

"Master Sergeant Montague!"

"What's this I hear about you refusing to follow orders?"

Regaining his composure, the kid slumped back against the pillows. "The orders make no sense."

"Come again?"

"There's no point fixing me up."

"Since when does a grunt decide which orders to follow and which to ignore?"

Orlando turned away. A new maneuver was in order. He remembered the night he'd seen them at the fetish club in L.A., getting a screaming redhead off on the St. Andrew's cross, right before they'd deployed. Of course, when Adam had seen Doc and Orlando, he'd high-tailed it out as fast as he could. That would have been a real morale buster if the two could have held it over his head. Not that they had any business being there either.

"So, have you ever restrained a woman on a St. Andrew's cross?"

Orlando looked back at him. If the man could blush, he would have. "Say again?"

"I asked if you were into kinky sex—tying women up, spanking them, that sort of thing."

Orlando seemed unsure how to answer. "I tried it once—well, maybe a few times."

Well, hell. Adam had seen them the one time, but didn't know there'd been others. He'd just figured Doc had dragged him up there. This might be just the therapy the kid needed.

How the hell many Doms did he have in his unit, anyway? D'Alessio for sure. And he'd heard rumors Grant was a Domme, although he'd never spoken with her about it, sexual harassment regs and all. Serving with a female Marine was like dancing on eggshells and trying not to break one.

Right now, Orlando was the one needing a little dominating.

"Well, I can tell you one thing, grunt. I'd rather be with a sexy redhead right now making her round ass all nice and pink than to be looking at your ugly face." He watched as the kid's face did flame a bit at the mention of a redhead. Adam tried not to smile at the look of surprise on the young man's face.

Orlando got over the shock of Adam's words pretty quickly, though, and the defenses came up yet again. Stubborn wasn't the word for this one.

"Guess I didn't tie mine good enough. She got away."

Fuck. What kind of woman would dump a man while he was recovering from something like this? If you asked him, good riddance to her. Adam would find the kid as many women as he needed to get over her. But obviously, she'd sunk her claws in him pretty deeply. He wouldn't get over her very easily.

Joni would never have ditched him, no matter what had gotten blown off. That's what she'd told him—and he believed her.

"Come back to Denver with me. You can help me out with a little business I plan to start."

Orlando took a deep breath and let it out slowly. Adam could tell he was choosing his words carefully, afraid to disrespect his former master sergeant. "I don't need your charity, Top. When I leave here tomorrow, I'm just going to hole up in a motel in Solana Beach and get a good drunk-on."

Memories of his own two-week bender in Minneapolis after Joni died came back to Adam full force. He didn't want to count the number of times he'd come close to pulling the trigger of his sidearm, rather than go on without her. Would Orlando have access to a weapon? If not already, he'd have little trouble getting one.

No way was he letting this kid leave here alone.

"It's a BDSM and fetish club."

* * *

Damián wondered if he'd heard the man right. "Pardon, Top?"

"You heard me. I'm starting a kink club—bondage, domination, discipline, sadomasochism, fetish—any kind of kink you want to get on. Doc's joining me, but we can always use another good Dom."

Damn. His dick went into a full salute just thinking about it. First hard-on since before the grenade blast. "I'm no Dom. I'm not interested."

"Like hell you aren't interested." Montague grinned and directed his attention to the tenting of the sheets.

Damián adjusted the sheets to hide his hard-on and slid his leg out to reveal his bare, grotesque stump. "In case you haven't noticed, I'm missing a foot."

"Well, last time I checked, most of the ladies at BDSM clubs are more interested in a firm hand and a stiff cock. You still seem to have both of those in your inventory. Sure, there may be some chicks with a foot fetish, but you still have a good one, don't you?"

Damián was speechless.

How could he get the master sergeant to see he wasn't good for anything anymore? Even though his former master sergeant was out of uniform, wearing his Marine t-shirt and blue jeans, Damián couldn't just out-and-out tell him no. He'd spent more than a year under the man's command.

"I'm supposed to continue outpatient therapy for the prosthesis."

"Denver's got an amputee center for vets." The man got more serious. "But I'll damned well make sure you do as you're told. You won't be pissing around the way you've been doing out here."

Damián had only planned as far ahead as tomorrow—with a couple bottles of tequila and a sidearm. That's all he'd thought about for weeks. Months. So, why did the thought of starting over far away from all the memories of Southern California appeal to him so damned much? He sure had nothing to lose, certainly no more than if he stayed here.

"Look, Top…"

"Cut the Top crap. I'm retired. Call me Adam."

"I appreciate the offer, but…"

"Sure, there'll be plenty of butts for you to redden once we get you trained and open up the club."

Damián knew his former master sergeant was being deliberately dense, because the man wasn't stupid. No way. He threw his arms up in exasperation. "Fine! I'll go with you!"

The older man smiled. "I knew you would. I've booked our flights back with Doc tomorrow afternoon. You just do whatever they tell you between now and tomorrow."

*　*　*

Six months later, December 2005, Denver, Colorado

"Madre de Dios! No! No! No!"

Fuck. Another nightmare. Adam tossed back the sheet, jumped up, and ran across the hallway into Damián's room. The kid had been plagued with these fucking nightmares for months, just about every night. Adam went to the bedside and laid his hand on Damián's shoulder. He knew from experience any kind of pressure on the kid's chest would trigger a PTSD response.

"Damián, it's Adam. You're dreaming. Wake up!" The boy's arms thrashed in the air like a rattlesnake on the attack and one blow caught Adam on the cheekbone before he could block the punch. Adam winced. The kid had been working on his upper-body strength. Judging by that blow, he'd say Damián was getting back to his pre-injury conditioning.

"Sergeant! Don't you fucking die on me!"

After hearing how Miller had bled out lying on Damián's chest, Adam understood all too well what the kid relived day in and day out. Grant said Damián hadn't been unconscious at first. He'd seen Miller's brains…

Adam needed to bring him back to reality before the kid hurt himself. Using his master-sergeant's voice, he tried again. "Orlando! Wake up! That's a fucking order, grunt!"

Damián's body stiffened. He stopped thrashing and Adam finally was able to grab and hold Damián's wrists against the pillow at the sides of his head. He opened his eyes, his gaze darting around as if waiting for more incoming. His breathing was shallow and rapid as if he'd just climbed Mt. Evans on foot.

"You're okay, Damián. You're safe. You're in your own bed…in Denver." Adam kept up a litany of calming statements, waiting for the crazed look to leave the kid's eyes. Damián looked around as his pupils adjusted to the darkness. "It was just a bad dream."

The young man's eyes cleared. "Fucking nightmare." He continued to breathe rapidly.

"Yeah, it was."

"You can let me go. I won't punch you."

"Again, you mean?"

"Aw, shit. I did it again?"

Adam smiled. "Barely stung me. I'd like to see the day when a young devil dog like you can get the better of me."

"Why do you keep putting up with my shit? You haven't had a decent night's sleep in six months."

"Sleep's overrated. I've been a Marine for more than twenty years. My body doesn't need much sleep to function."

"You've had to put your club opening on hold, too. I'm costing you money."

Adam stood up to assume his maximum intimidation factor. He placed his fists on his hips, his elbows at a ninety-degree angle, and tightened the muscles of his bare chest. "Now hear this. We're Marines. We look out for each other—on and off the battlefield. Until you're ready, the fucking club can wait."

Damián closed his eyes, crooked his arm, and draped it over his eyes.

"You aren't going to get rid of me just because you can't see me." Adam sat on the edge of the bed. "Now, tell me about the dream."

Damián's therapist said the more he talked about the experience, the less power it would have over him. Joni had done that with him while he was on his medical leave recovering from the Afghan ambush. She'd held him, cried for him, and just let him talk until he was all talked out.

If Damián kept talking, more details might come out, especially the ones he was afraid to admit even to himself. Adam talked him down from the nightmares every time. Just in the last month, he'd gone from nightmares two or three times a night to only once a night. *Progress.*

"The same one. Grenade goes off. Sergeant Miller blocked the blast for me, but wound up…" Damián stopped rattling off the usual details, but his breathing became shallow and rapid again.

"Deep breath. Now!"

Damián responded, taking several deep breaths actually. "Should have been me."

Guilt had been eating the kid alive. Hell, he'd experienced that feeling firsthand often enough. No amount of therapy would help either of them lose that. They'd survived while others had not.

"You'd have done the same thing if you were in Miller's place. Hell, Grant and Wilson said you were trying to protect them. Stop blaming yourself for what some fucking insurgent is responsible for."

Damián lowered his arm and looked Adam in the face. His body began to shake, almost imperceptibly at first, then harder. Adam rubbed the scar on the back of his neck.

"I froze." The words came out in a whisper. Tears streamed unheeded down the sides of Damián's face.

Fucking breakthrough. This was the first time Damián had admitted to freezing. The kid's pain tore Adam's guts out. After what he'd watched him go through the past several months, he'd thought they'd never get at what was eating him. He never wanted to give the kid a hug more than he did now.

Where the fuck did that come from? He didn't need to baby him.

"Tell me what happened." Adam started to reach out and squeeze his arm in support, but backed off. Touching him might interrupt this confession of sorts. He needed to let him talk, release some of his demons.

Damián turned his head away and pulled his legs up, the right knee tenting under the sheet a few inches lower than the left because of the amputation. Lost in the memories, he remained silent for a moment. Then he groaned in anguish. "I saw the grenade first. I just stared at it. Oh, God!" He cried out and Adam couldn't help but reach for his hand, which Damián grabbed onto with a death grip. "I just fucking stared. I looked at the others. They didn't see it! But I couldn't move for like a minute."

"Just seemed like a minute. Grenades go off in seconds. You've just slowed the motion down in your head." Adam sure could relate to that. He'd had those same slow-motion memories from the ambush in Kandahar. Watching and not being able to protect or save his men.

Damián stared at the ceiling with unseeing eyes. "By the time I screamed for them to take cover, there wasn't enough time. Grant was talking with Wilson. She didn't fucking know. I nudged Sergeant Miller and we both moved at the same time. I thought he'd moved fast enough, but I didn't make sure. I went after the others. When I turned back, Sergeant Miller was right behind me, but too close to…" His body stiffened and he squeezed his eyes shut, as though feeling the impact of the explosion again.

Damián pulled his hand away and hugged himself, squeezing his eyes shut. Adam couldn't stand it anymore. He pulled him up to sit, wrapped his arms around him, and held him tightly. The kid began shaking harder, as if in shock.

* * *

Smothered. Even though he wasn't lying down, he felt the familiar crushing weight against his chest. Sergeant Miller. He struggled to get the body off him.

"It's me. Adam. You're safe, Damián."

Not Sergeant Miller. Adam.

"You did everything you could. It's not your fault."

"Oh, God. I tried. I fucking tried. I couldn't…" He wrapped his arms around Adam and held onto the man who had become his lifeline. Surprisingly, the smothering feeling receded a bit.

"You did everything right. You couldn't save everyone. No one could."

"Why? Why'd he have to die? Why not me?"

Adam continued to just hold him, but Damián noticed that his former Top's heart pounded hard. When he spoke, Adam's voice had become raspy. "That's above my pay grade—and a question I've asked myself a million times, too. But you have to quit blaming yourself."

Easier said than done.

"I will, if you will." Damián knew they'd both probably go to their graves asking themselves the same question.

Adam cleared his throat. "What you have to do is find something or someone that will make your surviving worthwhile. Find a cause that moves you. Find a woman who needs you. Just fucking find something you can do to make the world a better place for at least one other person."

Damián held on tighter. He knew tears were falling onto Adam's chest, but didn't want to ease away and reveal the evidence. The man had been like a father to him the past six months, taking care of him day and night. Making sure he did his PT exercises. Forcing him to wear the goddamned prosthesis until finally it stopped rubbing his stump raw.

The man had had no fucking life as a result. Adam should have been enjoying retirement, not babysitting him. Why hadn't he just left Damián in San Diego to finish off what the grenade had started? How could Damián ever repay him for the sacrifices he'd made?

Puckered skin? Damián's hands rested against what felt like puckered skin on Adam's back. *What the fuck?* He pulled back and felt Adam's body go stiff.

Damián looked him in the eye. "Turn around."

"You don't give me orders, son."

"What happened?"

"It was a long time ago. Kandahar. Ambush. I took some shrapnel to the back."

While he rattled off the cold, hard facts in a non-emotional way, Damián knew from the pain reflected in Adam's eyes that the man must have battled his own demons. From where Damián's hands explored, half the man's back must be riddled with shrapnel wounds. The master sergeant had been through just as much as Damián had.

How had he stayed so strong, so normal, so sane?

Was Damián his cause, to help him handle his own survivor guilt?

Maybe there was hope for Damián yet. He needed to quit feeling sorry for himself and find some worthwhile cause to dedicate himself to.

But what?

Section Five: The Club

The Masters at Arms Club

July 2011, Denver, Colorado

Adam would be glad to get this meeting over. Damián wanted to add live music to the club. They'd finally opened in 2008 and were doing well, so they could afford it. Adam just didn't go in for most of that heavy-metal stuff Damián liked.

"Edgy?" Damián asked.

He looked at Damián and Marc as they searched for just the right word for the classified ad. Well, Marc seemed about as much into the conversation as Adam was. What the hell ailed that boy lately?

Adam realized Damián was waiting for a response. "I like it." *As long as it doesn't put* me *over the edge.* Adam watched as the younger man he thought of like a son scribbled that addition onto the notepad on the desk between them. "Read me what we have so far."

"'Private club. Friday & Saturday performances only. Eclectic, edgy music—heavy metal and Goth welcome. Auditions start at 3 PM Wednesday. For location and additional info…' Then the phone number and e-mail."

"Sounds good to me," Marc said. He seemed distracted this afternoon. Actually, he'd been that way for well over a year, but refused to tell Adam what was eating at him. Probably hadn't gotten over that woman who had dumped him last year. What was her name? Pamela? He'd only brought her to the club a couple times. She seemed nice, but there wasn't much chemistry between the two in their play scenes.

Marc hadn't talked with him about the relationship, and Adam didn't go looking to butt in. Still, he thought the younger man could benefit from some advice, if he ever asked for it. Sometimes he came across as too arrogant and manipulative to suit most women. He seemed to have some kind of wall up that always kept them in their place, but that place was never quite as close as women wanted to get.

Marc stood. "Sorry but I need to get to the shop, so I'm going to have to hit the road. I trust whatever you both decide to do."

They said their goodbyes and Adam watched him leave. Maybe he'd try to have a word with him before the club opened Friday night. With Marc's SAR work and his schedule at his outfitter shop, Adam didn't see much of him, though.

Damián, on the other hand, practically lived here and helped run the club.

"Son, you're in charge of hiring the entertainment." Adam wouldn't know what young people wanted to hear if it hit him over the head. Besides, he needed to keep Damián busy so he wouldn't dwell on things outside his control. He said the nightmares were rare now, but Adam could tell when he showed up with circles under his eyes that he'd been visited by his demons.

Being a Dominant helped Damián regain some of the control he'd lost over his life, but Adam worried that he sometimes went a little too deep into sadomasochism. He knew it wasn't in the boy's nature to inflict pain to get off himself but just because that's what the masochist bottoms needed. To date he had remained detached emotionally, but what if he ever had feelings for the bottom he was servicing?

Damián slid the notepad across the desk toward Adam. "If we could hire two or three acts—have a mix of styles—we can rotate them and keep things from getting stale."

Adam pulled the notepad closer. "Sounds good. I'll e-mail the ad to the online newspaper."

After discussing some other business matters, mostly about ways to improve the experience at the club for members and their guests, Damián went to set up a new piece of equipment in one of the private playrooms.

Adam watched him leave his office. Damián wore his trademark black leather Harley vest and black jeans. He had long ago ditched the crutches, then his cane. He'd gotten used to walking on the prosthesis and, only when he was overtired, did he walk with a limp.

Here in Denver, Adam, Marc, and Damián had gotten to know each other as civilians and friends. Whenever he thought back to that day in Fallujah, he remembered how he'd nearly lost them both—and *had* lost Miller. Thank God they at least had managed to get the rest of the unit home alive.

And these two men had become his family. When he'd lost Joni, he hadn't thought he'd ever feel he belonged anywhere again.

The three of them were pretty much at the service of any of the subs at Masters at Arms who needed a top. A number of bottoms came to the club solo, just wanting to have a scene with one of them. Marc was the only one who'd seen anyone seriously and that had lasted only a few months. Usually, the three of them were able to accommodate the subs, which might be why so many of them kept coming back and bringing their friends.

Damián told him about a girl in San Diego he'd dated once. Savannah. Adam had heard him scream her name a number of times while he was recovering here. He seemed hung up on her, given the fact he'd told Adam he was still looking for her when he'd been home to visit his sister and her kids last Christmas. She must have been something to keep him thinking about her all these years.

Under Adam's and Marc's tutelage, Damián had become a knowledgeable and attentive Top. Good thing, because Marc had become more and more scarce at the club in the past year. A few months ago, Damián had taken over the training of the new unattached subs.

Even though Damián served the needs of the masochists when he wanted to get off, his gentle side seemed to come out with the more inexperienced trainees. He was very vigilant to the needs of the subs, knowing how far to push them without going beyond hard limits.

"All done," Damián said, returning to the office. "It's going to be fun trying that one out."

Adam smiled. Marc had recommended the new spanking bench. Said his SAR partner had made him one for his home playroom. He wondered when Marc had time to entertain anyone in that playroom. He didn't seem to have his heart in BDSM play these days.

"Son, have a seat."

"Yes, Top."

"When are you going to quit that 'Top' shit? It's Adam." He'd reminded the kid of that many times. Damián just smiled. He'd probably ignore the order this time, too.

"You're doing a great job with the trainees. The subs are raving about what an excellent trainer you are. And the Doms have noticed the improvement in the subs' level of discipline, too."

"Thanks." Damián looked away. He looked serious. Then his gaze met Adam's again. "Remember how you wanted me to find a cause—something that would help me make a difference for someone else?"

"Yeah."

"Well, I think I have."

"Great! Doing what?"

"The Patriot Guard Riders. They provide motorcycle escorts for military funerals and keep protestors far enough away they can't bother the families. I've been supporting them as a non-rider for a while now, but my Harley is just about ready down at the shop. I'd like to ride now, too, whenever the call goes out."

A lump the size of Minnesota lodged in his throat. As he came around the desk to sit on the edge in front of Damián, he cleared his throat before trying to speak. "I think that would be the perfect cause for you, son. I know you've worked hard restoring that hog, too."

Damián looked away, then back again. "It might mean going on rides when the club's open."

Other than the club and his work at a local Harley repair shop, this was the first thing the kid had gotten interested in since he'd moved to Denver. "To hell with the club. Any time you need to go on a ride, go. I can get people to help out here as needed. Hell, most of our members are ex-military. They'll want to support what you're doing, too."

"Thank you." He cleared his throat and surprised the hell out of Adam. "I also want to thank you for pulling me back from the edge."

Adam reached out and squeezed Damián's shoulder. "God didn't bless Joni and me with children. We lost a son…" Adam stopped until he could control the shaking in his voice before this turned into an all-out bawl-fest. He couldn't think about Joni or their stillborn baby boy without regret and pain. "I couldn't have asked for a better son. I'm proud of you for fighting your way back."

Adam cleared his throat before continuing. "I've told you this before, but I think of you more as a son than a business partner." He felt Damián's shoulders shake with emotion. The kid had been very close to his own parents. But his father had worked himself to death trying to support their family, dying when Damián was only twelve. Adam surmised the loss of his father and the need to protect his mother and sister had played a big part in what led him into trouble with the law before he joined the Marines.

Reminded him a lot of Adam's own fucked-up youth and reasons for joining the Corps.

But the Marines had turned Damián into a fine young man. One anyone would be proud to call son. Adam certainly would continue to think of him as his son until the day he died—even if Damián wasn't looking for a replacement dad.

* * *

Would the ache ever go away?

Karla plucked a tissue from the box in her lap and stared at Ian's photo lying beside her on the burgundy-velvet antique settee. Every day for the past two months, she'd fought to accept and understand Ian's death. *Fail.* She'd lost the ability to function on a day-to-day basis. Last night, she'd been fired from the club.

Escape. She looked around her Soho loft, the place where she'd lived since college. Five of her college roommate's oil paintings dominated one wall, their vibrant colors usually able to cheer her up. Not tonight.

She should be singing at the club. Ian had come to hear her perform whenever he was in the city. With the bright lights blinding her up on stage, these past two months she'd often imagined him sitting there in the front row, smiling up at her. But when the show was over, he hadn't been there. He would never be there again. Last night, she hadn't even been able to walk onto the stage because she was hit with a full-blown panic attack.

She'd never frozen like that.

A week ago, her contract with the record label had fallen through. She just couldn't concentrate long enough to write anything new. With her career sufficiently down the tubes, she needed to get away from the city and regroup. But where could she go?

Her parents kept trying to talk her into moving back home. They needed her, but being in the house where she'd grown up with Ian was too painful. Every time she passed his room or stared at the empty chair at the table, she'd think of him. Her chest tightened as tears welled in her eyes. No, she couldn't move back there.

Maybe a visit to her college roommate's mountain cabin would help. She usually showed up at Cassie's in the fall when the aspens were so beautiful. Her gaze moved to the painting of a stand of the trees with their yellow-gold leaves nearly quaking against the off-white bark. Karla remembered being with Cassie last year as she created the painting.

The artwork complemented Karla's mix-and-match style furniture. The wooden dining table with funky chairs of aspen yellow, azure blue, and crimson. The bar with its vinyl-covered red, green, and blue lunch-counter stools. No one could accuse Karla of being dull when it came to colors. Well, except for her wardrobe.

And yet, the joy she usually felt here was gone. Even the few walls of the loft were closing in on her. She looked at the bookshelf where Adam's framed photo in his dress blues had been displayed proudly beside Ian's portrait ever since she'd moved into the loft.

Adam, I need you.

Few days passed since that Thanksgiving weekend without some thought of Adam. Her heart ached remembering images of him kneeling down before her in the bus station's ladies room as she cleaned up the wounds he'd received trying to protect her from harm. Memories of his arms around her had infused her with the strength and courage to return home and face her parents.

The sight of him half-naked in her parents' kitchen in the wee hours of that Thanksgiving Day had made an indelible mark on an impressionable young girl's mind. The corner of her mouth lifted in a half smile. No man had ever measured up to Adam, not that she'd really seen many men without their shirts. She'd focused solely on building her career.

And now that was gone. Tears welled in her eyes.

The few letters he'd managed to write while deployed also were among her most prized possessions, along with the printouts of Ian's e-mails. Neither was a prolific correspondent, but she understood how busy they were. But after Adam retired from the Marines, he'd kept in touch with a letter every month. In recent years, he'd even e-mailed her. But she preferred the letters. More personal.

Adam had surprised her when he told her how much he loved listening to the music she'd sent him while he was in Fallujah. She'd hoped to send him a copy of the professionally mastered CD of her Gothic rock love songs. But that wasn't going to happen now.

Adam had always sent her a bouquet of roses dyed neon pink for her birthday, reminding her of that awful hair color she'd had when she met him. She smiled. He always seemed to have a genuine interest in what she was doing and wanted to make sure she was okay. He'd check to see if she needed anything. Offer advice whenever she'd asked on matters small or large.

Mostly small matters, she realized now. She hadn't been able to tell him about Ian.

Guilt plagued her for not responding to his last two letters. Karla couldn't find the words to tell him about Ian's accident. Tears stung her eyes again. She grabbed a tissue and blew her nose.

Go to Adam. He can help.

Karla needed Adam more than she'd ever needed anyone before. With nothing left to hold here her in New York, she picked up the phone and booked a red-eye flight to Denver. She'd find some small club where she could sing that wouldn't be as demanding as the one in Soho. Just enough to help pay the bills while she licked her wounds and healed.

Karla pulled out her suitcases and started packing. She'd keep the loft for now, until she decided what she'd do. Maybe she could sublet it to a friend. Only a few possessions would go with her, though. The two bundles of letters. Her performance costumes. Copies of the demo CD she recorded last year. Everyday clothes.

She placed Ian and Adam's framed photos safely inside her carry-on bag, wrapped in one of the long gothic dresses she'd wear for auditions and, she hoped, performances. No way would she risk losing their photos if something happened to her luggage. Three years of living in the loft and everything that meant something to her, except for Cassie's paintings, fit neatly into two suitcases and a carry-on.

She made out a check to the landlady for two-months' rent to hold the apartment, just in case things didn't work out in Denver. Then she called a cab and closed the door on her independent life in New York City.

Karla hoped she'd be able to find Adam once she got to Denver. She only had his e-mail address and a Post Office box number. She'd reply to his last e-mail once she got settled in Denver.

* * *

Damián listened as the metal band's lead singer spewed his gritty lyrics. He wasn't sure the band was quite what the club needed. Not that any of the others he'd heard audition this afternoon were any better.

His mind wandered back to his talk with Adam last week. Adam had pulled his bacon out of the fire in San Diego back in 2005, when Damián had been just a day or so away from putting an end to his sorry life.

Plain and simple—Adam saved his life.

Damián cleared his throat, then noticed that the offensive music had stopped. He looked up at the stage and saw the lead singer waiting for a response from him. When had they finished playing?

"Thank you. We'll be in touch soon." The rote response rolled off his tongue after an afternoon of horrendous auditions. As the band packed up its equipment, he looked down at his appointment sheet. He had a few minutes before the next audition.

Since coming to Denver, he'd managed to put memories of Savannah and all the pain she'd caused behind him. When he was awake at least. She still intruded on his dreams, but she was a better night visitor than the images from Fallujah.

Damián still couldn't believe he was a Dom now. He even found himself enjoying some of the scenes with the submissives he was training. But he had to rein in the beast in those scenes, for fear of hurting someone—well, someone who didn't want to be hurt, anyway. There were some nights he just had to decline a scene because the rage was too close to the surface.

Of course, being the resident sadist, all the masochists found their way to him at some point. Even with them, he only indulged if certain he could keep himself from going too far. Nothing compared to the euphoric high he got when he was in hypervigilant Dom space, tuned into the sub's every breath, every gasp, every scream.

But, since he'd started working with the submissives in training, he'd learned he still knew how to please a woman without inflicting severe pain. While it didn't do anything for him sexually, he'd long ago learned that sometimes it wasn't about him.

Working at the club also gave him plenty of time to pursue the other things he loved. He'd restored his own classic and never felt freer than when he was on his hog. When the physical therapists had told him he'd be able to ride again, they'd given him the motivation he needed to get his ass in gear and do what they told him to do.

He heard the door open behind him and turned to watch as a tall, slender young woman approached. He hoped she could hold his attention better than the last performers had.

"Come in, Miss..." he looked back down at his sheet, "Paxton. I'll give you a few minutes to get ready. If you have a background disc, just put it in the sound system over there."

Damián watched her prepare. Her long, wavy hair hung loose to her waist and she wore a medieval-looking dress with pointed sleeves. Her low-cut front exposed the inner sides of her breasts. No bra. Interesting look, although he'd like to see even more skin if she performed in the club.

Hell, at this point, he just hoped she could sing. So far, they hadn't found anyone he'd want to hire. He looked back at her e-mailed resume. Her background indicated she was way overqualified. What was a Manhattan club singer doing in a small weekend private club like this one? Maybe she was like him, just needing a new start. Or maybe she'd lied on her resume.

When he glanced up at her again, he watched her bite her lower lip. Her eyes widened as she surveyed the room—homing in on the unconventional furniture, complete with chains and manacles. Hadn't she understood what the ad in the alternative paper meant by a private club? If she thought the room looked wild now, she'd never make it through a night of debauchery this weekend.

Then she noticed him watching her. He continued to stare until she became uncomfortable and looked down at the floor. Shy? Or submissive?

It would be interesting finding out. Interesting indeed.

* * *

Karla nibbled at the inside of her lower lip. What kind of club was this? She'd been so rushed to request an audition when she saw the online ad while waiting for her flight at LaGuardia that she really hadn't paid much attention to the reply other than to get the address and time right. With her flight delayed, she'd changed into her costume in-flight, which had been an interesting feat. She'd barely arrived in time for the audition.

Karla looked around the room. She'd never seen anything like this place. A private club. For what? Or did she want to know? There was a full bar and stage area, right in the middle of someone's house. And the furniture! A few tables and chairs were scattered about, but what caught her attention were a number of ottomans positioned around the stage—each with manacles and chains attached to them. Talk about a captive audience.

A center pole in the middle of the house's great room sported several thick eye bolts—and more chains and cuffs of varying heights spaced at regular intervals. Along the wall were any number of implements of torture whose purposes she didn't even want to think about.

She cast nervous glances at the Hispanic man in the Harley-Davidson vest sitting at a table between the center post and the bar. While he studied her paperwork, she noticed that his shoulder-length hair was pulled into a ponytail. His mustache and goatee gave him the look of a—well, if she needed to put a word to it—"sadist." Or what she'd imagine a sadist would look like.

Then he looked up at her and his black eyes bore through her, causing her stomach to drop with a ka-thunk. Unsettling. No longer able to maintain eye contact, she looked down at the floor. Maybe she should run while she still had the chance.

No. She needed this job. She looked up again, but her eyes gravitated to the center post first. Her stomach quivered, sending a jolt to her clit.

Oh, my!

"Miss Paxton?" Her attention returned to the intimidating man. "Are you ready?" His voice was stern. No smile. Would this man be her boss? Would she be able to work with someone who put her nerves on edge as he did?

Well, it's not like you have a lot of options. The market for Goth singers was pretty small, especially in an isolated city like Denver.

"Y-yes." She drew her shoulders back. Why did she feel she should bow down before him? Lord, he intimidated her.

"I'm Damián Orlando, one of the owners of the club. Just call me Master Damián."

Her hand shook as she adjusted the microphone to her height. *Master Damián?* What had she gotten herself into this time?

"Nice to meet you, sir."

He smiled as if satisfied with her response. Why did the thought of pleasing him seem so important to her? "Begin whenever you're ready."

She walked over to the sound equipment and queued up her music. When she returned to the mic, his intense gaze sent butterflies into frenzied flight inside her stomach. *Shoot!* She missed her queue.

"I'm sorry. May I start over?"

"Certainly."

Come on, Karla. You need this job. Don't blow it.

She went back to the CD player to start Track One again. *Deep breath.* She ran her clammy hands against the brocade dress covering her thighs, then returned to the microphone center stage. Unable to sing while he stared at her with that all-consuming gaze, she closed her eyes and felt the music flow through her.

For you, Ian. She almost felt as if Ian was watching over her. Not the sadist club owner in front of her, but her brother.

Then she sang Tarja's *I Walk Alone*, as if she really could bring Ian back.

* * *

Adam closed the checkbook and carried it to his filing cabinet in the corner to lock it away. Aerosmith's *I Don't Want to Miss a Thing* blared from the speakers. He'd been trying to drown out the noise from the auditions, but that song put him even more on edge. *Damn.* One of Joni's favorites. She'd play it almost every night he was home on leave.

They said time would heal the pain of her loss. Nine years had only managed to dull it. Rather than the sharp knife point he used to feel jabbing into his heart, the pain now felt more like his heart being squeezed in a vise.

God, I still miss you, Joni.

A particularly discordant note from the latest audition brought him back to the present. He hoped he hadn't made a big mistake with this whole live music thing. He'd barely been able to hear himself think while trying to concentrate on his bookwork. How the hell would he be able to focus on his sub during Dom/sub demonstrations with that racket in the background?

Of course, there were the private rooms, but he liked to do demonstrations in the great room for some of the newer Doms. He usually worked with Grant as his sub. She'd shown up at the club six months ago, after hearing about it from Damián. She usually topped submissive women and men—but she liked to switch things up with her former master sergeant. Unfortunately, she wasn't submissive so much as subordinate. Not the same as what he'd shared with Joni, but he didn't expect to find that kind of woman again.

Now that his accounting was done and the bills paid for another week, he opened the door to his office and went back to the desk to check his e-mail account. If anyone had told him while he was in the Corps he'd become a keyboard jockey in retirement, at his laptop several times a day to keep his business records up to date or to cruise the Internet, he'd have shot them for a fool.

During a lull between his classic-rock station's tunes, new music wafted through the door from one of the acts auditioning in the bar. Nice. A woman's voice. He actually understood the words. For some odd reason, thoughts of Karla Paxton came to mind. He still pictured her as a pink-haired Goth, although she'd sworn to him in her letters that had just been a rebellious teenage phase.

Karla had written to him as promised since he'd said goodbye to her at the airport that Thanksgiving weekend. She'd often send something she'd made, including the most incredible chocolate-peanut butter brownies he'd ever eaten. He felt guilty, as though that thought was disloyal to Joni, who had never been too interested in cooking or baking.

Then, during Karla's senior year in high school, he'd received an MP3 player with a few songs saved on it that she'd recorded. Nearly every night in Fallujah, he'd lain awake in his rack and listened to her sweet voice through his earphones. She'd kept him sane, especially after the disaster there, reminding him there still was innocence and beauty left in this fucked-up world. Somewhere.

He'd been so proud of her when she went on to complete a music degree at Columbia. Thank God she'd found a safe way to get to New York without having to pull another runaway stunt.

He drew his brows together. Why hadn't she replied to his last two letters and numerous e-mails? That wasn't like her. If they didn't both keep such crazy hours, he'd have called to check up on her. Adam decided if he didn't hear something this week, he'd make sure she was all right. He worried about her singing late at night at that club in Manhattan. Although she said she'd taken martial-arts classes after her encounter with that shithead pimp and his friends in the Chicago bus station, she was still a tiny little thing.

The voice of the woman in the great room called to him like a siren's song. The quivering lilt reminded him so much of Karla's voice on her MP3, but then the woman auditioning belted out the chorus in a well-trained adult's voice. She stirred something in Adam. He picked up the remote and muted the stereo.

"I walk alone. Every step I take, I walk alone."

Damn. Adam stood up, drawn toward the open doorway where he could hear her better. His hand drew instinctively to the scar on his neck. *What the fuck did he have to worry about?* He forced his hand back down to his side.

The hallway to the great room wasn't that long and before realizing he'd even moved, he found himself standing at the side of the stage. The woman's thick, black curls hung in disarray over her shoulders and back. She looked as if she'd just tumbled out of bed. His cock throbbed at the thought of holding her beneath him by fists full of her gorgeous hair as he buried himself deep inside her.

Jesus. What's gotten into you, old man? She's a little young for you, isn't she? Okay, a lot young.

Still, unable to take his eyes off her, he circled around behind the table where Damián sat. He hadn't had a gut-wrenching response to a woman, well, since Joni. Sure, he'd participated with Grant in demonstrations for various scenes and techniques and occasionally took a submissive under his wing until she hooked up with her own Dom. But that was merely physical. No emotional attachments. Exactly as he planned to keep it. No one would ever stir his interest in being a committed Dom the way Joni had.

"Go back to sleep forever."

He stopped and stood in front of her, about ten feet away from the stage. Eyes closed, tears spilling down her cheeks. His chest tightened. He fought the urge to go up on the stage to pull her into his arms to comfort her.

Little girl lost.

A distant memory sent his hand to massage that spot on his neck again.

"No one can help you."

Tall, probably five-ten. She looked a little gaunt. Dark half-moon circles curved below her eyes. They didn't look like makeup, although it was hard to tell with a Goth. Her breasts filled out the dress nicely, her curves exposed. Lovely breasts he wanted to press his lips against. Her hips flared under the loose dress, as well. At least she wasn't gaunt all over.

If they hired her, she'd definitely need to wear something a little more provocative than this Maid Marian costume.

He tried not to think about removing the dress to expose her body to his gaze. But his mind had other ideas. He imagined taking her nipple between his teeth and tugging at it. With her gaze cast downward, much of her face hidden by her hair, he found himself wanting to push the curls away from her face so he could look into her eyes.

When the song ended, she drew several deep breaths, her breasts rising and falling gently.

"Well done, Miss Paxton," Damián said.

No. Couldn't be. No fucking way!

As if in slow motion, Adam watched her brush away the tears and raise her gaze to Damián's. She smiled. Just as he remembered, except that her blue eyes didn't sparkle anymore. Then her gaze shifted as she noticed Adam for the first time. Her smile faded. What little color she had in her face drained away.

"Adam?"

When she swayed on her feet, he rushed to the stage and caught her in his arms before she collapsed. His heart pounded. Had she been sick? Was that why she'd lost so much weight? A vise of a different kind clamped around his heart as he lifted and carried her to the loveseat near the windows. He laid her down, propping her head and upper back against the armrest and pillows there. Kneeling beside her, he framed her face with his hands, hoping to infuse some of his warmth into her. Her face was so cold.

He reached for an aftercare subbie blanket from the basket beside the loveseat and wrapped her in it. Her body began to tremble.

"Adam? How did you know I would be here?"

"I didn't." When she looked even more confused, he added. "You're in my club."

Her eyes widened and skittered from the chaining post in the center of the room to the manacled ottomans. *Good thing she couldn't see the theme rooms.* She shouldn't be in a place like this. Damn. Shifting from horny perv to paternalistic thoughts did nothing to shrink the raging hard-on in his jeans.

"So, I gather you two have met."

Adam had forgotten about Damián. When he turned to look up, his surrogate son held out a bottle of water. Adam noted a bit of disappointment in the younger man's face, but didn't want to think about Damián taking Karla under his thumb.

Mine.

Where the hell had that thought come from? Karla was just a kid. Hell, he was old enough to be her father, as he'd told her all those years ago when she'd professed her love. Adam took the bottle, then opened and handed it to Karla. "Yes. A very long time ago."

"He was my knight in shining armor." Adam didn't appreciate the look of hero-worship on her face. He'd never been anybody's hero and didn't plan to start now.

"I did what anyone would have done." She quirked the corner of her mouth, as if to say "*bullshit.*" No, she wouldn't use language like that.

When her full lips wrapped around the bottle, he tried not to think about them wrapped around anything other than the lip of that damned bottle. Still, his other head ignored his paternal censors. What in the hell was he going to do? No way could he hire her and have her so near while he entertained perverted thoughts about her.

"When can you start, Miss Paxton?" Damián's words felt like a sucker punch to his solar plexus.

Shit.

"Wait here," Adam said to Karla. Then he stood and turned to Damián. "I need to have a word with you." Damián followed him to the bar, then Adam turned to face him. "She's not working here."

"What?"

"She doesn't belong in a place like this."

"What's that supposed to mean? This is a decent club compared to most. Besides, she has a great voice. We need her. The other acts were crap. She's the last one on my list." Adam remained silent as Damián rattled off the list of reasons they should hire her. The younger man then pulled out his trump card. "You gave me hiring authority. I'm hiring Karla."

What the fuck am I going to do now?

"Who the hell *is* she?"

Adam shook his head, then ran his hand through his hair. He wouldn't go back on his word to Damián. Maybe he could just make himself scarce and avoid her. *Just how the fuck do you plan to do that? This is your goddamned club.*

Adam sighed. "Forget what I said. Make sure she's okay. Then send her to my office to fill out the paperwork." He needed to get his dick under control, even if he couldn't control anything else anymore. Not trusting himself to go anywhere near her, he escaped to his office.

Good God, what the hell are You doing sending her here?

Then again, maybe it wasn't God's fault. Maybe he was being punished for all the things he'd done wrong in his life.

* * *

Adam doesn't want you here.

Karla couldn't mistake how quickly Adam had run away from her. She'd made a royal mistake coming to Denver. Tears stung her eyes as she sat up on the loveseat, swinging her legs to the floor and pushing the blanket away. At the back of her mind she wondered why you would have blankets in a nightclub. Well, she was in Denver. Maybe it got cold here at night.

She wiped her eyes, trying to compose herself before having to face either of them again. A facial tissue dangled in front of her field of vision. She looked up to find Master Damián holding the tissue out to her. For someone who looked like a sadist, he sure had a gentle side to him. Somehow gentle and sadist just didn't go together.

She accepted the tissue and dabbed at her eyes. Good thing she hadn't worn full stage makeup. She'd look like a raccoon right now. Just as she had when she'd cried for Adam in the Chicago bus station all those years ago.

"Sorry. I'm just really tired. It took me all night to get here. I only arrived from New York early this afternoon."

"Well, the club won't be open again until Friday night. Your first set will be at seven o'clock. Get some rest between now and then."

"You mean, he wants to hire me?"

"*I* am hiring you, Karla. But Master Adam asked me to send you to his office to fill out the paperwork so we can get you on the payroll ASAP."

Master Adam. The title caused warmth to spread into her stomach, then lower. She didn't really know much about Adam at all. How had he lived this separate life and not even intimated at such in his letters?

Because he still thinks you're a kid.

Master Damián extended a hand and helped her to her feet. His grip was firm, warm. When she swayed, he steadied her by holding her elbows with both hands.

She wished Adam's hands were holding her. Another tear ran down her cheek. He obviously wanted to have nothing to do with her. How could she stay here?

How could she leave?

"Could you point me in the right direction?"

"Better yet, I'll take you."

"Is it okay if I leave my bags in the entryway for now?"

"Sure. They'll be safe there. I'll be locking up after I take you to Master Adam's office."

As they started toward the hallway where Adam had disappeared, Master Damián discussed what was expected of her as far as a new wardrobe.

Oh, dear. "I'm sorry, but I...I don't have any money for new clothes yet. Would it be okay if I wore my dresses from the Soho club until I get a couple paychecks under my belt?"

"Talk to Master Adam. He'll probably advance you some money for appropriate clothing. Where are you staying?"

She bit her lower lip. "I'm going to find a motel when I leave here."

"I think we can do better than that."

Karla wasn't sure what he meant, but by then they'd arrived at Adam's office. She preceded Damián into the office and saw Adam seated at a large walnut desk, staring intently at some paperwork before him. He dominated the room, which was decorated in dark wood and black leather. When she hesitated, Master Damián took her elbow and led her to one of the leather chairs in front of the desk. But she chose to remain standing. Looking down at Adam gave her a sense of power she needed to feel right now. She wouldn't stay if he didn't want her here.

"Top, Karla's just gotten to town and doesn't have a place to stay. She'll need one of the rooms upstairs."

Top. What an odd way to address Adam.

Karla noticed Adam's hand had tightened on the pen he held.

Adam doesn't want you here.

She blinked rapidly and swallowed past the lump in her throat. *Don't let him see you cry.* Taking a deep breath, she squared her shoulders and rose to her full height, which was just short of Master Damián's. Even so, the man intimidated the hell out of her. She needed to stand up for herself and stop being led around by him as if she were a puppy.

"That won't be necessary. I'm staying at a motel."

Adam looked up at her, his piercing green eyes short-circuiting her bravado. "Nonsense. You'll stay here." His gaze sent a thrill down her spine at the same time as it caused her heart to come to a halt. She'd yearned to see Adam again for so long. Now that she was here, she wasn't sure if she wanted to run to his arms, or run out the door.

To Damián, he said, "Take her things to the guest room on the east end of the house."

Master Damián chuckled. She wondered what was so funny, but couldn't ask. What had she gotten herself into? Live here with Adam? That was just wrong on so many levels. She just wanted to crawl back to New York and forget about this whole harebrained idea. When Master Damián left, she remained standing as Adam stared up at her as if he didn't have a clue how to deal with her.

"I was worried about you." His voice came out in a husky whisper that washed over her as if he'd gently stroked a finger down her bare arm.

Of all the things she thought she'd hear him say after the scene in the bar room, that was the last she expected. Karla blinked away more tears, her bravado evaporating quickly. She'd expected him to continue to be all businesslike and distant, not so…caring.

Her tearfulness reminded her of the time she'd wrecked the family car when she was eighteen. She'd been fine until her dad had asked if she were okay.

"Are you okay?" Adam asked, concern in his voice.

The same question. Now all the emotions she'd tried to bury the last two months resurfaced. She began shaking, unable to form a coherent response. She steadied herself with a hand against the back of the chair. Tears blurred her vision. Then she felt Adam's strong arms surrounding her, holding her up.

Safe. Adam.

She took in a ragged gasp of air, then a wrenching sob poured from deep inside her chest.

"Shhhh. It's going to be okay." He turned her around and pressed her against his rock-hard chest and his hands stroked her hair. She felt his heart beating against her cheek as she wrapped her arms around his back, holding on as if he were a lifeline. She wept grief-stricken tears mixed with tears of joy to be holding Adam once again.

She'd tried for two months to remain strong for her parents' sakes and to make sure everything was beautiful for Ian's funeral. Then she'd tried to continue to tamp down her emotions and grief so she could return to New York and function again.

Fail.

"What's happened, Karla?"

She shook her head, not wanting to put into words what she still didn't want to acknowledge. The tears she couldn't dam up any longer spilled onto his chest. *Oh, no!* She pulled away and saw the blackened spots on his white shirt.

She reached out to touch the stains as more tears spilled. "I'm sorry, Adam."

He cupped her cheek in his hands and tilted her head back until she saw his face swimming before her eyes. "It's just a f…goddamned shirt. Karla, tell me what's wrong. Come. Sit with me."

He led her over to a black leather loveseat she hadn't noticed before. He sat down and, rather than have her sit beside him, pulled her onto his lap. She'd fantasized about being held by him like this, but he was her new boss, wasn't he? Totally inappropriate.

Adam. Her friend. He knew everything about her. Over the years, in her letters, she'd shared more with him than she had with Ian, her parents, or her girlfriends.

He'd saved her once. She so needed saving again. But she was too broken this time for anyone to save her.

* * *

Adam hadn't felt this helpless since he'd watched Joni dying, except maybe for Fallujah and its aftermath. Something tragic had happened to Karla. He needed to know what, so he could make it better. Nothing rotted his gut more than feeling so fucking helpless.

"Are your parents all right?"

She nodded, but kept her gaze on her lap. Thank God. Jenny and Carl had taken him in that Thanksgiving morning and treated him like, well, a brother. He'd feared perhaps something had happened to one of them.

Then, was it Ian? No, her brother's deployment had ended a while back. He'd made it home safely from Iraq. But they were redeploying units so fast these days. Had he gotten hurt?

"Ian?"

She squeezed her eyes shut and wrapped her arms over her stomach, holding herself as she tried to curl over into a ball as if to contain the pain. She nodded her head and a mournful sob escaped her lips.

Oh, God no. Not her brother.

He wrapped his arms around her and pulled her against his chest. He held her as she sobbed. She adored her older brother more than anyone in the world. He'd seen that in her letters as she'd bragged about his commendations and activities.

"Tell me what happened."

He didn't want to hear the words, but she needed to speak them, just as talking about his nightmares had helped Damián. Again, she shook her head. The scent of her citrusy shampoo drifted to his nose. Adam brought his hand up and held her head closer to his chest. He stroked her face. Her hair. Her skin. So soft. She felt so right in his arms—and that was so fucking wrong.

God, she was so young.

So hurting. He'd never been able to resist reaching out to help a lost soul.

"Karla, tell me what's happened to Ian."

The sooner she got the story out, the sooner she'd be able to begin to function again. To heal. Whatever had happened, she'd already kept it bottled up way too long. She gasped for air, trying to control her sobs.

"Take a deep, slow breath, Karla." She did as he told her. At least she heard him. She hiccoughed and he felt his gut clench—and parts south tighten. "Again." He needed to keep his mind off how nice it felt having her curled up in his lap. If she didn't spill the story soon, he would embarrass himself—and probably scare the hell out of her.

"Tell me. Now, Karla." He didn't mean to sound so gruff, but it was all he could do to maintain control over his wayward dick.

As if a dam had burst, the words spilled out in a jumble, with sobs obliterating most of the details in the story. But he managed to get the gist of it.

Motorcycle. Rain. Semi.

Ian's dead.

Dead.

"Oh, God, no, Karla." Adam held her tighter, resting his chin on the top of her head, trying to envelop her in warmth and safety. "I'm so sorry." He ached for Karla and her parents. When tears burned his own eyes, he let them flow, knowing she couldn't see them. He cried for Ian, who hadn't been given a chance to live. He cried for Jenny and Carl, who had to be caught up in a living hell right now. He even cried for Joni, who he hadn't been able to cry for since that Thanksgiving morning in 2002 at Lake Michigan.

But mostly he cried for Karla. She didn't deserve this. Her world was supposed to be happy. Innocent. Full of hope. He wished he hadn't ignored his instincts. He'd known something was wrong and should have gotten in touch with her sooner.

He didn't know how long she continued to sob, then suddenly her body went limp, sinking against him. Her weight felt good against him. She'd surrendered the last of her defenses. Thank God she'd come to him. Someone else might take advantage of her vulnerability.

While he and Karla had spent only a couple of days together face to face, they'd forged a deeper connection that spanned nearly a decade. She'd pulled him back from the brink when he'd thought there was nothing left for him in this world. Her letters over the years were honest, as if she were sitting right there at his feet telling him about her day.

No, don't think about her sitting gracefully at your feet.

Her letters had told of her life, her dreams, her world. He knew her better than he'd known any woman other than Joni.

Something or someone had brought them together again. He'd taken care of Karla once before. He'd take care of her this time, too. And he'd refuse to give in to the baser thoughts running rampant through his mind since he'd watched her performing on the club's stage a little while ago.

When her weight relaxed against him even more, he figured she'd fallen into a deep sleep. He held her a bit longer, stroking her arm, shushing her when her body convulsed with a shudder. Then he stood and carried her out the door into the hallway. They passed the theme rooms. Thank God she slept, although she'd find them eventually, if she'd be working here.

Christ.

Damián came out of the medical theme room. He raised an eyebrow at seeing her curled up in his arms. *No, this isn't that kind of aftercare.*

The man he thought of as his son grinned and looked up at him, a question in his eyes. Adam wasn't ready to explain his relationship with Karla. He told himself it was because he didn't want to wake her by speaking. In truth, though, he didn't know how to explain her to Damián. He knew what their relationship had been before today. But how could he explain his feelings now without sounding like a fucked-up pervert?

"Go back upstairs and move her things to your old room." He kept that one made up, in case Damián ever needed it. His son's grin widened. The devil dog probably thought he understood the reason for moving her so close to Adam's own bedroom, when Adam had intended originally for her to be as far away from him as possible.

"I need to keep an eye on her."

"Sure. Let me know if I can help with that...Dad."

Why had Damián chosen now, of all times, to remind him he was so fucking old? Hell, his surrogate son was only a couple years older than Karla. Maybe he should encourage them to get together. They both needed someone right now.

The thought of Karla being with Damián or any other man at the club rotted his gut, though. He carried her up the stairs. As he walked into the room where Damián had fought his demons all those years ago, he hoped Karla's struggles would be much less. But in here, he'd be able to keep a close eye on her, just until she was ready to venture out and find a place to stay on her own.

* * *

Adam sat in the corner of her room and watched Karla sleep. He hadn't wanted to scare her by removing her clothing, but had taken off her slippers and pulled a blanket over her. The thick black curls fanning out over the blue pillowcase sent his thoughts careening down dangerous paths yet again.

Demons flitted across her face a few times, but whenever he'd stand to go to her to fight them off, she'd become peaceful again and fall back into a deeper, more restful sleep. She couldn't possibly be aware he was here, could she? He'd never admit he'd watched over her like this either. She'd think he was some kind of perv. But he was worried about her and she might not be as vocal as Damián had been when he'd battled his demons in that bed. Hopefully, she'd remain sleeping when he left her here alone.

Her black eyelashes flickered. Adam tensed. She moaned in her sleep and he was ready to go to her, to hold her until the nightmare ended. Then she sighed and returned once more to a deeper sleep.

Obviously, she hadn't slept for a very, very long time. When had Ian been killed? Her last letter was two months ago and didn't hint that anything was out of the ordinary. He probably should call Jenny and Carl to offer his condolences. Let them know Karla was with him. Safe.

Safe? Yeah, right. "Oh, don't worry, Carl. Your daughter's fine. She's performing at my sex club—oh, musical performances only. Nothing to worry yourself about. She's fine."

Just fine.

Thoughts of her performing in other ways at the club flashed through his mind. *Shit.* No way would she be engaging in any activities other than singing as long as he had anything to say about it. He doubted she'd even be interested in BDSM. And, if she were, she'd probably lean more toward the Domme side, given the way she'd managed to order him around in the head at the bus station.

He smiled. She seemed pretty taken with her ability to bring him to his knees, as he recalled. Well, Adam didn't bottom for anyone. If he remembered her in that role, perhaps he'd be able to put an end to his carnal thoughts about her.

Fuck. How could he be thinking horny thoughts about the Paxtons' daughter in the first place? God, Carl and Jenny had taken him in, patched him up, given him a place to rest. Hell, they'd even given him a plane ticket back to Pendleton.

He'd have a battle on his hands to keep from thinking about having rough, kinky sex with their innocent daughter.

Fucking A.

Total clusterfucking-A.

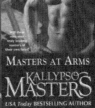

Rescue Me

Includes
MASTERS AT ARMS
in its entirety, the
introduction to the
Rescue Me series.

NOBODY'S *Angel*
KALLYPSO MASTERS

USA *Today* BESTSELLING AUTHOR

Praise for *Nobody's Angel*

Nobody's Angel is intensely sensual. While BDSM romance is not exactly my genre of choice, it seems to be handled quite well in this story, with an emphasis on safety and trust and not just kink. I also appreciated the fact that Marc does not want to participate in the lifestyle 24/7 but prefers to restrict it to playtime. I believe that we are going to find that his friend Adam is wired in a completely different manner.

~ **Bobby D. Whitney, Book Wenches**

~ ~ ~

I really liked this novel from beginning to end I cannot think of one thing that I would change! The plot is fast paced, its well written, erotic, exciting, gives you that emotional connection with your characters and more.

~ **Holly, Full Moon Bites Book Reviews**

~ ~ ~

I think I need to be rescued after reading this book! I don't know if I can take any of the sequels if they are as hawt as this one was. You may need to move to Antarctica to read the next ones.

~ **Trish, Night Owl Reviews**

~ ~ ~

Kallypso Masters did it again. Your DOM come true, this is the story of Marc and Angelina. Amazing plot, sexy and smart characters, and a loving story of trust, sex and passion. *Nobody's Angel* certainly brings the passion, and kinks, to a whole new level. Great read.

~ **Reading Diva's Blog**

Nobody's Angel

by
Kallypso Masters

(Book 2 in the Rescue Me Series)

Dedication

To my husband, who patiently and calmly puts up with my crazy writing obsession and loves me unconditionally regardless of the upheaval and chaos I create in his life.

And to three women—Jeri Smith, Fiona Campbell Cox, and Kelly Mueller—who made all the difference in how Master Marc's story turned out. I can't say how each of them helped without giving away the story, but they know what they did.

Acknowledgements

As always, there are so many people to thank, and my apologies to any I leave out.

First, I'd like to thank my editor, Jeri Smith, of Booksmith Editing. Your feedback on the earlier version of *Nobody's Angel* was extremely helpful to me in the arriving at the final version. And my thanks to Meredith Bowery, who edited *Nobody's Angel* for print and provided me with the analysis I needed to fix a some problems that had plagued me about this book from the beginning.

Fiona Campbell Cox, you're like having another editor. Your insights are spot on. Thanks for pegging the problems the "old" Marc had—and for always fighting for your Texan.

Carol Ann MacKay, your line edits at the eleventh hour saved this author much embarrassment and are greatly appreciated. And thanks also go to Christine Sullivan Mulcair who gave it one more look before going to audiobook format and found more things needing to be corrected.

Linda Lynn, my cover designer, is phenomenal. All I do is provide her with the photos of the characters and away she goes. I love how she alters the stock photos making them unique to my books.

Thanks to my beta readers, Kelly Hensley and Kathy Treadway, who provided valuable feedback for the scenes (including telling me what wasn't working).

Thanks to my fans and readers, affectionately known as the Masters Brats, for falling in love with Masters Adam, Marc, and Damián as I have, and for encouraging them (with your bratty behavior) to make regular visits on Facebook to keep you in line. Just one request: I'd love it if you would please stop asking them to get out their whips and floggers to keep me in my writing chair. Ouch!

Thanks to my many Facebook and Twitter friends. Your encouragement and support are great motivation. Thanks also for helping me solve major and minor plot and characterization issues. Specifically, my thanks to Ashlee Davidson, Jillian Schuler-Hall, and Laura Harnier for helping with the Denver and Colorado questions. Irene Eneri, M.C. Robb, and Joanne MacGregor for help with the Italian phrases. Patricia Wheeler and Top Griz (a retired Marine Master Sergeant) for help with Marine Corps questions. And everyone else who helped whenever I put out the call for help! (All errors are mine, of course.)

To my wonderful MPs, thank you for lifting me up, making me laugh, giving me delightful and informative inspiration into the BDSM lifestyle, and providing me with an awesome social-networking fix every day! You're the best!

Author's Note

If you haven't read the introduction novel for this series yet—*Masters at Arms*, please do so before you read this one. The e-book is free. *Masters* will give you a much deeper understanding of the bond between Masters Adam, Marc, and Damián. You'll also learn about key turning points in each of their lives leading up to their romances. And you'll see how Master Adam & Karla and Master Damián & Savannah met, as well as see some of Master Marc's prior experiences with women.

And if you or a loved one suffers from Post-Traumatic Stress Disorder (PTSD), please reach out to people who have been there and can provide support and advice. For military-related PTSD, contact the Wounded Warrior Project (https://woundedwarriorproject.org/) and other non-government organizations, as well as the Veterans Administration (http://www.ptsd.va.gov/). For non-combat PTSD issues like Savannah's, here are some web sites that can help if you need to talk with someone:

Crisis Services:
http://crisisservices.org/content/index.php/information-resources/

Rape Abuse and Incest National Network:
http://rainn.org/

To Write Love on Her Arms:
http://www.twloha.com/

Now I turn *Nobody's Angel* over to the good care of you, my reader. I hope you fall in love with Master Marc, Angelina, and Luke and that you will enjoy your visits with Master Adam, Master Damián, Karla, and Cassie, as well!

Chapter One

Marc D'Alessio put on the eye mask to maintain some anonymity. What Italian men didn't do for their mamas. No one from his earlier life in Aspen had ever shown up at his club, but he'd promised Mama he wouldn't be blatant about his alternative lifestyle. *Merda*, just having her find out about his interest in BDSM had been bad enough. If his little brother Sandro had just kept his mouth shut…

He wished he'd chosen a different mask, though. The damned wolf one just brought him attention he really didn't want these days from unattached subs and bottoms.

Marc donned the black leather vest over his bare chest and ignored the familiar hitch in his breath caused when he overstretched the adhesions in his side. He checked to make sure the vest pockets included the safety and first-aid items he might need while on duty tonight. The yellow armband he placed over his right bicep identified him as the club's Dungeon Monitor Supervisor tonight.

Marc stepped out of the dressing area and walked down the short hallway to where the great room at the Masters at Arms kink club opened before him. The scent of sweat and sex filled the air tonight. The club appeared to be at capacity, so he'd have to stay alert. He also was about an hour late and needed to find co-owner Adam Montague to get the lowdown. He scanned the room looking for his retired master sergeant.

Fellow Iraq combat veteran and Marine Damián Orlando, the youngest of the club's three owners, wore his trademark black-and-orange Harley leather vest and had a petite blonde chained to the center post where he delivered evenly placed lashes with his single-tailed whip. The center of the room had been roped off sufficiently to keep onlookers out of range, but many watched the demonstration with rapt attention.

Marc recognized the bottom as one of Damián's regulars, the expression on her face one of pure ecstasy, despite the red welts he could see on her back, ass, and thighs. No blood. Marc didn't get off on delivering that level of pain. Neither did this woman's Master, Victor Holmes, a local firefighter, who stood to the side just out of range of the bullwhip. The black man had a pained expression on his face as he watched Damián deliver what his woman needed. Damián sure was popular with the masochists who couldn't get what they needed any other way.

The tattoo on Damián's flexing bicep showed the rippling tail of a dragon, the body hidden by his vest. The tat covered a good portion of his friend's chest and back, Marc knew, because he'd gone with him for some of the sessions at the tat parlor. With his shoulder-length hair pulled into a queue, and his goatee and mustache, Damián had the look of a real badass.

Marc couldn't help but remember the shy kid he had been when they'd met at Camp Pendleton or that trip to the L.A. fetish club the week before they'd deployed to Fallujah. No, if he didn't know it for a certainty, he'd never believe this was the same man. The kid sure had come home from Iraq messed up. Marc and Adam had almost lost him during his deepest depression. Apparently, with BDSM he'd found a way to regain some level of control over his life again, even if it did mean he'd chosen to delve deeply into the sensual-sadist range of the lifestyle's spectrum.

Marc loved Damián like a brother, realizing he'd become closer to this kid from his Marine Corps training days than he was to his own little brother. The two of them had gone through some serious shit together in Fallujah. Damián had come out the worse for it. Marc wished he'd been able to do more, but was thankful that, as his Navy corpsman, he'd been able to keep him alive. His buddy's limp was hardly noticeable now and he seemed to be getting his life back on track.

Well, on track as well as any of the three co-owners had been able to since Iraq.

Continuing to look for Adam, Karla Paxton's final preparations for tonight's set caught his eye. She flinched each time Damián's whip struck the woman's bare and sweating skin. When Marc had first met Karla, he hadn't expected her to last more than her first weekend's performances. She sure as hell didn't care much for the lifestyle, even the milder stuff.

But Karla sure did care for Adam—not that his former master sergeant noticed. Shit, the man whose instincts and wisdom had kept a lot of Marines alive in combat zones was totally clueless when it came to Karla.

"You're here."

Well, speak of the devil. Marc turned to find Adam approaching him. After all these years of retirement, his friend still kept his hair trimmed to near-

Marine regs. Not a high and tight but close enough. There was a heavy mix of gray throughout his friend's dark brown hair now.

"Sorry. Got held up on…a mission."

Adam's intense stare bore through him saying he knew Marc wasn't being honest, which niggled at his conscience. Adam had gone back for him on that rooftop in Fallujah. He'd visited Marc in the hospital until they could ship him out of Iraq, often spending his nights watching over Marc as he slept. Most importantly, he'd helped ease some of Marc's guilt over the loss of his big brother, Gino, who had served under Adam in Afghanistan. He owed the man so much. Why was he trying to distance himself from him now?

Because you distance yourself from everyone.

No, that's just women. He did keep women at arm's length emotionally, but Adam would take a bullet for him before he'd ever hurt Marc. So, why didn't he let him in? Adam had been nudging him for months to tell him what was going on in Marc's head after he'd quit scening, opting to volunteer as a DMS most nights, well, when he showed up at the club. One thing was certain. Marc would continue as a co-owner of the club with these men; their band-of-brothers bond would never be broken.

Merda, he couldn't explain what was going on himself, much less tell his friend. He was just…unsettled since he'd left Pamela last year. She had been the first woman he'd gotten close to since Melissa all those years ago.

He had let Adam believe Pamela had dumped him, but he was in no mood yet to talk about what really happened. Marc deflected the man's unspoken questions. "So, what's the situation?"

Adam narrowed his eyes, paused a moment, then stood down, rubbing the back of his neck. "Keep an eye on Room Eight. They're new to the scene and I don't get the feeling they know each other very well."

The recent surge in erotic BDSM books had couples coming out of the woodwork to try out with their partners, some of them nearly strangers, what they had discovered in those romanticized stories. Too bad. Most of them should have stuck with the romantic version. They got off on the idea of BDSM, not the actual experience. Besides, most of their "Doms" had no clue. Too many used this as consent to abuse rather than any type of consensual power exchange.

Until the last few months, Marc had held a series of weekend training sessions when he wasn't on a mountain-rescue call and didn't have any wilderness expeditions planned with his outfitter company. Those Doms who truly wanted to learn to please their partners in the BDSM lifestyle signed up, but they'd represented a small fraction of the couples coming in to experiment on the equipment at the club. Of course, he hadn't given a class for quite a while.

"I'll keep an eye on them," said Marc. Adam filled him in on how many dungeon monitors were on duty tonight and where each was stationed. "Anything else?"

"No, pretty routine." They shared a grin. There was nothing routine about the Masters at Arms, now one of Denver's hottest kink clubs. They'd become so popular since hiring Karla to sing that they'd just started opening on Wednesdays, in addition to Fridays and Saturdays.

As Karla sang "*Song to the Siren*," Marc's and Adam's gazes were drawn to the young woman commanding attention on the stage. Her wardrobe sure had improved since she'd first started. Tonight she wore a black satin and sequin number that concealed her shoulders, but left a large oval on her chest exposed, showing off the swell of her breasts. Her arms were bare except for lacy black gloves covering her forearms and wrists. The hem of the dress was mid-thigh, showing off her sexy long legs encased in black mesh stockings. Definitely hot.

Marc turned back to Adam to finish up before getting to work. *Merda.* The look of intense longing on his friend's face bordered on pain. If Adam wanted her so badly, why didn't he just go after her? They shared some kind of history with each other from what he gathered, but Adam was doing his damnedest to treat her like a daughter. Hell, anyone with eyes could see that the looks Karla gave him were anything *but* those of a daughter's. Sure, there was a significant age difference, but she sure as hell didn't act twenty-five. She was mature, almost somber sometimes. Not that his fifty-year-old friend noticed—when he allowed himself to get anywhere near her. Maybe he was still holding on to the memory of his dead wife, but, after nine years, and with a beautiful woman like Karla wanting him, the man needed to wake up and smell the vino.

Like you're the expert on relationships.

Marc sighed. "I'll make the rounds."

"Hang around for a drink later on," Adam said. "I have Birra Moretti in stock."

Adam didn't drink alcohol, but just wanted an opportunity to grill him for information. He wasn't going to take much more of Marc's shit before he kicked him in the ass.

"Let me take a rain check. It's been a helluva long day. Now, I'd better go check on Room Eight."

Adam nodded and let him go, more than likely because he was worried about the couple in the private theme room than that he wanted to let Marc off the hook. Marc maneuvered around some couples gyrating on the dance floor near the bar, almost tripping over a sub kneeling on the floor beside her Dom at one of the tables.

The Italian woman, looking too damned much like Melissa for his taste, gave him a come-on with her eyes, then smiled. Totally disrespectful to her Dom, who seemed not to even notice as he spoke with Grant, another Marine vet, who stroked the head of the malesub at her side. Marc bent down to instruct the Dom to please keep his sub out of the walkway, and then he continued toward the theme rooms. He and the other monitors were spread thin tonight with a crowd this size.

The hallway to the rooms was painted red from the floor to the black ceiling. Flickers from the simulated-fire wall sconces caused his shadow to dance against the walls and gave the feeling he'd just walked into a sinister place. Not as bad as the dungeon, but...

Marc approached the fourth room on the right and stopped at the large window that gave DMs and voyeurs a vantage point over the scene inside the room.

Each of the theme rooms was set up with specific equipment. Some provided furniture and items that conjured up popular fantasies—the office, the medical examination room, the harem. He'd hired Luke Denton, now his Search and Rescue squad partner and the carpenter who helped renovate the club, to make the specialized BDSM equipment.

Room Eight focused on a number of spanking and whipping paraphernalia, including a spanking bench, a leather love seat, a sling, and the St. Andrew's cross. A muscular Dom dressed in black leather vest and pants held a leather flogger. His sub was tied spread-eagle on the cross, naked except for the blindfold. Her long black hair hung in waves halfway down her back. Thankfully, her hair stopped short of the gorgeous curves of her ass.

Focus, man. You aren't here to get off on the scene.

The blindfold impeded his ability to assess her condition. He switched on the intercom button to listen in. Her ass was red, and he heard her whimpers. Nothing out of the ordinary, except she was new to the BDSM scene and might not remember she could stop the scene if it went beyond her limits.

Slap!

The flogger struck her upper thighs, a particularly painful place to strike a novice.

"Acckkkkk!" Her lower body arched against the cross in an effort to escape the lash of the leather strips.

"Stop your crying, bitch," the blond man shouted at her.

Marc cringed at his tone. Was she into verbal abuse and humiliation? He'd monitor the scene a little longer and try to determine whether she was getting off on the scene. If not, maybe he'd take the inexperienced Dom aside and give him some suggestions for making the scene better for her. Perhaps the man would permit a demonstration on how to maximize her pleasure. Marc felt his cock come to life at the thought of working with this sub and her luscious curves. *Merda.* What was wrong with him tonight?

Slap!

More red stripes appeared across her upper thighs.

"Ow! Stop! …enough."

Marc couldn't make out all of her words. He became more alert.

"Don't top from the bottom, pain slut. You know you wanted to be punished. You made me wait so damned long."

Marc cringed. She didn't appear to love anything about the scene, unless her pleas and tears were part of her kink. Hell, it was hard to tell with someone he didn't know. He needed to check in with her, though, to make sure she wanted to continue. Marc turned off the intercom and slowly opened the door, slipping inside without a sound and keeping his distance as he tried to further assess her condition. Wrapped up in his scene, the Dom didn't even notice Marc. He delivered two more sharp blows, this time to each of her tender inner thighs.

"*Mio Dio!* Stop!"

Italian? *Well, shit.*

Not taking time to analyze why that should make a difference to him as a DMS who wanted nothing to do with another sub, he motioned to get the Dom's attention. Keeping his voice calm and low, he asked, "May I have a word with you a moment, Sir?" The man sighed heavily, but he had no choice but to obey a DM or DM supervisor. Not wanting the sub to overhear their conversation, Marc guided him to a corner of the room.

"I understand you're both new to the club," Marc whispered, "and I just wanted to make sure she understands about using her safeword."

"She's fine. She hasn't used her safeword." The Dom glanced away, making Marc suspicious as to whether he spoke the truth. "She just needs to get used to the flogger. This is her first time."

Damn. Adam was right. The Dom was riding her awfully hard for a first experience.

Marc noticed her feet straining on tiptoe because of how high he'd cuffed her hands on the cross. She clenched her fingers open and closed, as if trying to restore circulation. "I just came on duty. How long has she been on the cross?"

He looked at his watch. "About an hour. We reserved the room for ninety minutes."

Faccia di merda. This asshole was a real piece of…work.

"I need to check in with her before you can continue this scene. Then you might want to consider providing some aftercare during the rest of the time you have in here. It's pretty hard for a first-timer to have her body stretched and beaten like that for such a long time."

"She's fine." He ground the words out between his teeth. Now Marc understood why Adam was so worried about this couple. They'd both seen his type before. Thought he knew everything and wasn't one to accept advice. Abusive to boot.

"Excuse me." Marc left him and walked over to the woman. The rules forbade him from touching her without her Dom's permission, unless and until he put an end to the scene. He couldn't see her eyes, but the blindfold was soaked from her tears. She sobbed quietly. Was she in subspace? This could be serious for such a novice, but he couldn't really tell for certain until he saw her eyes.

Turning around to the man, he asked, "Permission to remove the blindfold and evaluate her condition?"

"I guess so."

Marc reached up and pushed the loosely tied sash up to her forehead. He stood in front of her face, wishing he could cup her chin and brush the tears away. *Focus. What the fuck has gotten into you?* Would she follow his command?

"This is the Dungeon Monitor Supervisor. Look at me."

Her eyes remained closed as she mumbled incoherently. No response. Damn. She was in too deep. Health concerns trumped no-touching rules. He pulled the flashlight from his pocket and lifted each eyelid in turn. Pupils unresponsive.

Shit.

"She's in deep subspace. This scene is over." Marc bent down and unbuckled her ankles as fast as possible.

"What's deep subspace?"

Asshole bastard. Her Dom would be fucking clueless about how to bring her back down safely, even if Marc were willing to let him anywhere near her. Which he wasn't.

He doubted these two would continue in the lifestyle together, but felt responsible for trying to explain the seriousness of this situation to Sir Asshole here, hoping to save the man's next unfortunate partner from a similar fate where there might not be a DM with medic training nearby to rescue her.

Marc reached up to undo the clips that held her cuffed wrists to the cross. Her hands felt cold. As he worked to free her, he provided a lecture to the scumbag. "For whatever reason, she didn't say her safeword when she reached her limit. Experienced submissives might have subspace as a goal, but she's too new to scening for that. Her mind disassociated from the pain when she could stand it no longer."

Turning his attention back to the now whimpering woman, Marc wished she'd had her first experience with a Dom who knew what the hell he was doing. *With me.*

Now, where had that thought come from?

"She agreed to this." The Dom went on the defensive and walked over to the dark leather loveseat in the corner to pick up a piece of paper that looked like the club's contract.

Sorry, Sir Asshole, but read the fine print about my right to shut your scene down.

After the last cuff clip was undone, she moaned as he lowered her right arm from its overstretched position. Her body collapsed into his waiting arms with a grunt, and he carried her to the loveseat.

Marc pulled an aftercare blanket from the nearby basket and wrapped her naked body in the microfiber cloth to quickly bring up her body's temperature. He covered her full breasts as quickly as possible, quashing an errant desire to bend down and take one of the delectable peaks into his mouth.

Merda. He hadn't been this attracted to a woman since…well, a very long time. *Why the fuck did she have to be Italian?*

Marc held her tightly against him. So soft. Her curves molded against his body. His breathing hitched as his cock sprung to attention without the use of his fist, a first in a long time.

Regaining some self-control, he continued his lesson for Sir Asshole. "Then the endorphins kicked in to the point where she could no longer engage her brain to make the decision to speak her safeword." He glanced up at the man in time to watch him look away once more. Guilt? Maybe he should double check. "*Did* she use her safeword or safe gesture?"

The man didn't meet his gaze. "Well, I'm not sure…"

Goddamned bastard ought to be flogged himself—but with a cat-o-nine tails instead.

Sir Asshole moved toward the loveseat. "Here, I should be doing that…"

When he reached down, as if to wrest her away, Marc growled. Remembering his role, he forced himself to speak in his calm DMS voice in no uncertain terms. "Don't touch her. If you want to learn how to administer aftercare properly, watch." *But don't think I'm letting you put your fucking hands on her again as long as I'm here to stop you.*

"I still have thirty minutes reserved on the room!" he wailed, waving the contract in his hand.

Obviously, he had no concern for her welfare. There wouldn't be any reasoning with the man—and no membership refund coming, either—but Marc really wanted to get rid of this asshole so he could focus on the woman. "Go discuss it with Master Adam."

When the wannabe Dom puffed out his chest and stomped from the room, slamming the door behind him, Marc texted Adam and told him what had happened in here—and that he should kick the sonuvabitch out of the club and ban him for life. Looking around the room and not seeing any bottled water, Marc sent another message, asking Adam to send over a bottle. As an afterthought, he added, *"and a dark Hershey bar."*

Putting the phone beside him on the loveseat, he looked down at the gorgeous woman in his arms. Olive skin, dark hair. He remembered her eyes were a rich chocolate brown. Yeah, definitely Italian. His cock throbbed, surprising him yet again. He'd avoided Italian women for years. Too close to home. Too emotional. Too strong-willed.

Too much like Melissa.

Marc wiped away the hot tears still flowing from her eyes. "You did well, *cara*. Shhhh. Just rest now." He kept his voice soft, soothing. Her body shook in response, or perhaps from chills. He pulled her head against his shoulder and laid his chin on the top of her head to keep more heat in her body. The scent of lavender surrounded him. "Shhhh. It's over. You were so brave, *cara*," he crooned.

He held her in his arms, for several minutes longer, savoring her weight in his lap, her delicious scent... Suddenly her mind and body reintegrated.

"Accckkkkkk!" The woman screamed and fought him, trying to pull away, to escape the pain, the blanket, him. The more she struggled, the more her back and ass would burn from the friction, so he took his hand and pressed her cheek against his chest to hold her still, but he wasn't able to keep her arms and hands trapped inside the blanket.

He needed to break through to her. What name had Sir Asshole called her? Oh, yes.

"Angie, lie still. You're safe now." He used a firm Dom voice, hoping to engage the sub's instinctive desire to please.

Her nipple beaded to a hard point against the underside of his forearm. She moaned—definitely not from pain this time.

"Ahhhhh!"

Oh, shit.

The newbie sub was going to come. He'd seen long-time submissives reach orgasm in subspace without being touched at all. This one would probably need a little help, though. Hell, if she were his little sub, he wouldn't hesitate to help her reach that level of satisfaction.

But she wasn't his.

She grabbed his vest and moaned in frustration, tilting her hips upward as she sought release. His cock bobbed against her ass. *Oh, hell. Why not?* She'd earned some degree of pleasure after all the pain she'd suffered with Sir Asshole. Why not salvage something from the disaster that was probably her first scene? Maybe then she wouldn't give up completely on exploring the submissive lifestyle with a responsible Dom someday.

With me.

Ignoring that stray and totally absurd thought, Marc's hand slipped inside the blanket, seeking the folds of her pussy and what he knew would be an erect clit. She wouldn't need much stimulation to fly apart for him.

No, he corrected himself. *Not for him.*

For her.

Chapter Two

Angelina Giardano floated. Free of pain. Free of her body. Free. Where had Allen gone? *Who cared?* She was free of him, too. She found herself staring down at what looked like her body being held by a dark-haired stranger. Definitely not Allen. This man's tanned and muscular, bare arms held her blanket-covered body. Even though she was unable to feel his arms around her, she knew somehow that it was her body. She marveled at the sense of security she felt.

Safe.

How strange. The delicious feeling left her without a single care.

Why didn't she open her eyes to look at his face?

"*You were so brave, cara.*"

Brave about what? She'd never been brave in her life. But his words made her want to believe him. He wiped away her tears. *Why was she crying?* She felt so incredibly safe. Blissful. Not a reason for tears. He'd even said she'd been good. Exactly what she'd been good at, she didn't know. She was just happy she'd pleased him.

A tremor shook her body and he pulled her closer to his chest, resting his head on top of hers, as if to keep her still. *You did well, cara.* He even used Italian endearments. *Cara.* Dear. Papa called her *cara.* She wished she could brush her fingers over the soft-looking black hairs on his corded forearms.

How could she be looking at him from above but feel him? Even though her eyes remained closed, she saw short black curls on the top of his head. Why didn't she open her eyes and look at him? *Mio Dio*, had she died? Was this heaven? If so, it was nothing like she'd been led to expect.

Suddenly a blinding flash of light engulfed the room. Oh, *Dio*! The pain!

"Accckkkkkk!"

The once strong, safe arms wrapped around her now only caused the pain to intensify. Her butt burned as if held over a flame. She screamed and fought to get away. From him, from the pain.

"Shhhh. I have you."

Safe? No!

His hand wiped the tears away from her cheek. When the underside of his forearm brushed lightly against her breast, she felt her nipple swell as if reaching out to him. *More.* Her skin tingled where he'd barely touched her, sending a zing to her… Why was she naked? Wasn't there a blanket a moment ago?

"Ohhhhh!" Both nipples hardened, as did her clit. She was going to come. How could that be without her or someone else stroking her clit? *Dio,* even with Allen touching her there, she'd never had an orgasm unless she took matters into her own hands. Now she was nearing orgasm without that stimulation?

Heat engulfed her—delicious, curl-your-toes heat. The pain in her butt receded as she reached up to hold onto his vest. The pecs she brushed felt like velvet-encased steel. She moaned, grabbing his vest tighter, frustrated as she tilted her hips upward seeking release. *More. Please!*

She needed him. So hot. Why did he have her lower body wrapped in a blanket? *Oh, good!* His hand pulled it apart. He was going to take the damned thing off of her. But he didn't. Instead, his hand reached inside the blanket, took her knee, and opened her wider, then his fingers moved to delve just inside the opening of her vagina. Oh! With two fingers, he spread her folds, and then a third finger slid up her cleft until he drew wet circles around the hood of her swollen clit.

"Oh, oh, yesss!"

Angelina's lower body bucked toward his hand. His finger moved faster. She wanted to feel him inside her. As if he'd heard her, his finger glided back along the path to her pussy and his finger slid deep inside her. So wet. Allen had never been able to do that without lubricant.

"That's right, *cara.* Just feel."

Oh, she felt him, all right. Her grip tightened on his vest. *Oh! Oh! Oh! Don't stop!* Had she shouted the words, or were they only reverberating through her mind? Thank God he continued, whether he'd heard her or not.

His finger slid out of her and back up to her clit again, this time directly touching the hard nubbin.

"Yes! Oh, *Dio,* yesssss!" Angelina pressed her forehead against his chest. The sensations were too intense. She was losing control, if she ever had any. Her hips bucked against his hand, harder and harder, simulating intercourse.

"*Mio Dio! Don't stop!*" she screamed as her release approached. Angelina pulled her head away from his chest and reached up, digging her fingers into the back of his neck. She pulled the stranger's head toward hers. Even with her eyes closed, she guided his lips to hers perfectly and tried to open his mouth with her tongue. His unyielding lips pulled away. She groaned, but didn't care anymore as she crested the waves of ecstasy.

"*Vola, cara.* Fly. Fly apart for me." His thumb rubbed her extremely sensitive clit as he rammed two fingers inside her vagina. She bucked up. "Yes, that's right. Ah, shit, *bella,* you're so damned tight."

His words and the friction of her motions caused her butt to rub against the blanket. Fire. She was on fire again. But the pain only added to the exquisite sensation. Pain mixed with pleasure.

"Yes, yesss, ohhh, ohhhhh, God! Yesssssss!" Her body stiffened with the intensity of the orgasm, then bucked and stiffened again, over and over. Her climax went on forever and her eyelids flew open as she clutched his vest, hanging on for dear life.

The wave receded much more quickly than it had built up. Tiny tremors shook her body as she floated. Her clit became hypersensitive and she moved away from his hand. He supported her back and readjusted the blanket over her hips and breasts, surrounding her with his arms and pulling her close against his hard body once more.

Her body began to shake, the muscles in her neck, arms, and legs spasming. *Oh, God, what was happening to her?*

"Shhhh. I have you, *cara.*" He tucked her arms inside the blanket again.

That voice. Her angel from heaven. The sexy angel with a Northern Italian accent. *Oh, Papa you were right. Heaven is in Italy!*

Fire burned in her butt. *No, this was hell!* Another chill wracked her body. Hot. Cold. The uncontrolled tremors caused her stomach muscles to contract, as well. He held her tighter.

"It's over now, *bella.* You're safe."

She crashed to earth violently. Disturbing images invaded her once-euphoric state. Allen. An X-shaped cross. Cuffs. Arms aching, stretched so high above her head. He'd used a flogger to beat her senseless. He wouldn't stop. She'd used her safeword. Hadn't she? Why didn't he stop?

Spasms gripped her calf muscles. She groaned and pulled her knees up toward her chest. The blankets trapped her arms, but she tried to reach down anyway to rub the knotted muscles in her legs.

"Hurts," she whimpered.

The angel took her calf in his firm hand and massaged the cramp away, first one leg, and then the other.

"Ow!" *Oh, Mio Dio*, the pain was more than she could stand. Tears wet her cheeks, hot against her skin, then cold. She'd never been in so much pain in her entire life. Not physically, at least.

Why had she agreed to come with Allen to his kink club in Denver? He'd used much more force than they'd agreed upon when they talked about doing a BDSM scene. At first, she'd tried to please him and not cry out, but the beating had continued for what seemed forever. She'd screamed, but Allen clearly had been getting off on her screams of anguish.

That bastard!

Where was he now? They had driven up here together. Had he left her at the club? Or was she somewhere else? How would she get home?

She heard a door open and close, seemingly far away. Her angel reached out for something, then tilted her head back. She missed the warmth of his chest against her cheek.

"Here, *cara*. Sip on this."

At last, she would be able to see his face. She opened her eyes, looked up, and gasped. Oh, God, he wasn't an angel at all. He was a wolf! She tried to back away, frightened again.

"Shhh. It's just water. You're dehydrated. This will help take care of the cramps in your legs, too."

An English-speaking wolf, with a Northern Italian accent, and intense green eyes. Was this a dream? A nightmare? As if in a trance, she opened her mouth and let him tilt the bottle until cold water trickled down her throat.

"Good girl."

Her insides melted. Why was it so important she please him? She didn't even know him. Some water dribbled down her face to her neck, but what she managed to swallow soothed her scratchy throat, raw from screaming, she guessed. She took his hand and tilted the bottle at a steeper angle.

"Whoa, easy, *cara*. Not too fast."

He smiled at her. He was only half wolf. Warmth pooled in her stomach. His mouth and chin were very human. A man, with a full lower lip and straight white teeth—no wolf fangs—against tanned, beautiful skin. Below his mask, his jaw and chin sported a shadow of scruff. As she sipped slowly, she wondered what it would feel like to be kissed by her angel-man-wolf. Why hadn't he let her kiss him moments ago? Would his whiskers abrade the skin on her face and neck—and other places?

He pulled the bottle away. "Now, have some chocolate. This will help you come back to us faster." He smiled.

She wasn't sure who he meant by us, then she remembered the door. She tensed. Allen! "Don't let him touch me again!"

"Shhh. He's gone." He clenched his jaw.

She relaxed again. *Safe.* He smiled. All she knew for certain was that she wanted to keep him smiling at her. As he broke off a piece of chocolate, she opened her mouth, waiting to be fed. He wouldn't have to force her to eat chocolate. When he looked down at her, his smile vanished and his hand went still just short of delivering what she craved.

"Please." Her voice sounded raspy to her ears. She wasn't sure if she was begging him for the chocolate or to smile at her again. She wanted both.

Used to taking care of herself, she reached up and pulled his hand toward her mouth, biting off a piece of chocolate, accidentally nipping his fingers in the process. He laughed. Bliss. The deep rumble from his laugh sent shivers down her body. She didn't know or care what was so funny. Closing her eyes, she sucked on the nectar of the gods while being held by an angel.

"Mmmm." The dark chocolate melted in her mouth. She licked her lips to get every bit. When she opened her eyes for more, his gaze was fixated on her mouth. Perhaps he wanted some of her chocolate. "I don't mind sharing."

He looked puzzled, his gaze straying to whoever was standing behind her, and then back at her. She looked down at the chocolate bar in his hand and licked her lips again.

He laughed, as if relieved. "Insatiable." She opened her mouth and this time he placed the flat rectangle on her tongue. She smiled at him and closed her mouth and eyes again, her lips surrounding his thumb and finger before he pulled them from her mouth. He lowered his arm and tightened it around her, holding her close again. If only she could stay here forever.

Not possible. The world intruded on her post-orgasmic state. She had to get back home. She had an event to cater on Wednesday. At least she thought it was this Wednesday. She didn't really care anymore. Her body became more relaxed and listlessness blanketed her. All she wanted to do was curl up in bed and sleep for a year or two. *Curl against her angel-man-wolf.* She smiled. As her eyelids drooped, she heard him speaking with whoever stood behind her.

He'd taken care of her. He hadn't hurt her. She deemed him safe enough to let down her guard. Angelina curled against him and felt his arms adjust to support her in sleep. If Allen came back, her angel-man-wolf would protect her.

Safe.

***

"I came in as soon as I could get rid of the shithead."

Marc looked up at Adam, bare-chested as well, except for his all-black leather vest. He stood with his legs apart, hands fisted on his black leather-clad hips. The man looked as if he held his beast on a tight leash. *Well, join the club.* He'd known Adam would take care of Sir Asshole. None of the Doms at the Masters at Arms tolerated abuse like what had been done to this woman.

Now, how did they keep it from happening again? Clearly, he needed to offer classes again, if it would keep her and others from going through something like this. He looked down at the beautiful angel sleeping in his arms and felt an unfamiliar tug at his heartstrings.

Dangerous.

Adam cleared his throat. "How is she?"

Marc tried to keep his voice low as he answered. "Better. Sleeping."

"I'm having a room prepared for her upstairs—the one next to Karla's."

Marc was familiar with every room in the house, of course. Adam had purchased the run-down mansion in Denver's Five Points neighborhood after he retired from the Corps. Seeing that Marc was going to be at loose ends after receiving his medical discharge, he invited him to join him in starting a kink club. Soon after, they'd discovered Damián needed a lifeline after the trauma he'd suffered at Fallujah.

The unlikely crew of three had embarked on converting Adam's monstrous house into a club and a residence for Adam and Damián. They'd worked over the next three years to refurbish the Victorian into the showplace it was today. Marc had learned how good it could be to work with his hands, and to be so proud of accomplishing something he'd set his mind and body to.

Luke had worked during the last year of renovations to do the cabinetry and trim. The man had become fixated by Marc's SAR work with the mountain rescue squad, asking a thousand questions. Then Marc had learned he'd lost his wife in an avalanche. Soon after, Luke began training for the squad and the two had become very good friends over the ensuing years.

He'd even had Luke make some equipment for a private playroom in the tower of that monstrous cave of a house his grandfather had bought him when he'd first come home from the Navy. He'd tried to convince Gramps it was more house than he wanted or needed, but the man had insisted the family's "war hero" accept it.

Marc was no hero. His brother, Gino, Sergeant Miller, and Damián were the heroes.

He couldn't disrespect the man by turning him down. Still, he sometimes wished he had someone else to rattle around with inside the mausoleum. He just hadn't found a woman he wanted to let that close—and probably never would. Pamela was long gone before Marc had been able to complete the playroom. Okay, so maybe the room wouldn't have helped their relationship and he did have commitment issues, as she'd accused him of having. Then again, maybe he was just discerning.

He wasn't the only one steering clear of commitment, though. All three of the club owners led pretty solitary lives outside of club activities. Adam lived upstairs, in the private west wing. Damián had lived here, as well, until a year or so ago when he got an apartment of his own—alone. He'd said he wouldn't put a woman at risk sleeping with him because he might hurt her if he had a nightmare or something triggered his PTSD. He'd had a tough time dealing with the amputation and Sergeant Miller's death. Marc guessed he still fought that firefight in his mind on a regular basis.

When Karla showed up for an audition two months ago and had been hired, Adam moved her into Damián's old room. He'd said he wanted to keep an eye on her, be there for her. His former master sergeant liked to make people think he was a hard-ass, but his heart was about as soft as they came. He was always rescuing the lost ones. Damián. Karla. Hell, he'd even rescued Marc on that rooftop in Fallujah, and afterwards, too, when he didn't know what to do with himself after his medical discharge.

Of course, Adam always kept rooms available in the east wing upstairs for club members who wanted their privacy. The bedroom in between was a sanctuary for someone who needed one, like his little angel here.

He glanced up at Adam again. While his friend kept his emotions in check most times, Marc saw the muscle twitching in his jaw. He was about as pissed as Marc had seen him since Fallujah.

They thought they'd done all they could to teach the Doms who frequented the place to behave responsibly, but despite putting Sir Asshole through their basic training, he'd broken most of the rules anyway.

"I'm glad you got to her in time," Adam said, unable to take his eyes off her.

Marc looked down and held her closer. *Mine.*

Whoa! Marc put the brakes on thoughts like that right away. He didn't know where that possessive thought came from, but looked up at Adam again. "We're going to have to address the problem of abusive Doms before someone else gets hurt."

"We'll discuss it at this week's meeting."

Marc nodded and looked back at the angel in his arms. He brushed the hair away from her face. Her eyelashes twitched and she grimaced. "Shhhh," he whispered.

He'd hoped helping her reach orgasm would take away some of the bad memories, but she'd probably be plagued with nightmares for a while, depending on how well she'd thought she could trust Sir Asshole. Marc brought his hand up to brush his fingertips across her full lips. His cock tightened, leaving him with the unfamiliar wish that he could stay with her tonight to hold her. Be there for her when the nightmares came. Help her forget.

Hold on. He hadn't spent an entire night with a woman in more than a year. Pamela. He'd moved too fast that time. He wasn't going to go there again, either.

"She'll be monitored closely during the night," Adam continued, as if he'd known the direction of Marc's thoughts. "Tomorrow morning, I'll see that she gets home safely. Karla has a friend who lives near where the sub's from, according to the guest form she filled out to enter the club tonight. I think Karla would like a chance to get away from…the club for a while. I'll ask her to take her home."

Marc wished he didn't have a five-day survival training excursion planned starting tomorrow at noon. He'd liked to have taken her home himself, to be sure she made it safely. But Adam's relief at being able to send Karla away for a while wasn't lost on Marc either. Adam liked to keep the young singer at arm's length—and sometimes even farther away.

Not his concern. He looked down at the sexy woman in his arms. Adam was trying to tell him to stop worrying about her and resume his DMS duties, but damned if he wanted to let her go. She brought out his most basic Dom instincts—to rescue and protect.

"I'll carry her upstairs soon and get back to work," Marc said to appease Adam.

"Stay with her until I send Karla up after she finishes the next set," Adam instructed. "We can switch to canned music tonight."

Karla would nurture the woman to the extreme, given the way she took care of the three Dom owners like a mother hen, despite her young age.

He stroked the soft cheek of the woman, who smiled in her sleep. His bone-hard erection grew even harder, if possible. The thought of training this little one into the lifestyle excited him a bit. Correction, she scared the living hell out of him.

No, she would not be his sub.

"Take as much time as you need. I'll send a sub in here to clean the equipment after you leave."

Marc nodded and Adam left him alone with her. Dark lashes lay fanned below her closed eyes. Serene again. She appeared to have returned from deep subspace fairly well.

A strong woman.

He didn't even know her full name. If she'd opted for confidentiality, as most guests and members did, he'd never find out who she was. Only Adam had access to membership and guest records. Good. He didn't want to have further contact with her anyway.

Of course, he didn't expect to see her back here again—ever. Not after the experience she'd had with Sir Asshole. He wondered if being someone's submissive was even her fantasy. Some women just went along with a kinkster boyfriend or spouse for fear of losing them to someone else who would be willing to share their kinky fantasies.

He brushed his thumb across her cheekbone again, unable to keep his hands off her. She moaned in her sleep and pressed her face into his hand. His cock tightened. No sense torturing himself with what might have been if they'd met under different circumstances. Still, he regretted refusing to kiss her earlier. Maybe just this once… He bent down and brushed his lips across hers.

He felt her lips curve into a smile as she snuggled closer to him. *Don't take advantage of her.* With a sigh, he pulled his face away, held her closer to his chest, and stood, leaving the room and making his way to the brick stairway. At the top of the stairs, he turned down the hall toward the private living quarters.

The door to her room was open. Marc carried her inside. The sheet and comforter had been turned down. He laid her gently near the center of the bed. It pained him to see her grimace and moan as her sore backside made contact with the mattress. She needed some lidocaine to help ease the pain.

Trying to keep a professional medic's demeanor, he unwrapped the blanket and turned her onto her stomach. *Don't ogle her gorgeous ass.* Reaching into his vest pocket, he pulled out the tube of soothing gel and a pair of latex gloves. She didn't appear to have any lacerations, just angry red welts on her ass and thighs, but he didn't want to chance infection.

He squirted the gel onto his gloved finger and spread it along the flogger lines on her thighs first. When she moaned, his cock threatened to rip through his zipper. Sweat broke out on his forehead. He moved as quickly as he could to cover the welts on her ass, too, and then blew on her skin to dry it more quickly, watching gooseflesh spread over her ass.

When he finished, Marc wrapped her in the aftercare blanket again, turned her onto her back, and pulled the sheet and comforter over her. In the morning, Adam would retrieve her clothes from her locker in the women's dressing room downstairs. Then she'd be gone.

As Marc looked down at her, she curled onto her side, burrowing under the covers. He wished he could crawl into bed with her and curve his body around her backside.

Cut that shit out.

He'd try to get back upstairs to check on her tonight, but with all the activity going on in the club, that would be hard to do. He sighed. Despite hiding in the role for months, tonight he wished he hadn't volunteered for DMS duty.

Oh, shit. He had it bad for this one. What was the matter with him?

"How is she?" Marc turned to watch Karla enter the room. She'd changed into black jeans and a "For My Pain: Fallen" Finnish band t-shirt. "Adam told me what happened." She shook her head. "Poor thing."

Marc smiled. Yes, Karla would mother her to death.

"I'll check back in on her later, if I can get away." Marc longed to bend down and kiss his angel again.

Hell, no! Not his. Still, he brushed a strand of hair away from her face, letting his finger trail across her lips before he turned and left the room.

* * *

Fire. Angelina's skin was on fire. She turned onto her side again, moaning at the pain. Something lashed at her backside, again and again, harder and harder.

"Red! Oh, God, please stop!"

"Shhh. You're dreaming."

Angelina opened her eyes to find a familiar, yet unfamiliar, woman standing over her in a strange bed. The woman was about her age, long black hair, heavy eye makeup, pale skin. Where would she have known her from?

The young woman held out a glass of water to her. "Can you take ibuprofen?" Angelina nodded and, with great care, scooted up to a sitting position. *Dio*, the pain in her butt grew even worse, definitely not the result of a dream.

A flood of memories washed over her. Oh, God! Allen. The St. Andrew's cross. Leather flogger. The man had ignored her safeword. Selfish, abusive bastard.

Angelina accepted the glass of water and two gel caps from the woman. "Thanks." After swallowing them down, she sank back against the pillows, too exhausted to sit up.

"How are you feeling?" the woman asked.

"Battered and stupid."

The sympathy in the woman's eyes touched Angelina. She didn't even know her, but the caring seemed genuine. Why did she look so familiar?

"Adam…I mean, Master Adam, is very upset about what happened downstairs. I haven't seen him that angry since he rescued me from a pimp in Chicago. When he dragged your boyf—I mean, the guy you were with—out the door, I thought he might change his mind and take turns with Master Damián to teach him a few lessons."

The woman smiled, her blue eyes sparkling, as she spoke about the altercation. Angelina wished she could have seen it herself. Allen didn't like to be pushed around. He was probably fit to be tied.

"I'm Angie Giardano."

"It's nice to meet you. I'm Karla Paxton. I sing here at the club."

Of course! The singer. That explained why she looked so familiar. Angelina hadn't recognized her without her Goth dress and stage makeup. "You have a great voice." Well, based on what little Angelina had heard while she was filling out the club's paperwork, before Allen whisked her off to her private torture session.

"Thanks." She glanced away, then back. "Master Adam said you live in Aspen Corners."

Angelina nodded.

"I have a college friend who lives about thirty minutes from there. I have some decisions to make soon and have been dying to see her. So, Adam's going to loan me his car so I can take you home today, after you've rested up a bit more, of course."

Angelina tried to follow the woman's conversation, but was so focused on the pain she only heard every other word it seemed. But the woman seemed trustworthy and kind—and didn't seem to be making a special trip just to take her home. One thing Angelina knew for certain—she wouldn't get into a car with a strange man at this point. She didn't trust any of them, not after what Allen had done to her. Seven months together. How could he just shatter her trust like that?

Karla was waiting for a response. She'd been talking about a ride home. Well, the sooner she got away from Denver, the better. "Thanks. I'd appreciate that."

Angelina looked down. The blanket wrapped around her had fallen, nearly exposing her breasts. Her very bare breasts. Her face flushed. She was naked underneath the blanket. She pulled the blanket higher. Where were her clothes? She looked around the room to find a cherry dresser and a matching footboard of an antique sleigh bed. The room seemed rather stark. Definitely not lived in by anyone. Was it used for sexual encounters with club members? At least the bed didn't smell of sex. It smelled of lavender, just like her Nonna's room in Sicily. Comforting.

Karla took a seat in a chair next to the bed, where she must have been keeping a vigil, waiting for Angelina to wake up. The woman looked away, but Angelina had the feeling she wanted to say something more. She'd learned to just wait people out. Usually, the silence made them uncomfortable enough they'd fill the void by saying something without the usual filters. Sure enough, the woman didn't disappoint.

Karla's gaze met Angelina's again. "Ad…Master Adam said you were new to this BDSM stuff." She cast her glance away, then sat up straighter and brought her gaze back to pin Angelina's. "Why did you want to try it? I mean, what made you think you were…?"

Angelina drew a deep breath. Okay, this wasn't the line of questioning she was anticipating. "Submissive?"

Karla nodded.

Oh, boy. How to answer, especially now that she knew she'd been so wrong. "Well, I'd been reading BDSM romance novels." She shrugged her shoulders and smiled. "Something about the whole exchange of power with a dominant man interested me. Giving up control, in the bedroom at least."

She glanced away, not sure how to explain what attracted her to try it. *Aha*. Her gaze returned to the woman sitting beside her bed.

"I own and manage my own catering business. I'm in charge of a small temporary staff and am responsible for all of the details. Everything. All the time." Angelina loved her business, even though things were a little slow in the Corners.

She took a deep breath before she continued. "I've always liked having the men I went out with make all the dating decisions. Where to eat. What to do. I just wanted a man who would take charge. Whisk me away on a date. Surprise me, rather than ask permission for everything. Allen was like that. How I ever let him talk me into this, though…"

"I'm confused. I thought it was about the giving and receiving of pain. Master Damián was really hurting someone tonight—and she was loving it."

Angelina shuddered. "There are some who get into the pain aspect. But for me, I wanted the feeling of being restrained. To give over control of my body to someone who would make me feel…I don't know what. Whatever I was looking for, I didn't find it with Allen—the Dom I came here with. He went too far down the pain scale for me. I thought I could trust him. We'd talked about what my limits were…" Angelina looked away, embarrassed that she'd gotten herself into a situation like this. "I'm not sure I would ever trust someone enough to let him restrain me like that again. I think I'm going to stick to my novels from now on."

Angelina looked over at Karla, who nibbled on her lower lip.

"I've never…I haven't really dated. I wanted a career first and foremost. But there's someone I like a lot who is really into this stuff. I just don't know how to tell if I could fit in. What if I tried it and hated it? He wouldn't want to have anything to do with me again."

Angelina felt sorry for the woman. She had it bad for someone, that's for sure. But who was she to be dishing out advice for the BDSM lovelorn?

"Does he know how you feel?"

"No. He thinks of me…as a kid."

Angelina thought she saw tears in her eyes. She wondered how much older he was than Karla, but didn't want to pry. There was one thing she could advise the woman on, no matter what kind of kink or vanilla sex life she wanted. "Talk to him. Communication is the basis for any relationship. You might be surprised that he likes you just the way you are." Changing herself for any man wouldn't work for long.

Karla's voice was barely a whisper. "But what if he doesn't? I don't think I could bear having him reject me again."

Again? Okay, that didn't sound good.

"I was only sixteen the first time," Karla was quick to explain.

Now this was getting weird. Angelina didn't get into the Daddy Dom stuff she'd seen online. *Ick*. Just how old *was* this guy?

Okay, to each her own. Who was she to judge? They were both adults. "I know it's a risk. But if you don't try again, how will he ever know you're serious about him, and not just in a teenage-crush way?"

"I guess you're right. I'll think about it. I'll talk to my friend Cassie after I drop you off, although she's had her own problems with men. Why do they have to be so complicated?"

Angelina laughed. That was the mystery of the century.

"Oh, I almost forgot! Adam said you could use chocolate. I made these chocolate-peanut butter brownies earlier today." She handed Angelina a plate of two brownie squares that set her stomach to rumbling. "They're Master Adam's favorite."

Had Karla blushed when she said the Dom's name? Was he the one she pined for? Oh, my! Angelina remembered him from when she'd turned in her paperwork. Tall, intimidating to the extreme, definitely older—at least mid forties, she'd guess, a generation older than Karla. Although he certainly was in better shape than Allen, who was at least twenty years younger.

Maybe Angelina should revise her words of advice to the timid young woman and warn her she'd be way out of her league with a Dom like him, especially if she wasn't even sure she wanted to be in the lifestyle. No way would he accept anything but a well-behaved submissive, Angelina was certain. Was Karla even sure she wanted to be in that role?

Stay out of it. It's not like you're an expert on BDSM.

Angelina munched on the best brownies she'd ever had. Who would have thought of adding peanut butter to a brownie? Holding up the last piece before popping it into her mouth, she said, "These are incredible."

Karla smiled and thanked her, obviously pleased.

An uncomfortable silence fell between them. This time, Angelina felt the need to end it. "You wouldn't happen to know where my clothes are, would you?"

"They're in the dressing room downstairs. Adam…*Master* Adam said he'd send them up after the club closed. He needs to wait to see what's left behind to determine which are yours."

"Listen, I can tell you exactly what I left down there, if you wouldn't mind retrieving them. I just want to go home and put this fiasco behind me as soon as possible. Would you be up for leaving soon?"

Her intense blue eyes lit with enthusiasm. "I'll need to throw some things into a suitcase. I'll get your clothes first, but we could leave within the hour. I'm sure Adam won't mind."

After telling her where to find her things, Angelina lay back down on the pillow and closed her eyes. Strange, disjointed images flitted through her mind. A wolf. An angel. And the most sensual lips she'd ever seen. Ever felt. Her lips tingled at the memory as if he'd just brushed them with his. Who was he? Had he kissed her, or had she only dreamed him up? Perhaps her mind had wanted to give her something with which to erase images of Allen.

If so, it worked for her! The sooner she forgot about Allen, the better.

Chapter Three

Luke Denton awoke with a start, most likely because of the pounding of his heart.

"Maggie?" he whispered, his hand reaching out to her. Empty mattress. He squeezed his eyes closed. The dream had been so real, as if she were right here in bed with him again.

When was the last time he'd experienced this hollow, sinking feeling after reaching out and realizing she wasn't there? That she'd never be sleeping beside him again?

All because of his stupidity and failing to take charge.

He looked around, not sure where he was. Dark room, strange bed, haunting images.

"It's time. I'm sending you an angel. She needs you."

Maggie. Her voice was as clear now as it had been in the dream. Images of a woman he didn't know—long dark hair, olive skin—near a stand of golden aspens quaking against an intense blue sky. Man, did he ever dream in color.

Luke blinked a few times, letting his eyes adjust to the darkness. He began to make out a desk beyond the foot of the bed, a small round table near the window, and a nondescript stuffed chair in the corner. Motel room. He raised his head and looked at the bed next to him.

Covered only in a sheet, his bare torso half exposed, Marc slept on his side, turned away from him. Then he remembered where he was and why. Aspen Corners. They'd rescued some hikers late yesterday up on the slopes outside town. He and Marc had been asked to stick around and do the media circus thing later today. They'd drawn the short straws because they'd been the ones to find the group of hikers.

Aspen Corners. Of all places, why'd it have to be here?

Marc insisted on staying over, rather than driving the three hours to Denver only to turn around and head right back. His partner didn't have another overnight wilderness trek to lead until Tuesday and had found someone to cover for him at the club. Luke didn't have anything urgent he was working on that couldn't wait till Saturday.

Still, he'd have walked to and from Denver if he could avoid staying in this town. But then he'd have had to explain why the town caused him so much anxiety. He'd never told Marc the real reason he'd joined SAR.

He just hoped to get out of this damned town before he ran into any of the Giardano brothers. Tony and Rafe also worked on mountain search-and-rescue teams, but had been in Colorado Springs training this week. That left only two, but they wouldn't know Luke or his problematic connection to their family.

The obituary had been branded onto his mind seven years ago. The fatal decision he and Maggie had made that day—one that had cost Maggie and a decent family man their lives—had haunted Luke every day since.

Veteran search-and-rescue worker Antonio Giardano Sr., 58, lifelong resident of Aspen Corners, died while attempting to rescue an injured hiker on Mt. Evans Wednesday. The hiker, Maggie Denton, a biologist from the University of Texas, also died in the accident.

Giardano is survived by his wife of twenty-seven years, Angela; four sons, Raphael, Franco, Matteo, and Antonio Jr.; and by one daughter, his youngest child, Angelina.

No matter how many lives he saved since joining SAR he'd always be haunted by the man whose death he'd caused—and the helplessness of knowing he hadn't been able to save his own wife.

* * *

"Vola, cara. Fly. Fly apart for me."

Fly, dear.

Angelina awoke with a start, her heart and clit pounding in alternating rhythm. Once again, her dreams had been filled with erotic images that had haunted her nightly for the last month, ever since she'd woken up in that bedroom at Allen's kink club in Denver.

Her nipples grew hard, aching for the touch of the man who dominated her dreams. His image was never clear, but often came to her as a wolf or an angel—sometimes both. How could someone who felt so real be a total figment of her imagination? Her creativity and imagination usually ended in the kitchen.

When she woke, the elusive encounters faded quickly, as if never there. But the feeling of strong arms surrounding her, a chin resting on the top of her head, made her feel safe.

You've been reading too many angel and shapeshifter novels, Angie.

She tossed the covers aside and sat up on the edge of the ornate wrought iron Italian bed that had belonged to Nonna and had been shipped over from Italy after her grandmother's death. Before last month, Angelina had found peace and respite in this bed.

No more.

Thank God she'd never let Allen Martin join her here, or she'd have had to burn the mattress to exorcise his memory. What a bastard. When she'd looked at her backside in the mirror in Karla's bathroom at the club and had seen what Allen had done, she'd been furious.

Just thinking about the creep caused her blood to boil. She jumped up and headed to the shower. She had a happy-hour event to cater and needed to get going. She'd also promised Rico she'd stop by tonight for a drink. For the past month, she'd been hiding away from her friend's bar for fear of running into Allen. Well, in a small town like Aspen Corners, the chances of meeting him were fairly good. But with the anger she'd built up since that night, she'd be able to handle him when the time came.

Never again would she give him her power.

In fact, Angelina would never put herself in such a vulnerable position with any man again. She'd had enough BDSM to last a lifetime.

* * *

Angelina's feet ached as she walked the two short blocks to daVinci's bar. At least, she'd thought they'd be short, but she definitely shouldn't have worn these damned heels, even if she did feel like dressing up "just because" for the first time in a long while.

She felt like celebrating. The cocktail party had been a great success. Her business was taking off. She couldn't hire any permanent staff yet, but each event put her closer to solvency.

And exhausted her. She loved being a caterer, but she often had to take on many aspects of overall event planning, as well. She'd much rather focus on what she loved to do more than anything—practice the culinary arts.

As she walked, her breasts bounced unrestrained, because the keyhole back in her new red knit dress forced her to remove her bra at the last minute. She kept meaning to order one of those backless bras, but never thought about it until she needed one. However, after her self-pity weight gain this past month, the new dress fit better than any of the others in her closet.

The breeze off the snow-covered Rockies loosened wisps of hair from her topknot clip. She pulled the gauzy black silk shawl over her shoulders and held her girls to keep them from bouncing. No need to attract attention.

These late days of summer could deliver a wallop of snow on the nearby slopes, as some teenage hikers discovered this week when the fury of the Rockies caught them by surprise. SAR teams had descended on the town for days until the hikers were found safely yesterday.

Damned careless hikers. When would they ever think about the rescue workers who had to risk their lives to save them all the time? All they could think about was their next adventure.

Angelina shook off the pain she felt every time she thought about the sacrifice her family made as a result of two careless hikers seven years ago. Her father had answered the call one too many times.

Miss you, Papa.

Her good mood quickly hit the skids. If only she hadn't promised Rico she'd stop in to see him tonight, she'd turn around and head back home to curl up with her e-reader and the newest BDSM novel by her favorite author. While she never wanted to encounter another real-life Dom, she loved to read about the near-perfect ones in her books. But she'd learned that reality bites in that alternative lifestyle.

Although she had to admit the Denver kink club's owner, Master Adam, had been very kind to her. Even solicitous. He was none too happy about her insistence on leaving in the middle of the night last month. But Karla managed to convince him to relent and he gave the singer his satellite phone, just in case they ran into trouble. He'd even called Angelina later that day to check on her and make sure she was okay. He seemed nice.

A nice Dom? Yeah, right. He was probably just concerned about her filing a lawsuit for damages she sustained at his club.

But the club's singer did seem like someone Angelina would have welcomed as a friend, if they didn't live so far apart. Karla didn't seem too keen on the kinkster lifestyle either. On their drive to the Corners last month, the two spoke about many things, but pretty much agreed that pain and sex didn't mix.

No thanks.

Angelina was surprised to look up and see daVinci's was just a few steps away. She'd made the two blocks faster than she'd expected and hadn't even noticed the pain in her feet for the last block. Until now. She strode into the dark bar.

"Angie! You made it!" Rico called from behind the bar. "Good to see you out again, baby!"

"Hey, Rico. I've missed you, too!"

While tame by Denver standards, daVinci's was the sole place for nightlife in town, especially on a Friday or Saturday night. Her high-school friend, Rico, the owner, would keep the creeps at bay while she reentered the social scene one aching toe at a time. Sometimes there were perks to being surrounded by overprotective Italian men. When it came to her social life, though, they were just a pain in the ass. But at least she'd have someone to talk with tonight. She didn't want to be alone with her thoughts any longer.

Or memories of her dream lover.

She sighed. The chances of a man anywhere near as exciting as her angel-man-wolf fantasy showing up tonight were slim to none. Not that she was ready for another relationship yet. After giving Rico her wine order and exchanging a few inane pleasantries, she waited for the conversation to turn to Allen. It did.

"He's been in here several nights a week since you dumped him. Different woman every time."

"Probably because they're smarter at recognizing an asshole than I was."

Rico looked guilty. "I wish I'd known, baby. He runs a good cleaning business. I've been a client of his for years. But I wouldn't have let you out of here with him if I'd known he'd ever hurt you."

Angelina's face grew warm with embarrassment. Rico didn't know the whole story. He thought her pain was emotional, not physical. If he knew what had happened at the club, he'd have told her brothers and together they'd have beaten Allen to a pulp. Not that he didn't deserve it.

But sweet little Angelina Giardano did *not* go to kink clubs.

Rico pulled her back from her thoughts. "I have to warn you, I think he's coming in here looking for you."

"Well, he may find me, but if he comes anywhere near me again, I'll…" She had no idea what she'd do, but it wouldn't be pretty. Her brothers had been good for one thing—they'd taught her how to fight. "I'm finished with men."

Rico laughed.

"I'm serious!"

"You just haven't found the right one, baby."

Yes, I have.

He just doesn't exist in reality. Why did her mind keep conjuring up thoughts of her dream lover? He had to be a spillover from a shapeshifter romance novel she'd read or something. The images lingering in her mind were so vivid—an angel who was half wolf, half man, with a delicious sprinkling of soft, black hair on his forearms.

She reached for her white zin and took a gulp. Maybe she should give up reading those novels that were warping her perspective on men and BDSM. And her libido. She picked up the cardboard coaster and fanned herself.

No, tonight she planned to enjoy Rico's company and hang out with any of her other friends who might show up. Woman-on-the-make wasn't her style, anyway. She'd dated Allen for months before she'd even let him touch her intimately. Of course, she thought she could trust him. She'd learned just the opposite.

Men were not to be trusted. Not only was she clueless about choosing the right man, but she was acquainted with every available man in Aspen Corners. By now, everyone had heard about her break-up. Hopefully Allen hadn't told anyone what actually had happened.

Not that there were all that many available men in town, and they all knew what her overprotective brothers would do to anyone they didn't deem "safe" (read: boring). Ironically, Allen had passed their inspection with flying colors. Successful businessman. Meek. Safe.

Boring.

Until he put on his leather pants and transformed himself into a sadistic bastard.

Angelina sipped her wine, nibbled on salty pretzels, and talked with Rico for half an hour about what was going on around town. She watched as Rico delivered two beers to a booth in the back—one, a bottle of Birra Moretti. Italian beer. She hadn't noticed the booth being occupied earlier, and couldn't see who sat there from this vantage point. One must be Italian, given the choice of beer.

Steer clear of that table, Angie.

Taking another sip, her gaze remained focused on the booth, anyway, through the reflection in the mirror behind the bar. She caught a glimpse of a man's white shirt sleeve rolled up to reveal a tanned forearm sprinkled with black hair. Just like the man in her dreams. Her clit responded as if he'd touched her. *Oh, come on.* Most Italian men have dark hair on their forearms. Was she going to think every man she saw was her dream lover sent from God?

As if the angel-man-wolf even existed.

Angelina took another sip of wine and bit into the last pretzel. Rico returned to refill the bowl and looked over her shoulder as someone came in the door.

"Uh-oh. Don't look now, baby, but Allen just strutted in."

Like involuntarily looking at an accident at the side of the road, Angelina's gaze went immediately to the mirror to find Allen with his arm wrapped around a very petite blonde with huge breasts. Surely they were implants. The air escaped Angelina's lungs.

"Rico, quick! Which man can I trust in here?"

She needed to move before Allen saw her sitting here—alone. No way did she want him to think she was without her own replacement model. Rico scanned the room and pointed to the booth in the back.

"Those guys should be safe. They were involved in the search-and-rescue yesterday up on the north slope."

Her gaze followed the direction of his finger. Mr. Sexy Italian Forearm— and a SAR man to boot. Along with his SAR partner.

Great. Thanks a whole helluva lot, Rico.

She scanned the barroom quickly, but only saw couples and Mr. Davis, who rented the apartment upstairs and looked as though he'd had a few too many—several hours ago.

Her gaze returned to the booth. What choice did she have? Drawing in a deep breath for courage, Angelina stood up, tucked her purse under her arm, draped her shawl over the same arm, and picked up her drink. She looked at Rico, "Cover me. I'm going in."

"I've got your sexy back, baby." He winked and Angelina wished she'd worn something less revealing—with a bra. Too late now.

As she approached the booth, she heard two deep male voices engaged in quiet conversation. Apparently, they'd been holed up back here since she'd arrived. She brushed a strand of loosened hair off her shoulder. Before she could see either man's face, another tanned, muscular forearm appeared. No surprise, given their line of work.

When she could see the face of the one in the dress shirt, she nearly stumbled over her shoes. His black hair framed the face of an Adonis. The white shirt contrasted starkly with his bronzed skin. A sprinkling of chest hair peeked from the opening at the collar of his shirt.

Why did he have to be Italian? Wasn't Adonis supposed to be a Greek *god?*

At least she had a bargaining chip to entice him into helping her. She'd yet to meet an Italian-American man who would turn down home cooking from the Old Country. If he'd help her out tonight, she'd offer to prepare a special meal for him as his reward.

The other man, whose face she couldn't see yet, wore a plaid flannel shirt, also with his sleeves rolled up. When his profile came into view, she saw he looked a little younger than the Italian. Clean-cut. Chiseled features. He could have been a model. His tanned arm was sprinkled with gold-flecked hair, kissed by the sun. His long fingers were wrapped around a brown bottle of Bud Lite.

Damn. Gold band on ring finger. Well, that pretty much ruled him out, even if all she planned to do was flirt and hang out. She did have her standards. She'd definitely have to win the Italian over to her cause.

When she arrived at the table, two pairs of sexy eyes looked up at her in unison. *Oh, man.* Her heart thudded, then halted momentarily. Way out of her league. Yes, she'd definitely have to offer them that gourmet meal. When they smiled at her, a frisson of electricity jolted from her now wildly beating heart to her clit, surprising her. These men had just turned her burner on with just their smiles.

What happened to the no-more-men rule, Angie?

The Italian had short, wavy black hair. His moss-green eyes narrowed as if he were trying to place her, then he smiled in the most disconcerting way. She'd never seen him before, but he seemed oddly familiar. He was the spitting image of Raoul Bova, from *Under the Tuscan Sun*. She'd seen the movie many times with Mama. That must be it.

His gaze devoured her, sweeping her length, virtually removing her dress. She shivered at the intensity of his gaze. Her nipples rose like a soufflé on steroids. Judging by the smoking-hot look he gave her as he smiled, he'd noticed her girls' response, too.

Definitely not a safe man. And why did her clit throb at that thought? She croaked a husky "Hi," then cleared her throat, remembering her mission. "Rico tells me you're SAR and I really need rescuing tonight."

Mio Dio. Did she really say that? How many times had women used that line on them? Well, desperate times and all.

The Italian broadened his smile. Her fingers twitched with the urge to stroke the five-o'clock shadow darkening his jaw. Unlike the clean-cut man, this man's kisses would leave abrasions on her skin. Her nipples tightened even more at the thought.

Angelina's face flushed. She took a gulp of wine hoping to cool down, but the liquid went down her windpipe instead. As she sputtered for air, both men jumped up and stood beside her.

"Cough, *cara*," the Italian ordered. The other man placed his arm across her midriff to support her as he patted her back.

Cara? A distant memory flitted across her mind. That and her close proximity with the two virile men caused her to go into a fit of coughing.

"Good girl." The Italian's hand stroked her back, skin on skin through the keyhole. Her fantasy angel-wolf-man had said that, too.

Snap out of it, Angie. He doesn't exist.

Heat radiated from both men's bodies, making her feel even hotter. She held a shaky hand to her throat and placed her glass on the table before she spilled or dropped it.

"Can you talk?" the non-Italian asked. She noticed a woodsy scent about him.

As the coughing spell ended, she croaked out, "I'm fine."

"How did we do, *cara*?"

Mamma mia. Northern Italian. Just like her dream lover.

Stop it! Stop it! Stop it!

The corner of his mouth twitched, breaking into a dazzling smile. She blinked a couple of times, stunned at his beautiful face, then grinned back. God, so much like the man in her recurrent dream, only ten times better. Unfortunately, they thought their rescue work was finished.

"Um, that wasn't the rescuing I had in mind." When she saw something akin to disappointment in their eyes, she rushed to assure them. "But you both did great!" Men had such fragile egos. Both remained poised to spring into action again at her very command. What power. Heady stuff.

"Do you mind if I sit?"..*before I fall off these damned shoes?*

"Of course! Pardon our manners." The man on her right had a Texas drawl. He gestured for her to have a seat—across the table from where he'd been seated. Happily married, no doubt. Angelina slid into the far side of the booth, the Italian joining her, heat from his body enveloping her. She took another sip of wine, a smaller one this time. The Texan sat down again, too.

The Italian leaned toward her and asked in a near whisper, "What else can we do for you, *cara mia?*" The timbre of his voice sent tingles over her entire body. The suggestive tone in his voice caused any number of lewd and lascivious acts to flit through her mind. He had short-circuited the electrical fields between her brain and her body, jolting places back to life that had long gone dormant.

She needed to bring her body temperature down before she caught fire. Good thing she hadn't put on much makeup, or it now would be sliding down her neck.

"I'm Angelina."

"Angel?" the Texan asked. He looked as if he'd seen a ghost.

Before she could correct him, the Italian said, "*Angelo mio.*"

My angel?

Taking her fingers, he brought her hand to his mouth, brushing his lips across the knuckles. His scratchy scruff tickled, causing gooseflesh to rise on her arms. Then he turned her hand over and brushed his lips across the underside of her wrist. *Mio Dio.* Her body grew weak. Thank God she was sitting. Taking a ragged breath, she pulled her hand back with great reluctance. Italian men and their damned sex appeal. He still reminded her so much of…

"Have we met?" she asked, suddenly needing to know why he looked so familiar.

"*Perdono.* Marco D'Alessio," he said by way of introduction, "but please, call me Marc." Pointing across the table. "This is my search-and-rescue squad partner, Luke Denton."

Still rattled by her body's reaction, she tried to distance herself from the disturbing presence next to her and turned her attention to Luke, reaching her still-tingling hand across the table.

"Angel, pleased to meet you," Luke said, shaking her hand and smiling as if he had a secret. He wore a braided leather bracelet on his right wrist that was well worn. His chestnut hair was disheveled, with a slight part on the right. Smoky blue eyes, perhaps gray, drew her in. There was a sadness there that tugged at her emotions a bit.

What in the hell was she doing sitting in a bar with a sexy married man and one who reminded her too much of her dream lover? Oh, yeah. *Allen.*

"This is really embarrassing," she said as she leaned toward them, motioning for them to lean closer as if she were spelling out a plot to overthrow the government. "I need your help. Did you see the man and woman who came into the bar a moment ago?"

Both shook their heads no, then in unison leaned outside the booth in a comical way to inspect the bar's latest arrivals.

"You mean the blond guy checking himself out in the mirror—the one with the skinny woman?" the Texan asked. He made skinny sound undesirable. If only he weren't married.

Marc clenched his fists and sat back in the booth, growing very still. He reminded her of a wolf about to pounce. *Stop it, Angie. Now! He's not your angel-man-wolf.*

"Um, yeah, that's him," she answered. "Well, I dumped him a month ago and really don't want to have anything to do with him. But this is a small town and… Anyway, this is my first night out since…"

Stop babbling. Seeing Allen again frazzled her nerves more than she would have expected. All her bravado went out the window. The man had hurt her and she didn't want him coming anywhere near her again. Before she said more than she wanted to reveal, she picked up her glass and took another sip, swallowed, then inhaled deeply. "I wondered if you would mind pretending to hang out with me tonight—just until he leaves, of course." She didn't want them to think they'd be saddled with her the whole night.

Oddly, being with these two strangers, she already felt safer than she ever had with Allen. That slug wouldn't dare approach her while she was surrounded by men who could beat him to a pulp. While the image of a bloodied Allen enticed her, she didn't want anyone going to jail—even if the bastard deserved a beating just as harsh as the one he'd given her.

Before they could say no, she rushed to assure them there was something in it for them, too. "I'll make it up to you for giving up your evening. I can fix dinner for you tomorrow night, if you'll still be in town. Or you can take a rain check for later. I'm an Italian cuisine chef. So, if you could just pretend…"

"He won't get anywhere near you again, *cara*." Marc seemed to be holding his anger on a short leash, then placed a protective arm along the back of the booth, surrounding her with his heat. Even though he didn't touch her, she felt as if he'd just enfolded her in his arms.

Safe.

Luke smiled, although a little reluctantly, it seemed. "Happy to have you join us." Then, he lifted his bottle to his lips and took a long draw. Probably a faithful husband nervous about what she had in mind tomorrow. His wife was a very lucky woman.

"This is really sweet of you both…"

Marc placed his right hand over hers on the table and brushed his thumb against her skin. Electricity shot up her arm, then zinged to the pit of her stomach.

"I assure you, *cara*, we are being totally selfish."

Oh, yeah. The dinner deal. Yet another jolt of electricity brought her body to full alert. A few hours from now, she'd be back in bed dreaming of her fictional angel-man-wolf, e-reader on the nightstand. Until then, she planned to have the night of her life.

Angelina sighed with relief. She leaned over and glanced at the mirror and saw Allen and Miss Blondie sit down near the pool table. When Allen looked up, his gaze met hers in the mirror. Surprise crossed his face.

Game on. She turned away from him and gave Marc what she hoped was her most sultry vamp look. But Allen couldn't hear her, so she'd keep the conversation safe. "So, Rico said you guys helped rescue the teen hikers."

They nodded, but remained silent. *Come on, guys. Help me out here.*

"Very lucky boys," Luke said finally, relief visible in his eyes. "This one could have turned out a whole lot worse, given how long it took us to locate them."

Sobered, Angelina said, "Thank God you found them." She shuddered to think what could have happened and took another sip of wine, knowing how thin the line is between victory and defeat in these mountains. "So, what kept you in town?"

"Media event went longer than anticipated," Luke said. "Otherwise, we'd have been back in Denver by now." She had the distinct impression he'd much rather be any place other than daVinci's bar tonight.

He stared at the nearly empty beer bottle between his hands. "It's weird," he said, as if talking to himself. "You hate for your pager to go off. You wish you didn't have to go out there ever again to try and find someone who's lost or injured. But you're glad you've trained to succeed…" He paused. "Well, we succeed most of the time." He closed his eyes in what seemed like regret before he lifted the bottle to his lips and drained it.

Angelina knew what Luke meant from the stories her father and two brothers told. The times they didn't succeed were the ones that haunted their memories for a very long time, sometimes forever.

"I appreciate that people like you are willing to go through all the training to volunteer to do what you do." Those involved in the rescue squads usually had some intensely personal reasons for doing so.

She wondered if they knew her brothers—and fervently hoped not.

"How'd you both get involved in SAR?"

Chapter Four

Marc thought it interesting that she pronounced SAR to rhyme with bar, rather than saying each individual letter as most unfamiliar with the search-and-rescue community would. Did she have a personal connection to a SAR worker?

He shot a worried look at Luke, and decided to deflect the question away from his friend. He didn't know all the details, but Luke didn't like to talk about his wife's fatal accident. Forcing a smile, he looked over at Angelina. "I joined the mountain rescue squad after I got back from Iraq."

"When were you deployed?"

"In 2004."

She placed her hand on his and squeezed. He envisioned her hand squeezing him a little lower and felt his groin tighten. *Merda*. Having her so close again and not holding her was torture of the worst kind.

"I appreciate your serving there, too. So, how'd you get from the desert of Iraq to the mountains of Colorado doing search and rescue?"

"I was a Navy corpsman—that's a medic for the Navy and Marines," he explained. Most civilians didn't know that the Navy provided medical support to the Marines, as well. "I was assigned to a ground unit of Marines and was able to make a difference for a few of them. So, I wanted to put those skills to use when I got my discharge. I didn't want to get an indoor healthcare job, though." That wouldn't have been any better than being chained to the desk at his family's resort, as he had been before he'd decided enough was enough and enlisted.

"I was born in the Italian Alps and my family now owns a ski resort in Aspen, so I just gravitated to mountain rescue when I was discharged."

Her eyes opened wide, "You're one of *those* D'Alessios! My God, that resort is one of the most exclusive ones in Aspen!"

Shit. Not another gold digger. He shouldn't have given his full name. Marc looked away, not even trying to hide his disappointment. When he'd looked up a few minutes ago to find his angel standing at their table, he couldn't believe his eyes.

Last month, as Marc went off DMS duty the night he'd rescued her—just barely—he'd been disappointed when Adam had told him his little angel and Karla had left a couple hours earlier. Not that he'd blamed her for wanting to put the flogging experience and his club behind her as quickly as possible.

But, over the past month, she kept invading his thoughts at unexpected times. No woman had ever obsessed him so completely, day and night, not even the two he'd nearly married.

"Um, thanks, Marc. I hope I didn't bring back bad memories or anything."

Marc turned back to her and smiled, but Angelina had shifted her focus back to Luke. "What about you?"

The silence stretched to the point of being uncomfortable. Marc looked at his friend. Just when he'd decided he ought to change the subject, Luke answered in a low, gravelly voice.

"I lost someone in the mountains once." He averted his gaze and twisted his wedding ring.

"I'm so sorry. I wouldn't be able to go into the mountain wilderness again if…" she trailed off and he heard a catch in her voice. When he turned, tears swam in her eyes, making him wonder what loss she'd suffered to cause her that pain.

She cleared her throat. "I'm so sorry," she said. "I didn't mean to pry." She reached out to touch Luke's hand and Marc felt an unfamiliar pang of jealousy.

Mine.

Shit, not again. He'd never had a problem sharing a woman before, so why did he want Angelina all to himself this time?

Normally, Luke would have pulled his hand away or waved her off. The man hadn't looked at another woman in seven years, despite Marc's attempts to get him into the club on occasion. He had no interest in the lifestyle. This time, he let her hand rest over his a few moments, just staring at it as if he didn't know what to make of it.

"Long time ago."

Marc could see the pain in Luke's eyes as clearly as Angelina probably could. His hurt was still close to the surface. Maybe he should talk about it more. Marc wondered what had happened, but hadn't wanted to push him to feel things that were too painful, any more than he wanted anyone pushing him.

"If I can keep others from going through that kind of hell, though…" He shrugged, then picked up his bottle, found it empty, and laid it back down, staring at it.

An awkward silence passed before Marc did change the subject. "So, *cara*, tell us about yourself." He knew nothing about her and had a definite interest in learning more.

"My life is pretty dull compared to yours. I graduated from culinary school last May and started a local catering business. Second generation Italian-American. I spent many summers with my Nonna in Marsala, where I learned all her culinary secrets. I specialize in her Sicilian recipes. Of course, I personalize them a bit."

Marc held his hand over his heart and gave her a pained expression. "Please, no more, or I'll have to kidnap you and chain you to my stove until you've prepared everything your grandmother taught you to make."

He saw her pupils dilate at the mention of chains and an image flitted across his mind of her wearing nothing but a skimpy French maid's apron, a smile, and an ankle cuff attached to the stove by a chain. Her jaw dropped open, as if she'd seen the same image. Hmmm. Culinary bondage? The thought made his cock stiffen. Fantasies of having her chained to his *anything* sent his cock to throbbing.

After a year of having no interest in the club or women, he found himself interested in playing with a submissive again.

* * *

Mio Dio! What was wrong with her? She wasn't into kink anymore, but the thought of being chained to Marc's stove just sent the wildest image into her mind. Her nipples hardened and she watched his gaze glance down at her chest. Her face heated as she wondered what he would do to her while she was in those chains.

Whoa! He wants you in… She supposed it could only be called culinary bondage. She reached for her glass of wine and took a huge chug, then sputtered when it went down the wrong way again. Would she ever be able to drink normally around these two?

Marc's warm, firm hand stroked her back through the open keyhole. "Cough, *cara*." She did and soon had herself back under control.

Anxious to move to a safer topic, away from the potent Italian sitting next to her, she asked, "So, Luke, where did you grow up?"

"All over. My folks moved around a lot. But I lived in Texas, near El Paso, during high school."

"Everything all right here?"

Angelina hadn't seen Rico approach the table. He stared at her, waiting for their prearranged signal. She smiled and winked twice. Satisfied she was fine, he took refill orders. She noticed Marc changed from beer to Perrier.

Over the next half hour, the three spoke about a number of other topics. She and Marc did most of the talking. She found him sexy as hell, but had to keep reminding herself he was just rescuing her in exchange for an Italian meal—chains optional. Besides she didn't plan to complicate her life with another man.

Marc reached out to brush a strand of loose hair from her face, sending her heart skittering. They may be annoying as hell, but Italian men certainly exuded sex appeal.

"Dance with me, *cara*."

Angelina looked over at Luke, who encouraged them both to go. She took a sip of wine for the courage to leave her hiding place. She'd be exposed to Allen's scrutiny on the dance floor. Marc cupped her elbow as she scooted out of the booth, and he helped her to her feet. While he fed the jukebox a few coins and made his selections, she waited on the dance floor. Allen's glare bore into her back, but she refused to make eye contact with him. She planned to make this act so convincing there would be no doubt…

The melodious strains of Dean Martin's "*Volare*" filled the air, instantly bringing tears to her eyes. She'd donated Papa's record collection to Rico for his vintage jukebox because listening to them was so painful. That particular song transported her back in time.

"*Papa, my prom's not till next year. Why are you giving me lessons now?*"

"*We never know how much time we have. My papa taught your Aunt Maria, and now I will teach you.*"

She didn't have the heart to tell him she probably wouldn't be dancing to music like Dean Martin's at her prom, but she didn't want to disappoint him.

"*Now, put your hand here,*" *he placed it in the center of his back,* "*and hold my hand like this.*"

"*Tesoro mio*, what is wrong?" Marc asked.

My treasure? Pulled away from her bittersweet memories, Angelina looked up at Marc. She hadn't felt like any man's treasure since Papa was killed.

She'd never slow danced with a man since Papa either. There had been no prom for Angelina. Her cheeks were wet with tears.

Marc's hand curled under her chin to tilt her face toward his. She tried to blink away the remaining tears, but more spilled onto her cheeks. He looked over at Allen. Did she just hear Marc growl?

"No, it's not him." She waved her hands in front of her eyes, trying to dry them. Her forced laugh sounded harsh, but she needed to lighten the mood. "I'm fine. The song just reminded me of my papa. Let's just dance." She tried to glance away from him, but he continued to hold her chin steady in his hand. Heat pooled in her lower abdomen.

Cupping her face in both of his hands, Marc brushed away her tears with the pads of his thumbs. After gazing deeply into her eyes, he seemed to accept that she wasn't going to divulge any more details and reached for her hand, placing it over the curve of his butt. Much lower than Papa had shown her. Then he wrapped his arm around her waist and entwined her left hand into his right one before he pulled her closer, pressing their intermingled hands and forearms between their bodies. Very intimate for a total stranger. So why did being in his arms make her feel so safe?

As the music slowed and wrapped around her, she closed her eyes and relaxed her head against Marc's shoulder. She wouldn't have thought it possible, but he drew her even closer, whispering Italian endearments in her ear. She wasn't as familiar with the nuances of the northern Italian dialect, but recognized enough to know he thought she was beautiful and sexy. His whiskers tickled her ear, causing yet another zing to ricochet through her body, going to ground on her clit.

Marc's free hand slid up her back and into the opening of her sweater dress. Goosebumps broke out on her arms and her nipples hardened against his chest as his thumb and fingers stroked her bare skin. She forced herself to take a deeper breath. Good Lord, all he was doing was touching her back! What if he were...

Don't go there, Angie! With her breasts pressed against him, she was thankful he couldn't see her body's response. But surely he felt the rapid pounding of her heart beating against the back of his hand, because she could feel his beating against her hand.

So right in his arms. If only this weren't just a show for Allen's benefit.

"That's right, *cara*. Just feel," he whispered.

Angelina stumbled and Marc tightened his arm around her. A memory having nothing to do with Papa or Marc flashed across her mind, of her being held safe and secure in the arms of her dream lover.

"*That's right*, cara. *Just feel.*"

As they moved, the music on the jukebox didn't match their movements, but they seemed to be moving to their own music. Marc's hand strayed down the back of her dress to trace circles over the curve of her butt. At first, she thought he'd wanted to make Allen jealous, but then she noticed he only touched her there when her back was turned away from Allen.

When the music ended, he continued to hold her, swaying in his arms. He seemed as reluctant to let go of her as she was of him.

As Dino's "*You Belong to Me*" began to play, Angelina shivered at the possessive message in the song's lyrics. Marc's arm tightened around her back and pulled her closer, but the thought of some man viewing her as his possession had a chilling effect on her. Was Marc a traditional Italian man, expecting his wife to stay home and raise babies? Mama had given up her dreams and her job to stay home and raise her five children. When Papa had been killed, Mama had barely been able to make ends meet. If Rafe and Franco hadn't dropped out of college to get jobs to help out, the family wouldn't have made it.

Angelina could never be that dependent on a man. She'd hold onto her independence, continue to build her career, and if that wasn't good enough for Marc or any other man, then they could just go find someone else.

"Relax. You're too tense."

His words caused her to give herself a mental shake and to relax her muscles. She barely knew Marc and already she was worrying about whether he would expect her to stay home and raise his kids? She smiled. Her biological clock must be working overtime tonight.

* * *

Angelina. What a perfect name for his little angel. *Dio*, she felt so damned right in his arms. Again.

Marc ran his hand over her satiny skin and trailed his fingers down the valley of her spine. Wisps of her long black hair strayed from the clip that held it captive. Longing to see her hair unrestrained as he had at the Masters at Arms Club, he reached up and released the clip, letting the thick tresses spill in waves over her shoulders and down her back.

"I love seeing your hair down like this." He slipped the clip into his pocket.

She laughed. "How would you know?"

Shit. Keep your wits about you, man. Obviously, she didn't remember him from the club. He didn't want her dwelling on those bad memories either. Not tonight, with Sir Asshole lurking so near. What had interested her in that man? Asshole looked as though he was well off. Was she a gold digger, after all?

Marc's cock remembered her, judging by the way it jerked to life as he ran his fingers through the silky strands. He detected a hint of lavender—heady when combined in the corners of his mind with the musky essence he remembered so well.

Images of her tied to his bed as he fully explored every inch of her delectable body caused him more than a little discomfort. What would it be like to have her submit to him? He couldn't help but notice how her eyes had lit up when he'd half-jokingly proposed chaining her to his stove.

He sighed. If he and Luke hadn't stayed behind to do media interviews today, he never would have found her again. Adam had been adamant, refusing to share her confidential information without her permission. He didn't know why she intrigued him so much, but he did want to get to know her better—find out what her kink was and how he could give her a better experience than the raw deal she'd gotten her first time at his club.

Marc and Luke could only stay in town until Angelina's dinner tomorrow night, though. Not enough time to establish the trust necessary for him to have her restrained to a bed or anything else. This little one would need even more time to overcome her bad experience with Sir Asshole before she'd trust any man enough to explore her submissiveness again with restraints. She'd take much more of a commitment than he'd be willing to give a woman.

Yet he wanted her. She had invaded his mind for the past month. Marc held her more tightly against him, guiding her around the small dance floor. After tonight, her sultry dark-chocolate eyes and delectable mouth would torture his sleep once more.

Maybe once he got through dinner tomorrow, he'd be able to get her out of his system. It had been his experience that, the more he knew about a woman, the less he wanted to stick around. KISS had become his motto—Keep It Superficial, Stupid.

She intrigued him now because he knew next to nothing about her. She was mysterious. She'd just shown up at his club with a boyfriend one night. Okay, he knew a bit more than that—like the expression on her face when she flew apart for him. His groin tightened.

He needed to put the reins on those thoughts.

But he had a real concern for her safety with Sir Asshole so close by. They probably both lived here in town. The thought of leaving her anywhere near the abusive man set his nerves on edge, but he couldn't exactly kidnap her and take her away to safety.

She stroked his upper back and shoulder, as if she sensed his tension and tried to knead it away. He forced himself to relax. What she ever saw in that arrogant ass, Marc couldn't understand. She deserved a man who would devote his entire being to bringing her pleasure and happiness. Adore her. Cherish her. Love her.

Not a man like Asshole.

Or Marc D'Alessio.

But he'd still be interested in exploring a Top/bottom relationship with her on a casual basis, if she didn't live so far away.

"So, what holds you to this place, *cara*?"

She didn't hesitate when she responded. "My family. My job. I've always lived here. I even commuted to and from culinary school in Boulder, except for my five-week externship."

"Everyone grows up and leaves their family at one time or another. What else holds you here?" She stiffened. Ah, he'd touched a nerve. "Is it some*thing*...or some*one*?" He was nothing, if not tenacious.

She laughed a bit harshly. "Well, it's not a man, if that's what you're thinking. I'm not looking for a serious relationship."

Ah, on that we can agree.

"I guess if I had to say one person, it would be Mama."

He smiled. Apparently, whatever hold Italian mamas had over sons, their daughters weren't immune to either. At least his own relationship with his Mama had improved since he'd been hospitalized in Germany after Fallujah.

"My papa died seven years ago and she depends on us to be there for her."

Marc's heart ached for her. He pulled her closer, rubbing her back when her body tensed. "I'm sorry about your papa." Angelina would have been just a teenager when he died. Marc admired her desire to take care of the woman who had given life to her. Angelina's mama sounded as if she were much more generous with her love than his had been while he was growing up, but her mama probably wasn't the fragile being her grown children imagined. Italian women held all the power in their families.

"How many of you are there?"

"Five, including my four brothers. I'm the youngest Giardano."

The baby and only girl in a close-knit Italian family. Oh, yes, he'd definitely steer clear of emotional ties with this one. "Your brothers live here still, as well?"

"No, only the oldest and youngest—Rafe and Tony—are in Aspen Corners. Franco and Matt live in Leadville, just an hour or so up the road."

Good. Angelina had two brothers in town to watch over her and keep Asshole away. But they also could take care of their mother's needs. She wasn't tied to this place—unless she wanted to be. Which apparently she did.

She sighed. Marc sensed restlessness in her.

"Have you ever considered moving to Denver? I'm sure your culinary skills would be in high demand."

He felt her spine stiffen again under his hand. She pushed at his chest and stepped back. "No. I have plenty of requests to cater and plan events here."

Easy, gattina. *No need to get your back up.*

Clearly, he'd touched another nerve. Then she laughed, releasing the tension as quickly as it had arisen. Her gaze bore into his chest, and she grew serious again. He pulled her back into his arms. She didn't let him hold her as closely this time as they swayed to the music. But he was happy she'd continued to dance with him because he loved holding her in his arms. Marc let the silence rest between them, giving her the time she needed to think.

"Sometimes it frustrates me, but I just can't leave."

Ah, so perhaps the door wasn't closed after all.

He smiled. If she were in Denver, perhaps she'd allow him to take her under his Dom wings and show her the ropes, so to speak. "Denver's only three hours away."

Marc felt her stiffen again before she drew him closer and tucked her face into his neck. Her breath hot against his ear, she whispered, "Shut up and dance."

He laughed aloud. Ah, the lady has a bossy side. His cock hardened as he imagined going head to head with her. No doubt in his mind he would come out on top, though. He smiled, his hand slipping under her hair to stroke her silky warm skin inside the hole in the fabric. He wished he had access to more than the tiny but tantalizing patch of skin on her back. He grew even harder at the memory of her sexy backside pressed against his crotch when he'd held her at the club. The need to bury himself inside her was stronger than ever.

As if coming to from a mental fog, he broke one of his primary rules, one that had kept him relatively sane for the past few years. No Italian women and their emotional drama.

Angelina would be high maintenance, wanting more than he could give her. He didn't mean financial maintenance either. Meeting a woman's financial needs was easy. Emotional needs? Not so much.

Perhaps it was for the best he'd be leaving town tomorrow before things went further than he intended to let them. This one could be dangerous.

But who said there had to be a long-term commitment? He'd had superficial relationships with women since he was seventeen. Only two had led to anything more than sex or BDSM play—first Melissa, then Pamela—and they had been separated by many years. He definitely wanted to be with Angelina in a superficial sort of way, though, to learn what turned her on, watch her bend to his authority in a bedroom or club scene, see her face again as she flew apart for him. But that was it.

Strictly sexual control. No commitments. No emotional strings.

He brought their joined hands up to where he could touch her breast without putting on a show for the entire barroom, especially Sir Asshole over there. The curve of her breast seared the back of his hand, making him want to touch even more of her. He reached out his fingers toward her other breast and brushed her nipple. Her sharp hiss against his neck only emboldened him. Keeping their hands entwined, he pinched the swelling bud between his thumb and forefinger. Her hips jolted toward him, pressing against his erection.

Dio, so responsive.

"Did you like how that felt, *cara*?"

"I..." Her breathy whisper was expelled as her chest rose and fell, making the contact against his hand even more tantalizing.

When she paused, he probed, "Answer honestly."

She pulled away and looked up at him, her brow furrowed. "I...I think that's enough dancing." She backed away, toward the safety of the booth—and Luke.

Before she turned away, he saw her nipples in sharp relief against the sweater dress. His own arousal was no less obvious, and he saw her cheeks grow even pinker when she glanced down at his bulging crotch.

Denying her arousal only made him want to entice her to explore her sexuality even more. A challenge. He wished there was time to take her in hand and show her what her body truly craved. But that couldn't happen—unless he could convince her to leave her safe little world here.

Marc decided to give her the space she wanted, for now, while he paid a visit to the head to regain control of his wayward cock. Lord knew she'd be safe from sexual advances with Luke. The man seriously hadn't looked at a woman the entire time he'd known him.

* * *

Luke watched as Angel came back to the booth alone, looking flustered—and sexy as sin. She stirred him back to life as no other woman had since Maggie. He couldn't take his eyes off her.

"It's time. I'm sending you an angel..."

"So, where'd you go to college?" she asked, picking up their earlier conversation as if there hadn't been a break.

"University of Texas—more to play football, than study, I'll admit. Wound up majoring in studio art." He smiled. The look of surprise on her face was one he'd gotten used to. He'd been ribbed about it since his football buddies heard what major he'd declared. "They didn't have the industrial arts program I wanted, but I wanted to work with wood. So, I wound up learning a lot about art that I didn't really need, or so I thought at the time. But the design, sculpture, and even the drawing classes have helped me with my current work. I do carpentry and make...specialized equipment that I design myself." He'd better leave it at that and not embarrass her by saying he made equipment for BDSM enthusiasts.

The conversation turned to her childhood and flowed naturally. When she told him about summers spent with her grandmother in Sicily, her eyes lit up. He envied her being part of a big, extended and close-knit family. Being an only child, his had been pretty lonely. His parents had followed one pipeline project site after another, leaving him to fend for himself. His shop teacher in high school had taken him under his wing and introduced him to woodworking. Then he'd met an art instructor in college who had let Luke use the woodworking shop in his garage. When he'd met Maggie, he abandoned his studies and his woodworking for a while. But he'd managed to graduate.

He couldn't keep his mind from comparing Angel to his wife. Both women knew what they wanted and went after it. But Maggie tended to be more introverted, interested in her research and not much else. He'd tagged along with a camera on her forays into the wilderness to help photograph her finds. She liked his artist's eye.

Angel leaned across the table and touched his hand. "You seem a million miles away."

Luke cringed. *Damn.* He'd spaced on her. Embarrassed, he sat up and said, "Sorry. Thinking about my wife."

She glanced at his ring and pulled her hand back as if bitten. *Double damn.* He'd forgotten he even wore the wedding band. At first, he'd kept it on because he didn't really want any more women offering him sex to "cure" his grief. Then it had just become a habit.

Maybe even a talisman. On every rescue mission, he felt Maggie with him, guiding him to the lost and injured. He didn't know why, but he felt a sudden need to tell Angel about Maggie.

"My wife died seven years ago."

Her look of surprise caught him off guard. "My God, I'm so sorry!"

He shouldn't have been so blunt but wasn't sure how to ease into the topic. "It was an…accident." He didn't really want to say anything more about what type of accident. But now what?

With a burst of nervous energy, Luke leaned forward. "Let's give that asshole something to look at, Angel. Play a game of pool with me."

He stood up to play it through. She deserved better than the deal she'd gotten from that scumbag across the room, whatever he'd done to hurt her. Not only was she sexy as hell, but sweet and beautiful. He loved the way she just plain seemed to enjoy life.

Luke reached for her arm to help her up out of the booth. He called the game. "Eight Ball." Ignoring her ex, even though they had to walk right past him to get to the pool table, he watched her go over to the wall and choose her pool stick while he racked up the balls and handed her the cue ball. "Lady first."

"Stripes," she called and proceeded to drop three striped balls in rapid succession into the table's pockets.

Hot damn. The woman was competitive. Game on.

"Luke, I think you've met your match," Marc teased as he rejoined them.

As she lined up a shot with the thirteen ball, Luke found himself riveted by the view of her curvaceous hips. "No problem. I'm enjoying the view."

She glanced behind her and met his gaze, blushing.

"Can't match my view," Marc countered.

Luke watched Angel look up at Marc, who zeroed in on her chest as she bent over the table to line up the shot. Marc had always loved women's tits. Her dress didn't show much, but the material fit her like a second skin.

Apparently they'd flustered her with their attention, because she made her move too soon and dropped one of the solid balls into the side pocket instead.

"Play fair, boys." Then a giggle burst forth and he saw a sparkle in her big brown eyes.

Luke studied the table and saw she sure hadn't left him any easy shots. "All's fair in love and Eight Ball, darlin'," he said, brushing her cheek with a kiss before he stepped up to the table. *Damn.*

Shaking off the feel of her soft cheek on his lips, he somehow managed to sink four solids in a row, two with one stroke and two singles. She must have realized the game was getting away from her, because Angel sidled up to him and let her fingernails dance lightly down his back.

Luke scratched his next shot. He stood and turned toward her. "Careful there, Angel. You're playing with fire now. I play to win."

He couldn't resist pulling her into his arms. Her pool stick lodged between them, but still he felt her heart beating against his chest. She looked up at him, expecting him to kiss her.

But he couldn't. He didn't know if it was because of Marc…or Maggie. Instead, he bent down to nuzzle her neck and whispered, "He's fuming, darlin'. He hasn't taken his eyes off you this entire game."

Chapter Five

Angelina had difficulty figuring out who Luke was talking about at first, so distracted was she by his warm lips burning against the pulse near the column of her neck. Electrical pulses ricocheted throughout her body.

Then she came back to reality. She did not have two sexy men making advances at her. This was just a show for Allen. She'd do well to remember that. She'd almost expected him to kiss her a moment ago. Angelina pulled away reluctantly, took a deep breath, and got back into character. She chalked her stick and sashayed to the opposite side of the table, leaned forward to give Allen the full rear view Luke had enjoyed moments ago, and lined up a nearly impossible bank shot.

Marc kicked their performance up another notch by following her around the table. Just as she prepared to strike the cue ball, she felt the heat of his body behind her seconds before he pressed his pelvis against her hips and leaned his entire chest over her back.

"Would you like me to show you how to make that shot, *bella?*" he whispered, his whiskers tickling her ear.

Mustering every ounce of strength she could to keep from melting into a puddle under him, Angelina wiggled her hips, feeling a definite bulge against her butt. *Mio Dio*, it was heating up in here! A bead of sweat trickled between her breasts.

"Not to worry, Marc. I can't miss." Where had that bravado come from? She took a deep breath and gave it her best shot, despite being pressed under the steel-hard muscles of one of the two sexiest men she'd ever met.

Mio Dio, yes! She stood and faced them. "And that, boys, is how it's done."

"Hot damn, Angel. That took skill, given the distraction you had to deal with."

Marc closed the space between her and him, and an expression of envy crossed Luke's face before he smiled to mask it. The man had missed his calling. He should have been a theatre major. Extricating herself from Marc, she set up her next shot. This should be the last. She wished the game didn't have to end so soon.

When she checked the trajectory of the ball, Luke placed his hands around her waist and turned her to face him. Her heart thudded to a halt, then jackhammered. She looked up at him, a mixture of uncertainty and excitement quivering in her belly.

Angelina reminded herself to breathe as he bent down and brushed his lips across hers. She sucked in a shallow breath and Luke teased his tongue between her lips. Not deep, bold strokes. Just playful forays. Her lips tingled deliciously.

No one had ever kissed her in such a playful way before. She felt her insides clench, followed by a throbbing in her clit. Too soon, he pulled away, but the wink he gave her reminded her that this was all an act for Allen. She forced a smile to her lips and tamped down her disappointment. This roller coaster ride of emotional highs and lows was exhausting her.

"Your shot, *cara*," Marc reminded her.

She turned to him and detected another hint of jealousy. They both were very good at playing up the rivalry bit. But tonight was only make-believe. A fairy tale. She didn't really have two men vying for her affections.

Not really feeling as interested in the game as before, she returned her attention to the table, took what should have been an easy shot, and missed.

Angelina stepped back to let Luke have access to the table and to put some distance between both of them so she could catch her breath. Even though it was just for show, having two men strumming her like a *mandolina* felt good for her ego. If Allen had been half as attentive toward her, maybe she'd have let him do whatever he wanted sexually—her four overprotective brothers be damned.

No, she had to admit Allen had never turned her on like this. He'd just been…safe. Or so she and her brothers had thought. Wondering what it was she'd seen in him, she glanced toward his table and found him watching her. The expression on his face scared her. Lust, sure. But a seething anger simmered just below the surface. She shuddered.

Stunned at the vehemence in his expression, she turned away, only half watching as Luke cleared the table of every remaining solid, including the eight ball.

Feeling sad that the game was over, in more ways than one, she went to the wall and hung up her stick. "Well played, Luke," she said.

Having Marc's body pressed against her and Luke's tongue playing with her lips had shaken her to the core. If she'd been alone with either man, she wouldn't have told him to stop. But two men at once? That was a forbidden fantasy best left to her ménage novels. Those kinds of relationships didn't happen in quiet little Aspen Corners. Did they? Before she embarrassed herself by asking for something they probably weren't interested in, she'd best remember the script for tonight.

With a sinking feeling, she walked back to the booth. Her feet hurt again. Funny how sometimes she didn't notice them at all. She guessed it depended on her focus. Luke passed her on the way to the men's room and Marc headed over to the bar, probably to order more drinks.

No sooner had she sat than a familiar voice said, "Angie, it's good to see you out tonight. How've you been?"

Angelina's lungs constricted. She'd known Allen would approach her at some point tonight, but weariness and her confusion about her feelings for Marc and Luke had lowered her defenses. Taking as deep a breath as she could, she faced the man who had tried to break her, as he had put it that night during the flogging.

"Fine." She hoped the chill in her voice conveyed to him he wasn't wanted here. She looked at him, wondering why she'd dated him so long. His blond hair and tanned skin gave the appearance of an outdoor enthusiast, but he'd paid for his tan at a salon across town. His hawkish gaze once made her insides quiver, she thought because of sexual attraction. Now the fierceness in his expression only caused her to shrink away in revulsion. He intimidated her, as much as she hated to admit it. Her hands began to shake. The man had shattered her trust and taken advantage of her when she was at her most vulnerable. Unforgivable.

"I didn't think I'd ever get a moment alone with you."

"What do you want, Allen?" When she heard her voice quaver, she took a deep breath and continued, "I have nothing to say to you. Not that you'd listen to me anyway." She'd always believe he'd ignored her safeword. No way had she left the word unspoken.

"Look, honey, that night…you just misunderstood—"

"Oh, I understood perfectly, Allen. For days afterward. Now if you'll excuse me." Dismissing him, she picked up her wineglass and drained it. Her heart pounded so loudly, she was certain he could hear.

Out of the corner of her eye, she saw Allen's hand coming toward her, but before she could even jump back, a bigger hand with long, slim fingers grabbed his wrist in midair.

"You heard the lady," Marc said.

Allen yanked his hand out of Marc's grip, glaring at him. She felt the intensity of his hatred, but Marc never flinched. Allen took a step back.

"If you ever put your hands on her again, I'll break them," Marc didn't so much make a threat as a promise.

Allen stood up straighter, coming short of Marc's height by half a foot. His gaze shot daggers at the taller man, then gave him the once over. "Do I know you?"

"Doubt it."

Marc grinned at him in an almost deadly way. The level of testosterone around her had reached critical mass. Someone was going to get hurt. And, as much as she detested Allen and knew he would come out on the short end, so to speak, she didn't want Rico to have any trouble with the law at his bar.

"Marc…"

Allen looked down at her. "If I'd known you were into threesomes, Angie…"

She winced, but before she could form a response, Marc's hand snaked out and grabbed him by the throat.

"Apologize to the lady before I mess up that face you seem so fond of." His voice remained calm, but lethal.

Angelina's heart raced as Marc held him. Allen sputtered for air, his face turning red, eyes bulging from a lack of blood to the head. Eventually, he held up his hands in defeat and Marc released his hold on his throat…somewhat.

"Hey, guys, I don't want any trouble in here," Rico said. Angelina hadn't seen him approach them, so focused was she on Allen and Marc. "Allen, I think you need to leave."

"Not yet," Marc said, his voice as smooth as pulled taffy. "He owes Angelina an apology."

"Marc, it's not necessary…" *Please just let him go away.* She didn't handle confrontation very well, especially public ones. Luke slid into the booth and sat across from her. When her hands began to shake, he took both between his and held them tight. She smiled her thanks, her lips quivering.

"Oh, it is quite necessary, *cara.*" Marc's gaze captured hers and she felt her heart jump into her throat. Though outwardly calm, his eyes were spitting fire. Thankfully, his rage wasn't directed at her. "No man speaks that way to a lady."

Marc's gaze returned to Allen, who straightened his shirt where Marc had crumpled the collar in his hands. He kept his focus in Marc's direction. "I'm sorry, Angie."

"Don't tell me," Marc said. He nodded his head in her direction. "Tell her."

Angelina's face burned with embarrassment, but she couldn't take her eyes off Marc. Something warmed in the pit of her stomach as he defended her. He'd come to her rescue. She couldn't ignore how incredibly turned on she was now.

"I'm sorry for what I said, Angie."

Angelina refused to even look at the weasel. She nodded, "Apology accepted," but her gaze remained fixed on Marc's.

"Now, get the hell out of here. If you ever come near her again..." Marc began, and then let Allen use his own imagination. When the bastard didn't move away fast enough, Marc took a step toward him and Allen stepped back.

"Come on, Allen," Rico said. "Get your date and leave."

When he'd gone, Marc sat down beside her. He winced, then shifted and pulled her hair clip from his pocket, handing it to her. "I believe this is yours."

How did he just turn off all that power in an instant? Now that the confrontation had ended, Angelina began shaking even more. Marc wrapped his arm around her, pulling her against his side. She laid her head in the crook of his arm and shoulder.

"Shhhh. It's over."

Angelina froze, transported back once more to the words spoken by her dream lover. Had that been a premonition for meeting Marc? Was this predestined? No, the scene in her dream was nothing like this one. Her angel-man-wolf held her in his arms on a loveseat, probably at the same club in which Allen had beaten her. She shuddered as she remembered how she'd barely been able to function for days, and almost lost a client as a result.

Given what she'd learned about deep subspace on the Internet, maybe the dream was just part of a hallucination when her mind and body had separated. She'd created the Dom she wanted. Karla told her a dungeon monitor had found her in time. If not, she could have had serious hallucinations and other problems while her mind and body remained separated.

Like Marc, the man in her dreams was Northern Italian and the two often spoke the same words verbatim. Was it cultural? Or was Marc a Dom, as well? She hoped not. She'd had enough dominant men to last a lifetime. She tried to conjure up an image of the elusive dream man's face. All she really remembered were a mouth and a square chin. Right now, she was too exhausted to sit up and compare Marc's chin with that of her dream lover's. She felt so incredibly safe in Marc's arms and wanted to stay here forever. Angelina relaxed against him even more.

Rico came back to the booth. "You okay, Angie?" She nodded, but didn't pull away from Marc, or even open her eyes.

"I think the lady could use something a little stronger than wine," Luke ordered.

"I've got just the thing."

When the margarita was placed in front of her a few moments later, Luke leaned over and held it to her lips. "Here, Angel. Drink."

Angel. Was that an endearment or just a shortened version of her name? She let him hold the glass as she drank, but the act was over, wasn't it? She took the glass from him and drained it, then sputtered as it burned from her throat to her stomach.

Luke laughed. "Whoa, you might regret that come morning."

"She earned it," Marc said, then turned his attention to her and whispered. "You were so brave."

Her heart swelled at the familiar words. She searched his eyes. Green. Why did she think her angel-man-wolf's eyes were the same color? She really couldn't remember, though. The images were vague.

"I'm sorry he insulted you guys like that," Angelina said. "I don't want to go into what we broke up over, but…"

Marc grew serious and cupped her chin and jaw, lifting her face to meet his gaze. The pulse in her neck beat against his fingertips. Surely he must feel it. She pulled away.

Marc's eyes furrowed as if hurt by her retreat, but then he smiled. "You have nothing to apologize for, and I know *exactly* what he…is." He seemed to be about to say something else before correcting himself.

Angelina tried to smile at them both for being so supportive, but couldn't ignore her disappointment. With Allen's departure from the bar, her magical evening with them would come to an end. She looked at Marc, then

Luke. Both radiated concern about her well-being. Well, they were search-and-rescue workers, after all. And they'd certainly rescued her from Allen.

"Thanks so much for being here for me tonight. Despite how it's ending, I had a wonderful time." She reached for her shawl and purse.

"Who says the evening must end, *cara*?"

"I do. You've both gone above and beyond the call of duty."

Luke smiled. "Wish all our rescue missions were this much fun."

"We have no desire for this evening to end either," Marc assured her.

"That's kind of you to say," she began, "but if I'm going to prepare that feast I promised tomorrow night, I'm going to have to get to the farmer's market early in the morning."

Marc pointed to her empty margarita and two wineglasses. "One thing you will not be doing tonight, *cara*, is driving home."

She smiled at his overprotective attitude. "No worries. I walked."

"Well, then, we'll take you home, Angel." Luke reached in his pocket for his keys as Rico approached the table, his damned "big brother" notebook in hand.

"Fellas, can I have a word with you?"

Man, how'd he know what they were talking about? Italian radar, she guessed. Angelina sighed. "Now, Rico, don't go all big brother on me."

He grinned, but didn't budge. "Can I see some IDs?"

"Beg pardon?" Luke asked.

"Rico!" Angelina rolled her eyes, but knew from experience there was no way to get an Italian big brother—even a surrogate one—to back down once he got all overprotective.

"I just want them both to know that I'll be checking up on you later tonight. If you're not okay, I'll be reporting them to the police."

Marc reached for his wallet, laughing. "It's fine, *cara*. I would want no less for my sister." Why did his thinking of her like a sister bother her so much, when she didn't even want a relationship with him or any other man at the moment?

Luke opened his wallet, as well, and both men laid their driver's licenses on the table long enough for Rico to jot down their information into his notebook.

Ten minutes later, they pulled up to her curb. She said goodnight to Luke in the SUV. Marc cupped her elbow as he helped her out of the vehicle and escorted her up the short sidewalk to the porch of her bungalow rental. The evening air was chilly, but her pulse thrummed, warming her blood. Okay, the margarita might have helped, too. Not to mention the hot body walking beside her.

When she missed the top step in those damned shoes, Marc caught her in his arms before she fell and spun her toward him, pressing her against his hard body. The contact with her thighs and breasts triggered a red alert throughout her body.

Careful, Angie. This man could break your heart.

She stepped out of his arms, but her body swayed toward him with a will of its own. *Oh, man.* She backed toward the door and opened her handbag, hating to send him on his way tonight, but she didn't want to analyze why his leaving disappointed her.

"Thanks for seeing me home, Marc. I'll see you tomorrow for dinner. Sevenish. Come hungry." She looked up at his eyes, which crinkled with a smile. "I can't thank you and Luke enough for all the rescuing you did tonight."

"It was you who rescued us, *cara*—from yet another dull night in a strange town."

Marc leaned closer. Her heartbeat accelerated, leaving her short of breath. She opened her mouth to draw in more air just as his firm lips captured hers and all thoughts, happy or otherwise, fled her brain. His kiss was gentle, teasing. He nibbled at her lower lip, but didn't force himself inside.

One hand slid behind her to support her back, stroking her bare skin. She placed her hand against the back of his head and hoped he would deepen the kiss. At first, he seemed to grow tense. Just when she thought he would pull away, Marc's warm tongue delved into her mouth, causing a delicious heaviness to settle in her pelvis.

For the first time in her life, there was toe-curling—just the kind she'd read about in her novels.

Too bad someone wasn't supporting her legs, because they were about to give out. As if he'd heard her thought, he pressed her against the doorjamb, holding her upright with his body. Angelina wrapped both arms around his neck to hang on for dear life. The curling sensation moved to the pit of her stomach, then burst like fireworks, causing her nipples to swell and an insistent throbbing to begin at the juncture of her thighs.

Just when she knew she wouldn't be able to deny him anything tonight, he pulled away. His breathing was harsh and erratic.

"Sleep well, *angelo mio.*"

Drawing a ragged breath, she tamped down the feeling of regret. This was for the best. Thank God at least one of them had self-control.

When she just stood there panting and staring up at him, Marc chuckled. "Let me unlock the door for you, pet." She didn't move, so he took her handbag and retrieved her key.

Well, as endearments went, it was lousy. An independent woman like herself should have been offended by his calling her pet. So why did the word cause butterflies to flutter in her stomach? If he *was* a Dom, she should be running far and fast. But at this moment, she would have submitted to him if he'd asked. Maybe not for kinky BDSM play, but sex wasn't out of the question, something she'd never dreamed of engaging in with Allen anywhere near this soon.

Thrown completely off balance, she continued to lean against the doorframe for support as he unlocked and opened the door. Being a possible Dom was bad enough. The man also was a D'Alessio. So out of her league. And Luke? She'd been ready to fall at his feet when he kissed her at the pool table.

What was the matter with her tonight? Was she just on the rebound? Man hungry?

So, how had she gone from wanting no man to wanting two? Despite what Allen had insinuated, she'd never been involved in a threesome.

Oh, Angie, who said anything about a threesome? Get the hell inside before you embarrass yourself.

"Well, um, good night, Marc." Her words sounded rushed, breathless, and lame, but before she changed her mind and dragged him inside with her, she scurried into the living room and closed the door. Breathing a lungful of lavender-scented air to replenish the oxygen his nearness had deprived her brain of, she leaned her forehead against the door and sighed.

"Lock the door, *cara*," he whispered.

A tingling danced down her spine as if he'd whispered a sexual command in her ear. Like "kneel, *cara*." She grinned, then turned the deadbolt and locked the doorknob.

Marc chuckled. "Good night, *bella*." His footsteps sounded as he crossed the wooden planks of the porch. Moments later, the car ignition turned over, and they drove away.

Tomorrow they both would be inside her house for the dinner they had earned. With sudden awareness, she realized that Marc's kiss a few moments ago hadn't been a show for Allen.

Mio Dio! What was she getting herself into?

* * *

Angelina applied lip gloss and pressed her lips together, then stepped back from the full-length mirror on her bedroom door. She hoped she hadn't overdone it, but the white Manoush party dress hid her wide hips. Twirling to hear the swish of the petticoat, she couldn't keep the grin from her face. Returning to the closet, she slipped into the stilettos, knowing they were sexy as hell. At least she wouldn't have to walk much in them tonight.

Time to get the bruschetta ready. The guys should be here within the next half hour. The smells of Nonna's kitchen permeated the rooms of her tiny bungalow, transporting her to summer nights in Marsala, Sicily.

Angelina made her way back to the kitchen where she'd prepared many of her family's favorites, hoping Marc and Luke would enjoy them, as well. Judging by how snugly the waistline of this dress fit, she wouldn't be able to eat much tonight herself.

Her stomach knotted every time she thought about Marc's kiss last night, which had left her aching for something more. Her defenses had crumbled like a fortress made of cards, her conviction that she was finished with men buried in the rubble. Luke's kiss during the pool game had sent similar thoughts into her mind. But that was just for show.

Dressed like this, she certainly didn't look like she was planning to put the brakes on whatever either of them wanted. Thoughts of their hands on her body sent a flush to her face. What had gotten into her?

She spread her homemade roasted garlic and golden tomatoes onto the slices of bread and heard the doorbell ring as she drizzled it with imported olive oil. A quick glance at the wall clock showed it was only six-thirty-five. They'd come early. She smiled at their eagerness. She'd serve them a glass of wine while she finished up in the kitchen. At least she was dressed. After rinsing and drying her hands, she nervously smoothed imaginary wrinkles from her dress. Her heart raced in anticipation before she even reached the door.

Knowing who she'd find there, she opened it without checking first and came face-to-face with Allen instead. Her heart plummeted. He smiled an insipid smirk. Funny she hadn't noticed what a weak mouth he had before.

"Angie, you look gorgeous."

Looking around his shoulder toward the curb, she hoped to see Marc and Luke pulling up. No such luck. She turned her attention back to the unwanted man standing in her doorway and willed her voice to remain calm. "Allen, I'm expecting company."

A shadow crossed over his face and his smile faded. "Those guys from the bar?"

"None of your business. I really don't have time to talk now."

She moved to close the door on him, but he shoved it out of the way, forcing himself inside. Caught off balance, she retreated a step or two, trying to regain her equilibrium on the wobbly stilettos.

"Get out, Allen! I told you I don't want you anywhere near me again."

His gaze roamed over her, making her feel dirty from head to heel. "You let those two men paw all over you last night, but you barely let me touch you in seven months. Then when I do, you get all hysterical."

Angelina's heart pounded as warning bells went off in her head. The look in his eyes told her he wasn't going to take a simple "get lost" for an answer. Something in his face wasn't right. She tried to remember the lessons her brothers had taught her about fighting off overly amorous boyfriends, but she'd never really had to use them before. Most guys respected her "no" as a no.

"Allen, leave now or I'm calling 911."

If I can remember where I put my damned cell phone.

He reached out and trailed a finger across her bare shoulder. She cringed, and pulled away from his cold fingers, her stomach churning. "You were so gorgeous on the St. Andrew's. I can't wait to see you there again. Only this time, I'll make it even better for you."

Mio Dio! Bile rose in her throat. "Get away from me, Allen." She wished her voice didn't shake, but damn, she was more frightened than she'd ever been in her life. He wasn't acting sanely.

Allen's hands gripped her bare shoulders as he pulled her against his body and one hand began mauling her breast. Adrenaline surged through her. When he lowered his mouth toward hers, instinct—and a well-aimed knee—kicked in. She connected solidly with his groin at the same time she thrust the heel of her hand upward toward his chin. But he moved his head and his nose took the full brunt of the intended chin jab.

"God damn you!" His hand flew out and he backhanded her across the cheek, causing her neck to snap as she hurtled backward. Falling in slow motion, she would have been sprawled on the floor if she hadn't hit the back of the sofa. Allen doubled over, one hand on his crotch while the other covered his nose, blood seeping through his fingers. She needed to act. Now!

Taking advantage of his momentary inattention, she charged head first with all the force she could muster and tackled him, pushing him through the open doorway. His bloodied hand reached out for the doorjamb, but he never regained his balance and fell backward down the steps. Not waiting for him to come at her again, she slammed and bolted the door.

"You're going to regret this, Angie!" She heard his muffled shout from the other side of the door. His voice sounded so close. He could so easily break down the thin door. *Dio, please help me.*

A car started, and she peeked out the curtains on the door to find the porch empty. Closing her eyes, she laid her burning right cheek against the curtain. The windowpane beneath felt cool to her flushed face. Her head began to spin. *Breathe, Angie!* She tried to fill her lungs before she passed out, but her legs began to shake violently. The tremors soon spread throughout her body. She kicked off the shoes and stumbled around the chintz-covered sofa, collapsing facedown and curling into a ball on her side.

She had no idea how long she lay there before she heard the doorbell again. Allen had come back! Her heart thudded, and then halted. *Run!*

Where was her damned cell phone? She tried to rise too quickly and winced as her stomach pitched. *Don't get sick.* Hair tumbled in her face and she pushed it back and groaned as the muscles in her shoulders and neck protested.

Her numbed mind registered the murmur of deep voices. Marc and Luke, not Allen. Relief flooded her senses, until she looked down at her blood-splattered dress. Tears pricked the backs of her eyes and she blinked several times.

How could she answer the door looking like this? She'd certainly get a visceral response from them both—just not the one she'd hoped for when she'd chosen to wear this dress. Her anticipation of another fun evening with them vanished. Maybe if she pretended she wasn't here, they'd think she'd stood them up and go away. At this moment, all she wanted to do was crawl into bed—alone—and hide.

Chapter Six

As he stood on Angelina's porch, Marc remembered the kiss he'd given her here last night. What had possessed him to kiss her like that? He never kissed the subs he played with. Shit, she wasn't even one of his subs. A kiss was too intimate, giving more of himself than he was comfortable sharing.

Tonight, he wouldn't let his libido rule his actions. This evening was about Italian cuisine from the Old Country. Nothing more. He shifted the bottles of wine in his hand, along with the Hershey bar. After watching her eat the chocolate during aftercare at the club, he'd fantasized about feeding her an entire bar. Images of her naked in his arms again caused his cock to stir to life.

Merda. Reining in his wayward thoughts might not be easy. If only he hadn't kissed her. The damned kiss had changed things, for the worse.

He looked at the bouquet of roses Luke had picked up on their way here tonight. They'd actually gone back to Denver this morning so they could dress appropriately. The clothes they'd packed for the hiker rescue this week weren't special enough for the occasion.

He glanced over at Luke, noticing the band of white skin where Luke's wedding band had once been worn. Well, shit, the man was ready to move forward. About time. Knowing his friend was interested in Angelina both pleased and disturbed him. But if Luke wanted to pursue her, Marc would step back before he got in any deeper with her.

He looked at the door. What was taking her so long to answer?

"Something sure smells good, Angel!" Luke called out. "Don't make us wait much longer!"

Luke reached out and rang the doorbell again, as Marc looked down at the porch, then stepped back. Dark droplets. He took the toe of his shoe and smeared it. Looked like fresh blood. Looking up, he noticed more blood on the doorjamb.

Marc pointed out the stains to Luke and pounded on the door. "*Cara*, open this door. Now."

"I'm coming!" Her muffled voice reassured him she was alive at least, but held an edge that didn't sound like the Angelina from last night. Her voice was strained, as if from pain. If she didn't open this damned door soon, he was going to bust it down.

What the hell had happened?

* * *

Angelina used the coffee table to pull herself to her shaky feet. The slightest movement caused pain, even in places Allen hadn't touched her. Overextended muscles screamed as she put one foot in front of the other and made her way slowly toward the door.

She wished she'd gone to the bedroom first to put a robe over her ruined dress. But they'd soon know something had happened if her cheek looked as bad as it felt. In addition to the burning, the skin on that side of her face was growing taut from swelling. Short of putting a bag over her head, Angelina would have to tell them what happened. Each step took an exponentially greater amount of energy than the one before. She had no reserves left after the burst of adrenaline she'd expended fighting off Allen's attack.

After what seemed an eternity, but was probably no more than a minute, she reached the door.

"Angel, darlin', if you don't open this door, we're going to…"

"I'm here," she called out. Taking a deep breath, she unbolted the lock and opened the door. Marc stood holding two bottles of vino and an enormous Hershey's dark chocolate bar. Luke carried a bouquet of champagne-colored roses. She watched as their expressions changed from concern to disbelief as their eyes opened wider.

Safe.

Her knees crumpled beneath her. Luke dropped the flowers and caught her in his arms, carrying her inside to the sofa. Marc placed the wine bottles on the coffee table and their triage training apparently kicked in as they began examining her for injuries.

"Where are you bleeding, *cara*?" Marc began checking her scalp and neck for injuries.

"There's blood on the porch, too, Angel. What happened?"

The questions overwhelmed her. Angelina dropped her head against the back of the overstuffed sofa, the effort to remain upright more than she could achieve at the moment. Her lower lip trembled as she tried to find words to explain what had happened. Someone's thumb grazed her injured cheek and she winced as he probed gently where Allen had backhanded her.

"That sonuvabitch from last night did this, didn't he?" Luke's voice.

"Where did that asshole cut you, *cara*?"

"He didn't." Every word took a phenomenal amount of energy. "Not my blood." Angelina's voice sounded as if it came through a long tunnel. Not wanting them to worry, she smiled then winced as even that tiny movement radiated more pain across her cheek. Salty tears stung her eyelids. "And his name is Allen Martin." Although "asshole" was growing on her, too. "Believe me, he's in worse shape than I am. I think I broke his nose—and he won't be having sex anytime soon either."

One of them squeezed her upper arm. Simultaneously, Marc and Luke praised her in their own ways:

"Good girl."

"Good for you, Angel."

Angel. She was nobody's angel, but she liked when Luke called her that anyway. And Marc's "good girl" was equally endearing, making her melt like Marc's chocolate bar sitting on a hot stove. Something niggled at her brain, but she didn't know why the stove was significant.

As Luke continued to check her arms and legs for injuries, she heard Marc walk into the kitchen. He came back and pressed what felt like ice cubes wrapped in a wet linen towel against her cheek.

"Tell us what happened, *cara*."

"I don't want to talk about it."

"You'll need to make a police report, Angel."

She opened her eyes and raised her head from the sofa, wincing as the ice pack Marc held against her cheek put painful pressure on the injury. "No police. If my brothers find out about this, they'll kill him."

"Not if we get to him first, *cara*."

"Marc, no one's going to do anything. I don't want anyone going to jail over this. I said I took care of him. It's over."

Angelina wasn't sure if she was more afraid of someone going to jail for assaulting Allen or of her brothers finding out she'd been in a kink club, which they most certainly would at some point if they got anywhere near Allen. He'd squeal like a tea kettle.

Luke sat down on the coffee table in front of her. "I don't think anything's broken."

"Go take a shower and change, *piccolo angelo*. You'll feel better."

Little angel. She'd never been considered little by anyone's standards and her binge eating for the last month hadn't improved that condition. Allen often cautioned her to watch what she ate when they went out. Asshole. He should be very happy with Miss Blondie from last night and her size-two ass.

"Stay with us, *cara*."

Angelina looked at Marc; her mind had wandered. She looked down at her ruined dress and blinked back hot tears. "Damn him. I wanted to look nice tonight." Why was she crying over a silly dress?

Before she started to bawl in earnest, she motioned for them to help her up. She needed to be alone. Each man took an elbow and Marc wrapped an arm around her back as they lifted her to her feet. Cosseted between them, she felt comforted, but she groaned at the effort it had taken just to stand. Her muscles were getting stiffer by the minute. How could she hurt all over when he'd only touched three places on her body? Tomorrow, she'd be hurting even worse.

Brushing the hair away from her face, Marc said, "*Cara mia*, you are beautiful no matter what you are wearing." Angelina half-smiled, favoring her sore cheek, as her mind filled in what Marc left unsaid—*or even if you're wearing nothing at all*.

"That's a brave girl," he added.

Tears burned her eyes again. She didn't feel very brave. "Look, I'm really sorry, but I don't think I'm going to be much fun tonight. You don't have to stay."

"Nice try, Angel, but we aren't leaving." She looked up at Luke, who just smiled, still holding her elbow.

"Not until we're sure you're safe," Marc assured her, "and we've had our fill of your Nonna's dishes that smell so fantastic."

"Oh, no!" Her special dinner! That's why the thought about the stove was important. She'd completely forgotten.

Angelina scooted on bare feet to the kitchen as fast as she could to open the door of the stainless-steel range. With her oven mitt on, she pulled out the rack and removed the lid from the pot inside, sighing in relief. Thank goodness the wine hadn't all evaporated.

"Don't lift anything," Luke admonished. "We'll take care of dinner. You go take care of you."

Normally, she wouldn't let anyone into her kitchen, but if she was going to rescue this evening, she'd need all the help she could get.

"In about five minutes, could you take the *braciola* out and put it on that platter?" She pointed to Nonna's oval blue-and-yellow stoneware platter waiting on the counter.

"I think, between the two of us, we can manage that, *cara*." He grinned.

Her smile faded quickly; her cheek now hurt even more. Luke placed his hands around her waist, pulling her away from the stove. "Go, Angel."

Looking back over her shoulder, she caught his worried expression. "Um, I'll finish the—" What had she been doing before Allen arrived? Oh, yeah, "... the bruschetta—when I get back."

"I'll take care of the bruschetta," Marc said, placing an arm around her back and guiding her to the doorway. Her body tingled at his touch. "Go. Now."

Why the rush to get rid of her? Were they going to report the incident with Allen to the police? She pointed her finger at each of them. "Promise you won't do anything stupid while I'm gone, like call the police."

They exchanged a glance that didn't reassure her in the least, but both nodded her toward the hallway, saying "Go," simultaneously. She'd have to trust them to respect her wishes. But would they just go after Allen themselves when they left here tonight?

Dio, *save me from overprotective men!*

Leaving her dinner's fate in the seemingly capable hands of Marc and Luke, she shuffled down the hallway. The hall had never seemed so long. Inside the bedroom, she went to the closet to choose something that would be easy to get into. The peasant blouse and skirt would be perfect. When she reached up to unzip the dress, pain stabbed through her shoulder. *Ow!* Her muscles ached as she tried to stretch farther than they'd allow.

Damn!

Embarrassed, she headed down the hallway again to the kitchen, entering just as Luke walked in from the dining room and Marc placed his black iPhone into his pants pocket.

"What are you up to, Marc?"

"Wrong number." Marc stared at her, clearly daring her to challenge him.

Yeah, right.

"What else do you want us to put on the table, *cara*?"

Angelina glanced from one to the other, knowing they'd ignored her request. Damn them. If her brothers found out, there would be hell to pay. "I told you, I've taken care of Allen."

Marc's expression grew solemn, "No more mention of him tonight, *cara*. I forbid it."

His order sent a funny sensation through her. She hadn't taken orders from anyone other than her mama and oldest brother, Rafe, for a very long time. Her other brothers had given her lots of orders too, she just hadn't taken them.

Yet those stern words coming from Marc produced a strange, but definite, sexual response in her. Unbidden, images of the culinary bondage he'd mentioned placing her in last night returned. Her brain must have gotten rattled in the assault, because just as she'd closed the book on Allen Martin, she'd done the same thing with BDSM.

Shaking her head, she remembered what had brought her back to the kitchen in the first place. She turned her back to them and asked, "Could someone unzip me, please? I'm afraid I can't perform any contortionist moves at the moment."

"Love to." Marc's fingers felt warm against her skin as he glided the zipper latch down her spine. He sure took his time as his fingers grazed her skin in the wake of the zipper, sending a delicious shiver through her body. When his warm lips pressed against the nape of her neck, she fought to keep from melting against him. Her nipples hardened, making her thankful he couldn't see them.

"Thanks," she said, voice raspy. Without turning to gauge his response to the sensual contact, she hurried back to her bedroom in half the time it had taken moments before.

There would be no seduction unfolding here tonight. She'd get through dinner and send them on their way. Then she'd curl up in bed and nurse her wounds—both those on her bruised body and those inflicted against her battered spirit.

* * *

Luke watched her leave the room. "She's on to us."

Anger boiled to the surface, an emotion he hadn't felt in a long time. Thoughts of what her ex-boyfriend had done to her churned in his gut. Men didn't hit women. Period. Luke vowed the man wouldn't get away with it either.

"No way is Asshole laying another finger on her. He needs to be locked up."

"What did you find out?" Luke asked. While Marc called the sheriff, Luke had been retrieving the roses from the porch. Memories of her battered face and tears twisted his gut into a knot.

"Not much, but the sheriff promised to do a background check and see if there's anything on him."

They had met the sheriff during the rescue operation for the lost hikers this week. Despite being in a small, rural outfit, he appeared to be well trained and professional.

Marc picked up the hot pad. "He's going to get a judge to issue an emergency protection order and will serve Asshole as soon as he finds him. After what Angelina said she did to him, I told them to check the local hospital first."

Luke felt bile rise in his throat when he remembered seeing blood drops and smears on her porch and worse on Angel's dress. Thank God the blood hadn't been hers. Still, that red spot on her cheek was going to result in one helluva bruise, maybe even a shiner, by tomorrow.

What kind of man would hit a woman? Hell, Asshole wasn't a man. He was a slug. If he came within a mile of her again, there would be hell to pay.

"I'll check back with the sheriff later," Marc said. "Now, let's see if there's anything else we need to put on the table."

Marc opened the enormous refrigerator and pulled out a tossed salad in a covered bowl. "Ah, here's the antipasto." He handed both to Luke, who carried them to the dining room.

Angel had set the table with colorful stoneware dishes in shades of rust, blue, and yellow. He'd placed the roses at the end of the table so they wouldn't obscure anyone's view. Maggie had loved only red roses, but Luke thought this off-white color would complement Angel's olive skin and chocolate-brown eyes.

Remembering how her eyes sparkled when she laughed, his balls tightened. How had she gotten to him so fast? Was it the dream? Maggie's telling him she was sending him an angel, or was her vulnerability pulling at his heart?

Last night, he'd fought the attraction, but she kept tackling his defenses anyway. Since Maggie's death, he'd barely looked at another woman. Yet, last night, he'd lain awake thinking about a woman he'd first seen in a hazy dream but who had very much come to life.

Returning to the kitchen, he found Marc leaning against the counter waiting on the meat dish.

"I see you've taken off your ring."

Or maybe he was waiting for Luke. Looking down at the white strip where his ring had been worn for more than nine years, Luke said, "Yeah. It's time."

"*It's time. I'm sending you an angel...*"

"Wouldn't have anything to do with Angelina, would it?"

Luke met Marc's gaze. "Yeah," he smiled. "I'd say it has a lot to do with her."

He couldn't help but feel Marc sizing him up. They'd never competed for a woman before, but Luke had never been interested in dating since Maggie's death. But Luke wasn't blind; his partner had strong feelings for Angel, too.

"The night before we met Angel in the bar, I dreamed of Maggie." Luke shuffled his feet and looked down. He'd never told Marc about the visits he'd had from Maggie over the years on their rescue missions. "I know it sounds crazy if you don't believe in this kind of stuff, but she said she was sending me an angel. That it was time to move on."

He glanced up at Marc, who didn't seem to disbelieve him. Maybe the idea of hearing from a dead loved one wasn't foreign to his partner either. "When Angel walked up to our table and looked just the way she did in my dream, I knew she was the one Maggie was talking about."

He didn't mention that he'd dreamed of Maggie again last night and she'd repeated that she was sending him an angel. That confused him a bit. Angel had already come into his life. She'd added that he shouldn't worry about her anymore; he still had the rest of his life to live.

Other than during rescue missions, he hadn't felt that close to Maggie since the weeks after her funeral. Marc had tried to get him back in the game and even dragged him to the club a couple of years ago, and he'd played with Marc and one of the bottoms there once, but the thought of restraining anyone but Maggie just didn't appeal to him. He'd never even told Marc that he and Maggie had experimented with bondage in the bedroom, because Luke just didn't feel all that confident at the BDSM club level. He didn't need to be in control to get off either, like Marc did. He and Maggie each had played both the top and bottom roles.

After seven years, he was ready to develop a relationship with another woman, with or without ropes. He smiled. He had no doubt Angel was that woman. Maggie had as much as told him, and she sure had an inside track on these things. Luke couldn't help but hope selfishly he'd win the jackpot this time and Angel wouldn't be hardcore into BDSM, though. He couldn't compete with Marc in that arena.

He watched Marc's face, but couldn't read him. If any kind of rivalry developed between the two of them, how would the tension affect their ability to count on each other during a mission? They'd worked well together the past four years. Hell, Marc had been responsible for Luke's going into SAR training in the first place. His new friend had been on the squad a couple of years longer, having joined soon after being medically discharged from the Navy. The man had been decorated for saving Damián's life at the risk of his own. Luke respected the hell out of him for making a difference like that. All three of the club owners were heroes in his playbook, but Marc had been Luke's partner since soon after he finished his training and their bond was tightest.

Marc cleared his throat. "I won't let a woman come between us." He grew uncharacteristically serious. "I made that mistake once. I can live with her choosing either one of us—or neither of us." He shrugged. As if the two hadn't just come to a monumental understanding concerning Angel, he turned around to open the oven door and pull out the pot as she'd instructed them to do earlier.

Marc might have tried to look nonchalant, but they'd both been affected by her tonight. Nothing brought out a SAR worker's emotions faster than rescuing someone. Still, knowing he wouldn't lose Marc's friendship if he pursued Angel tonight helped him relax a bit. Marc had become like a big brother to him over the past four years—or what he thought a big brother would be like.

Oh, what was he worried about? Marc's women came and went. Surely he'd see that Angel deserved better than that. Luke didn't want to see her get hurt. She was too special.

Marc opened the lid of the pot. "I've been transported to my Nonna's kitchen."

Luke's stomach growled. "Damn, that smells good!"

Luke was going to make his best play for her tonight. Angel seemed too innocent to go for whips and chains anyway. She needed a good ol' boy who wanted nothing more than to please her. Time would tell.

* * *

After her shower, Angelina pulled on the white peasant blouse and green handkerchief-hemmed skirt. The ruined dress lay on the floor because she hurt too badly to bend over and toss it into the laundry—or the trash, which might be more appropriate.

She waved the blow dryer at the mirror to clear the steam before scrutinizing her cheek, which was swollen and red. No sense masking it with makeup; they'd already seen the damage. After drying her hair, she started to pull it up into a clip, but the effort was too painful, so she let her hair loose and brushed it as best she could to fall over her shoulders and down her back. Marc had preferred it loose last night, anyway.

Bending over to put on panties caused her muscles to riot, so she decided to skip them altogether. Who would know the difference? Angelina pulled the elasticized neckline of her blouse off her shoulders, slipped barefoot into her flats—choosing comfort over sexy this time—and took a deep breath. Time to rejoin the guys.

As she entered the kitchen, Marc uncorked the bottle of pinot noir he'd brought. He looked up and gave her an appreciative once-over. She felt her insides grow warm, melting into a puddle in her lower abdomen as if she'd already downed a glass of wine too fast.

Luke came in from the dining room and smiled at her, as well. "You look beautiful, Angel."

She smiled back at them both. "I guess I clean up pretty good."

Marc crossed the room and handed her a glass of wine. He then poured glasses for Luke and himself and raised his in a toast to her. "Like a ray of light, you have brightened our day."

Angelina looked away, a little embarrassed, and then took a healthy sip of her wine. She set the glass on the counter. "Now, out of my kitchen so I can finish getting dinner on the table."

"Dinner's already on the table," Luke wrapped an arm around her waist, short-circuiting her brain. He placed her glass in her hand again, then steered her toward the dining room. Marc followed.

When she saw the table, the waterworks nearly started again. Not only had they brought out the dishes she'd stored in the fridge, but the roses she'd seen Luke carrying earlier had been placed in a vase at the opposite end of the table.

"Thank you so much for rescuing our evening and for bringing these beautiful flowers." She walked over to breathe in their delicate fragrance. "Mmmm. And for the wine, Marc." Angelina held up her glass and took another sip. "*Delicioso.*" He smiled.

When she thought about how close she'd come to canceling their evening, her lips began to tremble. She brought her fingers up to still their quivering. Marc put his wineglass down and came to stand in front of her. He tipped her chin up and searched her eyes. "The rest of the evening is just about the three of us. No more unhappy thoughts are permitted in this house tonight."

He pressed his fingertip against her lip to still her trembling. She leaned back and felt Luke's body pressing against her. He wrapped his arms around her, cradling her, his hands resting below her breasts, warming her to her core.

Angelina felt protected, but in a good way. She pulled away from Marc, whose eyes smoldered. For her? His breathing sounded erratic. Or was that hers? Or Luke's? She turned to Luke, reached up on tiptoes, and kissed him on the cheek. She gave him a quick hug and broke away.

Feeling awkward all of a sudden, she announced, "Um, I think we'd better eat before everything gets cold."

Not that she'd be able to cool down for a very long time.

Chapter Seven

When Luke pulled out the chair for her at the head of the table, he noticed the red smudges where Asshole's fingertips had dug into Angel's shoulders. Those shadows would turn to bruises by morning. Damn that bastard for putting his filthy hands on her. If only he and Marc had arrived earlier, they could have made *him* suffer instead. They shouldn't have gone back to Denver today. If they'd been holed up at the motel, they'd have gone stir crazy and probably come over earlier.

Well, he and Marc would pay the slug a visit before they left town. The thought of leaving her unprotected burned his gut. Chances were high the rat bastard would come back—and be even more pissed. He wondered if they could talk Angel into going back to Denver with them until they could convince her to press charges. If not, he'd get in touch with her brothers and make sure they kept an eye on her.

Aw, hell he couldn't do that. Angel made him promise not to bring her brothers into this. He and Marc would have to handle the situation.

Marc took the seat on Angel's left and Luke moved to her other side. After they'd finished their salads, Angel cut and served the…he couldn't remember what she'd called it, but it looked like beef rolls stuffed with ham, salami, cheese, and hard-boiled eggs, of all things. Strange thing to do to a perfectly good piece of steak, but then he took a bite and thought he'd died and gone to heaven. Just melted in his mouth.

"Mmm, that's fantastic!" Luke said after he swallowed. Marc added his praise, as well, with moans and gestures. Then Luke noticed Angel had cut a very small portion for herself. Not that the size mattered, because she wasn't eating it anyway. Surely the salad hadn't been enough to fill her up.

"You aren't eating," he said, pointing to her plate.

She stared longingly at the meat dish, hiking the corner of her mouth up as if in regret. "I don't have much of an appetite."

"*L'appetito vien mangiando.*"

"Hey, Marc, I bet I can translate that one, because my Mom used to say 'Appetite comes with eating.'" He'd hung out with Marc long enough to pick up some of the Italian words, like *mangia*, that the man liked to sprinkle in his speech.

Both Angel and Marc smiled at him. Hell, yeah. He'd gotten it right. Luke reached out and took her fork from her hand, cut off a piece of the meat, and lifted the fork to her lips. Her sexy mouth opened as she accepted his offering, her eyes on him rather than the food.

He tried not to think about how it would feel to kiss her mouth or feel her lips around his...*whoa there, buddy*. Watching her eat brought that long-neglected appendage to full attention. He'd never thought about how sensuous feeding a woman could be. She closed her eyes and moaned as if in the throes of sex. Her face was so damned expressive. She clearly enjoyed eating. So, why had she feigned no appetite?

Next, Marc broke off a piece of the bruschetta and brought it to her lips. "Open." She opened her eyes and smiled, then accepted the crusty bread. "How is your appetite now, *cara*?"

"Improving." She smiled at Marc.

Angel didn't seem anything like Maggie. His wife had been a biologist and took everything so seriously, especially herself. Angel seemed to know how to let her hair down and have fun. To be spontaneous, not plan everything to the nth degree. Maggie had never veered from a plan once it was made.

Which is probably what got her killed. He'd spent seven years blaming himself for her death, but damned if Maggie didn't own a share of the blame, too.

Luke took another bite from his own plate, but didn't taste the food any longer. He glanced at Angel who, at the moment, was eating out of Marc's hand. *Damn*. If he wanted to stay in the game and not just hand her to his partner on a platter in short order, he needed a hurry-up offense.

"Please, stop! I can't eat another bite!" She laughed, a deep, rich laugh that sent electricity arcing from his chest to his cock. "You all are the ones who are supposed to be eating. This dinner is for you!"

Jeezus. Too late. He needed to stay on his toes tonight.

* * *

Angelina stood, feeling a tightness in her shoulders, and reached for a plate to begin clearing the dishes from the table. They had agreed to save dessert for later, but Marc and Luke banished her to the living room. Needing to calm her nerves, she placed a CD in the stereo and soon the sounds of their rinsing and stacking dishes were drowned out by Mary Chapin Carpenter's *Time*Sex*Love**.

While waiting for them to join her, she stretched out, leaning her head against the armrest and shut her eyes, letting the music wash over her. Despite their earlier admonition to put Allen out of her mind, images of the attack and the memory of his threats caused her to worry at her lower lip. What if he came back later, after Marc and Luke left? What if he was outside now, just waiting for them to leave?

"I haven't eaten like that since…" Marc began, but then stopped. "Worrying again, pet?"

She averted her face in guilt. When she felt the edge of the sofa cushion sink under his weight, she started to open her eyes.

"Keep your eyes closed."

Okay, no argument there. She was exhausted. The pressure of firm fingertips smoothing the worry lines from her brow caused her to sink back against the armrest, no strength left in her body. Yet, despite her outward appearance of relaxation, her insides were strung tighter than a *mandolina*.

"Tell me what you're worrying about, *cara*."

Why did she feel a strange compulsion to answer him honestly? She opened her eyes and he removed his hands. "I said eyes closed." She complied and he trailed his fingers along her cheek, relaxing her a bit, but she soon began worrying again.

"I, um…I'm afraid Allen might come back after you leave." Before he could reassure her with empty promises, she continued, "I hate to ask this, after all you've both done already, but if you don't have to head back to Denver tonight, would one of you mind staying here?" She prepared herself for rejection, knowing they had to get back to their own lives.

Rather than answer, Marc leaned closer and whispered into her ear. "*Cara*, we won't let him anywhere near you ever again."

Ever? She pushed him away and opened her eyes, despite his orders, and searched his eyes. How could he make a promise like that? They couldn't stay on guard duty forever. And yet he looked so certain, she wanted to believe him.

When Luke came into the room from the hallway bathroom, Angelina tried to push herself up. Marc stood and helped ease her into a seated position in the middle of the sofa. He sat on one side of her and Luke the other.

"We're both staying, darlin'." He sounded as though the two of them had already made up their minds before she'd even asked.

She turned from one to the other. "Thank you," her voice sounding husky. Strangely, even though they couldn't keep their promise to protect her forever, she hadn't felt this secure since…well, since Papa died. Her world had tilted on its axis that day and had never righted itself.

She laid her head against the back of the sofa and closed her eyes, the heat from their bodies warming the chilled air around her. "I'm sorry you two are always having to rescue me."

Luke leaned over and whispered, as if for her ears only, "That's what we do, darlin'."

"I'm not usually so needy."

The two chuckled at the same time, and then Marc nuzzled her neck, his scruff scratching in the most delightful way, sending a series of zings shooting straight to her clit. She didn't even know the two areas had a direct-current connection.

"What else do you need from us, *cara*?" Marc's fingertips grazed her bare shoulder in feather-light strokes, causing chill bumps to rise over her entire body. Her nipples beaded. Only she didn't feel the least bit cold anymore.

Luke ran his fingers through her hair, then lowered his head and nuzzled the right side of her neck. A tingling raced down her spine, settling into her pelvis.

"Mmmm." Her moan seemed to embolden him because Luke's fingers trailed lightly down her arm.

"Well, *bella*?"

What was the question? She opened her eyes and turned toward Marc, who lowered his lips toward hers, then stopped and pulled back. He blinked and she regretted it when he pulled away. Hadn't he just been about to kiss her? Hadn't she wanted him to?

Definitely yes on both counts.

But those weren't the questions he was waiting for her to answer. "Can you tell me what the question was again?"

When Marc remained silent, Luke reminded her. "What can we do to make you feel better tonight?"

Kiss me.

"Love to, darlin'."

Mio Dio! Had she spoken the words out loud? All ability to form a coherent thought fled as Luke leaned forward and brushed his lips against hers. While she'd spoken the words for Marc, the tingling in her lips spread down the length of her body. When the tip of Luke's tongue flicked across her lips, she opened and welcomed the teasing of his tongue in a sexy mating dance. This time, her clit pulsed in response to Luke. Apparently, it didn't have a preference between the two men.

When he pulled back, she looked at Luke and smiled. There was a sweet vulnerability in his eyes. He really did tug at her heartstrings, even though he didn't cause her to go weak in the knees as Marc did. She reached up and brushed a lock of hair off his forehead. To have lost the love of his life at such a young age must have been devastating.

"You're so beautiful, darlin'. I've been dying to kiss you again since last night."

Luke's hand stroked up and down her arm, his callused fingers sending delicious waves of heat through her. Then his fingers started downward again, brushing over one breast. Her nipple hardened and her body actually became uncomfortable, needing his touch. She tensed. She wasn't about to admit what she needed right now.

"Relax, *bella*. Let us bring you pleasure after all you've given us tonight?"

Bring her pleasure. She'd never been one to accept pleasure without giving it. All she'd done was cook and serve them a meal. But she wasn't about to serve herself up as dessert. She'd made a perfectly delectable Italian cream cake for that.

"I don't think I can do this."

"We aren't going to jump your bones, darlin'."

"*Cara*, we just want you to fly apart for us a time or two. That would please us immensely. Anytime you tell us to stop, we will do so immediately."

"Angel, you've been through a lot tonight. You need to release some of the stress."

They just wanted to please her? Her dream lover had commanded her to fly apart, as well. Now she found herself wanting these two gorgeous men more than she'd ever wanted anything in her life.

She smiled. What would they say if they discovered she was sitting between them without any panties? That was supposed to be her little secret, but if she let them go any further…

"Does that smile mean what we think it does, *cara*?"

"Probably not. Depends on just how much pleasing you plan to do."

"Ah, the lady offers us a challenge, Luke." Marc's hand massaged her neck and shoulders, so sweet to avoid the sore areas. There must be visible marks for him to know where not to touch her. She grimaced, remembering…

"Your muscles are too tight. Relax, pet." His fingers worked their magic, pressing the knots out of her neck, stiff from when Allen had backhanded her. She closed her eyes and moaned.

"Like that, do you?"

"Oh, yes."

Luke's hand reached down to cup her breast, gently rolling the nipple between his fingers. When he began to lower his mouth toward her chest, she felt the momentary return of her good judgment and was about to stop him when he took her nipple between his teeth right through her blouse. *Mio Dio!* Her chest developed a will of its own, pressing toward his lips as she arched and threw her head back. The cloth of the blouse added to the friction against her engorged nipple, sending runaway electrical current ricocheting throughout her body.

She squirmed in her seat. Not used to such intense sensations, Angelina gasped and reached out to move Luke's head away, but Marc intercepted her hands and held them against the back of the sofa above her head.

"Just feel, *cara*. Stop thinking and feel."

The removal of her hands gave Luke easier access, but also removed more of her inhibitions in some strange way. Luke cupped her other breast and tugged at the already aroused bud there. His hand continued to explore, roaming down to massage her thigh. She tried to draw her thighs closer together.

"Open yourself up to receiving pleasure, rather than always giving it. Tonight is all about your pleasure, *bella*."

He meant more than opening her legs. Could she lower her inhibitions long enough to let two men please her at once? *Hardly.* But what harm was there in letting it go just a little further? As if she could have stopped Luke now even if she'd wanted to. But she was a sensible, good girl. She'd come to her senses—in time.

Luke's mouth left her breast—the cold air against the wet cloth causing her nipple to harden even more. As if sensing her surrender, he smiled at her. Marc turned sideways and moved until his back was against the armrest.

Then they both helped swing her around lengthwise on the sofa until Marc pulled her against his hard body, cradling her in his arms.

His erect penis pressed against her butt, telling her she wasn't the only one aroused. Oh, my! She started to get up, when he chuckled.

"I'm not a teenager, *cara*. A thirty-three-year old man can control the urges of his body. You're safe."

Safe. This was not the kind of safety she'd been taught to need or want. And yet, with these two men, she'd felt nothing but safe since she'd met them.

"Keep your hands here, *cara*." Marc bent her arms at the elbows and tucked her hands snugly against the back of her neck. The position caused her breasts to jut out. She could move her hands at any time she wished to, so she felt no fear. Well, not too much.

"Close your eyes."

Angelina obeyed Marc's instructions, her ability to deny either one of them dwindling. She wanted more. Much more. After years of giving more than she got out of relationships, she decided to let herself experience the kind of pleasure she'd only read about. They'd said this wasn't about their getting off. Well, good.

Because she was going to be totally selfish.

The thud of her heart confirmed her need. Marc gathered her hair away from her chest and face, pulled it around the back of her head, and let it cascade down her left arm. He positioned her head and arms against his chest and placed his chin lightly on the top of her head. Though the pressure of his chin was gentle, she felt even more restrained. The only other time a man had placed his chin on her head like that…no, this was no time to conjure up a dream lover. Two real men were more than enough.

Just as she began to wonder what Luke was up to, she felt him remove her ballet flats and massage her feet and ankles. Marc's fingers feathered along the undersides of her arms through the blouse, raising gooseflesh wherever he touched her. When he continued the path downward, he brushed against the sides of her breasts. She sucked in a breath, her chest and hips arching upward, toward which man she didn't know.

Luke's lips brushed over her calves, trailing kisses as he continued to blaze a trail.

She'd never experienced so many sensations at once. When Marc's fingertips skimmed down to her abdomen, she nearly kicked Luke in the head as her leg reflexed.

Marc laughed. "Ticklish?"

"Sorry."

Luke looked up at her and grinned. "I think I might need to hold these babies down for my own protection, darlin'. He wrapped his arms around her calves and pressed his lips and tongue against her, moving upward. The muscles at the opening of her vagina clenched in anticipation.

Marc's hands moved again, slowly cupping her breasts, covered only by the cotton blouse. *Ah!* She let out a pent-up breath, but sucked air back into her lungs again as he pinched her nipples—hard. He pulled at the taut peaks, and then released them to let them spring back. Embarrassed at how flabby her breasts were, she tried to move her hands to cover them, but couldn't.

"I'm sorry," she said.

"About what?"

"They're kind of, well...soft."

"They're real, *cara*. Perfect. *Bellissima*."

Beautiful? He cupped them again. They filled his hands and then some. Well, who was she to argue with the man? He'd touched a lot more women's breasts than she had. Now why did the thought of him touching anyone else's breasts bother her? But when he repeated the pinching and pulling motion several more times, a moan escaped her throat and jealous thoughts vacated her mind. Marc wanted to touch her breasts at the moment. That's all that mattered.

"Enjoy that, do you?"

"Mmm-hmm."

He laughed and the rumble in his chest reverberated against her back. He continued to torment her now-tender nipples. When he stopped abruptly, she felt the absence of his fingers, until he stretched the elasticized neckline of her blouse downward, tucking it below her breasts. The cool air against her bare chest caused her nipples to tighten even more.

Luke's lips pressed against the insides of her knees as his hands spread her legs open wider. She fought the urge to close them, having never felt so exposed before. When her clit zinged, her knees jumped in reaction, pressing her lower back against Marc's growing erection. *Mio Dio!* She was getting beyond the point of being able to stop them, even if she wanted to. She started to move off of Marc's chest, but he halted her, holding her upper arms still.

"Stop worrying, *cara*. Trust me." Marc placed his hands against her breasts and pulled her back against him, pinching her nipples even harder.

She sucked in a breath. She was putty in their hands now. If they wanted to worship at her altar, she wasn't about to reject their offerings.

Then in a case of lousy timing, "The King of Love" began to play on the stereo.

> *He wants to own your heart*
> *He already owns your soul*
> *No matter what you do*
> *He's always in control*

"I approve of your choice of music, pet." She heard rather than saw his smile and flushed as images of Marc in black leather pants and a leather vest flashed across her mind. *Wrong choice of CDs, Angie.* Oh, dear. Was that a flogger she heard in the background percussion?

Well, that's what she imagined a sensual flogging would be like, from what she'd read in her erotic romances. Not the slap of the hard strokes Allen had used, but gentle flicks just licking the nerves on the surface of her skin, making them oh so sensitive. Her face grew even warmer, if possible.

But she'd learned that reality bites. How could she be turned on by such an instrument of torture? Still, her clit pulsated as images of Marc wielding a flogger on her tender backside flashed through her mind. What was happening to her?

Luke's hand skimmed along her right leg, up to her thigh under her skirt, drawing ever closer to her pussy, then retreated. Teasing. She surprised herself when, wanting more, she opened her thighs wider. She'd never behaved so wantonly in her life. But guilt over taking pleasure without giving anything back assailed her once more. She should try to slow things down so she could touch them, too. If only she could move.

Luke's fingertips slid along her outer pussy lips. Her bare pussy lips.

"Hot damn, Angel."

She smiled and her pelvic area warmed. "It hurt too much to bend over to put panties on."

She felt Marc's erection throb against her lower back as he leaned down to whisper in her ear, "Is that the only secret you have kept from us, *cara*?"

She smiled. "That's for me to know and you to find out."

Oh, my! What had gotten into her? What other secrets could she possibly possess?

When Luke's finger delved between her very wet folds, she hissed and her smile faded as she focused on the sensation of his finger easing deep inside her pussy. Her pelvis bucked upward, taking his finger deeper.

Angelina moaned.

"That's it, *bella*. Let him know how much you love what he's doing to your pussy."

She flushed hearing him say the word. She didn't use such sexually explicit language out loud, but hearing her body discussed so openly shocked—and stimulated—her.

Luke withdrew his finger but soon reentered her with two fingers sending heat rising throughout her body. Her hips bucked upward as she moaned again. Marc tilted his own hips up, raising her pelvis higher into the air. He took one of the chintz sofa pillows and wedged it under his hips to elevate their lower bodies—not for her comfort but to give Luke better access to her pussy.

Mio Dio!

Luke's head moved toward her pussy. She anticipated what his lips and mouth would feel like, although she'd never been touched in that way before. Allen just made a face when she'd indicated her interest in him trying it, even though he'd certainly enjoyed her going down on him.

"What was that thought, pet?"

"I, um, nothing important. I don't think…" She lowered her hands to push Luke's head away and to try to close her legs, which was impossible with Luke wedged between them.

"No, pet. Your body tells me what you were thinking was very important. Tell us."

She bit her lower lip. She didn't want to speak the words out loud—and certainly didn't want to bring up Allen's name. "No one's ever…" *Mio Dio*, she couldn't finish the thought.

Luke looked up at her and smiled. "Angel, I'd be honored if you'd let me be the first." She looked down at Luke, who gazed up at her. "Darlin', I need to taste you. Please."

"Don't deny him, *bella*. Share your treasure with Luke."

How could she refuse when he looked as if he actually enjoyed doing this? She relaxed just a little in acquiescence and Marc took her wrists, crossing and tucking them behind her head again.

"Don't move your hands again, pet."

Oh, no! She'd forgotten about moving her arms. Why did disobeying Marc disturb her so much? Trusting her once more to keep them where he placed them, Marc's hands returned to playing idly with her nipples.

Her face flamed. What if no man ever offered to please her in this way again? How could she miss out on what might be her only chance to experience something she'd only read about? Angelina nodded with a whimper letting her legs fall open wider. Closing her eyes, she tilted her head back, and relaxed against Marc's hard chest.

His chuckle reverberated against the back of her head. "*Cara*, you act as if you're offering yourself as a sacrifice."

"Shhh. I'm preparing to just feel."

Taking her relaxation as consent, Luke crooked her right leg and placed her foot along the back of the sofa and her left foot on the floor, spreading her knees wider and lowering his mouth once more to her pussy.

Marc pinched her nipples as Luke nipped at the insides of her thighs with his teeth, causing a rapid intake of breath in response. Luke's lips drew closer to her folds, and then pulled away, trailing kisses and his tongue from her thighs to her knees. He repeated his teasing torture of her body until she bucked toward him each time his mouth approached her center.

More! She wanted more. *Kiss me…lick me…there.* How could she put into words what she wanted without embarrassing herself or sounding like a slut?

"Please!" It took her a moment to realize the needy plea had come from her lips. She opened her eyes to find Luke grinning up at her.

Chapter Eight

Hot damn!

His Angel was begging him to continue. "Much obliged, darlin'." Her close-clipped pussy called to him and he lowered his mouth. Her clit was erect, protruding from its hood, but he avoided it as he pressed his tongue against the opening of her wet pussy. Shit. Clearly, she was turned on. So was he. He adjusted his legs to keep from strangling his erect cock.

Flattening his tongue, he stroked her sex firmly at first but then lightly brushed over her clit. He grinned when she tilted her hips and pressed her pussy toward his face. The lady liked that and wanted more.

Not yet, darlin'.

Continuing to avoid putting firm pressure on her clit, he licked the sides of the hood, holding her hips down so she wouldn't be able to control where he touched her. Her groan of frustration succeeded in turning him on even more.

No longer able to resist—or deny her—he pulled the tiny erection into his mouth with his lips and flicked his tongue over the tip, gently at first. Her hips fought to buck upward. Emboldened, he placed his teeth over the hard nubbin and pulled gently.

"Oh, God!" Like a trigger, her hips bucked up into his face again. "*Mio Dio*! I can't take any more!"

Marc laughed. "Hush, *cara*. He's only just starting."

Damn straight.

"The best is yet to come, *cara*. Lie back and enjoy the ride."

Luke pulled back and, with his fingers, opened her outer lips to allow himself a chance to look at her. Her pussy was so beautiful, like the center of a flower. A very wet, pink flower. He lowered his face to her again, wrapping his hands around her thighs to hold her down as his tongue lightly circled her hood. Her thighs alternately relaxed, then tried to clamp against his head like a vise grip. His cock strained against his jeans. Shit, it had been so damn long.

He paused to take a breath and looked up at her. She lay slumped against Marc, her eyes closed with arousal written all over her face. She opened her eyes and smiled down at him, waiting. Time to take her the rest of the way on that ride Marc had promised. Luke went down on her again, holding her pussy lips open with his thumbs and preparing to finish what he'd started. He still couldn't believe his head was between Angel's thighs pleasing the hell out of her. He smiled.

As he lapped at her sweet juices, he heard her tiny mewling sounds reminding him of a litter of kittens. He could tell by the tremors in her thighs she was getting closer. He took his middle finger and plunged inside her wet pussy. She held her breath and squeezed his finger with her vaginal muscles. How much longer could she last? He plunged two fingers inside her. *Damn, she was tight.*

"Stop!"

Aw, shit, darlin'. Don't do this to me. You're so close.

But the lady told him to stop. Luke took several deep breaths in frustration, inhaling her scent before he pulled back to look at her. Her brow was creased in confusion. Hell, if this was her first time with oral, he didn't want to leave her hanging like this. Still, he couldn't force her to enjoy the experience either.

"No, don't stop!"

He smiled. "You sure, darlin'?"

"I don't know." He could almost see the warring factions duking it out across her face.

Luke watched Marc stroking her breasts and squeezing her nipples and wondered what it would be like to suck on them, but he had another project to complete first. Maybe she was just on sensory overload. He was pretty damn sure she'd never been with two men at once before. Hell, sharing a woman was pretty damned new for him, too, except for that one time at Marc's club. But he loved pleasing Angelina and, if she wanted two men loving on her at once, she'd get it.

"Tell me what you need, Angel."

"I need…" A look of frustration crossed her face and she closed her eyes.

Don't shut me out, darlin'.

When she opened those big brown eyes again, she looked as if she'd come to a decision. He held his breath, waiting.

"I need to come."

He released the pent-up air from his lungs with a laugh. "Damn right, you do. Hang on, baby girl." Luke lowered his head yet again, hoping he wouldn't raise it again until she'd exploded against his mouth. Backtracking a bit, he opened her up and licked the opening of her sex, and then resumed his tender assault on her clit as he built up quickly to firmer strokes. Her tremors told him she was ready.

"Oh, *Mio Dio*!"

"*Vola*. Fly apart for him, *bella*."

Luke felt her body stiffen. So close. He rammed two fingers inside her as he flicked her tiny erection with his tongue. She arched her back. When he pumped three fingers into her pussy like a piston, her walls clenched and spasmed around them. Shit. So tight.

"Oh, my God! I'm coming!"

Damn right you are, darlin'.

Luke increased the motion of his fingers and tongued her clit faster. When he sucked her nubbin into his mouth, Angelina exploded.

"*Mio Dio*! Don't stop! Oh, ohhh, ohhhhh! Yesssssss!" Her body bucked and jolted like a bronco just out of the gate. He wrenched every ounce of the orgasm from her, convinced that, if he and Marc hadn't been holding her down, she would have flown right off the couch.

He'd done that for her. He smiled as he sat up and looked up at the look of ecstasy on her face.

Hot damn.

* * *

When Angelina collapsed against him, spent, Marc looked down at Luke and made eye contact as his friend leaned back grinning in awe like the cat that had eaten the canary. Only Luke had eaten something much more delightful. His friend's lips and chin were covered in Angelina's sweet essence. Marc had no doubt the experience had been as exhilarating for Luke as it had been for Angelina.

Shit, watching Luke going down on Angelina had been pretty damned hot for Marc, as well. She flew apart like no other woman he'd ever known. Total abandon. Shock and awe, as if this was the first time she'd ever come. He remembered when she'd come for him at the club. Would she ever fly apart like that for him again?

No, he needed to back off. Luke needed her. For Marc, she was merely a want. But could Luke give her what she needed? Could he dominate her? Doubtful.

"Am I dead?" Angelina asked.

"Just a *petite mort*, my pet. The best kind." He really shouldn't call her that. She wasn't his pet. Probably never would be. Yet it seemed so natural.

She raised her head slightly. "That was…" she paused as she searched for the right words, then shook her head. "I have no words to describe it. I never…just…thank you."

He watched Luke's chest swell with pride, and then his friend reached up to stroke her cheek. "Don't thank me, Angel. Having you explode for me like that was…well." He shrugged and grinned at her.

Well done, my friend. Welcome back to the game.

Still, witnessing the exchange, Marc felt something twist inside him. He'd participated in scenes with multiple partners on many occasions, so, why did it bother him now, with Angelina and one of his best friends?

Mine.

Bullshit. He had no claim on her. Marc shook off the possessive thought and watched as Luke laid his head on her thigh and stroked her other leg from thigh to calf. Angelina tucked her head into Marc's shoulder. Eyes closed, she hung onto the waning effects of her release, fighting against the inevitable return to earth. Her well-sated body pressing against Marc's entire length caused his cock to throb.

He felt her stiffen. "Ignore it, *cara*. My cock has a mind of its own. Just relax." She sank against him again, smiling as he idly stroked the undersides of her breasts. Her nipples had begun to relax to their pre-orgasmic state, then he squeezed and watched them start to swell and harden again.

Dio, she felt so right against his body. He loved her generous curves sprawled open in licentious satisfaction before him. Her head lolled against his upper arm and he looked down at her. She smiled, keeping her eyes closed, and reached her hand up to stroke his cheek. Marc's cock tightened as his hand skimmed over her abdomen toward her pussy.

She laughed, pulling her legs up in a protective manner, closing herself off to him. Ahh, damned ticklishness. He smiled.

"Please, no more! Have mercy, I beg of you!" He returned his hand to her breast, but *Dio* help him, he couldn't stop touching her. Having her in his arms again was heaven on earth. He'd thought he'd lost his little angel forever and here she was, lying on top of him.

No, not his angel. If anybody's, she'd probably be Luke's angel. Marc needed to keep that in mind tonight, because he wouldn't let hard feelings come between him and his partner over a woman, even though Angelina wasn't just any woman.

Luke stood up, lifted Angelina's legs, and pulled them together as he sat again, laying her knees over his thighs. He pulled her skirt down over her knees and stroked her legs. Definitely a leg man. Marc watched as he slid his hand under her skirt to her thighs. She smiled and opened her eyes to look at Luke.

Marc experienced another pang of jealousy. He wanted her to look at him in a post-orgasm moment like that. Again. He wanted her all to himself.

"I think you two are the very guys my brothers warned me about all these years." Her eyes opened wide and she sat upright with sudden realization, turning sideways to face them both in turn. "Wait one minute! Have my brothers been off having all this fun while I've been threatened with life in a convent if I so much as let a man touch me?"

They both laughed. The double standard as old as time—what was good for the gander wasn't good for the gander's sister.

She soon lost her sense of outrage and slumped back against Marc, laughing.

"You're past the age of needing their approval, *bella*. It's time for you to have some fun, too."

"No, now it's *your* turn." She tried to sit up again, but Marc pulled her back against him.

"You have pleased us more than you know."

She sighed. "I don't know what kind of magic spell you two have cast over me. I've never been able to do that without…" He watched her face flush. Ah, so orgasms didn't come so easily to her. Maybe that explained the shock and awe. And yet, she'd come for both him and Luke. Well, his making her come was dubious under the circumstances. He wished he could experience the power of giving her an orgasm totally under his control.

Angelina probably didn't realize she'd been able to come so hard because he and Luke had restrained her arms and legs. If he could, he'd have shown her how this makes a difference, but it wasn't his place. If Luke wanted her, Marc wouldn't stand in his way. He reached down to pull her blouse back over her breasts. The sight of them had become too painful for him.

Her body became heavier against him as she seemed to fall asleep. Luke eased himself out from under her legs and placed a crocheted blanket over her. He went into the head, then the kitchen. Now, wasn't this the utter definition of torture. To hold a beautiful woman in his arms and know he couldn't have her?

He watched her sleep and when her eyelids began to flicker and she moaned in pain, Marc's fingers brushed against the furrows on her forehead, smoothing them out until she relaxed again. She'd been through a lot. He wished he could have protected her from all the pain she'd suffered at the hands of that bastard.

Guilt plagued him for not showing up earlier tonight, but most especially being late for his dungeon monitor duty the night she was beaten so badly. He'd failed her. Twice. Thank God she hadn't recognized him. There really was no need to tell her who he was or what role he had played that night. Even if she and Luke pursued something beyond tonight, they'd never show up at his club. Luke just wasn't into that scene.

* * *

Luke set out to wash the last of the dishes from supper, placing them in the dishwasher to drain. He hadn't wanted to wake Angel to explain how the machine worked and, well, having something to do to keep his hands and mind busy had helped.

Remembering Angel on the couch exploding beneath his lips such a short time ago, he regretted he hadn't been more insistent in convincing Maggie to let him please her in that way. They'd been married two years, but he'd never gotten past her inhibitions on that front—and many others. He had no doubt he'd have figured out a way to introduce more spice into their love life sooner or later, especially after he started tying her up. But there hadn't been enough time for them.

Angel seemed to have no such inhibitions; well, once she overcame her initial shyness. Knowing she wasn't promiscuous made her even sexier. He poured a glass of wine and took a swig, letting it mingle with the essence of Angel still on his tongue.

He reached for a towel and dried his hands and walked over to the refrigerator to put away the leftover meat. His hand froze as he stared into the face of Tony Giardano. The man was dressed in a suit, but no doubt about it, that was Tony. So, what was his picture doing on Angel's fridge?

He looked at some of the other photos there, until he found a snapshot of six people—an older woman and five adults of a younger generation.

Looked like they were dressed for Easter or Mother's Day or something. There was Angelina—standing next to Tony.

Luke closed his eyes. *God damn it all to hell.* He felt the wine reflux into the back of his throat. She was a Giardano? What kind of twisted fate would bring Angel into his life only to take her away so fast? What the hell was Maggie trying to do to him?

He didn't know how long he stood there in the kitchen…numb, heart aching as he thought about what he was going to do. He ran his hand through his hair.

Antonio Giardano's daughter.

…and by one daughter, his youngest child, Angelina.

Fuck. What were the chances she was anyone other than Angelina Giardano? Now he could put a face to the other names in the obituary—Angela, the mother, Raphael, Franco, Matteo, Antonio Jr.—and Angelina.

Oh, this was rich. He'd come to town worried about running into Tony or Rafe Giardano. Just his dumb luck, he'd met and fallen—hard—for their baby sister.

He'd been so wrapped up in the message in Maggie's dream that, when she introduced herself, all he heard was Angel. He didn't even consider the notion she could be *that* Angelina. She hadn't given a last name, which was understandable for safety reasons in a bar with strangers. She didn't need a stalker…well, another one.

Marc had to have known her full name, though, in order to call in the report on Allen Martin. Luke had never told his friend the whole story about Maggie's death, so Marc wouldn't have made a connection between the names. Luke ran his hand over his face and reached for the bottle of wine.

He just wished he'd been clued in before he'd taken things too far with her on that damned couch. Why hadn't he been the one to take the food out of the fridge? Maybe he would have seen the photo and put a halt to the attraction then. Regret for what he'd done twisted his guts. At least there was some relief in knowing he hadn't gone all the way with her.

Still, how could Maggie have sent her to him? Was this her idea of some kind of cosmic reconciliation? She'd never liked conflict or to leave things unresolved. Well, no thanks. He'd owned up to his responsibility by becoming a SAR worker and trying to make amends. He sure as hell didn't need to confess to the woman he'd deprived of a father.

He filled his wineglass, then picked up the glass and the bottle and headed back to the living room. Not able to even look at the two of them stretched out on the couch, he sat on the overstuffed flowery chair in a darkened corner of the room.

"What's wrong?" Marc whispered.

"Nothing. I plan to sit here and get rip-roaring drunk." Then he'd figure out how to walk away from the best thing that had happened to him in seven years.

* * *

Marc's gaze narrowed on Luke. Something had happened. Had he talked with the sheriff? Was there news about Martin?

He looked down at Angelina sleeping soundly and didn't want to disturb her but definitely needed to know what was going on.

"Before you get too far into that bottle, help me get her to bed."

Luke looked at him as if he'd asked him to pick up a coiled rattler. What was going on? Marc managed to swing his legs off the sofa and then lifted Angelina into his arms before heading down the hallway. He heard Luke following and waited for him to pull down the comforter and sheet so Marc could lay her in bed and cover her up. He stayed to make sure she didn't awaken, but the flickering of her eyelids told him she was still in a deep sleep.

"Pleasant dreams only, *cara*." He stroked a finger along the side of her face.

Marc turned around only to see that Luke had already left. He was going to get to the bottom of whatever was going on. Leaving her door open, in case she needed him, he walked down the hall, hitting the head for a much-needed stop after all the wine before returning to the living room. Luke had returned to the chair and poured a second glass of wine, which he downed swiftly. Had he even tasted the expensive Lombardy wine from Marc's wine cellar? Then he poured another glass.

Merda. He'd never known his partner to drink to excess. Was Luke upset with Marc for holding Angelina? What was he supposed to do? She'd fallen asleep on him. Or was it… His lungs constricted painfully, reminding him of his recovery from the hemopneumothorax he'd suffered in Fallujah.

"Have you heard something?"

Confused, Luke cocked his head and leaned against the back of the chintz chair.

Marc was losing patience. "What the hell did the sheriff say?"

Luke nodded in understanding. "I just checked, hoping they'd arrested the bastard and we could leave. They found him in the ER—and she did break his nose, by the way." Marc smiled, but Luke remained serious. "Served him with the protection order. Warned him to stay away from her." Luke shrugged.

For now, their hands were tied unless and until Asshole violated the order. By then, it could be too late to protect her.

"She's not staying here alone," Marc said.

Luke sobered, well, his expression did. "We're leaving in the morning."

"She's coming with us." *Even if she doesn't know it yet.*

Now just how did he plan to pull that off?

"No!" The wine in Luke's glass sloshed over the edge and onto his fingers and his jeans. He placed the glass to his lips and drained it, then looked at Marc. "We'll call her brothers. They'll keep an eye on her."

Like hell they will.

Marc needed to find out why his friend was trying to get drunk, which was totally out of character for him. Apparently, he'd started before talking with the sheriff's department, so something else had happened.

Marc crossed the room and sat on the armrest of the sofa, near Luke's chair. He hated to see his friend suffering like this. "What's wrong, Luke? You're hitting that stuff pretty hard." Was this about Angelina? "Look, we agreed to leave it up to her to decide, but I told you I wouldn't pursue her if you wanted her."

Luke dangled the now-empty glass between his knees and waved his other hand dismissively. He shook his head. "No need. She's all yours."

What the fuck was he thinking? Luke never walked away from something he wanted—and Marc had no doubt he wanted Angelina. Marc had admired his persistence and determination. When he set his mind to something, he damned well achieved it. Of course, Luke hadn't gone after a woman since his wife had died—until now. Maybe he was just scared.

Dio, she scares the hell out of me, too.

But Luke would have to be blind not to notice that Angelina had feelings for him, too. "Don't you think she should have something to say about who she wants?"

"No. We...aren't compatible."

Marc would have laughed, if his friend didn't look so fucking miserable. "If you were any more compatible, she'd have been jumping your bones, as you say."

Luke raised his head to meet his gaze. The ache in his eyes squeezed the breath from his lungs. "That was before." Marc came close to shaking some sense into him when he heard him say, "She can't find out what I did."

"What are you talking about?"

Luke shook his head in defeat and closed his eyes, laying his head in the crook of the wingback chair. He looked like he'd aged a decade since he'd pleasured Angelina an hour or so ago.

Marc stood and reached over to take the glass out of Luke's hand and set it on the coffee table, then grabbed the blanket that had been covering Angelina and used it to cover his friend. Given how much he'd had to drink in such a short time, it was probably safer if he remained upright, so he'd let him sleep it off in the chair.

Maybe Luke would see straighter in the morning—if he wasn't too hung over to see.

* * *

"Red!"

Marc opened his eyes and waited for them to adjust to his surroundings. Where was he? He straightened out his cramped legs and hit the footboard. What the…looking down, he saw it wasn't a footboard but an armrest. He was sleeping on a sofa.

He remembered where he was at last. Angelina's living room. *Merda*. Some watch guard he was. Sleeping on duty. He looked over at Luke, who was passed out in a chair. What had awoken him?

"*Mio Dio!* Stop!"

Angelina! Marc sprang off the sofa and bounded down the hallway before his mind registered anything other than that Allen Martin had returned.

Please don't let me be too late this time.

He entered the open door of the bedroom, expecting to find Asshole attacking her. She was alone in the bed.

"Hurts."

Her whimper reminded him of when she'd come out of deep subspace. Oh, *Dio*. A nightmare. He crossed the room to the bed and touched her shoulder.

"Wake up, Angelina. You're safe now."

When she didn't respond, he scooped her into his arms and sat on the edge of the bed, cradling her.

"Shhh. It's over."

She shook her head. "Not real."

"That's right, *cara*. Only a dream."

"But I wish you were real. My first Dom."

He smiled, because he'd been wishing the same thing ever since he'd met her. So, apparently, she wasn't thinking about Sir Asshole anymore. Did she remember Marc holding her that night at the club?

Ha! Dream on, man.

But wasn't it interesting she'd been dreaming of a Dom. He hoped Luke could give her what she longed for sexually. The thought of her needs not being met made his chest ache. She'd be an awesome woman to train. Perhaps he could help her learn to express her interest in kink and maybe even offer to talk with Luke on her behalf, if she was too shy at first. Marc just didn't know if Luke was interested in pursuing the lifestyle. He had some Dom tendencies, but had been uninterested in the club visit. Maybe it had just been too soon after his wife's death.

She stirred restlessly in his arms and he held her tighter. He brushed his hand over her hair, feeling his groin tighten. "I have you, *cara*."

But only for tonight.

Luke would come to his senses soon and see she was the most perfect woman in the world. Every man's dream. Marc closed his eyes. She certainly fulfilled his dreams. He regretted he would never be her Dom.

Shit. He had it bad. What the hell was he going to do about her?

Nothing.

"Open your eyes, pet."

She blinked and looked up at him.

"Marc?"

"Yes, *cara*. You had a nightmare."

"Allen and my d...never mind."

Had she been about to say "my Dom"? Or someone she wished was her first Dom?

"You can tell me, *cara*. I have been the keeper of many secrets." As the Navy corpsman for this unit, he'd been trained to be someone the Marines came to for advice or just to unload their anxieties.

"Sometimes I'm angry at him for spoiling my fantasy."

"What fantasy is that?" He wondered if she'd mention the club.

"It's too embarrassing."

"Fantasies are supposed to be a bit illicit. Forbidden. That's what makes them so exciting." Her breathing grew more rapid and shallow. Thoughts of her fantasy clearly turned her on. He wished she would share it with him.

"I read...well, erotic books a lot. Romances, but with a kinky side to them."

"What type of kink?"

Her body grew tense and he stroked her arm to relax her. This could be an interesting conversation.

"Promise you won't laugh or get all weird? It's not my fantasy anymore."

More's the pity. Asshole bastard ought to be horsewhipped for destroying her desire to explore her fantasies.

"I assure you your fantasies would be tame compared to mine."

She laughed. "Probably so." Her hand played with a button on his shirt front. "I used to be excited about being...tied down. Restrained. By someone...a man who is dominant."

He felt his groin tighten and his own breathing grow shallow. *Control yourself, man.* "Why do you say used to? Fantasies usually are deep-seated and don't vanish very easily."

"Well, this one got beaten out of me."

Chapter Nine

Angelina's heart thumped loudly. What had possessed her to tell him something like that?

"Oh, *cara*. I can't tell you how sorry I am that happened to you." He held her tightly, placing his chin on the top of her head and enveloping her in his strength and warmth.

"Let's put that fantasy and bad memory on the back burner for now. Tell me about another fantasy. One you haven't experienced yet. Perhaps something you've read about…or even seen."

"Um, there was this one time when…I was at a private club in Denver."

"What kind of private club?"

Oh, she didn't want to admit she'd gone to a kink club. "Um, one where adults…couples mostly…do…things to each other."

"Just what kinds of things do they do?" She could have sworn by his voice he was smiling, but didn't want to pull away from his comforting arms to confirm her suspicions. Just what did he find so funny?

She sighed. "Well, pretty much anything you can imagine."

"I can imagine a lot, pet."

Oh, damn it all, apparently the man had never been inside one before. He was going to think she was a slut, but obviously, she was going to have to tell him now. He was like a dog with a bone. "Promise you won't think badly of me?"

"It's rather difficult for me to promise when I don't know what you've done yet."

Well, what did she expect, unconditional love from a near stranger? One who happened to be cuddling her on his lap on the edge of her bed? *Oh, Nonna. I hope you aren't watching!* Angelina decided to just spit it out.

"I…*We* were…in a kink club." She held her breath and steeled herself.

"Ahhh, I see. What was it like?"

He certainly didn't seem to be judging her. But he wanted her to talk about it? Oh, God. This just got worse and worse on the embarrassment scale.

"I didn't see much."

She'd unbuttoned his shirt and her fingers played idly with the springy chest hairs in the vee. She didn't want him to think she'd gone to a sleazy one, though. "It seemed like a nice place. Karla, she was the club's singer, was very kind to me after…well, later. She brought me home. And the club's owner, Master Adam, was very nice, too."

His hand stopped stroking her hair. "Were there any other nice people you met there?"

"No. Mostly I just watched."

After a moment, his hand began stroking her again, but she felt tenseness in his body. Maybe he *was* judging her.

"What did you see?"

"There were several couples in the great room who were engaging in different…activities."

"Which activities interested you?"

Her mind returned to the main room of the club where two of the Doms had caught her attention while Allen was filling out guest papers on her. One wore a Harley-Davidson vest with the tail of a dragon tattoo curled around his bicep, the rest of the mythical creature disappearing under the vest. Very lethal looking—both the dragon and the man who held a coiled whip against his leather-clad thigh.

"There was a Dom with a whip." She felt Marc's body tense even more, but wasn't sure if it was the mention of the Dom or the whip that bothered him. Well, he asked, so she was going to tell him what she liked. "There was another Dom, too—a bald, black man. Kneeling before them was a blonde woman who looked up obediently at the Dom with a whip, waiting for him to do…well, whatever he wanted to, I suppose." *The man had a whip, for Christ's sake!*

"Did the whip excite you?"

She pulled out of his arms, bumping his chin against her head in her haste to get away, but she wasn't going to let him entertain the notion she was into whips. "God, no! Don't even go there!"

He relaxed visibly and smiled. "Duly noted, *gattina*."

Angelina felt the tension leave her, as well, and took a deep breath, releasing it slowly. He seemed as relieved as she was, although she had no idea why.

"So, tell me what it was about them that interested you so much."

She blushed. It was pretty lame as far as fantasies went, but she'd been so turned on. "The bald Dom put his middle finger deep into her mouth and, with the other fingers and the thumb of his hand, he…I guess you'd say caged her chin, forcing her mouth open." Angelina felt herself getting wet just remembering. She shrugged and smiled.

"Do you know what it was about the scene that excited you?"

She shook her head. "I'm not sure. It just did."

She lowered her gaze to his bare chest where her fingers were buried in the light sprinkling of black chest hairs. She liked touching him. He waited, expecting more of an answer, she supposed.

"The woman's expression for both men was…well, she looked up at them with such, I don't know the word—adoration maybe? Devotion? Trust?" She swallowed. "Or maybe it was the way the one took control of her mouth like that. Of her." She shivered. "I don't know, but it blew me away."

Marc's gaze went to her mouth and Angelina's clit throbbed in response as if he'd taken control of her mouth the way the Dom had done with the blonde at the club. Angelina squirmed on his lap; her gaze locked on his lips. She wanted him to kiss her again, only rougher than he'd kissed her last night.

She'd never tried to seduce a man, usually letting him make the first move. But then she wound up with guys like Allen. If this wasn't the opportunity of a lifetime—sitting in the lap of one of the sexiest men she'd ever met—there might never be another one.

Her fingers glided across his chest, stroking his firm pecs and wishing he wasn't wearing a shirt. His muscles were hard, too, and tight. She brushed the nail of her thumb across his nip and felt it grow even harder, but nothing compared to his penis pressing against her bottom.

He stilled her hand by pressing it against his chest. "*Cara*, you're playing with fire."

She searched his eyes. "What are your fantasies, Marc?"

His lips curled into a smile, but his eyes remained hard. "I don't think I'll be in town long enough to tell you about all of them."

"Which fantasy would you like to fulfill with me?" Had she just asked that? What had gotten into her? She'd never been brave, or brazen, in her life.

"None."

Angelina felt his rejection like the jab of a knife into her chest. *Oh, God!* What had come over her? She wasn't some sex goddess men fantasized about. Since Friday night, he'd made her feel so…beautiful and desirable. How had she misread his interest so badly?

Embarrassed, she tried to get off his lap. She needed to get away. "I'm sorry. I don't know what…"

His arm tightened around her waist and he held her forearm to keep her in place. "Remain still."

His tone of voice made her freeze in place, causing her stomach to drop, leaving her breathless. She blinked against the stinging in her eyes, overshadowed only by the stinging blow to her ego. He took her chin and turned her head to face him.

He seemed to struggle within himself for a moment, then a determined look flickered in his eyes and he looked down at her mouth. She felt his penis throb against her butt and held her breath until his fingers wrapped around her jaw and he stared into her eyes. His thumb pressed against her lower lip. Never breaking eye contact, he pushed at her lower teeth until her jaw slackened, and invaded her mouth with his thumb. Her clit jolted in response, and she gasped. Her breathing increased as she responded to this show of control.

Marc's thumb went deeper inside her, pressing against her tongue. He continued to watch her eyes as if waiting for some response. Her private bundle of nerves began to pulsate as if he'd touched her there. He smiled. Surely he hadn't felt it, too.

Her mind went back to the kink club in Denver. Angelina wrapped her lips around his thumb and sucked, just as the blonde had done. His smile faded and when he began to remove his thumb, she used her teeth to apply gentle pressure and keep him from moving. This fantasy wasn't over yet.

As if he came to some decision, Marc's thumb and fingers caged her chin and opened her mouth wider. She could have sworn her uterus just spasmed, because that spot in her lower belly grew warm and tingly, the muscles melting like butter. The very act of touching her this way was so primal.

So…dominant. She sucked air into her lungs, realizing that was exactly the reaction he'd intended. Her gaze remained locked with his. Why hadn't she realized all along he was a Dom? He'd taken control of his surroundings from the moment they'd met—of Allen, even Luke to an extent, and most definitely of her. *Mio Dio*, she hoped he wouldn't be able to tell the effect he had on her. She didn't want to submit to anyone ever again.

He smiled. Damn him. He knew she was turned on by his he-man display of authority over her. Then his thumb was gone and his hand gripped her lower jaw opening her farther as his mouth came down hard against hers. His other hand went to the back of her head, gripping her hair as he tilted her head back, forcing her mouth open farther. As if she could have denied him access at this point.

His whiskers scratched her cheek and chin, sending flashes of sizzling energy in a beeline to her clit, which began to throb in earnest now. His tongue plunged inside her thoroughly restrained mouth, plundering her. She no longer had the will to resist him.

Marc sucked her tongue into his mouth, released her, and invaded her mouth again. When he pulled his tongue out to let her breathe, he captured her lower lip between his teeth and tugged, once again looking deep into her eyes. She released a breathless gasp. Not wanting to reveal any longer whatever he was reading in her eyes, she closed them. He bit her lip indicating his displeasure, not breaking the skin but hard enough to sting, bringing tears to her eyes. She opened her eyes again and he smiled in victory.

His hand skimmed teasingly down her jaw, over her blouse leaving a wake of gooseflesh, only to grasp her nipple through the fabric and roll it hard between his fingers, sending her hips jolting upward in response.

Angelina pulled away, panting, and stared into the deep green pools of his eyes. Her chin burned where his whiskers had abraded her skin. Chest heaving, she tried to regain control, as if she ever could have control in this man's presence.

He released her and pulled away.

"Wow. How did you do that?"

He laughed. "Do what, pet?"

"Go all Dom like that. Take control." *Turn me on more than I've ever been before.*

Gentle now, his thumb stroked her cheek, avoiding the area where Allen struck her. He brushed his thumb pad over her swollen lower lip, sending more jolts to her pussy. His hand still held her head by the hair and her clit responded as if touched.

"Did you like that?"

Well, hell to the yes, I did. "I'm not submissive."

"Answer the question."

"Mmm-hmm." She felt her face go hot and glanced away.

"Look at me." He waited until she complied, and she was powerless to do anything else. "Why does being submissive scare you so, *cara*?"

"I trusted someone once. He...broke that trust."

"He wasn't worthy of your trust. Will you trust me to help you break free from that memory?"

Trust him? A knot formed in her chest. Allen had ruined her for being able to trust any man again. Even someone she was attracted to, like Marc. Tears burned her eyelids.

"Look at me, *bella*."

How many times had he called her beautiful? Maybe he just meant her face. She had a pretty face because she'd been told so all her life. Compensation for having a body that wasn't beautiful by any stretch.

So how could she trust Marc? Her brothers had told her since Papa died that men wanted one thing—sex—and would say whatever they had to in order to get it. Was Marc just trying to get her into bed?

Mio Dio! She became aware of where she was sitting with him—and how she'd nearly stripped him and had her way with him a moment ago. She wanted Marc. But not as Sir Marc or Master Marc or whatever a Dom was called in real life. She wanted him because she was attracted to him.

"Your mind is going a mile a minute. Look at me."

His command sent butterflies in frenzied flight in her tummy and she met his gaze once more, with reluctance. Oh God, she didn't want him to be displeased with her, but she couldn't do what he asked. "I don't know you well enough to trust you."

He smiled, his moss-green eyes lighting up. "Good girl." Puzzled by his unexpected response, she waited until he explained. "Trust has to be earned over time. We're just getting to know each other. But we *have* developed some trust. You invited me into your home. You let me hold you in my lap—albeit with some token resistance." He grinned, and she responded in kind.

She hadn't really thought about it that way, but he was right. He hadn't raised her hackles or her radar. Of course, neither had Allen. So, maybe her radar was on the fritz. Still, she'd learned to be cautious.

"I'd like to help you regain your ability to trust, whether it's for Luke or someone else, if you'll let me."

Her heart thrummed. He didn't promise anything in the future with him. Only tonight. "Just what did you have in mind?"

"A demonstration."

He wanted her to be a guinea pig? Okay, this set a few warning bells off.

"I want to explore something with you tonight. I will not inflict any pain you do not agree to or break the trust you place in me."

He paused as she considered his words and bit the inside of her lower lip. *Well, she certainly wouldn't agree to any pain whatsoever.*

"Do you remember how you flew apart for us in the living room?"

"How could I forget coming like that?"

"No, not *that* you came, but *how* you came?"

She creased her brow. "Sorry, I was too busy coming to overanalyze it."

He smiled.

Her insides melted and she grinned back.

Marc grew serious again. He stroked her cheek, the one Allen hadn't hit. When he smiled at her again, she felt her tummy turn to jelly.

"I believe you're sexually submissive, pet."

Angelina grew stiff and pulled away from his hand. She fought the urge to run to the mirror to see if "SUBMISSIVE" was stamped across her forehead. She was an assertive business woman. She lived independently and was in charge of everything in her life. Hadn't she even tackled Allen last night, leaving him bloodied and achingly sore? No, definitely not submissive.

After all, she'd already explored submission with Allen, and it was the worst experience she'd ever had with a man. Angelina pulled out of his arms and rose to her feet.

"I don't need cuffs and floggers to get aroused. Last night, I came with Luke because I was stimulated out of my ever-loving mind." She didn't want to analyze the experience on the sofa now either. "It wouldn't have been any different if I were restrained."

"Oh, but you *were* restrained last night. Think back."

What was he talking about? She definitely would have noticed if she'd been tied down. She tried to replay what had taken place in the living room. For one, she'd never been so responsive with any man before. Images flickered across her mind's eye of having her arms placed above her head by Marc. Okay, sure, he'd ordered her to keep them there, but he hadn't used ropes or cuffs or anything to restrain them. She could have moved them anytime she wanted to. In fact, she *had* moved them, to stop Luke at one point.

Suddenly she remembered that Marc had sternly ordered her to return her hands behind her head and she'd complied without question, just as she followed his orders a few minutes ago. When she'd tried to move her hips to get Luke to lick her where she'd wanted and had nearly kicked him in a ticklish response, even Luke had restrained her by holding her thighs in a way that made it impossible for her to move. Was Luke a Dom, too? Her heart pounded at the implications. Did they run in packs or something?

"But Luke didn't force me to give anything I didn't want to give. He even stopped when I screamed for him to do so."

Marc closed his eyes a moment and sighed. When he opened them again, he took on a patient demeanor, as if teaching a child. She should find that very offensive, shouldn't she?

"Being submissive doesn't mean you need or want to be taken by force. It might be a fantasy you want acted out, but isn't a requirement. The Dom/sub relationship actually is consensual to the extreme. You would discuss which acts you will—and will not—be experiencing with your Dom or Top in advance of a scene. You'll discuss the limits you're willing to allow in a scene."

He paused. Waiting.

Submissive? Why couldn't she get beyond that word? Bottom didn't sound much better. Marc couldn't be right. Could he? She looked back at him. He seemed to be waiting for her to catch up with him.

"Your sexual release can be heightened when you are with the right Dom."

"I don't want another Dom."

"I don't think you've ever had an authentic Dom. I think you were with someone who used BDSM to mask his abusive nature."

She couldn't explain to him what happened with Allen, not only because of the embarrassment of putting herself in such a position, but because it would just add fuel to the fire. She had a feeling Marc was ready to beat Allen to a pulp. Knowledge of what happened in Denver would put him over the top.

Marc seemed to come to some decision. "Go to the bathroom and wash your pussy, thoroughly dry yourself, and come back here and lie on the bed."

Where was he going with this? If this was his idea of a great way to get this woman into bed, he wasn't as sexy as she thought. He waited for her to move, rather than guiding or forcing her to do so.

Okay, fine. She'd humor him then prove him wrong. She went to the bathroom and did as he'd ord…no, *suggested*, before coming back into the bedroom and plopping onto the edge of the bed, sitting upright.

"I said lie down."

His tone let her know he was displeased with her. Now why did that cause her stomach to knot? "Sorry." Wanting to get beyond this silly demonstration, experiment, or whatever it was—and certainly *not* because she was submissive—she did as he instructed. Scooting to the middle of the bed, she reclined and waited for him to join her.

"Open for me, *cara*."

Not knowing exactly what he wanted her to open, she gave him a quizzical expression until his gaze went pointedly to her legs, which tingled as if he'd touched them. She raised her knees with some hesitation but spread her legs open for him, as if she no longer had control over them.

Marc pulled the hem of her skirt up over her knees, her thighs, her hips. Heat suffused her face. She wasn't used to being so exposed. His fingers touched her pussy as if inspecting her. "Good girl."

She hated how her body responded to his praise as if she was a dog, and he had just pet her on the top of the head for bringing him his newspaper or something. If she could wag her tail, she would. She stifled a giggle.

Before she could anticipate what would happen next, he lay down beside her—fully clothed, as she was. Well, more or less. Feeling exposed, she pulled her legs back together.

"I did not say you could move your legs."

Her heart pounded, and her knees fell open again as if pulled by invisible marionette strings. Okay, that was just weird. Why didn't he make a move? She waited for him to touch her or to tell her where he wanted her to touch him, but he simply propped himself up on his elbow and looked down at her, staring at her face. After a few moments of scrutiny, she began to squirm.

"You are such a beautiful woman. *Bellissima*."

Angelina looked away, uncomfortable with his words. For whatever reason, Marc and Luke hadn't noticed her more-than-ample pounds or that she didn't have…

"Do not contradict me, pet."

Her gaze flew back to his, her heart pounding in her ears. He wasn't happy with her. "I didn't say…"

"You didn't have to speak. Your body is very expressive, especially your eyes." His finger stroked her face from temple to chin. "If a man says you are beautiful, *cara*, what gives you the right to disagree with him?"

"I don't know what you mean."

"Since we were at the bar Friday night, you have made faces every time Luke or I complimented your beauty, your body, your breasts. You have, in effect, called us liars."

She propped herself up on her elbows. "No! I didn't mean to…"

"Lie down, unless I tell you to move."

Her stomach quivered at his firm tone and she plopped back down onto the mattress. He reached out and brushed the hair away from her face. "*Cara*, believe me when I say that a man could become lost in your eyes and never wish to be found again. Your gorgeous breasts fill my hand and are so damned responsive to my touch." To demonstrate, he cupped her breast, brushing his thumb over her nipple, which sprang to life. "You have the most delicious curves," he continued, letting his hand roam over her waist to her well-padded hip. "I could spend a lifetime worshiping your body and never grow tired."

Tears burned the backs of her eyes. She couldn't express how his words made her feel. Marc and Luke both appreciated her just the way she was, extra pounds and all. So what if they weren't the norm in American culture. They both wanted her. A tear trickled from her eye and made its way to her ear.

When Marc lowered his head toward hers, she closed her eyes, expecting his kiss. Instead, his tongue followed the path of her tear, as if to take her hurt away. He pulled back and she opened her eyes to meet his gaze. After scrutinizing her long enough to make her squirm again, he lowered his face toward hers once more and she closed her eyes, waiting for him to kiss her. Nothing. She opened her eyes and found he hovered just above her face, his gaze boring into hers.

"What is it you need, *cara*?" he whispered.

She forced her body to relax, even though he was invading her personal space—and not in a comfortable way. "Nothing. I just thought…you…" She wasn't used to expressing her wants or needs. "I just thought you were going to kiss me."

"What is it you need?" he repeated. "If you aren't submissive, tell me what it is you do need. What you want even."

Well, for one thing, she didn't want to be called a submissive. What was he trying to prove with this demonstration? Or had it even started? All they were doing was talking. Maybe he was waiting for her to take the initiative. Well, she could do that. Reaching up, she put her hand behind the back of his head and pulled him toward her again. Her tongue pressed against his closed mouth, trying to force him to open his lips to let her gain entrance. At first, he refused, just as her angel-man-wolf had done.

Eager to show him just how assertive she could be, she pressed harder until at last he opened for her. She entangled her tongue with his. After what seemed forever, his tongue answered hers, stroke for stroke. She fanned her fingertips down his neck and across his shoulders. His muscles strained against his shirt. What would he look like naked?

His hand returned to her breast, gently massaging the flesh through her blouse. *Pull my nipples again, Marc.* But he didn't read her mind and she waited in vain. Hoping to show him the needs she couldn't express verbally, she reached out and pinched his nipple, feeling the hard pebble through his shirt become even harder. Yet he continued to touch her breasts in an almost reverent way. This so was not what she wanted or needed.

Frustrated, she decided to turn up the heat. Her hand strayed down to his pants, boldly taking hold of the erect penis straining against his zipper. *Mio Dio!* His size filled her hand, heat emanating from the rigid member. He wanted her. She felt emboldened.

But he took her hand and placed it at her side. "Keep your hand here if you don't want this demonstration to go further than you need it to."

How could he know what she needed? Maybe she needed to have him make love to her. Wasn't that where this was leading? Uncertain, she pulled back just as Marc's hand moved from her breast across her abdomen, stroking her gently along the way. Nervous, she couldn't keep her knees from jerking toward her abdomen at the ticklish sensations his touch brought.

Oh, no. He'd told her not to move. But who died and made him a god? Besides, the movement was involuntary.

He grinned and her abdomen melted like jelly. "Your ticklishness might create some...interesting results."

She didn't want to think about what that meant.

"Lower your legs, pet."

And why did he keep calling her pet? The word sounded so...demeaning. So why did her stomach quiver every time he said it? When she did as ordered, her gaze never leaving his, Marc's fingers delved between her outer pussy lips, making it obvious she wasn't wet the way she'd been with Luke. He guided her knee outward, opening her more fully to his touch, but meeting resistance at the dry opening of her vagina. His hand stilled.

Embarrassed, she pushed him away and turned her face from his. "Maybe it's too soon," she said, hoping he wouldn't be disappointed in her.

Even when she played with herself, once a day was about as often as she'd been interested.

He laughed quietly. "My pet, I assure you, a woman as responsive as you are is capable of multiple orgasms in a very short time. Do you want me to tell you what is wrong, *cara*?"

No, the last thing I want to hear is that I'm sexually repressed or, even worse, a sexual deviant who needs pain to get off.

But earlier, on the sofa, she'd have begged to be filled with Luke's penis. Now, she didn't feel ready to make that step with Marc. Maybe she could only respond to Luke. Or did she need both of them loving her at the same time to achieve an orgasm?

Or, yet another possibility was that she needed to be restrained, whether with imaginary bindings or real ones? Damn it, she'd thought she'd finally hit her sexual stride on that sofa, only to stumble again in bed with Marc. Well, a threesome wasn't an option for this Italian Catholic girl.

She tried to push herself up to avoid this discussion and what she was sure would be a litany of her shortcomings. She'd just have to be content with the memory of her solitary orgasm.

"Lie down, pet." The authoritative way he spoke to her ended her retreat from the bed, but she remained upright.

"Look, you've had your fun. This demonstration is over."

"Oh, no, pet. The demonstration has only begun." He paused. "I…said…lie…down."

Chapter Ten

Angelina looked at Marc, who waited patiently on the bed for her to obey his order.

"Lie. Down. Now."

His calmly spoken, yet firm, command set off a flurry of butterflies in her stomach and increased her pulse exponentially each time he repeated it. She eased back onto the bed. Her gaze never broke contact with his. Determined to show him how submissive she was not, she refused to give him the downcast gaze of a doormat. Of a submissive.

Marc took her wrists and held them above her head with one hand, sending an immediate jolt of electricity to rejuvenate her clit.

Mio Dio! He hadn't even touched her there and already her body had responded just by having her hands restrained by him. *No!* She was *not* interested in being his submissive! Even while her mind screamed the denial, signals to the contrary pulsed through her body.

He lowered his mouth to her right breast and she closed her eyes as he took her nipple between his teeth and bit her through the cotton peasant blouse, tugging her nipple to the point of pain. Her knees bucked up as her pussy contracted.

Oh, God, yes!

Looking down at the top of Marc's head, his short black curls caused an image to flash before her eyes of her dream lover holding her safely in his arms—with a wooden St. Andrew's cross visible out of the corner of her eye so like the one she'd been tortured on. Marc raised his head and met her gaze and smiled, pinching her nipple. His jawline and mouth looked so much like…

Oh, *Dio*, no!

What if those images were some kind of premonition? If so, then that was a dream she never wanted to come true. She did not want to be strapped to his or anyone else's whipping post. Her body began to shake and Marc grew serious as he stretched out again, pulling her against him, holding her down with his arm across her abdomen, his leg over her thighs.

"Stay with me, pet. Tell me what's going through that busy mind of yours."

She shook her head, too embarrassed.

"I can't meet your needs if you don't talk to me. Now, answer me."

No!

Talk to him.

Angelina looked away as the two sides of her brain dueled for supremacy just as hard as Marc battled to dominate her body. She tried in vain to sort out the confusing messages her mind and body sent. His finger crooked around her chin, forcing her to face him again.

"Don't shut me out, pet."

Angelina opened her eyes. She did not want to react sexually to pain, even minor pain. Allen had made her feel like a freak at that BDSM club. She'd suffered the physical effects from the beating for days—and still fought the emotional ones from having her trust shattered. Marc said she'd even had a nightmare earlier, probably stemming from that incident, if not the attack last night.

Did she want to be demeaned by such labels as pet? To be convinced she was a pain slut, as Allen had called her? She groaned.

"Now what are you thinking, little one?"

Angelina shook her head. She couldn't speak the words. Some thoughts were best kept private, or he'd think she *was* some kind of freak. Lord, maybe he already did. Maybe he was into pain freaks. But he hadn't seemed interested in whips. That was something at least. Still she didn't want to be his…

"Talk to me, *cara*. I have a feeling your mind is conjuring up half-truths at best. Ask me questions. What do you want to know about submission?"

"I came for Luke and he didn't hurt me."

"Submission isn't about pain. It's about training your mind and body to surrender authority to a Dom who wants to meet your needs and protect you. For tonight only, I am that Dom."

Did he have someone else? Why hadn't she asked before? "Are you married?"

He threw his head back and laughed. "No, pet. I'm not the marrying type. Not even dating anyone at the moment."

Then why would he want to be her Dom for only one tonight? *Wait!* He was confusing her. She didn't want a Dom for even one night.

Her mind latched onto what else he'd said. Training. On the drive home from Denver last month, the club's singer, Karla, had told Angelina how desperate she was to get the owner, Master Adam, to notice her.

"Master Damián trains unattached submissives at the club to please the Doms," Karla said. *"I'm thinking about asking him to train me."*

"Why not just ask Master Adam to 'train' you to be what he wants?"

When an immediate response wasn't forthcoming, Angelina glanced across the car seat at the woman driving the SUV. Karla bit the corner of her lower lip.

"I'm afraid I might not be submissive." She spoke barely above a whisper. *"I don't want to disappoint him or embarrass myself. If I can't be a submissive, then I'll never attract his attention."*

Karla's voice had broken, probably along with a piece of the young woman's heart. Angelina wondered where love entered into a BDSM relationship. So what if Karla wasn't submissive? Couldn't the club's owner find her attractive anyway? Why couldn't they just have a normal sex life, without the dominance and submission stuff?

Angelina felt so sorry for the woman. She had it bad for someone who didn't even know she existed unless she could fit into the cookie-cutter shape of a submissive. Karla could have this crazy stuff if she was that desperate to have her man, but Angelina would never let anyone restrain her or beat on her again.

Anxious to put distance between them, she pushed him away, surprised that he let her up without resistance. She bolted upright and stood in one motion, feeling dizzy for a moment, but moved a few feet away before turning to face him as he rose to sit on the edge of the bed and sighed.

"I won't be anyone's submissive, Marc." When he only smiled back, she screamed, "I am not your pet! And I most certainly am not anyone's pain slut!"

He spoke calmly, not letting his voice rise with emotion as hers had. "*Cara*, are you trying to convince me…or yourself?"

He got up from the bed and came to stand a few feet in front of her. "You are spending too much time in your head, ignoring the needs of your body, blocking your body from feeling anything. Someone hurt you, Angelina, but I am not that man." He came closer to her, towering over her as he rubbed warmth into her cold arms.

"If I promise you I will not cause you pain, will you let me show you how your body responds to dominance?"

She remembered back to when she'd tried and failed to seduce him on her bed only minutes ago. No response from her body at all, and not for a lack of attraction. She found him very sexy, but she'd been too busy trying to figure out how to please him—trying to get him excited—to pay attention to her body's wants and needs.

No flames ignited. Not even a flicker.

Because you were too busy trying to analyze it in your head, Angie.

Oh, God. She had been, hadn't she? Then he'd restrained her arms, bit her nipple, and… Dear Lord. Just thinking about the scene sent her clit into spasms again. Was she a pain freak?

Wait. He said he could show her if she was submissive without pain. Maybe she should at least give him a chance to try. Under her terms.

"No restraints."

He smiled, as if he'd won some victory. "No restraints—as long as you obey me."

Obey? The seemingly minor clarification sounded like semantics, but just what commands did he plan to deliver?

She had two other criteria. "No pain, no humiliation." She felt like she was ordering a sundae—double scoop vanilla, peanuts, no sprinkles, please.

Only this kind of sex wasn't vanilla—and it was all about the sprinkles.

He grew serious. "Let's clarify pain."

"What is there to clarify? Pain is pain."

"When I bit your nipple a moment ago, was that painful? Be truthful."

Her face grew warm at the memory and her body responded to the sensory memory. *Oh, yes. It had hurt—hurt so good.*

"No. It…it excited me."

"Good girl. Thank you for your honesty." She felt her stomach turn to mush at his praise. "Now, let's get started." She had a feeling he was afraid she would change her mind—a valid concern, given how shaky her resolve was at the moment.

"I'm going to gather some items we'll need for our scene. This might be a good time for you to take care of any bathroom needs you have. You're going to be tied up for a while." When she flinched, he added, "*Figuratively* speaking, pet. Don't worry. I take your trust very seriously." His hand reached out and stroked her face, causing her insides to quiver.

"Now listen carefully, pet." His smile faded. How did he switch from gentle to authoritarian mode so seamlessly? Dom mode. "When I return, I want you kneeling on the floor." He walked over to the bed and took one of her pillows, placing it on the floor about two feet from the bed. "Here," he said, pointing to the pillow. "Back straight. Head down. Hands clasped behind your back. Facing the bed. Completely naked. Is that clear?"

"Ye—." The word didn't quite make it past the lump in her throat. She cleared it and tried again. "Yes." Would she remember all of his instructions?

"During this scene, you will refer to me as Sir."

She swallowed down the uprush of fear at the thought of being naked and vulnerable before him. Could she submit to him? It wasn't as if he hadn't already seen and touched her girly bits. But she'd still had on her clothing then, and she hadn't given up control. Well, not entirely.

But, truth be told, what she felt wasn't fear alone. His words excited her more than when he'd touched or bitten her. She swallowed hard.

"Yes, Sir."

He smiled, satisfied with her response.

Dear Lord, what had she just agreed to?

* * *

After watching Angelina walk into the bathroom through the closet—a bizarre architectural concept, to say the least—Marc crossed the short distance to the closet himself and searched for…*ah, yes. Perfetto.* He chose a wide satin sash and pulled down a few other cloth belts from the rack, in case he needed them later. Her being so ticklish might present a problem. One last check, but he didn't see anything else he could use.

Too bad he hadn't thought to pack his toy bag while he was in Denver yesterday afternoon, but he hadn't expected things to progress to this level with Luke in tow. He tamped down the momentary rearing of his conscience. This wasn't about sex. This was strictly about control and giving Angelina a lesson in how a Dom should treat her, should she ever dip her toe into BDSM waters again.

She needed him now, so he'd just have to improvise for this sensation-play scene. Quickly. She would feel vulnerable as she knelt waiting for him to return. *If* she knelt. He wasn't completely certain she'd submit to him yet. While he wanted her to wait long enough to begin to surrender some of that tight grip she had on her control, if he waited too long, she would get too deep into her mind again and talk herself out of going through with the scene.

What else could he use? There should be plenty of implements in the kitchen. She was a chef, for God's sake. He left the bedroom and headed down the hallway and found Luke asleep in the chair where he'd left him.

Marc shook his head. What his friend really needed was a wake-up call. If they managed to get her to Denver, would Luke come to his senses?

With Asshole lurking in the shadows, surely Marc could convince her she'd be safer at his house in Denver—for her own protection, of course—until the threat of Sir Asshole died down. His place was much larger than Luke's, had a security system, and would give Angelina her own living quarters. Marc's house had nothing but space. What would it be like to share it with someone—even a house guest? The only people who'd ever shared it were his brother and sister, Sandro and Carmella, on their forays into Denver to market the resort at various trade shows.

Marc heard a buzzing sound and walked around the sofa to look for the source. The purse Angelina had carried last night had vibrated off the table top onto the floor. When he bent down to retrieve it, he spied an antique sewing basket under the small table. It reminded him of his grandmother's basket.

He grinned, knowing just what he was looking for when he opened the lid. He lifted a neatly rolled, but frayed, tape measure and a scrap of green fabric out of the way and there it lay. Filigreed silver handle. Whoever owned this one had been a serious seamstress. Judging by its age, he surmised the tool was a family heirloom. Her Nonna's?

Forgive me, dear Angelina's Nonna, but she needs this for another purpose tonight.

He lifted the pattern-tracing wheel out of the basket and ran it along the back of his hand. The tool had fascinated him as a young boy in Italy in his own Nonna's sewing basket. The teardrop handle of this one fit well in the palm of his hand, its weight perfect. Oh, yes. This would do nicely in place of his Wartenberg wheel.

Marc went into the kitchen to grab a bowl and to take some ice from the freezer. Turning, he saw something he'd forgotten about and picked it up. Smiling, he carried his cache into the living room. When the phone buzzed again, he picked up her purse and added it to the items in his hand, then crossed the room toward the hallway. He glanced over at Luke, who snored softly, still sitting upright. Tomorrow, they'd have a talk. Marc intended to find out what was going on in his friend's head—and pound some sense into it if he hurt or disappointed Angelina.

Merda. He'd left her inside her busy head long enough. She'd be wound tighter than a two-dollar watch by now—naked, kneeling, and waiting for him. God help him, his cock throbbed at the image. Dawn was just a few hours away. He needed every bit of his self-control to give her what she needed most during his brief time as her Dom.

Tomorrow, he'd have to step aside for Luke. Marc had enough respect for the hereafter, after many years of catechism lessons about saints and angels, to know you didn't mess with messages like Luke had received in his dream.

Apparently, she'd been sent to Luke, not him.

* * *

Angelina could no longer control the trembling in her body as she waited for Marc to return to her. The air in the chilly bedroom caused her nipples to stand at attention. She'd placed the long strands of her hair over her breasts to cover them, feeling a little less exposed.

But the state of arousal she was in had more to do with imagining what Marc had planned than it did the cold. Kneeling as he had instructed, she hoped, and waiting for so long was doing something very strange to her mind. Anticipation warred with fear for supremacy in her head.

Anticipation had been winning for a while, but fear seemed to be edging it out at the moment. What did he plan to do? Would he keep his promise not to hurt her? He had wanted—no demanded—that she be naked. Kneeling.

Submissive.

Fear reared its deadliest weapon. Could she give up control and do whatever he commanded of her? How could he control her without restraints? She'd thought that would be a deal breaker, but he hadn't batted an eyelash when she'd given her restrictions. Would she be able to surrender her mind and body to him? Could she trust him? For heaven's sake, she'd only met the man Friday night, although it seemed as if she'd known him much longer. She felt so comfortable with him.

Well, comfortable might not be the operative word at the moment.

Mio Dio, what was she doing? She couldn't do this! As she prepared to get up and flee to the bathroom, she heard the doorknob turn. Her heart skittered into a rapid tattoo. Too late to escape! She tried to fill her lungs, but the tightness in her chest made breathing nearly impossible.

"Good girl."

That odd warmth flowed over her again, relaxing her taut nerves. Why did that simple, almost condescending expression set her all aquiver? Knowing she had pleased him made her feel good inside.

She heard him place items on the nightstand and started to turn to see what he was doing.

"I did not say you could move."

His sharp tone froze her in place and she returned her gaze to the rumpled covers in front of her. She'd practically memorized the pattern on the floral comforter. He walked into the bathroom and came back moments later to place something else on the stand; her heart thudded as fear returned.

Marc's legs and the crotch of his pants came into her field of vision as he stood before her and then sat down on the edge of the bed mere inches away. He still wore his black slacks, but had removed his shirt. Keeping her head down as instructed, she allowed her eyes to venture upward to stare at his gorgeous chest. His well-defined pecs were covered in a soft sprinkling of black hair. She longed to touch him, but hadn't been given permission to move. She didn't want to displease him, although she'd think most men would welcome having a woman touch them the way she wanted to.

His abdomen was taut, not an ounce of flab, his waist narrow. Again, she fought the urge to touch, or even lean forward and lick him. Her face grew warm at the thought. She'd never licked a man's abs before. But she'd never seen anything so beautiful in all her life. If he hadn't ordered her to remain on her knees, she'd have stripped him naked and taken his penis into…

Mio Dio. She could feel the wetness between her nether lips. She smiled at the knowledge she wasn't submissive after all. Why, she could get turned on just looking at a man's chest.

"Will you trust me not to hurt you, *cara*?"

She tilted her head back to raise her gaze to his. His expression was serious, but not frightening.

"Did I say you could raise your head?"

Confused, she quickly lowered it again. How many times would he put up with her little mistakes before he put an end to this role-play? His erection strained against his pants, riveting her attention. Apparently, she hadn't caused him to lose interest yet.

"I'm sorry, Sir."

Her mind registered that his hands were held behind his back, but before she could process why that should concern her, he brought his right hand out to reveal what he had hidden.

"No! I don't need that!" Her voice rose an octave, because the sight of the red satin sash she'd worn on her dress last Christmas instilled panic in her. She sat back on her heels to put more space between them.

"Do not move again, pet."

No! She didn't want to be restrained. Not after what happened at the club. Marc had promised. Already he was going back on his word?

Marc's voice remained firm. "Look at me."

She squeezed her eyes shut, trying to regain some sense of control, then opened them again as she raised her gaze to his. Tears welled in her eyes. "Please, Marc," she said on a whisper. "I can't be tied up. Trust me. You don't want to do this."

Something in her tone or expression seemed to get through to him. A shadow crossed his face and he laid the sash on the mattress beside him and reached out to stroke her hair and brush his thumb over her cheek. "Believe me, pet, I do understand." She could almost see the frustration and hurt in his eyes. "Please, trust me."

Angelina relaxed a bit. Even though she had known Allen many months longer than Marc and thought she could trust him, Marc seemed different. Of course, she'd read enough books to know one of the cardinal rules of bondage was to never let someone tie you up unless you trusted them completely. She wasn't at that level of trust—far from it.

Why couldn't they just have hot sex like a normal couple?

"Come." He stood and placed his hands at her elbows to help lift her to her feet.

"Oh!" When she swayed on legs left wobbly from kneeling so long, he steadied her and helped her to step off the pillow, which he kicked aside.

He moved his hands to her upper arms and gazed down at her. "I haven't gone back on any promise to you. I said I wouldn't use restraints if you cooperated and you have done everything I've asked. I am well pleased."

Pride swelled inside her. She'd pleased him, even though she'd forgotten herself a couple of times. Like now! Was she supposed to be looking up at him? She lowered her head, in part so he wouldn't see her tears, which now spilled onto her bare breasts.

He took her chin and lifted her gaze to his again as he gently wiped the tears from her cheeks. "First, let's work some more on trust. We're going to try something called honor bondage."

Angelina had heard of honor killing. Somehow that correlation didn't give her peace of mind.

Marc turned her sideways, took a step away from the bed, and extended his hand toward her. "Give me your hands."

Her heart fluttered, taking her breath away. Angelina stared back at him for the longest time, but her feet remained glued to the floor, her hands at her sides. She wasn't ready for this. Was she? Her body began to shake.

Oh, dear Lord, help me.

She couldn't go through with this.

Chapter Eleven

Marc couldn't resist reaching out to cup her breasts, brushing his thumbs across her nipples. His cock throbbed as the peaks became more erect. *Focus, man.* He leaned down to whisper in her ear, "Trust me, *bella*."

She closed her eyes and nodded, taking a deep breath. "I'm trying."

"I know you are, *cara*. Thank you."

Marc felt her tremble, whether from fear or excitement, he didn't know. Probably a little of each. He bent down and kissed her on her uninjured cheek, his hands brushing up and down her upper arms trying to infuse warmth into her cold limbs. Fight-or-flight reaction? She didn't try to escape his touch, so she definitely had decided to stay. Now the question was whether she'd stayed to fight.

If she would let herself experience the sensations he'd planned for the scene without letting fear consume her, she'd find it sexy as hell. Overcoming those fears and seeing they were unwarranted would help deepen her trust in him. He didn't want to think about why that was so important to him, given they only had this *one* night.

Truth to tell, he looked forward to experiencing the scene with her, more than he'd looked forward to anything in a long while. The woman brought out feelings deeper than any he'd ever felt before.

Marc chose not to explore those feelings at the moment. He reached down to pick up the sash, hating to see her begin shaking again. Definitely fear this time. He damned Sir Asshole to hell and back for making her feel such fear, because Marc didn't think she'd been fearful before the flogging last month. The BDSM lifestyle had piqued her curiosity if she'd agreed to go to a club. His job was to restore that curiosity and allow her to embrace the submissive trapped inside.

"I promised not to hurt you. Correct?" She hesitated for what seemed an eternity then nodded slowly. "Good girl. Now, one of the best ways to heighten your senses is to deprive you of the one you need the least." He took the wide red sash into both hands and stretched it in front of her. "This blindfold will intensify the sensation play."

Panic flashed from her eyes. "I don't think I can..."

"No more thinking, *bella*. From now on, you will only feel. It will be my job to do the thinking."

Knowing he needed to get this scene moving before she went into a full-blown panic attack, he walked around behind her and tied the sash around her head, covering her eyes, being careful not to pull too tightly because of her blackened eye and bruised cheek. *Asshole bastard.*

Marc took a breath to regain control of his anger and relaxed his fists as he reached for her arm. "You'll be amazed how much more intense your experience will be when you don't know what's coming next or exactly what is being done to you." He guided her onto the edge of the bed, then instructed, "Crawl onto the bed directly in front of you and lie on your back."

She held her hand out, as if not certain there truly was a bed in front of her. *Trust me.* But she did as he told her and he smiled. Her beautiful breasts begged to be touched again, but Marc held back. His heart hammered as adrenaline began pumping through him. He loved setting up and executing the perfect scene for a sub, and this was just what Angelina needed.

He knew how hard it was for her to trust him after Asshole had violated her the way he had. That she was willing to put herself in his hands, to place her trust in him, broke something loose in his heart.

Focus.

"With honor bondage, it is *I* who will have to trust you. Give me both of your hands, *amore.*"

He froze. *Love?* Why had he used that term of endearment? She wasn't his love. He'd do well to keep his emotions in check, as he would with any unattached submissive he was training at the club.

Marc's cock hardened as she lifted her hands toward him. Could this little sub be getting under his thick and scarred skin? He shook off the ridiculous notion. She merely needed him to help her overcome her aversion to the lifestyle and he wanted to get her to recognize and embrace her beautifully submissive sexual nature. Neither of them was looking for commitment. Even if she wasn't Luke's, just like all the women before her, he'd grow bored—or scared—in time. He always did, about the time she demanded more of him than he was able to give.

Melissa had caused him to lose control; Pamela had demanded more than he could give. He needed to be in control—of his body, his mind, his emotions. Most of all, of his life.

Anxious to exert his control right now, he said, "You will keep your hands where I place them, pet." With that, he took her hands and brought them to the intricate heart-shaped design of the Italian iron headboard. *Dio*, he loved that she had a bed tailor-made for bondage scenes.

"Hold onto the bed, here," he placed her left hand on the cold iron, "and here." She wrapped her fingers around the iron design where he had spaced her hands, about six or seven inches apart, over her head. When she released a pent-up breath, he grinned. She was strung tighter than a loaded crossbow.

Marc trailed his fingertip down the underside of her right arm, raising gooseflesh along his path. Her tiny gasp as he tickled her made him smile, but her knuckles turned white as she held on for dear life.

"Very good, pet."

Her chest rose, as if reaching out to him, begging him to touch her breasts. He didn't, but grinned at her neediness before his smile faded. *Not yours.* "You agreed that I could use restraints on you if you do not obey me. If you let go of the headboard, I *will* use sashes or belts to restrain you."

The pulse in her neck thrummed. She nodded her head. She'd find honor bondage preferable to physical restraints. His gut twisted as he remembered finding her bound and struggling on the cross at Masters at Arms.

Trust me, little sub. I won't let that happen to you ever again.

"If you want us to stop at any time, you will say 'red,' your safeword. If you say it, we stop and that's the end of the scene. Do you understand?"

Angelina nodded. "Yes, Sir."

She wouldn't need it for the sensation-play scene he had planned, but he wanted to convey she still had power. Without a doubt, she'd spoken her safeword with Sir Asshole, but the bastard had ignored her. Her body tensed. Was she lost in memories of the same scene?

Marc leaned down and whispered in her ear, "Stay with me, pet." He nipped the skin on her neck with his teeth. She whimpered. When he stood again and looked down, her nipples had become engorged. So damned responsive.

Marc stretched her legs open on the bed.

"The same is true for your legs. If you move them without permission, I will have to restrain them. It will be harder for you to control your legs than it is your hands, because they have nothing to hold onto. So beware. I will tie them to the footboard if necessary in order to proceed with this scene. The choice is yours."

* * *

Angelina held her breath. Choice? She had choice left?

Total darkness. Just like at the club. When she did remember to breathe, her breath hitched. *Marc isn't Allen. He wants to bring you pleasure. You can trust him. Marc isn't Allen...* The affirmations did little to steady her accelerating heartbeat and shallow breathing.

"Relax, *gattina*." Marc's lips brushed against her ear, his scratchy whiskers sending sparks throughout her body. "Remember, you need only say 'Red'—like the traffic light—and I will stop. But this isn't a pain session, pet. Only pleasure."

You can trust him.

"Are you okay to continue?"

Marc isn't Allen.

"*Cara*, answer me."

She took a deep breath. What was the question? She drew her lower lip between her teeth. What should she say?

"I asked if you're okay to continue?"

Oh, thank you, Sir! She nodded and said, "Yes, Sir." Now, she'd better stop letting her mind wander. Thankfully, he'd left her legs free.

He kissed her cheek, his whiskers scratching the curve of her neck. "I'm proud of you, pet. I know how hard this is for you."

His praise spread over her like warm honey. He didn't know the half of why she was freaking out, but he seemed very aware of her anxiety level and always brought her back down.

Back to him.

"Now, you will not argue with or disobey me. That will never be tolerated when we...when you are in a scene with a Dom."

Who me? Argue?

He never referred to anything beyond tonight. This was merely a training session, like Karla had said one of the masters at the club did with unattached bottoms and submissives. What if she did disobey him? Would she be punished, even though he wasn't her real Dom? Dread knotted her stomach. How? Spanking? Belt? Worse? She didn't want to incur any type of punishment, so she would definitely obey.

"Do you understand?"

"Yes, Sir."

"Good girl. Now I need to get to work so you won't wander off in your mind so often. Also, it would be best if you spoke only when given permission or if you need to use your safeword. Is that clear?"

"Y—" she stopped herself before it was too late and nodded her head instead.

"Excellent." Marc tweaked her nipple, causing her to suck in a breath as she felt blood rush to the sensitive peak. The heat in the pit of her stomach spread lower. Marc chuckled. "I love to watch your body respond to my touch, pet."

She wasn't sure what happened to turn on her body's sexual circuitry all of a sudden, but now she just wanted to bask in the light.

"I love seeing you stretched out for me, too. So beautiful."

Lying this way, as if tied, and wearing only the blindfold sent a thrill through her body. Even though he didn't touch her, she could almost feel his hands on her. With her hands stretched above her head, she imagined her girls were lifted and almost perky. She smiled, less concerned about how she looked and beginning to anticipate his lesson or demonstration or whatever this was with a little more enthusiasm now.

Marc's lips brushed her right ear. "That's right. Relax, *cara*." Marc's scruff abraded her cheek and ear in the most sensual way. Heat pooled in her core and she tilted her pelvis toward him, begging for his touch.

"Lift your hips."

Trying to keep her legs where he had positioned them made it impossible to do as he told her very easily, but she raised them as much as she could. His strong hand lifted her higher and he slid a pillow under her butt, leaving her pussy exposed even more. Her heart began to beat faster and her tongue licked across suddenly parched lips.

She felt the mattress sink under his weight then he straddled her hips and bent his upper body over hers. One hand cupped her left breast, teasing her nipple, while he brought his mouth down to her right nipple and suckled. Heat from his body enveloped her, the hairs from his chest tickling the skin on her torso and abdomen. He tugged on her nipple with his teeth, stretching her breast to the limits of comfort, and then let the tender peak go so that her breast bounced back into place. He repeated the motion again and yet again, just as he had done with his fingers on the sofa last night.

"I love your breasts, pet."

Gee, I hadn't noticed.

He gave her swollen bud another nip with his teeth, then, with a sigh, sat up again. His hand skimmed over her abdomen, just barely brushing the tiny body hairs and sending gooseflesh over her entire body. When his hand brushed lower, she pulled her knees up to protect her pussy in an instinctively defensive move. If he weren't sitting lightly on her thighs, she'd have disobeyed him.

"Ticklish there, are we?"

Her face flushed as she nodded.

He sighed. That didn't sound good. "Pet, I'm sorry, but more than likely, I am going to need to restrain your legs."

"No! I'll keep them down this time."

"I did not give you permission to speak, did I?"

Frustrated, she groaned and shook her head.

"If you defy my commands, I will gag you, as well."

She shook her head vigorously. Not that! How would she speak her safeword if she were gagged?

"Don't worry, *gattina*." His voice grew gentle again, as if he smiled. "When I...when your Dom introduces you to the gag, you'll be given a safe gesture to use instead of a word."

How did he always know what she was thinking?

"You aren't ready for that step, so if you simply do as I say, we can dispense with that tonight. But this is your last warning on both counts."

No leg restraints. No gag. And just what did he do, travel around with ball gags on him? Or would he improvise? She forced herself to relax her tensed muscles and sank back against the mattress and pillows. Marc moved off of her hips, stretching out beside her, and returned his finger to just below her breast where he began trailing it down across her abdomen. When he came close to her mons, her legs bolted up. *Oh, no!* How could she control the damned reflex if he kept tickling her like that?

Without a word, Marc got off the mattress and she heard his footsteps heading toward the nightstand. She grew tense once more as he took one of her ankles and she felt the coolness of satin or some other cloth quickly warm against her skin. He tied the sash or belt around her ankle then pulled her leg open wider than she thought comfortably possible. When he had secured her binding to the footboard, she tested her range of motion and found it to be less limiting than she'd expected. He really was trying not to scare the bejeezers out of her.

So sweet of you, Marc...er, Sir.

At least her hands were still free. She didn't feel as vulnerable knowing she could at least inflict some serious damage with her hands, not unlike what she'd done to Allen earlier tonight, if Marc so much as...

"Relax your leg."

She didn't realize she'd tensed up again and did as he ordered. After he attached another cloth belt to her ankle and restrained that leg, she felt his fingers slide between the sash and her ankle on each side as if testing the tightness. The mattress sagged under his weight on her right side moments later.

"Nod or shake your head. Are you okay with the restraints?"

She nodded.

"I'm proud of you, *cara*. You're being very brave."

Brave? He was only the second person to tell her that in her entire life—and the first one was a figment of her imagination. Before her mind could process his praise, his hand glided down the inside of her right thigh to her knee, causing chill bumps to rise in its wake. When he began a slow, upward advance toward her pussy, she held her breath. *Please, don't!*

Don't stop!

Pent-up tension built to fever pitch. Even though he had yet to touch her clit, the needy bit throbbed, waiting to welcome him. She'd been anticipating his touch for so long while kneeling on the floor that now when she was so close to—something she couldn't even name—the sensations were nearing torture. She would come at the slightest pressure against the place where she needed him most. She tilted her hips, begging silently. *Now! Please!*

Nothing. The hand touching her thigh left her. She arched her back, raising her chest toward him, hoping he would touch her nipples again. Bite them. Touch or bite her anywhere. Instead he got off the bed again and she ached at the loss.

Two days ago, if someone had told her she'd be tied to her bed—or half tied, in this case—craving a man's touch like this, she'd have told them they were delusional. When had she become so depraved? So wanton?

Dear God, she'd become a wanton woman.

No, a wanting woman. And what she wanted more than anything in the world, even chocolate, was Marc's touch. Where had he gone anyway? What was he doing? He climbed back onto the bed and his weight pressed into the mattress near her right leg. She relaxed her contracted muscles and smiled. It was a short-lived reprieve because, rather than feel his hands or mouth on her body, what felt like cold sharp steel traced lightly over the skin from her left sole, causing her to squirm at the ticklish, yet prickly, feeling. She heard a slight squeak, as if it were a wheel of some type, tracing a path from her ankle to the inside of her knee. Sharp, but not breaking the skin, although it probably could cut her if he exerted enough pressure.

She sucked in a gasp of air and held still, holding her breath, not wanting to be cut by whatever he was using. The pinpricks rolled up the insides of her knees, her thighs. Oh, God, not her pussy! She tried to close her legs against the invasion, but couldn't move them.

Exposed. Vulnerable. Restrained.

She couldn't stand the bite of that thing against her clit. Could she? Then the wheel rolled along the uppermost ridge of her hipbone and onto her abdomen. Her legs reflexively fought the restraints, but she was unable to defend against his ticklish onslaught. She gripped the headboard tighter, trying not to break into screams—or giggles. He rolled the damned thing lower, toward her mons, and she nearly came undone.

Mind over matter. In her mind, she prepared the batter for an Italian cream cake. After adding the first few ingredients, she was able to control her response to the ticklish stimuli.

"Very good, *cara*."

Warmth spread over her, then the wheel marked new territory again as it traveled upward. The ticklish sensation gave way to a more biting pressure as the wheel rolled around the edge of her right breast where it met her chest wall.

A finger from his other hand brushed the inside of her knee and moved upward, bypassing her pussy, as well. She moaned in frustration. His fingertip skimmed lightly over her hip, across her abdomen, unerringly along the same path the steel object had traced seconds ago, as if following a pattern across her skin. Was the instrument marking a path on her skin in some way?

The pinpricks skittered across the underside of her left breast and traveled over the space between her girls then onto the top of her right one, circling around the base of the breast and back to the other one. He was making repeated figure eights. Her nipples tightened, aching and waiting.

Please! Touch me there!

His fingertip traced the same figure eight around her breasts before returning the metal instrument to her skin again. This time, it came close to pricking one areola. Thankfully, the area wasn't as sensitive as other parts of her breast. Then the pricking spiraled closer and closer to one sensitive peak and she felt the bud rise up to meet the steel instrument, without even being touched directly. What was that about?

The steel was replaced by his warm mouth as Marc flicked his tongue over first one nipple, then the other. He blew air onto her nipple and it stiffened as the cool air kissed her wet bud. Angelina felt his soft lips almost reverently pull her nipple into his hot mouth again, just before the sharp-edged steel rolled over her other nipple, harder.

Angelina's lungs burned from the lack of oxygen, but she was afraid to breathe for fear of being cut. How could he do two things at once? The difference in the sensations between his soft, warm mouth on one nipple and the sharp, cold steel on the other caused her clit to spasm. Her hips strained upward, even though she cringed mentally at the thought of his using that sharp instrument on her more sensitive bits. She wouldn't be able to stand pain like that.

Would she?

Angelina had her safeword. Of course, she could let go of the bed at any time and remove the object before it did any harm. She hadn't agreed to cutting and no way could that touch her tender nubbin without cutting. But he hadn't broken her skin. Yet. She would wait and see what happened next before bailing out.

A niggling doubt plagued her. If she used her safeword, would he honor it? Should she test him? No. He said he'd end the scene immediately and, at the moment, the delicious sensations rampaging through her body made it clear she had no desire to end this anytime soon.

She was pulled out of her thoughts when the sharp instrument rolled over her nipple again. Surprised, her chest arched upward—toward the pain, rather than away—causing the sharp object to press deeply into her sensitive peak.

"Ow!" She cried out against the unexpected pain, then the torture device was gone, replaced with Marc's gentle hand on her breast and his warm tongue laving and flicking at her aching nipple until the pain receded.

Pain.

Pleasure.

She moaned and his mouth left her.

"I'm sorry, *gattina*. That was not intentional."

She whimpered, her self-control gone. How did he turn pain into pleasure so quickly? His words registered that the pain had been accidental.

He'd even apologized for the relatively tiny hurt. Allen had inflicted so much more pain and told her it had just been a misunderstanding on her part.

"Stay with me, pet."

His mouth sucked her tender nipple, but her pussy clenched in response, aching to be filled. She couldn't speak her wishes, but moaned as she tilted her pelvis upward, hoping he would take the hint. He released her nipple and cold air caused her well-loved peak to swell even more.

For a moment, he didn't touch her anywhere. She waited. What next? Her body missed the sensations of his hand, mouth, and even that painful metal device.

At last, he was touching her pussy, spreading her folds open, and exposing her tiny erection to the cool air. *Yes, touch me there!* His finger stroked directly against the sensitive nubbin, spreading something cold on her. He took his hand away. That was all? Why didn't he stroke her more? Help her to come? She could reach an orgasm now and wanted more, damn it.

Suddenly a strange warmth spread through her nubbin, which grew ever warmer, almost to the point of being uncomfortable. What had he just put on her clit? The sensation made her want to beg him to touch her again. Oh, God! She was on fire!

Then cold! What felt like wet ice brushed over her mouth, sending a trickle of water down her cheek and around her ear. Yes, definitely ice. And she smelled mint, which didn't make sense. Marc pressed the melting cube over her chin, gliding it slowly down her throat leaving a trail of cold as the runoff trailed to the back of her neck. He moved the cube at a glacier's pace. Would he ever reach his destination, wherever that was? Then the ice came to rest at the base of her neck, above her collarbone, where he left it to lie and melt, trickling cold water around her neck and to her back.

Her privates were on fire. Her upper body freezing. The mixed signals short-circuited her brain. She shivered, but whether from the cold or her burning clit, she didn't know.

His warm lips brushed over her cold ones causing hers to tingle and warm quickly; he trailed kisses over her chin and down her throat, stopping to press a kiss against her pulse before continuing on until he came to the pool of melted ice at the base of her throat. His tongue lapped at the water in the hollow and then the ice was gone.

His lips, colder now as they moved down her body, avoided her breasts, which confused her. As he reached her abdomen, his legs straddled her again. She could tell he hadn't removed his pants yet. Then all thought fled as his unusually cold lips brushed over her mons, closer and closer to her fiery nubbin.

No! Just as the thought occurred to her that fire and ice don't mix, his frigid tongue licked the hood.

Her hips bucked up on the mattress, then she tried to get away from his mouth, but movement was impossible. "Ohhh! Ohh, God, no!!!" No escape. The disparate temperatures, the sensations, the restraint were all too much, nearly sending her mind over the edge.

She'd spoken—well, screamed was more accurate—but he hadn't reprimanded her. She wouldn't be able to control herself if she tried, though. Maybe he'd make allowances for cries of passion.

Avoiding the most sensitive part of her clit, his tongue slid down to her pussy and he pressed it inside her warm vagina, leaving his tongue there without moving. As the coldness of his tongue disappeared, he flicked his tongue on a path toward her clit. This time, when he laved the area around the hood, his tongue was warmer, but still cooler than her most hidden place because of whatever he had put on her to make it burn.

Unable to remain still, she pressed her pussy toward his tongue. More. Oh, God, she needed more. He gently nipped at her. "Ahhh!" The pit of her stomach tensed as the sensation coursed through her, sending her ever closer to the elusive edge again. How much more could she take before he brought her the release she needed?

Please, Marc! I need you!

When she thought she could almost come without further stimulation, his mouth was gone and his weight shifted. She groaned as if in pain and tensed waiting to see what Marc would do next. She didn't have to wait long. His finger rubbed something cold onto her clit again. Seconds later, it began to warm. Only this time he removed his finger and began spreading even more of the first-cold-then-hot substance between the outer lips. He moved closer to the opening of her pussy. *No way!* Surely he wouldn't put that on her va...

The smell of mint reached her sensitive nose. What on earth was he using? She remembered he'd gone into the front part of the house, but there wasn't anything with mint there. The bathroom. Toothpaste? Who would think of putting toothpaste there?!?

Marc, apparently.

Slowly, heat spread like wildfire throughout her pussy. No longer capable of coherent thought, her head thrashed against the pillow. She was out of her mind with want. Why didn't he at least put his finger inside her? But she wanted more than a finger. She wanted him. Inside her. Now!

"Please don't make me wait any longer, Marc! I want you inside me."

Angelina froze. *Oh, God.* Had she spoken aloud? What would he do now? Tears of frustration filled her eyes. She wished she could see him. Judge his reaction.

Marc left the bed. "Pet, not only did you disobey by speaking, but you also neglected to respect me by calling me Sir. I will give you two choices as a means to help you learn discipline."

Her heart pounded as she waited for him to tell her what those choices were. What could he possibly do to her that wouldn't involve pain? But he'd promised not to hurt her. *If* she obeyed him. She hadn't. As she waited, her mind tried to imagine other punishments. Did Doms use timeouts like she'd had in kindergarten? Spankings, certainly.

Whatever he had put on her continued to burn, making her want Marc's touch more than she'd ever wanted anything. Her hips bucked upward as if with a will of their own. How much longer would he make her wait?

"Your first choice is for me to stop now, untie your legs, and let you go to sleep while I go back to sleep on the sofa."

More tears sprang to her eyes. How could he leave her wanting like this? Didn't good Doms always make sure their subs' needs were met? Well, she needed to come, damn it!

"Your second choice will give you the mind-blowing orgasm you crave—"

Yes, that one!

"—but you must submit to an over-the-knee spanking. Bare ass. Five swats."

Oh, God! No way!

Chapter Twelve

Marc paused, giving her time to process the image of her naked ass high in the air over his knee as he spanked her. Shit, the image was now branded on his brain as well. His cock strained against his zipper, as if he hadn't already been turned on. He'd prided himself in being able to control his body's responses, ever since he'd lost it that night with Melissa just before he'd enlisted. But with this woman, he wasn't sure he could.

He wouldn't be a responsible Dom, even if a short-term one, if he didn't show her there were consequences for a lack of obedience and self-discipline. He had to follow through.

Hopefully, forcing her to choose her own method of discipline—orgasm deprivation or a spanking with an orgasm—she wouldn't compare him to an abusive Dom like Sir Asshole who had left her with no choice. The first option didn't involve pain—well, not the physical kind she feared anyway. Guessing how inexperienced she was with orgasms in the first place, she might be content to just go to sleep and forget about getting off even once tonight. What a pity that would be.

Chances were slim she'd choose the spanking option, which disappointed him even more. Maybe someday she'd see spankings more as funishment than punishment, although another Dom would enjoy that pleasure long after Marc was gone from her life. Still, he was riding her awfully hard for a newbie sub, not cutting her much slack for things she just needed to practice and learn over time.

If she did choose the spanking, though, he couldn't go easy on her. Submission and power exchange meant showing discipline over herself and respect for her Dom. At this point, she wouldn't believe him if he told her she'd probably get off on the spanking. She'd have to experience that for herself. Would she be brave enough to trust him?

But she needed to learn that trust went both ways. If he promised something, he had to deliver on that promise, good or bad.

"Which do you choose, *cara*?"

She took her full lower lip between her teeth and her brow furrowed above the sash covering her eyes. The stain of tears on the red blindfold twisted his gut.

"Pet, your answer. Now." The longer she conjured up images in her mind, the more frightened she would become. Reality would be better than anything she could imagine.

Her chest rose as she inhaled a deep breath. "Please, Sir…," she drew another breath, "I want to come."

Oh, shit. "And?"

Her breathing stopped. "A-a-and to be spanked for speaking when I wasn't supposed to."

Marc's side hurt. He'd been holding his breath, as well. He relaxed his lungs and smiled. "You need to know what you're being punished for so that you won't repeat the bad behavior in the future—with another Dom. What else are you being disciplined for?"

"I called you a name other than Sir…Sir."

Good girl.

"Thank you for trusting me, *cara*."

Now to deliver her lesson without losing that trust. He returned to the bed and began to untie her legs. He didn't explain himself, deciding she wouldn't be able to enjoy herself if consumed by thoughts of her imminent spanking. The woman could hold onto a runaway train of thought, especially one that scared or worried her, longer than any sub he'd ever met.

To her credit, she didn't ask him what he was doing. She'd know soon enough. He released her other leg and went to the head of the bed. "You may let go now."

When she didn't move, he reached out to pry her fingers loose from the stranglehold she had on the headboard. He'd venture a guess she'd forgotten she could have let go at any point. Her mind and body hadn't been able to tell the difference between real restraints and invisible ones. *Good little sub.*

"Now, as your Dom, I need to show you that disobeying me has consequences."

She tensed and opened her mouth to protest, then snapped it closed again. Fast learner. Perhaps they could make even more progress than he'd expected in their short time together.

"In order for a Dom/sub relationship to work, we have to communicate fully and openly with one another. You need to tell me what you are thinking, what you like, what you don't like, what scares you, and so on. So, you are permitted to speak during your spanking. I want to know how it feels, how you are doing. Do you understand?"

She nodded her head.

"Speak."

"Yes, Sir."

"Good girl."

He reached down to push the blindfold off her eyes. She blinked several times to adjust to the light. Her wet eyelashes stuck together from her tears. He didn't usually let a woman's tears affect him, but this woman's did.

Not good.

He helped her sit up and massaged her shoulders where her muscles were tight from holding her hands over her head for so long. She moaned, definitely not in pain. She gathered her hair to one side and lowered her head, giving him easier access. Her beautiful olive skin was bruised from Asshole's attack, and he pulled away, afraid he would hurt her further.

Marc sat on the edge of the bed and motioned for her to climb onto his lap. When she started to crawl face down across him, he took her arms and guided her ass onto his lap. "We need to talk first, pet."

He read confusion on her face. Normally, he'd want to build up a healthy level of trepidation about what was to come, but given her high level of anxiety already, he found himself wanting to talk with her first.

He placed his fingers under her chin and raised her gaze to his. Her chocolate brown eyes were like an abused puppy's, and he felt a moment of disgust with himself for putting that look there.

No, he wouldn't accept that blame. Sir Asshole had put that expression there. Now Marc needed to try and remove it.

"You have asked me to give you five swats with my hand on your bare ass. What are your thoughts about that now?"

She cast her gaze away.

"Look at me, pet."

She met his gaze again and nibbled on her lip, causing his cock to bob against her ass. Her eyes opened wider, as if surprised by his sexual response.

"I know sharing your feelings and thoughts is hard, *cara*, but you must not keep anything from your Dom."

A flash of defiance crossed her face. "You're not my Dom."

Shit, were they back to square one then?

"Careful, pet, or you'll add the appropriate number of additional swats needed to teach you." He could smell the fear in her as her body prepared for fight-or-flight. "For this scene, I am your Dom and you will treat me with the respect a submissive owes her Dom, even in a short-term relationship." She clearly wanted to continue to smart-mouth him, but wisely lowered her gaze instead. "Now, tell me what you think about being disciplined."

Tears welled in her eyes again and her chin quivered, all signs her momentary lapse in judgment was receding. "I am sorry you feel you have to punish me."

"How do you address your Dom?"

Concern crossed her face as she worried about receiving additional swats, but she quickly corrected her gaffe. "Sir! I'm sorry, Sir."

He nodded. "You say you're sorry I have to punish you. But this isn't a punishment. That would be much harsher and for an infraction done willfully, not a mere lack of protocol while you're still learning discipline over your mind and body. Do you understand?" He could almost hear the gears turning in her head.

"I don't think you want to spank me…Sir." she added quickly. "Not as discipline, anyway. I'm sorry to put you in a position where you feel you have to, but I understand you're only doing it so that I can learn."

He was dumbfounded. His chest grew tight before he remembered to breathe. He'd only hoped she'd accept responsibility for needing the spanking, not that she would turn the tables on him and be concerned about his feelings.

Shit. Spanking a woman's ass had always been like foreplay to him. Now he needed to spank this one to help for the very reason she stated—to help her learn to discipline her mind and tongue—but he'd never wanted anything less in his life.

This spanking would be the turning point for them both.

Marc no longer feared she would reject him so much as he feared she'd want him, expecting more in return than he could give any woman. That she'd imprint on him as her Dom the way the Ugly Duckling imprinted on the mama duck in the children's story. Lord love a duck, his mind was addled now. What the fuck was he going to do with her? He needed to put some emotional distance between them again.

Her care for him touched him in places he didn't want touched.

* * *

Angelina wasn't sure what she'd said that had displeased him so. She wondered what she should have said, but had no clue. He visibly pulled away from her, even though she was still sitting in his lap. She wished she could stay here.

"Stand before me."

His command sounded like a decree from a king, then the words of the CD she'd just been playing earlier tonight came to her—

No matter what you do
He's always in control
And when he calls your name,
You have to follow

Oh, but she didn't want to follow him. She was afraid of him and of so many things, most of which she didn't want to put a name to. She slid off his lap to do as he'd told her, then turned and stood naked before him—more than naked of clothes.

"Place your hands behind your back and clasp them when you stand before me like this. This is how you present yourself to this Dom."

She followed his command, feeling vulnerable. Her eyelids stung, but she refused to let him see her cry again.

"You are correct, *cara*. I do not enjoy disciplining my subs. I'd much rather have play sessions. You may not enjoy it either—not at first anyway—because I won't go easy on you. I want you to know what you can expect in the future with whoever becomes your Dom. He may be even stricter. But you will learn to be more in control of yourself through discipline and, as a result, will not have to be punished very often."

He paused and she filled in the silence with a "Yes, Sir," but her focus was on trying to prepare herself mentally for the moment when he would ask her to lie across his lap for her spanking. Looking down at his lap, she saw the bulge against his pants. She'd felt it earlier against her. He was aroused. Perhaps she could win back his favor by giving him some relief.

"…and the duckling realized it had been a beautiful swan all along."

Angelina wondered how long this preparatory lecture would go on before he would actually begin the spanking. She'd never been spanked in her…

What did he say? A duckling? Why was he talking about roast duck or whatever when she was about to be humiliated? She raised her gaze. His patience was on a very short leash.

"What did I just say, pet?"

What had he said? "You don't like to discipline subs...Sir."

"What did I say after that?"

God, the only other word floating around in her brain was duckling. "Something about a duck, Sir?"

He took short, shallow breaths, seemingly at a loss for words, then reached out and took her arm, pulling her over his lap. "Oh!" After a stunned moment, she regained her presence of mind—and voice.

"Marc, I don't think I'm ready yet."

"What did you call me?"

Oh, God. She'd screwed up again. "Sir, I'm sorry. It's just that I'm scared."

He placed his arm across her back with his hand gripping her side to hold her in place. "To remind you, originally you incurred five blows for speaking when you were told not to and forgetting to use my title."

All she heard was *originally*.

"In addition to the first five, you've incurred three additional swats."

"Why?"

"For not listening to your Dom when he was speaking to you, and for, once again, addressing me without the proper title.

"But I only did two more things wrong. Shouldn't it be seven total?"

She heard him take a deep breath and release it slowly, as if he were counting to ten. No longer feeling sorry for him, she began to feel sorry for herself. She attempted to squirm from his lap, but he scissored her legs between his.

"Two of the swats were for ignoring your Dom. Place your hands flat on the floor."

"No! I don't want to play this game any longer. You aren't my Dom!" She reached back with one hand to shield her butt from him, but he only took her hand and moved it out of his way, pressing it into her lower back.

"I assure you, this is not a game, pet. You will receive eight swats. Count each one as it is delivered and thank your Dom for each." He rubbed her bottom as if warming her up. Then his hand was gone.

Smack!

Before she had time to prepare her mind, the echo of the first blow reverberated around the room. Outraged at the humiliation of being treated like a child, she couldn't even scream. After a moment, she felt the sting from his open palm against her butt, surprised it didn't hurt as badly as she'd expected.

"I am waiting, but my patience is wearing thin."

"One, thank you."

"Let's begin again."

Smack!

His hand hit the same spot, the sting worse than the first blow. "One, Sir. Thank you, *Sir*." There. Surely she'd given him enough of his precious titles this time.

"Your tone requires that we add two more swats to the count. If you want to get to your mind-blowing orgasm this evening, stop behaving like a brat."

Smack!

This time, his hand landed on her other cheek. Again, it stung, but not to an unbearable level.

"Two. Thank you, Sir."

Smack!

Smack!

Smack!

The blows fell rapidly, alternating between each of her cheeks and hitting in the same places over and over, each time harder than the last. Her butt cheeks began to burn now, as if stung by a wasp.

"Stop! You're hurting me!" Then she remembered to count and regained control of herself. "Three, four, five, Sir. Thank you."

If she'd just behaved, this could have been over by now. As it was, she was only halfway there. Obviously, Allen was wrong. She wasn't a pain freak. This spanking proved it. His hand hurt her! She didn't like this one bit.

He released her ankles from between his own. Seeing her opportunity to escape, she tried to maneuver one leg outward so she could stand up.

Smack!

Smack!

Smack!

Mio Dio! All she'd managed to do was expose her pussy to his brutal hand. Each intense blow struck her labia, the last falling against her now exposed clit.

Her very erect clit.

She sobbed silently in humiliation. How could her body betray her like this? And how much more did he think she could take? Her butt cheeks and pussy burned. Where was the gentle, caring man he'd been earlier? Just like Allen, he'd turned into a monster when she was at her most vulnerable.

"Have you forgotten something, pet?"

Her voice was raspy as she counted, "Six, seven, eight. Thank you, Sir." She emitted a ragged sob, her shoulders heaving as she sucked air into her lungs.

Then, as she awaited the last two slaps of his hand, he surprised her by stroking her butt and blowing cool air across her flaming cheeks to ease the raging fire. She whimpered. He slid his finger down her crack and between her folds, gliding easily between her pussy lips. His finger slipped easily into her vagina.

Angelina sobbed even harder at the humiliation.

"You're so wet, my pet."

She shook her head, her hair dancing on the floor below her. Then his finger slid to encircle her clit. He stroked the sides of the sensitive nubbin's hood, increasing the pressure and speed. She gasped. *No! She didn't want to come like this!*

Keeping her in a state of confused excitement, he'd alternated pain with pleasure. Angelina felt the pressure of the coming release building. Her body craved both sensations, which she wanted more she couldn't say. His hand delivered everything she wanted. Every stroke, every blow brought only pleasure now. Even faster than she'd come before with Luke, she drew closer to what she anticipated would be a cataclysmic release. She had to stop him. If she came, she'd be what Allen had said she was.

But the words wouldn't travel from her brain to her mouth. Instead, she heard a moan of passion, horrified it came from her own traitorous lips. When she thought she would explode into a million pieces, he removed his finger.

Smack! As his hand stung her butt again, tears spilled in frustration.

"Nine, Sir. Thank you." She continued to sob, unable to control herself. "I don't want to any longer, Sir."

Stroke. Rather than deliver another blow, Marc stroked her butt cheeks and pussy again, causing her ass to bob up and down. More. Oh, God help her, she wanted more.

"Don't want to what, *cara*?" His voice sounded strained.

She shook her head, unable to tell him what she feared most. "I don't want to come, Sir."

Smack!

He delivered the hardest swat yet just over her pussy.

"Ten, Sir! Thank you! Oh, God, no more! Please, don't touch me anymore."

Stroke. He gently stroked her butt as he had before, then his hand was gone and she felt empty, longing for his touch, whether to be spanked or stroked, she wasn't sure.

"Why don't you want to come, pet?"

No! She wouldn't confess such embarrassing thoughts. Suddenly she knew what she wanted. "Please, just stop!"

"The second part of your discipline choice was to receive a mind-blowing orgasm. I won't deny you the full session, pet. But I do want to know why you don't want me to continue."

She groaned. Why did he keep harping about it? He had to know exactly what she'd been thinking. Her arousal made that obvious. Sometimes he knew her thoughts before they even registered in her own mind. Except for now, when he seemed to have no clue how badly she wanted to crawl into a hole and hide.

Oh, Mio Dio, Allen was right. Another sob escaped her. He was right. Tears streamed from her eyes and her nose started to run.

"I will count to five and if you haven't told me by then, I will add five more swats."

No! That was just what her sick and twisted body wanted. "All right, I'll tell you!" she screamed. "I'm a freak!" Her throat felt raw from a combination of crying and screaming, but she couldn't stop the flow of words now. She twisted around to look up at him as best she could. "There, are you happy now? I'm a pain slut, just like Al—just like *you* said. I have to be restrained or in pain before I can enjoy sex." After her admission had been torn from deep inside her, Angelina's body slumped, her head hanging limply. A dry sob escaped her.

Marc muttered an earthy Italian curse as he pulled her up into his arms. The pain in her butt as it made contact with his lap caused her to hiss and fight to get away from him—the scene a mirror image of the one with her dream lover.

His arms tightened around her as he tried to control her movements. "Sit still, pet. You'll only hurt worse if you squirm around."

His words sank in after a moment and she stopped moving. Just as he said, the pain in her ass receded but not the ache in her heart. She lowered her head, ashamed to look at him. Tears dripped onto her thighs.

"Shhhh." He brushed her hair back, tucking it behind her ear so he could see her, she supposed. See her humiliation. "It's over. You were so brave, *cara*."

No. He wasn't her dream lover. He'd hurt her. Angelina pushed out of his arms and stumbled to her feet. Without a backward glance, she ran to the bathroom. Oh, God. She was going to be sick.

Slamming the door behind her, she hovered over the toilet, holding her hair in her fist. Nothing but dry heaves. She wasn't going to be sick after all. But she still felt sick, nonetheless. Standing, she went to the mirror, seeing red splotches and a bruised cheek. God, she was a mess. She pulled several tissues from the box and blew her nose. Running water, she took a washcloth from the shelf and wet it, then held the cold wet cloth against her face.

"*Cara*, open the door."

"Go away...*Sir*."

Angelina's hand began shaking and soon her entire body trembled. She needed to be held, but didn't want to go to Marc. He'd promised not to hurt her—but he'd only promised not to hurt her physically. He'd never said he wouldn't hurt her emotionally. Like now. She drew a ragged breath. She needed Luke who would be tender and gentle, only wanting to give her pleasure.

Putting the cloth on the vanity, she avoided looking in the mirror again—so she wouldn't chicken out—and went to open the door to find Marc leaning against the doorjamb, surrounded by all her frilly, colorful clothes on hangers. He looked so out of place.

"*Cara*, we aren't finished."

"Oh, I think we are more than finished. Sir," she added, as an afterthought. She started to walk past him, but there was no way to do so without brushing his body. Her clit began to ache for his touch and when he reached out to enfold her in his arms, she struggled to keep her distance.

She held up her hands to ward him off. "Don't touch me. I can't do this Dom/sub thing."

The look of hurt on his face tugged at her heart. "Pet, you left before the best part. Let me hold you."

His arms reached out to her. *Hold me, Sir. Please just hold me.* Her entreaty sounded so damned needy. Oh, God, she wanted him, but was too confused about the aching push-pull churning inside. She hated feeling vulnerable and fought the need to feel his body against hers.

"I need some space right now. I'm going to go check on Luke."

Ignoring her, Marc reached down to scoop her over his shoulder like a sack of potatoes. "Put me down!"

"Not until we're finished." He held her in place with a hand on her sore bottom. "Your disciplinary lesson isn't over yet."

She struggled in earnest, beating her fists against his back. He sat on the bed and pulled her into his lap once more, wrapping his arms around her and holding her tightly against his hard chest until her struggles ended in exhaustion. Why did his arms have to feel so good around her? She just wanted to cry on him in frustration.

Before she lost it completely, she pulled away. Not making eye contact, she tried to get off his lap, but he just kept his arms secured around her. Pulling her against his chest, he laid his chin on the top of her head and she stiffened. So familiar. Just the way she'd felt the angel-man-wolf in her dream. *Oh, God. It had been just a dream, hadn't it?* Why did it seem so real sometimes?

"*Cara*, there's nothing wrong with you. You are perfect for m…the man who will be your Dom someday."

Unable to fight him any longer, she laid her head against Marc's shoulder. A ragged hiccough escaped her. She sniffled and Marc reached for a couple tissues from the box on her nightstand. Lying next to the box she spotted Nonna's pattern-tracing wheel, the one with the filigreed teardrop-shaped handle. Memories of those sharp points pricking her breasts while she was blindfolded earlier caused her nipples to swell. She groaned in embarrassment.

Marc had raided the sewing basket she kept displayed in the living room. Well, he could have found far worse things in Nonna's basket, Angelina supposed. She remembered seeing someone at the Denver kink club having long, thin needles inserted into his nipples by a dominant female. Angelina shuddered. Even though they'd used special ones that were safe, no way was anyone ever going to play with needles around her.

Marc sighed. "What are you thinking now?"

Should she be honest? Oh, what was the point in telling him her limits? Their time together would end soon. She wiped her eyes, blew her nose, and tossed the tissue in the wastebasket beside her bed.

"Look at me, pet." When she refused, he repeated. "Look. At. Me."

Afraid she might incur further discipline or even punishment if she didn't obey, she turned to face him, blinking away tears.

He smiled. "Very good, pet."

"I wish you wouldn't keep calling me that."

"It's part of your training, *cara*. But I never called you a pain slut. I believe you when you say you aren't into pain."

She thought back to their earlier conversation and finally agreed he hadn't called her the name. He'd only asked if she was trying to convince him or herself that she *wasn't* a pain slut. Well, the answer to that question was pretty clear now.

"Why do I need humiliation to get off?"

"Ah, pet. It's not the humiliation that excites you. It's releasing that tight rein you have on your mind, your self-control, and letting someone provide what you need, sometimes something you didn't even realize you needed. It's quieting that busy mind of yours that keeps trying to analyze everything all the time, and just giving yourself a chance to feel again. To experience what's happening with your body."

She remembered the many sensations she'd felt on the bed such a short while ago, blindfolded, restrained, and screaming for him to take her. Her clit throbbed at the memory.

A shudder wracked her body, causing her stomach muscles to contract. He pulled the comforter from the bed and around her shoulders, wrapping her snugly and pulling her tighter against him. His hand stroked her hair and rocked her back and forth, making her feel cherished.

She was too exhausted to even want her mind-blowing orgasm anymore. All she wanted was to be held in his arms.

"Tonight, you gave me the most precious gift any Dom can hope to receive—your sweet submission." He stroked her hair, comforting her. "I want you so badly, Angelina." His hand stopped and his body grew rigid.

Had she heard him correctly? He wanted her? And he'd called her by her given name, rather than the many Italian endearments he so often used. Her heart melted just like the ice he'd pressed against her skin earlier.

"I want you so badly to embrace the beauty of your submissiveness. It's nothing to be ashamed of or to hide."

Oh, she'd misunderstood. Why couldn't she listen more carefully? She didn't want to think about why it disappointed her that he didn't want her as his submissive. It was just as well. They wouldn't see each other again probably—but the chances of finding another Dom who would want to take her on weren't good.

She needed to enjoy what little time she had with the Dom of her dreams.

Chapter Thirteen

S<i>hit, what was wrong with him?</i> He'd admitted he wanted her before he managed to correct himself. He hoped he'd saved himself, at least. Her surrender had nearly been his undoing. Holding her in his arms again felt so right.

And so wrong.

How had Angelina gotten under his skin so quickly? He'd only wanted to help her overcome her aversion to BDSM, not to declare he wanted her. The admission somehow made him feel weak. He wouldn't give Angelina or any woman that kind of power ever again.

He remembered the scene that September morning in 2001 when he'd found Gino and Melissa in bed together. He'd come off the slopes early, planning to ask Melissa to marry him. His best thinking happened out in nature, but as soon as he'd made up his mind, he couldn't wait to ask her. To find her naked, straddling his older brother, had so enraged him. After telling her to get dressed and leave, he'd torn into his brother with a rage he'd never known before or since.

He'd said some vicious things. Words that probably had been festering inside him since he was a kid. Gino had always been the one to shine brightest. The one who did everything so fucking right. Graduated top of his class at one of the best MBA schools. Groomed by their mother to take over running the family's ski resort. Marc had never been able to measure up.

Gino swore he had no idea Marc and Melissa were in a relationship. Melissa had told him she was just a friend from college. In retrospect, he realized Melissa was the one who had pursued Gino. Rejected again, as he had been his whole life except for the cougars he provided with Dom scenes in his "Master Marco" persona at the resort. He'd decided then that one-night stands and superficial relationships were safer. No messy emotions to deal with.

Marc had left home that weekend. Then came Nine-Eleven. His brother had enlisted in the Marines. Five months later, he was dead.

Marc could never forgive himself for that. Even though Adam, who'd also been his brother's master sergeant, had sworn Gino had been a good Marine and loved his service to his adopted country, Marc couldn't help think he'd still be alive today if Marc hadn't made remaining at home so uncomfortable for his brother.

Angelina stirred in his lap and moaned as the pain in her ass registered again. He needed to put distance between them but also to push her just a bit more to open up to him while her defenses were down.

"Who called you a pain slut?"

Every muscle in her body tensed and she shook her head. "I don't want to talk about it."

"Well, I do. Tell me who called you that name."

* * *

Angelina's heart pounded in her ears. His tone told her he wasn't going to let her remain silent this time. She really didn't want to talk to him about Allen, too embarrassed that she'd trusted him and even thought he was a Dom.

He wasn't anything like Marc, and Marc had been able to get responses from her body…

She'd just have to get him to drop the subject. "Someone I used to date."

He waited, expecting her to say more, but she turned her attention to his firm, but gentle hand stroking rhythmically against her hair again. His touch could be gentle one moment, stinging the next. And she loved both kinds of touches. But she especially loved what his hands did to her body when she was spread open for him on this bed. Maybe Angelina wanted her mind-blowing reward tonight after all.

"Tell me how your being a pain slut became a topic of conversation with A…with this person."

Oh, God, just let it go already! He was like a dog with a new rawhide bone, not content to let it go until he'd torn it to shreds and devoured it. She shuddered. She didn't want to be devoured by him or anyone else.

Well, maybe she did want Marc to devour her just a little, right here on Nonna's bed. Nonna would approve of Marc. Her grandmother had never been shy about her appreciation of good-looking Italian men, even in her later years.

"Give that busy mind a rest, pet."

She pulled away to look up at Marc expecting him to be smiling, but he wore a solemn expression. She reached up to stroke his cheek, but he stayed her hand before she could touch him. She smiled, hoping he would, as well. She missed his smile. Sometimes it was like a little boy with his hand caught in the cookie jar—she wondered what he was like as a boy. Probably full of mischief. Other times, he smiled like a man who knew how to enjoy life to the fullest.

But he remained so serious now.

"This conversation took place where?"

She sighed and pulled her hand out of his grip, tucking it back inside the comforter, suddenly feeling cold. Apparently, he wasn't going to let go of this bone until she told him. He already knew about her going to the club. How much worse could it be?

Nervous, she stared at his chest hairs and her hand ventured out of the comforter again to run her fingers through the springy black hairs.

"That kink club I told you about…"

Her heart thudded as images of the private room came back to her. She tried to remind herself the horrific scene was in the past. It had no power over her now. Oh, why did he want her to talk about it?

"Breathe, *cara*. Take slow, deep breaths." His hand pulled the comforter away from her shoulders to pool in her lap. He stroked her bare back in sweeping strokes from her neck to her hips, over and over, in a circular motion firmly enough not to tickle.

She focused on the movement of his hand and drew a ragged breath. "Please. I can't talk about it." She couldn't make eye contact, afraid he'd read her mind or something.

"You need to talk about it. Start at the beginning."

When she closed her eyes, she felt her breasts pressing against the wood of the St. Andrew's cross. "Tight. The restraints were too tight. My fingers were so numb. Cold." He continued to stroke her back, rhythmically. "Stretched out. St. Andrew's cross. Oh, God, I had a leg cramp." She'd forgotten about that.

"Did you tell him?"

She nodded.

"And what did he do?"

"Nothing. He told me to stop…complaining."

"A good Dom would have adjusted the straps, made sure you had enough to drink, even given you chocolate."

She didn't know any of those things might have helped. Allen just wanted to begin flogging her.

She flinched as she remembered the first few blows.

"What did he use?"

"Leather flogger. Oh, *Dio*, the pain. So intense, right from the beginning." She felt tears dropping onto her breasts. "The blows fell against my…butt. I tried not to scream at first. I didn't want to look like a wimp." Her breath caught on a sob.

"Shhh. I have you now. He can't hurt you anymore." He reached up and brushed the tears from her cheek. "Then what happened?"

"I began screaming, crying. I begged him to stop. I screamed 'Red!'" She looked into Marc's eyes. "You have to believe me. I said my safeword."

"I know you did, pet. He ignored you."

She nodded and drew a deep breath, relieved he believed her.

"He should have been whipped for abusing your body and your trust like that."

The image of Allen strapped to the cross with the Dom in the Harley jacket wielding his whip against Allen's already red-striped back brought a smile to her face. "Yes, that's something I'd like to see."

"Then what?"

The smile faded as he brought her back to the scene where she was the one strapped to the cross. "It went on and on. I don't know how long, but it became such a nightmare. Screams. Pain. So much pain. He said I should stop crying. Enjoy it. I'm a…pain slut." Meeting his gaze again, she said with some vehemence, "I did not enjoy it. At all."

"I know, pet." He stroked her cheek, brushing her hair behind her ear. His expression told her he believed her.

"There was no payoff. Just pain and more pain and then…suddenly all the pain left me." Her voice shook and more tears spilled down her cheeks. Realization dawned on her. "Oh, my God!" She needed to run. She needed to get away. She moved to get up, but Marc put his arms around her waist and held her in place.

"What's going on in your head? Talk to me, pet."

"Let me go. I don't want to talk about this anymore."

"I do. You haven't gotten to the core of what's bothering you. What happened when the pain left."

"Please, Sir. Don't make me say it."

Marc pulled her against him, even though she tried to keep her distance. "Shhh. I have you." He began stroking her back again.

His words brought her back into the club scene even more intensely. She wanted to forget what happened next. Her fingers idly stroked the black hairs on his forearm. So like the angel in her dream. But the dream lover seemed more real now. He hadn't just been in her dream, had he? He was the angel at the club.

"He stopped beating me and took me off the cross."

Marc tensed. "Who took you off the cross?"

"I don't know! Allen?" She tried to remember, but that didn't sound right. Marc's hand had stopped stroking her back and she missed the contact. "I don't think that's right. I was floating. Euphoric. It was like…heaven."

"That's called subspace."

"No, because if I was in subspace, that means I enj…" She couldn't finish the sentence.

"Not necessarily. There are levels. Some subs can be abused to a point where they go too deeply into subspace. That's not a good thing, especially for someone so new to scening like you."

"It felt so good at first. I was floating. Looking down on my body. Someone held me." Her fingers stopped pulling gently on his forearm hairs. "But it wasn't Allen. The man had dark hair. He held me like you're doing."

"That's called aftercare. Subs and bottoms give so much of themselves when they relinquish control that their Doms need to slowly ease them back into reality after a scene."

"Pain returned with a vengeance. Oh, God! It hurt so badly and he wouldn't let me escape him or the pain. He forced me to feel it."

"I'm sure he wanted to keep you from hurting yourself, *cara*. What then?"

"I can't say."

"Angelina."

"Please don't make me admit it. It's too humiliating."

"What happened, pet?"

He wouldn't stop until she admitted everything. With a burst of anger—at Allen, at Marc, at her angel dream lover even—she pushed away from his chest and met his gaze.

"I came! He didn't even touch me…not at first, anyway. And I came." Her face burned as hot as did her butt. "Oh, God, Marc. I *am* a pain slut." She pressed her face against his bare chest, no longer wanting him to look at her. Deep wracking sobs tore through her.

"What did the man who was holding you do?"

His words broke through her sobs and she pulled away. "I don't remember." And then the image she'd seen from the vantage point of the ceiling flashed through her mind again. He'd pushed the blankets aside. His hand had gone between the folds of the blanket and... "He touched me."

"Where did he touch you?"

"My clit. My... Oh, my! He's the reason I came. Not the pain. He stroked me until I came."

"Yes, he did."

Thrilled that he believed her, she pulled back and he wiped the tears away with the pad of his thumb. She grabbed a tissue and blew her nose very indelicately. Then she smiled. "Yes. He did." She giggled. Maybe she wasn't a pain slut, after all.

"I'm convinced you aren't a masochist. You wouldn't enjoy intense pain. If you negotiate a scene in the future, make sure your Dom knows that. There are lots of Doms, myself included, who don't like to administer severe pain either. While I don't think the Dom who abused you would have stopped without the intervention of...the DM or whoever stopped the scene. Clubs have dungeon monitors to keep an eye on things so they don't get out of hand. The DM should have gotten to you sooner."

He looked away for a moment then returned his gaze to hers. His look of sadness—no, more like regret—really touched her. He took the responsibility of being a Dom very seriously and almost seemed to be apologizing for the actions of others who didn't.

"Promise me you won't put yourself in a position like that again, Angelina, unless the Dom has won your trust—one hundred percent. No exceptions."

"I promise, Sir." Oh, why couldn't he be her Dom? "But there won't be any more Doms for me."

He smiled. "Never say never, pet. You're a sexual submissive. You're going to crave giving up control—again and again. It's not something you can just turn off like a faucet." He paused and looked down at her breasts. "Now, your Dom for the night isn't finished. There's the matter of completing your punishment."

Her heart thudded once and then stopped. She forgot to breathe. Marc stood, lifting her in his arms before pressing her down lengthwise in the middle of the bed. She winced as pain radiated from her sore bottom, reminding her of the first part of the punishment she had chosen to receive to learn better behavior. She lifted her hips off the bed to avoid direct contact. Without a word, he rolled her over onto her stomach and pulled the comforter away to expose her burning backside to the cool air.

"Don't move."

She heard him walk into the bathroom, run water, and soon he was climbing onto the bed beside her. The cold washcloth lay against her burning flesh, causing her to jump.

"Lie still." Her insides clenched at the command, but she forced herself to relax. He removed the wet cloth and dried her off with a soft towel. His fingers applied a cold substance to the places that stung most. Oh, God, don't let it be whatever he had used on her clit earlier because she didn't think she could stand to have her butt burning any more than it already did. But his tender ministrations actually removed some of the sting from her bottom.

"If I had my toy bag, I could have used lido to remove the burn, but aloe vera should work, too."

He blew cool air over her damp skin, causing chill bumps to rise, which, unfortunately, only made her butt hurt again, like gooseflesh on sunburned skin. Tears flowed again, not from the pain this time but rather from the gentle way in which he took care of her. She kept her face averted, too mortified to have him see her emotional response.

He popped the lid of the lotion container shut, then his firm hands glided over her back, raising more gooseflesh. When he touched her sides, she jumped.

"You and your damned ticklish spots."

She grinned and relaxed again. His hands became even more firm and he focused solely on her upper back. When he massaged her bruised shoulders, she groaned in pain.

"I'm sorry, *bella*. I forgot." He bent down and brushed his lips over the bruises, slightly abrading the tender skin, and her hips bucked upward in response.

Marc placed his warm hands under her and rolled her over. She blinked as she looked up at him searching her eyes before his gaze moved to her lips and eventually came to rest on her breasts.

She grinned. Definitely a tits-and-ass man. He lowered his mouth and took one peak into his mouth, sucking. His teeth gripped her nipple and bit gently.

"Ahhhh." Her hips bucked again. He held the tip of the bud between his teeth as he raised his head, pulling on her until she arched her chest to keep the pain from going beyond what she could endure with comfort.

But did she want comfort, or did she want it rougher? She reached up to keep him from pulling any harder and he let go. Her breast bounced back in place, her nipple exquisitely engorged and getting harder in the cool air.

"Hands on the headboard. Now."

Her pussy tightened at his firm order, but her hands moved without pause to the headboard where she entwined them in the intricate iron design, cool against her fingers.

His mouth descended on her other nipple and repeated the same torture. "Oh, Mar…Sir, I mean. Yes, Sir!" She stiffened, waiting to be chastised for using his name. And for speaking out loud. Were the old rules still in place?

He lifted his head and stared at her, very solemn. Oh, God. Don't let him stop again for another spanking—well, not a painful one, anyway. She wanted to come so badly. He'd promised. She waited to find out what he intended to do.

"Pet, I give you permission to be as vocal as you wish, because I am going to blow your mind in a few minutes and I want to hear how much you enjoy the ride." He smiled in a very wicked way.

"Yes, Sir," she said in an awed whisper. She relaxed, returning his smile. At last. The time had come—to come. She giggled. Something about his announcing what he intended to do made it much more thrilling. He had no doubt he would succeed, and neither did she, which also blew her mind.

He leaned up to kiss her, his hand reaching behind her head to pull her hair as he'd done earlier. The roughness of the kiss was exactly what she wanted. What she needed. His mouth blazed down to her breasts again, nipping her neck, tugging her nipples, but not lingering this time as he moved down to her belly. She cringed as the ticklish triggers went off.

I will not react. I will not react. First you sift the flour then add six eggs… She refused to give him any reason to restrain her legs again.

He stopped what he was doing and looked up at her. He wasn't pleased. "Was there a thought you neglected to share, pet?"

He wanted her to give a blow by blow of her thoughts? Embarrassed, she said, "I'm trying not to react to being tickled, Sir. Mind over matter."

"Well, you're so damned tense, pet, you aren't going to be able to feel anything. If I promise not to restrain your legs, will you let yourself relax enough to enjoy it?"

"How did you…? Um, yes, Sir!"

His smile warmed her entire body. "Good girl." He grabbed two pillows and told her to raise her hips, which she did. With her hips floating on a cloud of feathers, her pussy high in the air, he spread her legs wide as he lowered his head. He pressed his tongue against her wet vagina and, with his tongue flattened, slid it up and over her hood. She bucked toward his face. He pulled away making her afraid he would stop, but instead the tip of his tongue traced delicious circles around her clit, careful not to touch the tiny erection. Teasing her.

"Oh, God, yes! Touch me there!" She froze. Had she just said those words aloud? Dear Lord, she'd never talked during sex before.

He pulled away and waited for her to make eye contact. "That's right, *bella*. Don't hold anything back." Every muscle in her pelvis melted like chocolate in a double boiler. But she wanted to get on with the reward part of her discipline—her big O moment. She tilted her pelvis against his hand, urging him to get back to work, inviting him inside. He smiled and lowered his head again.

He pressed his fingertip against her opening, coating his finger with her pussy juices as he slid the wetness along a path to her waiting nubbin. Her mind screamed "*Mio Dio!*" when he touched her. "Please, lick me there again. Oh, on my clit!"

He ignored her pleas and she groaned in frustration. Two fingers spread her outer lips open. Exposed. She felt the cool air of the room and his warm breath touching her again. She throbbed with the need for direct stimulation. Open to him completely, his fingers glided between the open folds to her wet pussy and pressed against the opening of her vagina. Her very slick vagina. His finger pressed inside her, and then two, his knuckles ramming against her pelvic bone.

Yes! Finally! Please!

She remembered she could speak. "Please, Sir, I need you to touch me there."

As if she'd said some magic word, he lowered his tongue directly to her clit and flicked it rapidly. "Oh, *Gesù*, yes!" She gripped the headboard to keep from flying off the mattress, but her hips weren't restrained and did levitate, over and over.

His fingers slid in and out of her pussy like a piston as he tongued her. "Oh, God. I'm going to come."

He stopped moving his fingers and looked up at her. "No, you're not. Not until I give you permission."

What? Had he just said what she thought he'd said? She had to wait? "But you promised!" Her voice sounded whiny, needy, but she'd waited too long.

"Oh, I always keep my promises, pet. But in my time, not yours."

She groaned, even though she wasn't exactly in a position to argue. With a whimper, she tried to release the coiled tension in her body. He smiled and his fingers began to move in and out again, but he didn't take his gaze away from hers.

"You are so fucking wet and responsive, *bella*."

Heat flooded her face, whether from the compliment or the dirty talk, she wasn't sure. Instinctively, she tried to clench her legs together out of embarrassment. But his head and shoulders restricted her movement. He had, in effect, restrained her again anyway.

"Has any man ever discovered your G-spot?"

What? Her G-spot? Why did he have to talk about such things? *Just do it, Marc!* Did such a thing as a G-spot even exist? Her friends had joked about it, but none had indicated she or a partner had ever found the holy Grail-spot in their holy of holies, as they jokingly called it. Allen certainly hadn't. So, she had no idea what all the fuss was about but, if it did exist, she had no doubt Marc would know exactly where to find hers.

She hoped so, at least, because now she absolutely needed to find out if she had one.

"Answer the question—yes or no. Has anyone ever given you a G-spot orgasm?"

Closing herself off from him, whether physically or mentally, would be impossible. She shook her head. "No, Sir."

He pulled his fingers out, turned his hand palm up, and drove two fingers to the hilt inside her quivering core, taking her breath away. Her hips bolted upward as if attached to an invisible pulley in the ceiling. His fingers curled toward her pelvic bone and began massaging as his thumb rocked against her hood.

Waves of heat and sensation washed over her. "Oh!" She felt the pressure build and spread all the way to her lower jaw. He'd certainly touched a nerve. A delicious nerve. When he stroked her again, her pelvis bucked off the pillows. "Oh, God, yes!"

"You are not to come yet."

Chapter Fourteen

Before she could analyze why that sounded wrong on so many levels, his fingers curled even deeper inside her and she lost the ability to clench the muscles in her legs. They fell limp, as if paralyzed. Pressure from his thumb against her nubbin, alternating with the "come here" motion of his fingers inside her sent her body on a runaway roller coaster, riding toward the crest of the highest hill. The bucking of her pelvis increased and she writhed. The air in the room felt cold against her sweat-soaked skin.

"Oh, don't stop! Please, Marc! I want you inside me."

He stopped. "What did you call me?"

"Oh, please don't do this to me, Sir. I can't think. I need to come. Now!"

"No, that's not what you need right now, *cara*. You need to address your Dom properly."

But you aren't my Dom. She left those particular words unspoken, because she didn't wish to do anything to stop him for good. She looked up at him, begging him to fulfill her, and became frustrated when he just smiled. He held all the power. He even decided if she came or not.

He removed his fingers and spread the wetness to her clit. No! "Sir, please!" He smiled and his fingers thrust inside her again and she bolted upward, right back on the roller coaster, as he made contact with his thumb against her most sensitive spot.

The pressure began to build again as he pressed that incredible nerve, or bundle of nerves, inside her. Was that the G-spot? She didn't care what he called it, as long as he kept touching it.

"Yes, please, Sir. More. Give me more."

He lowered his face to her once more and took her erect nubbin between his teeth. Afraid to move for fear of being bitten, she tensed. He released her and flicked the tip of his tongue against the oh-so-sensitive tiny erection.

"Make me come, Sir!"

He pulled his mouth away and a third finger joined the other two that had already become intimately acquainted with her pussy. The fullness nearly undid her. His thumb rubbed her clit harder.

"Oh, yessss!!"

His fingers began to move inside her. She neared the crest of the hill, where she hovered. So close. She pumped herself against his hand, needing more.

"Don't leave me hanging, Sir!"

"I've got you, *bella*. Come for me, pet. Now."

The scream that escaped her lips, as she catapulted over the precipice and corkscrewed through Orgasm Curve, bounced off the bedroom walls, much as she bounced off the mattress and pillows.

"Oh! Ohhhhhh! Yesssss! Oh, God! Oh! Oh! Oh, God, yesssss!"

The spasms of her pelvic muscles came in waves, jerking her body as if she were dancing at the end of electrical wires. Her mind-blowingly explosive release exceeded anything she'd ever experienced before. She screamed, again and again, as the orgasm continued. Her body tensed, arched, and jerked over and over. Just when she thought it would never stop, her body collapsed like a wet noodle against the oh-so-wet sheet.

Marc stretched out over her, holding the bulk of his weight off of her by propping himself on his forearms, but still he pressed her lower body into the pillows. She felt his erect penis against her ultra-sensitive clit, which spasmed in greeting regardless of the pain. He bent down to press his lips against her mouth, capturing her groan of pain…or was it frustration?

She kissed him back, a sweet, gentle kiss that was about all she had the energy for. Spent, depleted, she lay for a few moments, gasping for air as her heart slowed its frenetic beating.

Marc cupped her breast and idly rolled her nipple. "You are the most responsive woman I've ever known. You can't imagine what a turn-on it was for me to watch you fly apart like that, *cara*."

Warmth infused her body, as if she needed to be any warmer. She hadn't realized he'd been watching her. She still felt his eyes on her. "That was, um, incredible."

"As are you, pet."

"I'd heard of the G-Spot before, but I had no clue what all the fuss was about. Now I know." When her heartbeat became steady again, she opened her eyes and looked up at him. "Please," she begged. "I need to touch you, too."

"You already have, *bella*. Watching you come almost caused me to embarrass myself without even using my fist."

She smiled, remembering her experience in subspace. "Is that called Domspace?"

Marc laughed. "Yes, pet. There is Domspace, as well—when your Dom is so tuned into giving you pleasure, meeting your needs, waiting for and interpreting your every visual and verbal clue to know if he is succeeding at his mission. Very intense for a Dom, just as being on the receiving end is for a sub."

A shadow passed over his face and he laid his forehead on her chest above her breasts, still keeping his weight on his forearms. She languished in the residual sensations and mini-tremors, thinking about how Marc had focused totally on her needs.

An overwhelming need to pull him closer bubbled to the surface. Cold tears trickled down the side of her face and around her ears, surprising her. Uncomfortable and shy about asking for what she needed, she let her tears of frustration continue silently until a broken sob escaped her and he raised his head up to look at her.

"Oh, pet. Shhh. I know it's intense." His hands stroked her face, careful to avoid her bruised cheek. She blinked, trying to clear the tears and focus. He moved up to hover over the top of her. Worry lined his forehead.

Tears spilled from the corners of her eyes and into her hair. Why was she crying? He'd given her the most beautiful experience she'd ever had, even better than when she came for her dream lover or for Luke on the sofa. So why did she feel so sad and lonely?

He brushed the tears away and curled her hair behind her ear. "You surrendered yourself beautifully. Thank you for trusting me."

She shook her head, not wanting to admit she'd done that. But he spoke the truth. He understood her better than she did herself sometimes. She gasped for air as another sob wracked her. Her throat ached, whether from crying or screaming, she wasn't sure.

He rolled off her and helped her turn onto her side, facing away from him, then pulled her tightly against him, his hard body curled against her back and legs, spooning her as he molded himself against her.

"I have you, *amore*. Just let it go."

Love? He'd used the endearment once before. Of course, Marc also called her dear and beautiful. Must be like an American southerner calling someone sweetie. It didn't mean anything. Marc further cocooned her, putting his leg against hers. Safe. She felt so safe with him. What was she going to do when he left her?

And what about Luke? Was he okay? She'd grown to need both of them so much in such a short time. In her efforts to become independent of her smothering brothers, she'd not allowed herself to let anyone get close for fear they'd smother her, too.

But she didn't feel smothered by Marc or Luke. Marc tugged the comforter over them. She sighed. She felt well loved. Special.

Cherished.

Marc's hand cupped her breast, not to stimulate her, but more as a possessive gesture. Safe in his arms, she let her eyelids droop. Just before she drifted off to sleep, he whispered in her ear, "Sleep, pet."

* * *

Luke poured a mug of coffee and stared out the window over the kitchen sink. Dawn was still a couple of hours away. He'd been awake since he'd heard Angel's screams, his muddled brain going on full alert at first, thinking she was in some kind of danger. But the screams resulted from passion, not fear or pain.

Marc walked into the room and filled himself a mug, as well. He looked like he hadn't gotten any sleep. "Any more news from the sheriff's department?"

"No. I checked in about forty-five minutes ago. They lost him after he left the hospital. He hasn't shown up at his house. I doubt they're going to keep looking long, unless he tries something that violates the protection order."

Luke had been thinking about what to do about Angelina for hours—on both fronts. He'd told Marc last night he didn't plan to pursue her any longer and didn't blame his friend for going after her. Hell, he'd have done the same thing. Angel was worth pursuing.

But he needed to come clean and tell Angel what happened on that mountain seven years ago. Guilt had been eating away at him ever since and he didn't want to keep it bottled up inside anymore. Besides, if Marc and Angel started dating, he'd have to see her.

First, he needed to make sure she was okay. "How is she?" Luke asked.

"Sleeping. Look, we need to talk about what we're going to do about Angelina before she wakes up."

Well, apparently they were on the same page. Best to talk about the personal-safety issues first.

"I'll call her brother, Tony, after daylight and let him know what's going on. We can stick around until one of her brothers can take over."

Marc slammed the mug on the counter, sloshing some of the liquid over the rim. "Like hell. She's coming with us. I'm not leaving her anywhere around that man."

Hell, this was supposed to have been the easier of the two discussions. "Just how do you plan to do that if she doesn't want to come with us? Kidnap her?"

"She'll come. I can be very…persuasive."

"Yeah, so I heard."

Marc's face didn't show any emotion one way or another, but the grip he had on his coffee mug told Luke his words had hit their mark. "She had a nightmare. Look, it's complicated, but there was nothing in there beyond the BDSM stuff. That's not always about sex. I just gave her what she needed."

Luke should have been there for her. "I'm sorry about last night. I'm glad you could be there when she needed someone."

"You ready to talk about what's going on?"

Luke took a swig of coffee and braced himself. There was no subtle way to ease into this conversation. His hand nervously twisted the braided leather bracelet on his wrist. He just needed to come right out and explain why he'd behaved the way he had.

"I'm responsible for the death of Angel's father."

While Marc wasn't one to show emotion as a rule, his eyes widened at Luke's confession. "What the hell are you talking about?"

Unable to watch his friend's reaction when he told him the truth, Luke turned toward the window again, but could see Marc's reflection in the glass pane. "Seven years ago, Maggie and I were hiking in a remote valley up on Mt. Evans, ignoring avalanche warnings from the Park Service." Luke looked down at his hands propped on the edge of the sink. The white band where his wedding ring had been goaded him on. "It was sunny and warm when we left that morning. She was on her break from the biology department at Texas. Early May." He drew a deep breath before continuing. "We were fucking clueless. She wanted to catalog and photograph some damned plant reported only to grow in that valley that time of year."

The backs of his eyelids burned. He didn't like remembering the events of that day, much less talking about them. Losing Maggie. Killing an innocent man who'd been charged with rescuing a novice hiker in a place she shouldn't have been.

Angel's father.

Can the emotions, man. He continued to let the details spill out, as if he were describing a scene from a movie. He'd rewound this scene over and over in his mind so many times he almost wished it *was* a movie.

"Maggie fell down a scree slope trying to get the damned photo. The scree rocks cut her up pretty badly, but she was conscious. I didn't have ropes or anything I could use to rappel down to her. Didn't even have a satellite phone to call for help. I had to leave her lying down there to hike back." Hardest thing he'd ever done in his life. He'd run to the car and then driven like a madman to the ranger station. "When I brought the SAR team back to her, I watched…"

Marc's hand on his shoulder brought him back from the nightmare a moment. Maybe he hadn't distanced himself from that day, after all. He shrugged Marc's hand off.

"For some damned reason, they let Angel's dad go down alone." Marc turned to face Luke. "You and I both know procedure. I've never been able to figure out why they let him go after her alone. But I guess if anyone else had been down there with them, they'd have died, too." God, the thought of any other life being taken that day…he squeezed his eyes shut, but the images didn't disappear.

"Then we heard the roar of ice and snow. Sounded like the whole damned mountain was coming down on us. The avalanche uprooted trees and headed straight for Maggie and Angel's fa…the SAR worker. He covered her, trying to shield her. I bolted toward her, but the rescue team pulled me back."

He drew a ragged breath into his tight lungs. "All I could do was watch. One minute they were there. Then gone." He stared at the floor.

"God, Luke. I knew it must have been bad, but I had no fucking clue." He paused briefly. "Does Angelina know?"

Luke shook his head again. He looked up at Marc, seeing some of his own pain reflected in the eyes of his friend, as if he, too, had been responsible for someone's death.

"She didn't recognize my name—but her brothers will. Tony and I attended a training session in Colorado Springs once. He avoided me the whole week."

Marc squeezed Luke's forearm. "Man, you've spent four years with SAR atoning for that accident. You two were just ignorant of the power of the wilderness. How many lives have you saved of equally ignorant people? If Tony blames you, he's a damned fool. Mr. Giardano knew the risks when he went down that mountainside. You and I would have done the same thing. It's what SAR workers do."

Luke shook his head.

"You need to forgive *yourself*, Luke. Until you do, it won't matter who else forgives you."

Luke shook his head. "I'll be atoning for this one until the day I die." He stood up, brushing Marc's hand away. "But I need to tell Angel."

"Why?"

"If we're meant to be together, we aren't going to get anywhere until that's out in the open."

Marc didn't say anything for the longest time, then said, "We've got to get her to safety and I don't want to give her any reason to refuse to go to Denver with us. Now is not the time to tell Angelina."

He stared at Marc, a man who wasn't one to be confrontational—ever—but was there more to it than that? Did he just want to keep Luke away from Angel? Is that what was going on here?

"Are you sure there isn't something more to you and Angel than keeping an eye on her? Sure sounded like more to me."

Marc looked down at the coffee mug. "Look, I just needed to help her get over a hurdle. There's nothing between us." His gaze met Luke's again. "But I don't want her to be alone. Which one of us is going to go in there?"

Hell, Marc had more of a claim on her at this point. He couldn't just show up in her bedroom like he had some right to be there.

"Go. She'll be more comfortable with you."

"Don't call Tony. She doesn't want her brothers to know, and I plan to honor that wish—unless they need to know."

It was a bad idea to even entertain the thought of bringing her to Denver with them. What were they supposed to do with her when they got there? Could he compete with Marc? Even if Marc said there was nothing between him and Angel, what about her? She'd sure sounded interested in him in there.

Damn.

What now?

***

Marc eased back into bed with Angelina and stretched out on his back afraid, if he touched her, she'd awaken. Or that she'd awaken parts of him best left sleeping.

His movements didn't cause her to move a muscle, so exhausted was she from the attack by Asshole—and more pleasant activities. She needed as much rest as she could get.

The coffee had revived him, not that he would have let sleep claim him tonight. Someone needed to watch over her in case Asshole returned.

But what the fuck was he going to do about Luke? He had no clue the man had something like that eating away at him. Hell, that kind of guilt could mess with a man's mind, as Marc knew all too well. He'd been counting on Luke pursuing her, if for no other reason than to keep himself away from her. Telling her about Maggie's death in connection with her papa's would just drive her away from Luke. Marc wanted his friend to establish some kind of relationship with her.

He wasn't sure when or how it had happened, but he'd begun to fall, and fall hard, for the little angel lying beside him. When was the last time he'd spent the night in bed with a woman—well, a sleeping woman, that is? He could easily have slept on the sofa and sent Luke in here. He told himself someone needed to be with her because of Asshole, but, in truth, he just wanted to be near her.

He covered his eyes with his forearm and images filled his mind of her smooth skin covered in gooseflesh as he'd traced patterns over her skin. Of her nipples puckering. Of her mouth open and gasping in wonder as he'd discovered her G-spot. His cock tightened. He'd been hard since dinner.

Why hadn't he buried himself inside her? She'd have welcomed him. Shit, she'd even begged him. So, when had he developed morals about such things? He told himself, it was because he hadn't brought any condoms. But, if he'd been determined to have sex with her, he'd have found a box of condoms somewhere in town, even if he had to hit every gas-station head within the city limits. No, a lack of condoms wasn't the issue.

Angelina was the issue. Vulnerable, curious, and very Italian Angelina.

What the hell power did she have over him? Was it about the rescue at the club last month? Or finding her bloodied and bruised in her doorway last night? His guts twisted at both images.

But Italian? That created a major conflict for him.

No, not because of Melissa. He'd never loved her. That had been carnal, pure and simple. Well, maybe pure wasn't the right word.

Fuck, he couldn't have loved anyone back then anyway. He was shit-hot, the Italian stallion of Aspen. Like some fucking gift from the gods to all womankind. He snorted in self-derision. Of course, it didn't help that the women had laid themselves out before him as if on a smorgasbord.

Angelina stirred and he turned to watch her sleeping. She wasn't a gold-digger like Melissa either. She was exciting, curious, and full of life. She also was sweet. Hell, she could have been his sister, Carmella. Okay, he wouldn't go that far. Then again, maybe the fact that she did remind him of Carmella made her so dangerous to him. He wouldn't want any man hurting his sister. With his track record, he had no doubt she would be yet another casualty of Marc D'Alessio's.

The thought of being dominated might terrify her, but he was equally terrified of dominating *her*. He'd failed her once, albeit unintentionally. But what if he did so again, this time intentionally or recklessly?

She scared him shitless.

But she wasn't his, so why was he even entertaining the thought of anything more? Marc suffered a pang of guilt that he'd unleashed the submissive buried within her tonight. If Luke didn't swing that way, it could create problems for them in a future relationship. But better they deal with it sooner than later. If she ignored her sexual nature and chose a safe marriage, she'd only have regrets later because she'd denied and closed off a vital part of herself.

Marriage. Marc certainly wasn't looking for those shackles. He'd come too close with Melissa and then Pamela to ever chance taking that path again. But Luke was the marrying kind. Angelina deserved someone like him. Stable, faithful, trustworthy. Hell, Luke would probably even play at being Dom if he thought that would please Angelina.

Not the same as being a born Dominant, but perhaps that would be enough for Angelina. Most men could get excited about bondage games, at least. He had no doubt she would surrender to restraints again, with a man she trusted.

Now how was he going to get her to trust him and Luke enough to agree to going to Denver and stay with one of them until things blew over with that abusive bastard Allen Martin?

Chapter Fifteen

A buzzing in her ears caused Angelina to swat at empty air over her face. The buzzing sounded again. Opening an eye to see what flying pest had invaded her bedroom on this early fall morning, she found herself curled up on an unfamiliar and very hard surface. The firm arm supporting her shoulders finally registered in her addled brain.

Mio, Dio! Heat flooded her cheeks and she fought the urge to spring up and run away. Marc's chest.

Buzzzzz.

The source of the annoying vibration registered in her head at last. Her phone. She rose up and spotted her handbag sitting on the nightstand. How had it gotten in here? Next to it sat a bowl of water, a washcloth, an enormous Hershey bar, and Nonna's pattern-tracing wheel. She remembered some of the items from last night. Too bad they hadn't gotten to the chocolate, though. Her stomach growled.

When the buzzing stopped, her attention was drawn back to Marc's massive chest. His right forearm covered his eyes. Was he sleeping? She couldn't tell. His breathing seemed slow, shallow.

Half sitting now, she tried to ignore the pain radiating across her shoulders and cheek, and in all of the muscles she'd used to fight off Allen's attack last night.

She brushed her cheek against the springy hairs on his chest, which tickled the whisker-burned skin on her chin. Last night, she'd run her fingers through those soft, coarse hairs. Unable to resist, she splayed her fingers open and dove into the sprinkling of hair again.

Her hand gravitated to his pec, and she flicked a thumbnail over a pebbled nip. She felt his heartbeat kick it up a notch under her cheek. Knowing he wasn't sleeping, she grew bolder and let her hand trail down his right side, until she brushed over what felt like puckered flesh.

Marc's body grew tense as her fingers explored the area—about the size of a silver dollar. Raising up, she leaned over and the sight of the angry-looking pink and white scar sucked every ounce of air from her lungs. The silvery ridges on the puckered skin told of a deep and violent injury. She touched it, wincing as if she might hurt him. Tears sprang to her eyes. Here she was complaining about some minor aches and pains, when Marc had been seriously injured.

"Long time ago," Marc said.

"What happened?" she whispered.

"Fallujah."

Oh, God, no. Iraq. He'd been wounded. "Oh, Marc, I had no idea."

"It's nothing compared to what happened to some of the men with me."

She scooted off and stretched out beside him looking into his sad green eyes. She'd reminded him of a nightmarish time in his life and now wanted to comfort him. Taking his arm, she pulled him toward her; eventually, he complied and rolled onto his side. Okay, he obviously wanted to turn, or she wouldn't have gotten him to budge. Once there, he stared, waiting, but said nothing.

Thoughts of the pain he must have experienced when wounded caused a tear to spill from her eye. She blinked rapidly to dry her eyes. "If you ever need to talk about it, I'm a good listener."

He remained silent, serious. She didn't think he would say anything. Didn't most veterans keep their private hell to themselves or share only with those who had been in combat as well? Compelled to find some small way to honor his sacrifice and his injury, she moved his arm out of the way exposing the scar to her gaze, and she bent over and kissed the puckered skin. She heard his sudden indrawn breath as her lips touched his warm and battered skin. With the tip of her tongue, she laved the area and placed tiny kisses all around it.

His hands grabbed her shoulder and pushed her away before cupping her chin and tilting her face toward his. "That's about the sweetest kiss I've ever received, *cara.*" His voice sounded husky with emotion and more tears spilled down her face. He brushed her hair back from her face and studied her for a long moment.

Needing more intimate contact with him, she leaned over and opened her mouth to capture his lips in an inquisitive kiss. In one fluid motion, he rolled onto his back, pulling her on top of him. Grabbing the back of her head to prevent her escape, he deepened the kiss. Just when she thought her lungs would explode, he broke away.

"*Buongiorno, bella.* I like how your body wakes up."

The phone buzzed again.

"Am I still your Dom this morning?"

"I'd better get that."

He chuckled, obviously aware of her evasion to his question. Was he still her Dom? Did she want him to be? *Oh, God.* He'd be leaving soon. Better that they just put the whole Dom/sub thing behind them. They'd only negotiated this one night.

She reached over to pick up her handbag, but the buzzing stopped. Still, she needed to see who called. She didn't have any catering jobs this week and sure could use one. Opening the handbag, she retrieved the phone and glanced down to see it had been Mama.

She laid the phone on the nightstand. Marc cupped her left breast and squeezed the nipple until it swelled, distracting her. He wrapped his arm around her back and rolled them both over until their positions were reversed and he propped himself above her chest on his elbows. As he had done last night, his lower body pressed hers into the mattress. His erection, very much concealed in his pants, bobbed against her mons.

Marc hadn't even come yet. What was he waiting for? Several times she'd offered to take care of his needs, but each time he had stopped her.

She didn't want their time to end but knew it must. Her heart constricted with regret. He and Luke had made her feel safe for the first time in seven years—and sexually alive for the first time in…forever. How cruel was fate to give her a glimpse of such carnal deliciousness, only to sentence her to a life of sexual blandness?

Marc pinched her right nipple again, reclaiming her attention, and her clit throbbed its response, eagerly awaiting his further ministrations. "Tell me what you're thinking."

"That I'm going to miss you and Luke when you're gone." She closed her eyes. No sense wondering what could have been. She was a pragmatist—and she wasn't going to Denver. Between Papa's death on the mountain there and her disastrous trip to the kink club with Allen, that city held nothing but bad memories. If she'd trusted her instincts and stayed away last month, she wouldn't have suffered at Allen's hands.

Marc bent down and bit her nipple.

"Ow! What was that for?"

"You were thinking unpleasant thoughts again."

Angelina rubbed her nipple. There were some things she wouldn't miss about Marc. He was dictatorial, domineering…

Attentive, adorable.

Whoa! Marc? Adorable? She really needed more sleep. Well, she had the whole afternoon to nap after they left. This morning, she didn't want to miss a thing by sleeping. But she needed to call Mama back. And find a toothbrush. And make them breakfast. And take a shower. Not necessarily in that order.

Marc's hand returned to stroking her breast. The man certainly had a fixation. He bent down to take her nipple in his mouth more gently this time, his teeth trapping the base of the swollen button as his tongue flicked over the sensitive tip rapidly. She inhaled sharply, grabbing the sides of his head and holding her breath. Her clit throbbed, answering his tongue stroke for stroke.

She closed her eyes, giving in to the sensations as she lifted her chest toward him. "Oh, God."

He released her nipple. When he didn't go further, she looked at him. He glanced up and smiled. "I'll never get my fill of your breasts."

His words suffused her with warmth from the top of her head to her curled toes. She still couldn't get used to the fact he found her so sexy. Of course, he'd have to get his fill very soon, because he'd be leaving in a few hours.

Sobered by the thought, she gave him a nudge. "I need to make a call."

He sighed and rolled off enabling her to sit up on the side of the bed. *Ow!* She couldn't stop the groan that escaped. Such a baby about pain. The exertion brought her hands up to massage the tender shoulder muscles. Marc knelt behind her and brushed her hands and hair aside. Gently but firmly he eased the tense and knotted muscles careful to avoid the bruises.

She sighed and picked up the phone again. "I really do need to call Mama back," she said, hitting the speed-dial number.

* * *

Marc smiled and reached around her arms to pinch her nipples again for good measure. He'd bide his time.

"Hi, Mama. I was in the shower. Sorry I missed your calls."

Ah. Lying to her mama. Not acceptable. Marc would find it difficult to respect a woman who would lie to her mother—especially an Italian one.

Time for some fun and games. Scooting back on the mattress, he got on his knees and positioned himself behind her, leaning forward and trailing kisses down her spine. When he brushed his lips and scruff against her love handle, she jumped. He loved playing with her ticklish areas.

He sat back on his heels and let the fingers of his right hand trace a path down her sexy back. He'd first been turned on by this view last month at the club. The catch in her voice as she chatted with her mama made him smile. She waved him away several times, as if he was a pesky fly. She might want to ignore or dismiss him, but he chose to ignore her wishes at the moment. His time as her Dom was dwindling and his newbie sub deserved his undivided attention.

He continued to explore her body, bending down to lick the dimple at the base of her spine. She scooted away toward the edge.

He skimmed his fingertips over her shoulders and down her arms. The bruising on her shoulders had darkened overnight. His gut twisted as his anger toward Sir Asshole resurfaced, but he tamped that emotion down—for now. The man would be taken care of in due time. Right now, his focus should be on Angelina and her immediate needs.

"Yeah, I went to bed early last night, Mama. Rough day."

Yes, and she also was too tied up to return your call, Mama.

That she was still able to carry on a normal conversation, told him he wasn't paying close enough attention to her. He needed to ramp it up. Placing one leg on either side of her, he positioned his hips against her backside and adjusted his erect cock against the crack of her ass. Too bad he still wore his pants. If not, he would definitely have had her squirming and unable to carry on this conversation.

When she tried to stand up to get away from him, he wrapped one arm around her waist to hold her in place. He brushed his lips lightly over one of her bruises. She hissed, and Marc pulled back. Had he hurt her? His thumb reached around to feel her erect nipple, and he smiled. No, she hadn't hissed because she was in pain.

"It was nothing, Mama. I'm fine. I, um, just saw a spider, that's all."

Marc's fingers danced a mock *Tarantella* from her elbow to her shoulders and then along the long, slim column of her neck before gliding down to cup her breast. She leaned against him, throwing her head back to give him better access.

Ah, I have you now, my pet.

He released her waist, no longer concerned she would flee, and brought that hand up to cup her other breast.

"Sorry, Mama. I can't make it to dinner today. Um, I have to work."

He pinched her nipples hard for lying to her mama again and her thighs clamped together in response. Did her mother hear that sexy hitch in her breathing?

"I know. But, something's come up."

Marc's cock throbbed against her ass. Well, she wasn't lying about that.

"I have to go to, uh…Denver today…for a class."

Marc grinned. That could be arranged. His playroom certainly could be converted easily for a classroom scene. He already had the principal's desk in there.

"No, I'll be gone all week."

Thoughts of her restrained on his spanking horse sent his cock into spasms. She pressed her ass against him in an automatic response, before scooting away again toward the edge of the bed.

"I promise I'll be there next Sunday. Tell the boys hi for me."

He slid his right hand down over her mons and his fingers slipped between the folds to encircle her clit. "Oh, yesss! I mean, yes, I will, Mama." She tried to elbow him away. "Love you, too. Bye."

He pulled his hand back. Why was he trying to start something with her this morning? Their "demonstration" was over. What had gotten into him? She wouldn't be in his playroom this week or ever. He just needed to get her to a safe place. He'd make sure she stayed with Luke. It would give the two of them a chance to get to know each other better.

Now why did that thought bother him?

She disconnected the call and stood up, spinning around to glare down at him, gritting her teeth. "There's a special place in hell for a man who would seduce a woman while she's talking to her mama."

"Oh, I assure you, *il diavolo* long ago reserved a special place for me, *bella*, for sins far worse than that one."

Memories of the fight he and Gino had had before his older brother deployed to Afghanistan flashed across his mind. He'd let a woman come between him and his own brother—and had never seen his brother alive again. A sin he'd never be forgiven for.

He didn't need to add one more to the list. Angelina deserved better than him. Yet, no sooner had the thought flashed across his mind than he reached up to catch her, pulling her onto his chest as he lay down. He rolled them until he lay on his left side and her on her back, then draped his leg over hers to keep her in place. Spreading her knees, he buried his middle finger into her pussy. She gave a breathless gasp as she tossed the phone to the bottom of the bed.

Dio, she was wet. He wet his thumb in her juices and slid it up to her clit, making slow, circular motions. Her pelvis bucked against his hand. The urge to bury himself inside her gripped him. He took a deep breath and tamped down his desire. Hearing her breathing increase, he rammed his finger inside her harder. Then two fingers.

"Oh, yes, Marc. Don't stop!"

"How do you address me?"

She fought for a deep breath and opened her eyes. "You're not my Dom now. Are you?"

There was a certain wishful sound in her question, which pleased him.

Shit. She'd done it again, slipped under his defenses. He didn't need a sub. He just needed to keep this woman safe. He needed to get her to Denver.

"*Cara*, I was pleased to hear you tell your mama you will come to Denver with us today." His thumb encircled her hood again.

"Oh, I didn't mean it. I just needed to give Mama a plausible excuse." Her voice hitched as he felt her nubbin harden. "No one misses Mama's Sunday dinners without a darned good excuse." She pointed to the bruising on her face. "I still can't go to Denver with you."

"I am very disappointed in you, pet." He felt her body tense against his and she opened her eyes, furrowing her brows. He fought the urge to grin at her stricken expression. She'd make some Dom a fine submissive someday.

"I am not your submissive."

"Are you trying to convince yourself or me?"

She glanced away.

I'm sorry, but I can't be what you need, cara.

"But if you don't come to Denver for the week, you will have lied to your mama. For such willful disobedience, as your Dom, I would have to punish you."

* * *

Angelina's attention was riveted once more to Marc's gaze. Was he still her Dom this morning? Was he serious? She wasn't a child. Besides, if anyone should be punishing her for lying, it was Mama, who didn't even know about the lie—yet.

So why did her clit pulse to life as she contemplated how he would punish her? Another spanking? Bare-handed or using an implement like a paddle, belt, or hairbrush? Or perhaps depriving her of the mind-blowing orgasms she'd been experiencing since last night? Or even torturing her with a rapid succession of orgasms?

Well, she'd read enough BDSM novels to know the possibilities were endless. Some involved pain. Some involved depriving a sub of something she wanted. Others, humiliation. And why did she feel her pussy contracting and getting even wetter just thinking about his punishing her again?

But he's not my Dom!

Her conscience battled silently. She'd never lied to Mama before.

Mama would understand this time.

No, Marc's right. You can't lie to your mama.

Oh, God. She needed to lay low for a week or so until things blew over with Allen. But she had no place to stay in Denver. No way was she moving in with Marc or Luke for a week. This weekend was extremely out of character for her. She'd never slept with a man in this bed before, for starters.

And certainly had never been tied to Nonna's bed with real or imaginary restraints—or both. Would she be able to go back to her safe, normal life after they left? Did she even want to? But why did they have to live in Denver, of all places? She'd managed to avoid Denver, except for that one disastrous nighttime visit last month, for seven years.

No, she wasn't going to Denver.

"I'm not sure I even want to know what all just went through that busy mind of yours, pet. You exhaust me trying to read your conflicting expressions."

Ah, so that's how he knew what she was thinking so often.

She breathed a heavy sigh. "Marc, if I show up at Mama's with a bruised cheek—something I can't hide as easily as the bruises on my shoulders—my brothers will be all over me to identify who hit me. I don't want any—or more likely *all*—of them going to jail defending my honor. They're Old World that way."

Marc brushed her hair away from her shoulder and breast. "As am I, *cara*."

She narrowed her gaze at him to see if he was serious. "I told you I don't want you or Luke going after Allen, either. I've taken care of him."

He smiled in an enigmatic way that gave her zero confidence he'd paid any attention to her warning. Dio, *save me from overprotective men, especially of the Italian variety.*

Maybe if she agreed to go to Denver with them, she could defuse the situation. Surely they'd forget about going after Allen in a week's time. And her brothers wouldn't accidently learn about the attack.

A sudden thought occurred to her. Had Luke slept in the living room last night—or had he gone after Allen? Macho Texans weren't any less overprotective of women than were Italians.

"Where did Luke sleep last night?"

Momentarily surprised by the question, he answered finally, "The wingback chair in the living room. Why?"

She didn't see any indication he was lying to her. If he was going to lie about it, the logical response would have been that Luke had slept on the sofa, not a chair. And didn't Marc say that Doms do not lie to their subs?

But he's not my Dom!

Or was he? *Mio Dio*, he'd been in control of her emotions, her body, sometimes even her thoughts, since last night.

And, dear Lord, she'd enjoyed it.

The thought of her boring, vanilla life stretching out before her turned her stomach. She knew what she wanted and how to get it.

Angelina wrenched herself away from him and scooted off the other side of the bed. "Excuse me a minute." She walked around the bed and picked up her phone, then walked into the bathroom.

Five minutes later, she returned to find Marc still lying in bed, his arm flung over his eyes. The angry scar on his side caused an ache in her heart making her want to kiss it better, but she couldn't.

He turned and looked up, and then quirked an eyebrow at her. The expression sent butterflies loose in her tummy. God, he was handsome.

Steeling herself, she announced, "Let's join Luke in the kitchen and get something to eat. It's going to be a long drive."

"You're coming with us." It wasn't a question.

"Yes, but only because I want to learn more about BDSM and being submissive." She paused then went in for the kill. "I want you to be my Dom this week…Master."

He stared at her as if she'd blindsided him with a two-by-four to the temple. She wasn't sure why, but that one night as his submissive wasn't enough. She wanted to know more. And she wanted Marc to be the one to teach her. Well, for the most part.

After some kind of internal battle, he nodded, his expression grim. "Very well, pet. But you won't be staying with me in Denver. Luke will have that honor."

Angelina smiled, but didn't correct him. She knew exactly where she would be staying—the perfect place to face her demons and learn more about BDSM.

He swung his legs over the side of the bed and towered over her. "The first rule you need to learn—never address me as Master again."

* * *

Luke's head ached worse than it had after the Texas football victory parties. His little head ached, too, and he gripped the steering wheel as he tried his damnedest to ignore Angel's body pressed against him. He noticed his white knuckles on the steering wheel and loosened his grip. What had possessed him to order the special center seat for his Rover? He couldn't wait to get her to Marc's house and make his escape.

Marc, riding shotgun, fumbled with the wrapper on an enormous Hershey bar. "One thing you should know about Angelina this week, since she'll be staying with you, is that she has a very special relationship with chocolate." Marc reached around Angel to hand it to Luke in a symbolic gesture not lost on Luke.

What the hell did he mean she'd be staying with him? He'd never survive a whole day with her, much less a week.

With reluctance, he accepted the bar and balanced it between his hands while keeping the heels of his palms on the wheel. He broke off a rectangle and extended it to Angel. "Open for me, darlin'."

Trying to keep his eyes on the road he missed the mark, but she took his hand and guided it toward her mouth, taking the tips of his fingers along with the chocolate. Her moan of ecstasy sent his dick into overdrive.

He knew she wasn't safe in her house alone, but he'd already let things go too far with her. He glanced aside at the nearly orgasmic expression on her face, then handed her the chocolate bar and returned his attention to the road, gripping the wheel harder.

As they ticked off the miles to Denver, he felt her body relax. Thank goodness her head gravitated toward Marc's shoulder and not his.

He hated not having choices or a well-thought-out plan. Bringing her to Denver wouldn't have been his first game plan, but how else could they keep her safe from Martin this week than for her to stay with one or the other of them? Why the hell did it have to be him? The more time Luke spent with her, the increased likelihood she'd discover his involvement in her father's death. He never wanted to have her look at him with accusation or even hatred in her big brown eyes.

Why the hell did she have to be a Giardano?

Regardless of whether Maggie, destiny, or Marc even, wanted to throw them together, Luke intended to steer clear of Angel this week. The best page for his Angel playbook would be to keep thoughts of Maggie front and center in his mind the rest of this drive—and week.

As they neared the metro limits, he saw Marc's hand roaming up her thigh, disappearing under her skirt. No, Angel certainly wouldn't be neglected with Marc around. She and Marc sure hit it off last night—and this morning. He was the logical one to keep her nearby, except for when Marc had treks to lead out on the mountain. He'd limit himself to guard duty on those occasions only.

She moaned in her sleep and Luke felt his dick tighten. *Damn.* Memories of his mouth on her pussy last night on the sofa just about undid him. Keeping his hands—and everything else—off of her this week would be the only way he'd survive.

Maggie, what the hell are you trying to do to me here, babe? Why couldn't you have sent someone else?

* * *

Marc enjoyed having Angelina's head resting on his shoulder most of the drive to Denver. He looked down at her, watching her breasts jiggle in the vee of her blouse as the SUV bounced along. She'd fallen asleep soon after Luke had fed her some of the chocolate bar. If he was smart, he'd have gotten some shut-eye himself.

But his head—both of them, to be honest—refused to give him any rest. Her turning the tables on him this morning still rankled him. He couldn't turn her down because he needed to get her out of Denver. But calling him Master couldn't have put a bigger damper on the words she'd just spoken—that she wanted him to train her.

Had she meant anything by it? Could she be satisfied with what he had to offer—this week only?

He looked at her eyelashes fanned beneath her eyes. Having her so close and not being able to do anything about it drove his cock to distraction, which, of course, short-circuited his other head. For most of the trip, he and Luke hadn't talked so as not to disturb her sleep, but they'd be entering the city limits soon. She'd have to wake up anyway.

Marc reached over and began stroking her thigh. She moaned in her sleep. His cock grew even harder, if possible.

"Mmm," Angelina spread her thighs apart and let her head loll against the back of the seat. Her eyes remained closed, giving the appearance she was sleeping, but she was faking. Well, there was one thing she'd better not fake with him this week. His fingers glided along the velvety skin of her inner thighs until he reached the short curls covering her pussy.

Very good, pet. No panties.

Her pussy had been clean-shaven at the club a month ago. She'd let it grow out since. He'd prefer to see her clean shaven. Marc slid his middle finger between her folds and into her wet opening. She hissed as he entered her without hindrance. *Dio*, she was so wet for him already. He withdrew his finger and drew circles around the hood of her clit. Her breathing grew more shallow and rapid.

"Who is touching you?"

"Marc," she whispered, her eyes remaining closed.

His finger stopped its motion. "Wrong answer, pet."

She grimaced in frustration, opened her eyes, and her sleepy gaze met his. "Sir."

His gut clenched at the word. God, he hadn't thought he would hear her say it again after their demonstration had ended. "Tell me what you need, *bella*."

"More."

"More what?"

"Marc, please." Her frustration grew.

"What did you call me?"

"Sir!" She ground the word out, which didn't please him at all. "You know what I need."

"Doms can't read minds. Now, tell me—respectfully."

She groaned, but needed to learn to respond properly to a Dom's questions. Most couldn't read minds. Bodies, yes, especially hers. *Dio*, she was so expressive.

"I need you to touch me, Sir. Faster."

"The speed is not up to you, *amore*, but your Dom. Touch you where?"

"There."

"Where?"

"My clit!"

He needed to work on her lack of proper respect, so he stopped and waited.

She sighed. "Sir, please touch my clit, Sir."

Better. He smiled at how she'd sandwiched her sirs and wondered if she would want to have another scene with Luke. He really needed to get the man into the game, if she truly was meant for him. And it sure seemed so, given Luke's dream the other night.

But he'd worry about Luke later. His finger resumed its movement, increasing the speed as he massaged the sides, always remaining outside her hood. Her breathless panting and *gattina* mewling told him she approached the crest. She leaned back against the seat and tilted her pelvis upward to give him easier access. He wet his thumb at her entrance then slid two fingers inside her, positioning his thumb over her engorged clit and his fingers on her G-spot.

"Oh, God, yes!"

This seemed as good a time as any to spell out a few more rules for exactly what he expected of Angelina this week.

"You will not come without permission, pet."

She opened her eyes, which held the glazed look of a woman about to reach an orgasm. Confused by the interruption, she asked, "What?"

"Just like last night, you will have to ask for permission to come, or be told by me when to come, or you will be punished. This time, I want you to ask."

"You're kidding, right?"

"Wrong question." He halted the motion of his fingers and thumb and her pussy muscles clenched around his fingers in frustration. "I assure you I would never joke about something as important as my toy's orgasms."

She shrugged. "Okay. Sir, can I come?"

He'd definitely have to work on her attitude. Not to mention her grammar. Why was it Americans slaughtered their own language? "*May* I come?" he corrected her.

"What!?"

His fingers remained motionless inside her. She tried to move against his hand. "Remain still."

She stopped moving and surrendered with a sigh. "*May* I come?"

"Sir," he reminded.

She looked over at Luke, as if he would rescue her. Luke shrugged. "Sorry, darlin'. That stuff's between you two."

She turned toward Marc and groaned. "*Sir*, may I come? Now!"

"Are you topping from the bottom?"

"No, actually, I'm begging from the bottom. Damn it, Sir Marc. Let Me Come!"

"You two are making it damned hard for me to keep this vehicle on the road," Luke complained. His knuckles whitened as he held onto the steering wheel with a death grip.

Marc laughed, but his focus quickly returned to Angelina's training. She had a lot to learn about how to speak respectfully to a Dom. But learn she would.

"You'll be punished for speaking to your Dom in that tone." Marc felt her vaginal muscles spasm around his fingers and he smiled. The thought of being disciplined again aroused her, whether she fully accepted the idea she should enjoy it or not.

"Sir, please. I need to come! Please don't bring me this close again and leave me hanging."

He heard the need in her voice. Yet, her request to come was far from where he wanted it. His fingers remained still.

"When you obey, you'll find your experiences will be much more pleasurable."

She bit her lower lip, taking slow, deep breaths as she fought for self-control. Damn her and that tight rein she kept on herself. But he could wait. He watched her breasts rise and fall. Lovely. Yes, he could enjoy this view all day.

"Please, Sir, may I come?" she pleaded sweetly.

He smiled. Much better. "Yes, pet." With his free hand, he reached up and pinched her right nipple—hard—then rolled her nub. Her pussy muscles clenched around his fingers and he resumed pumping in and out of her pussy, stimulating her G-spot, as his thumb rubbed her erect clit.

"Come. Now."

"Oh, yes!" She reached out to grab his and Luke's thighs and hung on for dear life. Her pelvis bucked against his hand as she crested, then tumbled over the peak. "Yesssss! *Mio Dio!* I'm coming!"

But of course you are. I permitted it.

He smiled as she flew apart for him. When her quivering pussy settled down to sporadic spasms, she looked over at Marc and smiled. "Thank you, Sir." After a short pause, she added, "May I have another?"

Marc laughed loud and long. Absolutely enchanting. Not to mention totally bratty. He was going to have such fun correcting her misbehavior. He regretted not letting her stay with him, but he'd still have time with her this week.

He grinned and leaned over to kiss her, when her eyes opened wide and she scooted her ass farther back on the bench seat.

"Oh!" Angelina reached on the floorboard to retrieve her purse and pulled out a piece of paper. "I almost forgot to tell you where to drop me off."

Marc's fingers pulled out of her pussy. "What do you mean, pet? You're staying with Luke, of course."

"Look, I like you both a lot and look forward to seeing you this week, but I'm not moving in with either of you, even for a week."

Marc had no intention of leaving her with someone he didn't know could protect her. One of the reasons he'd chosen Luke's place over his, apart from the intimacy issue, was that Luke worked from a shop in the garage of his townhouse. He'd be home tomorrow, while Marc had to lead a group of high-school reunion friends on a day hike to Summit Lake on Mt. Evans.

"Anyway, I made the arrangements to stay with a friend in the Five Points area. You told me I couldn't lie to Mama, Marc, so I called her this morning and asked if she'd like me to give her cooking classes in exchange for a place to stay. She agreed."

Angelina handed him the piece of paper. "Can you give Luke directions? I don't know Denver very well."

Marc hadn't seen this coming. Rattled, he accepted the paper and looked at the address. He blinked and looked at the words again. Angelina wanted them to drop her off at the Masters at Arms Club?

Oh, shit. This couldn't be good.

Marc needed to get a message to Adam telling him not to recognize him or Luke. And how was he supposed to clue Luke in not to mention their involvement in the club? Why didn't he just come clean now about being the dungeon monitor who failed her that night? Hell, no, because he wanted to make it up to her first. For reasons he couldn't explain to himself, he didn't want her to see him as a failure.

Chapter Sixteen

Angelina watched Marc pull out his smart phone, still holding on to the club's address. She was glad the building didn't have a neon sign out front proclaiming it to be a kink club. Karla had told her to go to the private entrance. Maybe Marc and Luke wouldn't realize what went on inside the place by looking at the exterior. Could she get them to just drop her off at the door without going in?

He held the phone in such a way that she couldn't see what he was doing. Probably checking for directions.

"I can put the address in the GPS here, if you like," she offered, pointing to the device mounted on the dash.

"No, that won't be necessary," Marc said. "I already...I have an app on here."

More and more houses and condos began popping up as they drove through Littleton. The closer they came to Denver, the faster her heart beat. She was looking forward to seeing Karla again, but wished her newfound friend didn't live in the very place she'd been beaten by Allen. Of course, Karla lived in the private living quarters, so she'd just avoid the downstairs club area and stick to the safer rooms in the house.

Like the kitchen. She couldn't wait to see what it would look like. She hoped there was decent equipment, but what were the chances a club like that would have a gourmet kitchen? She'd have to make do.

Despite her best efforts, she couldn't keep her mind from wandering back to that awful night last month or to Allen's brutal attack Friday night. She shuddered.

"Cold?" Luke reached for the heater control and turned it up.

"Thanks." Hardly, but she didn't intend to explain she'd been thinking of Allen. The sooner Marc and Luke forgot about him, the better. Maybe by next weekend the whole incident would have blown over and she could get her life back.

Marc wrapped his arm around her and pulled her closer to his side. She cuddled against him, struck once more by how safe he made her feel. Maybe there was something to be said for a dominant man. At least you knew where you stood. Marc said he'd never hurt her. While the spanking had hurt like hell, he'd intermingled the pain with pleasure. When he had semi-restrained her, he'd done nothing but provide her with the most diabolical orgasm known to woman. He seemed to only want to please her.

What's not to love about that?

Whoa! Nobody said anything about love. This was sex and submission, nothing more. At least, she hoped there would be sex this time.

What would it be like to submit to Marc—truly submit—not just playing like they were now. Well, *she* was playing; she wasn't so sure about Marc. How did he plan to punish her, she wondered. Was he into public scenes? The thought of returning to the club's playroom made her stomach churn. The room Allen had taken her to was more like a dungeon than a playroom, although she knew from her novels that a true dungeon was much scarier.

She'd spent years trying to become independent and to take charge of her life. With Allen, she'd only agreed to submit because she wanted to spice things up and see what all the fuss was about in her books. She'd felt nothing the few times they'd had vanilla sex. Then Marc and Luke had shown her how fantastic sex could be.

But Marc would want more than her body to submit. He'd want her mind—and maybe a bit of her soul. That was more than she was willing to give a man.

"What are you thinking so hard about, pet?"

"Lots of things."

"Choose one and tell me."

"Do all kink clubs have a dungeon?"

He laughed robustly. "Now, if I'd known you were thinking about kink clubs and dungeons, I'd have asked you to share more than one thought."

"I'm just curious."

"Yes, *gattina mia*. You are that." He chuckled then stroked her bare thigh in an affectionate way. "It is one of the traits I love most about you."

The mention of the word love scared her at first, but of course, he didn't mean love like that. She relaxed. No ties. Well, not the emotional ones, anyway.

"I don't know about all clubs, but the one I...the ones I've been to usually do. But it's in an area not accessible to any but those who are looking for one."

She shuddered at the thought of what went on in the dungeon. Did the Masters at Arms have a dungeon?

"What would someone do in a dungeon?"

"Don't worry, pet. You aren't going to be visiting a dungeon anytime soon—if ever. Not with this Dom, at least."

Angelina released the breath she'd been holding and relaxed against him again. She had no clue what Marc expected to gain from this week's lessons, but was too afraid to ask. Was he into having a woman be subservient to him twenty-four/seven, or only in the bedroom? And living room? And kitchen? And any other room in which he chose to make her obey?

How could she be an obedient submissive twenty-four/seven? She had no desire to submit to anyone that way. She got tired of Marc telling her what to do after a while. But she enjoyed hearing him tell her she had pleased him. Was that only because she wanted to avoid punishments like the spanking she'd received? How could she handle something more intense than that? She'd better stay on his good side this week, whenever they were together, at least. Well, starting now. She was already in trouble.

If she spoke her safeword, would he merely end the scene—or could they just hit pause? Marc hadn't really said what the consequences would be. She should ask him. Clarify things. Why was talking about sex so hard? Still...

"Marc? I mean, Sir?"

Marc's arm pulled her even closer to him and he placed his chin on the top of her head. She smiled, apparently having pleased him by remembering to use his title. "Yes, *amore*?"

Her heart fluttered at the endearment. "Um..." Oh, why hadn't she just kept her mouth shut?

"What is it, pet? Did you have a question?"

Why couldn't he just read her thoughts like the Doms in romance novels sometimes did? She took a deep breath. "Yes, Sir. I was wondering...what would happen if I used my safeword?"

"The scene would stop immediately."

"What if...what if I just wanted to pause and regroup?"

"Ah, you can designate a word for that, as well. Many use 'yellow,' like the traffic light. No, it doesn't mean floor it like some drivers interpret the yellow."

She smiled at his analogy. "Then what happens?"

"Whether you used red or yellow, we would stop and discuss what you're feeling and how we might adjust the scene to either continue or plan a future scene to make it less overwhelming."

"So, you wouldn't stop…um, being my Dom, if I used my safeword?"

Marc leaned back and cupped her chin to turn her face toward his. He smiled as if indulging a child. "No, pet. You've asked me to train you this week. I am committed to you during that time. Until I get to know you and your body better, I won't know all of your limits. I can only learn those by your being honest with me and telling me when you've reached one, so that I can pull back and renegotiate the scene. Communication is the most important tool in a Dom/sub relationship. You must always be honest with me."

His pupils dilated as he spoke, causing her breathing to hitch. Thoughts of giving up control and being dominated by him should have had her grabbing for the door handle to throw herself onto the side of the road and escape. Instead, she felt her clit throb as mental images flashed through her mind of herself kneeling before Marc, head bowed, waiting to be told how to please him.

Angelina thought he was going to kiss her, but he bent down and placed a chaste kiss on her forehead instead.

"Almost there." Luke's announcement interrupted her thoughts, and she broke away from Marc. She wondered if she'd see Luke this week. Considering he hadn't been able to even make eye contact with her this morning, that possibility seemed unlikely. Was he upset that she'd spent most of the night with Marc? She should explain to him the arrangement she had with Marc was strictly as a student of BDSM. No strings, no romantic attachments. Somehow, Luke seemed the more stable of the two.

But Luke confused her. Last night, she'd thought he was interested in her. The way he'd brought her to her first orgasm in forever made her squirm in her seat again. However, his constantly pulling away from her since then made her want to employ some domination tactics of her own. An image of Luke stretched out on the cross where she'd been flogged came to her mind, only he was facing away from the cross. The cross didn't seem so intimidating with him on it.

She was certain he would never agree to something like that, even if she could so picture him there. Still, he certainly wouldn't be able to run away from her there. She giggled.

"What's so funny, pet?"

"That's for me to know and you to find out."

"Are you keeping secrets from me, *cara*?" His tone grew very serious.

"Actually, this is more a secret from Luke." She felt both Marc and Luke tense. Angelina laid her head in the crook of Marc's arm and shoulder and laid her hand on Luke's thigh, looking ahead as they drove through a residential area with very expensive homes. Before she had time to explore that fantasy any further, Marc got a text message he read.

"Luke, maybe you should stop for gas."

"No, we're good."

"I really need to hit the head."

"Well, why didn't you just say so?"

"Trying to show some class around a lady."

She smiled, finding it humorous Marc could talk in great detail about sex, BDSM, and her girly bits, but then became embarrassed to talk about the call of nature.

"Besides, I need to show you the route map to where Angelina's staying."

A few minutes later, Luke pulled into a gas station and up to one of the pumps. She guessed he decided to fill up after all. They both got out, but Angelina stayed inside to just chill. As they came closer to the club, she became more on edge. She laid her head back against the bench seat and closed her eyes, trying to feign indifference.

How much farther? She wanted to get there—and at the same time to never go there again. This was going to be a roller-coaster week for her emotions.

* * *

"She wants to go where?" Luke's laughter only pissed Marc off even more. He needed to tell Angelina who he was, but after all his talk about honesty, he'd sure dug himself a deep hole. Until he could figure out the best way to explain his reasons for perpetuating this lie of omission, he planned to keep his mouth shut. But, just as Luke had felt the need to confess to him this morning, Marc needed to let him know what was going on, if for no other reason than to keep Angelina from finding out before he was ready to come clean.

"There's something you need to know." Marc waited for Luke to stop laughing. "Angelina and I met before—at the club."

"What are you talking about? She sure didn't act like she knew you."

"She doesn't remember me. She was in a bad place when I rescued her from an abusive scene. So she didn't recognize me—and I didn't fill in the memory lapse."

"Why not?"

Well, if I knew that, I'd probably tell her.

"When it started out, there was no need to dredge up bad memories. I didn't think I'd see her beyond that night at the bar. Then we went to dinner at her house, and you know what happened when we found her." Marc ran a hand over his face. "Look, I'm going to find a way to tell her. Just not right now."

"What about Adam? Is he in on the lie?"

Marc cringed inwardly at the word, but it was nothing less than a lie. "He knows. He's not too happy about my asking him to play a part in it. We may have to stick around at Adam's for a while after we drop her off so he can read me the riot act. He's been anxious to do so for a while now. I just handed him a full clip of ammo."

Adam's "WTF R U doing lying to her?" message left it clear he was in for a royal reaming out by his former master sergeant. Maybe Marc would feel better afterward. With any luck, Adam would know how he could extricate himself from the situation without damaging Angelina's trust in him…or, more importantly, a future Dom.

"Adam's going to talk with Angelina's friend, Karla, too. She was hired to sing at the club a few months back." Marc could just imagine how thrilled Adam was to have to talk to Karla, too. How the two could sleep across the hall from each other and barely speak boggled the mind. Regardless, Marc was in for the royal treatment, all right.

But having her stay here was worth it. She'd be safe from Asshole at the club. The man had been banned from the premises. Even if the bastard pursued her to Denver, this would be the last place he'd expect to find her. Marc wouldn't have let her stay with a friend anywhere else in town, but Adam would protect her as well as Marc could. Maybe even better, because he was retired and could be there twenty-four/seven.

They returned to the cab of the SUV and minutes later were pulling onto the street where the club was located. The area must have started to look familiar to Angelina.

"Karla said to use the back entrance."

Marc gave Luke directions as if he were reading them off his phone screen and totally unaware of where he was headed.

A minute later, Luke pulled into a short driveway behind the two-and-a-half story Victorian mansion. The black wrought-iron fencing and gates gave the red brick, rectangular building a militaristic look that suited the club's theme. On the second floor, a wrought-iron balcony surrounded Adam's private patio. A formidable presence drew Marc's attention in that direction, where Adam stood like a ship's captain at his helm. His hands fisted on his hips, the man was beyond pissed. When Adam turned and walked away, Marc steeled himself for the reaming out to come.

"Angie!" Karla ran down the back porch steps to greet Angelina. She wore a lacy black corset that barely contained her breasts and bounced to a stop just short of wrapping Angelina in a bear hug. Karla took her guest's hands between hers in greeting instead. "I'm so glad you're going to stay here this week."

While Adam purchased her stage wardrobe, he didn't have much say about what she wore in her off hours. But did she dress like this all the time? If so, was the man dead and had just forgotten to fall over?

Marc had never seen Karla quite so exuberant before. He didn't realize how being surrounded by three serious, non-active military men wasn't exactly conducive to much of a fun social life for her. She acted so mature and somber most of the time he'd forgotten she was only twenty-five, probably about the same age as Angelina.

Marc wondered how much younger Angelina was than his own thirty-three years. He watched as she gave Karla a hug, Italians being more demonstrative. The two sure hit it off quickly in the short time they'd known each other last month.

Marc wished he had his arms around Angelina right now. Touching her. Tying her to…something. Just when was he supposed to start her training—and where?

"What happened to your eye?" Karla looked over at Marc as if she were ready to deck him.

What had he ever done to make her think him capable of hitting a woman in the face like that? She didn't think much of the BDSM activities at the club, but that was a low blow, pun intended.

Angelina laughed at their expressions. "No, Marc and Luke rescued me. It was an old boyfriend. The one Master Adam escorted from the club during my last visit."

"Oh, my God! What a horrible man! I hope he's in jail now."

Angelina looked down at the ground. "No, but I took care of him. Between the chin jab that broke his nose and, well, a knee to the groin, he won't be bothering me again."

"Oh, sounds like you've had some self-defense training, too. Adam made me take martial arts before I went to college in New York City."

"I thought you only just met."

"Oh, we corresponded since I was sixteen." A shadow crossed her face. Clearly, times weren't as good as when they were pen pals.

Luke went to the back of the SUV to retrieve Angelina's suitcase and Marc hung back, waiting for Angelina to "introduce" them to her friend, but Karla took the initiative and came over to extend her hand to Marc.

"Hi, I'm Karla." He caught an almost imperceptible wink. Obviously, Adam had let her in on the ruse. He breathed a sigh of relief. Now why did it just add to his guilt to bring an innocent into his lie? Why didn't he just come clean and have a big laugh about the whole thing once they got inside?

He took her hand and shook it. "Marc D'Alessio. Nice to meet you."

"And my apologies for thinking the wrong thing about Angelina's black eye. I have no tolerance for men who abuse women."

When Luke joined them, Marc introduced him to Karla for real because Luke hadn't been to the club since Karla arrived.

A gruff voice from the back door caught everyone's attention. Marc looked up to see Adam standing there. "Come in and take a load off. Karla's made dinner for everyone."

Shit. So much for getting this over quickly. Marc turned his attention back to the ladies and motioned for them to go first. Luke fell into step before him and Marc brought up the rear, making his way up the wooden steps and across the porch. Adam stood by the door, greeting everyone as they went inside.

Marc appreciated the warm greeting and smile he gave Angelina, at least. She probably felt very uncomfortable being back here.

"Glad to have you back for a visit, hon," he said to her. She smiled up at Adam, thanked him, and walked into the kitchen.

Adam glanced down at Karla as she walked by but she didn't look up at him or say a word. Maybe Angelina could bring the two of them together this week so they could at least coexist without all the tension.

Next in the procession, Luke greeted Adam and whispered something Marc couldn't hear, causing Adam to nod and glance toward Marc. Coming to stand nearly at attention before his former master sergeant, Marc endured the man's brutal stare.

He'd do anything in the world before disappointing this man. But he'd not only disappointed Adam, he'd put him and Karla in an uncomfortable position.

Without preamble, Adam asked, "Who hit her?"

"Sir Asshole, or shithead as you called him after you kicked him out of the club last month. He attacked her again at her house Saturday night. I brought her to Denver to keep her away from him, but the police can't do anything unless he violates the protection order." Adam growled. No, he wouldn't have to worry about Adam keeping an eye on her while Marc was working. "I'll fill you in later."

"You'd better find a way to explain why you and I need to talk because your ass is mine just as soon as you can pop smoke after dinner." *Oh, shit.* Adam had reverted to Marine combat jargon. Yeah, Marc would be wishing he were in retreat all right—but Adam's office was where he needed to be retreating *from*. There would be hell to pay when he got there.

He deserved nothing less. Maybe Adam could tell him how to fix the mess he'd gotten himself into. As he walked by Adam, the man actually slapped the back of Marc's head. He wasn't looking forward to this talk. At least he'd get a last meal.

Marc walked into the kitchen to find Karla giving Angelina the grand tour. Well, grand might not be the right word. The kitchen certainly was utilitarian—but nothing to write home about for a gourmet chef like Angelina. He could tell from her expression she wasn't impressed, but trying to be polite.

When they'd done the renovations, Adam had barely known how to boil water so he hadn't fussed much about appliances or fixtures in here. He'd planned to eat a lot of takeout and delivery. The biggest expense had been the cabinetry, which Luke had made out of fine cherry. It gave the room a warm feeling at least. Not that he was getting any warm feelings from Adam right now. He avoided making eye contact with the man who had been his mentor for years.

"Angelina, you and Karla are welcome to have your cooking classes in my state-of-the-art kitchen." Marc certainly hadn't made much use of it. Like the rest of the house, the kitchen was mainly for show. He pretty much lived in the bedroom when he was home, where he had his books, his sound system, even a wet bar. Everything a man could want.

Except for someone to enjoy it with.

But wasn't that the way he'd always preferred it? Keep the women at the club? At arm's length? Well, it used to be.

Angelina smiled. "That sounds great...Marc." He could tell she didn't know how to address him outside the bedroom, so he smiled to let her know she could call him by his name now. Later he'd make it clear she didn't need to use the title unless they were in a scene or playing. He didn't want more than that.

"After you eat this, you'll see why I need cooking lessons," Karla said, as she pulled a covered dish out of the oven.

"Karla's tuna-noodle casserole is wonderful," Adam said. "So's her broccoli casserole."

She smiled at him before turning her attention back to the dish and removing the lid. "Yes, and you have had it at least twice a week since I got here, because I don't know how to make anything else, other than brownies."

"Cooking's easy. All you have to do is know how to read a recipe. How did you learn to cook those two recipes?"

A look of pain crossed Karla's face before she forced a smile and answered. "My mom's the baker in the family and taught me how to make the peanut-butter brownies for Adam and my brother while they were deployed." She glanced over at Adam and smiled, then continued on a near whisper. "My brother Ian taught me to make the tuna casserole on a visit to New York last year."

Out of the blue, Adam crossed the kitchen and, for the first time Marc could remember, wrapped his arms around Karla. He looked at Marc and the others and explained, "Karla lost her brother in a motorcycle accident a few months back."

"Oh, God, Karla! I'm so sorry!" Angelina crossed the room and rubbed Karla's shoulders, above Adam's arms.

Shit. Marc felt a stabbing pain in his chest, remembering how his own brother's death had affected him—for years. No wonder she'd been so somber since she'd come to the club. Her wound was still raw. Why hadn't

Adam said anything to him? Well, it might have helped if he'd been around more than just to work during club hours.

Marc cleared his throat. "Karla, I lost my brother in the war. If you ever need someone to talk to."

She brushed tears off her cheeks and pulled away from Adam's arms with some reluctance. "Thanks, everyone. I don't like to talk about it much. It's still too...hard."

Luke said, "Sometimes talking about it helps."

"Look," Karla began, "I didn't mean to start a sob fest here. If I haven't totally ruined your appetite, I'm sure my casserole will finish the job."

Adam picked up two potholders and the baking dish. "Nonsense. Everyone's going to love it. Let's eat."

* * *

Marc couldn't say that tuna-noodle casserole was something he could eat a couple times a week, but he liked it well enough. He'd certainly cleaned his plate. But he was sure Angelina would be able to bring out the hidden chef in Karla. "Thank you for going to all the trouble to make us dinner, Karla. It was great."

Luke put his fork down on his equally empty plate. "Karla, if I could cook that well, I'd look like a linebacker."

"Thanks, Marc and Luke. You're sweet."

Marc placed his napkin beside his plate. "No, we're stuffed."

Adam sat back in his chair and smiled at her. "I've tried to tell her that—after years of eating MREs in the field, this Marine appreciates home cooking...period. Thanks, Karla." Adam smiled at the black-haired Goth, who blushed and looked down at her half-empty plate.

Marc wondered if there was something developing between the two of them—finally. Adam had been a widower longer than Luke had. Maybe it was time for both of them to find someone.

Marc watched as Luke glanced over at Angelina and tried to tamp down the stabbing pain he felt in his chest. She deserved someone like Luke. But why did the thought of them being together bother him so much?

"This is one of my brother Tony's favorites, too. Easy to make and filling."

The mention of Tony's name brought a pained look to Luke's face. Should Marc have kept him from telling Angelina about his connection to her father's death? Why did he want to keep the truth from her on these two counts? She was a strong woman. She'd be able to forgive them both.

He hoped.

"Well tomorrow, I want to be challenged, up to a point." Karla glanced over at Angelina with something akin to worship. It was good to see the sparkle in her eyes that he'd seen when she'd first come out to welcome Angelina today. She seemed like a sweet person, but he could tell there was an inner resolve. The woman would get what she wanted out of life, once she'd recovered from her recent loss.

Angelina smiled. "We're going to start out early for the farmer's market and you're all invited to dinner tomorrow night to enjoy Karla's gourmet creation." When she turned her big brown eyes in his direction, Marc felt his groin tighten. "Marc, I hope it's okay if I invite everyone over to your place for dinner. It just makes more sense than transporting the food back here."

Marc grinned at her. "Absolutely. My place could use a little life. I'll be out on the mountain most of the day, but should be back by six or so. Adam has a…" he caught himself just in time before saying Adam had a spare key to his house. Damn, he was going to trip himself up yet. "I'll leave you a spare key so you can get in. Adam, if you have a GPS, I can program the address in it for you."

Adam glared at him. "Great."

Marc looked back at Angelina and then Karla. "Just make yourselves at home, but don't expect there to be any staples in the kitchen. I tend to eat out a lot. Navy corpsmen aren't much better at cooking than Marines are."

Adam cleared his throat. "I'll give Damián a call and see if he can join us."

Marc nodded before he remembered he wasn't supposed to know Damián either. *Shit.* Someone else to bring into the lie. "Damián?"

Adam was not at all happy at the moment. "Damián served with me in Iraq and is one of the co-owners of my club here. He's like a son to me."

"He used to live here in the same room I'm staying in now," Karla explained to Angelina.

"Just what kind of club do you run, Adam?" Marc asked. He watched Angelina take a sudden interest in her fork. Adam looked like he was ready to spit nails at Marc.

Adam grinned. "A BDSM club. Have you ever heard of BDSM?"

Angelina blushed at the mention of kink, and Marc smiled. "Yes, actually. I'm quite interested in the subject. You wouldn't happen to have any membership openings, would you?" He would so pay for this later, but was actually beginning to have fun with it now.

"Why don't we go have a little talk about it, Marc. In my office."

Shit. Okay, so he should have known Adam was just setting him up.

"Adam, what are the chances Angelina and I might use one of the theme rooms tonight?"

Adam glared at him. "If the lady is willing, she has full access to the house during her stay."

Marc looked back at Angelina, whose pupils had just dilated. He smiled. "Oh, I think the lady definitely is willing. We have some unfinished business to take care of from the ride up here."

The smile left her face as she nibbled on her lower lip and pleaded with him silently to forget about that. She clearly remembered the punishment she'd earned for disrespecting him. Just warning her ahead of time would have her on pins and needles tonight.

Adam stood. "Well, if everyone will excuse us, Marc and I need to work on some…paperwork."

Hoping for just a small reprieve, Marc offered, "Let me help clear the table first."

Luke smiled at Marc and said, "Don't worry. I can take care of it."

Traitor.

Chapter Seventeen

Marc sat down in the chair in front of Adam's desk, dreading the confrontation to come.

"You want to tell me what the fuck is wrong with you?"

Marc looked across the desktop to where Adam sat with his shirtsleeves rolled up and a laptop open to his right. Marc did his best to avoid eye contact. The screensaver showed photos of Adam and his wife, Joni. Marc stared at them a while—scenes of Joni and Adam on their wedding day, ones of her walking along an icy lakeshore, more couple shots in front of a lighthouse, on a sunny beach, and dressed in ski gear in the mountains.

A photo of a tombstone with the Montague name on it flashed on the screen for a second before Adam reached over and closed the lid on the computer, forcing Marc's attention in his direction. The man's wife had died of cancer nine years ago this November. Every year for the past five years, Adam had made an annual pilgrimage to her gravesite in Minnesota a few weeks before Thanksgiving. Damián and Marc had learned that date was non-negotiable on his calendar.

He usually came home and had some pretty dark days until he got past all the holidays. Marc and Damián had learned to steer clear of him during those dark times—and to not let the subs decorate the club for the holidays. They could never do it to Adam's satisfaction, which upset them because they wanted to please him. He'd thanked them, but asked that they not bother after the first year the club was open.

"I've been letting you stew in your own juices for nearly a year now." Adam's words brought him back to the dressing down he was about to receive. "What the fuck is going on? What are you thinking, lying to that woman? You said you cared about her when you rescued her last month. Prove it."

The man wasn't one to mince words. Marc met Adam's gaze. "I do. I swear to God, I don't know why. In the beginning, she didn't recognize me and there was no point reminding her of that time."

"When did you start negotiating scenes with her?"

"The next night. At her house."

"You should have told her then."

Marc ran his hand through his hair and looked down at the floor. "She insisted she wasn't a submissive. I wanted to prove her wrong, but I didn't want to tell her I had insider information."

"Is she?"

Marc looked up. "Is she what?"

"Submissive, damn it. Keep up with this conversation."

Marc smiled. "Hell, yes, she is."

"Well, you can do what you want off-premises, but you're not going OFP in here."

The man was channeling his inner master sergeant today, for sure, referring to the familiar Marine expression—OFP, going off on your Own Fucking Program rather than following the rules of the mission or group.

Of course, Adam had gone OFP on a couple of occasions, but those involved saving the men in his unit, including Marc on one occasion. But the BDSM community had established strict protocols, as well as general rules, that Doms and subs, Tops and bottoms, Masters and slaves were to follow. Made it easier to navigate the social waters when new people became part of the local Scene.

"Doms do not lie to submissives in this club. Now, tell me how and when you're going to tell her who you are."

"Give me a couple days."

"Why?"

Marc hated to admit this to his friend and mentor, but met his steady gaze. "I already failed her once." His voice was husky with unfamiliar emotion. He shifted in his seat. "I need to prove she can trust me to be there for her if she needs me."

"Come again?"

Marc looked away, remembering the night he just hadn't wanted to be here. "I arrived at the club late that night. By the time you brought me up to speed and I began to make the rounds, she'd already been on that damned cross nearly an hour. If I'd been on time, I would have ended that scene long before she went into deep subspace."

"You sound like Damián."

Marc looked at Adam, puzzled.

"Instead of blaming the insurgents for killing Sergeant Miller, he blamed himself. Well, I've got news for you both, Doc." Adam hadn't called him by his corpsman's nickname for years. "Shit happens. Sometimes diarrhea happens. There were other DMs on duty that night, too, and I'd been by to check on the couple. The scene went downhill fast. All that matters is that you were there in time. The only person to blame for what happened to Angelina that night is the shithead poser Dom she was with who went beyond her limits."

Marc wasn't convinced he could be absolved from guilt. He diverted his gaze to the wall to his left where a huge painting hung that Karla had given Adam, trying to brighten up his dark office—an oil on canvas with a stand of quaking aspens against a deep blue Colorado sky.

Adam captured his wandering mind. "Damián didn't believe me either. But deep down, you both know I'm right. I may not outrank you now—"

Marc smiled at him. "You'll always outrank us. Always be our master sergeant."

"Good to hear. Now tell me about this burr you've had up your ass for the last year."

Definitely a straight shooter. When Damián had been on the brink of suicide, Adam had given him a similar shock therapy session to wake him up and turn things around. Damián didn't laugh a lot back then, but he usually did when he recounted how he found himself recruited to become a Dom in a BDSM club.

So, it looked like it was Marc's turn. He sure as hell hadn't been able to sort out the problem in all this time. Maybe Adam could help. The man might not have gone to college, but he sure as hell had a wealth of wisdom about life.

"I was dating a woman last year for a few months."

"Pamela?"

Marc looked up. "Yeah. How'd you remember her?"

Adam smiled. "That was a track record for you, Doc. What—four months?"

Marc grinned. "Three. Well, therein lies the problem. She wanted to take it further than I could go." He grew serious and looked down at the floor. "I freaked, Adam. Not a full-blown panic attack, but close to it."

"Who was she?"

Puzzled, Marc looked up again at Adam. "Pamela?"

Adam sighed. Marc thought he'd been listening, but had better pay even closer attention.

"No, the one who still has you running."

Marc didn't want to talk about that part of his life. His heart pounded until he heard the blood rushing through his ears. "That was a long time ago."

"Judging by that jackrabbit pulse in your neck, I'd say not long enough for you to talk about her without another near panic attack." Adam paused then closed in for the kill. "What did she do to you?"

Marc could feel his throat closing. He really didn't want to talk about this. Getting up, he said, "Look, Luke and I haven't had much sleep and I'm sure he'd like to head home now."

"Sit down." The command was spoken in his normal voice, but was a command nonetheless. When Marc remained standing, he added, "Take that as a direct order from your former master sergeant. You're not leaving this office until you spill it." Adam leaned back in his chair and propped his feet on the edge of the desk. "I'm not going anywhere. Neither are you."

Marc tried to swallow, but his throat had gone dry. Adam had been there for him during one of the darkest times of his life. The man had never done anything but love and support him ever since. He didn't want Adam to think him less of a man for what he'd done.

Adam won't abandon you. He also wouldn't share anything outside this room. When Marc sat back down, Adam smiled almost imperceptibly. *Bastardo.* Marc gritted his teeth, trying to decide what to say. How much did he want to divulge about a time in his life he'd really like to forget?

He blinked. "She screwed Gino. The day I was going to propose to her, I found her and Gino together in my bed."

"That sucks, but it doesn't sound like a woman who's worth at least nine years of anxiety."

Adam would know exactly how long ago Gino had been killed. He'd been there with him in Afghanistan.

"What else?"

"Gino and I fought that day as only brothers can. We'd always had a rivalry, but so many ugly things were said—mostly by me. I was angry, hurt. Once again, he'd taken the thing I wanted most." Marc tried to swallow, but his throat was tight and dry. He studied his hands clenching and unclenching in front of him, and then forced himself to relax.

"I told him I wished he'd never been born." The words were spoken barely above a whisper, but sounded to his ears as if shouted through a megaphone. He'd actually said he wished he were dead, but those words somehow seemed too despicable to admit to his friend.

"Gino proposed to her that day and she accepted. I know he did it out of spite. He'd have come to his senses eventually—if there'd been time." Even though Adam knew Gino the Marine, he probably didn't know what Gino was like as a civilian. "Gino had been the studious one, driven to have a career. He didn't have a lot of experience with women, especially women like Melissa. I found out later she'd manipulated him into bed. She could see he'd have a higher payout than I would in life."

Marc was silent, lost in thought.

After a moment, Adam verbally nudged him. "Then what happened?"

"Nine-Eleven—a week later. Gino enlisted. I'd left Aspen after the altercation and didn't even return home to say goodbye before he left for boot camp. Never saw him alive again."

Adam let the words hang in the air a moment. "And the woman?"

"Yeah, well, she kept showing up like gum on the soles of my best pair of Gucci shoes. I was angry at Gino for dying. The funeral…I let her manipulate me into the bedroom just hours after we buried him." Marc hung his head, not proud of the man he'd been before he'd joined the Navy and later trained to serve with the Marines in Adam's unit.

"Any woman who'd take advantage of a man at a time like that should be horsewhipped. What else did she do?"

Wasn't that bad enough? Still embarrassed, he couldn't look at Adam. "I had a reputation as a Dom with women in the grapevine at the resort. I could give them what their vanilla-sex men couldn't or wouldn't. I became a Dom at seventeen."

"A little young."

Marc grinned. "Well, there was a persuasive cougar staying at the resort who made my training a personal hobby." He sobered again. "The women were older, had more power, and pretty much could tell me what they wanted. It was more a role to play than something innate that I felt." Marc glanced away for a moment, but wanted to see the reaction on his friend's face and turned back. "When Melissa showed up on my doorstep again almost eighteen months after the funeral, I…forced her."

Adam scowled. "You raped her?"

Marc sat up straighter. "Shit, no! She wanted to have sex. She even wanted it rough. But I'd never used a woman like that before to meet my needs. Had never taken out my anger on a woman's body like that. Spankings always had been foreplay until then. Never used as a punishment. I have no doubt she had bruises for a week after the paddling I gave her. And her clit was probably sore even longer from the forced orgasms."

"Doesn't sound as harsh as the punishment I'd have given her for that stunt after Gino's funeral. But I find most subs aren't traumatized by a good paddling or a little orgasm torture—once it's over anyway."

Marc remembered a demonstration in the club's medical room where Adam and Grant had shown the technique to a younger Dom who wanted to try orgasm torture on his sub. Grant, who had been temporarily attached to Adam's Marine recon unit and caught up in the firefight in Fallujah, wouldn't bottom for anyone but her former master sergeant. But if she hadn't been restrained so securely on that table, Adam could have kissed goodbye the ability to ever obtain an erection again, because she'd have delivered a well-placed kick to his cock and balls—somewhere after about the fifth orgasm in ten or fifteen minutes.

Adam waited for him to continue. "I went OFP that night. We didn't negotiate any of that scene. Hadn't been active in the lifestyle for a very long time. I did whatever I wanted, based on what she'd agreed to two years before." Marc paused. "I was out of control. I don't ever want to let that happen again."

Adam stared at him a few moments then said, "That's been a long time. What else happened with Pamela?"

Adam sure would have made a great interrogator of prisoners. Marc had glossed over his last regular sub, not even hinting that she'd been part of the real issue. "Nothing like that. She just started to get under my skin. I liked her a lot." In comparison to Angelina, he still hadn't lowered his defenses much, because he already was in a lot deeper with the woman in the other room.

"Pamela didn't manipulate me into doing what she wanted. She seemed like the perfect sub." Marc drew air into his constricted lungs. "I even proposed to her last year."

Adam didn't allow too much dust to accumulate on that grenade. "What happened?"

"Once she had me hooked, she asked me to be her Master in a twenty-four/seven after we were married."

Adam glanced at a framed photo of Joni across his desk. *Shit.* They had enjoyed that kind of relationship, well, when Adam wasn't deployed, anyway. Would Adam be able to understand why that idea freaked Marc out so much?

Adam turned his gaze back to Marc. "That kind of relationship isn't for most people in the lifestyle. Very intense and takes a lot of work, especially on a Dom's part."

Marc relaxed. "Exactly. I didn't want to live the lifestyle twenty-four/seven. Or to have to become a disciplinarian on a regular basis. If that was what she needed, then I knew she needed to find another Dom." Marc stood and paced in front of Adam's desk. "She wasn't too happy about that response. Tried to assure me she would be happy being my bedroom sub, but I knew she'd always wonder if she could change me. Or if she'd eventually go looking for someone who would give her what she wanted."

Adam nodded. "Now, tell me what all this has to do with you lying to Angelina That's no way to instill trust."

"She's haunted me since that night I rescued her." Marc cast an accusatory glance at Adam. "Not that you'd reveal her contact info so I could do anything about it. If she hadn't happened to show up in that bar—"

"I don't go OFP on the trust subs and bottoms place in me."

Ouch.

Marc sat down again. He had asked Angelina to trust him, but he hadn't opened himself up in return. In truth, he didn't know if he could trust anyone. Except maybe Adam and Damián. Possibly Luke, although he'd never tested him. But he could trust no woman he'd ever met. "She scares the hell out of me."

Understanding awakened in Adam's eyes, and his gaze shifted momentarily to the aspen painting on the wall, then returned to Marc. "What scares you most?"

Marc didn't need long to come up with an answer, but didn't want to put it into words. Adam's stare indicated the man could outwait him. Well, there were some things he didn't even want to share with Adam. Maybe he'd make a lesser confession to appease him. "I've never been a real Dom before. Not even in the bedroom."

"What the fuck does 'real' mean? That's like saying someone is a 'true' submissive. There isn't a one size fits all to this lifestyle. Hell, I knew you were dominant when I saw you in Jerry's fetish club in LA with Damián."

"Well, then, I haven't been a very good one. I've been topped from the bottom all my life, except for Pamela, but she needed more than I could give her." Maybe he'd just been playing the role of Dom all these years, but didn't really believe he'd been a Dom. "I'm filling Angelina's head with notions of a Dom/sub relationship as if I actually have a clue."

"Have you all talked about what each of you want or don't want—kinks, likes, dislikes, limits?"

"We've begun to, yes."

"In wartime, a plan is just a plan, Marc. Sometimes you have to determine conditions on the ground and proceed with your best intel." He reached up and rubbed the back of his neck. "But when you need to go Own Fucking Program, do it. BDSM is a spectrum. Some people get no further than tying someone to the bed. Others aren't satisfied unless there's blood drawn."

Adam swung his feet off the desk and onto the floor out of sight, then clasped his hands in front of him and leaned forward. "No one has to be in that bedroom but you two, well, unless you two want to bring someone else in there." Adam grinned. "Trust your gut. Keep talking with her, negotiating scenes, and getting to know each other. You've really only known her a couple days. Give it time. What's the hurry?"

"She's only here for the week."

"Oh, give me a fucking break." Adam struck the desk with his fist. "She only lives three hours away. Try having a relationship with your subbie when you're on the other side of the fucking world half the time."

He looked at Joni's picture again and the look of regret and something that looked a lot like guilt crossed his face. Even halfway around the world, he could tell Adam and Joni had been closer emotionally than Marc had ever been with any woman.

What if I can never let my guard down?

"Angelina needs someone who can meet all her needs. What if I'm not that Dom?" On a whisper, he added, "Not the man she needs?"

Still looking at Joni's photo, he said, "I've learned over the years the right woman can be awfully forgiving of her man's shortcomings." He looked at Marc. "Just treat her with love and respect. Don't take her for granted, unless circumstances prevent you from being there for her when she needs you. And never lie to her—that's the biggest one."

Adam cleared his throat. "You have exactly three days to come clean with Angelina about who you are, which is about three days longer than I hope you'll take."

"Then I have a favor to ask." Marc had no doubt Adam would gladly be on board with this request.

***

Luke munched on his third peanut butter-flavored brownie and watched Angel and Karla talk nonstop about all the things Karla had planned for the week. Well, good. The fewer interactions he had with Angel, the better. What Karla didn't orchestrate, he was sure Marc would.

"On Thursday, I'm going up to Cassie's cabin to pick her up for our annual overnight campout. This year, we're actually coming back up here to camp on Mt. Evans. There are some mountain goats there she's wanting to photograph."

Cassie sounded like Maggie, pursuing elusive bits of nature. He wondered who she was.

"Would you like to go with us, Angie?"

Angel flinched. No small wonder she had the same aversion he had to that mountain. He didn't have to guess at the reason.

"I'm not sure. I'm not much of an outdoorsy person. But don't change your plans. I'm sure Luke and Marc will keep me busy."

Marc maybe.

"Oh, believe me, you can't be less outdoorsy than I am. But Cassie's amazing. She knows the mountains like the back of her hand. I'll bet she knows them even better than Marc, well, except maybe for Mt. Evans. But he makes his living in that mountain wilderness."

"He does?" Angel asked. Hadn't Marc told her what he did? Well, there probably hadn't been time for chitchat last night.

Karla suddenly looked stricken and glanced at Luke for help. She'd forgotten she wasn't supposed to know Marc before today.

"Yeah, you heard him right at dinner. He takes people on wilderness treks. Bonding treks mostly, corporate executives trying to figure out what makes each other tick. I think Marc would live in the wilderness, if he didn't enjoy the finer things in civilized life so much."

Relief filled Karla's eyes, and disappointment, Angel's. "Don't worry, Angel. He wouldn't drag anyone out there who didn't want the adventure."

As if his words had thrown down some invisible gauntlet, she raised her chin. "I didn't say I wouldn't be willing to try hiking or camping. I just haven't had an interest in it…before."

The unspoken "Marc" hung in the air between them.

Still, she impressed the hell out of him. Even though the thought of going up on that mountain scared her to death, she didn't want to be seen as scared or weak. Strong woman, not that he hadn't figured that out in how she'd taken care of Martin the other night. He wondered how far her bravado would take her, though. Would she actually go camping overnight on the mountain that took her father's life?

As much as he'd like her to overcome her fears, and it would keep him from having to interact with her as much this week, he wouldn't goad her into going. But at least there wasn't any chance of an avalanche this time of year. Not that there weren't thousands of other dangers, based on the rescues he was involved in year-round.

* * *

Allen Martin watched as his cleaning crew prepared daVinci's bar for another week of debauchery. The clock over the bar read four-fifteen; Rico liked to have it cleaned Sunday afternoons. Allen didn't usually check up on his cleaning crews, and he was making them damned nervous right now judging by the surreptitious glances they kept shooting his way. Then the two workers headed to the restrooms. Good. He'd prefer they were at some other part of the bar right now anyway. He didn't want an audience.

Angie wouldn't be returning here tonight to whore in public for the two men she'd picked up the other night. No, she'd packed her things and left with them shortly after noon today. He'd been parked down the street waiting for their Land Rover to drive off so he could finish what he'd started Saturday night, Emergency Protection Order or not.

A restraining order sure hadn't helped his ex-wife any, either.

When he'd seen Angie come out with them and stow a suitcase in the back, he was stunned. The bitch had run off with them! If he didn't have a client appointment, he'd have followed them.

Well, right now, he needed to find Rico's big-brother notebook before his workers came back. He remembered the drill when he'd met Angie here back in January. No doubt Rico would have required the same info from those guys before he'd have let her leave with them on Saturday night. Allen hoped the book wasn't locked in the cash register or the office in back. He wouldn't be able to open that, well, not without leaving clues to a break-in. But he was reasonably certain Rico kept it on hand for when he needed to get all protective of his female friends.

Damn it. Allen didn't have time for this bullshit. He was supposed to be running through the books to make sure his accountant wasn't cheating him.

Nothing stood out on the top of the bar or in the area where the liquor was lined up three bottles deep. Maybe below the bar. Rico kept the notebook here, he was certain of it. But where?

He began rooting around under the bar, but didn't see anything familiar. *Aha!* Allen pulled the familiar hunter-green, leather-bound portfolio from where it had been tucked next to a bin of clean bar towels. His hand shook as he reached down and pulled it out. Not wanting his workers to see him, he turned around and walked to the other end of the bar where he opened the portfolio and flipped the pages up until he came to the last page with writing. Nothing. Just a liquor shopping list. He flipped back another page.

Bingo.

Two names stared up at him. Marco D'Alessio. Stephen Lucas Denton. He jotted down their license numbers and addresses. Then he closed the portfolio and returned it to its hiding place.

So, he'd be taking a drive to Denver tomorrow. Then it hit him. That voice had sounded so familiar. He looked down at his notes. Marco. The man had reminded him of some…that's it! The Dungeon Monitor Supervisor at the Masters at Arms who had ended his scene with Angie last month before it had barely gotten started.

Apparently, Angie's meeting him here last night was no accident. Had the two been seeing each other since last month? Is that why she hadn't been hanging out at the bar all this time?

No big surprise that they'd known each other intimately, given how they'd danced last night.

Slut.

D'Alessio had shut down Allen's scene with her that night just so he could get his kink on with her. The bastard had stolen her from him.

Well, we'll see who she'll be with…in the end.

Chapter Eighteen

Angelina was a bundle of nerves as she waited for Marc to return tonight for her punishment. He had so many more implements and devices he could employ this time. What would he use?

"Karla, would you walk through the club with me before Marc gets back? I want to see everything so I can know what to expect."

"Sure. Where should we start? The theme rooms?"

"No!" Angelina had to take a deep breath to decrease her anxiety. "I don't think I'm ready for that yet."

"How about the great room where I sing?"

She remembered the Dom in the Harley vest and the coiled whip. Maybe there was no safe place in the club. "I guess we could start there. Maybe you can describe some of the activities you've seen there."

A few minutes later, Karla flipped the lights on and the great room was illuminated before her. It looked so…normal without all the people in BDSM gear hanging around. She walked into the room filled with ottomans and tables. They were closer to the stage now than they had been the night she'd been here with Allen.

Angelina walked up to the center post and lifted up a cold, heavy chain with a leather cuff attached to it. Had the Dom in the Harley vest chained the blonde submissive here and used his whip on her? Still, she shivered when she thought about being restrained by them with Marc.

"Do the chains excite you, pet?"

The pit of Angelina's stomach dropped, and she turned loose of the chain as if it was suddenly on fire. It clanged against the center post and Angelina turned to find Marc standing in the entryway beside Karla. He wore black leather pants and a black leather vest, his chest bare, except for the tufts of hair over his heart. Dear Lord, her nipples hardened just looking at him.

His gaze went to her breasts. "Never mind. I can see your answer."

He stepped into the room and walked toward her like a wolf stalking its prey. Her heart pounded, curiously depriving her of oxygen that might have helped keep her mind from turning to mush. When he reached her, he stared until she squirmed in her skin, then took his knuckles and brushed them over her nipples, making them even more engorged. She hissed, gasping for air.

"Karla, Angelina won't be needing you for a while." He didn't even turn around to dismiss Karla. His gaze remained fixed on Angelina.

"Angie, will you be okay?"

No, never again. "Yes. I'll see you upstairs later." Karla was sweet to worry about her, but Marc wouldn't administer pain without pleasure. She wouldn't enjoy the first, but couldn't wait for the other.

"Did you miss me, pet?"

How should she answer that? Karla had kept her busy with unpacking and chatting, but Marc had dominated her thoughts all evening, mostly with her worrying about the scene to come.

"Answer me."

"Yes, Sir." Oh, God. She really had.

"Thank you for your honesty, pet. Now, strip."

Her eyes opened wider. Had she heard him correctly? She looked around to make sure Karla had left and that they were alone. They were, but someone could come in at any minute, couldn't they?

"I'm not sure…"

"I am. I said strip. Now. Or you'll add to the length of your discipline session."

"It's not a punishment?"

"No, pet. We're still training that mind and body of yours to submit. This is discipline."

Angelina sucked air into her lungs as she reached up to the vee of her blouse and began to slip each button through its hole, making her way downward to the hem. If this was how bad she felt to be disciplined, she hoped to never have to be punished. She spread the flaps open a bit and untied the peasant skirt belt, then shimmied the cotton over her hips until it pooled at her feet. She hadn't worn panties today, per Marc's explicit instructions before they left her house this morning. The cool air made it abundantly clear her pussy already was wet.

Marc motioned for her to continue. She reached up to spread open her blouse, pull it off her shoulders, and slip it down her arms to join the skirt on the floor. Her breasts were shielded in a skin-tone bustier that captured Marc's interest.

His hands reached up to cup her breasts, rolling her swollen nipples through the lace before he bent down to take one lace-covered peak between his teeth. He bit her with enough force to cause her knees to buckle. Marc caught her elbows to steady her.

"We can't have that, now, can we?"

Angelina wasn't sure what he meant, until he reached behind her and picked up the leather cuffs. "No! I'm not ready for that!"

Marc smiled and took each of the cuffs off the chain and rubbed them over her nipples, teasing her with the brass buckles. The sensations were delicious.

"What is your safeword, pet?"

"Red, Sir."

"Do you trust me to stop when you say that word?"

Did she? She liked to think so, but how could she know unless she actually used the word?

"Pet, I hope to enjoy your gift of submission all week. Why would I do anything to jeopardize that on our first night? I think you know I will stop immediately if you use your safeword."

She did. Didn't she? Oh, God. She could do this. She really could. Angelina extended her hands to him, palms up.

"Good girl."

His praise melted away some of the ice in her veins. As she held her hands before him, he wrapped each wrist in one of the cuffs and fastened them with Velcro. So the buckles were just for show, as she would be if he strapped her to the post. He slipped his finger between the leather in the skin. "Not too tight?"

"No, Sir. It feels fine."

"Well, let's see if we can do better than fine." He hooked the two cuffs together and pulled her hands over her head and placed his other hand on her upper right arm to begin maneuvering her into place before the post.

I can do this. I can do this. Oh, God. I can't do this. I can't do this!

Angelina's chest rose and fell rapidly. "Yellow!"

Marc stopped moving, but still kept her hands high above her head. With his other hand, he trailed gently down the underside of her arm until he reached her breast and rubbed his knuckles against her rigid nipple.

"Tell me what you're thinking, pet."

"I don't think I can do this, Sir."

"What frightens you?"

"My hands over my head. That reminds me of…" *the one who shall remain nameless.*

"When you were restrained before, were your hands together or apart?"

"Apart, Sir."

"Were you restrained to a post like this?"

"No, Sir. To a St. Andrew's cross."

"Good. I want you to focus on how this experience is different from that earlier one, not the least difference being who your Dom is this time. Will you trust me to continue, Angelina?"

Her name always sounded so lyrical when he said it and calmed her down more than when he called her pet or other endearments. She took a deep breath. *This is Marc. He doesn't want to hurt you.*

"Yes, Sir. Thank you for slowing down for me."

He rolled her nipple. "Thank you for remembering to use 'yellow' to slow me down. Now, we will continue." He guided her backward. Would he turn her around to face the post? Oh, God. Then she wouldn't be able to see what he was doing. Just like when Allen…

"Relax, pet. You're almost there."

She felt the wooden beam press against the expanse of skin between her shoulder blades and the cheeks of her bare ass. She still wore the bustier, although, with its front hooks, he could remove it whenever he chose. Apparently, he liked having her wearing it. For now.

"Keep your hands here."

Was he going to do honor bondage again? That wouldn't be so bad. Then she heard the rattle of chains and dread pooled in her lower abdomen. He knelt on one knee in front of her, the out-of-whack symbolism making her smile, and attached a leather cuff to each ankle.

After checking to make sure the bindings weren't too tight, he stood and walked to a wall where a variety of whips, paddles, and straps hung. He would remember she'd said no whips, wouldn't he? Before the concern became a full-blown panic, he bypassed them for a display of bars of varying lengths considering several before choosing one and bringing it back to her.

"Spread your legs. Wide." When she hesitated too long, he added, "Don't make me repeat my commands, pet."

She spread her legs and planted her feet about the width of her shoulders. "Wider." Her hips protested, but she complied. He knelt again and attached the ends of the bar to each of her cuffs. As he stood, he trailed the backs of his hands up her inner calves, knees, and thighs, until he reached the folds of her pussy. His right hand cupped her mound and, with his middle finger, he delved between the folds and thrust his finger inside her to the hilt.

"Ahhh," she gasped.

"You're so wet, pet. I see you enjoy having your body restrained for my pleasure."

So far, the restraints and what Marc was doing were giving her a lot of pleasure. He removed his finger and stared at her until she became uncomfortable again, then took this finger he'd just had inside her pussy and brought it to her mouth. He caged her jaw with his hand and forced the finger between her teeth, pushing her jaw down with pressure against her lower teeth until his finger was pressing against the back of her throat. Her pussy muscles clenched. He'd remembered her fantasy about having her mouth invaded by his hand, only this time she tasted herself on her tongue. He pushed deeper inside, his gaze never leaving hers, until she gagged and her eyes watered.

"I look forward to working with you to overcome your gag reflex."

That wouldn't happen in a week. But she didn't think he planned to use his finger for that particular bit of training.

He pulled out his finger and, reached up to take her hands in his again. She heard the rattle of a chain higher up the post and felt him attach the cuffs to either the chain or something on the post. She tested her bonds and heard the chain scrape against the post. She wouldn't be able to move her upper body much now.

A trickle of sweat trailed from behind her ear, down her neck, and between her breasts. Marc took his fingertip and followed the trail, then cupped her lace-covered mounds.

"I love your breasts."

She smiled, even though she hadn't done anything to provide him with this particular pleasure. His long fingers and thumb met in the valley of her breasts and unhooked the first of more than a dozen hooks. Then another and another until about half of them were undone. He pushed the lace aside and downward, exposing her breasts to his eyes and hands. Blood rushed to her nipples as the cool air hit them.

Marc lowered his mouth to one and suckled, as he pinched the other between his finger and thumb. Angelina's hips jolted away from the post and toward him. He pulled away, slowly tugging her nipples—one between his teeth, the other his finger and thumb. She arched her back as the pressure became painful.

"We can't have that much movement, now, can we?"

Before his words registered, she heard the rattle of another chain. This time, he wrapped the cold metal links around her torso, tucked just below her breasts so that their undersides rested on the links. He pulled the end tight until she felt the post against the length of her spine; he must have attached the chain to a hook or something on the post. She tried to move her upper body away from the solid wood.

Just when she realized she could still move her hips away, she smelled leather and felt the kiss of a belt of some kind on the bare expanse of skin between her hips and waist. He buckled the ends together snugly, but not too tightly. Yet another chain clinked as he threaded it through a loop above one hip and pulled it around her back to a loop on her other side. He moved behind her placing the post between them and tugged on the chain until she was flush against the wood.

She had very little motion left. Her breathing hitched and became rapid and shallow. He could do whatever he wanted to her now, and there was nothing she could do to stop him. Panic set in as she worried about what kind of discipline he planned to administer. He didn't have ready access to her butt. Why had he chosen to restrain her facing toward him?

"Breathe, pet. Slow, deep breaths."

Marc was standing next to her. She hadn't even felt him there. She drew a ragged breath into her lungs.

"Again."

This one wasn't quite as difficult. Her body relaxed, well, as much as she could relax while chained to a post. *Oh, God. She couldn't do this!*

"Again."

Breathe. This is Marc. He won't hurt you.

"Good girl." She looked up at him and he smiled. Her body melted, and she felt the chain above her begin to support her weight. "That's right, pet. Relax into the chains. Don't fight them. They're there to help you keep your focus."

Focus? All she could focus on were the chains. How could she...?

Marc stood in front of her and reached up, letting his fingers trail down the undersides of her arms. The sensitive flesh puckered in the wake of the feather-light touch. Her nipples puckered as well, even though he hadn't touched them, and her pussy clenched as if around his finger...or penis.

The strain on her arms wasn't painful, as it had been with... *No.* She wouldn't think of him. She drew a deep breath, relaxing further.

"Very good, pet. You're doing so well. I'm so proud of you."

She felt her insides turn molten and smiled. His fingertips brushed over her shoulders and with just the tip of his index fingers, he trailed across her upper chest until they met in the cleft between her breasts. They skimmed to beneath her full breasts and bumped along the links of the chain holding her to the post. He slipped his fingers between the chain and her skin, as if making sure it wasn't pinching. With the weight on her arms, she barely felt this chain until he drew attention to it.

"Now, pet, why are you restrained for me tonight?"

Her stomach muscles tensed. "To be disciplined, Sir," she whispered.

"Tell me why you want me to discipline you."

Want him to? But she didn't want him to. Did she?

"Because I was bad and I need to learn, Sir."

"What bad thing did you do?"

She felt a burning behind her eyelids and her throat closed up. She cleared it and whispered, "I didn't address you with the respect I wish to give my Dom." The thought that he was only her short-term Dom caused a lump to form in her throat.

* * *

Tears? Marc felt his gut clench that Angelina seemed moved to tears for having displeased him. Surely those tears weren't part of an act. When a teardrop fell from her right eye, he bent down to kiss it away from her cheek, careful not to put pressure on her bruise. Her remorse seemed genuine.

His chest grew tight. Why should he discipline her when she'd already shown him she was sorry? He much preferred role-playing with subs to actual power exchange where discipline was necessary in order to teach them. Would he ever grow into a Dom who could give a woman what she needed?

When he'd come into the great room and found her holding the chain with an expression of reverent awe, he'd immediately forgotten about the disciplinary flogging to come, wanting only to see her chained to the post for him to play with. That she'd let him get this far with her so fast tonight was a precious gift.

Her beautiful submission.

"Sir?"

She drew his focus back to the present. "Yes, pet?"

"I'm ready to accept my discipline session whenever you're ready, Sir."

Taking a step back, Marc breathed deeply himself and walked to the wall of implements. He hadn't planned to use this particular one tonight, because of her prior experience, but he'd set up the scene as differently as possible from her experience a month ago. Still, she needed to see that the same implement can be used for abuse, pain, or pleasure. She'd already experienced it as an abusive tool. Tonight he would show her its other uses.

He lifted one off the hook that had foot-long leather strips. He turned around and swooshed it through the air, watching as Angelina's entire body tensed. He continued to flick the strips in a circular motion as he came to stand in front of her. Her breasts rose and fell rapidly, her gaze riveted to the flogger in his hand.

"Breathe, pet."

She closed her eyes and drew a deep breath, then met his gaze. "Please, Sir. Not the flogger."

"I did not give you a choice this time, *cara*. You are to trust your Dom to know just what his pet needs."

"But I can't…not that one." She was nearly hyperventilating.

"Deep breath. Now, Angelina."

"I can't." She tried to fill her lungs, but failed.

"I. Said. Breathe."

With reluctance, she drew in a breath and looked at him again with pleading eyes. To her credit, she didn't use her safeword. But he needed to make sure she remembered she could use it, if needed.

"What is your safeword?"

"Red, Sir."

"Use it if you need it." Without giving her time to use it in her panicked state, he began flicking just the tips of the leather strips against her nipples. They grew even more engorged and sensitive, as if reaching out to the leather for more. Back and forth, he tortured her tits.

She closed her eyes and dropped her head back. She would surrender to the flogger, at least for pleasure. "That's right, pet. The flogger can hurt so good. Let it bite your tender skin as you think about how you will please your Dom in the future."

He stepped to her side and let the tips flick against the tender undersides of her arms. She hissed in a breath, causing his groin to tighten. He grew bolder and increased both the speed and intensity of the flicks as he moved down one side toward her abdomen. He watched her muscles clench in anticipation as he stood in front of her, never letting the bite of the flogger stop for a moment. He didn't expect to hear the giggle that escaped her lips when he slapped the tips against her abs. Damned ticklish woman. He fought to suppress a grin and flicked the flogger with more force.

Her gasp told him she was no longer being tickled by the flogger as he warmed her skin. The strands thudded against her mons, and he enjoyed watching the skin turn red under her close-cropped pussy hairs. He would order her to shave bare for him before their next session.

Her breasts bounced as she felt the lick of the leather. He wished he were licking her nipples, but first he had to deliver discipline to train her right for her next Dom. Maybe by showing her the flogger also could provide pleasure, she wouldn't always associate it with pain.

Needing to get beyond the disciplinary aspects of the scene ahead of him, he let the flogger drop to the floor and waited for Angelina to open her eyes. She did so after a moment, groaning her displeasure in having the flogging stop, her pupils large, eyes glazed. She smiled.

"Now for your discipline, pet."

Her smile faded.

Chapter Nineteen

Angelina furrowed her brow and quirked her head. "I thought that was the discipline...Sir."

Good catch! She'd almost forgotten his title.

Her skin tingled everywhere the flogger had struck, but the aroused nerve endings left her feeling so excited. Still, there had been pain, at first anyway, so she really thought he'd already begun the discipline.

"No, my pet. I prefer to see your ass grow red when I discipline you."

Another spanking? How could he do that in this position?

He came toward her and rubbed her breasts, her sides, all the places the flogger had touched. "Oh, my God." As if hit by a stun gun, her body collapsed and hung loosely from the chains above her. All of her muscles gave out as his touch on her hypersensitive skin sent her mind into near orgasm—euphoria. She closed her eyes and moaned.

Her mind was too far gone to give a coherent response. Eyes still closed, she relished the intense sensations. She wasn't sure how much time had passed when he reached up to unfasten the chain that held her arms.

"You enjoyed that, pet?"

She didn't want to leave that space and groaned when Marc spoke again. "Your shoulders are going to be tense and sore." He slowly lowered her arms, and her shoulder sockets screamed at the change of positions.

"Oh, God!" The painful burning in her joints brought her back to her reality with a vengeance. He lowered her still-bound hands to rest just below her abdomen and reached up to gently massage her shoulders, the pain compounded by the bruises Allen had left. But he was careful not to apply too much pressure there.

Her gaze became riveted to the hair on his chest. She wanted to move the lapels of the vest away so she could enjoy the sight of his pecs again. Her pain had receded surprisingly fast. He released the chain attached to the leather belt around her waist and removed the one that had restrained her torso just below her breasts. Expecting him to kneel and remove the bar spreading her legs open, he surprised her by bending down and pressing her abdomen against his shoulder. He lifted her like a sack of flour.

"Wait! Put me down!"

A hard smack against her butt told her what he thought of her giving him orders. He carried her across the room, one hand on her right thigh, the other holding her stinging butt in place. She had a feeling her butt would soon be stinging much worse.

He reached his destination and slid her down until her feet stood on the ground her legs open to him at a particularly dangerous position. "Wait here." He grinned at his ridiculous order and turned to walk back to the area near the center post where he picked up the flogger. Everything inside her screamed, *Nooooo!* She remembered that he'd shown her that the flogger was nothing to fear.

Deep breaths, pet. Oh, great. Now he had her calling herself that name.

"You earned ten lashes with the flogger for being insolent and rude to your Dom on the drive to Denver. Before we begin, do you have anything to say for yourself?"

"No, Sir. I just want to get it over with."

He smiled. "Show the flogger that you welcome its kiss against your flesh again. Kiss it."

He held it out to her and she looked up at him in confusion. Kiss the implement that would deliver her pain? Was he joking? From his somber expression, apparently not. She bent over and placed a kiss on the place where the handle and strips of leather were joined.

"Turn around." With his help, he turned her around to face a black leather loveseat. "Use your hands to catch yourself and bend over the armrest." Again, he helped her so that she wouldn't put too much of a strain on her shoulders. Why was he giving orders, then making them less difficult by bailing her out? He confused her.

She bent her arms at the elbows and rested her forehead on her wrists. Her butt and pussy were high in the air, exposed and vulnerable. Marc walked back over to the wall of implements, and then returned. Without warning, he let the soft leather strips of the flogger dance lightly over her ass cheeks.

"This is intended to bring the blood to the surface." Blood? She cringed. Soon, her bottom was burning and tingling. He stopped and rubbed his hand over the area where the flogger had just been flicking against her.

"Oh, yes!" The sense of euphoria returned, although not as intense, and she melted against the armrest, unable to control her body's muscles any longer.

"You will count and ask for your next blow. Other than your safeword, no other words will be allowed."

Marc stood to the side where she could see his black leather pants encasing a raging hard-on. To say he was excited by the scene would be an understatement. Angelina wondered if he would come inside her tonight. She clenched her vaginal muscles in anticipation.

Whack!

"Oh!" Marc's flogger landed with a thud across her butt cheeks.

"What did you say, *cara?*"

Say? She didn't say anything, did she? Oh! She was supposed to, though! *Think!*

"Answer me, pet."

Oh, yes! "One. Thank you, Sir!"

"You weren't listening, pet. I told you to count and ask for your next blow. Let's start again. The first one won't count."

Well, it sure counted to her! But she'd learned that good little subs didn't argue during a scene.

Whack!

Her butt stung already, and it was only the second one. Well, technically the first. This was much more intense than his hand on her butt had been during last night's spanking.

"One. Please may I have another, Sir?"

"Good girl. Yes, you may."

Whack!

"Two, Sir. May I have another?"

The flogger began to hurt like hell. And there were eight more to come? *Oh, God.* She'd never make it.

Marc's cool hand stroked her burning skin. *Yes, please touch me.* His finger slid between the folds of her pussy to rub against the sides of her clit hood. Her face heated as her bottom bucked up toward his finger. Had he changed his mind about ten? Was he finished? Just when she thought perhaps the session might end early, Marc removed his hand from her pussy once more. She steeled herself for the next blow to fall.

Whack!

"Ow!" Harder this time, he took her by surprise. Tears stung her eyes. "Three, Sir. May I have another?"

Whack!

Oh, God. Why did he keep striking the same place over and over? "Four. May I have another?"

"How do you address me?"

"Sir!" *Oh, please don't start over.* Tears spilled from her eyes at the very thought he might. How could she keep her mind on anything like titles when she was in such pain?

Whack! Angelina's butt cheeks flamed, then she felt cool air blowing against her skin, quenching some of the fire. What number was she on?

"Five? May I have another? Sir!"

"Yes, pet. Right on all counts."

Whack!

"Six!" She sobbed the word. "Please, Sir." She hiccoughed. "May I have another?"

She could no longer see him standing beside her. Marc's fingers spread her folds and his tongue trailed a path from her pussy to her clit. She strained upward to press against his mouth, but could barely move. She groaned in frustration. His tongue flicked her hard nubbin until it throbbed, sending delicious waves of warmth through her lower body.

"Perfect."

Angelina smiled, happy to have pleased him. She enjoyed her arousal, as well. It took some of the sting out of the lesson. But without his tongue against her, Angelina felt cold air against her wet folds. She waited, but nothing happened. What was Marc doing? When would he continue? And where had she left off in her count? She braced herself, no idea where the next blow would land.

Slap!

"Oh, sweet Jesus!" A stinging exploded against her erect clit and she clenched her hands into fists. Pain radiated throughout her pussy and thighs. She tried to draw her legs together, but the bar and her position over the armrest prevented her from doing so.

"Angelina. Have you forgotten something?"

What? Like my name? Oh, God. Count! Where was she? Seven? Eight? She wished it was ten. She couldn't take much more if the blows continued at this intensity. Guessing that if she said eight and it should have been seven, he'd take her back to one, she decided it was better to play it safe than sorry.

"Seven, Sir. Please...another?"

"Good girl."

Slap!

Before she could bask in the glow of his praise, another sting bit into her throbbing defenseless clit. *Please, no more!* "Eight! Please may I have another, Sir?"

You can do this, Angie. Almost there.

Tears dripped down her nose onto the cuffs at her wrists. She wished the session would end, but she still didn't feel nearly as much pain as she had when Allen had beaten her. That bastard had shown no mercy, no tenderness, no concern for her safety. Marc wasn't Allen.

Remember that, Angie.

"You're doing very well, pet. I'm proud of you for being so brave."

Marc's hands cupped each of her butt cheeks and she felt his tongue again on her sore and swollen clit. So close. She could come if he kept up this sweet torture. But she hadn't been given permission—and she wouldn't beg this time. The thought of being so turned on by pain still rattled her nerves.

She tried to fight the explosion bubbling up inside. He slid his tongue up her slit and pressed against her pussy hole. Angelina bucked against him as he pressed his firm tongue inside her.

"Oh, God. Please don't stop."

So much for not begging.

"Angelina, did you have permission to speak—other than to count?"

Noooo! Tears of frustration spilled from her eyes. Would he increase the number of blows remaining?

"Please, Marc...Sir. I mean Sir," she sobbed. "I'm sorry." Another sob tore from her. "I'm trying. Please forgive me."

She felt pressure on her lower back as if he were resting his head there. His hands held her hips. Then he was gone. She clenched every muscle from her shoulders to her thighs, anticipating the last two blows.

Whoomph!

Her thoughts were interrupted by a different kind of smack to her butt. Rather than the stinging blows of the first eight, it felt cushioned, even padded and fell against her upper thighs. The impact jolted her clit even though it wasn't a direct strike. Yet.

"*Cara,*" Marc cautioned.

So thrown off was she, she'd forgotten to count. "Nine, Sir. Please may I have another?" And then her other upper thigh received the same treatment.

Whoomph!

"Ten, Sir! Please may I have another?"

"Are you sure about that, pet?"

"No!!! I mean, no, *Sir!* Thank you. I got confused."

Marc rubbed the implement over her butt. Soft. Furry?

"Ahhh."

"I thought you might like that, *cara.*"

Finished. Oh, my God, she'd done it! She hadn't used her safeword either. And she'd stayed in the moment. Her body collapsed against the armrests after holding her muscles so tightly during the discipline session.

What next? Was she finally going to get to feel Marc's penis inside her? *Oh, please say yes!* She wanted him so badly. She felt his hands massaging her shoulders and upper back with firm yet gentle strokes. He ran his hands over her burning cheeks and kissed each butt cheek on the very spots where he'd hit her. Then his hands held onto her hips as if he'd settled himself on his knees behind her and he pressed his tongue against her clit. *Oh, God!* She needed to come so badly. Please don't let him torture her any longer. The eruption began to build in her belly and flowed through her chest, her thighs, her pussy.

"Please, Sir. I need you inside me."

Marc's tongue and lips left her. "No, that isn't what you need, pet."

Damn him. He was going to make her beg for it. Well, she had no pride any longer. "Yes, I do. I need you inside me. And I need to come, too, Sir."

"Half right—and not nearly as much as I need to make you come, *cara.*"

Marc's tongue pressed hard into her pussy as his thumb circled her. "Ohhhh! I can't stop!"

"Come." Marc's tongue flicked her clit.

Two fingers replaced his tongue inside her pussy, stretching her and causing her to buck up against Marc's hand. She hoped he would replace his fingers with his penis and penetrate her more deeply. Instead, his tongue laved her sensitive nubbin until screams were wrenched from her.

"Ohhhh! Oh, *Mio Dio*! I'm coming!" Angelina's orgasm neared its peak. "Yessss! Yesssssssss!! Oh, God, yessss!" Her body exploded, sending her flying to pieces. She convulsed against the restraints holding her earthbound. "Oh, God! Oh, God! Don't stop! Oh! Oh! Ohhhhhhhh, yes! Yes! Yessss!"

She jerked with each aftershock. When at last the world stopped trembling, Angelina collapsed like a wet noodle against the armrest again. She gasped for air, only managing to irritate her raw throat. God, she didn't know she was a screamer, but each time she thought she'd reached her most explosive orgasm, he took her to even greater heights. He hadn't even made love to her yet. God, she needed to feel him inside her.

Would Marc take her like this—on the armrest? She hoped not. "I need to touch you. Now, Sir!"

"Is that an order, little sub?" Marc laughed and smacked her butt.

"Ow." Was she in for another spanking? Then he rubbed her sore butt cheeks.

"I am pleased with how you took your discipline, pet."

Her body warmed—in a good way—at his words. "Because this was your first serious offense, I went easier on you than I will the next time. Discipline sessions will escalate in intensity as the week goes on, so try not to disobey me again."

"I'll behave, Sir." But what if she couldn't? This session had been bad enough, but the next one would be worse?

Even though Marc thought he'd gone easy on her, her ass still stung as if fire ants were having a picnic there. Her clit felt sore. What device of torture had he used on her clit? What was that fuzzy object at the end?

Snap. What was that sound?

"Relax. I was just putting on a latex glove. The Navy instilled in me the importance of not spreading germs. I want to put some lido on your ass to help with the burning."

She felt his cold fingers squirting the lotion on her and gently rubbing it into her burning flesh. She heard him pull a couple tissues from a box, then moaned as he slid a finger down her wet cleft to press into her pussy. She bucked against his hand when a second finger entered her. Then both fingers pulled out and slid upward, toward her asshole. She tried to pull away. "No. Not there!"

Ignoring her, he continued to move closer. "Have you ever let a man touch you there, *cara*?"

"Sure." If she weren't lying face down on a loveseat, she would have tilted up her chin in false bravado. Then she admitted to truth. "My gynecologist."

Marc chuckled. "I assure you what I plan to put there will be better than anything your GYN has inserted."

Her anus clenched at the thought. What did he mean? A finger? Two? His penis. Her asshole clenched again.

"Ah, I see the thought excites you."

Her face flamed and her nipples became engorged as her wicked, traitorous mind latched onto the fantasy.

"*Dio*, your willingness to consider new experiences enchants me. Clearly, the thought of anal play, and maybe even anal sex, will be on the table this week. Would you like to explore that with me?"

One part of her mind screamed a vehement *No!* So why did her head nod in response like a bobblehead doll sailing down a ski slope? She didn't even know what he wanted to do to her. How could she agree to an unknown?

"Answer me, pet."

She forgot he couldn't see her head from where he was. No, but he had a perfectly clear view of her anus. This was too embarrassing for words.

"Stop analyzing it to death." He seemed annoyed with her. "Just answer yes or no."

"Yes, Sir."

"Excellent. Well, if that's a fantasy of yours, I know just the place to act it out. And you're in luck. There was a time when I was known as Doc for my superior medical skills." She heard him rustling around for something. "But, first, a little preparation."

She felt cold liquid squirt against her anus and jumped. *Oh, God!* "No!"

"Did you wish to use your safeword?"

Did she? The idea of anal sex caused her clit to throb. But it was so wrong, so dirty. Why then did the thought of it have her mind and body aroused?

"Answer me, pet."

"I'm just scared." Her voice was so low, she didn't know if he heard her. "It will hurt."

He stroked her lower back and butt cheeks. "Thank you for being honest with me. I'm going to start stretching you so that it won't be as painful. There are four plugs you'll wear in succession over the next couple days."

Butt plugs? Oh, God.

"Tonight is the smallest. Now relax. I'm just going to start with my finger."

The thought of him scrutinizing her asshole at the moment sent an odd thrill through her. *Dio*, why did that make her feel like such a slut?

Marc's finger tried to enter her tight opening. "Press against my finger."

She did as he instructed and he entered her. *Oh, God! So tight.* No pain, just an odd pressure. She bucked against Marc's finger, taking him deeper.

"You're doing great, *cara*." She glowed at his words of praise and clenched her anal muscles. Marc chuckled. "I think you're ready for a second finger." The thought of being stretched by two fingers sent her into a swift retreat.

She raised up on her elbows and tried to scoot off the armrest.

"Remain still." Marc's stern warning caused her to freeze. Another cold finger pressed against her, seeking entrance.

"Relax for me, pet." Hearing his sweet, sexy voice made her want to please him. Remembering how pushing against Marc's finger had made taking his first finger easier, she adjusted her position and pushed against him, feeling his second finger stretching her farther.

"Oh, God!"

"So fucking tight."

The burning surprised her—but still in a good way.

"Slow, deep breaths, *cara*"

She'd forgotten how to breathe. The feel of two fingers inside her asshole short-circuited her brain.

"I said breathe. Now."

She drew a ragged breath, then another.

"Good girl."

His other hand began stroking her back and her butt. *Relax. Yeah, right.* Burning pain.

"Stop worrying. I'm not going to fuck you there—yet. You're too tight for me yet, *cara*."

A mixture of feelings warred inside her. Relief that she wouldn't have to take him inside her anus. Regret that she wouldn't *get* to take him inside her anus. Oh, God. What was the matter with her?

"To help prepare you, I'm going to have you wear this plug tonight. You took my fingers so well, I think you're ready for the second plug already."

He pulled his two fingers out and she felt empty. "Press against it." Already? God, he must have planned this all along. Something cold and wet pushed against her opening as his fingers opened her butt cheeks wider.

"Now." Marc said.

She closed her eyes and tried to push against the object, but it had only gone inside her a small bit before the burning pain became unbearable. "I can't!"

"You're doing great, pet. Push."

She started to hyperventilate.

"Deep, slow breaths, pet."

He ignored her distress and just kept pressing the damned thing against her. Wider and wider it stretched her, working its way through her rings of muscles. As the plug went deeper, it seemed to surpass the diameter of his two fingers. She clenched her hands.

"Relax. It will go in easier if you don't tense up."

She ran her tongue over her lips, which had become so dry, forcing herself to breathe more slowly, deeply. The plug continued its invasion. How the hell big was the goddamned thing?

"Almost there, pet."

Wanting to get it over with, she tilted her butt toward the offending object and felt it plop into place. The feeling of being stretched to the max remained. This was beyond burning; it hurt.

"You did great, *amore*.

Breathe. Just breathe.

She heard the glove being removed and the sound of tissues pulled from a box again. The tissues pressed against the plug as he wiped away the excess lubricant. His attention sent her clit to aching for him again. Then she felt his finger pressing against the plug and his tongue flicking her clit.

"No, I'm not ready!"

He pulled away for a moment. "Oh, you will come when I tell you to come, pet."

But I just did!

And yet, the pressure against her anus, his tongue against her clit, and the added sensation of his finger curling inside her pussy and pressing against her G-spot created the perfect storm.

"Oh, please, Sir! No more. No, I mean, don't stop!" She made no sense whatsoever, but rational thought had long since been eradicated. A second finger entered her and she screamed. "Please, Sir! I need to come."

His tongue left her clit again. "Yes, you do. Come for me, pet."

When his tongue returned to her clit, she came undone. "Oh, dear God!" Angelina's body was primed for takeoff so much faster than ever before. She was bucking against the three pressure points and gasping for air in her oxygen-starved lungs.

He increased the speed of his tongue and fingers and "Oh, Marc! Yessss! Oh, please don't stop!" She made mewling sounds as her body bucked and jolted against him until he wrenched every ounce of orgasm out of her. When the tremors stopped, she collapsed.

At the back of her mind, Angelina registered that he unhooked the bar from one ankle, then the other, but her hips wouldn't work when she attempted to move her legs together again. Besides, she feared the plug would hurt more if she pulled her legs together.

"Let me help you up."

Marc's erection pressed against her stinging butt and the plug he'd just placed inside her as he bent over her to lift her up. On her feet, she swayed as blood drained from her head. He caught her by her elbows and smiled down at her.

She felt as if she had a stick up her butt. How was she supposed to wear it all night? She looked down at the floor to see a flogger similar to the one Allen had used. How had Marc had managed to make it feel so much better? Next to it lay a miniature version of the flogger with a leather-bound handle and blue-colored leather strips, each about six inches long protruding from one end. Lying there, it seemed as innocuous as a feather duster. But it was capable of extreme pain when used on her clit.

But what had delivered those final, softer blows? A leather bag lay open beside where Marc had been standing filled with any number of objects she probably didn't want to know about. Laying on top was a red, fuzzy heart-shaped paddle. She giggled. It had to be the silliest thing she'd ever seen. No wonder those blows had resulted in only pleasure, no pain.

"I didn't think I could use anything else for those last two," Marc said, brushing the hair back from her eyes. She looked up at him. "I'm so proud of you, pet. That was an intense lesson…for both of us…and you took it very well."

She'd forgotten he didn't enjoy disciplining her and felt badly she'd put him in a position to have to deliver yet another one. She hoped this would be the last.

He brushed away tears from her cheeks she wasn't even aware she had shed.

Marc's hands then rubbed her butt cheeks, his hands cool against her heated flesh. Her muscles clenched around the plug. Chill bumps rose, causing her butt to sting even more. Standing on tiptoes, she placed a kiss on his lips. "Thank you, Marc. That was incredible." The look of surprise on his face was priceless.

"Come, pet. I need to cuddle."

She still wore the wrist and ankle cuffs, but actually liked the way they felt. He took her hand and guided her to the front of the loveseat where he sat and then pulled her onto his lap.

"Oh!" The plug pressed against his thigh as she sat on his lap. He smiled as he pulled a blanket from a basket at the other end of the loveseat. She hadn't realized she was cold until he wrapped it around her and pulled her against his chest.

Home.

Safe.

"Don't worry. You'll hardly know the plug's there after a couple hours."

Yeah, right.

She felt the warmth of his body surrounding her. All she wanted right now was to be held in his arms like this. To be safe. Loved.

Whoa! Nobody said anything about love. This was lust. Discipline. Sex. Nothing more.

Chapter Twenty

"Karla, it looks great!" Angelina watched as her new student pulled the thermometer from the Florentine roast pork and put the pan back into the stainless-steel gas range. "Won't be long now."

While Karla wiped down the jade-green granite countertop, Angelina surveyed Marc's kitchen. State of the art didn't begin to describe this place. The expensive countertop material covered a number of surfaces around the room—from the appliance island to underneath each of the many cabinets. What would it be like to work in a kitchen like this every day rather than the tiny one she used now?

The island contained the gas stove and a wide prep space. On the back side was a second tier of granite countertop and three bar stools. What a great place to cook and entertain at the same time. The appliances all were stainless steel and professional grade. What a crime this phenomenal room hardly looked as if it had been touched.

"Adam's not going to believe how much I've improved with just one lesson." Karla's blue eyes sparkled. The change in her just since she'd first met her a month ago, when she was still reeling from the recent death of her brother, was quite noticeable.

"You're a fast learner. We should go shopping for some cookbooks that will give you lots of ideas after I go back home."

Karla reached out to squeeze Angelina's hand. "I'm going to miss having you around. It gets kind of lonely at Adam's place when the club isn't open. Adam…kinda sticks to himself most of the time." She glanced away and Angelina could see how much that disappointed her. "I know he's just busy managing the club. Damián and…his other partner aren't around as much to help as they used to be from what I gather."

"Let's face it, guys just don't have a clue how social we women are."

Angelina looked at the clock—almost five. Still plenty of time to work on the salad, with two pair of hands. Angelina went to the fridge and pulled out a bottle of wine, along with the bowls of vegetables they had washed earlier.

"Might as well relax with a glass while we work." She found the wineglasses and poured them each a generous amount before they sat down on the bar seats with the tomatoes, carrots, cauliflower, lettuce, spinach, and other items they'd purchased at the market this morning.

Karla's interest in Adam certainly hadn't waned. Maybe Angelina could orchestrate something to get them together.

"Are you still curious about BDSM, Karla?"

The woman's alabaster skin flushed a pretty pink. Karla looked over at her with a confused expression on her face and reached for the carrots and a paring knife. "The jury's still out on that one. So, you were pretty quiet last night after you came upstairs."

Angelina felt a blush of her own start in her neck and crawl up over her cheeks. "Yeah, it wound up being later than I expected. I fell asleep in his lap. Actually, I think maybe we both fell asleep." Waking up to find his arms still wrapped around her, and the soft snore coming from him, she'd felt disoriented at first. When she rose up off his chest, he awoke and was at full alert with a speed she'd never witnessed before. Must be his military training. One thing led to another and…

"If you don't mind me asking, did it hurt much?"

For a moment, Angelina wasn't sure what Karla was referring to. What she remembered best about last night was being strapped to the post and flogged in such a sensual way, the mind-blowing orgasms he'd given her while draped over the armrest, and the ones he'd given her while stretched out on the loveseat.

"You mean the discipline lesson?"

"Any of it. Everything about it looks so painful."

How could she explain it to a novice? This wasn't her area of expertise either, that's for certain. She'd heard BDSM described with the expression "hurts so good," but that just didn't give her a clue until she'd met Marc.

"Karla, I think it's something you have to experience yourself. Yeah, some of it starts out painful, but then, something clicks in your brain and all of a sudden, you're hypersensitive and so…horny, you can't stand not being touched or spanked or flogged or whatever he wants to do to you." Heat pooled in her lower abdomen. "Have you ever fantasized about anything you've seen at the club or read about?"

Her cheeks grew redder before she grinned and replied. "Ropes. Being tied. Not *to* something. Just tied. Adam did a demonstration once with Grant…" A pained expression crossed her face at the mention of whoever Grant was, but the sparkle returned quickly. Obviously, she was thinking about whatever Adam had done to the sub. "My stomach just went ka-thunk. It was the most beautiful thing I've ever seen. Almost like art. The knots. The way he wrapped her breasts, restrained her arms behind her. Oh, my!" Karla released a nervous laugh and reached for her wineglass and took a large swallow. After taking a deep breath, she smiled at Angelina and shrugged, as if embarrassed about what she'd shared.

"No, Karla, don't be ashamed of it. That's it exactly. I think for me, too, it's more about giving up control than it is about pain. Being restrained. Having a Dom read your body's responses like a book and know just what you need. I'm sorry I can't explain it better, but I've certainly changed my mind about it in the last few days. I am definitely submissive."

"Ah, music to my ears, *cara*."

Angelina's heart thudded and she looked up to see Marc standing in the doorway smiling at her with more than a bit of arrogance. The man needed a bell around his neck so he couldn't keep sneaking up on her like that. She blushed, even though Marc already knew exactly what she was. Somehow admitting it aloud to him made it reality.

It also made her more vulnerable to him. This man could hurt her, because he wasn't one to commit to anything more than the present. Wait! I don't want anything more than that either. So, in that way, we're perfect for each other. She smiled.

Marc smiled, too, as if he'd just read her mind. "Something smells wonderful."

She dragged her attention back to the kitchen. "Karla's a wonderful cook."

"Angelina's an awesome chef and teacher."

"And, Marc, if the offer to put me into culinary bondage is still open, I'll be your slave for life. Just chain me to your incredible stove anytime."

Marc grew tense and she squirmed at how he might have taken her words as asking for more from him than what they could ever have. "I didn't mean…"

"Where's Adam?"

"Right behind you." Adam walked under the brick archway and into the kitchen.

Angelina watched Marc visibly relax. Oh, maybe she'd misread his change of mood. Marc probably had asked Adam to be her bodyguard, which would explain why they hadn't been able to shake the man all day. Clearly, Marc hadn't forgotten about Allen. Well, he needed to, because she would be going back home, alone, on Saturday night—or Sunday morning at the latest. She could take care of herself.

She didn't want to think about why the thought of leaving Denver bothered her, so she tamped down those thoughts with an idea that might help her new friend with her own relationship. Angelina turned to Karla and apologized silently for not clearing this with her ahead of time, but her grandmother had always told her to strike while the iron was hot. Okay, she didn't want to think about hot steel in connection with BDSM, but…

Angelina turned back to Marc and Adam. "Karla and I were just discussing how much we'd like a demonstration after dinner of the finer points of restraining someone with ropes. Would either of you happen to have any rope—and expertise in that area?"

Marc smiled. Adam growled. And Karla reached for her wineglass again and drained it.

* * *

Allen tailed Denton from his townhouse. Angie wasn't with him. Maybe she was with the other one—the Italian. He hoped Denton would lead him to her soon, because he'd spent the day driving in circles trying to catch a glimpse of her at the home of one of these two men.

As they entered the ritzy neighborhood of McMansions, Allen's anger grew. When he'd seen where D'Alessio lived this morning—a fucking mansion surrounded by towering spruce and fir trees, totally secluded—he'd figured out what she saw in that one, at least. A dollar sign. The man was born to money, according to the research Allen had done. He hadn't had to work hard every day of his life, unlike Allen who had to carve out a niche building a business from the ground up.

The only thing women cared about was landing a rich man so they wouldn't have to work or support themselves. Well, Allen might not be as rich as this guy, but he could offer Angie a damned comfortable life. His business was growing, too. Of course, it would be good if he were back home overseeing it now, rather than having to chase her down all over Denver to get her to admit he was the perfect man for her. The perfect Dom.

When Denton pulled into the familiar driveway, Allen noticed in front of the garage a Harley and a Ford pickup truck that hadn't been there this morning. Was there some kind of party tonight? He could just imagine Angie servicing all the men at a private kink party. She might have played innocent with him, but she liked it rough.

Soon, very soon, he would give her just what she wanted.

* * *

Marc had avoided eye contact with Angelina throughout dinner. He'd been excited to hear she wanted to try rope bondage tonight, but her mention of being his slave, even the joking way she'd said it, worried him. Marc had no interest in the baggage that came with Italian women, always wanting drama, babies, commitment.

Who'd said anything about babies?

Babies or not, he wouldn't be trapped into a relationship he didn't want. If she wasn't content with a casual Dom/sub relationship, then he needed to make tracks and soon.

Maybe if he hadn't monopolized her time this week, she could have gotten to know Luke a little better. Of course, he'd been decidedly absent since they'd returned from Denver, claiming some out-of-town house renovation project.

Marc could feel the noose tightening around his neck, but then the conversation veered off in a direction that opened the door for his escape.

"So, which of you gentlemen would let me practice rope tricks on you?"

Rope tricks? Obviously, this was some kind of game to her. She'd never been restrained with Shibari, the Japanese martial-arts practice that took rope bondage to the level of art. But none of the Doms at the table seemed anxious to take her up on the idea. No big surprise there. Then she homed in on Luke.

"How about you, Luke? Being from Texas, you must have been around a lot of rope." She winked at him.

"Well, like the other men here, I've usually been the one doing the tying, not being tied, Angel." To say Marc was surprised by his friend's words would be an understatement. "Maggie, my wife, and I did enjoy playing with ropes. But she did do the tying a time or two. I'd be honored to let you practice on me."

Shit. The man had been holding out on him. Maybe this was what he'd needed to get Luke and Angelina together. So why did the thought of throwing her at his friend bug the hell out of him? When he'd thought them incompatible, he hadn't had a problem with it. Now that there might actually be something that could bind them together, so to speak, he was less interested in pushing her in Luke's direction.

But he was getting too damned attached to her. Too comfortable. Falling asleep with her in the club last night surprised the hell out of him. He'd never trusted a woman enough to allow himself to be that vulnerable.

Marc glanced over at Angelina and decided to strike while the iron was hot, a favorite expression of his grandfather's. "Great. So, Adam and I can demonstrate on Luke and Karla." Already knowing the answer, because Adam had spent many hours showing him the ropes, so to speak, Marc still had to play ignorant. "Damián, are you any good with ropes?"

He grinned at Marc, but played along. "Actually, yes. But I have to head to the shop. Still trying to catch up after taking time off to be at my niece's sixteenth birthday party in California last week." He'd grown up in a town—something or other Gardens—between San Diego and Camp Pendleton and had strong ties with his sister and her kids. Damián turned his attention to Karla and winked. "I'd be happy to give you some advanced lessons later, though. Maybe after your sets are over Wednesday night?"

The chokehold Adam had on his fork as he glared at Damián made it clear to Marc that wouldn't be happening. He grinned. If Adam wanted her, he'd better mark his territory soon before Damián moved in. Marc had a sudden desire to see Adam practicing rope bondage on Karla tonight. Angelina on Luke? Well, maybe not as much, but it was time to get this show going.

Marc smiled across the table at the two chefs. "Thank you, Karla and Angelina. That was a wonderful meal." A round of praises went around and everyone carried the dishes to the kitchen and loaded the dishwasher. The leftovers were stowed in the fridge and Damián took his leave.

"So, let's see this playroom you were telling me about," Adam said.

"Sure. Luke's worked hard on equipping the space. Glad to show you around." It was too pathetic to admit he and Luke were the only ones who'd been there, but that was about to change.

Angelina reached out and touched Luke's forearm. "You make furniture, too, Luke?"

Marc tamped down the jealous feelings that reared up. This was what he wanted, wasn't it? He'd try to keep his distance from her tonight and give them a chance. He'd been monopolizing her since Saturday night.

"Yeah. Equipment might be a more accurate description."

Marc led the group up the staircase. On the first landing a panoramic view of Denver spread out before them and the ladies stopped to look and comment on it. The lights twinkled as twilight set over the city. Marc preferred the western view from his bedroom to this one, though. Mt. Evans dominated that view, one of the prettiest sights in the world, next to Angelina. He watched her looking out the window in awe and wonder.

Marc cleared his throat. "This way," he said as they continued up to the second floor hallway. He led them down the hall to his bedroom and walked up to what probably looked to them like a closet door and opened it. He flipped on the light switch, illuminating a staircase to the tower room. Standing aside, he motioned for them to enter. "Last set of stairs." The narrow stairway forced them to go single file. Marc noticed Angelina had been holding Luke's hand, which she released before stepping through the doorway.

Marc was the last to head up the stairs and closed the door behind him. When he reached the top, Karla's eyes were wide open taking it all in, and Angelina looked as if she'd tackle him to get back downstairs before taking another step into the room.

Shit. He hadn't thought about her intense response to seeing the cross that was identical to the one at the club, because Luke made both of them. Tonight certainly was not proceeding as planned.

* * *

Angelina came to a halt beside the king-sized bed sitting in front of thick red velvet drapes, but the sight that riveted her was the St. Andrew's cross on the other end of the room. Frighteningly like the one at the Masters at Arms Club, it brought back memories of being beaten by Allen. Suddenly wound tighter than Uncle Guillermo's *mandolina*, her body began to shake.

Oh, God, I can't do this! She backed away.

"Easy, pet." Marc stood behind her and his hands went around her, encircling her waist. He nuzzled her neck. "I don't want you to fall down the stairs and hurt yourself." Marc's arms tightened around her and she closed her eyes, lowering her head. His warmth soaked into her cold skin, making her feel safe. Marc whispered in her ear, "I'm here, *amore*. Don't be afraid."

She nodded. Tearing her gaze away from the floor she looked up to find Adam, Karla, and Luke staring at her with concern. Her face grew warm. She'd called this party together, so she'd better get with the program.

She pulled away from Marc and turned to force a smile of thanks. When she left his arms, her body felt chilled again. "So, where are the ropes?"

Marc reached out and tapped his index finger against the tip of her nose. "Watch out, Luke. This one's rather anxious." Marc grinned, but the smile didn't reach his eyes. "Come, everyone. Let me give you the ten-cent tour first."

Marc took her hand and led her over to Luke and then released her to him. She had the distinct impression he was pushing her toward Luke, who gave her a look of sympathy and took her hand in his, squeezing it. She smiled up at him and followed Marc to the right. A wooden desk and what looked like the examination table in her doctor's office, complete with stirrups, were along one wall. Her face flamed and her butt clenched as she remembered his words last night about knowing of a place where they could play doctor.

Angelina hadn't been listening. *Focus.*

"Of course, there are more theme rooms at the club, but these just happen to be a couple of my favorites. Luke made the desk, too."

Angelina went over to run her hands over the gold-streaked walnut desk. The detail was amazing, for something that would just be used for…oh, don't think about what kinds of fantasies were played out on that desk. She wondered how many women he'd restrained on it.

Don't go there, Angie.

"I'll get the rope." Marc went to a cabinet in the corner. The rest of them walked across the room and Karla went up to the cross Angelina had been trying to avoid staring at. Karla ran her hands over the cherry wood, so like the one at the club. Angelina shuddered.

Karla looked at Adam. "How does she support her head on an X-shaped cross?"

When Adam just stood there as if he'd been turned to stone, Luke started to move forward to answer Karla's question, but Angelina pulled his hand back. When he looked down at her, she shook her head. He looked back at Karla then at Adam as realization dawned. Luke smiled and nodded.

When it became clear to Adam that no one was going to answer the question for Karla, he stepped closer to her and reached down for her wrists. He lifted them over her head and when he took a step toward her, she instinctively stepped back and came up against the cross. Her eyes opened wider and she stared up at Adam. Angelina could see the pulse in her throat throbbing. Is that how Marc judged her response to him, by watching for tells like that? Adam pressed her wrists against the wood where one might attach them if wanting to restrain them.

"Your hands go here. Now, are you thinking about where your head goes at this moment?"

Karla shook her head.

Adam cleared his throat and stepped away, releasing her hands. "Don't worry. The sub can keep her head upright, let it drop to whatever position is comfortable for her—or do whatever her Dom orders. Same for malesubs."

Angelina watched as Karla continued to stare as if mesmerized, leaving her hands exactly where he'd placed them.

Oh, Karla. Don't look at him like that if you don't mean business.

Angelina needed to bring her friend back to the present, so she ignored her aversion and walked up to the cross. "Believe me, Adam's right. If you're strapped to one of these, the last thing you'll be thinking about is what to do with your head."

Karla blinked and focused on Angelina, her eyes wide in wonder. Clearly, Adam's touch had affected her more than she'd expected. Angelina leaned forward and whispered, "Are you okay, sweetie?"

Karla whispered a one-word description. "Ka-thunk." Angelina chuckled. Karla leaned away and made eye contact, smiling. Angelina loved seeing her eyes sparkling. She just hoped Karla knew what she was getting into if she decided to pursue Adam.

Marc joined them near the cross and took Angelina's hand. Her stomach muscles clenched when he stretched her shaking hand out, forcing her to touch the cross. The wood was smooth, warm. Her heart jumped into her throat. Which way would he restrain her to the cross? Her stomach churned. Why, then, did she feel her pussy getting wet thinking of what he might do?

He smiled. "The cross isn't all that different from the center post. Just a device for restricting the movement of the submissive. If your Dom is trustworthy, the experience will be very erotic and one you will…enjoy.

Keeping her hand in his, he walked over to the equipment next to the cross. Angelina hadn't even noticed it until now, but she looked more closely.

Good God! The contraption was made of leather and wood and looked like something out of a Victorian dungeon. Velvet pads provided a place to rest her knees, along with cuffs to restrain her ankles and thighs. A narrow bench-like expanse would support her trunk. She noticed a wide leather belt over the middle of the bench for her waist. At the other end was a round cushion much like the face rest on the table at her massage therapist's office.

Total restraint. She imagined herself kneeling, face down, arms outstretched and strapped to the armrests that gave the appearance of those on a lethal injection gurney. The numerous leather straps with shiny brass buckles would keep her arms, legs, and even her waist restrained so she couldn't interfere with the lesson.

Angelina began to shake. Her clit stirred to life. How could something like that turn her on?

She looked at Marc. He smiled. "This is a spanking horse. Luke made this, as well as the cross."

Luke? How could such a sweet man make such devices used for torture? Okay, to be fair, they were only torture devices when in the wrong hands. But still! Angelina couldn't get over how much the cross looked like the one at the club. She hadn't seen any other crosses used for this purpose, but wondered if there was a standard pattern all BDSM craftsmen used or something.

She turned to Luke who shrugged. "It's become a kind of hobby since I met Marc."

Angelina was baffled that there were so many otherwise normal people involved in this subculture. She'd definitely led a sheltered life.

Marc handed Adam two bundles of rope still in the store packaging. Good to know he hadn't used them on another woman.

* * *

Adam took the silk rope bundles from Marc and tried to think what he could demonstrate on Karla without getting too close. Well, how the fuck did he plan to tie her up without getting close? But perhaps he could minimize contact.

How the hell he'd gotten wrangled into this scene still baffled him. But the thought of Karla and Damián doing a Shibari bondage scene together rotted his gut. He looked over at Karla, who was intently watching Marc show off his spanking horse.

When had she gotten interested in this stuff? At the club, she could hardly watch most of what went on while she sang in the great room. Now she was curious about rope bondage *and* spanking?

Don't be thinking about spanking her, old man.

No, he'd tie her up. That was it. Then he'd just go right back to avoiding her. That had worked for the last couple months, although he didn't realize until dinner yesterday how much she needed someone to talk to about Ian.

"Well, who wants to go first?" Angelina asked.

Adam looked up to see her looking between him and Marc. Wanting to get this over as soon as possible, Adam stepped forward. "Karla, are you ready?"

When she looked at him and smiled, a sparkle lit her blue eyes that he hadn't seen since he'd been with her at her parents' that Thanksgiving weekend nine years ago. He'd been so intent on avoiding her that he hadn't provided her with an ear for listening or just a hug when she needed one. If he wasn't always thinking such perverted thoughts about her, he could have been the friend she'd come to Denver looking for.

Man, he'd sure fucked up this mission.

She stepped toward him and his eyes zeroed in on the red bustier she wore that left her shoulders and arms bare. Her breasts filled out the cups of the top telling him there was no fucking way he was going to demonstrate tit bondage. He'd keep those breasts pointed in the opposite direction for this tutorial.

"Do I call you Master Adam or just Sir?"

Aw, hon. Don't ask me to pretend to be your Top. What are you trying to do to me?

"If you need to address me, Adam will be fine." The disappointment in her eyes caused him to amend that. "Or Sir will work, too." The smile on her face reminded him how much he'd missed her smile over the years.

"Turn around."

So much for her smile. Using his Dom voice, he'd wiped it right off her face. Karla didn't strike him as particularly submissive, so her immediate response surprised him. She turned around and presented him with her gorgeous black curls cascading down her back. He wanted to run his hands through those thick locks, but restrained himself.

How was he going to narrate what he was doing when he couldn't keep his mind on the task at hand? He'd done numerous demonstrations of Shibari at the club with Grant and others over the past few years and hadn't had any trouble concentrating.

Focus, man.

"Shibari is the name Westerners use for the ancient art of Japanese rope bondage. In their culture, it actually was used for non-sexual purposes."

Fuck. This is definitely non-sexual, too, Karla. Don't get any other idea in your head.

"Most often, for restraining prisoners."

Adam could see that he couldn't begin the Teppou technique until he first wrangled her hair into submission. *Don't be thinking about getting her anything into submission, old man.* He finger-combed her hair from her scalp to the nape of her neck. When Karla moaned, his dick went into a full salute. Total clusterfuck.

"It feels so good having you play with my hair, Sir."

Adam closed his eyes and took a deep breath, trying to regain his focus. "I'm not playing with it. I just need to get it out of the way before I can start."

"I'm sorry it's in the way, Sir."

Damn. Now he'd hurt her feelings with his gruff tone. He reached down for one of the rope bundles and unwrapped it until he found the end piece. How had he gotten into this situation again? To go from not touching her and barely interacting except for small talk at chow, to touching her hair and making her moan as if he'd touched her…somewhere else, was more than he could take.

With unnecessary roughness, he gathered her hair into a ponytail at the nape of her neck. Unwanted images of pony play came to his mind. He'd never been into having a submissive act like a pony, although Joni had liked puppy play once in a while. His dick throbbed at the image of inserting a puppy tail plug into Karla's… Adam's hands began to shake. How was he going to get through the demonstration if he couldn't even tie a fucking ponytail without nearly coming?

"Angelina, can you help by holding her hair until I get this hair corset started?"

"Yes, Sir." Her impudent grin deserved some attention from a Dom, but Adam literally had his hands full with Karla.

With Angelina doing the job of a hair tie, Adam was able to make the lark's head knot to anchor the rope onto Karla's hair at the nape. "Thank you, hon." Angelina nodded and took a step back, but continued to watch with rapt attention.

Marc surprised him by reaching down for a bundle of rope himself and began mimicking Adam's moves, taming Angelina's hair. She moaned, as well. What was it with women having their hair "played with," as Karla put it? Joni's hair had been short, so he'd never really thought much about it being sensual to have it touched. Joni just liked having it pulled. Adam wondered what it would be like to grab two fists of Karla's hair while he…

Fuck. Good thing he didn't have to think while he repeated the same knot over and over, because his mind had gone south. Too soon, he got to the end, knotted it off, and reached down for the paramedic shears to cut off the ends. Trust Doc to have all the right equipment.

"There." He filled his lungs as if he'd just run a sprint. Now it was time to run a marathon.

"Thank you, Sir." Adam heard the catch in her voice.

Aw, hell. She sounded as if she'd been crying. Feeling like a heel, Adam slung the rope over his shoulder and walked around to stand in front of her. This most likely was Karla's first time in bondage of any kind and he wasn't even treating her with the respect he'd show a favorite dog. Time to put his wants and needs on a back burner and focus on the wannabe sub standing before him.

He placed his finger under her chin, and tilted her head up to meet his gaze, but she kept her eyes averted. He cupped her cheeks and used his thumb pads to wipe away the tears. She must have found waterproof mascara, because there was no trail this time, as there had been so many times before when she'd cried. He grinned.

"Look at me, Karla."

She blinked several times and raised her gaze.

"I apologize for speaking so harshly. This is your first time, isn't it?"

Karla blinked again and her eyes opened wider. After a moment, as if understanding finally dawned, she nodded.

"Thank you for allowing me to be your first. I'll do better binding your arms than I did your hair. I promise."

When she smiled, the vise that had constricted his heart for nearly a decade began to loosen a bit. His groin only grew tighter, but he had enough control over his body not to let his dick rule his other head.

Hell, he was supposed to be demonstrating for the others, but his focus shifted to Karla. Only Karla. Her big blue eyes looked at him with so much trust.

"As I'm tying, don't let me pull farther than your comfort level. If it hurts or is too tight, just say 'yellow' and I'll back up a bit. You understand that pain isn't the goal here?"

"Yes, Sir."

"Good girl." Her smile quavered and he tried to keep his attention away from her lips. He stroked her bare arms in long, gentle strokes. "I want you to relax. Take a slow, deep breath and release all the tension from your body."

Adam watched her breasts rise as she followed his instructions, visibly relaxing her shoulders and arms. He took a slow deep breath of his own.

"The technique I'm going to use is called Teppou. It means gun because, when I'm finished, the shape of the tie and the placement of your hands will look like a gun slung diagonally across your back. Now, are you ready?"

"Yes, Sir. Thank you."

Her appreciation before he'd even started warmed some cold place inside him. "Good. I want you to embrace the rope. Find release through restraint. I think you'll understand more as we go along. Give me your right wrist."

She presented her arm to him, a most precious gift, and he accepted it, taking her delicate wrist in his hand. Her skin was cool and he wrapped his hand around her tiny wrist a moment to infuse his warmth into her.

Taking the rope from his shoulder, he released her wrist and made a single-column tie, secure but not tight. He stepped behind her and lifted her arm until it was at a forty-five degree angle, her fingertips pointing toward the corner of the ceiling. He supported her outstretched upper arm just below her elbow, took the loose end of the rope, and pulled, gently drawing her wrist backward and down as if she were reaching behind her to draw a bow from a quiver. The gracefulness of the movement and the trust she placed in him touched him beyond words.

"Are you okay?"

She nodded.

Adam pulled her elbow outward, away from her face, and bound her wrist to her upper arm. Her flesh trembled—or was it *his* fingers? Once he had secured the tie there, he took her left hand and gently twisted it behind her back, extending it upward until it was directly below her other hand, separated by about six inches, with her palm facing outward.

"Are you in any pain or discomfort?"

"No, Sir."

"If you become uncomfortable, what do you say?"

"Yellow, Sir."

"Good girl."

Adam pulled the end of the rope from her upper arm and wrapped it around her forearm and then around her upper arm. He adjusted the rope, pulling tighter as he repositioned her upper elbow to keep the line of the "gun" right, and made several more loops around the right arm and elbow.

She had an incredibly flexible body, probably because she was still so young. She would make an excellent demonstration partner at the club.

Fuck. Like that was going to happen.

He brought the rope back down to her lower arm, weaving it through the pattern numerous times and making quick work of the remaining loops. The sooner he finished, the better. He secured the end and his hand caressed the ropes and her hands. "Beautiful, pet."

Realizing how he'd addressed her, he was shocked out of the scene. He circled around to stand in front of her. Her breasts were pushed out even more from the position of her arms, nipples hard, pressing against the bra cups of the low-cut top. If he'd thought this position would be less intimate, he'd been sorely mistaken.

"You did well, hon." He cupped her cheek and she leaned into him, closing her eyes and causing his dick to throb.

Angelina whispered, "If I smoked, I'd want a cigarette right now. That was incredibly...hot."

Adam turned in time to see Marc swat her backside and whisper, "Quiet, *cara*. Don't intrude on their scene."

Adam cleared his throat. "It wasn't a scene, just a demonstration." The hurt in Karla's face made him feel like a shithead, but he needed to put some distance between them again. Stepping away, he said, "Marc, take a picture for Karla to see later."

Because I don't plan on having another demonstration with her anytime soon.

Chapter Twenty-One

Watching Adam tie Karla earlier this evening had been incredibly erotic for Angelina. She'd also loved Marc's binding her hair, clearly an erogenous zone. His fingers combing through her hair had sent Angelina's clit into spasms.

While Marc and Adam had shown her a much simpler technique for binding Luke's arms and hands behind his back—they called it the hogtie—she hadn't been as turned on tying up Luke. She'd been thinking about what it would be like to have Marc tie her up the way Adam had tied Karla.

She was so turned on by the time the gathering was winding down, after Karla and Luke had been untied, she felt as if she would explode. But Marc had only spoken to her as needed during the demonstration of the rope-bondage technique. Now he'd retreated into himself, as if he expected her to want to be with Luke.

But she wanted Marc. Hadn't she made that clear?

"I think it's time to get back to the house," Adam said. "Karla and Angelina, are you about ready to go?"

Angelina looked at Marc, hoping he'd ask her to stay. But he just bent down and picked up the rope they'd discarded, ignoring her. Tears stung the backs of her eyes.

Luke came over to her and rubbed her back. "Angelina, I can give you a lift back to Adam's, if you'd like. Might be a little crowded in the pickup."

"Thanks, Luke." She thought it might be good if Karla and Adam had some time to themselves anyway, although Adam seemed to have retreated as far as Marc had.

Were all Doms this distant?

As she watched Karla, Adam, and Luke head for the stairs, she glanced over at the bed and wished Marc would finally make love to her. But clearly he wasn't interested in that kind of relationship. Participating in BDSM scenes didn't necessarily lead to having sex. He'd only agreed to the BDSM stuff this week.

Well, she'd take what she could get. She walked over to Marc and looked up, forcing him to return her gaze. "Thanks for everything. It's been a lot of fun." His sad smile took her by surprise. Nothing ventured... "If you want to play tonight, I'd like to stay."

He stroked her cheek. "No, pet. I have a trek out on the mountain tomorrow, so I'd better get some sleep."

"When will I see you again?" She could barely get the words out from the tightening in her throat.

"This one's an overnight, but I'll be at the club Wednesday night. Maybe we'll give that medical room a try." Her butt clenched at the reminder of the anal play he'd promised her. Even though they were alone, he bent down and whispered, "Wear the next sized plug for four or five hours tomorrow, then move up to the last size on Wednesday, if you're ready." His scratchy whiskers brushed against her skin as his lips planted a very chaste kiss on her cheek.

"Yes, Sir. Good night."

Angelina turned and walked toward the stairway to follow the others.

"Angelina."

Hope swelled in her chest as she turned around to look back at Marc. Had he changed his mind? Did he want her to stay, after all?

"Take the leftovers with you. They'll go bad before I have a chance to eat them."

Tears welled in her eyes and she turned as she nodded, unable to say anything. She held onto the railing so she wouldn't miss a step, and ran into Luke's chest as she walked through the door into Marc's bedroom. When he wrapped his arms around her, she let him hold her for a moment, then brushed the tears away and pulled back, not making eye contact.

"You okay, darlin'?"

She nodded, unable to speak. Taking his hand, she walked with him to the kitchen. Adam and Karla were nowhere in sight. She went to the refrigerator and pulled the dishes of leftovers out and set them on the counter.

"Marc wants us to take these over to Adam's." After determining that Luke didn't want to take anything to his place, she picked up her purse and carried one dish while Luke took the other and they headed out the door. The nearly full moon bathed the driveway in light and made it easy to walk to the SUV and put the leftovers in the back. Feeling someone's eyes on her, she looked up to find Marc's silhouette in the window of the tower. Then he was gone, but the feeling of his watching her remained, a little niggling at the nape of her neck.

Luke opened the passenger door for her and she got inside. Her mind played over the events of the night. What had been one of the best nights of her life certainly had ended on a sour note.

* * *

Luke walked around to the driver's side of the Land Rover, feeling a bit like manure on a boot. Clearly, Angelina wanted to stay with Marc, but his friend had been pushing her at him all night. Not that he didn't appreciate the effort, but Luke had begun to realize pretty damned quick Angel was made for Marc. He didn't know what Maggie's dream meant yet but clearly this woman wasn't his angel.

He got behind the wheel and glanced over at her, but she kept her gaze out the window, looking up at the tower. Was Marc standing there? Luke was pissed that Marc would treat Angel so badly, but didn't expect to have a chance to talk with him about it anytime soon. He'd be out on the mountain until Wednesday afternoon.

Luke wished he had the words to make her feel better, but he didn't understand Marc's behavior. Why was he running hot one minute and cold the next? The man loved women. Angel was what every woman should be. Was he blind? If she'd been anyone but Antonio Giardano's daughter, he'd have…

That was a dead horse. He turned the engine over and backed out of the driveway and onto the darkened street. No lights out here. Funny, Marc managed to find a place close to the city but close to the wilderness, too. Out of nowhere, a vehicle came up behind him, it's headlights on high beam. Jerk. So much for wilderness.

Luke looked over at Angel. "You okay?"

"Yeah. Just tired, I guess. Thanks for taking me back to Adam's."

"Not a problem."

They drove for a few miles before Angelina broke the silence. "The Shibari was pretty amazing. How did you like being tied up?"

He laughed out loud. "I think I prefer being on the other end of the rope."

"Me, too."

"I wish I had the skills Adam does, though. He and Karla moved as if they were in a choreographed dance."

"They're good together. I know she likes him."

"Well, good luck with that. He hasn't really looked at anyone since his wife died, from what Marc's told me."

"But that was so long ago. Oh, I'm sorry, Luke. I wasn't thinking."

Luke waved her hand away. "It's been seven years for me and even longer for Adam. But I don't think you can tell someone to grieve X number of years and then have them just get back into the game when they reach that magical limit. It's different for everyone."

"How about you? Think you'll ever remarry?"

"Not really looking for a wife at the moment. But I think I'm maybe going to date again sometime. If I meet the right woman."

I'm sending you an angel.

"I hope you do, Luke. You'll make someone a wonderful…date." She grinned, and he was happy her mood had lifted some. They drove on in silence; traffic picked up as they neared Adam's house.

"Oh, my God."

Luke eased off the accelerator. "What's the matter?"

She turned to him. "You said Marc had told you about Adam's grieving for his wife. You and Marc didn't just meet Adam for the first time on Sunday."

Oh, damn.

Luke drew a lungful of air, trying to think how he should answer this without sharing things it wasn't his place to tell her. "No, I met Adam when I did the carpentry on the house while they were renovating it for the club five years ago."

"They?"

Okay, he was just digging the hole deeper. Marc needed to be the one to come clean to her, not Luke. "Adam and Damián?"

"Are you asking or telling me?"

Clearly, she already suspected. He'd only make matters worse if he continued the lie at this point.

"And Marc."

She gasped. *Shit.* He needed to get Marc over here.

* * *

Blood pounded in her ears as she processed what Luke had just told her. Marc had lied to her. Why? What difference could it make to her if Marc was in some kind of partnership at the club?

All that mattered was that Marc deliberately lied to her.

What else had he lied about? How could she ever trust him? He'd demanded that she trust him and always be honest, and yet he hadn't been decent enough to show her the same courtesy. Angelina wanted to go home, nurse her wounds.

Maybe Karla could drop her off Thursday morning when she went to pick up her friend Cassie for their camping trip. Angelina felt a mixture of regret and relief over not having to go out in the wilderness with them. But she couldn't wait to get inside and talk with Karla tonight. She needed some advice about what she should do.

Luke pulled into the driveway and cut the engine. "Angel, talk to Marc before you do anything. I'm sure he has his reasons."

"Thanks for the ride home, Luke." She reached for the door handle, and Luke put his hand on her shoulder.

"He's scared about something, Angel. I don't know what, but I don't want to see him hurt either. Just talk to him before you do anything. Don't go back home alone, either. You know that scumbag can come after you again at any time."

Angelina nodded, mainly to end the conversation. "Can you help me get the leftovers inside?"

When they walked into the kitchen, they put the dishes in the fridge and Luke said goodbye.

"Please don't say anything to Marc."

Luke looked away.

"I mean it, Luke. I need time to think, and I can't do that when he's around me." He would just fill her with more of his lies or, worse yet, short-circuit her brain so that she would blindly obey any command he gave her.

Only she no longer wanted him to pretend to be her Dom. Clearly, he'd only been playing some kind of game with her. He had no intention of ever being her real Dom.

After Luke left, tears stung her eyes, and she started toward the hallway. On the stairs, she passed Karla on her way down, her eyes red probably from crying. The two of them made a lovely pair tonight.

Apparently Karla noted Angelina's distress, as well. "What's wrong, Angie?" She squeezed Angelina's forearm.

"Marc lied to me. Everything about him is fake."

When Karla's gaze shifted away, Angelina realized her new friend knew this already. Adam had to have known, too. They'd all lied to her.

Angelina started up the stairs again. "I'm going to bed." She couldn't get away from everyone fast enough.

"Wait, Angie! Let me try to explain."

Angelina turned and looked at the woman she'd thought would become a good friend. "I'm listening." Her voice sounded cold, and she hated to see tears in Karla's eyes, but her stomach churned. She really wanted to be alone.

Karla stood several inches taller than Angelina, so she took the next step up to be able to come face to face and avoid having to tilt her head back. She needed to be able to run the bullshit meter on whatever Karla was going to say.

"Oh, God. I don't even know what's going on! Please believe me, Angie. All I know is that Adam told me not to recognize Marc—and I'd never met Luke before, so that was easy enough."

The distress in Karla's expression seemed genuine. "Let's talk to Adam. I'm sure he can explain. I think he had a talk with Marc. He wasn't happy at all about the lie; that much I know. He doesn't get angry often, but he was angry when he told me Sunday. From what I know about Marc, he must have had a good reason for doing it."

But Marc had told her repeatedly that a Dom and his sub could have no lies between them, no secrets. And yet, he'd blatantly lied.

"Thanks for that, Karla. I'm tired. I just want to go to bed. Is it okay if I use your shower?"

She wanted to just wash the lies down the drain—and escape in sleep.

* * *

Oh, merda.

Marc disconnected the phone and set it on the nightstand. He'd gone to bed right after everyone left. The house was his silent tomb once again, but for a few hours tonight, there had been life inside these walls. He hadn't felt that in…forever.

He tried to lose himself in the latest Carofiglio novel, but not even Guido Guerrieri's new case could hold his interest. He had put the book aside and turned off the light when Karla called to tell him Angelina knew he'd lied to her and asked what he planned to do to fix it.

Had Luke told Angelina, or had she just figured it out on her own?

No matter. In a way, he was glad she knew, because trying to pretend he didn't know Adam and Damián had been a nightmare. He'd probably slipped up any number of times tonight alone. No wonder she'd figured it out.

But now what? Should he go over to Adam's and tell her why, or was this the opportunity he needed to back away from her without things getting…complicated. Hell, it was only Monday and he'd already started dreading her leaving this weekend to go back home.

Even so, he'd found it so damned hard to push her toward Luke tonight, even though it was the right thing to do. Maybe he should call Luke and have him go over and be there for her right now.

He told himself he just didn't want the tears and drama of being confronted by Angelina tonight. Italian women could be…emotional.

In reality, he had no business being with her. She deserved someone solid. Someone who wasn't missing the commitment gene. Someone like Luke. Marc knew he was being a shithead, but he picked up the phone and speed-dialed Luke.

"What's up?" There was an edge to Luke's voice. Was he feeling Marc out to see what he knew? So, had he been the one to tell her?

Marc cut to the chase. "Angelina needs you."

"What the hell are you talking about?"

Marc closed his eyes. "She found out I lied to her."

"Then why aren't you over there right now telling her whatever the hell is going on in that thick head of yours?"

"Because I'm not going to make excuses. We weren't meant to be. You're the one with divine intervention on your side. You said you had a message from Maggie that she was sending Angelina to you. Now's your time to be there for her. Karla said she's hurting."

Dammit, I don't want her to be hurting.

"I don't think Maggie's message meant Angel."

"Oh, come on! You two are perfect for each other. You can give her everything she needs. Hell, you're even into BDSM. I had no fucking clue until tonight."

"Marc, for once in your life, stop running. Get over there and talk to her. I'm telling you, she wants you and will probably forgive you, if you'd just explain yourself."

But there was no explanation he could give her. No, it was better that she hated him than that she got any more attached. He couldn't be the Dom she needed.

He sure as hell wasn't the man she needed either.

After listening to Luke call him a few choice names, words he'd never heard Luke speak before, he hung up the phone and laid his forearm over his eyes. Unfortunately, he couldn't block out the images of her.

Angelina's smile. Or the way she nibbled her lower lip when she was overanalyzing something—which was often. How she dominated his kitchen and made him want to see her there every night when he came home. The way she flew apart with such abandon under his hand.

Shock and awe. His cock stirred to life. She'd woven herself into his life so insidiously he didn't know how he would ever be able to look at another woman.

But she deserved a lot more than he could give. He'd shut down emotionally a long time ago. She was bursting with a joy for living, an exuberant curiosity, and more love to give than most men deserved.

Certainly not this man.

His phone beeped to indicate a text message and he picked it up to read: "Get ur fucking ass down here. Now."

He smiled ruefully. *Sorry, Adam. Not following orders this time. She doesn't need me in her life.* He punched in the words "Tell her whatever you want. I don't want to hurt her any more" and hit send, then turned off the phone, as well as the light, and went to bed.

The alarm went off six hours later, and he awoke feeling as though he'd only slept ten minutes. He hadn't been this restless since Iraq. After a shower and breakfast, he got into the Porsche and drove to his outfitter store downtown to meet his six clients for today's trek. Brian Maxwell, his business partner, had seen they were equipped to within an inch of their lives. The man could sell firewood to a snowman. He could also balance the books, which made Marc happy, so he could devote himself to trekking.

They loaded into the 14-passenger van, Brian driving, and headed west on I-70. Brian would meet up with them over on Torrey's Peak tomorrow afternoon. The group planned to hike Gray's Peak then proceed to Torrey's, camping overnight somewhere in between. He welcomed the strenuousness of the hike. He needed to expel a shitload of frustration today. Two Fourteeners ought to provide the level of exertion he needed to make a dent, at least.

Reports indicated the roads were open to the trailhead for Gray's, not always the case at this time of year because of snow. But there would be snow at the summits. The Knife's Edge at Kelso Ridge ought to be interesting even with a dusting.

Bring it.

* * *

Angelina's eyes were gritty as she rolled over to see what time it was. Eleven. Good God, she hadn't slept that late in forever. Well, slept might not be the best word to describe what went on in this bed last night.

She picked up her phone and called Tony. The sooner someone could take her home, the better. Adam had refused her request last night, probably because of Allen. But clearly there was no reason for her to stay here. She'd handled Allen before and would again.

The man she couldn't handle seemed to be Marc. She felt tears burn her eyes again as Tony answered.

"What's up, baby?"

"Don't call me that. You know I hate it."

"That's what makes it the perfect name for you."

She could just imagine his grin. She walked over to the dresser and picked up her brush and looked at herself in the mirror. The bruise. Oh, God. She'd forgotten all about that. No way would she be able to cover it without looking like an actress in full-stage pancake makeup.

What had ever possessed her to call her brother?

"I was just calling to see how Mama is."

"Fine, as far as I know. I was over there Sunday. We missed you. You will be there this Sunday, won't you?"

She looked at the bruise, which was only just beginning to turn shades of yellow. "I think so."

"How's Denver? Mama said you were doing cooking classes?"

Denver sucks and I just want to go home.

"Denver's fine. The first day of class went well." Oh, God, would Karla be wanting another lesson today? In Marc's kitchen? She didn't want to go anywhere near him, although he'd said he would be out on the mountain today. Overnight.

"What did you learn?"

Never to trust men like Marc D'Alessio.

"I'm actually the instructor."

"Wow! I'm impressed as hell, sis."

She sighed. "Yeah, well, class is about to start. I just wanted to say hi."

"Well, hi and bye. See you Sunday. Knock 'em dead, baby."

I'd love to, but he's out on a mountain right now.

After saying goodbye and disconnecting, there wasn't anything she could do but go downstairs and face Karla, and possibly Adam. The two of them had tried to engage her in conversation last night, but she'd retreated to her room after her shower and cried herself into a fitful sleep.

Why she'd let herself want Marc so badly in such a short time baffled her. No, not a want—a need. How could she come to need someone so fast? But the thought of his not being around to continue her training made her physically sick.

What happened to her being independent and not needing a man for anything? And yet he'd made her need even more than a man. He'd awakened her body to its need to submit. For her mind to be dominated during sexual encounters, at least, by a Dom who would make sure all her needs were met.

Oh, Angie. That perfect Dom only exists in your dreams.

At the bottom of the stairs, she turned down the hallway to the kitchen. The smell of coffee and cinnamon assailed her as she entered the room, one or both causing her stomach to churn. Better not attempt to eat anything this morning.

Karla sat facing her at the table, with Adam's back to her. The woman's eyes looked like they could spit fire. Angelina wondered if she should leave.

Then Karla noticed her and smiled, her demeanor softening immediately. "Good morning, Angie." She got up and came over to greet her, just as Adam stood and turned around. The look of pity in his eyes just made her feel worse. She didn't want anyone's pity, even if she deserved it. She also saw a bit of remorse there. Now that she'd accept. He could just wallow in it. Doms weren't supposed to lie to subs. There was a rule about that somewhere, wasn't there?

But you're nobody's sub, Angie.

Karla stopped in front of her and stood awkwardly, then seemed to come to a decision and wrapped her arms around Angelina. At first, Angelina just stood there, arms at her side. "Please forgive me, Angie. I never wanted to hurt you."

Karla had just been trying to please Adam. All subs tried to please their Doms. Not that Karla was any closer to finding her perfect Dom than Angelina was. They'd never get there if they kept choosing emotionally unavailable men like Marc and Adam.

Feeling something squeezing her chest, Angelina hugged Karla back. She decided she didn't want to lose the woman's fledgling friendship. When the hug ended, they just looked at each other, speaking volumes without saying a word.

"Have some coffee." She looked over at Adam who extended a mug of the brew toward her. "You can doctor it up any way you'd like." He pointed to the sugar and creamer on the counter.

"Black's best. Thanks." She avoided making eye contact and brought the mug to her mouth, inhaling the aroma as she took a tentative sip. Hot.

"Karla made some cinnamon rolls, if you're hungry."

"No, thanks. Coffee will do it for me."

Adam motioned toward the table. "Let's all sit down?"

Without anywhere to escape to, Angelina had to get to where she could at least be civil with Adam while staying in his house. She hoped the conversation wouldn't turn to Marc, but those hopes were dashed soon after she sat down.

"I'm sorry about the lie that was perpetrated against you in my house," Adam began. "I told Marc I wanted him to come clean—and soon—but, for whatever reason, he didn't do so."

Surprisingly, no tears threatened. Maybe she was getting over him already. "It's okay. I…"

"No, it's not okay, hon. You need to get pissed and yell and scream or something. I don't want you thinking you deserved to be treated this way."

Okay, if he didn't stop talking like that—and soon—she would start crying again, and she wasn't going to go there. She looked down at the black liquid in her mug, a reflection of her mood. Maybe he was right. She didn't usually get silent. She fought back.

Angelina raised her gaze to meet Adam's. "Why did you go along with it?"

"Because sometimes I'm a damned fool." He rubbed the back of his neck before meeting her gaze again. "But Doc's…Marc's trying to sort some things out right now. He's been at some kind of crossroads for a while now and you just steamrolled over him while he was standing there deciding which way to go." Adam smiled. "I thought if he took a couple more days to process whatever's going on in that thick Italian skull of his—sorry, no disrespect to you—but I thought he'd come to his senses by now and do the right thing."

Angelina smiled. "Italian men do tend to be thickheaded." She sobered again. "But I trusted him, and I don't trust easily. Why did he lie to me, when he demanded honesty from me?"

"That's something you're going to have to ask him. But I've known Marc as a friend for seven years and I can tell you lying isn't in his character. He's an honorable man. Stubborn, arrogant, and domineering, too."

"I hadn't noticed," she said, hoping her voice dripped with the sarcasm she intended. "And why didn't he come over here and explain himself last night?"

"Marc will climb a Fourteener to avoid confrontation."

Apparently, that's not all he liked to avoid.

Karla leaned forward and touched Angelina's hand. "I've only known him a couple months, but I've never seen him so taken with any of the women at the club. I think he does care a lot about you, Angie."

Adam cleared his throat. "I want you to hear this if you hear nothing else, hon. I have no doubt that man would lay his life on the line for you, just as he did for Damián and others in Iraq. He's a good and decent man. Whatever is going through that confused head of his, he just needs some time to sort it out. Maybe he'll find some answers up on that mountain. He does his best thinking out in the wilderness."

The thought of Marc thriving in the wilderness was just another wedge between them. She could never share that with him. Being out in those mountains terrified her, even though that hadn't been the case before Papa's death. The Giardanos had enjoyed camping, hiking, and skiing every chance they could. Angelina was the only one with an aversion to those activities now.

"Look, I'm not saying look the other way. You go ahead and hold his balls to the fire." Adam looked away. "Sorry. Once a Marine…" He returned his gaze to her and grinned like a little boy. *Like Marc.*

"I'm just saying, demand honesty, hear him out, make him bleed a little, if you need to. But if you want a man to go to the ends of the earth for you, they don't come much finer than Marc D'Alessio."

Chapter Twenty-Two

The wind whistled through the pass and Marc pulled his parka tighter around his face. The blowing snow stung at his cheeks, but the goggles kept his eyes clear. They'd arrived at Kelso Ridge, the trickiest part of the route, and he needed to keep his wits and his senses clear.

When he arrived at the Knife's Edge on the ridge, he waited for the six men to catch up. Angelina had been trying to dominate his thoughts since he'd set out this morning. Luckily, the group wasn't one for chitchat and they had experience, so he could lead them without worrying too much. They were single-minded in their goal of ticking two more Fourteeners off their bucket lists. Sadly, they hardly stopped to take in the incredible beauty around them.

His majestic mountains, where he was restored. Renewed. Rejuvenated. Here on the top of his world, all of the disappointments and failures in his life faded away and the future spread out before him like snowy peaks shimmering in the late afternoon sunlight. Magical. Up here, he experienced peace. Freedom.

The mountains didn't confine him. One thing he hated more than anything was the feeling of having no options, being forced into something that wasn't right for him.

Trapped.

He'd run away from managing the family resort in Aspen, where that same trapped feeling had nearly strangled him, pulling him away from the mountains where he belonged. He'd not only lived in the shadow of the mountains then, but in the shadow of his dead brother. He could never measure up; he'd never done anything to make his parents proud of him for who he was back then.

In the Navy and while training and serving with the Marines, he'd done a lot of growing up, found himself, and started thinking about someone other than himself for once. He'd found people who needed him, respected him for who he was, and, in Adam and Damián, people who loved him unconditionally.

A place where he belonged.

When he returned to Colorado, these mountains beckoned like a siren to this sailor. Here, his mind and body healed. Climbing and hiking were nearly impossible at first, while still healing. But each day, he'd climbed a little higher, growing stronger. The freedom was exhilarating. No cares or concerns.

On top of his world again.

Nothing had ever given him the same feeling. Not even sex, which was too fleeting. These mountains were eternal. Not a care in the world. Escape.

Until today.

The restlessness that hounded him during the night had stayed with him for the entire hike. The farther up the mountain he climbed, the more drained he felt. Anxious. Today, the mountains pulled him away from where he wanted to be, rather than gave him that sense of belonging.

Angelina. Even the wind seemed to whisper her name.

He needed her here to experience this beauty with him. Without her, it felt…empty. All of the meaning was gone. He wanted to be with Angelina, whether in the middle of a crowded, busy city like Denver or up in his peaceful mountains.

But he'd fucked up any chance with her. If he hadn't been running scared last night, he would have gone to her and explained. He'd hurt her and had done nothing to comfort her afterward.

He was no better than Sir Asshole.

How could she ever forgive him? He ached to be with her, hold her in his arms, and bury himself so deep inside her they wouldn't be able to tell where one ended and the other began.

He belonged with Angelina.

They belonged together.

One.

Not telling her who he was before he entered the temporary Dom/sub agreement with her had just been his way of sabotaging any future relationship they might have. He'd been running scared all his life.

But not anymore. Maybe he couldn't get back to her until tomorrow, but by God when he did, he'd make amends. He'd find some way to show her she was made for him—and he for her. Would she be at the club tomorrow night? Adam had assured him via text he wouldn't take her home while Allen Martin was around.

He pulled out his sat phone and had to laugh. There really were few wilderness places left anymore where modern technology couldn't reach. While he carried the phone for emergencies, he'd never been so happy for technology than he was right now. If this wasn't an emergency, he didn't know what one was.

* * *

Angelina and Karla carried their packages in from the car. Adam had insisted they go to Denver's "hootchie" clothing shops, as Karla called them, on Broadway. Apparently, he took Karla there often, because all of the shopkeepers knew them by name and even pulled out special items they'd ordered with Karla in mind.

Adam told her Luke would be escorting her to the club tonight. Being escorted seemed a bit superfluous, considering she'd just walk down the hallway to a separate section of the house she'd been staying in, but she'd go along with whatever. She really didn't care. It would fill the time until she could convince Luke to take her home this weekend.

When Adam chose several outfits that would fulfill every man's fantasy and told Angelina to try them on, she'd balked. But he gave her the "Dom" look and, after a ka-thunk moment of her own, she found herself loaded down with outfits and accessories, heading for the dressing rooms.

School girl. Nurse. Harem slave. French maid. At least he didn't insist on seeing how they looked on her. Adam said there was a costume theme at the club on Wednesdays in October, but that she would be wearing the nurse's outfit tonight. No discussion.

Karla had chosen a black latex, skin-tight short skirt and a red corset. She'd added over-the-knee stiletto patent-leather boots with five-inch platform heels, a black hat with a pheasant feather, and a red-feather eye mask to finish the ensemble. Well, Angelina supposed it was a costume.

Angelina and Karla had followed Adam's instructions to a T. The club owner certainly enjoyed telling women how to dress. Of course, it made sense he would care about how Karla dressed, because she worked at his club. But he'd taken just as much time to make sure Angelina's purchases fit whatever fantasies he thought Luke might have.

Adam also chose their shoes, stockings, and lingerie. She blushed at the level of detail the man knew about women's undergarments. Well, he'd probably undressed many of them over the years. At least the shoes didn't have five-inch fuck-me heels. He specified she was not to choose anything higher than three inches. Very considerate of him, but she was secretly happy because anything higher killed her feet. She also chose a white-feather eye mask to go with the nurse's outfit.

Lordy, if her mother could see how she'd be dressed in a semi-public setting, she'd have started a novena of prayers for the redemption of her soul. Angelina never would have chosen those items—singularly or together—especially at the obscene prices they charged for such skimpy outfits. But Adam insisted there was no limit on cost, provided they selected items he approved.

She'd actually had fun shopping, though. Not that she had a clue where she'd ever wear any of the costumes back in Aspen Corners.

After they had finished shopping, Adam had taken them to have a late lunch at a restaurant near the club. Unfortunately, the Italian cuisine was uninspiring and very little of it was fresh. They needed a new chef.

By the time the three returned to the club, it was after five and she and Karla went upstairs to dress. She couldn't wait to see Karla perform tonight.

Angelina stood in front of the mirror. No way. The bustier under the nurse's uniform created lots of cleavage that spilled through the deep-cut vee. The skirt barely covered her butt cheeks, accentuating her wide hips. Sure, it had been short when she tried it on at the shop, but she hadn't tried it on with the bustier—and having the white garters peeking out, holding up the white-mesh stockings, just made it look…too sexy. And white open-toed mules? Like a nurse would wear something like that while on her feet all day long. She'd pulled her hair up into a clip hidden underneath the vintage 1960s nurse's hat.

A knock at the bedroom door captured her attention.

"It's me, Angie." She opened the door to find Karla in her funky outfit. "Oh. My. God! Angie, you look fantastic! I love it!"

"Oh, please, Karla. No way am I going into the club looking like this."

Karla's eyes grew wide. "But Adam said to…I mean Master Adam—I keep forgetting that's how I'm supposed to address him on club nights. You can't disobey him."

"He's not my Dom." *I don't have a Dom anymore.*

"At the club here, he's kind of everyone's Dom—the über Dom, if you will. Or is it Alpha? Whatever, you're coming with me. Now. Let's go."

Angelina sighed. Karla sometimes acted more like a Domme than a sub. But what option did Angelina have? If she didn't wear this, she could choose the school girl outfit with an equally short plaid skirt, or the harem slave costume that was practically see-through.

"Fine. Let's go. I don't want you to be late for your first set."

They walked downstairs and into the kitchen, where a cowboy and Zorro stood chatting near the table. The two turned as they came into the room. Adam was Zorro, bare-chested under his cape, and Luke wore jeans, chaps, a vest, but also was shirtless. Luke's pecs and abs, or what she could see of them, were well-defined. She wondered why she couldn't have been attracted to him.

"Hot damn! You both look incredible," Luke said, grinning. He came over to Angelina, and she had to tilt her head back to maintain eye contact. "Darlin', you're mine tonight."

Angelina felt a little shiver. Not the same response as with Marc, but he wouldn't have the nerve to show up while she was here. Taking Luke's elbow, she genuinely smiled for the first time since Monday night. Luke was a nice man. Even though he didn't feel very Dom-like, he'd certainly lit her fire on Saturday night on her sofa. She could do a lot worse. And had.

Tonight she just wanted to have fun. She let Luke lead her to the hallway and they went by the theme rooms, Adam's office, and then into the bar and great room area. His spurs jangled as he walked. Adam and Karla walked behind them silently. She avoided glancing at Room Eight, but kept her gaze straight ahead of her.

"What can I get you to drink?"

"An Italian tickler, please." When Luke quirked an eyebrow, she grinned. "Amaretto and club soda."

As she waited for Luke, she surveyed the scene in the club. The costumes worn by the women were skimpy—whether they were Tops, bottoms, Dommes, or subs, it didn't seem to matter. Angelina didn't feel as self-conscious as she had upstairs. One Domme looked like Catwoman and kneeling beside her, his cheek against her over-the-knee boots, was Robin. Angelina smiled.

Several subs or bottoms were dressed as animals—puppies mostly, although there was a cat and even a pony. In addition to their animal ears and paws or hooves, they had tails attached to their butts by…oh, God! Butt plugs! She averted her eyes to where Karla prepared to sing.

Luke handed her a drink. "Why don't we go up near the stage?"

Angelina looked in that direction, but each of the small tables only had one chair. Luke took her by the elbow and led her to one and sat down. "You have two choices, darlin'. Kneel at my feet or sit in my lap."

Luke smiled at her discomfort. Angelina flushed. There were no pillows to cushion her knees here like the one Marc had put down on the floor in her bedroom. Not knowing how long she'd be here, she made up her mind rather quickly. "Lap."

She set her drink on the table next to his longneck and decided to wipe the smirk off Luke's face. When she straddled his lap, facing him, clit to crotch, his jaw nearly dropped. He glanced nervously toward the entrance, or perhaps he was looking for an exit. She smiled at the power she felt. Clearly, she'd surprised him. Well, good, because she had a feeling this night was going to be full of surprises for her, too.

Angelina Giardano was going to be nobody's angel tonight.

"I've wanted to do this since I came into the kitchen and saw you tonight." She reached out and touched his chest, running her fingers under the flaps of the vest, over his taut skin, until she flicked the tip of her thumbnails over his hard nips. She felt his erection pressing against her bare clit. Master Adam hadn't included panties in her wardrobe purchases.

"Oh, Luke, I think you might be getting a fever. Where would you like Nurse Angelina to check your temperature—orally or rectally?"

Angelina had never role-played or played the vamp before, but was having fun watching a bead of sweat break out on Luke's forehead. He looked as if he were about to explode. Then he regained his authority and reached for her hand to keep her from touching him.

"On your knees, Angel."

The forcefulness of the command took her off guard. "But I thought—"

"I said kneel. Don't make me repeat myself."

Ka-thunk. Her stomach seemed to drop a few inches. The change in his demeanor puzzled and excited her. Were they supposed to be on a real date? She just thought she was a mercy date because he felt sorry about how Marc had treated her.

"One. Two."

She swung her leg off his lap and knelt on the floor beside his chair. Thankfully, the floor was made of some material that had some give, which would help a bit on her knees if she were to have to kneel long. She remembered Marc had asked her to remain upright and keep her head bowed, so she assumed the same position.

"You can sit on your heels. You might be there a while. Keep your eyes on my boots."

Karla began singing "*Poison*" and Angelina wondered if Master Adam had a clue she was singing to him. She might as well be singing for Angelina and Marc, as well. That man was equally lethal to her.

After Karla finished that song, mind-numbing boredom set in. Angelina surreptitiously looked around the room, trying not to raise or move her head much. Master Adam spoke with a dark-haired Dom dressed in green scrubs with a stethoscope around his neck. She could tell he was a Dom just by his stance—legs apart, hands on his hips, laden with testosterone. But she couldn't see much more than the outline of his body without turning her head.

"I asked you to keep your eyes on my boots."

"I'm sorry...Sir." She returned her gaze to his feet.

"So am I, darlin', because I'm going to have to put this on you."

He held a black silk sash. A blindfold. "No, Luke! I'll behave. I was just...curious."

"Well, curiosity just got my nurse blindfolded. You need to learn some manners, too. Tonight you call me Sir."

Angelina's heart pounded as the room went dark. Why hadn't he given her another warning? Marc usually had repeated his commands, at least until she'd gotten used to them. Luke insisted on perfection right from the start. Would she survive the night with him without a severe punishment?

Karla sang "*Spellbound*," a song she recognized by an Italian Goth metal band, but the words had new meaning for her tonight.

Tell me who you are...You cannot have this control of me...I would break the spell you've put on me.

"Open your mouth and take a sip."

She opened quickly, not taking any chances on earning a punishment if she didn't move fast enough. His hand grabbed the ends of the blindfold sash and pulled her head back slightly—not enough to impede swallowing, but far enough to exert his dominance over her. He held the glass to her lips and she sipped, the liquid tickling her nose.

When she pulled away to indicate she'd had enough to drink, she heard the glass being placed back on the table beside her. His finger pressed against her wet lips and forcefully entered her mouth while his hand caged her chin and pushed her jaw down to allow his finger deeper access. Memories of Marc doing the same thing in her bedroom caused her clit to throb. The finger slid along her tongue, deeper and deeper, until it hit the back of her mouth and she gagged, tears springing to her eyes. He pulled back immediately and with his other hand stroked her cheek gently.

"Sorry, darlin', for being such a clumsy oaf."

Oomph.

Luke sounded as if he'd been kicked or punched. Before she could figure out what happened to him, she felt his hand cup her breast just before his finger and thumb pinched her nipple. Hard. Her head went back of its own accord as her chest jutted closer to his hand.

"Like that, I see."

"Yes." Did all Doms have a fixation on nipples and breasts?

Luke squeezed both peaks, eliciting a moan from her.

"Did you forget something, darlin'?"

Angelina furrowed her brows. "Oh, Sir! I'm sorry. Sir."

"Well, that's the second time now. I think maybe you might need a little discipline to help you remember how to address your Dom properly."

"Please, Sir. I'm just a little rattled tonight. Give me another chance. I'll do better."

"Oh, you'll do better all right. Because I'm going to make sure you don't forget it."

How had Luke gone from nice guy to cruel Dom in such a short time? Angelina regretted agreeing to be his date tonight. She just wanted to go back upstairs and read an erotic romance or something.

"I want to try something different. I'm not going to speak commands or instructions, but only use my hands and body to convey what I want you to do. So pay careful attention." He chuckled.

Two hands gripped her upper arms and helped her to her feet. Before she could steady herself, an arm went around her back and another behind her knees and she was suddenly lifted into his arms.

"Oh!"

She heard Luke's spurs below her as he carried her. Where was he going to discipline her? Dread began to churn in her stomach and she thought the amaretto might come back up. They hadn't discussed limits or anything. As Karla's voice receded, she realized they were going to the theme rooms. But which one?

Please, not the St. Andrew's cross.

He carried her into a room and the sounds of the club disappeared when he kicked the door closed. Her heart thudded then stopped before resuming its fast pounding again.

"Luke, I mean Sir, I'm scared."

He eased her feet to the floor and she felt his erection pressing against her abdomen. Her clit pulsed in response. He pressed his finger against her lips as if to shush her. Why didn't he speak, say something to calm her nerves?

Why couldn't he be like Marc, explaining everything along the way?

With his hands firmly on either side of her waist, he indicated he wanted her to move backward. She took one awkward step, then another, trusting him not to put her into danger. She had taken three steps back when something hard pressed against her butt and shoulders. A hand flat against her chest told her to stay put.

She heard the jangle of spurs and then buckles, making her wonder what would come next. He lifted her left wrist and wrapped a cuff around it. Then the right. Next came cuffs on both ankles. As if afraid she would bolt, he swiftly raised one arm and fastened it to something at a forty-five degree angle, and did the same with the other.

The cross! Her breath came in shallow spurts and he stroked her upper chest slowly, conveying that she needed to slow down her breathing. She took a deep, shaky breath, then another. His hand cupped her chin as his thumb stroked her cheekbone.

She could almost hear Marc saying *"Good girl."*

Disappointed that it wasn't Marc with her, but Luke, she tried to relax. Then he grasped both ankles and pressed outward, forcing her to take side steps until she could spread her legs no farther. The clicking of the cuffs being attached to the cross sounded like the clicks of an empty revolver as the trigger was pulled.

As he stood, his hands roamed up the insides of her calves, knees, thighs. She tried to raise her leg as a reflex against the coming invasion, but she couldn't move. When he reached the garter, he pulled it away and let it snap against her thighs, stinging her.

She thought he would touch her pussy, instead his hands slid along her hips to her sides. She couldn't control a giggle when he touched her hypersensitive sides near her breasts. He sighed. Apparently, Luke was just as thrilled with her ticklishness as Marc. Well, deal with it. She couldn't change who she was. And she was ticklish.

His fingertips trailed lightly along her cheeks, her ears, and she felt him removing the hairpins from her nurse's hat. Next came the hair clip and he shook her hair out until it fell over her shoulders and breasts. Apparently, both men liked her hair loose. His fingers massaged her scalp, and she felt herself relaxing.

He stopped, and his hands were gone until he began undoing what few buttons there were on the skimpy uniform. He spread the fabric open and exposed her bustier. The air was cool against the tops of her breasts, which spilled over the top of the lacy garment.

His lips came down on the hollow of her neck and, if her arms weren't holding her body up, her buckling knees would have left her in a puddle at his feet. She realized the cross was actually helping her not to have to worry about silly things like standing upright.

He pulled away and tapped her forehead and then pressed a finger against her lips again.

"Give that busy mind a rest, pet."

Marc's words rang loud and clear and she tamped down any other thoughts. Feel. *Just feel.* His lips pressed against the beating pulse in her neck and he suckled, then his tongue blazed a trail to her breasts. He lifted her breast out of the dubious confines of the bustier and took her rigid peak into his mouth.

"Oh, Sir. Please. Suck me hard. Bite me."

He groaned, sounding so much like Marc, then took one peak between his teeth and the other between finger and thumb, clamping down hard on each. Her body jerked away from the cross and toward him.

His hand left her breast and trailed over her side and abdomen until he cupped her mons. She tilted her pelvis as much as she was able and silently begged him to touch her. His fingers spread open her folds and slid between her wet cleft. Without stopping, his finger thrust inside her, then another.

"Oh, God, yes!"

With his thumb he stroked her clit. She took off like a Roman candle as he stroked her faster and faster.

"I'm going to come. Please, Sir, may I come?"

His answer was to curl his fingers around to stroke her G-spot.

"Oh, yes! Oh, God! I'm coming! Her body convulsed against his hand. Don't stop, Marc!" He stroked her until the sensation was too painful, and she pulled away.

No, not Marc! "Oh, Luke. I'm sorry!" How had she forgotten who she was with? She wished he'd say something, or touch her so she'd know he was okay.

Nothing. No sound. No touch.

Tears stung her eyes. She hadn't meant to hurt Luke, but wished Marc had been the one to restrain her on this cross tonight. How could she ever be anyone else's submissive? She only wanted him to be her Dom.

Luke reached up to untie the blindfold. Clearly, this scene had ended, just as abruptly probably as her last one in this room. She had no other words to say to convey how sorry she was, but it was probably for the best if she didn't get involved with Luke. His friendship with Marc would only force them to be in each other's company from time to time, and the thought of being with Marc and not being able to touch him would be the worst form of torture she could imagine.

The blindfold came loose and he pulled the ends away. The air felt cool against her wet eyes. She blinked, afraid to look up and see the hurt in Luke's eyes. He placed a finger under her chin and forced her to look at him.

Angel. Man. Wolf.

Her dream lover.

Her knees gave way and she hung supported by her arms until he placed his hands around her waist to relieve the strain on her arms until she could stand on her own again.

"Marc?"

He nodded. He removed the wolf mask, not that she didn't already recognize him. Apparently, she didn't even need her eyes to know it had been Marc touching her. Her body had known all along.

"It was you that night?"

He nodded and reached up to remove the cuffs from the cross. Her joints were stiff as she lowered her arms. Then he knelt down and unhooked the ankle cuffs from the cross. He scooped her up in his arms and carried her to the loveseat in the corner, his spurs clanging on the floor. She smiled. He'd certainly gone to great extremes to make her think he was Luke. He pulled a blanket from the basket, but Angelina waved it away. She wasn't cold in the least.

Sitting on the leather seat, he brought his finger up to trace the line of her jaw.

"I'm sorry I didn't get to you in time that night, *cara*. I've been haunted day and night by images of you being flogged so badly by that asshole. If only I'd come to the club on time, I could have saved you from much of that pain."

Is that why he'd lied to her? He was ashamed for not rescuing her soon enough? All she could think was that he *had* rescued her from Allen's cruelty. Not once, but twice. More importantly, he'd started her on a journey of sexual self-discovery as a submissive and she wanted to continue that—in the bedroom and out, with or without him. No, only with.

Angelina needed to tell him these things, not just keep them inside. She reached out and ran her finger along his collarbone and down to the vee in his scrubs to touch his chest hair.

"You did rescue me, Marc. And I, too, have been haunted by that night, but my dreams were filled with an angel-man-wolf dream lover I thought I'd imagined. You reminded me so much of him so many times, but I didn't think he existed. Yet, here you are."

"When you left the club that night, I thought I'd never see you again."

Marc leaned forward and pulled her face toward his, teasing her lips with tiny nibbles until she opened her mouth, allowing his tongue entrance to thrust in and out in simulated lovemaking. When she sucked him deeper inside, his hand brushed across her nipple, then pinched the tip until she squirmed in his lap. Her clit throbbed, needing him to touch her there again.

She pulled away, gasping for air. "I need you to make love to me, Marc. Now."

"Not yet."

She groaned. "Marc, please."

He chuckled. "First, I want your hot mouth on me, Nurse Angelina. Give ol' Doc a blow job."

She grinned at his crude language. Well, he'd turned her down so many times she'd wanted to please him, she didn't think he'd ever let her get this close, so she wasn't going to wait around for him to change his mind. Scooting off his lap, she knelt between his knees and lifted his scrubs, then pulled the drawstring on his pants to free his penis.

Mio Dio. So long and thick. How would she ever get him inside her? Well, that was something to worry about later. Staring at him, she felt some performance anxiety. She wanted to please him so much.

Angelina placed her hand at the base of his penis and he hissed, throwing his head back. She smiled. He hadn't come with her before. More than likely anything she did would get him off. She brought her fingers up to play with his balls, gently pulling the hairs and skimming her fingernails over him.

She lowered her mouth to him and ran the tip of her tongue around the head of his penis, tasting the salty pre-cum.

"Ah, *Gesù, amore*, you're killing me."

Empowered, she wrapped her lips around him, sucking him into her mouth, pulling her head away at the same time. He scooted farther down in the loveseat, closer to her. She pressed her mouth down his shaft and pulled back. With each thrust, she pressed him a little farther into her mouth, until he'd gone as far as the back of her tongue. Oh, God, she still only had half of him inside her.

He placed his hands on her head and held her there as he pumped his penis into her mouth. With each stroke, he went deeper until he hit the back of her throat and she gagged. He didn't stop and each time he hit her throat, she gagged a little less. His hands controlling her head made her want to try and take him deeper. She relaxed her throat. He continued to pump into her face and she placed her hand around the base of his penis and fisted him.

When she felt him start to pulsate around her hand, he reached down and pulled her face away.

"I'm sorry. God, your mouth is so hot. I didn't want to stop you, but I want to come inside your pussy. Put a condom on me." He pointed behind her and she turned to find a bowl of condoms on the table. Picking up one, she grinned seductively as she slowly tore open the foil package with her teeth.

"Pet, if you don't get that damned thing on me now…"

She laughed and took the condom out and placed it around the head of his penis, then slowly rolled it down his bobbing shaft.

"Straddle me. Now."

Angelina pulled the short skirt of the nurse's uniform up and placed a knee beside each of his hips. He took her bare butt in one hand and his penis in the other and rubbed himself along her cleft.

"So fucking wet for me, pet."

She leaned forward and pressed her mouth against his, nibbling and biting at his full lower lip. When his penis found her entrance, he pushed himself against her. Would he just ram himself inside? She held her breath.

"Relax. I haven't lost all control. Yet." He placed both hands on her butt and held her in place as he thrust his hips up and down a little more each time, stretching her opening, lubricating his penis by entering, pulling out, entering and going a little deeper, and then withdrawing and repeating the motions over and over as he worked himself inside her.

"So tight. So perfect."

His words warmed her and she lowered herself farther onto his penis. "Oh, Marc. I mean, Sir. Oh, God."

"At this moment, I'll answer to any of the above."

His hands left her butt and went to her breasts. He kneaded and pinched them into a frenzy. She threw her head back with abandon.

He continued to ease his length into her. How much more? She reached between their bodies and felt he still had several more inches not yet inside.

"Touch yourself, pet. Play with your clit."

In front of him? She shook her head.

"It wasn't a suggestion. Touch yourself the way you do when you're alone."

Her face flamed. He wasn't supposed to know she did that.

He pulled out of her and she was afraid she'd displeased him, but then he took the head of his wet penis and slid it along her well-lubricated cleft. He slid his penis back down until he was at the opening of her pussy again and pressed halfway in with one thrust.

"Oh, God." Her insides melted.

"Touch yourself. Now, pet. Don't make me punish you for willful disobedience."

With reluctance, she let her finger slide to her now very wet clit. She closed her eyes and looked away, embarrassed.

"Look at me."

She groaned then opened her eyes.

"Pleasure yourself for me, pet."

She felt her pussy clench around his penis as he drove deeper inside. When his penis hit her G-spot, she felt her control giving way. Slow it down. He hadn't given her permission to come. She stroked harder, taking him deeper and deeper. Using her free hand on his shoulder and her knees on the seat to steady herself, she pumped up and down on her knees.

"Yes, *bella*. Fuck me. Fuck me hard."

Emboldened and close to coming, she flicked her finger over her erect clit. "Sir. Please, may I come?"

"Come, pet. Suck me dry."

She took herself over the crest. "Oh, God! I'm coming! Harder, Sir. Fuck me harder. All the way in."

"I thought you'd never ask." He grasped her hips and lifted her up, then slammed her down on his penis to the hilt.

"Oh, my God! Oh, Marc! Don't stop! Oh, yesss!" No longer needing her finger to come, she put both hands on his shoulders and they slammed against each other. The pressure built, each impact sending a frisson of electricity to her clit, her pussy muscles tightening.

"*Gesù*. I'm coming, pet." Ahhhhgggggg! Marc shouted his release at the same time she bucked and jerked against him in a simultaneous orgasm.

All coherent thought escaped her. She screamed as he continued to plow into her then glanced down at him. His eyes were closed, a look of ecstasy on his face. She'd made him feel that. The power left her weak, which didn't make sense at all.

His penis stopped pulsating. Unable to hold herself upright any longer, she collapsed onto his shoulder, gasping for air.

Marc stroked her back. "Incredible."

"Yes, it was."

She smiled, then sat up, his penis still inside her, and began buttoning her nurse's uniform with fumbling fingers.

"I had a whole scene planned for the medical room tonight, but I'll never make it across the hall. I've been hard for you since Friday night at the bar. That scene will have to wait for another time, though."

"Well, I did offer to do something about that on Saturday. And Sunday. And Monday."

"I know, *bella*. Sometimes I'm a damned fool." He looked up at her and stroked her hair. She thought he was going to say something else, but he just grinned and said, "Now I'm just going to have to make up for lost time."

This couldn't be good. Okay, yes, it could, but she'd already had two orgasms tonight. She was more than satisfied.

"You didn't happen to wear the butt plugs like I asked you the other night."

She shook her head. She hadn't wanted any reminders about what she'd lost with Marc. To have him back now seemed too good to be true.

"Well, maybe we can do a little demonstration of Doc's techniques some other time in there."

"You mean let people watch?" She tensed.

"Judging by the way your pussy just tried to strangle my cock, I'd say that's a definite possibility." Marc smiled. "How do you feel about that?"

She'd never thought about it, but wondered what kind of demonstration he had in mind.

"I can see from your eyes the thought interests you. I love your curiosity."

She couldn't believe the things she'd tried in less than a week. "I can't believe how different tonight's experience was from my first one in here."

"It's all in who you let Dom or Top you, pet. Trust. Negotiation. Consent. Safety."

Angelina smiled and almost didn't say it but decided to be brave for a change. "I want you to be my Dom. Not just for this week."

His eyes warmed to her. "I'd be honored. Thank you for trusting me." Then he grew serious. "Why don't you move to Denver? You can live with me. My house is enormous and you can have as much privacy and independence as you like. But I need you in my life, *amore*. You complete me."

Angelina froze and pushed away from him. Whoa! Moving in? This was happening too fast. "Marc, I appreciate how gentle and patient you've been with me as you explained this lifestyle to me and I want very much to be your submissive. No man has ever excited me the way you do."

"Angelina, once in my life, I want more than a Dom/sub relationship."

She placed her finger on his lips to stop his words before he said something they'd both regret. "I can't be anything more right now. Please don't ask."

The hurt in his eyes made her ache to know she'd put it there. But Marc was an adventurer; he loved the wilderness. She was afraid of everything about that part of his world. Eventually, he'd grow tired of her not wanting to share all of his world. Sex and lust could only last so long. While having a Dom/sub relationship would be enough for her right now, eventually, he'd expect more. She couldn't tie him down to her like that.

"You need someone who can share your love of the wilderness. That's a huge part of who you are and I wouldn't be able to be with you. I'm terrified of those mountains. They took Papa from me." She felt him tense. "He was SAR. There was an avalanche." Marc showed sympathy, but didn't seem at all surprised, which seemed odd to her.

"I'm so sorry, *cara*. To suffer a great loss like that, it's understandable to want to find a reason why. To blame someone—or something." He reached up and brushed the hair back from her face as he searched for words to say. "The wilderness can be unforgiving. She demands respect. But she can also embrace you and make you feel you've come home, as she does me. I could show you that world, too, just as I introduced you to this one." He waved his hand to take in the cross and spanking bench.

Tears pricked her eyes. "You see what I mean? You're at home out there, but I'd feel like a prisoner." Yet she wanted more with Marc, too. She touched his cheek, hoping he'd know how much she cared for him, but restraints were working against her now.

Maybe it was time to free herself. "Marc, you did rescue me in time last month. But now I have to rescue myself before I can be the woman you deserve."

Fear flitted across his eyes. "You're already perfect for me, *amore*."

She shook her head. "I can't explain, but give me a few days. There's something I need to try first."

He cocked his head and quirked an eyebrow, waiting for her to explain, but she needed to formulate a plan first.

"You'll just have to trust me, even though I think trust might be harder for you than it was for me."

"Touché." He smiled, but his eyes remained filled with hurt and disappointment.

Would she survive this trial by fire she needed to put herself through to see if she could move forward in a relationship with Marc?

Chapter Twenty-Three

Marc felt his guts twist in a knot at Angelina's announcement in Adam's kitchen a few hours later.

"No fucking way."

"Marc, I'm going. This is something I have to do."

"Not with Martin lurking out there somewhere. The sheriff's department hasn't been able to locate him since he left the hospital Sunday morning. For all we know, he tailed us to Denver and is just waiting for his opportunity to find you alone so he can attack you again."

"But I won't be alone. I'll be with Karla and Cassie."

"I forbid you to go."

She put her hands on her hips and stood her ground. "You and what army?"

"No way are three defenseless women going to be able to stave off an attack if Martin goes after you, Angelina."

"Cassie and I are black belts in Taekwondo," Karla offered.

Marc glared at Karla. *You're not helping*. His attention returned to Angelina, who put forth her argument, as well.

"You know I fought him off Saturday night, so I have a few moves of my own. My four older brothers taught me well."

Marc felt control slipping away from him. He didn't like to feel out of control, but she was putting herself in a place where he couldn't protect her from harm. If he was her Dom, he had to protect her. If he ever wanted more than a Dom/sub relationship with her, he'd have to give her freedom outside play scenes. She was a stubborn, independent woman. Italian. She controlled the relationship, their future. He couldn't really stop her from trampling his heart if she decided to.

That thought scared him to death.

"I'll be fine, Marc. But you know why I have to do this."

Yeah. Marc pointed a finger at his chest and she smiled at him. She had to prove some damned thing to him. If it got her killed or hurt, he'd never forgive himself. "Let me show you the wilderness. I take novices out there all the time."

She shook her head and the noose tightened even more around his neck.

"If I lose it out there, I'm not going to embarrass myself in front of you." She smiled again. "Relax. It's just an overnight camping trip. Nothing's going to happen."

Karla tried to reassure him. "We're just going to be up at Lincoln Lake on Mt. Evans. There will probably be lots of other people hiking and maybe even camping, as well. Cassie's determined to get some wildlife shots and the mountain goats are pretty easy to find there."

Adam walked into the room, still wearing his cape, but he'd lost the mask and hat. Luke followed. The tenseness in the room was palpable.

Adam's hand went to the back of his neck, a nervous response Marc first noticed back in Fallujah. "What's wrong?"

Adam could help. He could at least control Karla a little bit, if he chose to. "These two women think they're going camping overnight on Mt. Evans. They're planning to leave at daybreak, after they run up to get Karla's friend."

"Yeah, Karla said it's something she does every year with Cassie."

"Well, Angelina's my concern and with Allen Martin still out there, she's not going anywhere without one of us watching over her."

"Karla, hon, why don't you and Cassie postpone the trip until things settle down here? Or let one of us go with you?"

"No, Adam. Cassie and I have been planning this for weeks, and now Angelina wants to join us, which is great. But this is a female bonding adventure. Cassie's not comfortable around men, especially the dominant types like you guys." She looked away. "I won't make her uncomfortable like that. This is our annual ritual and we're going to do it without men, like always."

Shit. Adam had no better control over her than Marc did over Angelina. God save them all from strong, stubborn women.

Chances were they'd be safe. There were fewer nutcases per capita in the wilderness than there were in the city here. Martin was probably off nursing his broken nose and lying low after realizing what a total asshole he was.

Yeah, right.

Marc sighed. He had to let her go. As with Shibari, the rope could embrace or strangle. He had to let go of the tight rein he wanted to place on her—or he'd lose her. But he didn't have to leave everything to chance.

"Let me take you down to the shop to get the gear you'll need."

* * *

Angelina stretched out her aching legs. She'd never hiked so long in her life. The boots she'd gotten at Marc's store were comfortable, but all she wanted to do right now was take them off and wiggle her toes.

Karla and Cassie were off gathering firewood while there still were a couple hours of daylight left, giving Angelina a chance to chill and recover from the strenuous hike. The wind blew constantly up here, no trees to slow it down. She got used to it after a while and it became like white noise, blocking out all other sound.

Such a sad and desolate place. In the distance, she could see snow-covered mountains. She shivered. At least the snowline was above them here. Still, it was cold.

Lonely.

She wished Marc was sitting here beside her. Sure, Cassie and Karla would be back soon and it sounded as though they had some fireside rituals they would go through tonight to burn away painful memories from their pasts. For Karla, it had something to do with her brother's death. For Cassie, it sounded as though she had some demons of old to release, but Angelina hadn't wanted to pry.

Angelina didn't want to release anything, well, except maybe Allen. More importantly, she wanted to embrace someone. Be tied to him forever. All she wanted was to feel his arms around her, their bodies becoming one again.

A stinging on the side of her neck brought her hand up to swat whatever had bitten her this time. Didn't insects migrate or hibernate for the winter or something? She'd been pestered by them all day.

After struggling to pull off her boots, straining muscles in places she didn't know existed, she leaned back and let the warm afternoon sun kiss her face. It really was peaceful up here. A good place to come and think.

Not that she couldn't think in civilization, too.

She certainly had some thinking to do. Like about where her relationship with Marc was going to go after this. She didn't expect any earth-shattering wilderness epiphany or anything, but would be happy if she just survived unscathed and didn't become a wuss at the first sign of wildlife. Didn't the animals leave you alone if you left them alone? Well, not so with bears or mountain lions, she supposed. But up here, they were more likely to see bighorn sheep and mountain goats, according to Cassie.

Even though she was from the mountains of Peru, the woman had become one with her surroundings here in Colorado. It was an almost mystical experience to watch her move. Angelina couldn't understand how anyone could experience that sense of being. Of belonging. Did Marc feel that?

Cassie would be perfect for Marc. Well, if she liked men. Some man must have hurt her deeply.

Angelina felt a cramp tighten in her calf and stood up to put pressure on it. A movement out of the corner of her eye sent her heart into her throat. She turned expecting to find a grizzly bear only to see the blur of something tall and brown lunge at her, hitting her head and knocking her off her feet. When the back of her head hit a hard surface, she was momentarily stunned. Whatever had attacked her was straddling her, cutting off her ability to fill her lungs. When her eyes cleared she looked up at the bandaged face of Allen.

He pinned her wrists to the ground and hovered over her face. "Hello, Angie. Did you think I wouldn't find you eventually?"

She struggled to get him off of her, but his weight was solid and her legs couldn't make contact with anything but air. He moved her arms above her head, taking both wrists into one hand, then reached down and began unzipping her jacket. His hand went inside to squeeze her breast until she screamed.

"I've missed hearing you scream for me, Angie."

"No! Get off of me, you fucking asshole."

Tsk-tsk. "You've been hanging around that sailor too long, picking up such foul language." He brought his hand up and slapped her, hitting the bruise he'd left there Saturday night. Black spots blinded her for a moment. "Now, we're going to get out of here before your friends get back."

He pulled a roll of duct tape from his pocket and ripped off a piece. She managed to open her mouth before he placed the tape over her. Perhaps with a little mobility in her jaw, she'd be able to work the tape off. How far had Karla and Cassie gone? Did they hear her scream?

He pulled her to her feet and dragged her over to her backpack. "We'll just take your pack, because I didn't know we were going camping when I followed you out here today."

She had no idea what was in there. Marc had packed it while his manager added a few items to Cassie and Karla's already well-equipped packs. His grip on her forearm hurt and she felt stones digging into the soles of her feet. She tried to tell him she wasn't wearing her boots, but he paid no attention. His intention was to get her away from her friends. From safety.

Angelina fought and tried to pull away from him, but he only stopped and turned her to face him. He put her pack on her back and then tackled her, his shoulder digging into her abdomen, until she was slung over his shoulder.

Dio, this couldn't be happening. She looked back at where she'd been waiting for Karla and Cassie, but soon it disappeared as he turned in another direction. The path below her and Allen's feet filled her vision as he took her farther and farther away.

She screamed, hoping someone would hear her despite the duct tape. Allen laughed at her feeble attempts.

"Save those screams for later, Angie. We have some catching up to do."

* * *

Marc's phone beeped indicating a SAR emergency. When he saw the GPS coordinates, the air whooshed from his lungs. He hadn't felt this breathless since his collapsed lung.

Marc sent text messages to Luke, Adam, and Damián. "Attack on Mt. Evans. Lincoln Lake. Might be the girls. Cougar. Meet at the trailhead." He gave them the coordinates. "Adam, bring your laptop. Damián, your rifle."

Marc grabbed his gear and headed for the Porsche, knowing he could ride shotgun with Luke once they met up. Damián had been the best sharpshooter in his Marine recon unit. Marc hoped he'd be able to traverse the terrain up there, but if he could get within a mile of the cougar, he'd be able to take it out.

Please, God, don't let anything happen to them.

Why hadn't he been more forceful and refused to let her go up there? He was supposed to protect her. He'd taken what precautions he could, but his mind had been so focused on the human threat, he hadn't even considered a cougar attack.

When his phone beeped again, he looked down. Adam didn't mince words. "Karla says Angelina's gone."

The Porsche swerved as Marc lost control. Before he killed himself or someone else, he pulled over to the shoulder and dialed Adam. His heart hammered loud in his ears. He screamed at the top of his lungs, "No!

Goddamn it. You can't take her away from me!" He rested his forehead against the steering wheel.

Mio Dio, not now. I just found her. I can't go on without her.

When Adam answered, Marc asked, "What's happened? Was it the cougar?" His voice rasped in his ears.

"No. It's that fucking shithead, Karla thinks. Damián and I are on our way with the gear you asked for."

Martin? Who was attacked by the cougar? He signaled to merge and got back onto the highway.

"I have GPS monitors in all three packs. Find out if she has her pack still."

"She does. But no boots. That's why they don't think she just wandered off on her own." He paused and added, "There were signs of a struggle."

Stay strong, amore. *I won't let him hurt you again. I promised you—and I keep my promises.*

God help me. Please, don't let me fail her again.

* * *

As the sun sank lower on the horizon, Angelina wondered if he'd ever stop. Her bones and muscles were screaming as he jarred her along the trail. Where was he taking her? He stopped abruptly and let her fall to the ground with a grunt.

Would anyone be able to follow their tracks? She wished she'd had something to drop along the path for them to follow. That worked in the movies, at least.

"We can't start a fire and call attention to ourselves. I'm sure your sleeping bag will keep me warm, though."

She closed her eyes, hoping he'd leave her outside to freeze rather than have to touch him. Allen started pulling things out of her pack—flashlight, rope, trail mix, the water purifier Marc had shown her how to use.

Angelina edged away from him, toward a pile of fist-sized rocks. Maybe if she could get one of them, she'd be able to hit him. She wished they were larger, but these would be easier to conceal. She just hoped there weren't any snakes concealed by the rocks.

"Don't move."

Damn. He was onto her.

"Sit down."

Maybe not. She moved just a little closer to the rocks before sitting on the ground. When he turned his attention back to the pack, she reached out to grasp one stone in each hand, the biggest she thought she could handle.

"That fucking bastard."

Angelina looked at Allen who held a small black box in his hand, not much larger than a matchbox. Allen stood and threw the box off the side of the mountain with as much strength as he could.

"Your rich sailor boy thinks he can outsmart me. Well, I'll show him who's smarter." He began repacking the items. "Get up. We have to keep moving so we can lose their track."

Track? What had the box been? Some kind of tracking device? She smiled ruefully. *Thank you for trying to protect me, Sir.*

If she let Allen take her any farther into the wilderness, Marc would never find her. She needed to make her move. Now.

She tried to speak through the tape to attract Allen's attention and get him to come closer.

"What is it?" He was exasperated, which might play in her favor. He wouldn't be thinking clearly.

He stood and walked toward her. When she made no move to stand, he reached down and grabbed her by her upper arms. She assessed her options and decided on her best target. Bringing her hands around to her chest, in one continuous movement she slammed both rocks into his bandaged nose. The sound of bone crunching against bone gave her some satisfaction. Hearing him squeal like a pig provided the rest.

"Goddamned bitch."

Once more, she watched the blood spurting from between his fingers and she scrambled to her feet. She ran to the pack and pulled out the rope and flashlight. Returning to where Allen lay huddled on his knees, she swung the heavy-duty light against his temple, sending him sprawling face down on the ground.

Before he could recover his senses, she dug her knee into his back and took the rope, executing the hogtie technique Marc had shown her at his house the other night. She'd never thought she'd use it for non-erotic purposes. While the tie didn't look as nice on Allen as it had on Luke, he wouldn't be getting loose anytime soon.

She reached up and pulled the tape off her mouth. "I'll be sure to send someone back here for you, Allen. If they can find you without the tracking device—and before a bear or mountain lion does." The look of fear on his face brought a smile to her face.

Angelina looked around. Having no clue where she was, she grabbed the now-bloody flashlight and her pack and started up the same trail Allen had taken her down. As she walked along, she began to hear sounds. The wind, always. But now her senses were heightened. Birds chirped. Burrowing animals scurried for food as they took advantage of the last bit of sunlight. She stopped and looked out across the landscape, seeing the mountains stretching out forever.

Majestic.

Marc's world. She found that she did want to know more. Explore more.

Sweat broke out on her forehead and trickled down her face. The air was chilly against her wet skin. That probably wasn't a good thing. With the sun just above the mountain peaks, she had to get back to her friends as soon as possible. The thought of being up here alone at night terrified her.

"Angelina!"

Marc? As if her thoughts had conjured him up, she looked up from where she'd been watching where she placed each footfall, hoping not to hurt her feet any more than she already had. Her eyes blurred and then cleared. He smiled and she dropped the pack and sailed into his open arms.

"Oh, *angelo mio*. You're safe."

"I am now. I've never been so happy to see someone."

She let the tears flow as she held on, afraid if she let go she'd find she'd only dreamed him to her again. But his solid arms around her were definitely real. He pulled away, lowering her to the ground, and took her face between his hands. When she winced, he inspected her cheek.

"Did he hurt you, *cara*."

"He's worse off than I am."

Marc smiled. "Good girl. I'm so proud of you."

His praise warmed her. She was proud of herself, too.

"How far back?"

"Fifteen minutes or so?" She had no idea how long she'd been walking. She'd just put one foot in front of the other, over and over again. God, her feet were aching.

"Damián's waiting for us about 500 yards up the trail." Marc turned around and spoke. "Luke, escort the ladies to meet up with him while Adam and I go back up the trail to pack out Angelina's trash."

She smiled and relaxed, relieved not to have to go back there with them. Leaning around Marc, she found an entire search party—Luke, Cassie, Karla, and Adam. She hobbled over to Karla and gave her a hug.

Karla squeezed her tight. "I was afraid I wouldn't see you again."

"I'm like a bad penny. I'll always keep turning up."

Karla let go and put her pack down and unzipped it. "You forgot something." She pulled out Angelina's hiking boots.

She smiled and sat down to put them on. Her feet were swollen and sore, but at least she wouldn't ding them up any more on the hike back.

"Angelina, will he be hard to spot?"

"No, he's in a small clearing right next to the trail. Hogtied."

He smiled. "Good girl."

She grinned back. "I had a great teacher."

Marc reached down and gave her a hand up. "We won't be long. I'd like to get you all back to your campsite before it gets too much darker."

"You'll let me stay?" She knew she didn't need his permission to stay, but just assumed Marc wouldn't leave the decision up to her after what happened.

"If that's what you want to do, I want you to stay. The threat is gone now."

She smiled her thanks. He trusted her to make her own decision. Maybe he wasn't into the total domination thing after all. She could still remain independent and be with him.

Except in the bedroom or at the club, when she so wanted him to control her, rather than be an equal partner. She could accept that type of relationship.

"I love you, Marc."

He looked stunned a moment, as if he were about to bolt. Then he grinned and brushed a strand of hair from her face. "I love you, too, Angelina."

Without warning, he grabbed a hank of hair at the back of her head and pulled, opening her mouth to prepare for the onslaught of his kiss. Her clit went into overdrive as his lips crushed hers. He drove his tongue into her mouth without preliminaries, performing a mating dance with her own tongue. She reached up and held onto his shoulders to keep from melting into a puddle at his feet. Grabbing the hair at the back of his head, she gave him a little of what she'd gotten. His hand lowered to her butt and he ground their pelvises against each other.

Suddenly he broke away and looked down into her half-open eyes, which probably were glazed over with lust.

With love.

"I'll let you decide if you want to stay up on this cold mountain tonight—or sleep in my warm arms."

* * *

Shit, Marc thought, his woman was a fast learner. Not only had she trussed the pig, she'd rebroken the asshole bastard's nose, as well. If the wilderness thought it could get the best of her, it had another think coming.

"If you fucking let this one get away, you're a damned fool."

Marc grinned. Adam wasn't referring to the man suspended from the makeshift pole between them as they made their way back up the mountain. "Don't worry. Even if I have to hogtie her, I won't be letting her get away anytime soon."

"Karla! Watch out!" Angelina's shout brought them to a halt, and then they heard the growl of a cougar split the night air. Women's screams followed and Luke shouted, "Don't move, Karla."

Adam and Marc dropped Martin unceremoniously to the ground, ignoring his scream of pain as he probably landed on his broken nose, and ran up the trailhead until they came around a bend to find Karla pinned with her back against a boulder. An adult cougar stood mere yards away from her, poised to strike.

Angelina stood frozen in the middle of the trail. Luke held onto Cassie, who kept trying to lunge at the cat, or escape Luke's grasp, he wasn't sure which. Adam didn't pause, but ran down the trail trying to get the attention of the cougar.

"No, Adam!" Karla seemed more worried about him than herself.

Marc cupped his hands around his mouth and yelled: "Damián! Can you make it down here! We've got big-cat trouble!"

"I heard! I'm on my way!"

If Damián could get a clean shot, the cougar would be neutralized. He hated to have to destroy something so beautiful, but the Park Service would come after and kill any cat that attacked humans. If they could take care of it before Karla or Adam got hurt, that's just the way it would have to be.

"I'm scared, Adam." Karla kept her gaze on the cat that growled again.

"I know, hon. Just keep your wits about you while I try to distract it."

Adam turned to run up the trail. Much more interested in a moving target, the cougar took off after him.

"Adam! No!" Karla scrambled off the rocks and ran after them. Marc and Luke followed, after telling Angelina and Cassie to stay put.

Marc shouted, "Karla, stay back!" She ignored him. The cougar sprang into the air and crashed down onto Adam's back, sending him sprawling to the ground. *Shit.* Its teeth tore at his bare neck, immobilizing him immediately. In a flash of speed, Karla latched onto the cat's tail and singlehandedly tried to pull it off Adam. *Gesù.* Didn't she know how powerful that creature was?

But the cougar hardly noticed her, so intent was it on tearing the jacket and shirt off Adam's back and biting into his neck. Adam struggled under the weight of the cat.

Damián shouted, "I can't get a clean shot! Get Karla away from there!"

Marc looked down the trail where Damián was poised to shoot, his eye on the rifle's scope, waiting. Marc caught up to them and grabbed Karla around the waist, dragging her away. She screamed. "Adam! Don't die, Adam! Please! I need you!"

Marc carried her behind a boulder, out of range. Damián wouldn't miss. There would be no ricochet. One shot, one kill, just the way he'd done with insurgents in Fallujah. When the rifle blast rent the air with its report, Karla jumped. The cougar fell silent. Karla slumped against him for a moment, then recovered quickly and pushed away from him to stumble back up the trail. Marc followed. The cat had to weigh nearly as much as she did, but before he could catch up to her, she'd half dragged the animal by its bloody head off of Adam's back. Adrenaline surge.

Luke called out, "The EMTs are coming; ETA twenty minutes."

Karla stretched out on the ground beside Adam, touching his face, which didn't have a scratch from what Marc could see. "Adam. Don't you dare leave me. I need you." She continued talking to him, trying to keep him from drifting away. Sometimes Marc had seen it help with cases he'd have thought were goners for sure.

Adam groaned, a pool of blood forming near his neck. Marc's training kicked in and he unstrapped the medical pack he kept in his car. He'd strapped it on earlier in case Angelina had been hurt. He quickly put on gloves and searched for the puncture wound or wounds causing the blood loss. If it was an artery, Adam could bleed out in no time.

There it was!

"What can I do to help?" He looked up to see Angelina kneeling down beside him.

"Put on a pair of gloves and take a four-by-four—gauze—and fold it into quarters. Then I need you to put pressure against this neck wound. You aren't afraid of blood, are you?"

"No. I have four brothers. Remember?"

Once he'd shown her the amount of pressure to use, Marc searched for other deep wounds. None on his neck. He pressed his fingers against the carotid artery and found a weak pulse. Adam's now limp body had probably gone into shock. Marc wished he had his corpsman's pack and could start an IV.

Luke came over and spread a Mylar blanket over Adam to try to maintain body temperature. Marc took out the paramedic shears and, lowering the blanket to Adam's waist, cut through the shredded and bloodied jacket and shirt. The blood loss was significant. Had they stanched it in time? Adam's shirt also was filled with streaks of blood. Marc wouldn't have enough bandages to cover all of the cuts on his back, but he could debride, clean, and cover the deepest wounds.

He glanced at Luke. "I need antiseptic and cotton gauze. Lots of gauze." Luke reached into the medical bag to find the items.

Marc splayed Adam's shirt and jacket open to expose his back and froze. Old scars marred his upper back. Shrapnel wounds. Christ, was there even an inch of him that hadn't been ripped apart? The puckered skin ended at the white scar across the back of his neck, the place Adam often touched when anxious. The shrapnel wounds had been laid bare again by the teeth and claws of the cougar.

Farther down his back, where the skin hadn't been damaged by combat or cougar, Marc found a tattoo depicting the Fallen Soldier Battle Cross—boots, rifle, and helmet in the traditional combat zone memorial to those who had been killed. Beside the image were tattooed three names—Carlos Garcia. Gino D'Alessio. Thomas Miller. Sergeant Miller's name had been added later, evident by the slightly different lettering.

After Fallujah.

Garcia must have been the one who was killed with his brother, Gino. Adam must have been haunted by the deaths of these men every day to have memorialized them on his body like this.

"My God!" Angelina's gasp brought him back to what he needed to be focused on. "What happened to him?"

"Enduring Freedom."

Focus, man.

Luke had his gloves on and had removed several packets of gauze from the packaging and handed them to Marc who took the antiseptic and soaked them, then cleaned the deepest wounds. At least there were no rocks or dirt to compound problems, but with a cougar, chances of infection were high.

As Marc worked cleaning the wounds, his mind returned to what he'd seen on Adam's back. He'd had no fucking clue what this man had been through in Afghanistan. He'd felt guilty for not bringing Gino and Garcia out alive, but that was just his being a Marine. They always tried to bring every Marine out alive—or die trying—but seeing what Adam had gone through trying Marc thought it insane for him to carry any guilt.

Marc had an occasional hitch in his side from his wound, but his former master sergeant must have had days where he went to hell and back with the pain—and the memories. How did he get through those days without complaining? Why didn't he have PTSD? Hell, maybe he did, but hid it better than most.

"Adam, you listen to me." Karla kept up her non-stop litany, trying to get some response. "You're not meant to leave yet. I waited nine years for you. I came back to you. You will not leave me. Do you hear me?" No response.

Nine years? Where the hell had those two met? She would have been what…sixteen? No wonder Adam treated her more like a daughter. He probably still saw her as a kid.

Marc continued to clean the wounds in the order of severity. Where the hell were the EMTs?

"Is he going to be okay, Doc?"

Marc looked up to see Damián looking like he was about to drop. All the blood had to be triggering PTSD shit for the kid, from that rooftop where he'd lost his foot to a grenade blast and had Sergeant Miller bleed out lying on top of Damián's chest.

"I hope so. Why don't you start down the trail and meet the EMTs? You don't have to return with them. Just let them know where we are. Your stump might be rubbed raw after all this hiking."

"I'm fine. Don't let him die, Doc."

Damián thought of Adam like a father. Despite the fact that Marc and Adam were a little closer in age, emotionally, Adam had been like a father to him, too.

God, don't let us lose him. Not after all he's already been through.

Adam had to have one of the strongest constitutions and wills to live to have fought back from Afghanistan. But he had Joni then. Marc glanced over at Karla as he continued to clean and cover the cat scratches.

Tears streaked her face. She closed her eyes. "Ian, don't you let them take my Adam away from me. It's not his time. He's mine. God sent me to watch over him." She sobbed the last words.

He hoped Adam had the will to keep fighting, because he was going to have to deal with a long recovery from these wounds—the fresh ones, true enough. But more importantly the reopening of old ones—both physical and emotional.

Karla would be up to fighting right alongside him, pushing every step of the way. The two were a good match, if only Adam would get his head out of his ass long enough to realize it.

First, though, Marc had to keep him alive until the EMTs arrived.

Chapter Twenty-Four

Angelina lay curled in Marc's arms, her head against his shoulder. She couldn't let him go. After seeing what happened to Adam, she just wanted to be as close as she could. Marc went out into that wilderness nearly every day. The thought of him laid open like that made her sick to her stomach. Angelina shuddered when she remembered Adam's back.

"Cold, *cara*?" He pulled her closer and laid his chin on the top of her head.

Safe. Protected.

Loved.

After a few minutes, she pulled away and sat up, meeting his gaze. "I love you so much, Marc." She'd said it at least a dozen times in the last few days, but needed to make sure he knew.

He smiled, as if he understood, as well. "And I you, *angelo mio*." He brushed his thumb over her lips, making them tingle.

She could read the worry in Marc's eyes. She'd watched him work so hard to save Adam's life—and she had no doubt Adam would have bled to death on that mountain if Marc hadn't been there.

What a nightmare for everyone. Adam was the glue that held this family of sorts together. Angelina looked around the waiting room at the odd assortment of people, all here because of their connection to either Adam or Karla.

Poor Damián looked shell-shocked, staring blankly at the floor, flexing his fist as if he just needed to pound something to make everything all right again. She remembered him at the club last month, his whip coiled at his side, ready to take the hide off that poor blonde. He'd scared Angelina at first, but now she knew what a gentle person he was inside. The way he was with Karla these past few days touched her, too. Karla would need all the support she could get to nurse Adam back—if he…

No, she wouldn't think like that. He was going to make it. The fever that had consumed him since yesterday was no match for Adam...or Karla, for that matter.

Luke sat next to Damián and grinned at her when she met his gaze. Angelina couldn't believe it had only been a few days since Luke, Karla, and Adam conspired to perform the elaborate mindfuck Marc had orchestrated to win Angelina back. He'd planned everything from wardrobe to script.

When would this nightmare end so everyone could get on with their lives, most especially Adam?

Luke cast a worried glance over at Cassie, who sat huddled in the corner, alone, brushing her pencil in rapid bursts over the sketchpad on her lap. The woman wasn't comfortable being around all this testosterone, but Cassie had refused to wait at the house. She was worried about Karla. The two shared a special bond that Angelina envied.

The last three days had been exhausting for them all, but no one had wanted to leave the hospital. Poor Karla had barely left Adam's side in three days. When they managed to pull her away to get something to eat, she barely touched a thing. She needed to keep her strength up if she was going to help Adam fight back.

Angelina heard the ding of the elevator around the corner and a moment later the distinct aroma of her mother's lasagna. She looked at the doorway where Mama, Tony, and Rafe had come in carrying a thermal baking dish, bread, plates, silverware, bottled water, and plastic cups.

Angelina jumped off Marc's lap and ran across the room to them, pressing a kiss on Mama's cheek. "What are you doing here?"

"When you called to tell me why you couldn't make it to dinner today, we decided to bring dinner to you. Franco and Matteo are parking the car."

Tears welled in Angelina's eyes. Luke and Marc cleared the magazines and silk-flower arrangement off the coffee table to give them a place to lay everything out.

Angelina turned to Mama and wrapped her arms around her. "Thank you so much." She pulled away. Tears swam in Mama's eyes. Then anger as she reached up to lightly brush the bruise on Angelina's cheek.

"Who did this to you?"

She heard Tony and Rafe growl and looked over to find them glaring in turns at Marc, Luke, and Damián.

"No! Allen Martin did this, but he's in custody now. I'll definitely be pressing charges to make sure he gets locked away for a long time." She took a breath, registering the curious expressions on their faces. "Come, let me introduce you to everyone."

She introduced Cassie, Luke, and Damián to Mama and two of her brothers, and couldn't help but notice some tension between Luke and Tony, but was more intent on introducing Marc to her family. She released Mama's hand and walked over to him and wrapped her arms around his waist. "And this is Marc D'Alessio."

He squeezed her waist, then pulled away and walked over to Mama. Bending down, he wrapped his arms around her and kissed her on each cheek. "I am honored to meet the woman who gave life to the woman I love."

Mama's face grew as red as Angelina's flushed face must be, and now they both were crying. Mama smiled and pinched his cheek, then looked over at Angelina. "I like this one." Everyone laughed, releasing some of the tension in the room. "Now, let's eat before this gets any colder."

As Mama went to dishing out her fabulous meal, Marc took Angelina's hand and pulled her aside. "We're going to get Karla out here. See if you can get her to eat something, too."

Angelina nodded and watched as he and Damián went toward the entrance to the unit. She noticed Luke had retreated to the opposite side of the room and went over to him. "What's going on between you and Tony?" A cloud passed over Luke's eyes before he turned away.

Luke drew a deep breath. When he turned to face her again, despair and turmoil filled his eyes. Had he and Tony known each other through SAR? How could that be a bad thing?

"Angel, I should have told you this a long time ago, but couldn't find the words."

No. Wait! Her heart thudded loudly. She didn't want to hear any more bad news, but it was too late to rescind the question.

"I was on that mountain the day your father died."

"I didn't know you'd been with SAR that long." She thought he'd said it had been four years.

He turned away. "No, I'm the reason he died."

Angelina's heart pounded in her ears and she swayed. He stood up and grabbed her arms to steady her.

"Take your hands off my sister."

Angelina looked over to see Tony, eye to eye with Luke. What on earth was Luke talking about? And why was Tony so angry?

"I don't understand. The newspaper said Papa was trying to rescue a novice hiker who'd gotten lost." Luke looked down at her, filled with self-loathing and guilt.

No! Luke knew the mountains. He saved lives. He wouldn't have been stupid enough to head out on a hike with the threat of an avalanche. The warnings had been clear from what she'd heard.

"My wife, Maggie, and I had come up from Austin on vacation."

His wife. Maggie Denton. Why hadn't she made the connection?

"We didn't know enough to listen or look for warnings. It was sunny and warm. We thought nothing of it." Luke seemed lost in the memory of that day seven years ago, his gaze unfocused. The words tumbled out of him. "We got lost. Then it started to snow. Hard. Maggie wanted to keep going. She wanted to photograph some damned plant to share with her students. Then she slid down a scree slope. The rocks cut her up badly and she injured her ankle. I couldn't get to her, so I hiked out for help."

Angelina's Papa died because of Luke? Her throat closed as the emotions of losing her father all those years ago resurfaced. She wrapped her arms around her waist and closed her eyes, withdrawing from him. Tony encircled her with his arms, his body tense.

Luke shuffled his feet. "I know it's lame. Nothing can bring him back. But I'm so sorry, Angel."

Tears blurred her eyes, and she closed them. Warm lips brushed her cheek. She turned to find Marc. When she gave him a curious look, he said, "We're waiting for Karla to come out."

Angelina was never so happy to see anyone and wrapped her arms around him. He whispered, "Shhhh, I've got you, *cara*. Just let it out." And she did, but after a few moments, he said, "*Amore*, I know you're hurting, but so is Luke. He lost his wife that day—and he's blamed himself every day since."

"But if he hadn't gone up on the mountain that day—"

"Your father signed onto the SAR squad to help people, no matter if it was their own stupidity that got them into danger or not. Hell, most rescues involve someone making a stupid, potentially fatal mistake. Luke grew up in Texas. He didn't know the mountains then. Remember what we said about respecting the wilderness?"

Angelina hiccoughed then nodded.

"He's spent the last four years atoning for his mistake. He's saved dozens of others who got themselves in similar predicaments, including those hikers last week. He doesn't judge them. It's his duty to rescue them."

Angelina looked up at Marc.

"Just like it was Papa's."

Marc reached out and stroked her cheek with his thumb, careful to avoid her injured one. "We know the risks when we go up there. Your father volunteered to go down that scree slope to get to Maggie. He knew the dangers. He knew the threat of an avalanche was high. He went anyway, because that's what we do."

Oh, God, no! As if Marc's being in the wilderness for recreation and his business wasn't enough, he also faced danger on the search-and-rescue missions. She'd worry sick every time he left the house alone. She wanted to be out there with him every chance she could, when she wasn't working wherever she found a job as a chef or caterer.

But Luke had saddled himself with the guilt of the deaths of his wife and her father all these years. She turned to him, embarrassed at the way she'd reacted. New tears sprang to her eyes and trailed down her cheeks.

"Luke, I'm such a child sometimes. I'm so sorry. For your loss. For the guilt you've carried. For being so…"

Tony came toward Luke, his gaze intent, and she feared a physical altercation. Angelina's heart pounded as Luke eased himself away from her side, setting her away from him and steeling himself.

Tony spoke to her instead. "You're not the only one who behaves like a kid sometimes, baby." Then Tony surprised them both by extending his hand to Luke, as well. "I'm sorry, too. No more hard feelings."

* * *

Luke felt some of the guilt ease away from him at Tony and Angel's words. He shook Tony's hand. Nothing would bring back the life of the innocent man who had died on the mountain attempting to rescue his wife. But he needed to extend his deepest regrets at long last to the woman he'd deprived of her husband's love, comfort, and protection all these years.

He crossed over to where Angel's mother stood riveted watching the scene, tears streaming down her plump cheeks. "Mrs. Giardano, your husband will always be a hero in my eyes."

She wrapped him in her arms. Two other tall Italian men walked into the waiting room and Luke pulled away. Matt and Franco were introduced by Mrs. Giardano who drew everyone over to her.

Luke looked at Cassie, who hadn't glanced up from her sketchpad since introductions had been made earlier. Her hand flew over the paper as she captured something from her imagination onto the paper. Her long brown hair fell in loose, wispy braids over her breasts. Her olive-colored skin indicated European heritage, and her high cheekbones, her native Peruvian ancestry. Something niggled at his brain, but Mrs. Giardano brought his mind back to her.

"I haven't told any of you this before, because I didn't think you needed to know," she said, her gaze taking in each of her five children. "I thought it best to let you believe…"

He heard Angel whisper, "No, Mama," and Marc wrapped his arm around her to hold her close. Luke was happy the two finally realized they belonged together.

"My Antonio was indeed a brave and caring man. He loved his family. He loved his work." A tear trickled down her cheek. "But he also was proud and stubborn."

Rafe walked up to put a supportive arm around his mother. Luke handed her a couple tissues from the box on the table and she brushed the moisture away from her face. She seemed like a sweet woman, not unlike her daughter. She dearly loved her family and they loved her.

"Antonio didn't like to go to the doctors." Angel flinched and Marc held her tighter. Mrs. Giardano continued. "He smoked too much. I'm so glad none of you picked up that habit," she said as an aside, smiling through her tears. "But one morning, he coughed up blood. I insisted he go to the doctor's and they found stage-four lung cancer that had spread to his liver."

Angel gasped and Marc held her up when she would have collapsed. Luke wasn't sure why her mother was telling them this, especially with so many non-family members listening, but she seemed to need to get something off her chest.

"They told him they could do radiation and chemo, but that would only buy him another six to twelve months. His quality of life would be…" She looked down at the mangled tissue in her hand. "Not good." She took a deep breath and then Luke felt her gaze on him once more, as if her next words had special meaning for him. His heart drummed in his chest. "Luke, that was a week before your wife was injured on the mountain."

Luke's mind returned to that life-altering day. He'd spoken with Antonio before the man had gone down to Maggie's side—to let him know she was three months pregnant. The man had promised to do everything he could to bring her back—and had insisted on going down alone, which Luke later learned was against SAR procedures. Everyone had known the avalanche threat that day. He'd argued privately with his chief for a couple minutes, which had frustrated Luke no end. He had just wanted someone to go get Maggie. Then the chief had nodded in agreement and Antonio had loaded up the gear and rappelled down the scree slope toward Maggie.

As understanding of what had happened that day dawned, Mrs. Giardano smiled at him. "Chief Morgan told me at Antonio's visitation of my husband's insistence he be the only SAR member to attempt to save your wife." Tears flowed down her cheeks unheeded now.

Rafe patted her shoulder. "You don't have to do this, Mama." She laid her hand on his and stilled his movements.

Damn. What more could there be?

"Antonio didn't want a lingering death filled with suffering and medical bills. If it were his time to go, he wanted to die performing his duties. To die a hero. I'm convinced if he hadn't died that day, he would have continued to volunteer for other impossible missions until his time did come, one way or another." When she finished, she broke into sobs and held onto her eldest son.

"Oh, *Dio!*" As Angel broke down and sobbed, Marc sat down and pulled her into his lap, letting her cry against his shoulder.

Luke reached out to Angel's mama, squeezing her forearm. She broke away from her son and turned to him. Luke's heart swelled as he felt the love emanating from her every pore.

"But I want you to know this. I'm certain he tried his best to save your wife. And your baby. The captain told me she was pregnant. I'm so sorry..." Her voice broke. She sounded anything but certain about her husband's death.

Luke met her gaze and held it steady. "Mrs. Giardano, I was there that day. Antonio did everything he could to get Maggie out safely. He followed every procedure, well, except going down to her without a partner. If not for the avalanche, he'd have succeeded."

She smiled and wiped her cheeks. "Thank you, Luke, and I'm so sorry about your wife and baby."

Then she blinked and raised herself to her full five-foot-six inches or so and announced, "If anyone still has an appetite, please eat up all this food."

Strong woman, just like her daughter.

* * *

Angelina held onto Marc.

"Shhh. I have you, Angelina."

Memories of her dancing lessons with Papa flooded back. It was the weekend before he died. He'd said she'd need to know how to dance so she could go to her prom. She was only seventeen, and the prom was a year away, but she'd stayed with him instead of hanging out with her friends. She'd always been glad she had made that choice. Papa teaching her to dance was one of her most precious memories of him.

He'd known he wouldn't be there to teach her later.

"Your papa didn't want you to see him waste away," Marc said. "He wanted to face death on his terms. He was a very brave man."

Instead of more tears, Marc's words, along with Mama's and Luke's, brought some peace to her heart. Of course, the floodgates had already been released and Marc's white silk shirt was wet where her head rested against his chest. Mama's revelation hadn't just opened old wounds, they had shifted her world back onto its axis.

The wilderness hadn't controlled Papa. He'd faced her on his own terms. And, while he would have done everything in his power to bring a young pregnant woman to safety, she was glad he'd been there to provide her with comfort in the end.

Angelina had been insecure since her Papa's seemingly senseless death, never certain about anything in life, afraid to make important decisions for fear they would be the wrong ones with equally disastrous results. Lord knew she'd made many foolish decisions in those years and suffered the consequences—Allen Martin being a major case in point.

But she'd also avoided the joys of the natural paradise her father loved so much. She'd lived in fear, locking herself away from such an important part of her world here.

And Marc's.

They were both strong Italians and there would be lots of emotional upheavals in their lives—probably more than Marc wanted to deal with. He kept himself so closed off emotionally.

But the only emotion that mattered was love, and they had that in abundance for each other. There was still a lot of work to do, but she'd take a chance with Marc.

He needed her to complete him. And he, in turn, would give her wings.

To fly.

Per volare.

Epilogue

Karla slid her hand under the thermal blanket and laid it on Adam's bare chest, over his heart. The monitors beeped his heartbeat at steady intervals, but she needed the reassurance that only came from feeling his heart beating against the palm of her hand.

His skin was so hot, dry. They couldn't keep the fever down. She pulled the blanket up to the bandage on the side of his neck that continued to seep blood, especially when he thrashed around as he had been doing since last night. The cougar also had clawed his side, which was covered in a bandage under the blanket. But most of the damage had been to his back and neck.

Tears blurred her eyes. He lay so deathly still now. They kept him heavily sedated because of the painful wounds he'd suffered, but she longed to see those crinkles in his eyes when he smiled. To know he had the resolve to fight his way back to her. To hear him growl or give her that special look that told her she'd gotten through to him, good or bad.

He stirred in his sleep. Since last night, he'd been restless, mumbling and thrashing about as he appeared to fight old battles in his head. She'd stayed by his side for three days and nights, occasionally letting the others in, but Marc said she was probably the one he needed most. The one who could pull him back.

She didn't understand why he'd said that, but didn't argue either. Adam was only allowed two visitors at a time and she hated to give up her spot here for even short breaks. The nurses, as well as her friends, tried to get her to leave from time to time, but rarely succeeded.

Adam always took care of everyone else; he never thought about himself. That was going to change. "Adam Montague, you'd better hear this," she whispered. "You are precious to me and I'm going to take care of you, whether you like it or not."

Adam needed her. He'd risked his life to protect her. Just as he'd done in that bus station, only this time, he'd nearly died. Now he needed her to protect him, watch over him. She wanted to be the first person he saw when he awoke.

If he ever woke up.

She laid her head on his arm, the one that didn't have the IV tube puncturing his hand. Just one more wound on his battered body. She hadn't been able to look at his back at the scene or when they'd changed the bandages. From Marc's and Angelina's reactions, it sounded really bad. She couldn't stand to see his beautiful body so horribly mutilated.

All to save her.

Again.

"Garcia! D'Alessio! Report!"

Karla sprang up to look at Adam's face contorted in sleep, his head thrashing about on the pillow. His hand flung up and would have hit her in the face if she hadn't caught it in midair and held on tight.

"Shhh. It's okay, Adam. You're safe. I'm here."

Her voice seemed to calm him, which made her feel good. Did he know she was here with him?

"I lost them, baby."

She smiled. He'd never used any endearment other than "hon" or "honey" with her before, and he used that with other women, as well. But the despair on his face caused her to reach out and stroke the worry lines from his forehead.

"Oh, God, Joni. I lost so many of them."

Joni. Her hand stilled. He thought she was his dead wife. Tears stung her eyes, but she blinked them away. Well, if he wanted Joni right now, she would be Joni.

"You did everything you could, Adam. You were a brave soldier."

He growled. "Marine...know better."

Karla smiled. She'd forgotten that he'd told her while writing to her from Iraq that calling a Marine a soldier was an insult. "I'm sorry, sweetheart. I forgot myself." His eyes remained closed and she leaned closer. "You're my hero, Adam. Don't you forget that."

"Nobody's hero." She thought he'd fallen asleep again, he'd become so still. "Lost you, too, didn't I?" he whispered.

Tears stung her eyes. "No, Adam, you'll always have me. God brought us together" Forever.

"And our baby boy."

Oh, God, he'd never told her that he'd lost a child. Adam kept so many of his hurts bottled up inside. She cleared her throat to get past the tears. "There'll be other children." She hoped. He would be such a wonderful father.

"Too late."

No, we have all the time in the world—if you'll just stop pushing me away.

The days of her letting him ignore her were over. She'd waited for Adam for nine years and, by God, she was going to have him. If that meant becoming a submissive for him, she'd learn how to do that.

When he'd bound her in ropes the other night, rather than feel constricted, she'd actually felt freed. Release through restraints, he'd said. She'd felt so precious and cared for. Adam had been so incredibly gentle, considerate, and tender. Long ago, she'd wondered what kind of lover he would be. Well, that night had shown her he could be gentle, even with the BDSM stuff.

"Excuse me, Miss." Karla looked up to find a nurse's tech. "Two family members would like to come back for a quick visit." She looked down at a piece of paper in her hand. "Marc and Damián. This might be a good time for you to take a dinner break. Something smells really good out in the waiting room."

Karla didn't want or need a break right now. But Adam needed to have time with Marc and Damián, too. She sat up, ignoring the protesting muscles that had been cramped for too long in the uncomfortable chair. Leaning over, she placed a kiss against his lips.

"I love you, Adam."

"Love you, li'l subbie."

Tears welled up in her eyes. Joni was the luckiest woman in the world to have been loved so well by this man.

"I won't be gone long." She squeezed his hand and left his room.

Karla met Marc and Damián at the entrance to the waiting room for the Tertiary Care Unit. "He's been having a lot of dreams and nightmares. Incoherent. Fever hasn't broken yet."

Inside the waiting room, she was surprised to see what was left of an Italian feast spread out on the coffee table. The food probably smelled delicious, but it just churned her stomach at the moment.

After being introduced to Angie's family who were about to leave, she homed in on Cassie, sitting alone with her sketch pad, lost in her special place. The crowd must have set her nerves on edge. She walked over to her sweet friend. "Cassie, what are you still doing here?"

Cassie looked up, blinking her sad brown eyes as she shifted her focus from the drawing she'd been intently working on back to the real world. Wisps of hair had come loose on her forehead and at her temples from her braided pigtails. She smiled, her lips always looking as though she'd painted them with a pale pink lipstick. But Cassie didn't wear makeup. Ever. She tried to make herself as unattractive to men as possible, which was totally *im*possible, because she had a natural beauty that couldn't be hidden or denied.

"I wanted to be here for you, Kitty. How is he?"

Karla sat down beside her. Cassie was the only one of her current friends who called her Kitty, a nickname she'd picked up in high school for reasons she couldn't even remember. In college, she'd matured and the name seemed so childish.

"He's still out of it. Talked in his sleep a little bit tonight, but he thought I..." She glanced away. "He gets confused. I think he's having nightmares about things from the past, probably because of the fever and narcotics."

And maybe a little bit because his guard has been relaxed for the first time in...well, forever.

"How are you doing, Kitty?"

Why did that question always lead to tears, whether it was her dad, Adam, or now Cassie asking? Her friend reached out and squeezed her hand. "I love him so much, Cassie, and he doesn't even know I..."

"You'll let him know, when he gets better. Show him."

"He's so stubborn, honorable, proud. And he still loves his wife so much. I don't know if he can ever love anyone else again." Her heart squeezed tight.

"Breathe, Kitty. Right now."

Karla remembered Adam's giving her similar instructions on the nights she'd found him at her bedside after particularly vivid nightmares about Ian. *Deep breaths. Now.* She smiled.

But her smile faded quickly. When he regained his strength, the steel wall would go back up and he would shut her out again.

"I don't know how to break down the wall, Cassie."

"If anyone can figure it out, you can, Kitty."

Cassie laid her forehead against Karla's and the two shared a quiet moment, then Karla lifted her head and looked down at the sketchpad. Cassie had drawn the image of an angel—a woman holding a tiny baby.

"Who's that?"

Cassie looked down as if seeing it for the first time. She picked up the sketchpad and examined the angel and child more closely. "I have no idea. I don't even remember sketching it."

"You were intently working on it when I came out. You didn't even notice me at first. May I?" Karla reached her hand out.

"Sure."

Karla looked closely at the angel's smiling face, but didn't recognize her either. She wondered if it was Joni and their baby. Maybe Luke would know what Joni looked like. There was a photo of her in Adam's office, but Karla had never brought herself to look. The woman's ghost had such a strong hold over Adam. Right or wrong, she felt a little jealous of the woman's chokehold on Adam's heart. But perhaps seeing a sketch showing Joni and his baby boy were happy on the other side would ease some of Adam's pain.

Maybe Luke could help. She carried the pad over to him.

"Any change, Karla?"

She shook her head and gave him the report she'd given the others. "Luke, do you know what Joni looks like?"

"I've seen a picture of her in Adam's house, but it's been a while."

Karla extended the sketchpad to him. "Could this be her?"

* * *

Luke took the sketchpad and his blood ran cold.

Angel, seated next to him, placed her hand on his tense arm. "What's wrong, Luke? Who is it?"

"Mag…" He had to clear his throat to speak past the lump that had formed there. "It's Maggie, my wife." *With our baby?* Luke blinked several times so he could see the sketch clearly again.

Karla's hand covered her mouth. "Oh, my God. How can that be?"

Good question. How could Cassie, who'd never met either of them, draw such a perfect image of his dead wife? Luke looked over at Cassie, who became self-conscious under his scrutiny and moved her left hand up to brush the tendrils from her forehead in what clearly was a move to hide her face from him.

Luke turned back to the sketchpad, unable to stop looking at this smiling Maggie holding their baby. He'd forgotten what a beautiful smile she had. He had no doubt she'd wanted him to know both of them were okay.

"It's time. I'm sending you an angel. She needs you."

He closed his eyes, but couldn't block out the image of the woman he'd seen in his dreams. Olive skin. Long brown hair. Sketching outside a mountain cabin. Cassie fit that physical description and was a recluse who lived in a cabin in the mountains.

She needs you.

Was Cassie the one she'd sent? The message seemed even clearer this time, but he'd mistaken Angel Giardano as being the one, too. He wouldn't jump to conclusions too fast this time. Hell, Cassie was so skittish, he didn't know how he'd be able to get within ten feet of her anyway.

You always did have a warped sense of humor, Maggie.

Karla didn't take the sketchpad away from him when she returned to Cassie. Karla apparently told her, because her heard Cassie gasp just before she glanced furtively toward Luke, pain and confusion in her eyes. He held her gaze a few seconds then squirmed in her chair as she looked down at her clenched hands.

Well, Maggie, you know I've always liked a challenge. If she's the one, I won't give up.

He smiled.

* * *

Karla had never felt so rattled before in her life. For Luke to have such a precious glimpse of heaven and his lost loved ones was such a godsend. But why Luke? Cassie had never met him before in her life. Why hadn't she sketched a picture for Karla showing Ian happy on the other side? Smiling. Raising a little hell maybe.

And Adam. What would it have meant to him to have received a similar sketch of Joni and their baby boy?

She shook her head. "Why Luke?" She hadn't realized she'd spoken aloud until Cassie responded.

"I told you, Karla. It just came to me out of the blue. What do you think it means?"

"I have no clue. You're sure you've never met Luke?"

Cassie glanced surreptitiously across the waiting room at him and Karla thought she noticed a blush on her cheeks. "Never. I'd have remembered him. He looks like…" She turned her gaze to Karla. "Never mind."

Before she could ask any other questions, Marc and Damián came out and her focus reverted immediately to Adam. They approached her and she wanted to get back to Adam now. When she stood, the blood rushed to her head and she swayed on her feet. Damián was by her side in a second and wrapped his arm around her, supporting her.

She'd grown very fond of him, since he'd intimidated her to death during her audition at the club. He teased her the way Ian had and usually managed to bring a smile to her face. Only he wasn't smiling much these days either.

"When's the last time you ate, *chica*?"

"I'm not hungry."

"That's not an answer. C'mon, look at all this food. You need to eat."

Karla pulled away and glared at him. "I said, I'm not hungry."

Damián grinned. "Me-ow. The *gatita* has claws."

"Stop calling me kitten."

He grew serious. "You can't be strong for Adam if you don't take care of yourself."

The sadistic bastard knew just how to draw blood. How Damián could go from playful tease to sensual sadist in the club, Karla never could understand. But he knew what would inflict the most pain and the thought of not being strong enough for Adam led her to walk over to the table and dish out some lasagna and pull off a piece of crusty bread. She sat and ate, growling at Damián, who just grinned back at her.

I'm doing this for Adam, not you.

Minutes later, she was beside Adam's bed again. He slept fitfully, having kicked the blanket off again. Karla covered him and took up her sentry position in the chair at first. She stroked his arm, which felt sweaty. Maybe his fever was breaking.

"Just rest, Adam. Everything's going to be okay. I'm here."

Suddenly needing to feel closer to him, she laid her head on the bed, placing her hand across his blanketed chest. She drifted off to sleep and was awoken by another one of Adam's bad dreams.

"I'll be good. Don't lock me in there, Mommy!"

He sounded so scared. His voice was high-pitched, like a little boy's. *Oh, God!* What horror was he reliving now? What kind of mother would lock a little boy up? Anger welled up in Karla and she wanted to slay the dragons of his past, whoever they may be.

Adam cried out, a most pitiful, keening sound, and her heart broke for the little boy locked inside him. What horrors had he endured? Karla stood and reached up to stroke his whiskered cheek.

"Adam, listen to me. You were a good boy. And you're a good man. No one will ever hurt you again."

Not if I can prevent it.

Needing to hold him, to keep the most insidious of the demons away, Karla crawled up onto the narrow bed and stretched out beside him. She laid her head on his chest and her arm and leg over his chest and thigh, sliding her hand under the blanket and splaying it over his heart.

She'd first fallen in love with Adam's bare chest at the age of sixteen, there in her family's kitchen as her mother had patched up the wounds he'd received rescuing her at the bus station when she'd been stupid enough to run away from home.

But if she hadn't run away, she never would have found Adam. Fate. Just like the voice she'd heard later that day telling her to go after Adam when he'd left the house to walk. *Watch over him.* She'd followed him to the lake and watched as he stood braced against the elements, lost in his thoughts. When he'd turned toward her, she'd seen tears in his eyes and, much later, she'd learned Joni had died just a couple weeks before that.

When Karla had professed her love for him on her front porch shortly after, as only a sixteen-year-old with a crush could do, he'd let her down so gently, not wanting to hurt her feelings. She grinned. The look of terror on his face had been priceless—in retrospect. But she'd never forgotten his words.

I still love my wife.

Now, nine years later, Karla could see his love for Joni was as strong as ever. How could she make him see her as a living, breathing woman who loved him? She needed to show him she wasn't that immature sixteen-year-old runaway. She needed to…

"Karla?"

Her heart thudded to a halt. *Adam!* The rumble of his beautifully raspy voice against her cheek brought her head up and she met his gaze. He recognized her! She smiled and reached out to stroke his scruffy cheek. "You've come back to me, Adam."

"What the fuck are you doing in my bed?"

About the Author

Kallypso Masters writes emotional, realistic Romance novels with dominant males (for the most part) and the strong women who can bring them to their knees. She also has brought many readers to their knees—having them experience the stories right along with her characters in the Rescue Me series. Kally knows that Happily Ever After takes maintenance, so her couples don't solve all their problems and disappear at "the end" of their Romance, but will continue to work on real problems in their relationships in later books in the series.

Kally has been writing full-time since May 2011, having quit her "day job" the month before. *Masters at Arms* was her debut novel (published in August 2011), followed by *Nobody's Angel*, *Nobody's Hero*, and *Nobody's Perfect*. A change of plans for the series will make *Somebody's Angel*, the continuation of Marc and Angelina's romance, the next in line.

Kally lives in rural Kentucky and has been married for 30 years to the man who provided her own Happily Ever After. They have two adult children, one adorable grandson, and a rescued dog and cat.

Kally enjoys meeting readers at national romance-novel conventions, book signings, and informal gatherings (restaurants, airports, bookstores, wherever!), as well as in online groups (including Facebook's "The Rescue Me Series Open Discussion" secret group—send a friend request to Karla Montague on Facebook to join; she also visits the Fetlife "Rescue Me! Series Discussion Group" regularly) and in live online chats. She hopes to meet you in her future travels! If you meet her face to face, be sure to ask for a Kally's friend button!

To contact or interact with Kally,

go to Facebook (http://www.facebook.com/kallypsomasters),
her Facebook Author page
(https://www.facebook.com/KallypsoMastersAuthorPage),
or Twitter (@kallypsomasters).

To join the secret Facebook group Rescue Me Series Open Discussion, please send a friend request to Karla Montague (https://www.facebook.com/karla.montague.1) and she will open the door for you. Must be 18 to join.

Keep up with news on her **Ahh, Kallypso…the stories you tell** blog at
KallypsoMasters.blogspot.com
Or on her Web site (KallypsoMasters.com).

You can sign up for her newsletter (e-mailed monthly) at her Web site or blog, e-mail her at kallypsomasters@gmail.com, or write to her at

Kallypso Masters
PO Box 206122
Louisville, KY 40250

Get your Kally Swag!

Want merchandise from the Rescue Me series? T-shirts and aprons inspired by a scene in *Nobody's Angel* that read: "Master Marc can put me in culinary bondage anytime." A beaded evil stick similar to the one used in *Nobody's Perfect*. Items from other books in the series will be added in coming months. With each order, you will receive a bag filled with other swag items, as well, including a 3-inch pin-back button that reads "I'm a Masters Brat," two purple pens, bookmarks, and trading cards. Kally ships internationally. To shop, go to:
http://kallypsomasters.com/kally_swag.

Excerpt from

The Embattled Road
(Prequel, Lost and Found Series)

The Embattled Road (excerpt)

Copyright 2012, J.M. Madden

In the harrowing prequel to The Lost and Found series, three embattled Marines must deal with their devastating physical and emotional injuries in a world that seems to have turned against them.

When the rescue helicopter crashes into his convoy in Iraq, Marine First Sergeant Duncan Wilde struggles with the loss of men, his career and the use of his body. Things can't get much worse. Until his fiancée decides she has to move on with her life, and that of her unborn child by another man.

Sergeant Chad Lowell knew when he went to war that it would come with a price. And it did. A young Marine under his command is killed by a landmine. Chad's left with one less leg and a mountain of recriminations. That doesn't mean he wants to be a pitied by every female he comes in contact with.

Gunnery Sergeant John Palmer is furious at the hand he's been dealt. He's served his country faithfully, if not without antagonism, for many years. Now they're turning him out like a relative who has overstayed his welcome. And, since he's not even a real man anymore, maybe it is time to move on permanently.

Can these wounded warriors use a friendship borne out of adversity to form a partnership rescuing others? And can they find real love in spite of their challenges?

And now a special excerpt from J.M. Madden's *The Embattled Road*, free at all outlets. Also available in trade paperback in a combined volume with the next book in the series.

* * * *

Chapter One

June 2007

Duncan could not wait to get the fuck out of this sand pit. He had grit in his junk, his armpits, the creases of his eyes. It didn't do any good to try to rub it away because all you did was scratch yourself. Fucking desert.

Jungle fighting would be welcome right now, and that said a lot. He hated the jungle.

Three more months before he reached the end of his tour and could go home. His last tour. He'd already decided to go on drill instructor duty when he was done, so he could train recruits at Parris Island in relative comfort instead of here. He'd served his time. Perhaps he and Melanie could actually build a life together.

The Humvee rattled over a rock, bouncing him in the seat.

"Monroe, you gotta hit every damn rock on the road?" Bates groused. "My ass is killin' me."

The driver grinned and glanced behind him at the other two Marines. Bates always complained. "Dude, you've been here long enough to know the damn rocks breed like crazy. Scrape 'em off and they're right back with a new layer. I'm following the tracks exactly."

The men snorted in the back and Duncan looked out the window. The monochrome, hilly landscape stretched for miles, leading to the mountains in the distance. Rocky outcrops dotted the land, interspersed with scrub grass clumps, perfect ambush points they had to pass to get to the northern base, where they were due to relieve the current MP force rotating out. The convoy had been traveling for hours. It was slow going through this rough terrain. Driving in Iraq wasn't like driving in Colorado. You had to be aware of everything and follow in the path of the truck in front of you. Too many men had died already by IEDs this year, and more died every day.

Beauchamp had been the most recent. Blown to hell by a young Iraqi on a motorcycle that pulled alongside his window while he was talking to a group of kids. Three of the kids had been blown away as well, but insurgents didn't care about them. They were supposedly blessed by Allah for dying a glorious death. He wondered if the mothers felt the same way as they gathered up pieces of their children.

The radio squawked to life with men yelling. His ears were hit with a reverberation of sound and he knew immediately that an IED had been triggered. Duncan gripped his weapon, ready to jump to the ground as he searched for the source of the explosion. Monroe slammed on the brakes, sending the Humvee skidding in the loose gravel. Duncan glanced in the side mirror. The vehicles behind them had disappeared in a cloud of smoke and fire. Burning debris rained down in chunks on their vehicle. Black smoke swirled upward. Duncan saw the vehicles were still there, but heavily damaged, all shoved akilter. The men's screams reached his ears before they were drowned out by rifle fire.

"Out of the vehicle! Bates and Clark, cover fire! We've got men down!"

He threw himself out of the Humvee and shouldered his M16. There was a copse of rocks several hundred yards to the west. The attack seemed to be coming from there so he fired in that direction. Smoke obscured his vision as he took cover behind the truck, but he could still hear men screaming. "Monroe, get on the horn and make sure we have air support coming!"

Crouching, Duncan ran across the open expanse of ground between his vehicle and the one behind him in the caravan, the M16 barking in his arms. Bates and Clark laid down cover fire as he ran. The first Marine he reached was already gone, a gaping hole in his sternum. Duncan circled the truck, which sat at an odd angle, flipped with the roof to his side. The front passenger's side wheel was in a hole, but the ass end poked in the air. He tried to follow the sound of screaming while staying under cover. At the back of the truck, he found another young Marine trying to crabwalk around the vehicle. The distinctive chatter of the enemy's AK47s echoed through the air, and the answering response from the Marines. Ignoring the heat of the smoldering truck, he surged to grab the kid beneath the armpits and drag him around the vehicle. Bullets struck the dirt in front of him and he jumped, rolling with the kid out of the line of danger. Monroe was there, then, laying down cover fire as Duncan dragged the Marine out of reach of the bullets.

The passenger side door of the Humvee fell open just above them and two men tumbled out to the sand. One hustled to the front of the vehicle, raised his weapon and started to fire. The second fell to the ground and didn't move. Duncan glanced down at the kid he'd just helped. His tag said Fallon. He gasped for air but Duncan didn't see any obvious blood or breaks. "Hey Fallon, looks like you skinned by with this one. You're fine, you just need to breathe. Just breathe. I'm going to check on your buddy."

Fallon blinked and nodded his head. He still had his helmet on.

The Marine who had fallen to the ground did not. Duncan scrambled across the sand, ever conscious of how close the little puffs of dust around him reached. Some were within inches of his feet. The insurgents had planned this ambush perfectly. Before he rolled the kid over, he felt for a pulse. There, but faint. Again, he didn't see any obvious blood but in situations like these what you couldn't see was more dangerous. The impact of the percussion to the body and then the body against the vehicle could kill a Marine in minutes. Not an easy death. He called for a Corpsman, but all he saw was swirling smoke.

Pulling the kid over enough to look at his face, Duncan leaned in. Shit. Parker. Newest of the bunch. He'd only been here two weeks. Poor kid had a hell of a dent in his head that Duncan hadn't seen at first.

A bullet pinged off the undercarriage inches from his face and he knew he needed to move him whether he wanted to or not. Slinging the rifle around to his back, he grabbed him by the pits and pulled. Parker didn't rouse at all. Bad sign.

The Corpsman dropped down beside him as he lowered Parker to the ground, twenty feet from the overturned Humvee. He motioned to the young Marine's head. "Head wound!"

Scrambling back to the truck, he pulled his weapon forward and took position behind Monroe, firing toward the rocks. The gunfire slowed and he wondered if the enemy had retreated.

Eventually the firing dwindled away. Duncan stayed put. Sometimes the enemy stopped shooting and waited till the Marines relaxed, then set in on them again. This time, though, they seemed to be gone. Or dead. Several bodies littered the outcrop.

He clapped Monroe on the back, impressed that the young grunt had done exactly what needed done.

The medic shook his head when Duncan returned to him. "I don't know if he's going to make it or not First Sergeant. He's got serious swelling on the brain. I've called in a 9-Line Medevac but I've got other wounded to eval."

In other words, there was nothing more he could do for him.

Duncan nodded and waved the man away. Monroe helped Fallon over to sit with Parker. Fallon still wheezed and held his gut, but he'd probably be fine. Duncan followed Doc to the next vehicle in the convoy, obviously the epicenter of the blast. Bodies lay strewn behind the burning carcass of the Humvee. The transports were armored, but only to a certain extent. Obviously, this one had been deliberately targeted, fired upon repeatedly after it had hit the IED. Did they think he had been in it? The driver's side was ripped open like the lid off a can, with its guts strewn everywhere. The men in the fire team were all men he knew and had spoken to hours ago. Now, they were all gone. The gruesome sight was enough to turn his normally cast-iron stomach. It had been his responsibility to get the men in these squads to the camp safely.

His throat tightened as he went man to man, cataloging names when he could see them. Six dead, total, from two different teams. Six families he'd have to call when he got to base. Sorrow threatened to drop him to his knees, but he had to shove it aside.

The third Humvee affected by the blast had little to no damage and the men were fine, though banged up. One had a bullet hole through his leg but was conscious and calm as the Doc bandaged him up.

Duncan sent out a squad to secure their position. A few minutes later he heard the distinctive thwop-thwop-thwop of the Medevac. Shielding his eyes from the sun, he watched the chopper roll in.

It was a couple hundred yards away when a surface-to-air rocket blasted out of the hills from the west and struck the side of the massive two-rotor machine, sending it floundering in the air. Rifle fire sounded, three shot bursts, but it was lost in the whine of the overtaxed engines as the pilot tried to recover the craft.

Too close. The thought registered as his feet began moving. He tried to get the men up before the chopper came down right on top of them.

Even as he started shoving Marines out of the way, he knew it was too late. The monstrous machine hit the ground behind him and blew. For a heartbeat of time, everything stopped—sound, motion, thought. Then the blast struck him in the back, flinging him into the air. It seemed like he flew forever before landing with a sickening crunch on top of one of his men. Heat seared his body from shoulders to toes.

His burning world went dark.

Duncan jerked awake, then realized all he did was open his eyes. Reality smacked him in the face as he focused on the beige tile floor. Yep. Still at Walter Reed. Landstuhl Hospital's floor had been pale blue with darker flecks in it. He remembered that much. Somebody had turned the page of the automotive magazine for him, but he was still strung up like a marionette, arms stretched out to his sides, in the medical contraption immobilizing his spine and protecting his burns. The mattress beneath him was hard. After three weeks in the same position, you'd think he'd remember. But no. Every time he woke up, he wondered why God hadn't just killed him and gotten it over with. At least then the pain would end.

One of the nurses squeaked her way into the room. Pink rubber Crocs stopped beside his bed. What was her name? Lacey? Or Lainy? Something like that. He glanced into the edge of the mirror not covered by the magazine. She smiled at him, that professional nurse smile meant to conceal how very desperate his situation actually was.

"How do you feel today, First Sergeant?"

He rocked his head as much as he could and closed his eyes. If she was going to ask stupid questions like that he wasn't going to answer her. She circled the bed and he felt her tug at the sheet over his burnt back. "How is your pain right now?"

He sighed. She wouldn't leave until he answered her. "About a seven." She hummed under her breath and moved to the IV stand, adjusting something there. Within seconds he felt a blessed wash of numbing heat roll through his body. Seemed like the only thing that made him happy anymore was morphine. He closed his eyes and tried to sleep his life away.

* * * *

And connect with her on social media! She loves talking books!
www.jmmadden.com
www.jmmadden.blogspot.com
FB – https://www.facebook.com/jmmaddenauthor
Twitter – @authorjmmadden

Or
Email her directly – authorjmmadden@gmail.com

Angel Payne presents

SAVED BY HIS SUBMISSIVE
The W.I.L.D. (Warriors Intense in Love & Domination) Boys of Special Forces, Book 1

Available Now!

Excerpt

Okay, so Zeke had been right in grilling him before the mission. It was a little harder to keep his head in the game on this one, especially as they'd arrived and surrounded the hut—especially because he knew what they'd find inside. Or at least prayed they'd find.

Turned out their timing was better than perfect. They'd gotten here in time, and the women were safe. That didn't mean he had to stick around and help Zeke with the head count. He was glad to be out of that cramped room, with all of those women crying in relief—and ripping his gut out in the process.

But now the asshat wanted him back in there? Zeke had to know this wasn't the easiest fucking thing for him. Which meant that whatever the reason for the callback, the beer tab was on Z tonight.

"This'd better be good," he growled, stomping back into the Quonset hut. "Your panties have been twisted more times today than—"

A fist in his gut would've been less painful. And joyful. And terrible. And incredible.

Zeke had just helped the woman to her feet, though it was doubtful she'd continue standing on them. She looked weak as a fawn and shaky as a newborn colt.

She also looked exactly like Sage.

He gulped painfully as he glared at Zeke. His "friend" didn't even bother to look back. Z was too busy cutting free the zip ties that had cut purple welts into her wrists. When the woman winced from the fresh flow of blood to her hands, the cavity in his chest filled with pain too.

Forget the beer tab. Zeke was going to pay for his whole three-day bender after this. He didn't bother asking the guy what kind of a sick joke he thought he was pulling, because Zeke knew—*knew*—that some pots didn't get stirred. So if that wasn't his friend's purpose, what was?

Zeke gently helped the woman lift her head. They'd zip-tied a filthy rag into her mouth, and his friend started exploring how to best cut that free as well.

After two seconds, Garrett barely noticed the thing.

She looked past it, directly at him. No. She looked *into* him, just as she always could. Just as she always *would*. She cut him open from sternum to scrotum, filling every vital organ in his body with life again, blinding him with that brilliant green light that had haunted his dreams and been a relentless ghost in his soul.

She was a ghost no more.

Shit. Holy, heavenly shit.

He didn't remember how his legs carried him, or how many steps he took. It only mattered that he yanked the knife out of Z's hand, palming it himself. He had to be the one who set her free. He needed to be the one who saw her face when the last disgusting piece of her captivity got peeled back.

He cut the tie with a savage jerk. She reacted with a little cry, but he knew he hadn't hurt her. The sound was one of need. Of release. Of love.

When he pulled the rag free from her face, tears ran through the dirt underneath. In wordless wonder, he cupped both sides of her jaw and kissed each tear until he got to her lips. She sighed against his mouth, opening to him, inching her shaking arms around his neck.

"My heart," he said against her lips.

"My hero," she whispered back.

Garrett stiffened and swallowed. The words entered his gut and twisted it like scarab beetles. Hero? Right. Some champion he was, buying the story from the CNO hook, line, and fucking sinker. No skeletons in the van merely meant the rebels had moved the bodies as some kind of a sick fuck-you to God only knew who. There was no sense in jeopardizing extra American lives to look for two charred corpses. The region was unstable and unsafe now.

Goddamnit, he'd believed every line they fed him. He'd settled for saying goodbye to her photo on a tripod as they tossed flower petals off a cutter in the Sound, instead of demanding they all look harder, deeper, further for her.

Never again. He vowed it now with every cell in his being. He'd never again give up on her. The angels had given her back to him, and he sure as fuck wasn't blowing the chance. He'd never again let her go, and he'd never again rest before knowing she was safe, secure, completely protected.

He began making good on that oath that moment, clutching her close and claiming her mouth with a kiss so deep and consuming, they both dragged air in harsh, heavy breaths afterwards.

He kept her pressed against him, still barely comprehending that her heart beat beneath his and her arms actually trembled against his neck, before he murmured, "Welcome back, Sage Weston."

Sage pulled back a little. She tilted her face up at him, her chapped lips tremulous with the question that tumbled off them. "Welcome back…to what?"

"To life, sugar." He brushed her lips softly with his own again. "To life."

* * *

Website: www.angelpayne.com
Facebook: www.facebook.com/angelpaynewrites
Twitter: @AngelPayneWrtr
Pinterest: angelwrites

The *Rescue Me* Series

Masters at Arms
(First in the *Rescue Me* Series)

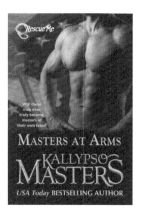

Masters at Arms is an introduction to the Rescue Me series, which needs to be read first. The book begins the journey of three men, each on a quest for honor, acceptance, and to ease his unspoken pain. Their paths cross at one of the darkest points in their lives. As they try to come to terms with the aftermath of Iraq—forging an unbreakable bond—they band together to start their own BDSM club. But will they ever truly become masters of their own fates? Or would fate become masters of them?

Masters at Arms & *Nobody's Angel*
(First and Second in the *Rescue Me* Series)

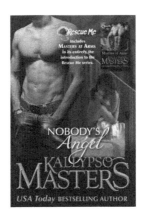

Masters at Arms is an introduction to the Rescue Me series, which needs to be read first. The book begins the journey of three men, each on a quest for honor, acceptance, and to ease his unspoken pain. Their paths cross at one of the darkest points in their lives. As they try to come to terms with the aftermath of Iraq—forging an unbreakable bond—they band together to start their own BDSM club. But will they ever truly become masters of their own fates? Or would fate become masters of them?

Marc d'Alessio might own a BDSM club with his fellow military veterans, Adam and Damián, but he keeps all women at a distance. However, when Marc rescues beautiful Angelina Giardano from a disastrous first BDSM experience at the club, an uncharacteristic attraction leaves him torn between his safe, but lonely world, and a possible future with his angel.

Angelina leaves BDSM behind, only to have her dreams plagued by the Italian angel who rescued her at the club. When she meets Marc at a bar in her hometown, she can't shake the feeling she knows him—but has no idea why he reminds her of her angel.

Nobody's Hero
(Third in the *Rescue Me* Series)

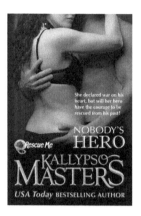

The continuing romantic journey of Adam and Karla, which began in *Masters at Arms* and continued in *Nobody's Angel*, and ended in a dramatic cliffhanger that sets up the opening scene of *Nobody's Hero*.

Retired Marine Master Sergeant Adam Montague has battled through four combat zones, but now finds himself running from Karla Paxton, who has declared war on his heart. With a twenty-five-year age difference, he feels he should be her guardian and protector, not her lover. But Karla's knack for turning up in his bed at inopportune times is killing his resolve to do the right thing. Karla isn't a little girl anymore—something his body reminds him of every chance it gets.

But their age difference is only part of the problem. Fifty-year-old Adam has been a guardian and protector for lost and vulnerable souls most of his life, but a secret he has run from for more than three decades has kept him emotionally unable to admit he can love anyone. Will she be able to lower his guard long enough to break down the defenses around his heart and help him put the ghosts from his past to rest? In her all-out war to get Adam to surrender his heart, can the strong-willed Goth singer offer herself as his submissive—and at what cost to herself?

Damián Orlando and Savannah (Savi) Baker also will reunite in this book and begin their journey to a happy ending in *Nobody's Perfect*.

Nobody's Perfect
(Fourth in the *Rescue Me* Series)

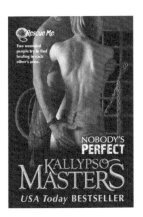

The continuing story of Savannah Gentry (now Savi Baker) and Damián Orlando from *Masters at Arms* and *Nobody's Hero*.

Savannah/Savi escaped the abuse, torture, and degradation forced upon her by a sadistic father for eleven years and has made a safe life for herself and her daughter. When her father threatens her peace of mind—and her daughter's safety—Savi runs to Damián Orlando for protection. Eight years earlier, young Savannah shared one perfect day with Damián that changed both their young lives and resulted in a secret she can no longer hide. But being with Damián reawakens repressed memories and feelings she does want to keep hidden—buried. At Damián's private Masters at Arms Club, she discovers that sexual healing might be achieved through sadomasochism administered by a loving Service Top named Damián.

Damián, a wounded warrior, has had his own dragons to fight in life, but has never forgotten Savannah. He will lay down his life to protect Savi and her daughter, but doesn't believe he can offer more than that. She deserves a whole man, something he can never be after a firefight in Iraq. Damián also has turned to SM to regain control of his life and emotions and fulfills the role of Service Top to "bottoms" in the club in need of catharsis by whipping or other SM practices he is skilled at delivering. But he could never deliver that level of pain to Savi, who needs someone gentle and loving, not the man he has become. But when Savi witnesses a cathartic whipping scene on her first night at the club—delivered by Damián—she begins to wonder if Damián could also help her regain control of her life and reclaim her sexuality and identity.

Connect with Kally on Substance B

Substance B is a new platform for independent authors to directly connect with their readers. Please visit Kally's Substance B page (substance-b.com/KallypsoMasters.html) where you can:

- Sign up for Kally's newsletter
- Send a message to Kally
- See all platforms where Kally's books are sold
- View excerpts of Kally's work on your web browser, tablet, or smartphone
- Download free samples of Kally's eBooks

Visit Substance B today to learn more about your favorite independent authors.